A.C. DONAUBAUER

The Order – Book 1

The Order - Book 1

A.C. Donaubauer

First published as ebook in August 2015
Paperback
2nd edition

Copyright © 2019
       Astrid Donaubauer-Grobner
       Waltenhofengasse 3/3/3302
       1100 Vienna, Austria

The author online:
       www.ac-donaubauer.com
       www.facebook.com/acdonaubauer

Cover: Biserka Design

Editing: Jürgen Donaubauer, Hannes Ohrlinger
Proofreading: Philip Scott

Video trailer: imageIn Media

02/2019

ISBN 978-3-904142-05-2

To Jürgen – my friend, my lover, my partner.

Thank you for giving me wings and roots.

CHAPTER 1

Eryn

The air was chilly and smelled of the snow that was yet to come. This winter was already harsher than the last few she could remember, even though it was only beginning.

Eryn watched her breath condense in pale clouds before her face and looked up at the star-strewn night sky. Though it was a sight to behold on such a clear, cloudless night she looked forward to returning home to a cosy fire and a warm drink. She hated the cold, always had. Her time of the year was the hot summer months, no matter how exhausting many tasks became in the heat. It certainly was preferable to this chill.

Hugging her bag of roots close to her side, she hurried through the dark main street of the little town. She was supposed to have been back before dark, but the roots were hard to find this year. She suspected that some of the villagers went out themselves to look for them to sell on the markets.

Her father would already be waiting impatiently and be looking out the window every minute or two. He kept pointing out how dangerous being out in the darkness alone was for a fifteen-year-old girl, and Eryn always suppressed a sigh when he started one of his tirades about the many hazards that lurked around every corner. Her late arrival would earn her another one, she was absolutely sure.

Just two more houses and she would reach the narrow path that led to the secluded little house she shared with Treban, her father.

Treban was the town healer, an excellent one, whose reputation had spread all around. The ill and injured came from remote places to seek his help, hardly ever in vain. He took great pride in his work and had never sent anyone away because he or she didn't have the means to pay.

However, those he treated nevertheless were always eager to find a way to compensate him, even if it took them a while to do so. It was not wise to make a bad impression on somebody like her father; it might be they had need of his services again one day. Sometimes packages arrived with written notes that

1

thanked him, blessed his generous heart. Her father never kept any records who had paid and who hadn't. He simply didn't care about that.

He said that healing was not just something he did to put meat on the table, but to serve and take care of people who would in turn take care of him. While to some his altruism seemed rather naïve and they sneered at him for it, his attitude did not keep him from seeing people the way many of them truly were. He just had made the decision himself not to be like them. He was a man who wanted to believe the best, but was very well aware of human nature at its worst.

And Eryn knew that this was exactly why he kept trying to impress on his daughter the need to keep herself safe.

A twig snapped somewhere behind one of the houses, but this was just one of the noises that accompanied life in the countryside. She told herself it might have been a small animal or just somebody who was taking in some chopped wood for cooking.

Nothing to be nervous about, she assured herself, cursing her father for making her see danger in every shadow, portent in every noise around her.

The next sound was closer, behind her.

She swallowed, took a deep breath, turned around – and sighed with relief when she spotted Krion, the baker's son. He was a few years older than her - a tall, good-looking young man who always had a smile and a wink for Eryn when she came into his father's shop for bread.

He had started flirting with her some time ago and Eryn felt flattered by his attention. Some of the other girls her age and older had tried to catch his eye, and she was very pleased that he had singled her out. At least, she hoped she was the only one he flirted with… Finding out that this was just how he talked to all the girls as soon as he had a quiet moment with them would devastate her.

A few other boys had started noticing her, but none of them left her stomach feeling tied in knots like Krion.

She beamed when he came closer, as she always had to when she beheld him. "What are you doing out in the cold? Shouldn't you be home?"

He smiled, bright teeth glinting in the darkness. "I could ask you the same, little Eryn. It's dangerous out here in the darkness."

She rolled her eyes. "You sound like my father!"

He laughed. "Why don't I accompany you home so nothing happens to you that would upset your father?"

She felt her palms starting to sweat. He was offering to escort her home! She would walk with him all the way to her house, having him to herself! This meant he liked her, surely? He wouldn't walk with her if he didn't care for her, would he? Or did he do it because this was the kind of chivalrous thing that was just like him?

He waited for her answer. "You are not afraid of me, little Eryn, are you?" he teased her.

Afraid? She was almost dizzy with happiness and smiled. "No, of course not. Thank you, I would like that very much."

They walked in silence until they had left the town behind them and reached the little path that led to the healer's house.

"How do you like working with your father? The healing? I mean; your father is teaching you to be a healer, isn't he?"

She nodded. "Yes, he is. I like it a lot. Sometimes it's really hard to stay up all night to help somebody who needs to be cared for and watched over and then after only two or three hours of sleep to carry on with your daily work - though luckily enough, that's not too often. But seeing people come in and feeling really bad and then watching them leave looking so much better is really great." Don't babble, she warned herself, you'll just drive him away.

He stopped before the curve that would bring the house into sight. He came very close, putting his hands on her shoulders and pulling her even closer. Her heart skipped a beat. Would he really kiss her? Her face felt hot despite the cold. What a shame that she could only see his silhouette in the dark.

His lips were cool as they met her own, cold lips, but his tongue was warm. She slipped her arms around his middle and leaned into him, melting.

When she felt his hand on her breast, she pulled back and brushed it aside firmly. He put it back and made to pull her close again.

"No," she said breathlessly, shaking her head in the dark.

"Why not? You do like me, don't you?" She could hear the smile in his voice.

She pushed harder when he grabbed one of her wrists to stop her from retreating. "I don't want this, let me go!"

"All of a sudden you're playing hard to get? We both know that's what you are doing!" He sounded irritated, as if he had not really expected any resistance. He seemed to consider it a personal insult.

Instead of answering she tried to kick him where her father had shown her. He barely avoided her foot and cursed when she kicked his thigh. When he grabbed his leg with both hands, Eryn turned towards the house and started to run.

She felt his clutch at her elbow after only a few steps… it almost made her stumble backwards.

"Let me go, you brute!" she screamed, fervently hoping for her father to hear her and come to her rescue.

He slapped a hand over her mouth and pulled her down onto the cold, hard ground, fumbling with one hand to pull up her skirts. She squirmed and writhed under him, kicking, trying to bite his hand, to get him off her. She felt his cold hand on her stomach, working its way down, and felt tears running down her temples. Tears of betrayal, of anger at herself, of utter despair at her helplessness.

Then suddenly his weight on her was gone from one moment to the next. She heard him yelp in surprise and heard what sounded like somebody being hit. There was a sickening crack of what had to be a broken bone and then she heard Krion's voice retreating, wailing curses.

She didn't see the man, but recognised her father's scent of herbs before she felt his warm hands close around hers to pull her up and back on her feet.

"Father," she snivelled, "he wanted to…"

"I know exactly what he wanted," her father's disconcertingly calm voice interrupted her. She recognised the barely contained wrath in it and pushed closer when he put his arm around her shoulders to lead her back to the house with him.

"The roots…" She stopped, trying to see where the bag had landed. Her father saw it first and bent down to pick it up before he put an arm back around her shoulders to pull her close again.

"Come, girl," he said. "You need to get inside. You are cold as ice."

Cold was exactly how she felt, chilled through and through. It went deeper than outside temperatures could reach. Not even the welcoming fire she could soon see through the windows of the house promised any relief.

She expected him to reprimand her, scold her for her carelessness in walking alone with a boy in the darkness, but her father said nothing. He merely took the cloak from her shoulders and neatly hung it on the hook at the door beside his own. He had not worn one when he had come for her.

Then he took her hand and led her to his comfortable chair in front of the fire. He went away again and she heard the clinking of earthenware. When he returned to her side, he crouched in front of her, pressing a cup with a clear, dark, sharp-smelling liquid into her hands and brushing away the tears that kept running down her cheeks as she sat, wordless, in the chair.

She made no move to drink, so he lifted her hand with the cup until she took a sip. The sweet liquid burned its way down her throat and made her cough. She almost instantly felt the warmth spread in her stomach.

She looked up into her father's face that swam in and out of focus between tears. She didn't speak, still waiting for his tirade that must begin.

For a few long moments they just looked at each other, then her father finally spoke, but to her surprise not to reproach her as she had expected. "I am sorry, child. This is my fault."

She stared at him, feeling as if she was trapped in an absurd dream. "What?"

He shook his head. "I should have warned you. I should not have sent you out for the roots when it gets dark this early. I should have gone instead. I…"

She grabbed his hand, finding it unbearable that he of all people was blaming himself for what had happened. Or rather, for what he had prevented from happening.

"You *have* warned me!"

4

"No." He freed his hand to rake it through his greying but still full hair. "I did not warn you about *him* in particular."

She had not thought that she could freeze even more inside. "Him in particular?" she repeated almost inaudibly.

"Last year I was called to a young girl in town. She had been waylaid and..." His voice drifted off. "She said it had been the baker's son," he continued after a while. "I've kept my eyes and ears open since then to learn about it in case something like that happens again. And now *you*, you were almost..." He broke off again.

Too stunned to speak, she sat rigid, only one thought circling in her head: the young man she had been falling in love with was no more than an animal who made a habit of forcing himself on helpless young women. Every last bit of regard that might have survived his assault dissolved, evaporated to be replaced by something hard and cold.

"I will make him pay for this," Treban hissed out from between clenched teeth.

She looked up at her father, surprising him when she said, quite calmly, "No." The tears were still drying on her cheeks, but the glimmer in her eye had turned from injury to cold steel hardness. He was about to object, when she just said, "*I* will."

* * *

When Eryn rose the next morning, she was surprised at how late it was. The sun was well up already, and normally her father would have woken her quite some time ago. She was grateful that he hadn't. The night had not been a peaceful one; it had taken her hours to fall into a restless sleep, despite her father's nightcap.

When she dressed and went downstairs she saw him sitting in his chair, staring into the fireplace. He had let the fire burn down - only a few glimmering bits of wood remained to give off a little warmth. He looked up when she approached him.

"Sit, Eryn. There is something I want to talk to you about."

She turned around and fetched a chair from the table to sit opposite him. Then she waited for him to speak.

"I should have done this some time ago already, but I have always deferred it in these last few years, not wanting to see that you are growing into a woman instead of continuing to be my little girl." He sighed. "But still, knowing what kind of people are out there I should have been keener to do it when you were little."

Eryn frowned, not having the slightest idea what he could be talking about.

"I see I am confusing you," he smiled. "You know how the internal organs of a woman work. I showed you several times, you have even healed minor problems yourself. You are blessed with the gift, my dear girl, and this makes it possible for me to do something that will make sure that nobody can ever do to you what this beast tried yesterday."

She looked slightly uncomfortable.

"Don't be afraid, Eryn. I am talking about a magical protection that prevents any man or object from entering your body unless you wish it. I can place it there without any pain and it will never be a burden to you. You alone will decide who may pass beyond it."

Unlike other girls her age, she had no problem talking about matters such as this with her father. The human body was nothing mysterious or shameful, for her it was like an open book. The magic she could perform enabled her to just close her eyes and look around, to see how everything worked, find out what didn't and administer whatever was needed, either a nudge of healing energy or a herbal cure.

"What happens if somebody tries it without my permission?" she asked curiously.

"It would be a rather painful experience for whoever tried it," he smiled thinly with a slightly malicious glint in his eyes.

"Anything that would leave permanent damage?" she asked hopefully.

"You know very well how I think about using our abilities to harm people," he said with an undertone of warning.

She sighed. Of course she knew. It was that just sometimes it would be so much more satisfying to be allowed to cause a little discomfort at least. An itch here, a rash there… Where was the harm?

When they moved here about five years ago, after migrating from one place to the next for about the same length of time, she had needed to adapt to a completely different life from the one she had known. She was the awkward new girl that the other children had teased and called names. A little revenge every now and then would have been nice - especially as they wouldn't have guessed where it came from.

She had been confused when her father had told her that in this country there were no women with the gift, only men. When she had asked him why, he had told her that he didn't know.

The next unusual thing had been all these people with the same light hair colour. She dimly remembered that her own natural colour was a lush, dark brown. Here one didn't find a single person with dark hair. Her father had magically altered their hair colour from a rich, shimmering brown to one of the many shades of blond here.

Keeping it blond, however, had not been so easy. The change was not permanent and as soon as her body did not actively provide the magical energy, the hair changed back again to its original colour. It had taken them weeks to train her subconscious to keep supplying the necessary stream even when she was asleep. She had been and still was too young to learn how to do it herself. It was a highly complex technique.

But the memories of life before coming here had faded so much in these last ten years that she remembered hardly anything now.

"Do you agree?" he father spoke impatiently into her thoughts when she didn't respond.

"Yes." She didn't really need to think about it. Her father wouldn't propose it if it were dangerous or unnecessary. "How does it work?"

"I will place some protection around your lower abdomen that will remain as long as you have life force in you to power it. All your fluids will still be able to leave your body without any problems."

"Nobody can remove it?" she asked.

"Only a magician stronger than myself. And there shouldn't be many of those around," he added, with a confident smirk.

Eryn wouldn't know, she had never seen any other magicians, but he himself knew that he was extraordinarily strong. Which was why he had lost his companion to a stupid game of power and had to flee with his daughter into another country where he lived a simple life, hiding his and his daughter's abilities, passing as no more than a well-educated apothecary. The fact that Eryn was beginning to show the first signs of being an apt healer herself didn't pose any danger, even if, thanks to her hidden abilities, she did turn out to be uncommonly good at it.

Everybody here knew that women didn't have any magical powers, after all.

* * *

Eryn took a deep breath when she looked out the window and saw Prowel, the baker come down the path that led to their house.

"Father," she called out urgently, "Prowel is on his way here. He doesn't look happy."

Her father went to the door and opened it abruptly before the baker had a chance to bang the fist he had lifted against it. He all but stumbled inside.

"What do you want?" her father asked calmly.

"You!" Prowel pointed a finger at the healer, "You have broken my son's arm!"

So that had been the cracking noise, Eryn mused. She smiled, knowing that carrying bags of flour would really hurt for a while.

"He attacked my daughter." Still no sign of emotion.

"He told me all about it – kissing her is no justification for your breaking his arm, you ignorant fool!" The baker had started shouting.

Not a good move, Eryn mused. Her father did not respond well to loudness. That he was dead set against harming people with magic didn't stop him from doing so physically if necessary. He might seem bookish in his grey robe and long hair, smelling of plants, but he chopped his own wood, did all repairs in and around the house. He was in very good shape.

"Kissing is not what I saw. How could he when his hand was covering her mouth to keep her from screaming?" Now she could hear steel in his voice. "You know very well what he was trying to do and what he's done in the past. If you do not put a stop to this, nobody in your family will ever receive any medical help from me again."

Prowel's entire head had gone completely red. "I demand that you come at once and take care of that arm that you broke!" It clearly was an immense effort for him to keep himself from screaming.

"I just told you that you and yours are no longer entitled to any healing from me. Leave now. Don't come back before you have taken care of this." He made to close the door but the baker drew back his fist. As he made to punch the healer in the face, he felt himself dragged forward and then a sharp pain erupted in his back where he hit the floor. When he was able to move again he staggered to his feet and out the door.

Stumbling on unsteady legs, he turned back to the house and raised his finger. "This is not over, *healer!*" He spat out the last word and wobbled back to the town.

* * *

People talked, of course. The baker's son had his broken arm in a sling around his neck, telling everybody who wanted to hear it, as well as those who didn't, that he had obtained the injury when he had jumped out of the way of a cart that would otherwise have surely killed him.

But the reason for the gossip was rather why he had not seen the healer to tend to it. The baker could surely afford to pay for medical treatment for his son, especially as Treban's rates were more than reasonable and he generally accepted payment in kind. But Krion declined with a depreciating snort, declaring it was just a scratch and that the quality of the healer's services was grossly overrated anyway.

That made people's ears prick up. Talking about their healer in a derogatory way was not something that was done. It was an unwritten law. Not only was there hardly ever a reason for it, but it was also a great stroke of luck for the town that the man had decided to move there and provide affordable, high quality medical services when he could instead easily have made a fortune in a larger city.

It was further noticed that neither the healer nor his daughter seemed to come to the baker's shop any more to buy bread. When they tried to get some information out of Treban he would just reply in his usual good-natured way that Eryn had developed a liking for baking, and thus he indulged her by letting her experiment. And now they had so much bread and cake at home all the time that there was no more need to buy any.

Many were satisfied and, just as he had intended it, amused by the little story. Others, however, knew Eryn a little and not entirely unjustly hardly took her for the baking kind.

Whenever Eryn saw Krion somewhere in town she forced herself not to avert her eyes but meet his coldly and steadily. First he had sneered when he encountered her somewhere, clearly confident in the knowledge that he had done something punishable and had got away unscathed, but after a while his bearing seemed to be confused. She wasn't acting as he was expecting her to: no sign of timidity, anxiety or even hatred. Just coolness.

For many weeks, ways of punishing him were coursing through her head, some of them public, others in a private setting, some which left no visible marks, others which were bloody and for everyone to see, some dealt with the aid of magic, others with nothing more than a heavy object hitting his easily harmed places.

Her father would object to her using magic, she knew. She understood his philosophy of not using a powerful advantage to harm others, but it was not as if Krion had the same scruples that kept him from using his physical strength against somebody weaker than himself. Why did he deserve any lenience – especially when he had already got away unpunished with hurting a woman before?

She almost bumped into Krion when she crossed the road lost in thoughts of how to torture him. He was with a group of boys the same age, most of whom she knew.

"If it isn't the healer's daughter," he drawled. "I have heard that you have discovered a liking for baking. Not to compete with my father and me, I hope?" His companions looked uncomfortable when he laughed. One didn't mess with the healer's family, it just was not prudent. But while they didn't join him, neither did they try to make him move along.

"Well, what can I say?" she smiled sweetly. "The bread has just not been up to standard lately." Touch me, she thought. Give me an opportunity to harm you while you are trying to harm *me*.

But he merely ground his teeth together and glared at her through narrowed eyes. She wondered how she could ever have found him appealing.

"Forgive me, my high-born Lady, that our humble country baking is not to your distinguished taste."

She saw that he had clenched his fists. Good, she thought gleefully. Just a little further now…

"Oh, don't worry about that. I know you try as hard as you can," she cooed patronisingly. Krion quickly cut off a boy's snicker with an angry glare.

"How is that arm of yours doing?" She made her voice ooze with a delighted malice, this being the last thing she could think of that might provoke him enough to lay a hand on her in bright daylight.

Triumph surged through her when she suddenly felt the fingers of his intact hand dig into her upper arm. It was no direct skin contact, but better than nothing. A few thin layers of fabric were no trouble. She could work with that.

She stretched her inner senses and used the diagnostic skills her father had taught her to look inside his body, following the weak pulse of energy she had sent up the arm that held her. Concentrating on his forearm she slowly instructed his body to reduce the substance of the healthy, strong bone inside at one particular point. Not entirely, nothing he could feel, but enough to cause the next extra strain to make it snap.

It was the exact reverse technique for healing a bone, yet worked a lot more quickly. Funny, she thought, how doing damage was so much easier than mending it.

His friends had finally decided that he was going too far and had grabbed his shoulders to pull him away from her.

"What are you doing?" she heard one of them whisper. "Are you totally mad?"

Krion just freed himself from their grasp and turned around to stalk away wordlessly.

She hid a smile when she watched him disappear into the tavern, closing the door behind him none too gently.

* * *

The door to the little house was pushed open violently and banged against the wall with an ear-splitting crack. Eryn flinched and looked up from the dried herbs she was sorting on the table.

Treban looked furious. He was beyond angry, she could tell it from the way the blood pulsed through the bulging blood vessel at his throat. That did not bode well and there was only one reason she could imagine that might have put him in such a mood.

"What do you have to say for yourself?" His voice had taken on a threatening, forced calm that barely contained the rage that she could see in the eyes glaring at her. He still stood in the door frame. It didn't even occur to him that she might not know what he was talking about.

So Krion had finally broken his other arm as she had intended. And now she had to pay the price for her revenge: facing her father.

She covered the herbs on the table with a clean cloth to stop the cold breeze that came in through the open door from whirling them around. Then she swallowed and rose. Better to do this standing up.

"He has received what he deserved," she said quietly, knowing for sure that he would not take this well.

"What he *deserved*? What he DESERVED?" He flung the door shut with a forceful movement of his hand, making the little picture frames with the dried herbs on the walls tremble slightly. "You should be glad I don't bestow upon you what *you* deserve! You are no better than that animal! You used your power to harm somebody who was helpless to defend himself against it! I am ashamed of you." The volume of his voice had subsided with every sentence until he had almost reached his usual pitch.

She flinched at his words, even though she had expected them almost word for word. The lessened volume had not made them easier to listen to. Quite the opposite. She waited silently for him to continue. He didn't look as if he was finished yet.

"I told you of the dangers of misuse, of how power like ours can corrupt souls. How people who think they are superior thanks to their abilities can cause immense misery for themselves and those around them. You just made the first step towards that abyss." He sounded empty, resigned. She was almost relieved when his anger flared up again.

"Did you listen to nothing I have told you?" He had stepped close to her and accompanied his words with smashing his fist down on the table hard enough to make the herbs jump. And Eryn.

She swallowed hard and remained standing in front of her father, lowering her gaze under his furious one. This was not the first time she had seen him this incensed, but never before had she been the target. She wondered if he was going to hit her for the first time.

He took a step back as if to keep himself from doing just that. Then he turned around. "I can't look at you just now," he said and opened the door again. "We will talk later." And he was gone.

Eryn stared after him feeling her mouth dry. She wondered if she should run after him to apologise and beg him to forgive her. She decided not to for two reasons. Firstly, he was certainly not in any mood to accept an apology right now and secondly, it would be a lie.

She was positively *not* sorry for what she had done and she was convinced that she had not set foot on a dark path that would lead to perdition and damnation. But she was sorry about her father's grief and felt the rejection burning inside her.

She would make up for it somehow. Maybe cooking him a good dinner would be a start. She put on the cooking apron and started cleaning vegetables.

* * *

Eryn kept glancing towards the door whenever she thought she heard a noise from outside. Her father had been gone for many hours and it was already dark outside. Was he angry enough at her to stay away from home for the night? She hoped not.

Trying to keep herself busy she continued working on medicines, decanting herbal concoctions into small glass vials, grinding herbs into a fine powder to be mixed with hot water directly before use and tipping it into small leather pouches.

Her father would be pleased with her efforts, she knew. She had saved him several hours of work, after all. And she hoped that would make him better disposed towards her and forgive her more easily. Of course he would see right through her reason for working on the herbs, but that didn't matter. He wasn't usually one to spurn a sensible attempt at bribing him when it was done well. He had that kind of humour.

She was almost finished when she saw torches emerge from behind the hill that hid most of the path to the town. She counted five of them. Her heart started beating harder in her chest and she felt unease creep up on her. Where these men from the town bringing her drunken father home? The thought was dreadful, but the nearer they came the more she hoped that this was all it was about.

When they were close enough for her to recognise the men's faces, she opened the door. Her father was not among them.

They looked at her, their pale expressions masks of grim misery. She could read in their eyes that something was terribly, horribly wrong, and tears sprang to her own even before the oldest of them, the glass-maker who supplied them with vials for their medicines, began to speak.

"Your father is dead, child." His voice sounded rough and sad.

Her vision blurred behind tears and the sudden pain in her chest forced her to her knees. She felt two pairs of hands at her shoulders, lifting her up and guiding her back inside the house into her father's chair in front of the fire place. Fighting for air, violent sobs burst from her.

Gone! No - this couldn't be. He couldn't be lost forever when they had just talked a few hours ago. The last words between them... His had been that he was ashamed of her, and her last words were spoken in defiance of his beliefs. Never again a chance to set it right, she would have to live with this burden.

She didn't know how long she had sat there with the men trying to talk her into sipping the strong drink they held to her lips.

When her sobs had lost most of their force, the glass-maker exchanged a look with the others before he spoke again. "Your father was killed, Eryn. Prowel stabbed him in the back with a knife. He accused your father of breaking Krion's other arm. He must not have been right in the head."

She stared up at him, hardly comprehending the words she heard. When the full meaning of the message sank into her consciousness, coldness gripped her and slid deep until it had reached the very core of her being, deeper than warm blankets, fires and potent drinks could ever reach.

Her father had warned her that nothing good could ever come from using magic against the unprotected, the ones unable to defend themselves. He had been right, she realised with a dreadful, numbing clarity.

Her actions had cost him his life.

CHAPTER 2

Enric

He sat on the roof of the bakery nearest to the palace, watching the sun rise. That was not typical for him. He usually avoided rising before the sun unless there was no other choice. He wondered if today's exception might have something to do with what awaited him in a few hours, but dismissed this quickly. He blew a strand of his slightly overlong hair out of his blue eyes. Not wearing it the way he was supposed to was a minor act of rebellion he delighted in. One of many, in fact.

A few passers-by looked up at the young man in his early twenties who had chosen such an unusual spot for staring up at the sky, but moved on when they recognised the robes the young man wore. Magicians. It was best not to interfere with whatever they were up to.

All his fellow magicians who had finished their training with him this year would be tested to gauge their magical strength and then apply for a suitable position in the Order. In an institution where hierarchy was defined by the amount of magical strength a man could wield, this was practically an evaluation of personal worth, Enric mused. He had never been a friend of evaluations, be they magical or intellectual.

And thus he had never been a particularly attentive student. He had enjoyed the comfort his status as magician conferred. He came from a family of wealthy merchants and had not exactly been raised as a pauper, but joining the Order had still been a step up in living circumstances.

His parents were thrilled when they discovered his abilities and had sent word to the Order immediately. He was twelve years old then. Amazing, he pondered, how mind-numbingly tiresome the ten years since then had been. Not that he would have preferred spending them with his father, though.

His parents' excitement and pride had quickly turned into anger and frustration when they kept receiving reports of his less than productive attitude. His father, a merchant through and through, had tried hard to sell to him the idea of being an important man with important duties, making his family proud, accomplishing great things. Which was all to no avail.

14

The Order of Magicians was dedicated to the defence of the kingdom, even if only history teachers knew about the last time there had been an actual need for that. The fighting skills training had been fun, Enric had enjoyed it even if Lord Orrin, his teacher, was not exactly thrilled with his laziness and lack of respect.

The rest of the lessons from the last years merged into some kind of blurred sphere of information. He graduated one year late, as his approach to learning had not exactly been an ambitious one and he'd needed to repeat several exams.

Today was the day when his place in the Order's hierarchy would be decided. He was not tense as such - more curious. He knew that he was stronger than most – if not all – of this year's graduates, but it would be interesting to see how far up he could make it. Not too far, he hoped. The more responsible positions came with requirements. He was not a great fan of requirements, rules and the like.

Most of his teachers had reprimanded him for his laziness when it was apparent that he had a talent for magic and its use, but didn't want to bother with spending the time and energy that would have made him proficient. They tried to impress on him that magic without the knowledge of when and how to use it would hold him back, but he had never planned on going far.

A nice position as a clerk or assistant in the Order would suit him just fine. Something that left him enough spare time to pursue his interests: hunting and spending time with his friends.

* * *

He stood together with a group of young magicians his age. Most of them were edgy. Some of them admitted it openly, others were trying to hide it with grandstanding or rudeness.

"Not much to be afraid of, eh, Enric?" his good friend Kilan asked. "You are pretty much the strongest one this year, I imagine. Maybe there is a nice place waiting for you in the upper ranks?" He spoke the last words with a smile, knowing fully well that this was not at all what Enric was striving for.

"Yeah, wouldn't that be nice," Enric replied without enthusiasm.

Kilan was the next who was called in to be tested. It didn't take him very long to return. He looked pleased.

"Category D. Not too sloppy," he grinned. He had known that there was no way for him to make it any higher than C, and he had hoped not to be classified lower than E. So the golden middle was absolutely fine.

"Congratulations, mate." Enric turned when the double doors were opened again and his name was announced. "See you in a moment."

He walked into the hall and bowed before the assembled magicians who in turn inclined their heads.

Enric let his gaze wander over the ten men. He knew them to be selected from the different strength categories, the strongest one of them Lord Poron, a B as far as he knew and the second strongest magician in the Order and thus the kingdom. He fit the picture of second in command nicely, Enric had always thought. He had to be in his sixties, his thinning hair bound together in a short tail at the nape of his neck, his eyes intelligent and sharp as if he was constantly analysing the world around him.

Several of the magicians were known to him by sight only, a few were his former teachers.

Their expressions were not exactly enthusiastic when he entered. With the exception of Lord Orrin, his fighting instructor, who had been the only one who had never taken any cheek from Enric, none had very fond memories of him.

"Shield yourself," Lord Poron's instruction echoed off the high stone walls.

He did so and moments later the first bolt of energy hit his barrier. Two more were sent his way without any effect. A second magician, his old history teacher if he remembered correctly, joined his colleague and started attacking Enric's shield. Nothing happened.

More magicians joined them, one after the other, until seven of them shot strikes in quick succession. Enric saw them frown. Then Lord Poron lifted his arm to stop them. He breathed in, pointed the palm of his outstretched arm at him and fired a clear bolt at the shield.

It didn't penetrate the barrier. Lord Poron looked pale and troubled and motioned for the scribe who was there to note down the category of each magician. He whispered something into the young man's ear, who then went off at a swift pace.

Enric waited, still holding his shield in place. This playing around was a waste of time - why didn't they start the real thing so he could join his friends for a cool drink?

"Am I finished? Can I leave? What category am I?" he called out to the assembled magicians that had started whispering amongst themselves and occasionally gave him an apprehensive glance.

Lord Poron walked towards him. "We must ask you for a little patience, young man. We need to wait for somebody. I am sure he will arrive soon."

Enric frowned in puzzlement. "What is this about? The others before me were in and out in a matter of moments. I am not in any kind of trouble, am I?" He couldn't remember having done anything recently he ought to feel guilty about.

"No." Lord Poron's smile seemed rather forced. "No trouble, rest assured." Then he returned to the other magicians, leaving the young man standing alone in the centre of the great hall, waiting.

Not much time had passed before the double doors opened again and the man who came in caused Enric's brows to shoot up in surprise. It was Lord Tyront, the big man in the Order. What was he doing here?

Lord Tyront was in his mid-forties, a tall, formidable looking man with first streaks of grey visible in his beard. His pale blue eyes darted to Enric instantly and stayed there when he approached him without talking to the other magicians first.

When he was only a few paces away he stopped and raised his booming voice, "Shield yourself, boy."

Enric did so hastily and took a step back, whereupon a volley of strikes was sent from Lord Tyront's palm at his barrier. They were stronger than what had been thrown at him before, very much so. The older man continued to send bolts towards him, increasing their strength with every salve. Soon his shield started to waver and he quickly poured more energy into it to keep it intact.

Lord Tyront stopped, looked at him thoughtfully and then without warning unleashed a white flash that cut through Enric's barrier and threw him on his back.

The young man swallowed an exclamation of pain. It wouldn't do to show any sign of weakness in front of the Order's mighty leader. He struggled back to his feet and frowned at the man who had struck him. Surely that had not been necessary.

When he looked at the magicians in the back, he saw a few mouths hanging open, others were pressed into a thin line. One thing they all had in common: stony silence.

"Am I done *now*?" He demanded from no one in particular.

Lord Tyront smiled without humour. "Oh no, my young friend. You are not done. In fact, I think you will not be done for quite a while."

Enric stared at him in puzzlement. "What?"

"Category A," the leader announced loudly for everyone in the hall to hear. "We have a new second in command." Then he turned around and left the way he had come.

Enric stared after him uncomprehendingly, even after the heavy doors had closed behind him with a loud boom.

He shook his head. Something had to be wrong with his ears. Category A? What nonsense. Nobody was that strong, apart from the Head Magician, of course.

But the way the magicians gawked at him in disbelief let the truth dawn on him gradually.

They had called for Lord Tyront because Lord Poron, the second-strongest magician in the Order, had not been able to break Enric's shield. All colour drained from his face when he started to grasp the full impact of what had just happened.

"Oh no," he moaned, closing his eyes.

* * *

Tyront sighed and felt how the tension was slowly building behind his forehead when he read the reports about his future second in command. The boy had been causing him headaches for weeks now.

Considering Enric's past education it was hardly a surprise that he had not responded very well to the training plan that had been assigned to him and cooperated no more than was necessary to avoid the accusation of outright disobedience. It had been nearly one month now, and it didn't look as if his attitude was about to change anytime soon.

Not only did he have to learn a whole lot of new things and improve sets of skills, but he was also meant to repeat every single test he had passed barely or in which he had merely scored average marks during the years of his magician training.

In his new position he was supposed to be a role model, a respected pillar of the Order, a well of wisdom and knowledge and, if need be, a strong commander to lead others into battle. He needed to leave behind him the lazy scallywag image he had cultivated in these last years.

Orrin was the only one who had something remotely positive to report about him. So at least the fighting was going comparatively well. Unfortunately, that was only a minor comfort and by no means enough to consider the training in its entirety a success.

His thoughts wandered to Lord Poron, his current second in command. As was to be expected, he was anything but thrilled about being displaced in general and particularly by somebody like Enric. He was not the vengeful type, Tyront mused, and wouldn't make life harder than necessary for his successor. Pity, he thought. A reason to fight, even if only against a disgruntled predecessor might have provided the motivation for finally making an effort. It seemed like he would have to take care of that himself.

It was time to have a little chat with Enric.

* * *

Enric swallowed when he read the note on the soft, expensive looking light brown paper a servant had delivered only a minute before. It didn't say much, only *My quarters, nine o'clock. Lord Tyront.*

That was in less than one hour. Not enough time to prepare sufficiently, but enough time to become really nervous. Which was probably the idea, he suspected.

There was not much doubt as to the reason for this summons. His progress, as he was very well aware, was anything but satisfactory, which was fine for Enric as he had never wanted the honour that was forcefully bestowed upon him.

The Order's leader would hardly be pleased with how things were going. Being called upon to justify his poor performance had really only been a matter of time.

So far Lord Tyront had not shown any interest in him since the day of the testing. This message was the first time he had seen or heard anything from him. Obviously the great Lord only gave his attention when something was amiss. Like now.

Enric looked around in his new quarters in the King's palace, still feeling a little lost. They were to his former abode what a sapling was to a tree. Four large rooms, all to himself. And a lot more than he really needed. But being high up in ranks was not about only having what was required, was it? His quarters were supposed to reflect his importance, be representative.

Representative they were, he sighed. Yet the question was what they represented. Certainly not his personality.

The apartment was furnished elegantly and luxuriously, leaving nothing to be desired. The parlour alone was larger than the two rooms he had lived in before. And he was assigned his own servant who cleaned, fetched his food from the palace kitchen and took care of his every whim.

Enric had always been one to enjoy luxury, but not to a degree to motivate him enough to make the effort they expected. There was too much attached that he simply didn't want. All this responsibility, the consequences if he failed, the hard work to get there... No.

That was not what he had planned for himself. What he had wanted, and still did, was a nice, uncomplicated, comfortable life with none too hard work, enough time for his friends and being more or less left to his own devices.

His friends. That was another matter that worried him. Most of them had kept away from him since the big announcement. And even with those that still met him, the frequency had decreased considerably. Even his closest mate, Kilan, who was used to dealing with influential people thanks to his father's position, had started withdrawing noticeably.

Enric stared out of the window unseeingly.

How was it possible that he of all people had turned out to be the second-strongest magician in the kingdom? What a joke.

* * *

The door opened after Enric had finished knocking. An elderly male servant bowed slightly and stepped back to let him enter the parlour - a room that looked very much like his own apart from the clearly visible female hand that had been at work here.

Lord Tyront rose from his seat by the window and looked his guest up and down. He didn't bother with a greeting of any sort but motioned to a dark red settee in front of a small round table.

"Sit."

And a good evening to you, Enric thought, annoyed, but did as he was told.

"Please leave us alone now," Tyront addressed the servant and waited until the man had retreated. Then he turned back to Enric and scowled at him.

He remained standing and began without introduction, "Your performance keeps falling short of my expectations. Justify yourself." Even though the words were harsh, his tone was not.

Unconsciously Enric sat up a little straighter, an ingrained habit from his days as a boy when he had been expected to show respect when he was scolded.

"I'm sorry, Lord Tyront."

"No, you are not. I didn't ask you to lie to me, I asked you to give me a reason."

"I… I have to admit, My Lord, that I am not very happy with the current situation."

Lord Tyront sighed impatiently. "Stop pussyfooting around, boy. Say what's on your mind."

The young man lifted his chin defiantly when he said, "I do not want to be forced into this position. Neither have I asked for it, nor am I interested in it."

"A clear statement, finally," the other one commented dryly and finally took a seat opposite his reluctant guest. "What is it that puts you off?"

Enric sighed and lifted and dropped his arms several times in search for words before he replied, "All of it."

"Would you care to elaborate? This is not exactly helpful," the older man said patiently.

"The responsibility. I mean, what exactly qualifies me to take a position to command much older, more experienced magicians than myself? This doesn't make any sense! What if I do something wrong or make a wrong decision? The consequences!" His voice had become agitated.

"What qualifies you is firstly your superior strength, as it serves the Order's primary purpose of defence and secondly, the knowledge and special training you are receiving." Lord Tyront's voice was calm. "What else?"

"The work. I want to be independent, not being told what to do and work all night long for nothing, no time for myself and…" He stopped himself.

"And your family? Like you father, the successful merchant, who always worked almost around the clock to chase the next business opportunity? Who left you and your siblings in the care of an unhappy companion unless he had demands you had to obey?"

Enric stared at Lord Tyront. How could he possibly know about that? He had never told anybody about it, not even his closest friends. He felt exposed, vulnerable, as if his private life had been trespassed on by this man whose face was of course known to everybody in the city, but who was basically no more than a stranger to him.

Lord Tyront continued while he remained silent, staring gloomily at the carpet. "And you just contradicted yourself. If commanding other, older magicians is such a great issue for you, why would you worry about being told what to do yourself? You can't have both, positions of neither giving nor receiving orders are not in accordance with the nature of our institution. Or of our society, for that matter. Though being high up in the hierarchy considerably reduces the number of people that may order you around."

"There is you. And the King," he replied sullenly. "There might not be as many above me, but the ones that are left do not respond well to having their orders questioned."

A problem with authority, Tyront thought. But that was no surprise after insights which recent and older reports had given him. "True. There is not much room for questioning the King's orders. But I assure you that *I* will listen to what you say and might even act on it if it is halfway sensible. It is, in fact, your duty to advise me."

"Me, advise you?" Enric shook his head in desperation. "How can *I* advise you?"

"You will start by growing up and working hard to meet the Order's and my expectations." His words contained only a hint of threat. "You will learn to think before you speak and act. You will show respect and demand it in return. Before that you will have to turn into somebody who *deserves* respect."

"I don't want this," the young man whispered.

"The trouble is that nobody asks us what we want," Tyront replied sympathetically. "But let me tell you something: Men who strive for great power are usually the ones least suitable to wield it. Hunger for power is not a requirement for this position, quite the opposite. This is the great thing in your favour, my boy." He leaned closer and caught Enric in a penetrating stare. "Dealing with your issues is something that you will have to come to terms with by growing up quickly. You might consider the upper ranks as a bunch of harmless old men, but let me tell you that weaklings do not survive long among us. The air is thin up here, as you will learn soon enough." And then he uttered what he was confident would work: a challenge.

"Are *you* weak, Enric?"

CHAPTER 3

Handed Over

12 years later

Eryn climbed up the steep, for want of a better word, *path* and pulled a cloth out of the canvas bag she had slung over her shoulder across her chest to wipe her perspiring forehead. Collecting herbs was usually a task she enjoyed but not when it was that hot and there was no shadow in sight.

Unfortunately, the plants she needed were rather high up and required a lot of direct sunlight, so there would not be a cool spot coming along anytime soon.

She stopped to pull out the sturdy leather drinking pouch filled with water and took a generous swig. It was lukewarm and not exactly refreshing, but served well enough to moisten her dry throat.

Judging from the receding tree line to her left side the rest of the way would only take her another hour. She walked a few steps to a nearby boulder and sat down to rest for a short while. She knew better than to overexert herself in this heat.

The memories of the first time she had walked this way more than fifteen years ago came suddenly and unbidden. Her father had been with her that autumn day, constantly asking her to identify this tree, that flower, testing her as to the procedures of turning them into medicines, correcting her if she got a detail wrong or supplying bits of information that had slipped her mind.

Father. The pain of loss had dulled over time, so had the desperation of guilt. Twelve years had managed that. She had fought to keep the pain alive, it was the only thing that still linked her to him, the only person in almost all her life that had been close to her. But it had become more and more difficult to keep it with her, to fight the dulling effects of time.

At first, looking at his books, his drawings, the things he had built to conjure up memories had worked perfectly well. Tears had welled up in her eyes in seconds and had provided the illusion of closeness, no matter what the hurt.

Today the pain was almost beyond reach, and so were many of her memories of him. But there still was the emptiness, the loneliness.

At the age of fifteen she had been little more than a child, and twelve years later she still would have liked to have had somebody older and wiser around, somebody close to her she could fully trust.

She had stayed in their small wooden house at the edge of the forest, carried on her father's work as the town healer as well as she could. This was her duty, her penance, her life's purpose. She would continue his mission as long as she was able to.

The last time they had walked this very path together had been a few weeks before he had been killed. They had replenished their herb supplies and she had been thinking about Krion, planning to eat up all the bread so she had a reason to return to the baker's shop soon.

Krion. She shivered. He, too, was part of her penance. Facing him regularly in town after all that had happened, that they had caused together. Her father was not the only one who had died that night.

What the men that had come to her house to tell her the terrible news had not mentioned was that the townspeople had lynched the baker after they had found him crouched over the dead healer's body, still holding the bloody knife in his hand.

Justice had been swift and final. Or what the townspeople had considered as such.

She had been torn between amazement at the reverence people had felt for her father and horror at the merciless slaughter of a man they had known all their lives.

Not one, but two men had died due to what she had done. And nobody but her knew about it. Her father had always been adamant about her never revealing her gift of magic to anybody, and other than his directive of never using magic to harm anybody, this one she had never broken.

She wondered if Krion had ever felt any guilt about their fathers' deaths, or if she was the only one carrying that burden.

It had been several days after her father's ashes had been given to the wind that she had sought out Krion in his bakery. She had gone there after dark when the bakery that was now his had been closed for business for the day. The picture of his face when he had opened the door at her knocking was one she would probably never forget. Shock and horror had contorted his features.

At that moment she had realised that he was terrified of meeting the same fate as his father, being considered the cause of the whole situation by the townspeople. He had let her in without a word and she had entered, not afraid any more of what he might do to her alone.

She had turned to him, stepped really close, and grabbed his collar to pull him down to her height so close their noses had almost touched. His eyes had been puffy from crying and she remembered wondering at it as she had in her mind deprived him of the ability to feel anything remotely human, made him into a monster. She remembered the sour smell of days-old sweat on his skin, a sign of him having neglected his hygiene.

She had stared him in the eyes and told him that, should she ever hear that he had so much as looked at a woman against her will, she would come for him and maim him permanently so that two broken arms would feel like a warm embrace by comparison. Then she had left, not at all gratified by the additional fear she had seen in his eyes, a fear she had put there.

It had worked. Not a single incident of that kind was told to her in all these years.

So she had been faced with the challenge of following in her father's footsteps at fifteen, years before she would have completed her training. Reading Treban's books had helped her to improve her medical knowledge, but he had been very careful and had not kept any magical books that might have led to the discovery of his powers. So her magic training had stopped with his death. She had considered experimenting on her own, but discarded the thought over and over again for fear of discovery. One never knew who was watching, her father had always said.

Eryn sighed, snapping out of her reminiscent mood. She took another gulp of the tepid water and tucked the water pouch away. There would be another five hours of daylight, and she planned to be back home before darkness, which she wouldn't if she kept sitting around. There was another hour to walk yet, about one or two hours of collecting plants and another three hours of walking back.

At first the plan had been to start her journey in the morning but there had been a patient, and then another and before she knew it the afternoon was there and she had hastily packed her herb-gathering bag and left.

If she found enough herbs, she deliberated, she might be able to prepare enough medicine to get over the next three months. She would have to talk to the glass-maker about the last delivery of vials and how the opening was too narrow for the viscous concoctions to get out again without the aid of a thin wooden stick.

She cursed when her shoe got caught in a tree root and she almost fell forward. A quick grasp at a thin tree prevented her from landing on her knees. Leaning on the tree she wiggled her foot to free it from the root and sucked in a sharp breath when she heard the brittle wood crack and break, dropping her down the steep escarpment.

Frantic grabs at trees, roots and rocks rushing past brought her no more than scratched and bloody palms. She opened her mouth to scream but not a single sound came out.

Please - no head injuries, her last thought was before her head hit the moss-covered rock that stopped her descent, and then she lay motionless on the shadowy ground.

24

* * *

Firelight blinked through the trees as seven men walked through the forest, each of them carrying a lit torch and searching the ground for any sign of their healer. She had been gone too long. She was a careful person, always leaving word when she was off to one of her gathering trips, letting one of the women in the town know where she was headed and also telling them when to expect her back.

When she wasn't back five hours after her designated return, two groups of men had set out to look for her. The smith frowned when he saw a brown boot stuck under a tree root.

He called for his companions. They discussed the broken tree and what looked like a trail where a person might have slid down the bank.

Treading carefully, half of them climbed down and soon found the motionless figure of a woman. They recognised her face easily, even though one temple was covered in blood. They would have sworn that this was the woman they had known since she had been a child and who had been offering her services as a healer for many years.

But there was one little detail that left them utterly speechless and more than a bit scared: Her hair, that now held a mix of earth, small twigs and leaves, looked different. It had turned from shiny blond to dark brown.

* * *

She tried to turn her face away from the sunlight that shone directly on her face, penetrating her lids. The movement was painful and she moaned softly while she slowly opened her eyes. Pain in her head, more pain when she lifted her arm to cover her eyes.

She closed them again and did a quick survey by sending a pulse of magic through her body that brought back information on the damage it had taken. A sprained ankle, a broken arm and an injury to the head. Nothing too serious that couldn't be repaired in a few minutes, even if it would take a few pauses to recover in her current state.

Finally she opened her eyes fully, staring up at a stone ceiling that did not at all look familiar. Her eyes wandered slowly to the source of the light, a small window high up in the wall – with bars in it. Her gaze darted to the bare stone walls and the heavy door with a small barred window in it.

She was in a lock-up, she realised with a jolt. Why ever would anybody lock her away? Especially as she was injured from the fall!

"Hello?" she called weakly, her voice rough.

"She has woken up," said somebody at the other side of the door. "Inform the mayor."

Then there was silence.

She must have drifted off again, because the sound of a key being turned in the lock gave her a start. Three men and a woman entered, the mayor, the smith, the smith's oldest son and the mayor's companion. They looked at her with an expression she couldn't quite decipher.

"Why am I here?" Eryn croaked, causing the mayor's companion to fetch a glass of water and hold it to her lips before stepping back hastily.

Her voice sounded clearer when she asked, "What is the matter? Why did you lock me up?"

Instead of an answer, the mayor handed her a small hand mirror.

Eryn gave a small yelp of horror when she saw her own face framed by a tangled mass of unfamiliar brown hair. She almost dropped the mirror and touched her head, feeling the familiar texture of her hair mixed with the leftover debris from her slide in the forest. It didn't feel any different under her fingers and yet the change was plain enough to see.

Thoughts began racing through her already throbbing head, increasing the pain. Why had this happened? How was this possible? Her father had trained her hard to prevent exactly that from happening, so why had it for the first time in all these years stopped working?

Then the truth dawned to her. Because she had not been merely asleep but her consciousness had drifted far deeper, too deep to respond to any training or ingrained habit. Her carelessness on the path had damaged far more than a few bones and tissue. She had lost the protection of being the same as all those around her. Now she was different. Different was dangerous.

"We have notified the King of this," the mayor said gravely.

"The King?" she replied weakly. "But... why?"

"You know well enough why. You are not from here. The King needs to decide what must be done with you."

"What must be done with me?" Her vision started to blur, the headache kept increasing even further from a dull throb to a hammering. "What do you mean, what must be done with me? I have taken care of this town for the last twelve years," she sobbed, helpless against the tears of anger, fear and desperation that ran down her cheeks. "After everything that happened I stayed here, and this is how you thank me for it?" She tried to stand but sank back on the hard bench.

"It was not easy for us," the smith spoke this time. She heard regret in his voice, saw it in his eyes. "We have always considered you one of us, we don't want to lose you. But..." He just pointed at her hair, helplessly searching for words that didn't come.

"The punishment for harbouring spies is death," the mayor said, his voice hollow. "We can't risk that. What will happen with you is no longer in our hands."

When Eryn raised her knees to her chest to bury her face in them, they left quietly, wondering how it could feel so wrong to do the right thing. And following the law had to be the right thing.

* * *

Two days had passed since they announced to her that the town was giving her up to the King when she heard the commotion. The window was too high up in the wall to look out. They had provided food, water and had brought some of her clothes to change out of the dirty, torn, bloody ones. She had not exchanged a single word with anyone. Not that they had been eager to converse with her.

Healing her injuries had taken her longer than she had anticipated. Of course she could only take care of the invisible damage inside her, healing the wound on her head completely and thus exposing herself as a magician would make the colour of her hair her smallest problem.

She had desperately tried to come up with some possible use of magic that would free her from her cell, but healing was not exactly an offensive skill. Well - only if one didn't consider the damage it could do to the human body, of course.

But she had no idea whether or how heavy stonework or wooden doors could somehow be removed, turned into air, made to fly away or do whatever else would help her get her out of the cell.

She braced herself when she heard several pairs of feet approach. No show of fear, she reminded herself. She wouldn't give them the satisfaction of seeing her afraid.

The key in the lock turned and shortly after the mayor entered and was followed by two men dressed in what clearly were uniforms of some kind. They exchanged a glance and nodded, obviously confirming to each other that this was definitely the woman they had come for.

Then one of them stepped closer to her, lifting his hands in which, as Eryn noted only now, he was holding a pair of steel manacles. She considered refusing out of pride, knowing fully well that she had no chance of succeeding. But being dragged kicking and screaming was not how she wanted to leave here. She wanted to go away in dignity, showing them that in contrast to their cowardice she knew what courage was. That what they were doing to her was by no means more than she could deal with.

Raising her arms she allowed the man she considered a soldier to shackle and lead her out of the holding cell. In front of the small building a coach was waiting. She had seen several coaches in the past. Wealthy people from further away places in need of medical help tended to arrive in them.

This one was different, though. It had the usual wooden doors but they were on the outside reinforced with metal bars and sporting a large lock. Well, she thought, at least they didn't intend to throw her over the back of a horse like a sack of flour.

Only now did she notice the crowd that had formed around the coach, watching silently from a safe distance. She let her gaze wander over their faces, fighting hard to keep her emotions to herself, presenting to them no more than an expressionless mask. She saw the glass-maker, looking pale with his mouth set in a thin line; the smith with his arms folded, frowning; Krion, with a pretty young woman beside him clinging to his arm, looking serious when instead she would have expected smugness. Eryn wondered if the woman knew what she was getting herself into with him.

She was led to one of the coach doors and climbed in, before they could use force and escaped the sight of these people that had handed her over just like that, before they could see the tears she could no longer contain.

One of the soldiers or whoever he was got in after her and sat down on the opposite bench to keep watch on her. She didn't care if he saw her tears as long as the townspeople didn't.

Her father wouldn't have been surprised at this, she thought, and felt tears well up again. After all, he had worked hard at preventing it, never taking any unnecessary risks of exposing his magic power. He had been very aware of the downside of human nature.

* * *

Two days of travelling in the dark coach, one of the guards always with her, gave her plenty of time to think of what might await her in the city and let her imagination run wild with unpleasant options such as being locked up for the rest of her life, tortured to obtain whatever knowledge they might suspect her of possessing, or even sent into slavery. Or a nice combination of two options. Every combination would work, except for one and three, which probably excluded each other. An imprisoned slave surely wasn't really useful.

Apart from her mind's exploration of the potential horrors to come, the journey was not exactly an exciting one. The King's red crest tended to keep trouble away so there was no entertainment such as highwaymen or other criminal elements.

They spent the nights at inns, each time in a room with two beds, one for her, the other for one of the soldiers to rest while his colleague stayed awake on a chair to watch her.

The soldiers were not very talkative, which was fine for Eryn as she herself was not in a sociable mood. What was more important to her was that they kept their hands to themselves and never even once touched her in what might have been considered an inappropriate manner. Wasn't discipline a beautiful thing in a soldier, she mused.

Unfortunately, it did not only keep their hands *off* her but also their eyes *on* her at all times. There was no such thing as giving in to the urge for a quick nap to give her an opportunity to try and climb out the window silently.

How immensely inconsiderate of them.

Day three brought them into view of the royal city of Anyueel, capital of the kingdom of Anyueel. Nobody ever referred to the country as anything else than *the kingdom,* though. Probably because there was no need to distinguish between the names of countries when there was no contact with any others. And it would only lead to confusion about whether somebody was referring to the city or the kingdom.

Eryn had never before been there and stared at the grey stone wall that surrounded it. It was larger than she had imagined. She could see a tall building towering over countless roofs. Surely the King's palace, she guessed.

Many dark columns of smoke rose into the air from a great number of chimneys.

She watched the city draw nearer and nearer, and it was not long until the coach stopped in front of a large gate. She heard the soldier on the coachman's seat exchange a few brisk words with the guards on duty before the vehicle was set in motion again.

Eryn tried to take in as much as possible from the little window when they passed the gate. Her heart sank when she saw that there was not only one thick stone wall but another one a few paces inside as well. The outer gate had two heavy looking doors on mighty metal hinges, and the inner one could be blocked by a portcullis that was currently open and had a great number of metal spikes pointing downwards like a dire warning. She imagined what they would do to the bones and tissue of a person or animal caught under them and shuddered. Very probably more than one or even two healers could repair in time.

Then the coach stopped in front of the tall building she had spotted from the coach window before and the vehicle's door was opened.

The soldier sitting opposite her motioned for her to get out first, just as he had done every time in the last two and a half days. She supposed that they were trained not to present their unprotected backs to a prisoner. Which certainly made sense.

Heads turned on the large square in front of the palace when she emerged from the coach and countless eyes were drawn in amazement by her unusual hair colour. She heard whispering from different directions and saw children's fingers pointed at her.

The soldiers were about to lead her into the building, but two men in dark brown robes approached them from across the square with quick steps. Both of them were rather young and one had lifted his arm to stop them.

When they were within earshot, one of them called, "We will take her. She will be questioned by the Order."

The Order wanted to talk to her? That was a surprise, a worrying one. Her father had frequently expressed his views about it in the privacy of their home. They had not been fond ones. A bunch of oafs, he had called them, who rather played around with their magic, fighting each other instead of doing something useful with it.

Her heart had started beating faster. Why would they take her to the magicians? They couldn't possibly know about her powers, could they? Had she revealed anything in her sleep in these last two days? Or when she had been locked up in the town?

The soldiers nodded and followed the men into the palace. Were these two robed men magicians? Was that how they dressed?

The shadows inside the building made it hard for her to make out her surroundings at first. When her eyes had adapted to the change in light she saw that she was in a large entry hall with various columns, each as thick as an old tree and at least as high. Four corridors started between two columns and stretched away.

The robed men turned into the first one on their right and then stopped in front of medium-sized double doors that seemed almost too modest for this place.

The slightly taller one of the men opened both doors and motioned for the soldiers to bring Eryn in. She swallowed and was pushed forward when she didn't move of her own accord.

This was very likely the room she would be questioned in. Looking around she noted with relief that no torture devices were visible at first sight. It was a rather large room with a single chair at its centre and a massive table at one end.

At the table five robed figures of different ages were seated. One of them was completely grey and looked to be in his sixties, the others seemed much younger and between their mid-twenties and late thirties. They were all clad in brown robes that made them look oddly indistinguishable from each other.

They didn't rise when she entered. She reminded herself that the respect that she had enjoyed as a healer for the last one and a half decades was not what she could expect here. In this place she was no more than a stranger suspected of being a spy.

The soldiers escorted her to the chair, pushed her down on it and left without a word. The two magicians that had led them here took up position in front of the door.

She'd had plenty of time on the journey here to consider what to say when the time came. She decided to stay as close to the truth as possible. Surely the mayor had informed them about everything he knew about her. Which was not a lot. There wasn't really a reason for her to lie to them; her story was harmless enough and she knew only little about her own past before they had left their home country. She didn't even know exactly where she was from. The only thing she had to keep hidden was her magic, the rest didn't matter.

If they saw that she cooperated, would they let her leave again? Where would she go if they did? Returning to the town was hardly an option. How could she bear living near them again?

No, she decided, she would return at night to get her things and then never look back. She could settle anywhere else - healers were not exactly in great supply in this country, so it shouldn't be too hard to find a place where her services were valued higher than the colour of her hair.

"What is your name?" the oldest one asked into her thoughts.

"Eryn," she replied obediently.

"Where are you from?"

"I am not sure. I think from the west."

The old man frowned. "How can you not be sure where you come from?"

"Because I was no more than a child when we left."

"We?"

"My father and I. He brought me here."

"Where is he now, your father?"

"He is dead. Has been for twelve years."

"Why did he bring you here?"

"I don't know."

They started muttering amongst themselves. Then one of the other four asked, "So you have no idea where you are from and why your father brought you here? This sounds rather implausible."

Eryn remained silent and just looked at them. Protesting would hardly win her any points.

"Where is your mother?"

"She is dead. Has been since before we left."

This went on and on. They seemed very interested in her father and how it was possible that the townspeople had never seen her brown hair before her accident in the woods. Now the dangerous part started. She needed to diffuse any suspicions about magic.

"My father knew how to mix a powder that made it possible to change the colour of our hair. He just wanted to live in peace and not be troubled," she explained calmly.

"Why had your hair then changed back to its original colour when you were found?" another one enquired.

"Because I was climbing a path up a hill for several hours and it was very hot. My sweat must have removed most of the powder."

She had been prepared for that one and was relieved to see that they seemed to accept her explanation.

"We heard that your father was a healer."

"Yes, he was a very fine healer."

"Apparently he was not merely fine but extraordinary."

"Yes, he told me that he had been trained for many years back home."

"Ah yes, the mysterious home you don't remember." The old man smirked and then continued, "You took up your father's work as a healer after his death."

She nodded. "Yes."

"He trained you, then?"

The hours seemed to stretch. They took turns in asking her questions, sometimes they wanted to hear again what she had answered before and she wondered if they were trying to make her contradict herself.

The afternoon had already started to turn into early evening when the oldest of the robed men rose and stepped towards her. She was exhausted, thirsty, hungry and sick of this whole situation. But she had sat through it and now it looked like this would finally come to an end.

"There is only one thing left," the man said, coming closer. She eyed him nervously. What did he want now?

"What?" she sighed with tiredness.

"Just a little test if you are telling us the truth."

She frowned. "What test?"

"I will ask you some of the questions again. This time I will use a little magic to keep your mouth from saying anything untrue."

Her head started reeling. That did not sound good, not at all. She pulled her arm away when he made to take it, jumped up and backed against the wall.

"No, I don't want this," she shouted. "Stay away from me!"

The man stepped closer, cornering her. "I'm afraid you don't have much choice in the matter, considering why you are here."

He grabbed her arm and gripped it tightly so that she couldn't free herself.

She forced the panic inside her down. Maybe it wouldn't work on her. Would she be able to use any magic of her own to block his? But how? She had never even heard that such a thing was possible, let alone how to counter it.

She felt the trickle of warmth from his palm move up her arm.

"Now, tell me again why your father brought you here," he demanded.

She shook her head, desperately. "I don't know! I really don't. I think he was hiding." That was not good. She had not intended to say that last bit.

"Who from? And why?"

"I don't know!"

"Was your father a spy?" The grip on her arm grew stronger.

"No!"

"Are you a spy?"

"No, I am not!"

If his questions kept following this path there would not be any imminent danger of revealing her secret.

The next one, however, destroyed that illusion quickly.

"Was your father able to use magic?"

She drew in a sharp breath and was about to negate it, when her mouth refused to let out the words. The man's eyes flashed in triumph.

"Aha!"

That was enough! She kicked him in the shin and ripped her arm away from his grip. He cursed under his breath and instructed his colleagues, "Hold her!"

Fresh, hot panic welled up inside her. She breathed hard and retreated slowly into a corner, watching the magicians approaching her steadily. She kicked the first one to come into her reach in the knee and made him jump back hastily with a yelp of pain.

"We should probably stun her. That might be safer," one of them said. "A weak stun should keep her conscious and able to answer our questions."

Moments later something shot towards her and hit her directly in the chest, making her gasp for air.

The magician frowned, shaking his head. "That should have taken her down! She should not be standing anymore!"

"It must have been too weak," another one said and this time she saw how the bolt of energy curved towards her without being able to avoid it. This one hit her in the stomach, nearly doubling her over.

She stared at them uncomprehendingly at such unprovoked readiness to hurt her, hate, fear, desperation erupting from a tight knot inside her. When another one lifted his palm, she raised her arms protectively in front of her and prepared for the next impact, willing herself not to feel the pain it would cause.

When indeed she didn't feel anything, she looked up again and right into seven astonished faces staring at her. Then suddenly half of them raised their hands and unleashed streaks of magic against her, but they were somehow stopped and dispersed in front of her body without hitting her.

She searched frantically for an explanation of this unexpected phenomenon and after a few seconds noticed a faint shimmer in the air right in front of her. She raised her fingertips to touch it and hastily pulled them back again when she felt a slight charge tingle on her skin.

Somehow she had managed to protect herself with magic! And it seemed like they couldn't get through to her.

Now all of them aimed their palms at her, letting loose strikes. Every single one of them was stopped before they could harm her. They tried again and again, but to no avail.

They looked pale, she saw. Afraid? She didn't want to wait around to find out but instead inched slowly towards the door, which two magicians still guarded with panicked expressions.

"Run! Get Lord Enric! NOW!" the old magician's voice boomed urgently.

The two of them were frozen in shock for a moment longer, then took off instantly, leaving the door open behind them. Eryn slipped through it and started to run, aware that the magicians were following her closely.

She turned left where she remembered the entrance had been, slithering along the smooth floor. She had to get out of here quickly before they managed to stop her somehow.

She heard another volley of bolts hit her shield and looked back to the men who quickly ducked into a niche as if afraid that she would return the attack.

Realisation dawned on her. That was exactly why they were hiding – they had no idea she didn't know how to return the attacks! For all they knew she could be shooting back any moment.

She had almost reached the large entrance hall when several more bolts hit the barrier without any sign of disrupting it. She wondered why they didn't stop when it was obvious that it had no effect on her.

Then it suddenly occurred to her that it *had* an effect. They were stalling her. Hadn't they sent for somebody? A lord or some such? And it was working, too: she had slowed down each time they had attacked her.

Determined not to accommodate them any further, she hastily grabbed the heavy iron ring to pull one door wing open when she heard a loud, authoritative voice behind her shout, "Cease your attacks!"

A quick glance over her shoulder revealed the source of the voice. A man in his mid-thirties, tall and slim, clad in blue robes approached her briskly, apparently not fearing an attack like the others.

He radiated confidence, wore it like a second skin. And he looked determined. He stopped between the pillars, raised his palm and without even a moment's hesitation released a strike of energy.

She stared in utter disbelief at his resolutely set face, the lips pressed into a thin line, the frown between his brows, taking in all these meaningless details with impossible clarity, and slowly folded at her knees.

The pain where his bolt had hit her right in the chest was already being dampened by the blackness that had her in its grip even before she hit the floor.

CHAPTER 4

The Testing

The young King watched both of them incredulously, his blue-grey eyes narrowed. "What was that?"

The older of the two robed figures, Lord Tyront, spoke again, "The captive, she has magic abilities."

The King shook his head in disbelief, making the few blond curls that escaped the short ponytail at his neck dance with the movement. "How is this possible? There has not been a gifted woman in more than three hundred years... You are absolutely certain?"

Well, Enric, the younger magician thought laconically, at least the boy knew his history even if his lack of trust in his highest-ranking magicians left a lot to be desired. He still found it hard to look to this man of twenty-five years and see the sovereign of an entire country.

But thinking back, King Folrin had been twenty-two years old when he had taken the throne after his father's death. Exactly as old as he himself had been when he had been elevated to the place at Tyront's right hand.

The King's advisors Marrin and Loft exchanged glances and Loft then enquired, "How strong is she? And how old?"

It cost Enric quite some effort to refrain from rolling his eyes in annoyance. Subtlety had never been one of Loft's character traits. He was obviously already planning to strengthen the royal bloodline with a magically gifted heir to the throne – despite the laws against it and their historic foundation. The idea was doubtlessly to help the future rulers to more independence from the magicians and thus weaken the Order.

Politics, Enric sighed within himself. He was not a great fan of it, but one could hardly survive in his position without paying close attention to it. Tyront was much better at it, but then he'd had two decades' more experience.

"She must be a few years younger than Lord Enric and is unusually strong," Tyront answered. "It's hard to say exactly how strong she is, but she withstood several magicians who tried to stop her."

"How then did you manage to subdue her?" Marrin enquired.

"Lord Enric was able to penetrate her shield and stun her."

The King nodded slowly. "So at least we know that she is not stronger than the two of you. That is a great relief."

"Yes," Enric agreed, "but there are probably not too many of us stronger than her."

"How many of your men did she hold off?" Loft asked.

"Seven," he answered and was secretly delighted at Loft's obvious discomfort. He just didn't like the man.

"When she is so hard to control we should probably kill her if she doesn't cooperate."

Enric forced himself to remain impassive. Ever-so-careful Loft, if something or somebody couldn't be exploited in a way that fit his limited view of the world, then one better got rid of it quickly.

"That might be premature and rather extreme," Tyront retorted with a disapproving frown. "This is the first time in many generations we have encountered a female magician. This is a very rare chance for us, there is so much we can learn."

"Well," Loft conceded airily, "there is always the chance to shackle her in gold to make her cooperate."

"Being shackled in gold will hardly make her cooperate. It will just make her helpless, angry and bitter," Tyront said mildly. Enric envied him his patience.

The King started to show first signs of impatience. "Well, if she is so strong, she might be dangerous to us. Can we find out how strong she really is? Don't you usually test young magicians by setting them against a few older ones to gauge their strength?"

Tyront nodded. "Yes, though we don't let them fight, as fighting skills and experience can still lead to a stronger magician's defeat. The one to be tested raises a shield and magicians then try to break through it. And according to the amount of strength necessary to do that the magician will be classified and then assigned his place in the hierarchy."

Marrin pursed his lips. "This would mean that she might be entitled to a high position among your magicians if she is as strong as you suspect."

"Only if she willingly joined the Order."

"You can hardly consider this seriously! She might be a spy, a criminal!" Loft flourished his hands in wide dramatic gestures.

Tyront's quiet voice gave away nothing of the anger churning inside him. "She has been questioned as to that and has answered truthfully. We used magic to make sure of it. We would be honoured to have her. It has for five hundred years been our duty to protect the kingdom. Pushing strong magicians aside is not how we have accomplished this in the past. Strong magicians mean a strong kingdom."

Marrin silenced his colleague with a piercing look before he could reply and said, "As your Order's first duty is the protection of the kingdom, fighting skills have always been a priority."

Tyront saw where this was heading. "Yes, we would have to train her so she could join us. Though of course there are two major considerations. First, is it wise to train a captive in the art of fighting and second, will she agree? We did not exactly make a favourable first impression on her, I dare say." Not entirely without reason, he had to admit. People did, after first being interrogated and then struck down, have a tendency to react in a *slightly* irritated manner.

Marrin nodded. "Well, I don't really see how the second point can be much of a problem, as people are queueing to be accepted into the Order rather than trying to avoid it. But for reasons of safety I admit to having objections to training a captive who would in time easily be able to defeat many of the other magicians. Letting her escape is too dangerous already, let alone when she is trained." Then another thought came to his mind. "You said she had a shield up? Does this mean she already has the mastery of combat skills?"

Enric shook his head. "I don't think so. She never once returned the attack. The shield seemed to be more a matter of luck than skill, from what I was told. She was clearly surprised that she could conjure one and even more so that it was tough enough to withstand so many of us."

"She discovered shielding *by accident*?" Marrin was obviously not very happy about that.

Tyront tried to conciliate him, "This is not unusual. When under considerable stress, magicians sometimes instinctively discover certain skills that ensure their survival."

Marrin shot him an annoyed look. "Don't use your placatory voice on me. I am well aware of how rarely this happens. The last time was twenty years ago, when a certain young boy," he nodded at Enric, "had a chance epiphany of how to look through solid stone walls by making them transparent. Though I fail to see how his survival was dependent on that skill at that time," he added dryly.

Enric grinned at Marrin. He remembered it well. They had found him out when he and Kilan had used his newly acquired skill to satisfy their adolescent curiosity about the other sex. Watching through walls at the women bathing had been a marvellous but brief pleasure before they had been caught and disciplined. What he had realised only too late was that if they were in a position to look inside, those in the bath were just as able to spot him and his friend. Still, he hadn't regretted a moment of it.

The day he was tested and named second in command of the Order couldn't have been a very joyful one for Marrin who had always considered him a bad influence on his own son.

Enric remembered seeing him cover his eyes in exasperation when the results were announced twelve years back. But since then they had learned to work together and even respect and rely on each other to a certain degree.

Marrin tried to maintain a serious expression but could not suppress the slight smile and humorous glint in his eyes completely.

The King folded his arms. "Then the next step would obviously be to test her strength. Where is she now?"

"She is still unconscious from Lord Enric's stun, but we expect her to wake within the next three hours. We should be ready to test her by then."

King Folrin nodded. "Good. I want to see this. We will do it in the throne room." He lifted his hand when Loft took a breath to object. "And don't tell me it's too dangerous. I dare say she will not be stronger or faster than all present magicians together, even in the unlikely case she decides to attack me."

* * *

Eryn woke with a light headache. It took her a few seconds to figure out what had happened. She remembered magic flying through the air, towards her. The first strikes hitting her full on and bringing her to her knees, the subsequent ones being unexpectedly deflected by what turned out to be a magical barrier she herself must have raised. Her slow retreat, when she had realised that the confusion and urgency on the robed figures' faces meant that they couldn't stop her. Her relief that she had been able to withstand their attacks and then, all of a sudden, the tall figure in dark blue robes who had entered the hall, targeted her with a stare and barked a command that had the other magicians stop their attack. Then he had unleashed a single pale bolt of force from his palm that had curved towards her and right through her barrier.

Her last memories before collapsing on the cold stone floor were of pain and of the tall man moving towards her with long tense strides while the world around her was beginning to tilt.

They had put her in what appeared to be a cell. The windows were barred and apart from the plank bed she sat on, the only other thing to break the monotony of grey stone around her was a wooden door with a small barred aperture at eye level.

Only then did she look down and saw the golden manacles around her wrists. Golden manacles? Why would anybody chain their captives in gold? It was too soft a metal and, of course, too expensive. Was this meant as a blatant demonstration of wealth?

But maybe there were not solid gold but just covered with a thin layer thereof. Still decadent, but a lot less costly. She tried to scratch away a little with her fingernail to check, but to no avail. Was gold even soft enough for that? She knew that a few metals were.

She examined the shackles and was surprised to find no seam or clasp. How had they got them onto her wrists? Had they forged them on? There were no burning marks or the like on her skin, so if they had, the smith must have learned to do this with immense precision.

A few calming breaths released enough tension for her to focus on the internal damage survey she tended to do whenever she fell or was ill.

But this time there was nothing, complete emptiness. The signals her head sent downwards did not trigger the usual response. She felt her heartbeat quicken. What had they done to her? Had it even been them or had she lost her magic for some other reason? Was it maybe a shock reaction or some such? And if yes, was the effect reversible? Would her powers return to her or be gone forever?

She forced herself not to give in to the panic that wanted to burst out. First she would try to get somebody to talk to her and ask a few questions. There would very likely be enough time to panic after that. And maybe create panic, as well.

She slowly got up from the bed and carefully approached the door. Just as she was about to raise her fists to bang them against it, the key in the lock was turned from the other side and she jumped back a step when it opened wide. Two men in dark grey uniforms embroidered with the royal crest beckoned for her to step between them.

"Where are you taking me?"

"To a room where you can wash and change your clothes."

That didn't sound too bad, she decided. It would probably not make much sense to ask them why her magic was gone. They either wouldn't know or not be allowed to tell her. So she followed the first guard silently while the second one trailed behind her.

They left the underground prison and entered what had to be the passageways of a palace. They stopped in front of dark wooden double doors and opened one wing for her to enter.

"Come out again when you are finished." With this they all but pushed her inside.

This was something completely different from the cell before. It was a luxurious room for a high-ranking guest with tall shining furniture and a bed that would comfortably provide sleeping space for a family of four. The tall windows let in the dull light of a rainy evening.

On a small round table underneath a broad mirror framed in the same dark wood stood a large bowl filled with steaming water, as well as a piece of soap, clean towels and a hair brush. On the bed lay a dark green linen tunic with brown leggings and a pair of black leather boots stood on the floor next to it.

Further investigation of the room showed another small table with a tray of food on it. She dismissed the chunk of bread, meat and vegetables. Eating was the last thing on her mind.

It seemed they wanted her presentable, so there was a good chance she was meant to meet somebody who could answer her questions.

Looking around to make sure she really was alone, she quickly undressed and started washing. The manacles were an annoying obstacle but she managed to work around and under them. A look into the mirror made her sigh at the dusty rumpled mass of hair that seemed now rather grey than brown. She washed it as well as she could and then dressed in the clean clothes. With nimble fingers she braided the freshly combed hair into a long plait that fell down her back. After a last glance in the mirror she decided she was ready and opened the door.

*   *   *

The entire room filled with fair haired men of different shapes and ages fell silent when the guards opened the doors to lead her in. She swallowed and looked around. The giant hall had to be three stories high. A quick assessment showed that it had to be the throne room and the young man with the small band of gold around his head standing on the dais surrounded by a group of people seemed to be the throne's current occupant. King Folrin.

Robed figures stood to one side of the hall and kept talking excitedly among themselves. She could read different expressions in what she estimated had to be at least 30 pairs of eyes. Some showed curiosity, others worry, many eyed her suspiciously and a few seemed nervous.

A man with grey streaks in his yellow hair, clad in dark red robes approached her and dismissed her guardians with a nod. Then he turned to her. Pale blue eyes inspected her and he seemed satisfied with what he saw.

"My name is Lord Tyront," he introduced himself. "I preside over the Order of Magicians in this kingdom. We have brought you here to test you."

"What?" Her voice echoed eerily through the large room.

"We will test your magical strength."

Her eyes wandered once more over the assembled figures and an unpleasant suspicion started to rise.

"How?"

He followed her gaze. Her last encounter with magic had been only few hours ago, and it had been far from pleasant, he mulled. She would undoubtedly not be enthusiastic about having it repeated like this. But that couldn't be helped.

"You will form a shield in front of you, just like you did last time. My magicians will try to penetrate it and from the amount of strength that is necessary to break it we will see how much power you have."

"There are a lot of you," she said dryly, hoping that sarcasm would cover the panic that threatened to overwhelm her. "I suppose this time I will take a lot more damage. There is no more power in me."

He smiled. "No, this time we will be more... careful. As for the other..." His hands reached up to her manacles and opened them with a quick stab of energy.

She inhaled deeply as she felt the familiar flow of energy return into her.

"How is this possible?"

"Gold has a naturally balancing effect on magic. This in combination with the right enchantment effectively blocks the magical abilities of the wearer."

She then closed her eyes and did the internal examination that had not worked in the cell. Everything was as it was supposed to be. He could see the relief in her eyes when she opened them again.

"I thought I had lost it."

Then she saw *him*, standing tall in blue robes, looking at her. She took a step back.

"My shield was broken without any effort by a single man," she said, flustered.

Tyront didn't have to turn to know who had put that expression on her face. "True. But he is no ordinary magician, he is the second most powerful one in the kingdom. We need to know how big the gap between your power and his is and how many of us are stronger than you. You have managed to keep seven of us at bay with no apparent effort. That makes us rather nervous, as you might imagine."

Now she tore her appalled gaze away from Enric and looked back at Tyront.

"I promise you, I do not intend to harm you or anybody else. If you just let me leave, I will stay out of your way," she pleaded.

He shook his head in regret. "I'm afraid that is not possible right now. Raise your shield now, child. We are about to begin."

Raise her shield? How had she even done that? Fear for her life and anger must have triggered some kind of reaction, she thought and remembered the pain when she had been hit by magic. Pain that was about to be inflicted on her again as she lacked the knowledge how to consciously protect herself.

"No," she panted, "leave me alone! You have no right to do this to me!"

Her voice was shrill from fear and she started to run for the door through which she had entered the hall.

Only a few steps before she would have reached it, the impact of what felt like a punch knocked her back and to the ground. She looked up in confusion and could only then sense more than see the pale blue, shimmering barrier in front of her.

A heavy hand closed around her wrist and pulled her back to her feet with considerable strength. Tyront's faintly lined mouth was set in a grimace.

"You had better raise your shield now or this will get very painful for you." With this he dropped her arm and stepped away from her.

At his signal the first magician across the room aimed his palm at her and loosed a stream of light and energy that hit her directly in the chest.

The exploding pain knocked her to her knees and she didn't see Tyront's hand signal that stopped the attack. He waited for her to get back to her feet before he gave the signal again.

She saw the magician, who had to be about her age, frown and hesitate. Attacking an unprotected target did not seem to sit well with him. Tyront shot him a stern look and the man gave in and resumed his assault.

Fresh waves of agony soared through her and took her breath away. She frantically searched her memory for how she had done it last time, but to no avail.

A few seconds later the onslaught paused again and Tyront grabbed her by the shoulders and shook her angrily.

"You foolish woman, you either raise that shield NOW or I will make sure..." He stopped when she whispered something weakly. "What?"

"I can't. I don't know how," she forced out.

She still trembled slightly from the streaks of energy that had been shot at her.

"What do you mean, you can't? You did it before!"

He sighed exasperatedly and let go of her shoulders. Could it really be possible that she had no idea how do it again? In this case he had just unnecessarily exposed her to pain and humiliation.

After breathing in and out slowly to calm himself he said, "Alright. Listen carefully and do what I tell you. Close your eyes. Imagine in the centre of your body a small protective ball of energy." He gave her a few seconds to envision it before he continued, "And now make it expand in all directions by feeding it with magic. Let it pass through your skin and increase in size until it engulfs you completely." He watched the barrier that had emerged around her with relief. "Very good. Now shape the shield. You don't need it behind you and at your sides right now, only in front. Let your energy flow into it and strengthen it. When a strike takes away some of the energy, replenish it from within you." He stepped away from her again. "And now protect yourself."

She saw him once more give the signal and winced when energy was thrown towards her again, only this time it was dispersed along her shield with a crackling noise.

Relieved that the pain was over for the moment, she concentrated on keeping constant the level of energy on her slender protection.

Tyront then pointed his finger at two more robed figures who added their bolts of energy to the first magician's. She felt the power of her barrier drain away more quickly now and concentrated on keeping it strong enough to deflect the attacks. Another two men were added and shortly after two more.

Seven, she quickly counted and swallowed. About that many she had been able to handle before. She shot a hurried glance towards the tall blue-robed man and was relieved to see him standing there with his arms folded without any sign that he intended to join the trial.

The bursts of energy stopped suddenly and Tyront motioned for seven more men to come forward while dismissing the others from before. Now one after the other started battering her shield until all seven of them were firing at her. These were noticeably stronger than their colleagues, and she had to pour new energy into her shield more rapidly now.

Tyront once more gave the halt signal and considered her for a moment before motioning forward a middle-aged man of sturdy built and unusually short hair. The way the others reverently stood aside made her suspect that he was more powerful than he looked.

At his leader's nod he now began striking at her shield and she felt the steady increase in power he put into his attack until he took a deep breath and shot a bright bolt at her.

She raised her arms protectively before her face, but the shield held, even though she had to correct the energy level quickly to keep it from faltering.

The man frowned at her and pursed his lips. He had obviously counted on his last shot to break the barrier around her.

Now Tyront instructed all fifteen magicians to resume their attack and Eryn felt her heart skip a beat. Seven weaker magicians, seven stronger ones and the final strong one. That did not bode well. She put all the strength that was not necessary for standing upright into the shield and felt a wave of relief when she realised that it held. The sizzling and crackling of the magic that was thrown at her prevented her from hearing the commotion that had started but she could see the men whispering and talking frantically.

Enric followed the proceedings mesmerised. It obviously cost her more effort now to stem the flood of strikes, but her shield remained steady and hadn't even flickered once to indicate an imminent collapse. She truly *was* an immensely strong magician.

Tyront caught his eye and gave him a nod.

Eryn swallowed hard and felt her heartbeat quicken even further when she saw him unfold his arms and approach until he stood next to the other fifteen. Immediately after he had started adding his bolts to the others', she felt the drain of energy increase dramatically. Now it was only a matter of time until her barrier would give in. He had been able to break her last one alone and with one single shot. She imagined the combined power of the strikes hitting her and cringed in anticipation.

Tyront looked at her, his expression tense. "How do you feel?"

She shot him a nasty look and hissed, "Like I am being attacked without provocation by cowards in superior numbers."

The anger inside her turned into wild rage and then grew further into something new.

Her vision blurred and she felt how her hands started shaking slightly with the wrath that gathered inside her like a cyclone, whirling and potent, gathering more strength with every moment.

How dared they! Dragging her from her home, shoving her in here, battering at her with their magical powers and expecting her to endure it like a defenceless cornered creature!

She would show them, she swore. She didn't care what damage to herself this would result in, if she would survive it. There was no space left for such considerations, the ferocious urge to act in a way that would displease them, take away some of their power over her, pushed aside even the powerful instinct of self-preservation. Nothing mattered anymore. Better to die quickly than be their plaything for who knew how long.

A strange calm had come over her, detaching her from the situation around her. It was like floating in the eye of the cyclone, watching the goings on around her, but not being part thereof.

Straightening her shoulders, she pressed her lips together. And dropped her shield.

* * *

Enric observed her closely. His approach seemed to have increased her fear considerably. Small wonder, he thought. Their first and only encounter so far had consisting in him knocking her out. There were better ways of introduction, admittedly.

She held off the streams of energy directed towards her even though doing so seemed to become more and more strenuous for her.

Then he saw it, a flicker of defiance in the setting of her face, the squaring of her shoulders and he immediately stopped the flow of his magic and desperately cast a strong barrier between her body and the one she let drop.

* * *

She staggered back when she saw the bolts of energy unexpectedly reflected away from her instead of diving into her body. How…?

Tyront cut off the attacks with an imperious hand gesture and shot her a deadly look before sending a curt nod of approval to the tall blue-robed man who accepted the sign of appreciation silently.

Well, she thought dumbfounded, that was obviously where the second shield had come from.

Tyront's strong hand clamped around her upper arm and all but lifted her off the ground when he whirled her around to face him. She valiantly swallowed a yelp of pain when his fingers dug into her flesh.

"What has gripped you to do such an immensely foolish, idiotic, imbecile thing?" he shouted. The words were reflected from the high domed ceiling which increased the already impressive effect of a powerful voice raised in anger even further. His pale eyes seemed to emit sparks of fury when he continued roaring, "The shock of these combined attacks could have killed you!"

She felt lightheaded, dazed and stared for a few silent moments at him, before to the amazement of all present, she began to laugh. Her guffaws were the only audible sound in the great hall. Only the hand still fixing her upper arm like a vice kept her from doubling over. She dashed away a tear with her free hand and shook her head at him when she felt composed enough to speak.

"Really? You are scolding me because I did not *cooperate*?" Her voice was about to crack. "You drag me in here to scrutinise me, have me panting from pain on the floor and scold me because I do not *comply*? I suppose I should be ashamed of myself and apologise!"

Again she burst out laughing, recognising first signs of hysteria in her own voice.

Tyront's face bespoke of wrath wrapped in iron control to keep his fury from erupting. Enric quickly stepped forward and retrieved the golden manacles that had been fixed around her wrists when she had been brought in.

He didn't know how much longer Tyront would be able to contain himself before lashing out. He caught her hands easily and fastened the golden bands back on with a quick push of power that made the seams of the metal disappear.

She stared at her wrists, then at him and tried to get away, forgetting that Tyront's grasp on her arm made that impossible.

Enric moved his hands smartly, pressing one to her forehead and sending a pulse of energy into it and then keeping her from collapsing to the floor by grabbing her around her centre when her consciousness drained away.

Damn, her last thought was when her knees buckled under her, not *him* again.

Enric looked up at his superior. "Well, that was fun," he commented dryly, shifting her in his arms. "We should definitely repeat that on occasion. Can I do the shouting next time and you knock her out?"

CHAPTER 5

Combat Training

Tyront shook his head, still feeling remainders of the rage which had nearly burst forth, out of control down in the throne room half an hour ago. He sat down in his study while Enric closed the door and took a seat opposite him.

"Third strongest. This is not good, not good at all." Tyront drummed his fingers on his desk restlessly. "You and I are the only ones strong enough to contain her. We can either lock her up, shackle her in gold or act as her wardens around the clock. Neither option is very attractive."

"No," Enric agreed. "Especially as we want to find out more about her abilities. Shackling her and thus stopping her from using them would not make that any easier. But there is not much choice, I am afraid. From what happened today I dare say she will not be too thrilled about the idea of cooperating with us."

"Not thrilled? That's quite an understatement. She almost got herself killed today in no more than stubborn defiance. It's like having an even worse version of the young *you* on my hands again." He rubbed his face with both hands. "I should have taken better care. It was a stroke of luck that you did with that shield of yours."

"Don't blame yourself. Suicide attempts are not usually something we need to be prepared for when magicians are tested. They are more likely afterwards, if they don't make it to the category they wanted," he added laconically. "And I resent your comment about me. I was never suicidal, just lazy and unwilling."

Tyront shook his head. "How can you joke at a time like this? We need to decide what to do with her. Letting her leave is out of the question, even if we can pretty much eliminate the possibility of her being a spy."

"Unless she knows a way how to circumvent a truth block somehow," Enric tossed in.

The older man dismissed that possibility with a hand gesture. "No, I doubt that very much. She could have lied instead and thus kept the secret of her father's and her own powers to herself. That brings us to the question why her father had never considered joining the Order."

"She said something about their having fled from their home country, didn't she? He was probably not sure if we would have sent him back. It might have been a nice way for us to revive our diplomatic relationship with the Western Territories after all that time."

"Probably. And I dare say the King is considering doing exactly that with her now. We might only be able to prevent this by either convincing him that she is more use to us here for the moment or getting her to join the Order. Though I imagine that we have better chances with the King than her."

Enric snorted. "We might have better chances of making Loft shave his head and dance naked in the palace square than making her join us."

"Thank you very much for that image," Tyront replied wryly. "We need to buy time. We should learn as much as possible about her. It has been centuries since anybody has encountered a female magician. She might be able to help us find out why."

"You heard Loft," Enric said. "He is thinking about using her to provide a magical heir to the throne. This is not good and I don't really see how we can prevent it. She might be unusually strong, but if they insist on shackling in her in gold that will not make a difference."

"Yes. That is something to consider. History has shown us that magic powers and the Crown are not something we want to have embodied in the same person again. But we don't know if the King himself is thinking about it. Let's hope it is just one of Loft's little ideas that will be forgotten soon enough."

The younger man stretched his long legs and crossed his ankles. "The King is awaiting our report about the testing. What do you want to tell him?"

"The truth, of course. It's not as if I could tell him anything else. He was there and witnessed everything, after all." He smiled. "And I will add that she would be a valuable addition to the Order and that it will be no problem at all to keep her here until she has decided to join us, as you and I are both stronger than her."

Enric rolled his eyes. "Yes - a nice and cheery prospect with no downsides whatsoever. So one of us will always be at her side to keep her from running?"

"That will not be necessary. We will put her in a room at the warriors' quarters. There will be plenty of magicians around her to at least slow her down until we arrive in case she tries anything. And I will have a pair of eyes on her at all times so we would be notified as quickly as possible if our intervention is required. I assume the King won't have objections to this. Unfortunately, we need to seek his permission for everything pertaining to her as long as she has not joined us."

"Whose custody do you want to place her in, then?"

"I was thinking about your old fighting trainer, Lord Orrin." He smirked when Enric started laughing.

"Very good. He will be so thrilled. Too much time has passed since he had to train an unwilling magician who was stronger than him and showed no respect. Can *I* tell him?"

Tyront shook his head indulgently at this rare display of youthful joy. "No, I think rather not. Watching your delight, I am convinced that might not be such a good idea. We wouldn't want him to think he is being punished for something. And that's definitely the impression *you* would convey."

Enric sighed in mock hurt. "Your low opinion of me pains me. I would never make him think it was something as petty as a punishment. I was thinking more along the lines of good old revenge. Do you have any idea how often he has made me polish the damn practice swords? All of them! There must have been a hundred or more of those bloody things."

"I seem to remember a little… accident where all of them were somehow melted into a great puddle of metal?" Tyront commented with raised brows.

"True," Enric smiled at the memory of Orrin's reaction back then, but when he remembered the consequences the smile disappeared. "A lot of good that did me. He sent me to assist the smith with forging new ones. I was stuck in the hot, stuffy, stinking smithy for almost an entire month. Never before in my life have I sweated that much. And not since. That was when I decided that a nice position in administration or archiving would be just the thing for me." He chuckled. "But I did learn a lot about forging weapons. The smith even helped me craft a very nice sword for myself. He had received quite a large order for new swords due to me, after all. I think it was a roundabout, non-official way of thanking me."

"Yes," Tyront retorted, "where would our craftsmen be without wilful, adolescent rebels bent on destruction?"

"Underutilised, I dare say. And yet I have never received any thanks for my efforts to serve the common good, but was scolded and punished instead."

"Well, what can I say, dear boy? The world is unjust."

Enric grinned broadly. "Not anymore. Justice is about to enter Orrin's life."

* * *

Eryn opened her eyes slowly, staring at yet another stone ceiling. Somehow she managed to stumble into situations that resulted in her waking up from unconsciousness in unfamiliar surroundings. This was the third time in less than five days. She really needed to work on lowering that frequency.

She slowly turned her head and looked straight into the bright green eyes of a sturdily built, middle-aged man with a thin scar running down his right cheek. He looked familiar.

She thought for a few seconds and then remembered seeing him at the testing. He was the one with the strong bolt. The scar had not been visible from the distance.

After spending two nights in a room with the two soldiers that had brought her here, waking up with a stranger looking at her did not alarm her much.

What a long way she had come in such a short time, she mused sleepily, still a little slow after just waking.

A few days ago she would probably have jumped up in terror and started throwing things at an intruder. How quickly attitudes could change. She was not at all thrilled about the direction these changes took, though. She shuddered at what kind of things she would probably get used to after a few weeks in their tender care here.

She returned her attention back to the man with the scar and noted that he wasn't wearing robes but was dressed in dark brown leather armour.

"Welcome back among the living," he said with a reverberating voice. It was the voice of either a singer or somebody who was very used to bellowing loudly. She doubted very much that he was the artistic type. Judging from his attire and the muscles outlined under his shirt he definitely appeared as more like the fighting kind.

Memories of her father talking angrily about the Order of Magicians and their waste of magic for fighting rose up again.

Sitting up slowly, she took in the very small room she was in. "Where am I this time?"

It didn't look like a prison cell as there were no bars in front of the small window, but it was hardly larger or more comfortable than one.

The bed was narrow and hard and, apart from a small table with a bowl for washing and a small mirror above it, contained not much more than a chest that was obviously intended for clothes and a few personal belongings. Right now the man was using it as a seat due to the absence of alternatives.

"These are your quarters for the time being," he answered and smiled at her reaction of displeasure.

She thought back at her little house with its bright wooden floors, the dried herbs in picture frames on the walls, the blankets and soft cushions, the fireplace with her father's old, comfortable chair placed in front of it, the shelves filled with numerous books and the ever-present scent of drying herbs in the air.

"Cosy. You certainly know how to make newcomers welcome. If I had known this was waiting for me I might have given myself up years ago."

"Think of it as an alternative to a dungeon cell or sleeping out in the street. This is a regular room for a trainee magician. So you are not the only one who has to put up with this, if this is any consolation."

"Great. This will doubtlessly warm my heart when I wake up here in the morning. Misery does so appreciate company. I suppose you don't reside in one of those charming little closets yourself?"

One corner of his mouth curved upwards slightly. "No. I live in very nice, spacious quarters. I was, in fact, about to offer you a nice hot drink there if you would care to join me."

She stared at him. "Join you? I don't even know who you are! I don't normally have a habit of following strangers into their homes even if they promise me nice things. In fact, *especially* not if they promise me nice things."

"I should probably have introduced myself. My name is Lord Orrin. I will work with you on your fighting skills." He rose and waited for her to do the same.

"My *what*?" she asked flatly. This had to be some kind of surreal dream; he could not possibly have said what she had understood. What sense did it make to teach a prisoner how to fight? Where they even crazier than her father had thought?

"The Order has decided that we need to learn more about the nature of your magic and the best way for us to find out how you handle it is by comparing it with what we are good at. And that is combat."

Yes, definitely crazy, she decided.

"Come now," the man who called himself Lord Orrin said and stepped outside into a dusky corridor, "Let's talk in my quarters. I promise you have nothing to fear from me."

She remained seated for another few moments while she considered his words. He could hardly be more dangerous to her in his quarters than in this very confined space, could he? And why take the trouble of bringing her somewhere else for any dark deeds if this here was an enclosed, undisturbed space already?

Not a great risk then, she decided, and rose to follow him out of the depressing cell into a hardly less dismal corridor. If his quarters really were as comfortable as he said she could at least spend some time in more pleasant surroundings.

"You are a fighting instructor, then?" she asked when she walked one step behind him. They reached a junction after which the way became broader and less gloomy.

"No, I'm a stable boy," he replied sarcastically without turning around. "Of course I teach fighting."

So much for conversation, she thought, and decided to keep her mouth shut for now.

They climbed a flight of stairs and then another before they finally stopped in front of a large door. He gripped the handle, turned it and entered first, waiting for her to step inside so he could close the door again.

She looked around curiously and decided immediately that his lodgings were definitely superior to the ones she had been given. The room they were in was large, and bright daylight streamed in through two large windows. Several broad leather chairs were grouped around a heavy looking stone table. The overall colours were brown, black and dark red. Definitely a man's place, no female hand visible here: no flowers, embroidery or the like.

Suddenly one of four doors that led from the room opened without warning and a lean boy of no more than fifteen years stormed out.

"Father, have you seen my…"

His voice trailed off in surprise when he saw Eryn. He stared at her with his mouth open until Orrin cleared his throat loudly enough to snap him out of his rigid pose. Blinking rapidly a few times he seemed to find back to himself and remember his manners.

"Good day to you. My name is Vern, Orrin is my father."

He bowed and beamed at her. They were about the same height, only he looked like he was not fully grown yet. His limbs seemed slightly too long for his body and he had yet to grow into his large ears and teeth.

"Hello. I am Eryn." She gave him a polite nod.

"Is it true that you are a spy and have defeated twenty magicians?"

She felt almost sorry to disappoint the boy with the hopeful shine in his eyes and the delighted voice.

"No, I'm afraid I am no more than a humble healer with no inclination whatsoever towards spying. And I didn't defeat anybody. Sorry to disappoint you." She smiled despite herself.

He dismissed this with a generous wave of his hand. "Oh no, not at all." His gaze flicked to her unusual hair colour and then returned to her eyes. "But you have magic, don't you?"

"That I do, yes."

His grin widened again. "I have never seen a female magician! Nobody here has for more than two hundred years!"

"Three hundred years," his father corrected.

His son shot him an annoyed look as if he did not at all appreciate being corrected and thus exposed in front of the woman everybody was currently talking about.

The son seemed so young, she thought. Had she ever been that young? She was fifteen when her father had died. That had been her final push into early adulthood, even though she had started her training as a healer much younger.

Vern smirked when he saw a way to pay his father back. "Won't you take a seat and have something to drink, Eryn? It seems my father has forgotten his manners."

Eryn suppressed a smile when she saw Orrin roll his eyes. "Yes, thank you very much, Vern. Your father has so far not impressed me as somebody who bothers much with manners."

This seemed to please the boy immensely, judging from his grin. He indicated one of the chairs for her to sit in and turned around to prepare a drink for her.

"That's what our servant Moran says," he informed her conversationally. "She thinks he needs a companion to keep him connected to civilised people that sometimes talk instead of attacking each other with swords."

Orrin took a seat as well and pinched the bridge of his nose. "I think that's enough, son. What was it you were looking for?"

"What?" He stared at his father, drink in hand. In the excitement of meeting Eryn, Vern obviously had forgotten what had been troubling him before. "Oh," he said, remembering, "just for my new blue vest. I want to wear it tomorrow when we meet Lord Tyront."

Orrin saw her stiffen at the mention of the name.

"Moran had to take it away to have a stain removed." He shot his son a disapproving glance. "Its colour seems to shed light on the matter of my missing wine bottles from last month."

Vern turned pasty and swallowed. "Why don't I leave you two alone? I'm sure there is a lot you need to discuss."

Self-preservation had won over curiosity, but only barely. He placed a steaming cup in front of Eryn and his father both and gave her a crooked smile before disappearing swiftly back into the room he had walked out of before.

Orrin lifted the cup and took a careful sip. It seemed the encounter with his son had relaxed her a little, he noticed.

"So, you are from the Western Territories, they say," he remarked.

"No," she smiled sweetly, "I just rub dirt into my hair to seem more exotic in a place of fair-haired people. I do so enjoy the attention."

It was a small triumph to see him scowl, but in a situation like hers even small things such as getting even for a sarcastic remark were worth having.

"Your training starts tomorrow morning. To start with I will teach you separately until you have mastered the basics and then continue with..."

He stopped when she shook her head and lifted her hands, palms facing away from her.

"I have no intention whatsoever to learn fighting. In my opinion, it is a gross waste of time. Furthermore, I am a captive here. Why should I be concerned with complying with your demands? So I will save you the trouble of waiting for me tomorrow." She downed the rest of her drink with a quick motion, and rose. "You can put me back in that cell now or transfer me to a dungeon or whatever you do here with troublemakers."

"Sit down."

Orrin spoke quietly but she could hear the authority behind the words. Her knees wanted to buckle obediently and make her sit down again, but she forced them to withstand the impulse and remained standing, folding her arms in front of her.

His gaze turned to steel when she didn't move and almost too quickly for her to see he lifted his palm and she felt something intangible push her back and off her feet so that she landed in the seat again, not able to move. He looked at her coldly and folded his fingers.

"This is what will happen if you refuse," he said mildly as if talking about the weather. "You may be very strong, but as long as you are wearing the gold, this will not make any difference."

Then he got up from his seat and walked around the little table between them to where Eryn was still pinned helplessly. He leaned forward until his face was close enough for her to see the flecks of grey in his green eyes.

"Don't make the mistake of thinking I am soft or weak because you saw me with my son. I will come for you tomorrow morning. I will be at your door at sunrise. If you don't open it at my knocking, I will break it down, throw you over my shoulder and carry you to the training grounds. Do you understand?"

He waited a few moments for her to speak and when she only stared at him blankly, he gave a tiny smile.

"You will not get up from this chair until you have answered me. Do you understand? I will not ask a third time."

"Yes, Orrin," she hissed. "I do understand you. I am neither deaf nor stupid."

He straightened again. "Good. And it is customary to address a high-ranking magician using the title *Lord*."

She smiled acidly. "Is it now? Thank you so much for enlightening me as to this charming little custom, *Orrin*."

He had to admire her guts. She was pinned down under his force field defencelessly and yet still defiant.

Returning to his seat, he kept the field, and thus Eryn, fixed in place.

"We will start with the basics such as using a sword, building your muscles, working on your speed and agility. This will keep us busy for the first few months."

He noted how her eyes widened at his last words. It seemed that she had not really counted on being kept here for such a long time.

"After this," he continued, "we will start using magic to further improve your skills."

Months, she thought numbly. She would have to stay here for *months*. Wearing these infernal golden manacles for months. Sleeping in this confined little cell for months. She swallowed and closed her eyes for a moment. No forest, no healing, no freedom.

Orrin watched her. "It will be easier if you work *with* us instead of fighting us, Eryn." The acerbity was gone from his voice.

Then he lifted the field and she regained control over her muscles. He rose and motioned for her to follow him.

"Come. It's getting dark and you should go to bed early. You will need all your strength tomorrow."

They didn't speak on their way back to the room she had woken up in. When they had reached it he opened the door for her, waited until she had entered and closed it behind her. As an afterthought, he created a shield in front of the door to keep her inside in case she got any wayward ideas.

* * *

She listened for his steps until she was sure that he had left the corridor, then she waited a little longer before opening the door as quietly as possible and leaning forward to see if anybody was there. She recoiled when she felt something hit her forehead and cursed colourfully when she realised that he had penned her in with a magical barrier.

She paced the small, narrow room as far as this was possible without constantly hitting her knees and shins.

"Think!" she commanded herself. There had to be a way out of here.

She looked at the small window. Would she fit through it if she squeezed hard enough? Probably. But what then? With her ability to shield herself blocked she would not make it very far. And if that blue-robed bastard was anywhere close, not even that would help.

She inspected the manacles again, and just like before saw that the metal was smooth and in one piece. Gold was soft, wasn't it? She started rubbing it hard against the bedstead and checked to see if she had made a dent, a scratch, anything. Nothing. The gold remained unblemished. So the spell the leader of the Order had mentioned seemed to have strengthened the gold. That was unfortunate, but hardly a surprise.

She let her head sink into her hands and felt tears building behind her eyelids. She was used to solitude, to the necessity of staying away from others in order to protect her secret.

But the emptiness inside her due to the block on her powers hurt almost physically. It was as if the very thing she had worked on protecting all her life was out of reach, taken from her, vanished. Just like everything else she had ever possessed.

* * *

Eryn was awake long before sunrise. She sat on her bed, her back leaning against the wall and waited with her eyes closed.

She had been sitting like this for quite some time before the first knocks came. She could feel the tension in the pause that followed while the caller waited for her to open the door. A second series of knocks came, this time more of a pounding.

She had moved the chest in front of the door. It was not exactly a serious obstacle, though - more of a gesture of defiance. Symbolic. Just in case ignoring the caller didn't convey the message of her unwillingness to cooperate emphatically enough.

The door flew open with a loud crash and hit the wall, revealing Orrin, whose expression was not in the least surprised, but instead determined. Without a word he glanced at the splinters of wood between the door and the wall that had once been a chest and then back at her.

His smile was grim when he stepped into the cell, grabbed one of her wrists and pulled her without any apparent effort up to her feet. He bent down, yanked her close and when he straightened again, she felt his shoulder push against her abdomen and lift her off her feet.

When she started kicking, he caught the backs of her knees with his forearm and pushed them down to stop it. The fists hammering on his back he simply ignored, like the unflattering names she was calling him.

True to Orrin's word, he carried her all the way to the arena. She saw early risers on the adjacent streets and the training grounds stop whatever they were doing to turn and watch the unusual sight of the combat trainer carrying a strange-looking and obviously displeased woman over his shoulder.

* * *

Enric and Tyront each stood with a warm drink in hand in Enric's study as the window afforded a clear view of the training grounds.

Both of them narrowed their eyes when they saw the familiar figure of Orrin step out the door, a writhing brown-haired, female slung over his shoulder.

Tyront whistled through his teeth. "It looks like those two didn't get off to a very good start."

"No," Enric agreed with a thin smile, "and he hasn't even given her a weapon yet. That is going to be fun to watch."

That earned him a frown. "You should not rejoice in Orrin's difficulties. We are all on the same side. Or supposed to be," he scolded, but Enric did notice that he, too, couldn't help watching the spectacle unrolling on the other side of the square.

They saw Orrin bend down and put her back to her feet. When she tried to kick him, he quickly jumped back and then swept her legs from under her with a nimble movement. She landed hard on her back and looked up at him standing in front of her, his legs astride and his arms folded.

A young student of his came running from one side, holding two wooden practice swords in one hand and hurriedly offered them to the waiting magician.

Orrin grabbed both and tossed one of them on the ground next to Eryn's hand. She struggled to her feet, ignoring the blunt stick completely.

"Oh dear," Enric shook his head. "This is going to be painful for her."

One moment later they saw the magician hit her with his training sword on her upper arm. They were too far away and more guessed than actually heard her outcry, but both of them contorted their faces in sympathy. That had looked painful.

"Do you think she will pick up the training weapon?" Enric asked after taking another sip from his cup.

"I dare say she will. The question is how many of his strikes she will take first."

"I bet one gold piece that it will be no more than four. She is a fast learner."

Tyront chuckled. "Alright. I say she will take at least seven. She may learn quickly, but her pride is quite the obstacle to overcome first."

Both of them fished a small gold piece from their pockets and put it on the windowsill in front of them.

"The winner is the one closest to the actual number," Tyront said.

"That was number two," Enric commented when Eryn had taken another strike on her right upper leg.

"Three," Tyront counted the hit on her right hand and added "Four," when Orrin hit the other hand as well as she clutched them together.

"She starts moving out of the way," Enric noticed her narrowly avoid a hit to her left shoulder.

"Five," Tyront said. That had been the right shoulder.

"Six," Enric sighed when she still had not picked up the wooden sword and he had thus lost the gold piece. "That was the same thigh as before. Ouch."

They saw her then crouch and quickly grab the sword to inexpertly block the next strike that was aimed at her side.

"And again he has managed it." Tyront smiled. "I dare say the young lady will sport quite a few bruises. Six of them, to be precise, which is just a little closer to my number than yours."

He grabbed both gold pieces and let them disappear into his pocket with a satisfying jingling noise.

CHAPTER 6

Desperate Measures

Eryn dragged herself back to the little room after yet another day of torture. The third day, to be precise.

She had more bruises than she could count and her muscles were sore from the unfamiliar exercise. There was not a single movement apart from breathing and blinking that didn't hurt somewhere. And, of course, the gold around her wrists prevented her from healing herself.

Orrin had started the day just like the two before them by hitting her to make her block his attacks and then in the afternoon had switched to throwing small pointed objects at her to make her jump out of the way and increase her ability to react, as he had explained.

The first thing she did after returning to the cell each afternoon was to wash her hands and wrists to remove the sand, earth and sweat that clung there between skin and metal and which would otherwise chafe her skin open.

She stared at the bowl of clean water that waited for her every time she returned. It seemed even prisoners were entitled to certain services.

What would they do if she *did* let her skin chafe until it was inflamed and raw? Leave the manacles on? That would increase the pain so much that she would soon be unable to continue her training. They would want to avoid that, wouldn't they?

If they forced her to go on despite the pain, this could seriously endanger her health and if they let it go on for too long, even her life.

She stepped away from the clean water. The logical thing for them to do, then, would be to remove the shackles for at least a short time - so she could heal herself - or to bandage her wrists. And that would return control over her powers to her.

A slow smile spread on her lips. She moved the manacles up as far as possible, drew in a deep breath and started rubbing the skin underneath against the stone wall. She clenched her teeth to keep herself from voicing her agony when the sharp edges cut open the tender skin and forced herself to proceed despite the pain. The burning sensation made her break out in a sweat that clung to her forehead in cold beads.

* * *

Orrin frowned when she dropped the wooden weapon and clutched her wrist in apparent pain. Lowering his own stick he stepped closer and pulled her hand up to inspect it. When she tried to pull away, he just shot her a look and she remained still while he moved the manacle slightly down to catch a glimpse of the skin under it.

He sucked in a sharp breath at the sore and bloody mess underneath. A quick examination of her other hand showed the same injuries.

"What happened to your wrists?" he demanded. "That was not there yesterday!"

She glared at him. "No. It gets worse every day. Have you tried wearing these overtight things for days at a time and then cleaning away all the dirt that has chafed your skin all day long? I have. And let me tell you: it doesn't work very well."

He let go of her hands and stood frowning, considering what to do. Something had to be done, there was no doubt about that. But what? Removing the manacles would return to her the ability to heal, but unfortunately also to shield herself.

Then there was the question of how to proceed after she was healed. The manacles were not usually worn continuously for such a long time. Putting them back on afterwards might lead to the same result in another few days.

He would have to talk about this to Lord Enric. He stepped away from her and lifted his hand to beckon a young boy who was leaning against a wall to come over. Orrin exchanged a few words with him too quietly for Eryn to hear and then the boy ran off across the square towards the palace.

Orrin waited until he saw Lord Enric's tall figure emerge from the palace portal and looked down at Eryn again, who just frowned at him and wondered what he was waiting for. She stood with her back to the palace and didn't see the man approaching from there.

When the warrior raised his hands and removed the shackles, she felt the blocked power flood her body with a force that almost brought her to her knees. She had been put in the damn things before, but not for that long. Once she felt the energy more as a steady flow than a violent rush, she created a shield around herself.

Orrin just sighed and shook his head. "You don't really think I wasn't prepared for that, do you?"

He nodded his chin to something behind her and when she turned, there *he* was, blue robes, grim expression, halfway across the square and getting closer quickly.

Her thoughts raced. Now she had to hurry. A direct confrontation was not an option, but if she managed to keep some obstacle between him and herself, he would most likely not be able to hit her directly.

She looked at the messenger boy who had just returned and grabbed him to pull him inside her shield with her, positioning herself right behind him so his body would protect hers if there was an attack.

"Move and don't do anything stupid, or I will hurt you very badly," she hissed into his ear when he became stiff with fear. She tried to pull him with her but that was no use. He was too afraid and just stood there, shaking and wide-eyed.

A quick scan around helped her estimate a route towards the plainly visible city gate that would cover her as much as possible. She pushed away the boy and started running towards the broad building where the fighters' meals were served three times a day. When she rounded the corner, she heard the impact of strikes hitting the stones of the wall behind her, where she had been only a moment before.

A short sprint brought her behind the next building and thus closer to the gate. A hectic search made her realise that there was no cover available for the wide stretch from her current position to the gate, it was completely open and unprotected. There was nothing. Apart from people.

She heard steps coming closer behind her and started running.

People were, after all, better than nothing. She would stay behind and between them as well as she could, so they instead of her would be hit by the bolts aimed at her.

That was not a merciful thing to do, she knew, especially as a healer was supposed to protect people from damage instead of exposing them to it, but she hoped very much that the blue-robed one wouldn't shoot to kill but, as before, just to incapacitate her. She pushed the question aside of whether he was ordered to kill her if she couldn't be stopped otherwise.

The gates were close enough now for her to see the confused faces of the guards. They had to be aware that they couldn't stop her but she supposed it would nevertheless not look good for them to abandon their posts. So they just stood there, staring at her rapidly approaching form, not daring to take any action.

Fortunately, they had in their stupor not thought of the one thing that would have posed a real problem to her: closing the city gates.

And sure enough, close behind her a loud voice shouted, "Close the gates, now!"

That shout had been much too close, he had gained on her quickly.

The guards remained frozen for another moment, then all at once jumped into frantic action, almost tripping over one another.

She darted between them out the first gate, aiming straight for the opening of the second outer one that they wouldn't possibly be able to close in time to block her exit. Only a few more paces, she thought and ignored the pain in her still unhealed wrists. First things first.

She saw the light shimmer in the air only moments before she would have collided with the barrier. It blocked the entire gate. She turned right into a little turret, expecting stairs or a ladder inside that would enable her to climb the outer wall. But once inside, there was nothing, not a single opening. It was a dead end.

She whirled around to run back outside but the narrow door was blocked. A figure, now unpleasantly familiar, stood in the doorway with folded arms, showing no sign of exhaustion from the chase, even though his blond strands of hair looked a little ruffled.

They stared at each other for a few seconds before he spoke softly. "I would suggest you heal those wrists of yours now before we put the manacles back on. That does look rather painful."

It was over. The thought hit her with aching finality. She had failed. The tension drained out of her muscles and she leaned against the wall behind her, sliding down onto the cold stone floor.

Enric looked down at her without coming any closer. She still had the shield in place, even though she had to be aware that it would not help her at all against him. But who was he to deny a captive a false sense of safety?

He waited. She pulled her knees closer to her chest and looked intently at her lacerated wrists. Then she closed her eyes and he stared spellbound at the wounds that slowly began to regenerate in front of Enric's eyes.

Firstly, the red and bloody flesh smoothened, then a thin layer of skin seemed to grow on it. When the wounds were completely covered with tissue, he watched the last signs of reddened skin disappear and leave her wrists flawless again. His eyes fell on the bluish-green bruises at the back of her hands the first training lesson with Orrin had left. They, too, faded slowly.

When he looked back at her face, he saw her staring at him tensely, especially at the golden shackles he held in one hand. He himself had never worn them for more than a few uncomfortable hours at a time during training lessons. He imagined that having them on for several days was not at all pleasant, being cut off from what was such an essential part of a magician.

He needed to talk to Tyront about it. Keeping her manacled like this was not a permanent solution. He wondered if magicians could go insane if they were deprived of their powers for too long. Better not to test it. But for now there was no other way if he or Tyront didn't intend to guard her personally every minute of the day.

He stepped closer to her and watched her shuffle away from him into a corner, climbing back to her feet awkwardly and looking around frantically in what he assumed was a quick search for any object she could use as a weapon against him.

He narrowly avoided her foot that had aimed for a very painful spot, and caught it without difficulty, making her fight for balance on one leg before dropping it again and grabbing her wrists instead, pinning her into the corner at her back.

He turned them around easily despite her efforts to free herself and let his thumb glide over the smooth skin that had looked raw only minutes before.

"Impressive," he murmured. "What else can you do?"

Break your bones while you are gripping me, shot through her mind before she could stop it. She cringed back from the unbidden memories welling up inside her when she had last done this, and what it had cost her.

He saw her flinch at his question and wondered why such a simple, harmless enquiry seemed to cause her pain.

It was the first time he was so close to her without her being unconscious and he took a few moments to study her.

Her features did not look exotic or foreign, and he could see how changing the colour of her hair had been enough to let her pass as a local woman. Her hair was longer than was currently in fashion among the ladies, probably because her priorities in maintaining appearances were not about drawing admiring glances but keeping them off her altogether.

She was attractive, he mused. Not in the delicate, fragile or carefully assembled way that was so typical for highborn women, but with an energetic radiance that kept her from falling in line with almost all other well-featured females he knew.

Eryn didn't like the way he studied her. He seemed thoughtful and his grip on her wrists was too firm, almost painful. Her shield had not even slowed him down, he had reached right through it. That was not good. He could break her defences even without attacking. How strong did a magician have to be for that? Or was it just a matter of the right technique? But then Orrin, too, would have been able to do it which he clearly wasn't.

Enric seemed to snap out of his deliberations and fastened the manacles back on. The now familiar drain of power inside her and the emptiness it created took away all energy to continue fighting. There was nothing she could accomplish now.

She didn't resist when he took her upper arm and led her outside the turret, where Orrin, six guards and a number of curious onlookers awaited.

Enric handed her over to Orrin, who didn't seem in the least surprised that his superior had been able to apprehend her.

"Meet me in Lord Tyront's study in an hour." He glanced at Eryn. "And make sure she is locked up safely."

Orrin nodded and nudged her to set her in motion towards the dark looming building at the other side of the square, back to her tiny, grey cell with the hard plank bed.

* * *

When Orrin entered his leader's study, Enric was already there and toyed with a small dagger while leaning against the bookshelves that covered three out of four walls from floor to ceiling.

It seemed the younger man was just telling his superior about the interesting morning they'd had.

"We need to do something about the guards on gate duty. There is some training in order. When I told them to shut the gates, they lost precious moments standing around and staring. Without my magical barrier she would have left the city. We should not have to depend on one of us two being around when she tries to walk out of here next time."

"Yes, I see your point. Good morning, Lord Orrin. It seems we have just identified some need for improvements among our guards."

"Good morning to you, Lord Tyront." He inclined his head. "I have already arranged for a training plan." He'd gained first-hand insight into their incompetence, after all.

Tyront nodded in approval. It was typical for the man to notice such details and take care of them immediately, even if he had a larger problem on his hands, such as a powerful magician in his care trying to escape from the city.

"I have watched her heal herself in the turret," Enric continued. "It was impressive. Wounds, bruises - everything just disappeared. That is a very handy skill. I wonder how hard it is to learn. After all, she was trained for several years by her father so it's probably not something you pick up quickly."

"I should think not," Tyront agreed. "We had the books from her house packed up and brought here." He nodded to a pile of wooden creates behind his desk. "I have leafed through a few of them, but I understand hardly anything, they are full of what seem to be medical expressions and drawings. Many of them contain side notes, comments and additions. It seems she or her father or both of them figured out new things and added their own knowledge."

"We need to do something about the manacles," Enric pointed out. "We have no idea how it affects a magician's mind if his powers are blocked for too long. My impression is that she seems to suffer more from the blockage than her captivity. I think we should change the enchantment, weaken it to grant her limited access to her power. Enough to be aware of it and also be able to heal the damage she takes every day during her training."

Orrin frowned. "For this we would need to know how much power healing really requires. If it is too much, she would also be able to shield herself against me, and that would hamper me somewhat," he concluded dryly.

"I suppose asking her does not make much sense. She would try to make us make the blockage as weak as possible. I suggest we reduce it by one third and see what happens. This way you will still have a considerable advantage," Enric said and twirled the dagger between his fingers.

"We should also have the smith reduce the manacles in size. The ones we have were made for the arms of fighting men. That might also reduce the chafing." Orrin waited for them to consider his words.

"Well," Tyront replied, "that should not be a problem. The strength of the binding does not depend on the manacles' shape, so I don't see how making them appear as jewellery should be a problem. Or... just wait a moment."

He rose from his seat and left the study.

They heard him call his companion's name, and after a few minutes he returned with two identical simple, but elegant gold bangles with intricate engravings.

Orrin smiled. "Vyril gave up her jewellery voluntarily?"

Tyront snorted. "I wouldn't say *voluntarily*. She blackmailed me ruthlessly and made me promise her another pair plus earrings."

"Well done, Vyril! Next time make him add a nice necklace," Enric shouted to the still open study door and won a high, clear laugh in reply.

Tyront shook his head at him and closed the door. "What happened to solidarity among men?"

"I don't think there is any between single and attached men. It usually is sacrificed either in favour of envy or pity," Enric laughed and added quickly, "In my case, of course, it's pure envy."

Orrin inspected the golden pieces. They looked nice enough, he supposed, not too fancy for a down-to-earth person and yet not so simple as to look cheap. He nodded in approval and handed them back to his superior.

Tyront took one in each hand and closed his eyes for a moment.

"There you are," he said satisfied, presenting the freshly enchanted bangles. "Let's see how these work."

"Apart from minor setbacks such as attempts to flee, how is the training going?" Enric enquired, hiding his smile.

Orrin just lifted an eyebrow. "Why don't *you* tell me, Lord Enric? I seem to recall that your study window overlooks the training grounds. Your window has been open more often than usual since, let's say, three days ago?"

Enric chuckled unabashedly at having been found out. "True enough, but unfortunately the distance and the fact that I can only watch you for minutes at a time prevent me from learning all the details."

"She is unwilling, to put it mildly. Fighting is to her the most useless waste of time and magic she can imagine, as she keeps pointing out to me. This rather dampens her motivation," he concluded laconically.

"But not her progress, from what I can see," Enric commented.

"Not entirely. But I suppose your reason for choosing *me* to take over her training is my experience with unwilling students," he said with a meaningful look at the younger man.

Tyront smirked. "That was a thought that had occurred to me, yes."

Orrin sighed. "All in all, she is neither stupid nor slow. But her attitude towards fighting will very likely keep her progress slow. I am not sure how to overcome her stubborn resistance without breaking her."

Enric nodded. Tyront had indeed chosen the right man for the task. Not breaking her was essential, and other warriors might have put their personal need to prove themselves before the Order's priorities.

Orrin, however, was beyond such petty needs for demonstrating his strength; he was comfortable in the knowledge that his power was considerable and didn't care who else knew. That had to be true confidence.

"How can we change that attitude? I suppose not every woman is as easy to bribe as my companion," Tyront said with a sideways glance at the study door.

A slow smile spread across Orrin's face. "I might have an idea here."

CHAPTER 7

Vern

Eryn lay on the uncomfortable bed and stared at the ceiling. The dusky light that came in through the small window did little more than cast shadows.

She wouldn't have believed that anything could dampen her spirits even further. Yet the failed attempt at escape had done exactly that. Though she had to admit that her physical state was much better after she had been able to do some basic healing. No more aching muscles when she moved, no more bruises that stung.

She lifted her head at the hesitant knock at her door and wondered. That was definitely not Orrin. Not his usual assertive way of announcing his presence, she thought. He would probably have kicked in the door by now. Curious, she got up on her elbows.

"Yes?"

"Eryn, it's Vern. Orrin's son, you remember?" The boy's voice sounded muffled through the thick door.

She swung her legs off the bed and got up. He smiled at her when the door had opened.

"Vern. What are you doing here? I'm not sure your father would approve," she said frowning.

"Oh, don't worry, he sent me to fetch you."

"Why? Where did he tell you to take me?"

Not back to the training grounds to catch up for the time lost today, she hoped.

"To our quarters," he said cheerfully and looked at her in a puzzled way when she didn't seem too thrilled about that. "You don't like them?"

"No, they are very nice."

"You don't look like you want to go there. Why?"

Ah, she thought, the refreshing openness of youth. "The quarters are not the problem. It's more about a conversation your father and I had there last time. It was not very pleasant for me."

He wrinkled his nose. "I know what you mean. I have the same feeling about his study. That's where he usually tells me off. Whenever he calls me in there, I start sweating, even when I'm sure I haven't been up to any nonsense recently." He grinned. "Or at least none he could know about."

Eryn chuckled. The boy had a way of making her smile in difficult situations. She appreciated how precious that was right now.

They reached the door to Orrin's quarters and Vern opened it for her, demonstrating once more his manners. The parlour was as tidy as she remembered it. The boy stepped to a small table and picked up a note that seemed to have been left for him.

"Oh," he said surprised, "my father has been called away. He writes he will be back soon and asks me to entertain you until then."

He was obviously very pleased with this turn of events, judging from the gleam in his eyes.

"Brilliant! I have so many things I want to ask you and he is not here to shut me up!"

Eryn grinned and had to admit that the prospect of spending some time in Vern's presence was more appealing than time in his father's.

She looked at him apologetically when her stomach rumbled loudly.

"Sorry. I haven't eaten since breakfast."

"Oh, that's easy to fix."

He went to a little tube in the wall and ordered two times something he called *the big tray*.

"Would you like something to drink?" he asked.

"Sure," she said and took a seat. "I'll take whatever you are having."

She heard him handle cups and some kind of liquid. When he handed her a bright blue drink, she frowned and looked up. He smiled and motioned for her to take a sip. She did and felt fruity sweetness expand in her mouth.

"Not bad. What is this?"

"It's made from berries. It's my current favourite." He leaned forward in his seat, eager. "Is it true? You tried to flee from here today?"

She groaned inwardly. That was not the most pleasant conversation topic she could imagine right now. But this would of course be exactly what a boy his age would like to talk about. Resigned, she leaned back and nodded.

"Yes. Not very successfully, though."

He smirked. "Obviously." He leaned back as well. "What went wrong?"

"The blue-robed magician. I had not been aware that your father had sent for him before he took off my shackles."

"Ah, Lord Enric," the boy nodded sagely.

"Is that his name? Then yes," she agreed without any enthusiasm.

"Why did father take off your shackles? That was not very smart of him, was it? You are stronger than him, right?"

"I was injured underneath the manacles. I was supposed to heal myself and let him shackle me again afterwards."

He snorted. "I see why you didn't. Bad thing, though, that Lord Enric is so strong."

"Tell me about it," she rolled her eyes.

"Why can you heal? Nobody here can. Is it a skill that can be learned?"

That was a nicer topic, she decided. "My father was a very good healer. He taught me for several years."

"Where is your father now?"

"Dead. He was killed when I was about your age."

She saw his eyes widen in sympathy.

"I'm so sorry. I shouldn't have asked."

"No," she smiled sadly. "It's alright. It was a long time ago."

"What things can you heal?"

She shrugged. "A lot of different things. It depends mostly on how long somebody has waited before coming to me and how serious the illness or injury is."

"What illnesses for example?"

"Pretty much anything, I would say. A few years ago there was a chest disease in my village. It was highly contagious has spread quickly through another two towns nearby," she remembered. "I managed to contain it after a few weeks, but doing that while keeping my magical abilities a secret was quite a challenge."

"So is there an immediate effect when you heal somebody? If I cut open my arm, you could heal that instantly?"

"Yes, normally this would be no problem."

"Can you show me?"

She could see the excitement shimmering in his eyes and reflected in his whole posture.

"I would love to. But..." she jangled her manacles, "right now I am a little incapacitated, I'm afraid." She leaned forward and smiled. "But if you can open them I will show you."

He laughed. "Nice try. Even if I could, my father would skin me alive."

At that moment there was a knock at the door and when Vern opened it, two servants brought in a large tray each filled with a number of plates and bowls. She inhaled the mix of rich scents and her stomach responded audibly.

Vern lifted all covers from both trays and smiled at her hungry look.

"Enjoy it! There is more where that came from."

They sat in companionable silence, eating. When she leaned back, full and content, he eyed her leftovers.

"Are you eating that?"

She saw his own plates completely empty and marvelled at the appetite of a growing boy.

"No, help yourself."

When he had finished off every single crumb, he seemed satisfied as well.

"That was nice."

He got up to put the trays aside for the servants to pick up later, when the door opened and Orrin stepped in.

He took in the scene and nodded at his son in approval. Hospitality was important to him, and judging from what he saw it seemed he had been a good role model for Vern.

"Good evening, Eryn," he said and watched her sit up straighter, tension returning into what had before been a relaxed posture.

"Orrin," she replied, again deliberately omitting the title.

"I have something for you." He pulled out the two thin bangles Tyront had given him.

She eyed them uncomprehendingly. "More gold around my wrists? Really? What for? Or are these for my ankles now?"

"They are not in addition to your current ones but in exchange," he explained.

"Why? I mean, they look nice, but my problem with them is not exactly one of design. I won't like the new ones better just because they are pretty." She looked up at him, frowning.

"There is another difference. They will not block your magic entirely, but enable you to access part of it," he explained patiently and lifted his brows. "Do you want them or not?"

She thought quickly. They had already blocked all her powers, so the new ones could hardly take away more than that. But what if they had added another spell? Could they force obedience on her, for example? She dismissed that idea. If so, they would very probably have done that already.

Orrin waited for her answer and smiled when she lifted her wrists up to him wordlessly.

"I thought so."

As she had expected he first fixed on the new pieces before he removed the older larger ones.

She felt the difference immediately. The void inside her was not filled completely, but she felt more like herself again. Closing her eyes, she sent her usual impulse downwards to see if that was possible.

The warrior watched a smile of relief form on her face.

"So, can you show me your healing *now*?" Vern enquired eagerly.

She opened her eyes and chuckled. "Why not? But let's not cut open any body parts. Do you have an already healed injury or a scar?"

He nodded and rolled up his sleeve to reveal a rough white patch of skin about the size of a palm.

"I burned myself there when I was a child."

He observed her closely when she put both her hands on his arm directly underneath the scar and closed her eyes. Within moments he saw the skin change and transform into ordinary tissue that did not look any different from the one around it. He exchanged a look with his father, who looked equally fascinated if less surprised.

When she opened her eyes again, she saw the boy staring with big eyes at where the large scar had been. Then he looked up at her when she removed her hands.

"That was… incredible! Can I touch it?"

"I should hope so. Every now and then you should even wash it," she said mischievously.

He carefully put two fingertips on the new skin and tested the surface. When everything seemed alright, he pinched it lightly.

"It looks and feels just like the other skin around it! Amazing! I have always hated that ugly thing, and they said it would stay with me for the rest of my life. And now it's just gone! Thank you so much!"

He lifted his open arms, but let them sink again after a moment's consideration, seeming somehow lost in looking for a way to express his gratitude in an appropriate, adult manner when his first impulse would have been to hug her.

She smiled at him, recognising his dilemma. "It was my pleasure. Maybe one day you can show me something you can do."

Orrin coughed. "Yes. Just make sure it is nothing that helps her escape."

Vern rolled his eyes as if this was self-explanatory.

Eryn pushed herself up from her seat. "I suppose that was what you wanted to see me about? The new manacles that look like jewellery? What will you give me next time I try to flee? Nicer quarters? Earrings?"

He gave a thin smile. "Hardly. This is not to reward you, it's just a way to make sure we don't have to take them off again anytime soon. It seems to give you silly ideas. They won't chafe and even if they do, you will be able to take care of it."

"I am touched by such generosity. Can I leave now or are there any other gifts you wish to bestow on me? Like a candle for my dark and depressing cell or a blanket that actually manages to keep me warm?"

She heard Vern behind her snicker and then hastily cough to cover it.

Orrin pursed his lips and narrowed his eyes. "Benefits, my dear child, are not granted for nothing. You need to earn them." Her displeased expression cheered him up a little. "Vern?"

He looked around and saw his son coming out of his room, looking too innocent by far.

"Yes, father?"

"Please accompany Eryn back to her room."

And if she tries anything, he thought, just hit her with the candlestick you are trying to smuggle out here under your vest. Amateur.

Youth, he thought, exasperated. Advancing age seemed to equal stupidity in their opinion. But right now that was alright for him. Vern was bonding with Eryn, and bonds could weaken resolves.

How could a woman, alone and in captivity, ever resist a boy who risked his father's fury by giving her candles?

He smiled.

CHAPTER 8

The Protection

Enric unfolded the message his servant had just handed him. Tyront wanted to see him.

He turned to his window and looked down across the square to watch Orrin and Eryn for some time. This had turned into a habit very quickly.

Orrin had brought his son to the training session today. Vern sat on a bench and watched his father, none too happily from what could be seen from the distance. Was he bored or did he object to how Eryn was being treated? Hard to tell.

Why had he brought his son anyway? Vern was not a great fighter, as Enric recalled, much to Orrin's chagrin. Did he hope to lift the boy's spirits by showing him an adult who was much worse at fighting than him? That, however, seemed very much unlike Orrin, increasing somebody's confidence by making him look down on somebody else.

He turned away from the window. It was time to leave, he didn't want to keep Tyront waiting.

When he arrived at Tyront's quarters, he was without delay shown to the study, where the older man was pacing nervously.

Tyront immediately created a soundproof barrier around them. This might be his home, but there was no such thing as too much caution.

"What's the matter?" Enric cut straight to the point.

"According to my sources the King is considering Loft's ambition for having an heir to the throne with magical powers."

Enric didn't have to ask what sources they were. Tyront maintained a complex and widespread network of spies and informants that provided him with a constant stream of information.

"So we need to dissuade him from dragging her into his bed? Splendid." Enric shook his head in disgust. "Is there anything in our favour? What arguments do we have against it? Historical ones won't count, he is as aware of them as we are. And willing to discard them carelessly as it seems."

Tyront shook his head in agitation. "We have nothing. As long as she is not in the Order, we can't do anything. She is not subject to the Order's protection."

"Maybe she will join the Order to avoid the alternative? I wonder what the smaller evil would be for her. There is only one way to find out."

"This might be a risk for us, Enric. She doesn't like us, thinks we are completely useless and waste magic in playing around. From her point of view the option of siding with the King to avoid us might be the more attractive one."

"Probably. But for now she is still the King's captive, not the Order's. Maybe a little reminder of this would help her judgement along in our favour."

"That is a big *maybe*. But I don't see what else we can do. And quickly, too. I will inform Orrin that we want to meet her in his quarters tonight. Bringing her here might arouse suspicion. As we frequently meet him in his home anyway, this should not be a problem."

Enric nodded in agreement and Tyront removed the barrier to sit down and write a note to Orrin.

* * *

Eryn yawned when she returned to her cell. She used the fresh water in the bowl to wash herself and then put on the clean set of clothes that lay on her bed. Another day of fighting was over.

Just when she was about to sit down on the bed, she heard Vern's knock and smiled. She had come to recognise his knocks and could even tell what mood he was in most of the time. Today the rapid tapping bespoke excitement.

When she opened the door, he quickly pressed two candles into her hands, which she hid away under her blankets immediately.

"Father says you need to come quickly."

"Why? What's the matter?"

Vern shrugged. "I have no idea. He just says it's important to get you there now."

"Get me where?"

He looked up at her as if this should be fairly obvious. "To our quarters, of course."

She followed his quick pace along the corridors, up the stairs and into the parlour.

She skidded to an abrupt halt when she saw Enric and Tyront rising from their seats at her entrance and was about to whirl around and flee back out the door, when Orrin, who had been waiting behind the door, pushed it shut with a finality.

He took his son by the shoulders and guided him to the study, then he closed the door behind both of them, leaving her alone with the two men.

"Good evening, Eryn," Tyront said calmly.

She swallowed, her heart beating rapidly, her throat tight. The last time she had seen him was at the testing, where he had shouted at her. She glanced at

Enric, but her last encounter with him had hardly been any more pleasant, either.

"Don't bother trying to leave," the latter said. "The door is secured. And so are the windows, just in case. Why don't you sit? There is something we need to talk to you about."

She folded her arms, wrestling her fear down with pure willpower. "Talk, then."

When she refused to sit, the men decided in silent agreement to stand as well. They moved closer to her and stopped when she was about to retreat.

"There is no need to fear us," Tyront tried to soothe her. "We are here to let you know that due to your uniqueness as the first female magician in several hundred years, there have been considerations of a rather delicate nature."

She smiled without humour. "You mean about the privilege of siring my offspring? Generating a new era of powerful magicians with both parents passing on their ability? Maybe even female ones? Or a magically gifted heir to your throne?"

Both men stared at her in surprise. Enric recovered first. "Yes, something along that line."

"Then I fear I have to disappoint you, My Lords. This will be absolutely impossible without my acquiescence."

"Even with your magic blocked?" Enric enquired carefully with a quizzical expression.

"Even then."

"How?"

"A little gift from my father. He protected me against unwanted intrusion." She watched them exchange an incredulous glance. "Well, what can I say? It's a cruel world and a woman needs every help she can get."

Tyront cleared his throat. "Do I understand you correctly - that your father placed some protection against unwanted, erm, attentions on you which works even if your magic is blocked completely?" He sounded doubtful.

"Exactly. It is connected to my life force, my very essence. Your shackles cannot break *that* connection. And if they could, I would not be standing here right now."

She smiled at them triumphantly, but frowned when she saw them exchange looks of relief as if she had just given them good news. What was going on here?

"Your acquiescence," Tyront asked, clearly not being all too comfortable with the topic, "is it a matter of physical reaction or merely of verbal accordance?"

She stared at him dumbfounded. "Are you asking me if I need to enjoy it or if just saying *yes* will be enough?"

Even Enric smirked at the older man's efforts at making talking about sex easier by paraphrasing it as much as possible.

Tyront sighed in defeat and lifted his gaze to the ceiling. "Yes, that's exactly what I was asking."

She grinned broadly, enjoying his discomfort. "I'm afraid it's the first one. So if you have any intentions, old man, you had better make it worth my while."

She looked at Enric, quite sure that the violent coughing fit he seemed to be dealing with was no more than an effort to cover an outburst of laughter he had not been able to control.

Tyront seemed to have reached the same conclusion as he shot his second in command a reproachful look.

"So there is no way around that protection?" he asked while Enric fought for composure.

She smiled sweetly. "No."

Her smile faded gradually, when she remembered a conversation with her father in their little house more than twelve years ago:

Nobody can remove it?

Only a magician stronger than myself. And there shouldn't be many around.

Oh dear. Now it would be tremendously useful to know how strong her father really had been. Stronger than those two right here? She hoped so, desperately.

Enric observed her change in expression with interest. So there *was* something. And it seemed that she herself had only just remembered it.

She renewed her smile, but it had lost its authenticity.

"None at all."

* * *

Five days later Enric knocked at Tyront's study door and waved his summons from the King in the air.

"Are you ready? We should leave now or we will be late. Any idea what this is about? I wish he would sometimes write a bit more than a time and a place."

Tyront nodded and rose. "It's about Eryn as far as I know."

Enric snorted. "When has it not been about her in these last two weeks?"

"This time the King has sent for her as well."

"I see. Then this should get interesting."

It didn't take them long to reach the throne room and they were already expected by King Folrin and his ever- present advisors.

"We are almost complete. I have also sent for our… guest. She should be with us shortly," the King announced.

Marrin seemed unusually quiet, Enric noted, while Loft seemed to vibrate with energy. That was not a good sign.

"She has not expressed a wish to join the Order as yet, I assume?" Loft asked sweetly, knowing fully well that she had not.

"No," Enric replied simply.

It didn't take long for Eryn to arrive. She was escorted by two palace guards and Orrin so he could intervene in case she tried to hurt them. Even if the greater part of her powers was blocked, she still posed a danger to non-magicians.

Loft dismissed Orrin with a hand gesture and the warrior bowed stiffly and left the great hall with the guards.

Eryn looked around and scowled when she saw the two magicians. Seeing one or both of them usually meant bad news.

The little man fighting baldness cleared his throat.

"King Folrin has sent for you to discuss the matter of Eryn's future. As she is, despite her magical abilities, not a member - and thus, not subject to the Order of Magicians but the Crown..."

Eryn rolled her eyes at such pompousness and interrupted loudly. "Excuse me, could you come to the point? Unless, of course, your point is that I am to provide you with magical offspring. It seems to be a common misconception that this is the best use to put a woman with unique qualities to. I will not agree to any such plan and I am telling you this to save you time and pain."

She knew it had been a wild shot, but after her little conversation with the two head magicians she was pretty confident that she had guessed the reason for this little meeting correctly.

All five men stared at her.

Marrin was the first to find his voice again. "I beg your pardon? Save us time and *pain*?"

"Yes," she explained, "consider it a gesture of goodwill. Any man who tries to conceive children with me without my permission will suffer rather painful consequences to his nether regions. I have a powerful magical protection inside me put there by my father before his death. And no, shackles will not make any difference as the effectiveness of the protection does not depend on my magic, but on my life force."

There was silence. It stretched on for quite some time until Loft, controlling his voice with an effort, addressed the magicians. "Is this possible? Is this true? Can you verify this?"

Enric stepped forward. "I couldn't say. Magic pertaining to the inside of the body is known only marginally to the Order. It seems her father was an experienced healer. I think it is possible that she speaks the truth."

Loft jerked his head towards Eryn. "That is not enough. Go and see for yourself. Now!"

Enric raised his brows. Loft was not in a position to give him any orders, but Tyront nodded once and he thus turned to Eryn.

She narrowed her eyes. Oh, no. That was not quite the response she had hoped for. The magicians had left peacefully when she had told them a few days ago. She had hoped that this would be pretty much the same here. In vain, as it seemed.

When he took a step towards her, she took one back. He, too, didn't look happy about this situation.

"Don't play around, take care of this," Loft shouted from behind them.

Enric ground his teeth and gripped her upper arm to stop her from retreating. He looked her up and down, not sure what to do, where to start. Was this mystical protection even detectable by somebody who was not trained as a healer?

She kicked him hard and he cursed and pulled her back, further away from the watchers until he could press her against a wall. At least her legs would no longer be a danger like this. He then caught her wrists and put them behind her, where he held them with one hand between her back and the wall.

"Stop this," he hissed. "This is hardly going to help you. Is it true? Is there really a magical protection inside you?"

"Yes," she snarled back.

"Then stop this childish behaviour and let me verify it to them!"

He had decided how to go about this now.

She sucked in a sharp breath when he lifted her tunic and placed his flat palm on her stomach. His bare hand felt cool on her warm skin.

His eyes widened slightly in surprise when he felt the low, familiar humming of – a shield. She saw the corners of his mouth curve upwards in a delighted smile no one but her could see.

"A shield," he whispered. "I had no idea it is possible to place one *inside* a body and leave it there."

He suddenly understood what she had not wanted to tell them in Orrin's quarters.

"But not insurmountable if you happen to be a magician stronger than the one who cast it." His face came closer and she could see the excitement in his eyes. "How strong was your father, Eryn? Stronger than me, or even Tyront?"

She swallowed hard, fear clear and plain in her eyes, and just stared up at him.

"Not sure?" He pursed his still smiling lips. "Why don't we find out?"

Moments later she felt warmth from his palm seep into her abdomen and tensed when she felt the barrier's energy level, that had been constant and familiar all these years, rise.

Her father had *not* been stronger than him. And the shield inside her was no longer hers. It had just been taken over. She could only hope he had done no more than strengthen it without changing its nature somehow. That could be very dangerous if certain functions were blocked.

She sunk slightly at the realisation, the tension in her muscles leaving. But being pressed between him and the wall, this hardly made any difference.

Triumph flashed in his blue eyes and instead of retreating, he kept feeding energy to the field.

His expression changed to one of annoyance when Loft's querulous voice demanded information.

"Is there a protection in place now or not? If you haven't found one by now, Lord Enric, there is none I dare say."

He smiled down at her one last time before he schooled his features into an expression of serious consideration and released her to turn back to the waiting men.

"Oh, but I *have* found one. A very strong one, too."

"Can you remove it?" The King asked calmly.

He shook his head in regret. "No, I don't think so. Not without damaging her organs permanently."

Loft's complexion had turned to what seemed a rather unhealthy shade of red. He wasn't one to take defeat well.

His eyes bore into Enric's, and then he addressed the older magician, "Lord Tyront, would you be so good as to verify Lord Enric's observation so we can be sure there was no... misconception or error?"

Tyront stared at him coldly for a moment, then turned when the King addressed him.

"What Loft *undoubtedly* meant, Lord Tyront," he explained with a pointed look at his advisor, "was that a second opinion on a delicate matter such as this would be valuable. He did surely not mean to imply that your second in command is not considered trustworthy."

The older magician nodded once and stepped close to Eryn, placing his palm on her stomach as Enric had done before, only he didn't lift the tunic. She didn't resist this time, just turned her head away from him. What difference did it make now?

He, too, reacted surprised at the nature of the protection. Then he turned around and nodded to the King.

"I can confirm Lord Enric's words. There is very strong protection in place."

Eryn noted dimly how both magicians had avoided using the term *shield*. They had both lied to the King. Each of them would have been able to remove the shield without any problem. It seemed as if they wanted to avoid a magician on the throne in the future.

"Lord Enric," the King spoke again. "If the protection cannot be removed without damage, can it be penetrated instead?"

He nodded. "Yes, Your Majesty. By any magician stronger than the one who conjured it."

"Am I right in assuming that her father must have been very powerful to put something like this in place?"

Enric nodded.

"And," the King continued, "am I also correct in surmising that you would - in theory only, of course - be strong enough not to be stopped by it?"

"Indeed, Your Majesty. *In theory* that would be the case."

"I see. You are dismissed for now."

He rose and turned to leave, his advisors close behind him.

The two magicians went to Eryn, who was still leaning against the wall, both hands protectively on her stomach.

Enric caught her wrist only an instant before her palm could connect with his face, then dragged her out of the throne room behind him.

"Bastard!" she shouted at him, furious, while the large double doors to the throne room were being closed behind them. "Do you have any idea what you could have done? You could have harmed me forever! Bastard!" she spat at him once more for good measure.

Orrin, who had been waiting for the audience to end so as to escort her back, quickly stepped closer and wrapped his strong arms around her from behind to stop her from going at Enric with tooth and claw. He had seen her in a foul mood nearly every day, but this...

He wondered what could have happened in there but knew better than to ask. If he needed to know, they would tell him. If he did not, they wouldn't answer him.

Enric eyed her, sizing her up, as she struggled in her trainer's strong grip.

"You know, Lord Orrin, I think today there is a good chance that she might fight willingly. Why don't you take her back to the training grounds?"

Orrin shot him a look of utter disbelief at the thought of handing her a weapon now, even if it was only a wooden stick. But as he was facing a superior magician, he could do no more than nod and comply.

Enric smiled widely when he watched him drag her away. Justice was a beautiful thing.

"She is right, you know," Tyront chuckled. "You *are* a bastard."

CHAPTER 9

Sightseeing

Eryn groaned loudly, lying on her side on the ground of packed dirt.

"Get up, you have not earned a break yet," Orrin jabbed her with his wooden sword.

"Go away, torturer. Leave me here to die."

She closed her eyes, then jerked up with a yelp of pain when he nudged her in her side with his boot none too gently and rolled her onto her back.

"Have I told you that I hate you?"

"A day without my hearing you say that is like a day without sunshine," he retorted.

"Father? That is no way to treat a lady!" Vern called indignantly from the side where he sat and watched.

"I will treat her like a lady when she starts behaving like one." Turning back to Eryn, he added, "And now get up. It's my son's turn to give you a good whacking."

Vern perked up and smiled. "Really?"

Eryn scowled at him. "I don't appreciate your enthusiasm." But she slowly got up, brushing the dust and dirt from her clothes.

The boy came closer unperturbed. "I'll be gentle," he promised solemnly.

"Yes, right," she snorted.

Orrin handed the practice sword to his son and stepped out of the way. He was curious about how this would go. She clearly had a soft spot for the boy, so she would very probably indulge him with some fighting practice to make him happy. And learn a thing or two herself.

He listened to Vern instructing her how to stand right, hold the stick correctly, move back when he did this, block when he tried that.

Eryn let him guide her through the moves, listened to his suggestions for improvement and even engaged in a short fight that she lost quickly.

Interesting, Orrin thought and looked up to the window where very likely another watcher was standing to take in the scene. He let his gaze wander back to the practice area in front of him.

So it seemed that his son had a certain talent when it came to teaching. That was definitely something he could use for the benefit of both.

If Vern kept training with her, his own skills would improve as well. And it was obvious that the interaction with *her* gave him far more pleasure than with the boys his own age. Or with his father, for that matter.

Vern had grown up without his mother. The only older female figure in his life was their servant who treated the boy well enough but was much too old and involved with her own family to take over a greater part in his life.

But Eryn, who was pretty much on her own here and enjoyed showing kindness as much as receiving it, was a different matter. He wondered under what category she would fall for his son: attractive older woman, big sister or young mother figure?

The second seemed the most harmless one, so he hoped for that option. At least that was how *she* treated him.

A new training plan, he thought, one that included Vern regularly. Vern would hardly object if he was allowed to miss the combat training with the other boys instead, quite the opposite. And Eryn would surely appreciate a more playful attitude every now and then. She still had to spend the mornings with Orrin for the more intense instructions, after all.

"Lower, Vern - you are neglecting your cover," he instructed absentmindedly.

He watched his son correct his stance and heard him point out the same problem to Eryn, showing her how it was done instead. Well, well, he thought, if that didn't look promising.

*　*　*

"He is using his son to soften her," Enric lifted one brow. "That's what I call commitment."

Tyront stood beside him, looking out the window with him at the scene. "From what I see he is using them both to get each other to do what he wants. That's not only commitment but ingenuity."

"What do you mean? Vern is not exactly what I would call a rebel."

"That's for all *you* know. He keeps smuggling candles to her. Not that Orrin isn't perfectly aware of it. But as it serves his purposes nicely he lets his son think that he has outwitted his old man. And there is the little matter of the mysteriously altered city maps in the library, where dancing naked women and men were painted onto all major streets."

"That was him?" Enric raised his brows in surprise. "I didn't know he had it in him. I saw the pictures, they were not at all bad." At Tyront's disapproving look he added, "A highly inappropriate demonstration of his talent, however. A despicable deed. Does Orrin know?"

"Of course not. You never know when you need a useful bit of embarrassing information on somebody in the future."

The younger man laughed. "So you are preparing for blackmailing him one day? That is rather devious, even by your standards. I shudder at the thought of what information on me you may be hiding somewhere."

"A thing or two," Tyront said smugly. He looked back at Eryn and the boy. "Have you ever heard of Vern picking up a sword voluntarily?"

"No. So that's what you meant. They make each other do voluntarily what Orrin would have to force upon either of them. They even look like they are enjoying themselves." He shook his head. "I keep underestimating him."

"You shouldn't. He is a very capable man, with or without a weapon."

Enric stepped back from the window to create a soundproof barrier around them. "What is our next step? We were no more than lucky the audience went as it did. If her father had not placed the shield in her, she might have been lost for the Order."

"The reason why it went as it did was less luck than your lying to the King."

"*I* lied to the King? What about you? I don't recall you rectifying matters."

"I was only asked to confirm that there was a protection in place, not that it was impossible to remove."

Enric snorted. "If you are planning to use this as blackmail material I have to warn you that this might not be a very convincing argument if the King asks you why you failed to inform him of my untruth."

Tyront smiled. "Well, in this case it should remain our secret. Back to your question. We need to give her a few months to develop proper fighting skills, otherwise there is no way she will be accepted into the Order. I don't worry about the King. The most interesting option for him was to impregnate her with his child. As he is averted from that idea now, the next best thing for him is to have Eryn in the Order. I don't expect any more resistance from his side."

"You think she will need no more than a few months to improve her combat skills sufficiently?" Enric sounded doubtful.

"With Orrin's attention focused on her alone for several hours a day? You are still underestimating him, my boy."

* * *

Vern's knocking woke her with a start. She groaned when she saw that it was only dawn. Sluggishly climbing out of bed, she slowly hauled the heavy door open.

"You are aware that your father grants me exactly one out of ten days for myself, right?" she said instead of a greeting.

He stood there, looking freshly scrubbed and full of energy, nodding.

"And you know that this day is today, right?"

"Yes, sure!"

"Then go away and let me sleep!"

She made to push the door closed again, but he held against it from the other side with more strength than she would have expected. He probably used a little magic to aid him.

He pressed hard and long enough against her resistance until the door was wide enough ajar for him to slip into the cell. Completely unperturbed by her unwelcoming attitude he gave her a toothy grin.

"I have never been in a woman's bedroom before," he announced matter-of-factly.

"Indeed? I'm sure your father would be very relieved to hear that." She let her gaze wander over the grey stone walls, the narrow uncomfortable bed, the bare floor and the simple table with the water bowl and smiled thinly. "I dare say that's not exactly what you expected."

He waved his hand dismissively. "I know that this charmless environment does not reflect on you as an individual. I appreciate that items of decoration are rather hard to come by for you."

Eryn raised her brows at his slightly pretentious way of expressing himself. "That is very generous of you."

"And after all, it's less the visible than the invisible allures in a lady's chamber that pose the attraction, I'm told," he continued suavely, then let his gaze wander down her sleepy form with an expression that made it obvious that he did not see a lot that qualified in that regard.

"Oh dear!" she sighed and rolled her eyes. There she was, standing in her rumpled nightgown, tangled hair and hardly able to fully open her eyes yet, and this boy was talking about the *invisible allures* of a lady's chamber.

"Don't tell me. Your father sent you here to torture me, right?"

"No," he beamed, "it is a reward."

"So he is rewarding me with sleep deprivation?" She stared at him in confusion.

"What?" He stared right back. "Not you. *Me!* Dear me, you are slow in the morning!"

She closed her eyes in exasperation and rubbed her fingers over the lids. "Please, can we start again? You are here because your father rewarded you for something by allowing you to satisfy your curiosity about women's bedrooms? I really need to talk to him. This is not exactly the right incentive. I shudder at this demonstration of his complete lack of parental qualities."

Vern stared at her incomprehensively. "You know, I think I will wait outside while you get dressed."

"Why would I get dressed? I want to sleep!" she lamented.

"Because, as I told you, my father has rewarded me with the permission to take you on a tour through the city," he said slowly as if talking to a difficult child.

"No, you did *not* tell me this!"

"I didn't?" He thought back, then shrugged. "Well, I've told you now. Hurry up!"

She stared at the door just closed behind him to give her privacy for getting dressed. A tour of the city? Interesting. So old Orrin was either trying to keep his son happy or using him to get through to her, she reflected.

Well, she could still use this to her advantage. Learning more about the layout of the city could be very useful to her and the boy could very likely be tricked into giving her more information than warier guide would. She smiled. That was definitely worth giving up her precious sleep for.

* * *

"King Folrin's grandfather ordered the reconstruction of the outer wall after fights between the nobility and the peasants in the south and added the inner wall," Vern lectured. "He was very keen on defensive architecture."

Then he nodded at the broad street they were currently walking along. "This is the main passage through the city. It starts at the eastern gate, the one you tried to escape through, and leads through the city centre all the way to the western gate."

That *was* interesting. "How many gates do you have here?"

"Three."

"I suppose they are all as well-guarded as they look," she said casually.

He shot her an amused look. "Yes, depend on that. Especially as they have now been warned to keep their eyes open for you." He laughed at her sour expression.

She lifted her nose when the scent of fresh baked goods wafted towards them and inhaled deeply. Vern stopped.

"I completely forgot that you haven't eaten anything yet. Come on."

He took her sleeve and tugged her into the small bakery where the smell originated.

"Pick what you like," he said generously. When she had chosen a small round loaf of bread and he had paid for it they continued their leisurely walk and he pointed out shops and buildings of interest to her, supplying what information he remembered from his classes.

Then he suddenly changed the topic. "Your mother - was she a magician?"

Eryn shrugged. "I don't know. It made my father sad to talk about her, so he didn't. And after a while I gave up asking. But I suppose it's possible. I imagine there might be more female magicians where I was born."

"Do you remember much about that place?"

She shook her head. "No, not really. There are memories of grand houses, people with different hair colours, and smells. But they are only fragments, I can't really combine them into a real picture."

He walked next to her silently for a while before he asked, "Did you become a healer because your father wanted you to?"

She took a moment to consider his question. "That's hard to say. I dare say that the way I was brought up had a lot to do with it. He raised me to consider healing the most worthy use of magic and to despise the exploitation of its more destructive possibilities. And, of course, there was not much choice for me to do anything else, as my father was the only magician around to teach me. I have no idea if I would have chosen a different path had I been raised among other magicians with different professions." She looked at him sideways, feeling that more than mere curiosity was behind the question. "What made you ask?"

He avoided looking at her. "My father is disappointed. My fighting skills are not exactly up to his standards. No matter how much I train, I don't achieve much. People keep telling me that I will find joy in it as soon as I have managed to improve, but I can't help thinking that this joy should be there in the first place to make me *want* to improve."

Careful, she warned herself. Encouraging him to rebel against his father would not be fair, however satisfactory hurting Orrin might be. Vern would be the one to bear the consequences, and if he did, it had to be of his own accord.

"I see," she said quietly.

He looked at her then, a tad reproachfully. "You see? That's all?" he said when nothing more came from her. "I thought you hated fighting! I would have expected you to understand my point of view."

"Oh, that I do, believe me. Very much so, in fact. Fighting and healing are to me exact opposites, so committing to one and being forced to practice the other is for me a violation of everything I believe. All my life I have learned how to undo damage, and now I am being made to learn how to cause it."

He stopped and shook his head. "And my father is the one doing it to you, every day, again and again." He looked pained for her. "I wonder why you don't hate me, too. I am his son, after all."

That made her smile. "I am not a great believer in blaming people for the sins of their ancestors. And as much as it pains me to say something remotely positive about that tyrant of a father of yours, he is hardly the only one doing it to me. There is the King, whose captive I am, and the Order, which fulfils the King's wishes in a way that serves their own interests properly." She thought of Enric's tampering with her internal shield that day and unconsciously laid a hand on her stomach. "Your father is only one of many who are doing this to me. But rest assured," she winked at him, "there is enough resentment in me for all of them, your father included. You have not yet earned a share in it. But if you keep waking me up on the only possible day where I can sleep in, that might change."

He grinned and she was relieved to see that his gloomy mood had changed back to a more cheerful one.

"I will keep that in mind. It's not as if seeing you directly after getting up is an experience I would want to repeat any time soon."

He laughed when she whacked him lightly on the back of his head, muttering, "Insolent brat."

* * *

Eryn watched Vern return from the bakery with two of the bread buns she had come to like so much. She didn't know what they did here to make them so savoury, whether they added any special ingredients or just followed a different procedure than the bakery in her little village, but the result was quite different. Amazingly different; they were light and sweet, juicy without being sticky. A work of art.

Eryn and Vern walked in companionable silence, munching their bread.

Vern stopped when they heard a shrill cry of what had to be either a very pained animal or a child. Eryn quickly swallowed her last bite and tried to discern where the sound had come from. The people around them didn't bother stopping their daily work, some of them just looked up for a moment and then continued with whatever they were doing.

The boy grabbed her sleeve and pulled her into a smaller street, where she could see a group of children throwing stones and laughing at another child, who was cowering on the ground, hands lifted protectively over the tucked-in head.

Eryn immediately raised a barrier in front of the child and the stones that were about to hit it were stopped and bounced off to ricochet against house walls instead.

The stone throwers looked at each other perplexed, until they turned around and saw the woman and the older boy.

"Hey!" Vern shouted. "What sort of cowards attack a single girl in greater numbers? You should be ashamed of yourselves!"

They regarded him with widened eyes. His clothes clearly marked him as a magician and he was with the brown-haired woman everybody had been talking about for weeks. The one nobody was really sure about how dangerous she was.

When they didn't move and just stared, Eryn looked them coldly in the eyes, one after the other and growled, "If I ever see you do something like that again I will make it so your arms and legs fall off."

That seemed to revive them. The few who still held stones let them drop hurriedly and then they all ran off.

Vern had been right, it was a young girl. At Eryn's touch at her shoulder she timidly looked up. Eryn gulped.

One half of the girl's face was pretty, delicate, perfect, and the other was in contrast almost like a cruel joke, disfigured by what looked to her like an immense scar of a burn that covered almost the entire side, slightly distorting the form of her eye, one corner of her mouth and nostril.

Eryn smiled, trying to reassure the timid figure. "Hello. My name is Eryn. What is your name?"

The girl stared at her for a few more seconds, then said something that couldn't have been longer than one syllable and had been much too quiet to be heard.

"Could you say that again, dear? That was a bit too quiet for me."

"Plia," the girl repeated, still staring at her.

"Plia. That is a pretty name. Tell me, Plia, did they hurt you?"

She shook her head, but Vern pointed at her hand. "She is bleeding."

Eryn crouched next to the girl and looked at her questioningly. "May I? I can make that better if you like."

The girl grabbed her injured hand and pressed it close to her chest, shaking her head vehemently.

Alright, Eryn thought. A young girl was not meant to trust random strangers she met on the street, especially after what the kids had done to her.

"How old are you, Plia?" she asked, trying to get the poor creature to open up a little.

"Twelve," she replied in a timid voice.

"Really? My friend Vern here," she nodded at him, "is fifteen years old. I am exactly as old as the two of you together. Do you know how much that is?"

"Twenty-seven," Plia replied almost instantly.

Good, Eryn thought, no hard blow to the head.

"Can you get up and walk a few steps for me? I would like to see if you are badly hurt."

The girl rose hesitantly and walked a few paces, not taking her eyes off the two strangers.

"Very good," Eryn said softly. "Does your hand hurt?"

Plia just looked down at the ground instead of replying.

"I really could heal this for you, if you like," she offered once again.

The girl looked up sharply, disbelief apparent in her eyes.

"Really," Vern smiled, "she can. I have seen it. She is really good."

Eryn stretched out her hand, offering it to her and waiting patiently. Only after more than a minute Plia lifted her small, pale fingers to touch them to the woman's hand.

Closing her eyes, Eryn let her magic enter the frail body and found the wound immediately. Only a slight push was necessary to make the tissue reconnect what had very likely been gashed open by a stone thrown at her.

She heard the girl's gasp of surprise at the edge of her perception and let her attention return to the physical world outside.

Plia stared at the unmarked skin and touched it lightly with her index finger, then her eyes wandered to Eryn's and she tried to speak, but was obviously speechless.

Poor child, Eryn thought.

"Where are your parents, Plia?" she asked. "Can we take you home?"

The girl shook her head. "I have no more parents. I live with Mistress Walchan at the orphanage."

"What happened to your face?" She regretted the question instantly when she saw the girl flinch. As a healer she was used to asking questions about ailments bluntly. People came to her to receive help, after all.

But this was not the case here, Eryn reminded herself. The girl had not come to her, she was no more than a stranger asking intimate questions, prying into matters that were none of her business.

Vern stepped closer to Eryn, whispering, "You can heal this, right? Just like you did with my scar."

"It might be a little more complicated than that," she murmured back when the girl didn't answer. "It depends on how deep the damage goes, if it is only skin that needs repairing or if muscles and even bones are affected."

She fell silent when Plia said, "I got the burns when I was a baby. That's what Mistress Walchan said."

"I see. Can I have a look at it with my magic? I don't have to touch it, I can do it if you take my hand," she added when she saw the reluctance in the troubled eyes.

Then the girl slowly lifted her hand and let Eryn take it into her own. Again she explored the small body, this time concentrating on the head, the area where the damage was. She sensed damaged skin, but intact bones. The muscles seemed slightly marred, but she couldn't be sure.

"Can you slowly open your mouth as wide as possible?" she asked with closed eyes, not wanting to lose the contact to the inside while interacting with the world around her. Muscles stretched just like they were supposed to.

"Now pretend you are chewing something. Make that same movement now."

There was a slight blockage in the jaw muscle, the upper one that connected the jaw to the rest of the skull. It was not bad - just a few damaged fibres that were now no more than mere vestiges but could be repaired easily enough. The skin around it would be a challenge, however.

She stopped herself. She didn't even know if the girl wanted to do this. Even though she was quite probably an outsider and the target of attacks, it was the only face she had ever known and she did probably not want to give it up just like that.

"Thank you, well done." She smiled. "I want to offer you something."

Plia looked at her unsure, waiting.

"I think I can mend the scars on your face. But only if you want me to."

The girl's mouth dropped open, her eyes widened and before Eryn could determine whether this was in amazement or pure shock, Plia started nodding, first hesitantly, then more emphatically.

Vern clapped his hands. "Excellent! I can watch, right? Please!"

Eryn chuckled. "I probably couldn't stop you if I tried." She looked around. "This is not a very good place to do this, I need somewhere quieter. Any idea?"

"Sure," the boy beamed, "we can go to our quarters. Father is in the palace today, at a Council meeting. He won't be back any time soon. They usually last a very long time. Lots of old men fighting over trifling matters."

"Vern, I'm not sure this is such a great idea…" she started but stopped when he raised his brows at her.

"You wouldn't want to do this in that closet of yours, would you? We would hardly all fit in there, and even if we did it would not exactly be comfortable, if you get my meaning."

Eryn sighed, feeling defeated. "Alright, then. But are you sure your father will not be there for some time? I don't know how long it will take."

He waved his hand dismissively as if Orrin was a minor factor, quite unimportant when it came to bringing strangers found on the street to his home in order to perform medical procedures on them.

Eryn turned back to the girl. "Can you come with us now or do you need to go somewhere? Would you like me to speak to your matron first?"

The girl shook her head, clearly not very happy at the mention of the woman she lived with.

"*No* you can't come or *No* you don't want me to speak to the matron?"

"I can come with you," Plia said quietly.

"Very good."

Eryn straightened again and offered the girl her hand. They went back to the warriors' quarters and straight into the parlour.

The girl looked around, clearly overwhelmed with the splendour around her. There wouldn't be any luxury in an orphanage, Eryn mused and led Plia to a settee that was long enough for her to lie down.

Plia stared in panic at the seating furniture, then at her own dusty clothes.

Vern realised her dilemma and smiled. "Don't worry, our servant knows how to clean this in case something gets dirty. You should see what stains I leave there sometimes."

When Eryn turned to him and grinned, his head flushed a deep red.

"Wait, what? No! Dirt, dust, mud! After the combat training…"

He gave up and just exhaled in exasperation when she kept grinning. Instead, he turned to the girl.

"Would you like something to drink? There is one bottle of my favourite juice left."

Without waiting for a reply, he turned to the small cabinet where Orrin stored numerous bottles and took out three glasses, which he filled almost to the brim and took them to his guests.

Eryn smiled warmly at him when he handed her a glass and another one to Plia. Kindness without calculation, she thought. He had asked her to heal the girl, offered his home to do it and shared the last bottle of his favourite drink with an orphan girl he had just met in the streets. He had also been the first one to turn into the alley where she had been attacked.

Pride welled up inside her when she looked at his animated face framed by tousled, blond hair that was slightly longer than what currently seemed to be the fashion among the boys his age and social class.

Plia carefully tasted the juice, then drank the rest quickly as if afraid that it might be taken away from her again.

"Please lie down now." She continued when the girl had followed her instruction, "This won't hurt you. Just close your eyes and think of something nice. You will feel a warmth in your face, this is completely normal. This is where the magic will be at work. Don't be alarmed if it feels a bit strange, like something is moving under your skin. Just relax and let me do my work. Are you ready?"

The girl gave a hesitant nod.

She let herself sink into a state of relaxation just like her father had taught her. For more complicated repairs it was important to be more careful and alert and release all tension inside her. When she felt calm enough to begin, she laid her hand on Plia's and let a steady trickle of magic flow through the girl's skin.

Muscles were usually harder to convince into regenerating than skin. She tickled them with energy until they responded lazily, slowly growing together again. Each of them had to meet their counterpart after bridging the gap the damage had left.

She watched the ends melt together, sent small impulses through them to make sure the connections were solid. When the muscle was repaired, she moved closer to the surface, where the muscles were covered by several different layers of skin.

She was familiar with the altered nature of scar tissue compared to undamaged skin and slowly coaxed the tiny blocks they consisted of to awaken and do her bidding. She fed them information of what needed to be done, provided the energy necessary for it and supervised the work, making slight corrections where necessary.

Twin impulses of energy kept running across the girl's facial muscles to compare the work of the damaged side with the forms on the unharmed half to make sure the visual effect was as natural as possible.

When Eryn opened her eyes, the room was aglow in the light of numerous candles. She looked out the window and whistled in surprise at how long it had obviously taken her. She felt the tension in legs remaining too long in the same position. She had been more or less blind and deaf to the world around her while her mind had been at work.

She looked down at the girl who seemed to have fallen asleep during the procedure. Her face was perfect. There was no other word for it. Symmetrical features, beautifully sculpted.

She turned when Vern laid a hand on her shoulder and smiled at his expression of wonder and amazement. When she saw behind him a dark shadow just outside the reach of the nearest candle detach itself from the wall, she took a step backwards, almost stumbling onto the sleeping girl. Vern caught her elbow and steadied her.

"It's only father - relax! He has been here for quite some time now. He says it's alright."

Now she could see Orrin's face, calm and without any sign of anger because his parlour had been used for healing a stranger.

"That was impressive," he said quietly, "This is quite a skill you have."

Appreciation from Orrin? That was new. And unexpected. She was not sure how to react to that, so she turned to the girl instead and tenderly took her hand to wake her.

"Plia?"

Her eyes fluttered open instantly and she sat bolt upright, obviously not comprehending where exactly she was, just seeing a strange room that she would hardly be able to recognise without daylight after having seen it for only a few minutes before.

Vern had brought a small hand mirror and handed it to the young girl, waiting patiently until her small fingers had safely closed around the handle. She lifted it to her face hesitantly. Mirrors had probably not been her friends in the past, Eryn thought with a sharp pang. But that, she hoped, would be different from now on.

The girl's hands had managed to lift the mirror high enough for her to see her face fully reflected. She gasped and almost dropped the mirror, but managed to hold on to it with an effort. She stared at herself, gripping the mirror with one hand, touching the newly smooth half of her face with the other.

Her eyes started to swim in tears and Eryn swallowed, fervently hoping that they were tears of joy and not desperation at seeing an unfamiliar reflection she didn't recognise.

Plia put down the mirror carefully on the small table next to the settee and fell to her knees in front of Eryn, hugging her legs and weeping unabashedly.

"Thank you," she managed to burst out between sobs. "Thank you so much. Thank you."

Eryn looked down at her, feeling rather awkward and slightly helpless in dealing with this emotional display of gratitude. When she tried to loosen the thin arms from around her knees, they just seemed to grip her harder.

Then the pressure suddenly stopped and she looked down into a pair of wide open dark green eyes that seemed on the edge of panic.

"What's the matter, Plia? Are you in pain? Is everything alright?"

She bent down and was about to send another magical impulse through her skin, when she heard the girl's teary voice.

"I have no money."

Uncomprehendingly, Eryn stared at her. "Of course you don't. Why?"

The girl frowned at the woman's lack of understanding of that rather obvious matter. "I can't pay for this. But," she added quickly when Eryn's brows rose in surprise, "I will soon be able to work and then I can pay you back a little every month! Please?"

The healer blinked a few times before answering slowly, "Plia, I didn't ask for money. And I won't. This is a gift for you." She stroked the tangled blond mane. "Come, I will get you back home. It's late."

"Vern will take her. You'd better go to bed so you are fit for the training tomorrow morning," Orrin said and opened the door for his son and the girl to leave.

When Eryn made to follow them, he closed it again. "You wait here a moment."

He went into what she supposed was his bedroom and returned shortly afterwards with a bundle in his arms.

"Congratulations," he said and pressed the soft dark blue package into her hands. "You have earned yourself a warm blanket."

With this he shoved her out the door, leaving her standing confused and slightly dazed in the corridor.

CHAPTER 10

Pointed Sticks

Orrin was waiting for her at the training grounds like he usually did. He tapped his foot impatiently.

"Where is your stick? No poking today?" she said with insincere regret.

Her mood was unusually good today. The first time since she had been brought here she had spent a halfway comfortable night wrapped in a warm blanket. That was not something she would in her former life have considered anything special but now it seemed like pure luxury.

"Later. We will have a look at something new today. You will learn how to use magic to improve your speed and physical strength."

She looked at him in surprise. That was the first time they actually would do something using magic. That might even be interesting.

"The first thing we will work at is speed. It is essential for good swordsmanship. If you are slower than your opponent, you will probably end up dead."

"Then all these weeks you have been badgering me for nothing? Didn't you say *that* was meant to improve my reactions already?"

He rolled his eyes. "Yes, it was for nothing. That's my sole purpose in life: tormenting you. You can only build on what's there already. If you use magic merely to raise yourself up to the standard a well-trained non-magician fighter can reach, you have given away an advantage that could very well decide victory or defeat. The faster and stronger you are without magic the higher you can push yourself."

"How high up are you, then?" she asked, folding her arms.

Before she could even blink she felt his arm around her neck a moment later, holding her in place from behind without any apparent effort when she instinctively tried to wriggle free.

"Fast enough for *you*, I would say. And we need to work on your reaction to an attack like this. Clawing at my arm is hardly an effective defence. You react like a girl."

He removed his arm and swiftly stepped away from her, just in case she decided to repay him for his words with a kick or punch.

She turned slowly, rubbing her throat more for effect than actual pain. "Well, the last time I looked I still was one."

"This doesn't mean you have to fight like one. In many animal species the females are more vigorous fighters than the males."

She frowned. "Haven't you just contradicted yourself? First fighting like a girl is a problem, and suddenly it's desirable?"

He smiled. "*Girl* is a decidedly human expression and stands for something soft, weak and defenceless. *Female* on the other hand is something completely different. We will work on your transition from one to the other."

Soft, weak and defenceless? Nice.

"Well, then introduce me to the secret of strength and speed, oh great and wise teacher."

He rolled his eyes. "I would rather introduce you to the secret of showing respect to your elders."

"This is not very likely, I'm afraid," she smiled. "And my way of showing respect might not be what the Order deems appropriate."

He was aware of that, very much so in fact. Respect was not necessarily something that had to be demonstrated by addressing somebody by a title. He didn't mind not being addressed as *Lord* by her and even enjoyed their mostly playful banter. It was something different for a change. Not many people around him dared talking to him like that.

And there was the way she treated Vern. That earned her a lot of points in his book. It did him good to be treated as an equal by an adult; it did wonders for his self-confidence.

Vern's fellow trainee magicians looked down on him, Orrin knew. The ultimate measure for worth was magical strength, and in that area Vern was not exactly gifted.

In addition to that he was the studious kind of boy, more interested in his books than his fighting lessons, which did not exactly improve his reputation among his peers.

"The first thing we will practice is how to infuse your muscles with magic in order to increase physical strength." He pointed to a large stone, its size in diameter about the length of her arm. "We will start by lifting that. Concentrate, focus on the muscles that you will need for lifting the stone. You can try to lift it first without magic to see which muscles are involved. Then you send energy right into those muscles, enough to provide sufficient strength for them to deal with the unusual strain. Take your time, it may need a while."

She just threw him an amused look, went to the stone, closed her eyes for a moment and then lifted it over her head without any apparent effort.

"Like that?"

Orrin's eyes bulged. That normally took the trainees about two weeks to learn. Even those who were quicker usually had to experiment a little to get the amount of energy right, figure out the right muscles to infuse and then keep the supply of magic steady for a while to avoid dropping the lifted stone on their own or somebody else's feet.

"Yes, that looks about right." He didn't manage to hide his surprise entirely.

She smirked and slowly lowered the stone back to the ground. Sending magic into precisely the right region of the body was the very first step in healing. That was something she had learned at an early age and constantly used for many years, even though not for enhancing her athletic abilities but to find and heal damage exactly where it was located. The principle was basically the same, only the amount of magic to be sent to the muscles was different.

"From what I can see I have mastered that lecture a bit faster than you anticipated. Does that mean I am free for the rest of the day?"

He sneered. "What do *you* think?"

"No?" she sighed.

"Smart woman. That just means we can progress to working on your initial problem: your slowness."

But if she once again managed to direct the magic with the same precision, that would not be too much of a challenge for her, either, he pondered. That was good, very good. Using her already developed skills would help moving along with others she was less eager to work on as well.

"Sure. And don't waste any words of praise on me. That would just make me conceited," she said slightly mockingly.

"I will praise you for results that take an effort, not for what is obviously no challenge for you. Now show me what you can do with speed. You see that building over there, where the young ones have their lessons? Run to it, touch the door and run back as fast as you can without using magic."

She shrugged and did as she was told.

"I counted to twenty. Now remember the muscles you used and infuse them with energy. Now run again."

She closed her eyes again, identifying the muscles that were now filled with more blood due to the sprint. How could she increase the speed of her steps? Increase the speed of the blood flow to provide more oxygen and thus energy? That would be dangerous for her heart, it was not meant to beat faster than a certain rate. That left infusing the muscles directly with magic. But would doing it like before only increase their strength instead of their speed? The only way to find out would be to try, she decided.

Sending energy into her legs, abdomen and upper body, she started running and immediately felt the effect of the magical infusion. She smiled when she realised why the same technique of magical enhancement worked for both strength and speed: The force she used to press herself off the ground and forward determined her speed, and that force in turn required increased strength.

When she returned to Orrin in what seemed like no time at all, he looked at her thoughtfully with pursed lips.

"So? How far did you count this time?"

"Eleven."

"Is that good? Your expression is not very helpful for determining that."

"It was surprisingly good, yes," he admitted.

She had almost doubled her speed despite wearing the manacles. What would that woman be able to do with more training and all her power at her disposal?

"Let's see if you can use some of that speed while you are holding a weapon."

He went to retrieve the two training swords from a bundle he had brought and tossed one at her.

She caught it easily and sighed. The fun part seemed to be over. She should have held back more to make it last longer.

"Now do what you did before and infuse the muscles you use with magic to react faster."

He stabbed at her and she yelped and jumped back to rub her side where the wooden stick had caught her.

Orrin shook his head. "Eyes on *me*. There is no use for fast muscles if you don't choose to move them. You don't have problems with your eyes, do you? You would have healed them otherwise, I assume."

She shot him an annoyed glare. "My eyes are perfectly fine, thank you. If I had to guess, I would say it's the lack of enthusiasm that slows me down."

"Lack of enthusiasm... That's an understatement if ever I heard one. Unfortunately, bruises and injuries are nothing to worry you for too long as you can take care of them very quickly. So there is no real reason for you to make an effort to avoid them. Unless," he smiled wryly, "it's not your body that's hurt but your pride. I think I have an idea how to motivate you."

She frowned suspiciously. That did not sound very promising.

He signalled for one of the gate guards to send a messenger boy who was stationed at the gate and upon his arrival told the boy to go and fetch somebody called Rolan and bring back two swords from the students' weapons depot.

Then they just stood and waited for several minutes until the boy came running back, followed by a magician in his early twenties with his eyes half closed in a look of permanent terminal boredom with the world. He wore his hair in a medium-length blond ponytail hanging down his back.

Orrin acknowledged his bow with a nod and took the swords from the messenger boy, handing one to the man called Rolan and held out the other one to her.

When she just folded her arms and looked at him with a raised brow, he shrugged. "You don't have to take it. But I would advise you to. Otherwise that might be rather unpleasant for you." He stuck it into the ground next to her.

Rolan looked her up and down and cast a doubtful look at Orrin. "With all due respect, Lord Orrin, I have seen her train. A first-year trainee could take her without any difficulties. May I ask why you have sent for me?" he said as if she wasn't present.

"To teach the lady a lesson which I thought would be the more effective if it was delivered by you, young Rolan." What he didn't say out loud was: Because you are an arrogant young chap and she will dislike you at once. And you are skilled enough with a sword to do what I need you to.

"Are you done questioning my orders?" The last words were sharp and made Rolan bow again, this time in apology.

"Forgive me, Lord Orrin. What is it you wish me to do?"

"I want you to try and touch her with the sword as often as you can. And in doing so cut her shirt a little every time without hurting her. The last part is not optional," he emphasised with a warning look.

"I understand, Lord Orrin."

Eryn swallowed and quickly grabbed the sword that still stuck in the ground, pulling it out and holding it defensively. It was noticeably heavier than the wooden training weapons.

So he had exchanged her blunt wooden stick against a sharp pointed metal one when he made her fight for her dignity. How very considerate.

He had chosen his tactic well, she thought morosely. She would try to avoid having her clothes cut off her body, as well as she could, by that young idiot that looked at her as if she was something he had found lying in the gutter.

Her opponent's first advance also brought the first cut in her tunic, directly above her elbow. Eryn cursed under her breath. She was not good at discerning first attacks. Somehow she was never ready for a fight to begin - as if refusing to believe that she would be attacked might actually prevent it.

Rolan looked at her, bored. It seemed as if he considered this an immense waste of his precious time.

When he made his next move, however, she was prepared and jumped back in time to avoid his blade. She managed this another three times before Orrin called a stop.

"You are not meant to merely run away from him. Parry his attacks!" Then he turned to the young man and nodded to signal that he could continue.

The second cut happened shortly after, directly underneath her collarbone. She cursed and put her fingers on the skin underneath. There was blood on them when she removed them.

Orrin shot the young man a cold look. "If this happens again I will consider it a refusal of a direct order. And don't even think of trying to convince me that it was an accident. Every cut you make that affects more than her clothes I will pay you back afterwards."

Rolan nodded once and returned his attention to Eryn. He blinked in surprise when the cut in her skin was gone and turned back to Orrin, frowning.

"No, there is nothing wrong with your eyes. She can heal herself. You can't," he added with a slightly threatening undertone. "That's why you would suffer from my cuts a lot longer than she does from yours." Then he turned to Eryn. "And you might want to start applying what you have demonstrated to me before."

She swatted his sword away without any elegance when it came at her again. She watched his every move carefully, remembering that infusing the muscles only made sense when it was clear what they had to do.

Blocking another two thrusts, she started to feel a little more confident. It probably helped that he had been warned not to draw blood from her again.

The third cut across her midriff came when he feigned to the right and then attacked from the other side. He sneered at her.

"How much longer are we going to do this?" she called to Orrin without taking her eyes off her opponent.

"Until either your shirt is cut to pieces or you manage to parry ten attacks in a row," he called back way too cheerfully for her taste.

Ten parries? She had managed two so far, and those had been more luck than skill. She growled something unintelligible.

If that boy in front of her were not such a twerp she would cut her tunic herself just to defy Orrin, but that would make that arrogant idiot sneer at her again, and right now she did not have the serenity to bear that.

Grinding her teeth in grim determination, she lifted her sword again, waiting for the next blow.

* * *

"Ten!" she called out almost an hour later and dropped the sword to the ground with feeling, challenging Orrin to make her go on despite his announcement before.

"Indeed. It has taken you long enough. And this is not how we treat a sword." He shook his head and motioned for her to pick it up.

She smiled without humour. "If it was up to me that wouldn't be the only thing I would do to that sword. With a little heat and a hammer I could turn it into something useful, like a door stopper or a spade."

His angered frown made her sigh and bend down to retrieve the weapon from the ground.

"Rolan, you are free to leave. I will send for you again when I need you."

When, she thought and gave a silent groan, not *if.* So it seemed she would have to endure the pleasure of training with him again, such an appealing thought.

Rolan bowed to Orrin, shot her another disdainful look and left.

When he was out of earshot, she eyed Orrin curiously. "Why did you bring that very charming, well-mannered young chap in? Don't tell me you have suddenly developed scruples that prevent you doing the dirty work yourself."

Dirty work? He shook his head in amusement. No, he thought, he could never have done it himself. Motivating her to fight with everything she had by trying to cut her clothes from her body was crossing a very delicate personal line and doing that himself was out of the question.

It would have changed the nature of their fragile relationship of grumpily bestowed respect and slightly tense bantering into, well, whatever the result was if a man who was more or less her guard and many years her senior tried to slice the clothes from her body.

Delegating this little task to somebody who she would have found trying under the best of circumstances was a much better alternative. But that was not a good thing to tell her.

"You are so used to being defeated by me that I dare say you wouldn't really have tried."

She snorted. "Yes, sure. I would just have stood there, waiting until snippets of my tunic surrounded my feet." She poked her fingers through one of many slits that had luckily not progressed far enough in number to be revealing. "What about the shirt? It's all cut up. Will I have to wear it the whole day until the servants have replaced it in the evening?"

"Yes. But you will wear leather armour on top of it so it doesn't really matter for now. You will continue your training with Vern when his lessons are over. And as you will continue to use the sword it is wiser to use armour. Even if you can heal yourself easily enough in most cases, I think it would disturb my son to see a weapon protruding from your body."

"Yes, let's definitely focus on how *your son* would feel if he stuck a sword into me, thank you very much," she retorted dryly.

He chuckled. "Don't be squeamish. I suppose you have seen worse than that back in your village. I hear accidents with heavy crafting tools can be quite gruesome."

"I have, yes, but not to *my* body."

"That's why I am generously granting you the armour to protect it. And I don't see any gratitude for that, I might add."

"Yes, right. Why don't you punish me by sending me off to my room for the rest of the day?"

He smiled good-naturedly. "Oh, I couldn't do that. It would be too cruel."

* * *

Tyront stood at the window that so conveniently overlooked the training grounds and followed Eryn's moves, which had started to resemble actual fighting.

97

"When did Orrin exchange wood for steel?" he enquired of Enric, who was leafing through a stack of papers to find a report.

Enric answered without looking up. "About ten days ago. Don't tell me your information network has failed to provide you with progress reports?"

"They are otherwise engaged. I usually wait for Orrin's reports, but he is not very reliable when it comes to paperwork. Warriors usually aren't. Is that young Rolan she is fighting? I would not have thought him the type willing to assist in that training."

Enric smirked. "He isn't. My suspicion is that this is the reason why Orrin keeps involving him. That and the fact that he is not the most pleasant person to be around. I think he wants to motivate her by making her wish that she can defeat him one day. I am not too fond of him myself, but he does know how to use a weapon properly."

"I thought Orrin had his son spar with her to make the training more appealing for her?"

"He still does, but only in the afternoons when the boy's lessons are over. Rolan usually comes every second or third day in the morning. I suppose that makes her appreciate Vern all the more."

Tyront watched her whirl out of the way of a thrust aimed at her shoulder with a speed that was clearly magically improved. "That is quite some progress she has made in the two and a half months she has been here."

"Well, that's why you commissioned Orrin with this task, to get quick results. Don't tell me *you* are the one underestimating him now?"

"No, not really. But knowing it and seeing it with my own eyes is still a difference. She hardly knew which end to point at her opponent when she came here, and look at her now. She is pretty fast already, despite the block on most of her powers."

"Yes, it took her only minutes to grasp the principle of infusing muscles with energy from what I have seen."

"Minutes? That is impressive. Although I assume that as a healer she would of course know where to send it and how much. Still, using it in a fight is surely different to healing I imagine."

"Speaking of healing, I suppose you have heard about the orphan girl?"

"The scars. Yes, of course. Something like that doesn't remain unnoticed for very long. It was half her face, after all. I haven't seen the girl before, but from what I have been told the sight was not exactly a pleasant one. I took a look at her and her face seems flawless." Tyront looked down at Eryn thoughtfully.

She had just blocked a thrust and successfully aimed a kick at Rolan's shin. The young magician bent down, wrapping his hands around his lower leg.

"Her fighting style is not what I would call traditional."

Enric smirked. "No, not really. I assume Rolan will have to adapt his own to be better prepared for her little manoeuvres. The day before yesterday she threw a handful of dirt in his face and then robbed him of his sword while he was blinded. I can tell you he was not pleased about that."

Tyront chuckled. "Not exactly the gentlemanly way of fighting he was taught."

"Hardly. Though that seems to be the *only* gentlemanly thing he has ever been taught," Enric retorted. "He is not known for showing his superiors a lot of respect. He keeps getting kicked out of his positions for that reason. And he treats Eryn with disdain and condescension."

"Then I say we look forward to the day when we can remove her shackles and let her teach him a good lesson."

Enric had finally found the sheet of paper he had been looking for and stepped next to Tyront, handing it to him.

"Here are the results of this year's testing. No surprises as you can see. The highest one this time was Berk, Lord Poron's nephew, a strong category C. He has expressed a wish to work in teaching."

"He has?" The older man raised his brows in surprise. "I recall a few incidents where he has proven to be less than dedicated to his studies. I wonder if this is the kind of influence we want on our children."

Enric shrugged. "I say we let him try. At least he has a realistic idea of what to expect of a bunch of disinterested and mischievous students. And it could have been worse," he grinned, "he could be a category A and thus be the kind of influence you wouldn't want on our Council."

Tyront shuddered at the thought. "Yes, that might be something to be grateful for. But I seriously doubt that something like that will ever happen to me again. First you, then her... if there is ever another category A or B magician as long as I lead the Order, it will surely be a compliant and uncomplicated person, eager to please and willing to listen. I mean, what are the odds of this happening to the same man three times? My predecessor never even once had to deal with anything like that in all his life."

Enric sighed in mock hurt. "And there I thought you considered me a great success in the meantime."

"I do. A tough one that took me a lot of hard work."

"*You* had to work hard? Amazing how our memories seem to differ from each other. If you think I was hard work I may direct your attention back to our guest down there." He frowned, then sucked in a breath. "Has she just kicked him in the...? Oh my, that is not what I call exemplary conduct in fighting. Now I do feel sorry for him after all."

"You and every other man. But I dare say his pride is the only thing that will suffer lasting damage. What I would like to discuss, especially after seeing her progress, is how to proceed here. If she keeps up that pace, her fighting skills in only a few more weeks should be sufficient for her to be accepted into the Order. We need to start working on making that an interesting option for her."

"What do you propose?"

Tyront stepped away from the window and took a seat. "Well, Vern's efforts are a very good start, even though he is not aware that they are aiding the Order. From what I hear she has also befriended the orphan girl. But I think she also needs an adult person she feels comfortable with; somebody from the Order would be ideal to soften the impression the two of us have made on her."

"I don't really see who would be suitable. Orrin is too much involved already. Befriending her would very probably make his task of training her even more difficult, if not impossible. And there is the question if a member of the Order could really get through to her. She is not too fond of the institution as such."

Tyront nodded. "Yes, I agree. How about women close to the Order? How about Valredy?"

Enric pondered this option. She was an uncommonly gifted musician and was pretty much the authority in the city when it came to anything remotely connected to music. Self-confident, stunningly beautiful and with the typical artistic temperament that made her rather erratic.

He himself had spent a few memorable nights with her in the past, but spending more than a few minutes with her any other way was a trial for his patience.

"I am not sure this is a wise idea. She is rather unpredictable. You never know where you are with her."

"Two women, both unique in their own way in the same city, close in age… I would assume that these are promising circumstances for them to get along."

Enric just snorted. If only it were that easy. "I don't know what I would be more afraid of, their getting along well or not at all. If they do befriend each other, Valcredy will be faced with a woman in distress because of her containment here, and might well decide to help her. Or they will hate each other as Val is not one to appreciate competitors for attention, which Eryn definitely is simply because of her unusual hair colour."

"I see. Well, I bow to your expertise here. I don't have any particular experience with either of them. Any other suggestions?"

"Not really. I think Eryn and Vern's strolls through the city should over time acquaint her with different people. It might not even be important if they are in favour of the Order or not as long they help turning the city into a more pleasant place for her to live."

"We might encourage young Vern to take her out to recitals, dances and the theatre. Isn't the next Freedom Night in only a few weeks? That might get her loosened up a bit."

Enric smiled. "Yes, but I would not recommend for him to accompany her there. He is not even old enough to be allowed to participate. And I doubt she would consider going there anyway."

"I was not suggesting for Vern to take her to the Freedom Night. Orrin would not appreciate that thought at all, considering his own experience, even if his son was old enough already."

"So we casually mention to Orrin what a nice idea it would be for his son to accompany his reluctant trainee to evening entertainments?" Enric sounded doubtful.

"No, that would be overstepping a boundary, I am afraid. Orrin might have his own reasons for letting his son spend time with her, but he will hardly grant us the same privilege to make decisions with regard to that. He is not normally one for subtleties but I imagine asking him if she has been to any entertainment will give him the idea of suggesting it to Vern anyway. I will see him tomorrow as the King is due another status report and I need to see Orrin before for that."

"Alright then. Would you like another cup? Plotting how to manipulate people must surely get you thirsty."

Tyront smiled lopsidedly. "Fortunately not. I wouldn't get any work done otherwise."

CHAPTER 11

Exhaustion

Eryn bit into the bread bun Vern had made a habit of buying for her whenever they took a walk through the city together. The weather was dull and grey today, but that didn't dampen her spirits.

After living in the countryside almost all her life, where the weather had to be braved in all its forms, be it to get to a patient in need or simply to restock empty food supplies, a little grey sky and the occasional drop of rain hardly impressed her.

But city people were less willing to leave their dry homes unless it was absolutely necessary, she had noticed. Of course they could afford the luxury of waiting for a short break in the rain to run wherever they needed to go. In the country, that break would have to be longer considering the distances that had to be braved and one could never be sure there was one to come anytime soon.

She saw Vern sending suspicious glances up to the sky as if expecting an assault by a raindrop any moment.

"City boy," she chuckled. "A bit of water will not hurt you, you know."

"Probably not," he admitted, "but it would soak me to the bones and give me a chill. And believe it or not, my father is not what you would call a compassionate nurse."

She had no problem believing *that*. He was not exactly someone she would call a compassionate trainer either.

"Do you know where the orphanage is? I would like to visit Plia and see how she is doing."

Vern nodded. "Sure. It's a twenty-minute walk, though." Another glance at the sky.

"Lead the way, then."

They walked along less crowded streets and alleys, and Eryn saw a part of the city she had not been through before. It was not as much dilapidated and in danger of collapse any minute, but there was a certain degree of increased shabbiness. This was not where the well-established businesses were at home. The alleys were narrower, the smells less pleasant.

She swallowed and looked around. She and Vern stood out in their clean, well-made clothes and she hoped that they would not make an attractive target for muggers. But then Vern clearly looked a magician, so that should make any intended thieves more careful.

The question was probably which the worse outcome of taking liberties with Vern would be: trying to rob him and facing his magical defences, or stealing from him successfully and running - and hiding from subsequent sweeps of the streets as attacking a magician would hardly go unpunished.

It seemed the local thugs had either not yet spotted them or had reached the same conclusion because they arrived at the orphanage unimportuned and unscathed.

She stared up at the two-storey building. The façade was dark grey and weathered, in many places the window panes either cracked or replaced by wooden boards. Shivering at the thought of being forced to grow up in a place like that, she swallowed and approached to knock at the worn-looking door.

It took a while until there was a response. They heard a shuffling noise behind the door, as if somebody was dragging a leg behind them with every step. When the door was opened by a large, elderly woman in a washed out blue dress and a stained grey apron, they saw from the crutch she was holding that the scuffing they had heard was indeed caused by a leg injury.

Her scowl lost some of its disdain when she noticed Vern's attire, but not completely.

"We are here to visit Plia," Eryn said before who she assumed had to be Mistress Walchan had a chance to speak.

The matron pursed her lips. "You would then be the healing woman who made her face whole." Her voice was raspy and deep.

"Yes, that would be me. Can I see her?"

The woman turned and let loose a hoarse cry that echoed along the narrow stairway before being swallowed up by the damp walls and floor. "Pliaaaaa!"

Only moments later the girl came running down creaking stairs, her face twisted in fear of what might await her. Being called like that was obviously not a good sign and failure to respond immediately probably made it worse, whatever the matter was.

Her face lit up immediately when she spotted her visitors, but Eryn's own fell when she saw bruises in different colours blooming along her jaw, cheeks and one eye. She had seen abuse before - as a healer there was not really a way to avoid that. But that didn't make facing it any easier, it just gave her the strength to force her voice into a casket of ice when she turned to the matron.

She heard Vern beside her gasp when he spotted her.

"What happened to her?" he exclaimed.

The woman just shrugged. "She is a clumsy, careless little thing, always falling down stairs, bumping against things."

"Indeed?" Eryn's voice had turned saccharine. "That is interesting. From my experience these are the kind of bruises physical abuse leaves."

The woman's stare turned hostile. "Are you saying I beat her?"

"No. I can hardly tell, can I? But what I can tell is that even if you haven't done it yourself, you didn't do anything against it. Some of these bruises are several days old, others are fresher. So she was hit repeatedly. That could hardly have escaped your notice."

Mistress Walchan narrowed her eyes. "I can't have my eyes on all of them all the time. So they gave her a beating. She will get over it."

Eryn felt the wrath inside her boil up. Her first impulse was to snatch Plia's hand and drag her out of this terrible place. But where to? Sense cut in. The only place she had was a tiny cell that could barely house one, never mind two people. And even if there had been more space, they would hardly let the girl live with her. Eryn was a prisoner, after all, even if the prison comprised an entire city instead of a dungeon cell.

So Plia had to stay for now. But there had to be something that could be done for her. Eryn took a few calming breaths. Angering the matron was not the way to do this. The girl would be the one to pay for it.

"I see you have trouble with your leg, Mistress Walchan," she said, keeping her tone neutral, professional.

"Yes, what of it?" The woman's voice had grown suspicious.

"Maybe we could make a bargain here. I will take care of that if you in turn make sure that my friend Plia will no longer... bump into things and fall down stairs."

She could see the thoughts work behind that broad forehead. "What if I can't stop it?"

Eryn gave her a cool smile. "I am sure your influence here is sufficient to make that happen. I have no doubt about that. Otherwise, if I had the impression that I was being taken advantage of, I might have to consider... alternatives." That was a bold bluff, she knew. What could she do, after all? Undoing the healing was harming by way of using her skills, and she had sworn to follow that path never again. But the matron didn't know that, did she?

"What if I don't want to take that risk?"

"Let me make this absolutely clear to you: The situation as it is right now is not acceptable. We either find a way to change this together, or I will find one on my own and I dare say you won't like it." She put as much venom into her voice as she could, making the empty threat as convincing as possible.

The woman swallowed. Good: a sign of weakening resolve.

"Alright, then," she said slowly and opened the door wider as a sign of permission for them to enter.

Eryn stepped inside the gloomy room and fought hard not to flinch. Vern was less successful in hiding his disgust and looked around as if afraid that unknown horrors might jump him from every dark corner. He made sure not to touch anything and stood rigid.

There was a grimy table at one end of the room surrounded by chairs of different heights and states of decay that looked anything but stable. Or comfortable. The stench of mould made her gulp, but she bravely approached the chairs and motioned for the matron to sit, taking a chair next to her and moving it to a position where they would face each other.

"I will come here regularly and check on Plia," Eryn said before holding out her hand and waiting for the woman to take it.

When she nodded and took it, Eryn closed her eyes and took some time to shut out her surroundings to reach that place of peace inside her. Then she sent an impulse into the woman's body.

It was like walking through a desolate building. The leg was just one of many things that needed tending to. The heart was weak and in danger of being starved of oxygen, the lungs were filled with more liquid than there should be, the blood vessels were in places all but clogged up and there were areas of some growth inside the body that should not be there.

Eryn fought for clarity. What to do? Healing all of it or sticking to the bargain of taking care of only the leg?

She could almost hear her father's voice scolding her for even having to think about the answer to that. He had impressed on her more than once never to let personal feelings for a patient influence the quality of her services.

When she opened her eyes again, it was almost completely dark. She tended to lose track of time when she was healing, but judging from the complexity of what she had just done, at least two hours must have passed, maybe more. She looked up and saw Plia and Vern sitting side by side on the dirty steps. The boy had obviously overcome his aversion to touching any surfaces in favour of resting his legs.

Both of them perked up when she moved.

Mistress Walchan opened her eyes as well. It seemed she had dozed off. That tended to happen with patients when the healing took longer. It made working on them easier.

"I upheld my end of the bargain," Eryn said tiredly and stretched her stiff limbs. And much more you will never know, she added silently.

The matron nodded, cautiously turning her leg to the left, then to the right and setting it on the floor when the pain was gone.

"Come, Plia. Let's take a little walk together," Eryn suggested and walked towards the door, eager to get out of this depressing building.

When the three of them had left the building, Vern breathed out heavily and looked down at Plia.

"You have lived in this place all your life?" He shivered when she assented. "When I brought you here last time, it didn't exactly seem friendly in the dark, but in daylight it's much worse."

A shame it was, nothing less, Eryn thought, for a society to treat its orphaned children that way. It was a sure way of bringing up a new generation of criminals. Neglect together with lack of education and nourishment were a reliable combination for that. But please not *her*, she thought, looking down at the girl.

"I am hungry, I need something to eat." Vern looked at both of them. "Can I treat you two to a hot meal? Is there a good tavern around somewhere?"

Plia's eyes widened in disbelief at such unexpected generosity. Eryn swallowed. Food didn't seem to be in such great supply judging from her reaction and her skinny arms and legs.

"That is a splendid idea," Eryn said with more enthusiasm than she really felt. She would have to find a way to feed the girl regularly as long as she was in the city.

However she would accomplish that without having any funds at her disposal was another matter. She didn't want to impose on Vern for that, he was spending part of his allowance on her bread buns already.

It took them only a few minutes in the dusky light to reach a tavern that had a good reputation according to Plia. That meant edible food not watered down too much, hardly any pickpockets and reasonably clean.

They found a small table not far away from the counter and waited for the server to take their orders for stew and drinks.

While they were waiting for the food, Eryn extended her hand to Plia and smiled. "Why don't we take care of your face, little flower?"

Plia smiled shyly and lifted her own hand into Eryn's.

When both of them opened their eyes, the skin on the girl's face was unmarked again. They looked up and into the face of a stocky, bald man holding three large bowls of stew, staring at them.

"So it is true. The foreign one with the healing hands," the man spoke quietly, his voice awed.

So that was why the publican served their food himself instead of the woman who had taken their order. He must have heard from the server about the brown-haired stranger coming to his pub and was curious to see her, she thought.

She waited for what his next step would be. People with knowledge of healing or herbs were generally treated well, for people could never know when they needed their services. But things were probably different in the city.

But she needn't have worried. The man put their stew in front of them and cleared his throat before he sat down with them. It seemed to take him a few moments to gather his courage before he looked at Eryn and spoke, his voice grave.

"My companion is ill. We have had the apothecaries here, oh, I don't know how often, but nothing they have given her did her any good. It keeps getting worse. She keeps coughing up blood and I have to force her to eat something." He lowered his gaze to the table. "I don't know how much you take for your services but I am willing to pay what I have."

Eryn nodded. "Don't worry about that. Why don't you take me to her and I have a look?"

The relief flooding the man's features was almost tangible. "I will take you as soon as you have eaten."

She shook her head. "No, it's better if I do it before I eat. It is easier for me to focus if my body isn't busy digesting." She rose and looked at Vern and Plia. "Stay here and eat up. I will pick you up as soon as I am finished." Turning to Vern, she added, "If it takes very long, please accompany Plia back to the orphanage and then return home."

The boy was about to object, but Eryn had already turned away and was following the publican to a staircase at the back of the room next to the counter.

As soon as he opened the door and she entered after him, she knew that the woman on the bed was nearing death. She stepped closer to the bed and looked at a woman only a few years older than herself, sweat covering her forehead, her breathing laboured. Her linen nightgown clung to her miserably thin body, her facial features sharp in the candlelight and so pale they could almost be called white.

She took a seat at the chair the publican had put next to the bed for her and smiled at the woman.

"Hello, my name is Eryn. Your companion brought me here to have a look at you."

The woman's eyes focused on hers and she shook her head weakly as if she didn't want to deal with another try at alleviating her suffering.

"I am going to go. He can't deal with it, but he has to learn. Go away... don't give him any false hopes." Her voice was weak and high pitched and her words were followed by a violent coughing fit that left the white handkerchief she had pressed to her mouth stained with blood.

Lungs, Eryn thought immediately.

The man bent down to take his companion's hand. "That one is different, Gara, she is a healer, a real one. I have just seen her heal a girl's bruises downstairs, she has the use of magic."

The woman named Gara stared up at Eryn, taking in the brown hair she had not noticed before in the dim light. "The King's prisoner..." she whispered.

"Yes," Eryn replied mildly, "that I am. But only due to what I am, not because of something I did. I am not a criminal, you have nothing to fear from me. May I examine you? It will not hurt, I promise."

The woman stared at her a few moments longer, before nodding reluctantly. Eryn took her clammy hand into her own and immediately found her suspicions confirmed. The lungs were badly damaged, clusters of dead cells hampering the function of the lungs for breathing.

And there was another problem: The illness was contagious, highly so. It had the same characteristics as the lung disease she had had to deal with back home. Healing that woman was not the only thing that needed to be done.

Fortunately, this would not be a problem here. There was no more need to hide her magical abilities.

When another fit convulsed the frail body in front of her, she sent it into a deep, relaxing sleep. Even with closed eyes she sensed the immediate panic of the man behind her.

"I have made her fall asleep, don't be alarmed. It is easier for me to work like this when the patient is suffering great pain," she explained calmly, her eyes still closed. "There is a good chance I will be able to heal her, but there is more to consider. The illness might already be inside you and all others who were in close contact with her as well. But we will deal with this later."

She returned to her patient and started to work.

* * *

Eryn woke when she felt a gentle hand brush over her hair, noting the ache in her back before she had even opened her eyes.

The room was bright with morning light and she looked into the face of the woman she had started healing… yesterday. Oh dear, Orrin would be furious.

Orrin be damned! she thought immediately, angry at herself for granting him that power over her. This here was more important right now than whatever he felt necessary to punish her with for missing her training.

She made her lips curve into a smile. "You look much better. How do you feel?"

Gara laughed and shook her head. "Amazing. I had forgotten how good it felt to take a deep breath without pain or coughing."

She did so right now, her chest expanding and deflating again, the smile on her face relieved and joyful. Taking Eryn's hands into hers, she pressed them against her lips.

"How can I ever repay you? And to think I wanted to send you away… You fell asleep, it must have been a terrible strain on you."

Eryn smiled and shook her head. "No, it was not so bad. Considering how serious your illness was, it was fairly easy to repair. The trouble is that I'd done another rather complex healing session yesterday and my body is just not used to this kind of exertion anymore and tires more easily." Especially with only a fraction of her magic available. Her tone grew serious again. "There is the danger of other people who were in contact with you having acquired the illness from you. I will test your companion and the people who work here. We should also look at anybody who has visited you in the last weeks. If anybody shows symptoms like yours, make sure to let me know. You can contact me through the girl I brought here yesterday, her name is Plia and she lives at the orphanage."

Gara nodded and was about to reply, when the door flew open and a willowy woman stood in the doorway, out of breath and her hair tangled as if she had just run here.

"Gara!" she gasped and took in the scene.

"This is my sister Junar," Gara chuckled. "She has obviously just learned about my recovery."

Junar stepped closer to the bed, touching her sister's face timidly as if afraid that the rush of colour there and the smile were just an illusion that might be gone at the lightest touch. When her cheeks were warm to the touch and not cool and clammy like before, Junar's tears started and she drew her sister into a hard embrace.

Eryn rose and then saw the publican in the doorway, smiling at her and motioning for her to come with him. He had prepared a basin of warm water, soap, towels and a hearty breakfast tray for her.

"My name is Roy, by the way. Somehow I didn't manage to introduce myself properly yesterday."

She took his hand and shook it, smiling. "And I am Eryn. Yes, I understand very well that etiquette was not your primary concern."

"We need to talk about your price, Eryn. I told you before, whatever I have is yours."

She was about to tell him that it was her pleasure to help him and that she didn't require any compensation, when a thought occurred to her. A publican, not too far away from the orphanage... Yes, she decided, there was something he could do for her. And he would probably be grateful to do her a favour in return instead of owing her one.

"The girl I had with me yesterday evening. She is an orphan and doesn't get fed too well. I would appreciate it if you had a bowl of something warm and nourishing ready for her every day."

Roy looked at her, trying to discern if she was serious. "Is that all?"

"Yes, taking the burden of worrying about her eating properly off my shoulders would be a more than acceptable compensation for me."

He nodded and smiled lopsidedly. "If this is your wish then she is welcome to eat here as often and as much as she wishes. I feel, however, that this is not equal to what you have done for me."

"It is for me, believe me. As your companion has pointed out, I am a prisoner. What would I do with money here? They would probably just take it away from me anyway."

He nodded in understanding and turned to leave, when a thought occurred to him. "Ah yes, your escort is waiting downstairs. But don't worry, take your time. As far as I am concerned they can wait."

She froze. Escort? Orrin most likely, she thought. Of course Vern would have told him where he would probably find her when she hadn't showed up for the training. Well, she supposed it was a good sign that Orrin had not yet come storming in and dragged her out of here.

When she walked down the stairs, she saw indeed Orrin and Vern seated at one table, each of them with a glass in front of them. They looked up at her,

Vern smiling broadly, very probably because he had been pardoned from attending classes today, and Orrin with a grim expression.

"Apart from the fact that you are meant to spend the nights in your room at the warriors' quarters, I would appreciate if you sent a message next time something keeps you from returning there," he started without greeting her.

"I hadn't planned on falling asleep here. And I had a very long day yesterday and not enough time to sleep, so just back off, will you?"

Roy stepped next to her, glaring at Orrin. "She has saved my companion's life. I have never seen either of *you* do anything like that for anybody. So if there is any punishment for her, I will take it instead." He lifted his head in defiance, his massive hands balled into fists.

Oh no, Eryn thought. From the looks of the patrons around them she could tell that provoking a magician was not usually something that ended well. She put a restraining hand on Roy's arm.

Orrin lifted an eyebrow at him. "I do not appreciate your tone, publican. But considering what you have been through I will let it drop this time. Your willingness to step in for her punishment is admirable but completely unnecessary, I assure you." He rose. "Come now, the both of you. It's time to return."

Vern walked a step or two behind them to give them the chance to talk, but not so far away as to miss anything.

"You look strained and exhausted. Your offer to help is admirable, but it can't interfere with your training," Orrin said sternly. "To make this clear to you we will start our training as soon as we are back. You have missed three hours so far and will add them accordingly afterwards. That, I hope, will teach you to restrict your leisure time activities to the time allocated to them."

"You are joking, right?" She shot him an incredulous look. "How can the life of a person be less important than a stupid training schedule?"

He stopped in the middle of the street, causing quite a block to the traffic flow, as nobody dared to run over, shout at or push away an obviously angry magician.

"What is for you no more than a stupid way to waste your mornings is something I have been commissioned to do, which I am responsible for! You are not the one who has to bear the consequences if I can't show any satisfactory results!"

She let out a bitter laugh at the absurdity of his statement. "Really? *I* don't have to bear any consequences? I have to bear them no matter what! I am stuck here, whether there is progress or not! So tell me - what exactly is my motivation in making your work as pleasant as possible for you so you can show the big lord and his Lordling how brilliant a teacher you are?"

"I don't have to prove myself to anyone! Having done so in the past is what got me stuck with you! We are not training you to make life as hard as possible for you, as you are well aware!" Orrin fumed and grabbed her by the forearm, dragging her with him.

Was she aware of that? Really? She frowned at him, trying to remember if any one of them had ever deigned giving her a sensible reason for doing this to her.

CHAPTER 12

Junar

Enric watched Orrin deal her an especially hard blow, one that sent her staggering backwards and ultimately landing her on her back in the dirt.

He shook his head. "Orrin does seem rather tense since the matter of her not returning for the night several days ago, or is this just my impression?"

Tyront sighed and shook his head. "No, you are right. They did get along quite well before, considering the circumstances. They had an argument about that incident. She is angry at having to spend her time fighting when she sees more use in healing instead. And Orrin - well, it seems even his considerable patience has its limits."

"Have we decided anything about her little healing excursions yet?"

"No, but as long as she keeps them brief enough not to interfere with her training, I don't see that there is anything to be decided. I think it is a good thing she has started to use these skills here. It gives her the feeling of doing something useful."

Enric nodded, then shook his head at Orrin sweeping Eryn's legs from under her and sending her roughly to the ground once more.

"What do the apothecaries say? I dare say they won't be too thrilled about a magician wandering around and healing people, and for favours instead of hard currency, too."

Tyront smiled thinly. "True. Especially as *her* healing really works compared to what many of those charlatans practice."

"So we don't worry about them for now?"

"I have my eyes on them. And they have not even applied for an audience with the King yet. Let's wait for that."

"What would be the King's most likely reaction to a complaint from the apothecaries? I dare say his reputation would suffer serious damage if he put a stop to her healing efforts. The people in the city have started to like her."

Tyront nodded. "Yes, that is very likely. I would be surprised if he let it come to that. It might be a good way of keeping them in line, though. The apothecaries have not exactly performed according to their prices lately. Or

112

ever, now that I come to think of it. A little competition for them might do the city some good."

Enric smiled when Eryn ducked under one of Orrin's blows and surprised him by jumping over a low wall and stabbing at him, forcing him into a hurried retreat.

He said thoughtfully, "I wonder how much longer she needs to be trained with her shackles on. The requirements of the Order say she has to prove her fighting skills, and even though she has mastered no more than the basics right now, her superior strength will soon enable her to defeat more skilled opponents. This should be enough to admit her into the Order."

Tyront nodded. "True enough. But this would also make it as good as impossible for Orrin to continue training her. She could just envelop herself in a shield and refuse to cooperate with him.

"Probably." Enric snickered. "I would love to see how the old warhorse would deal with that situation."

"Shame on you. You two are meant to be on the same side. I'm afraid we have to wait until she is good enough to defeat Orrin without the shackles. Then it would no longer make sense for him to train her anyway."

"You know," the younger man said slowly, "I think I rather look forward to that day. A nice challenge would do me good."

* * *

Eryn groaned in pain from Orrin's recent blow to her side and looked up at the upside-down face that bent over her from above. Mid-thirties, long, wavy hair, dark grey eyes. It took her a few moments to know where to place the face, and then she found the connection: a bedroom on the first floor of a certain pub.

"You are Gara's sister, aren't you?" Eryn croaked and rolled on her side so as to get back onto her feet with what only a very good-natured observer would have called a graceful move.

"Yes, I am Junar." She smiled. "I am not interrupting your lesson, I hope? I was told you usually finish at this time."

"Don't worry, he has hit me so often in these last few hours that even his fiendish joy in hurting others should be satisfied for now. There is a good chance he will release me for today." She turned to Orrin, who looked Junar up and down, frowning.

"Don't tell me you are receiving visitors now during your lessons," he growled.

"Calm down, torturer," Eryn shot back. "I dare say I have had my usual dose of beatings from you for one day. It's time to stop for today anyway."

His thin smile made her clench her teeth even before she heard the words. "When I last checked I was still the one to decide when we are finished. Now lift your weapon and try to cover your flanks for once."

"Slave driver," she muttered under her breath but loud enough for him to hear.

Instead of a reply he attacked and battered her weapon until he had once more managed to hit her side with the flat of his weapon.

"Well, at least it starts taking longer until you expose your flank."

"Oh, such praise," she snapped at him after she had healed the pain away. "Am I finished now or do you have any other unresolved anger issues you wish to take out on me?" She smiled at him sweetly.

He turned with a grunt and stalked away.

Sighing, she turned back to Junar.

"What can I do for you? Is everything alright with Gara? When I last saw her two days ago she looked fine to me."

"Oh yes, she is up and about, taking over her old duties in the kitchen and shooing everybody away who insists on taking some work off her hands." She smiled. "I have come to bring you something, a little token of gratitude for what you have done for my sister." A soft bundle was pressed into Eryn's free hand.

Eryn sheathed the weapon and went to a bench to sit and open it. It turned out to be a bright blue tunic soft to the touch. A far cry from the course linen shirts she got to wear for her training. She whistled through her teeth.

"This is beautiful, but you shouldn't have spent so much money."

Junar waved the objection away. "It was no more than the fabric, and as a seamstress I get a good price for that. I wanted to make you a dress, but I suppose you don't have much use for one of those at the moment. I thought you might want to wear something nice when you take your walks through the city with the young magician."

"That was very thoughtful of you, thank you. I will enjoy wearing something that reminds me that somewhere deep inside me I am still a woman."

Junar smiled. "I don't see how anybody could forget that, whatever you are wearing."

Eryn looked down at her dusty leather armour and shrugged. "My current attires don't exactly accentuate my female attributes."

"But they don't hide them completely, either. You would be amazed what tricks I sometimes have to resort to in order to make the boyish bodies of some women appear remotely curvy. I thank the stars for frills and ruffles."

"You can do that? Well, it seems I am not the only woman in the city with magical abilities," Eryn smirked.

The other woman smiled back at her. "Do you have a place where you can try it on? I have my sewing kit with me so I can make minor changes if you need it."

Eryn thought of her cell and shrugged. "Yes, though I'm afraid it's not the most comfortable place to entertain guests."

She jumped with a yelp when she heard Orrin's voice behind her. She hadn't realised he had returned.

"You will take her to my parlour, of course."

His tone warned her not to oppose him on this and accept it for what it was: a peace offering. She looked up at him, regarded him for a few moments and then nodded.

She got to her feet and motioned for her guest to follow her.

Orrin watched them both walking away, nodding to himself. This was a good sign. It was time for her to socialise with adults as well and not only children and adolescents. Junar seemed to be a few years older, he pondered, yet close enough in age for them to connect.

* * *

Junar waited patiently in the luxurious parlour for Eryn to return from cleaning herself up after the training and sipped at her fruity drink.

When the magician finally reappeared, her face slightly red from scrubbing and her hair neatly arranged into a damp braid, she was already wearing the tunic.

"It looks very good, I like it."

Junar shook her head. "No, it doesn't look *very* good. But I can make that happen." She set a few pins on both sides and stepped back. "Now take it off again."

She was already threading a needle while Eryn considered the wisdom of undressing in the middle of a parlour that belonged to the quarters of two men who could enter any moment.

"One moment," she said and disappeared into Vern's room. She returned with his morning robe and slipped into it after removing the tunic and handing it back to the seamstress.

Watching in fascination how the needle expertly glided in and out of the fabric, she sipped at her own drink.

"How long have you been doing this? Sewing, I mean."

"Since I was twelve years old; that would be about twenty-three years now. I learned the profession from my aunt. She had no children of her own, so I got lucky. But I'd started playing around with needle and thread when I was a lot younger than that. Almost before I could walk." She cut the pale blue thread with a small pair of scissors and handed the garment back to Eryn. "Try it on again."

Eryn discarded the robe and slipped into the tunic again. This time it clung to her body more tightly. She looked at her reflection in a glass cabinet and exclaimed in surprise, just as the door was opened by Orrin and his son, "Oh dear, I *do* have breasts! I was so worried where they had gone!"

Two pairs of male eyes were magnetically drawn to her chest only to be forced away again. Vern's face flushed red and he stammered something unintelligible and disappeared into his room. Orrin recovered more quickly and just raised his brows.

"Then I assume congratulations are in order," he stated dryly and walked to the cabinet to pour himself a drink.

Junar giggled and Eryn smirked. It seemed Orrin had got over the bad mood he'd been in over the last few days. Good. That would make the training with him less of a strain. She hoped.

"That they are. I have just rediscovered my femininity after wearing sackcloth for these last, what, three months?"

Orrin took a closer look at Junar. "Where have I seen you before?"

"At the public house where you picked up Eryn in the morning after she had healed my sister, My Lord." Junar swallowed and then added nervously, "I hope you don't hold a grudge against my sister's companion. He spoke out of turn, I know, but it was just a rather clumsy attempt at being gallant. He was really worried that Eryn would be punished because of helping him and Gara."

Orrin nodded. "Yes, I am aware of that. If I weren't, he would have been punished for it already." He tilted back his head to empty his glass. "I'll leave you now, ladies. There is some work I need to take care of." He nodded to both of them and disappeared into his study.

Junar stared at the closed door a few moments longer. "He is kind on the inside, isn't he?"

Eryn chuckled. "He has his moments, yes." She let her hands once more glide over her new tunic. "I think I should take it off now before I stain it."

"You know, I think you should leave it on and we present your newly discovered femininity to the world. What do you think?" Junar smiled.

Eryn grinned back. "Yes, why not?" It felt good to look like a woman again, even if it was only for a short time.

* * *

Enric slowed his steps when he saw the two women emerge from the building towards which he was heading to give himself more time for beholding the view. He didn't know the second woman, but Eryn he recognised immediately. He would have even without the dark hair. He had been watching her for several weeks from his window, after all, and her way of moving had become familiar to him. His brows rose at the clothes she wore. It seemed as if she had somehow acquired a well-cut garment that emphasised instead of hid her personal advantages as her usual attire did. Clothes made to fight in and protective armour were not meant to be flattering, but functional, after all.

He could tell the very moment she spotted him. Her steps grew rigid and she directed them in the opposite direction immediately.

But he was too close already and stepped in their way. Even if Eryn hadn't stopped, the other woman did and bowed to him. "Lord Enric, a good day to you."

Enric nodded to her. "And to you."

His gaze wandered to Eryn, who clearly wanted to take a step or two back but forced herself not to. Probably to avoid showing him any weakness.

"Eryn. It has been a while." His smile was faint and to his credit his eyes stayed on hers instead of wandering south where he felt them drawn.

"Not long enough," she snapped, then briskly turned away, taking the other woman's arm to drag her along.

He watched them all but run, shaking his head with an indulgent half-smile. It seemed she had not yet forgiven him for tampering with her internal shield.

Junar swallowed and turned to her, holding on to her arm to stop Eryn's rapid pace when they had rounded the first corner and were out of the Lord's sight.

"That was not very polite, I must say," she said reproachfully. "He is a very important man, you know. Angering him is hardly a smart course of action, he has means at his disposal to make you pay for it."

"He is a massive bastard as well," she growled, "and most of my encounters with him have left me either unconscious or a victim to some other action of his. I try to stay as far away from that one as I can."

"Really? He seems so… cool and civilised."

She snorted. "Yes, I suppose he would if he is not using you for target practice or the like."

Junar stared at her incredulously. "So they have been torturing you? But… that's terrible!"

Eryn sighed. "Well, that would depend on your definition of torture, I think. I have not been abused physically if you don't count Orrin battering me in my involuntary training and those accursed magicians knocking me out repeatedly after I was brought here."

"Now I am completely confused."

Eryn studied her for a few moments. This woman was more or less a stranger to her, yet the thought of sitting down and talking to her about the mess she was in was an immensely tempting one. And it was not as if she had to be careful to keep her abilities a secret any longer. What did she have to lose in confiding in the seamstress?

"You know, I could really use somebody to talk to and you seem to be willing to listen. Do you know a quiet place?"

Junar smiled, delighted. "I do. I happen to live in one."

* * *

Three hours later Eryn leaned back contentedly. It had done her good to share this weight she felt under. Junar was an excellent listener, making the right sounds at appropriate intervals, asking good questions and showing sympathy without letting it progress as far as pity.

Then Junar had talked about herself, about the man she had lived with until he left her due to her inability to have children and turned to another woman who bore him three children in as many years. After Junar's aunt's death five years ago she had taken over her business. This had coincided with the separation from her companion and provided a welcome opportunity to focus all her attention on something she could control and that was to be hers alone.

"I could have a look at you, if you want. Maybe I can find the problem and take care of it," Eryn offered.

Junar smiled and shook her head. "That is a generous offer, thank you, but I am alone and also getting a little old for children. And the way it is now I don't have to worry about unwanted surprises if I decide to become intimate with a man every now and then." She refilled her cup with the steaming herbal concoction, then continued, "I think it would be marvellous if you could do more healing in the city. The apothecaries are too powerful here, for whatever reason. Their remedies often don't help at all, and yet they take our money whether their medicines work or not."

"The apothecaries?" Eryn sat up and listened attentively. "They take care of all the healing in the city?"

Junar snorted. "After what you have done I don't dare call what they are doing *healing*. But that's what they would like to make people think they do, yes."

"What exactly is it they do?"

"Mostly they squeeze money out of desperate people who seek help. They look at a patient, tell you what they think the problem is and then pull out from their bulgy black leather bags a medicine that costs a small fortune."

"You seem to be rather out of sorts with them?" Eryn enquired cautiously.

"I have seen them treat my sister. Roy spent twenty-five gold pieces on medication and consulting. Do you have any idea how long they both had to save for that? And nothing has helped. When he returned to them time and again to tell them that there had been no improvement, but instead a worsening, they told him that he must have made a mistake in giving her the medicine." She shook her head in disgust.

Eryn bit her lip. That sounded like the kind of travelling medics she had encountered before. They pushed their carts from village to village and town to town to promise miracles, and they usually were gone by the time their victims found out that they had been conned out of their hard-earned money or goods. Only the ones here seemed to have reached another level of perfection: they didn't even have to run afterwards.

"You said you used to heal people in your own town. Why can't you do the same thing here? There are many who would trust a magician far more than any apothecary." Her eyes had started to sparkle. "And you could earn a lot of money with it."

Eryn shook her head slowly. "No. That is not what healing is meant to be: a source of wealth for a single person," she murmured, repeating the words she had heard her father use so often. "Healing skills are meant to serve *people*, not the greed of the one providing them."

"That's even better!" Junar had leapt up in agitation, pacing her little room. "You could really provide a service here, help people. I mean, what is to stop you from doing it?"

Eryn rubbed her face. "I hate to dampen your enthusiasm here, but there is quite a lot to stop me. Firstly, I am a prisoner in this city. Neither the King nor the Order would be thrilled about my building up a healing empire, kicking the law-abiding, tax-paying apothecaries out of business. Secondly, the apothecaries themselves would probably not observe my efforts quietly but demand the King himself remove me. And thirdly, Orrin was angry at me for more than a week after I missed one single morning of fighting training – can you imagine what they would do to me if I made this into a habit? They would very likely lock me up in no time. And not just inside the city, but in a rather more confined space." She bent forward, when Junar's face fell, taking her hands. "Believe me, there is nothing in the world I would rather do, but right now I can't do more than the occasional healing I happen to stumble upon."

"This is not fair. You sit here, these amazing abilities unused and people around us are taken advantage of while you are forced to learn swordplay." She let herself fall back into her chair, sighing in frustration.

Eryn smiled. Hearing this from a mouth other than her own for a change was balm for her soul.

CHAPTER 13

Vern's Talent

She let her legs dangle from the fence she was sitting on and smiled when she saw Vern approaching. Her smile slowly faded once she caught sight of his expression. It seemed as if he hadn't had a good day.

She jumped down to the ground and slung an arm around his shoulders when he was close enough.

"You look like a raincloud, love. Talk to your Auntie Eryn, tell her all about it," she cooed, hoping to make him smile.

He shook his head at her in exasperation instead. "You know, you are blurring that older friend/mother figure line. That really is confusing for a growing lad like me." He looked at her with a sagely look in his face that spoke of suffering.

She whistled through her teeth. "Been reading smart books again, have we? Come on, then you may buy me another one of these fabulous buns while you tell me why the world is a cruel place not worthy of your intellect."

That finally made him smile. "Oh my, may I really?" he asked in his best eager-little-boy voice imitation.

"Yes, my traumatised growing lad, I generously grant you the permission to buy me sweet pastries," she announced solemnly, head held high. "A privilege granted only to the smartest and bravest of men!"

That, again, seemed to have been the wrong thing to say as his face fell again.

"You know, I am kind of manoeuvring through a conversational field with a lot of traps. Why don't you tell me what's wrong before I inadvertently make you cry, explode or go berserk on me?"

He sighed and turned to her. "I just had a very disagreeable talk with one of my teachers. He told me that my lack of enthusiasm will make it impossible for him to let me progress to the next year if I don't improve quickly."

"I'm sorry, Vern." She tried to remember if he had told her about anything that he found particularly annoying. He was normally happy about anything that involved books. Fighting, she mused, was the big exception as far as she could remember.

"What is that terrible subject, then? Combat training?"

He looked at her sheepishly. "No. Botanical studies."

She looked at him with raised brows. "What? You are joking, right? A bookish lad like you can't find anything remotely interesting in studying plants? Do you have any idea what mysteries lie hidden inside plants? How immensely useful they are for healing? What amazing changes they go through? How they are part of the circle of life around us?"

"No, I don't!" he exclaimed, throwing his arms up in desperation. "All I see are poor pictures in old books, names that are too complicated to pronounce and useless knowledge that nobody knows how to use!"

She pursed her lips. "I see. So, why do you even learn about plants? I mean, there is no real use for them in fighting, is there? And that's pretty much all you seem to learn about."

"Not for fighting directly, but for surviving out there in the big wide world in case one day we are forced to march upon an army and stay hidden in the woods without supplies."

She smirked and shook her head. "Oh dear. That's it? Ignorant idiots, the lot of them. Come, I'll show you something. But first you buy me that bun."

* * *

He looked up at the tree, doubtfully. "What exactly is it that's so fascinating about a tree?" He managed to make the last word sound like an insult.

"Put your hand on the bark." Another unnerved look at her. She waited until he had complied. "Now close your eyes." When she had touched the tree as well and closed her own eyes, she continued, "Send a small magical impulse into the tree and explore the inside. Don't make it too strong or you might hurt it."

He opened his eyes again. "Magic? Into a tree? How is that supposed to work?"

"You do know how to send energy? I mean, you learn how to do it to improve your strength and speed for fighting, after all. This is hardly any different."

"But then I am only sending it inside my body! I have no idea how to do it otherwise. The only other way I send energy away from myself is when I am attacking somebody with strikes."

She opened her eyes again, considering what he had just told her. He had already learned how to deal strikes? Now, that was interesting... She forced herself to return to the tree in front of them, storing that bit of useful information away for later.

"You have learned how to infuse your own muscles with energy. It pretty much works the same with another person. Give me your hand."

When their fingers touched, she sent a surge of power into his calves that almost made him jump.

"Whoa!"

"Now send the energy back to me, adding a little of your own."

She felt a prickling in her upper arms. "No, too high. Lower." This time the energy flowed into her lower back. "Vern, stop guessing. Send an exploratory impulse into my body and locate my calves. When you know where they are, target them and sent the energy directly."

"What?"

She sighed again. "Find your calves inside your body. Have you found them?"

"Yes."

"Look at their rippled structure, their length, how they contract when you move them a little. Now send a small impulse of energy inside my body, but don't let it completely loose. Maintain a connection, like a piece of cord tied to an animal. You build and maintain this connection by adding small amounts of energy the further inside me you send it. Imagine this like spinning a thread with energy, the longer it becomes, the more energy it requires. It provides you with information about me. You need to actively collect this information and lead it back to where you touch me. It needs to pass from my body back to yours and back to your head where you identify and understand it."

She heard him draw in a sharp breath. "Is everything alright, Vern?"

"I... It... I mean..."

She opened her eyes and tried to find out what seemed to disturb him. He just stared at her, shaking his head slightly. "I have never seen this before... it's amazing! I have seen inside you, everything!"

She smiled at his reaction. "Incredible, how complicated it is, isn't it?"

"I want to do this inside my own body. How do I do it?" His eyes had taken on a feverish shine.

"It works just like before, only easier, as you can send the impulse from your head and guide it through your body and back to your head again."

She waited until he opened his eyes again after what had to have been several minutes. He exhaled and leaned against the tree.

"I look completely different from you. Especially, you know..."

"Our reproductive organs? Yes, quite a difference, isn't it?" She laughed when he blushed scarlet. "Would you like to try sending energy out again? It seems you know how to find you way around now."

He nodded and took her hand eagerly. Moments later she felt power flooding her calves.

"Very good - you are a fast learner. Now stop the supply or you'll make me walk up that tree."

She took his hand and laid it back on the bark of the tree. "Now send the same impulse into the tree, explore it. Be careful how much energy you use," she repeated her warning. "We don't want it to burst into flames."

"There is a flow of life inside," he murmured in surprise. "And not only the tree itself, but many, many little life forms as well. The inner part, it's not active any more, like it's dying." He frowned, his eyes still closed. "Only the outer part around the middle is active. This tree is ill."

"No," she corrected him. "This is how a tree grows. It is completely normal. You can go to other trees and see for yourself. Do you remember what the stump looks like when a tree is cut? The dark circle in the middle is the dead part. The outer circles that are still bright transport the nourishment up to the leaves."

He removed his hand, looking at it as if he still felt the strange sensation of being inside a tree and tried to determine where his own physical form ended.

Looking at Eryn for a long time, he finally said, "Can we do this again? Can you show me more? There is so much..." He broke off, his eyes darting from side to side as if his mind was overflowing with all this new information, of the new world that had suddenly opened up to him.

Eryn looked at him, slightly worried. Had she overwhelmed him? Should she have introduced him into this more slowly?

Then his head jerked up. "I need to draw this. Come."

He grabbed her hand and all but dragged her with him when he started running back to the warriors' quarters. She almost stumbled a couple of times when he raced up the stairs, not letting go of her hand until they were in his room. He searched frantically for a pen and a piece of paper.

Only then did he speak again. "Please sit still and don't move." He gently pushed her onto his bed, then put the paper onto his bedside table, held her hand, closed his eyes and started drawing something with his other hand.

Her eyes bulged when she recognised what the lines began to form. He was drawing the muscles in her calves, what they looked like when they were relaxed. She could see the fibres, how they built fascicles and stretched in neat alignments.

She could feel her heartbeat increase as the possibilities of the boy's amazing artistic talent started to dawn on her.

"What's the matter? Are you alright?" He sounded alarmed and opened his eyes. "Your blood, it has started moving faster."

She laughed, giddy with excitement. "Don't worry, this is a natural reaction. Go on, finish your drawing."

When he opened his eyes next time, the drawing was finished and he stared at it as if in surprise. He handed it to Eryn, who shook her head in amazement, even though she had seen it progress under his capable hand.

"This is a phenomenal talent you have here, Vern. What wouldn't I give to have it... what I could do with this." Her voice was quiet, awed.

Vern stared at her, looked alternatingly into each of her eyes to understand what he had just heard. "You are a healer, and you envy *me* the ability to draw pictures? But this is just..." He waved his arm through the air, searching for a word that aptly described the irrelevance of his capability.

She looked up at him, frowning. "You better stop right here. Whatever would come after *just* is nothing I care to hear." She grabbed his arm, leaning forward to lend her words more vigour, "You have a rare gift here. Something that has nothing to do with magic, something I bet not many other magicians or non-magicians could do. And then your magical powers in combination with this... If I had this ability, I would be able to teach people about healing, give them the chance to look inside the human body without magical abilities or cutting it open." She let go of him and leaned back, exhaling. "And you discard it as something worthless. This hurts me almost physically, you know."

* * *

She lay awake that night, tossing and turning and trying to find sleep. But her brain was overactive, it kept refusing to close down and give her the rest her body needed.

Thoughts of Vern's talent kept resurfacing, of the low opinion he had been taught to have of it for many years. Something people did at fairs to earn a few coins, or if they were good enough, to indulge the rich by painting their portraits. Nothing a magician should ever have to resort to, not an ability fit for one who was meant to reach higher, more dignified goals in life.

She lit one of the candles Vern had smuggled to her and had another look at the picture he had drawn. He had given it to her as a gift, touched that she had seen value in it he himself had not yet been able to fully grasp.

She traced the muscle fibres on the paper lightly with her finger, careful not to smudge the lines. Then she closed her eyes, relaxed her calf and examined it from within. She smiled again, marvelling how he had been able to transfer that inner image to paper without medical knowledge of the human body.

Knowing that he had that talent and was not encouraged or even permitted to use it, began to gnaw at her. She thought about the books back home in her cottage. The pictures which many of them contained, not a single one as well done as what she was holding in her hands right now.

Her father had brought the books with him from their home country. Artists and magicians, she thought, what a pity that the chance for finding both in the same person was rather remote. And now, that she had found one in this unlikely place she couldn't even make use of his talent as he was not supposed to indulge in it.

What a depressing situation.

* * *

She jerked awake when she heard the loud thumping at her door. This was not Vern, that much was certain. This sounded more like…

"Eryn, wake up! Now! Open the bloody door!" Yes, she sighed deeply, him exactly.

She opened the door a crack and jumped back hurriedly when Orrin pushed it open completely, almost squeezing her between it and the stonewall.

"You are aware that this is my free day, aren't you? You know, the one you yourself agreed to grant me after every nine terrible, excruciating, unbearable ones? Go away and let me sleep," she almost whined. "What is it with you and your son and your determination to begrudge me my well-deserved sleep?"

Then she saw Orrin's expression. "What…?"

But he had already grabbed her hand, very much like his son the day before but with considerably more strength behind it, and dragged her after him, not caring about her unkempt hair or her being in sleeping attire that barely covered her knees.

He only stopped when they had reached the door to Vern's room. He gave her a grave look before pushing it open, revealing pandemonium.

The bed, the floor, every available surface was covered with sheets of paper filled with sketches and drawings of the human body, inside and out.

Vern, hunched over another sheet, his hair standing up in all directions as if he had raked through it repeatedly, didn't even look up to acknowledge them but continued the hectic movements of his pen with closed eyes.

Eryn clasped both her hands over her mouth and stared at the scene in front of her.

Orrin grabbed her shoulder, spinning her around so she faced him. "What is the meaning of this? What happened to him?"

She stared at Orrin for a few moments with wide eyes, then deftly stepped into Vern's room, closing the door with a swift movement and turning the key in the lock before he had even reacted.

Orrin shook the door handle, knowing that it was useless but feeling the need to do it nevertheless, as if action - be it ever so futile - was better than doing nothing at all.

Orrin sat down on a settee directly opposite the door and gazed at it, wondering what to do. He had fetched her because he had been afraid for his son, that it might be a mental illness. He wanted her to have a look at him.

He was not even sure what exactly she had just done. Had Eryn locked herself in with Vern because he was dangerous? But what about she herself? Or had she done it because the world outside was dangerous for Vern in his current state? What state could that be? No mental illness, he hoped fervently even if from what he had seen there didn't seem to be any doubt about that.

But he had a healer with him. If there was a chance, then Vern was with the only person in this damned kingdom that could help him.

Was there anybody Orrin was supposed to inform? Lord Tyront? As long as this was only about his son, there was no duty whatsoever to do so, but now that Eryn was involved… Too much to think, not now…

He got up and went on shaky legs to the drinks cabinet, pouring himself the strongest drink he had into the tallest glass he could find and stumbling back to the sofa to wait.

* * *

About four hours had passed when Orrin decided that he had had enough. Repeated attempts at listening at the door had not revealed anything. At first he had heard the low sounds of murmuring but nothing he could have deciphered through the wooden door.

Then nothing. It was quiet in there and he had no idea if this was a good sign or a terrible one. He regretted drinking the entire tall glass and tried to get rid of the images of two badly maimed bodies lying behind the locked door out of his reach.

It didn't matter that here had been no sounds suggesting anything of that kind or other impressions to give ground to such fears; this was not logical thinking, but worry and anxiety.

He rose and had finally decided to resort to violence and break the door open, when a memory from long ago slowly made its way to the surface, fighting against agitation and substances that made thinking so damn hard right now.

The door to Vern's room. There was a mechanism that allowed it to be opened from the outside. The boy had managed to lock himself inside the room twice before, when he was very young, not knowing how to get out again, locked inside panicked and screaming. Orrin had then decided to do something to prevent this from happening ever again.

A broad smile spread across his face, and he raced into his own bedroom to fetch the tool the smithy had made for him when he installed the new lock more than ten years ago. He removed the outer handle and applied the tool, turning it slowly and leaned his forehead against the cool wood. Then he heard the click that signalled that the door was unlocked. Re-attaching the door handle with shaking hands, he swallowed and then pushed himself back to his feet to enter the room.

He blinked a few times. The scene presenting itself to him was nothing like what he had imagined. It was peaceful, cosy and somehow intimate. His son and Eryn both lay on the bed, covered with a blanket, Vern's back to her and her arm around his middle.

The mess of paper everywhere was gone, it had been stacked into neat piles on the desk.

Eryn stirred and looked up at him, sending him a withering look from under half-closed eyelids.

"Go away! We both had a long and restless night. Leave us alone." With that her head fell back onto the pillow and within moments she had drifted off again.

Orrin just stared at them, completely lost. Then, half-dazed, he shook his head and walked out the room just as he had been told. He stood in his parlour, wondering when exactly they had switched roles and she had become the one to take command and he the one to follow her orders.

They looked peaceful enough, he considered, and would very likely be asleep for several more hours. That meant he could take care of the work he had waiting for him.

CHAPTER 14

Teaching Vern

When Orrin returned to his quarters late in the afternoon he found his son and Eryn seated on the parlour floor, sorting through the flood of pictures that had been the result of what seemed like a frenzy of activity.

Behind them on a table stood the remainders of what must have been a hearty meal. Both of them looked up with a frown as if less than happy about the interruption.

Vern looked much better than in the morning, Orrin noted with relief. Gone were both paleness and the feverish expression in his eyes. Eryn was still wearing her night attire from the morning when he had dragged her here anything but gently, but had donned Vern's morning robe and a pair of his slippers that were too large for her feet.

Orrin straightened. He felt he had been patient enough with them, and now it was time for answers. Strolling over to them he cleared his throat. Each looked up to him, holding sheets of papers with drawings in their hands, as if waiting for him to speak and then be gone again to leave them to proceed with whatever they were doing.

"Talk to me. Now."

Vern glanced at Eryn and when she nodded encouragingly he rose and motioned for his father to sit with him at the table. His own son was looking for guidance to her before talking to him. When had that happened?

"Would you like something to drink first, father?"

"Stop stalling, Vern."

Vern breathed in and out a few times to brace himself, then looked straight into his father's eyes and said, "I have decided to pursue drawing."

"Drawing what?"

That question seemed to take him by surprise. He blinked a few times before answering, "Well… *things*. Everything. Whatever I want. For now, illustrations of the human body."

"Alright," Orrin said carefully. "Why?"

"Because I think I am very good at it."

"Yes, I can see you are."

Vern stared. "You can?" he asked dumbfounded.

"Well, it's not hard to see, is it? I have no idea what exactly it is I am looking at, but I can tell it's well done."

"Oh." That was obviously not the reaction he had expected. "Then you don't object?"

Orrin leaned back, folding his arms. "That I am not so sure about. From what I have seen in the morning it does not seem to be a healthy thing for you to do."

Eryn sighed. It seemed there was some clarification in order. "He told me yesterday that he had problems with botany and I wanted to show him how fascinating it really is. I showed him something about plants so he could learn about them, but it seems the inside of the human body is more to his liking." She could not entirely hide how pleased she was about that. Then she shot Orrin a withering look. "He was, in fact, so taken with it that something was unleashed inside him that has been forced into dormancy for quite a while as it seems: the talent for drawing. It erupted so violently last night because it had been suppressed for such a long time."

She stared at Orrin with her arms folded, and he couldn't get rid of the impression that she expected him to justify himself somehow.

"I never told Vern he couldn't draw. It is just not generally considered a fitting pastime for an aspiring magician," he replied with as much dignity as he could muster. He sensed a rising relief surging through him. It had been no mental illness, but a creative outburst! The boy could draw as much as he liked for all Orrin cared, as long as he didn't have to feel this withering fear about his son anymore.

Then he thought of something and glared right back at her. "What about your sleeping in one bed together with my son? You are aware that he is still a boy and not a plaything for you?"

A moment of silence preceded the laughter that then burst out of Vern. "What? Her plaything?" Vern held his stomach, convulsing with laughter.

Eryn raised an eyebrow when a tear rolled down his cheek. "You know, this reaction of yours is not exactly flattering for me."

Vern's guffaws died down to a chuckle. "Seeing your hair after you wake up for the second time had a sobering effect on me when it comes to the natural attractions of femininity."

"How charming you can be," she snorted. "Don't ever come to me when you need to talk about women. And with that attitude I'd say you will need every help you can get."

Orrin relaxed visibly at their banter and especially after Vern's reaction to his question.

Eryn nodded at him. "Not good enough for your son, am I? Lucky for you then the little brat doesn't want me because of my tousled morning hair. Pretty shallow attitude though, I would say. Especially when I look at his own style. I wonder how he dares even mention mine."

"What exactly are you two up to? What are these drawings for?" Orrin drew the conversation back to what he still couldn't fathom.

"No special purpose," Vern replied and stretched out languidly. "They just, you know, wanted to be out." He looked rather owlish, knowing fully well that this was hardly a comprehensible statement for his father who had never in his life felt the urge to draw a picture.

Orrin looked at her thoughtfully. "Are they good, his drawings?"

She shook her head. "No, they are not. They are more along the lines of fabulous, amazing and completely genius."

Vern beamed at her. "Keep talking about me like that and I might accept you as my plaything after all," he quipped and narrowly escaped the throw cushion she used for the purpose it seemed to have been named for.

Orrin rubbed his face with both hands and then sighed. "Can you two be serious for a short while at least? I am trying to talk to you here."

Both settled down again, though Vern wisely kept a safe distance from Eryn.

"What things have you been teaching my son? Why can he look inside his own body now?"

"This is a very basic skill - nothing dangerous. He can't harm himself with it."

"Now, that is a relief for a change. Anything else I should know?" He looked at both of them alternately.

"Nothing I am aware of," she smiled innocently.

"Yes, right," he grunted and looked down at the stacks of paper on the carpet. "Now tidy up your things, I am expecting Lord Tyront soon."

Eryn rose hurriedly. "That was my cue. I better return to my hole." She had no particular wish to meet Tyront, especially as she felt rather vulnerable in her current attire.

Vern looked up hopefully. "Tomorrow after your training? I'll pick you up?"

She smiled at him, "Sure. You do that," and then left quickly.

* * *

Junar turned when she saw Eryn and Vern walk down the street and hurried to catch up with them.

"Wait," she called before they were out of sight. She had been on her way to the training grounds, but it seemed she had been a little too late.

Both turned and waited for her.

"Junar," Eryn then said, "I suppose you don't remember Vern. He is Orrin's son."

Junar smiled. "But of course I do. You were waiting for Eryn with your father when you came to pick her up from my sister's place."

Vern was obviously pleased at that and bowed formally. "It is a pleasure to meet you again."

"Where are you two off to? I was on my way to you to ask you if you needed a dress for the Freedom Night. I suppose you don't have one yet, do you?"

Eryn took a step back and lifted her hands, palms out as if to ward off evil. "Hey, wait a moment! I have no intention of going there, believe you me."

"Why ever not? After what you have been through I am sure you could use a night of folly." She smiled apologetically when Vern's face took on a slightly darker colour.

"You can't be serious! I might end up in bed with..." She waved her hands around, desperately, "...Orrin or that terrible idiot he forces me to train with!"

"My father never goes there, so there is no danger of that," Vern stated quietly. Both women looked at him.

"Why does he never go there?" Eryn asked, suddenly curious. There had been something in the boy's voice, a tension that spiked her interest.

"Because when he went there the last time he got stuck with *me*."

Now that was an unexpected revelation. She had been wondering what had happened to Vern's mother.

Junar cut in before Eryn could continue her questions. "Why don't you two come to my place? It seems this is not a conversation fit for a crowded street."

Eryn nodded gratefully and off they went to the small apartment above her shop.

When they were comfortably seated, Eryn leaned forward, considering how to phrase her question tactfully.

"Now, can we go back to what you said before, Vern?"

He fidgeted about on his seat, uncomfortable. "If you must know..." he sighed, and started talking about a night sixteen years ago when his father had been to his last Freedom Night where he had met a young woman whom he had shared a bed with.

Several months later she had somehow managed to discover his identity, which was quite a feat considering the strict rules of anonymity, and decided to visit him. She had told him about the child inside her, that it was Orrin's and that she had no intention of raising it herself. Orrin had offered her to pay for all the child's expenses and also for hers, but she wouldn't accept the offer.

Then she had returned again a few months later with a small bundle, and, after pressing it into his arms, turned around to run off, never to be seen again.

Eryn and Junar both stared at him. Eryn recovered first. "Her loss, my lad. And your father's gain. You are aware that he loves you very much, aren't you? In the few months I have been here I have never once seen anything that made me think that he feels you are anything other than a blessing."

Vern nodded. "Yes, I know that. Yet it is strange not knowing anything about my mother."

She smiled sadly, knowing well enough how that felt. "I suppose she thought that your father could give you a better life than she might have. It couldn't have been easy to give you up." She ruffled his hair. "Even if you are cheeky and unbearable sometimes."

That made him smile again. "Father says it's the bad company I keep."

Junar laughed out loudly at that and with this the gloomy mood vanished completely.

"Now, about that dress you are going to need," she began, then and turned to Eryn, who rolled her eyes.

"I told you I have no intention of going there. I saw a few of these events back home and I think I can live a happy life without ever attending one again."

The older woman grinned. "I think you will find that the ones in the city are a bit more festive than those you have been to. It is quite a big event here. You don't have to go with anybody, just have a look around. The decoration is really a sight to be seen, the music is nice, the drinks are free and if you don't like it, you just leave."

"Why don't I save you the time and effort of making me a dress I can't even pay for to go to an event I don't want to be at?"

Junar gave a cool smile in return. "Instead, why don't you save your words, get up from your seat and let me take your measurements?"

Eryn shook her head and rose, defeated. "Well, you are a grown woman, it's your time to waste."

"There's a good girl. Now stretch your arms out. Higher. Good." She took a measuring tape from her pocket and jotted down the numbers on a small pad.

After a few minutes she motioned for Eryn to sit again. "I should be able to finish it within the next few days. I will send for you when it is ready for the final fitting."

"You know, it's not even as if I would be anonymous there." Eryn pointed at her hair. "Everyone will know who I am. I am the only person plainly recognisable amongst a horde of blond strangers."

"That should give you an edge, dear. I bet you will have a nice choice of interested men, of all shapes and ages, at your disposal. You just have to pick the one you like best and have a little fun for a change." Junar's smile was indulgent.

"You know, I really don't think this is an appropriate topic to discuss in front of Vern," Eryn sighed.

"Nonsense. He is almost a grown-up lad. In a couple of years he will be allowed to go there himself. It can't hurt for him to learn something in advance. I imagine his father would not be too comfortable talking to him about this."

Well, there was no denying that, but it still felt wrong somehow to talk about sex in front of a boy who was yet to be allowed to partake of it.

Junar disappeared into her cooking niche around a corner and they heard clattering and what suspiciously sounded like shattering pottery.

"Is everything alright? Are your hurt?" Vern called out.

"No, not really. It is a shame about the plate, though." She returned, sucking her thumb, holding a dangerously tipping tray with three cups and a jug with her other hand. Eryn quickly rose and took it from her to avoid more crockery casualties.

"You have cut your finger," Vern exclaimed with what seemed inappropriate pleasure in such a situation.

Junar eyed him with a raised brow, taken aback. "So it would seem, yes."

Eryn laughed. "Don't be annoyed, he doesn't mean it like that. He has just spotted another chance of witnessing a healing."

"You don't need to do that. It is only a tiny scratch, nothing that won't heal in a few days."

When Vern looked disappointed, Eryn sighed. "Why don't we take care of it nevertheless?"

The boy grinned happily. "Can I watch, you know, from the inside?"

"Well, we would have to ask Junar's permission for that. She might not be comfortable with a young man peering around inside her body."

Junar looked puzzled. "What was that?"

Vern turned to her eagerly. "I saw Eryn heal before, but now I have learned how to look at a body from the inside, too. I would absolutely love to see how it looks from there, what really happens."

"I think we can manage that," the woman said, smiling. "How does it work? Do I need to do anything particular?"

"No." Eryn shook her head. "Just relax. And Vern, you will keep your attention on the cut, no unauthorised exploring. It would be a violation of Junar's privacy. Understood?"

He nodded quickly and when Eryn touched the injured hand he took her other one and sent an impulse through it.

The cut was only shallow and was mended easily. She took more time with it, however, to give Vern the opportunity to have a good look. When the skin was knitted together again, both opened their eyes.

"This looks even more incredible from inside," he marvelled. "And so complicated! All the little things happening in there at the same time..."

"It's easier than it looks. Most of it would happen anyway, only at a slower pace. It's more or less a matter of providing the energy to speed it along." She looked at him thoughtfully. "You wouldn't, by any chance, want to try it out, would you?"

He sat bolt upright and stared at her in disbelief. "Try it? Me?"

She could see panic, fascination, excitement and uncertainty flitter across his face in a matter of moments.

"Don't be alarmed," she soothed him immediately. "It was just a thought. If you are not comfortable with it…"

He interrupted her agitatedly, "Comfortable? I would love to try it! But what if do something wrong?"

She smiled. "Then I would tell you and we would correct it together."

"Brilliant! Yes! Yes!" He jumped up, looking around.

"What are you doing? Sit down, my lad."

"I need something to cut myself with, don't I?"

Eryn sighed and shook her head. "No, you will not heal yourself. You need to be concentrated and focused, not distracted by pain at your first time."

She rose and went to where she had heard the pottery shatter and retrieved a shard from the floor. She saw both of them swallow when she slowly dragged the sharp edge across her palm and blood welled up. Then she held out her unharmed hand for Vern to take and closed her eyes.

When she felt his warm and now slightly clammy fingers wrap around hers, she gave him a few moments to orientate himself.

"Have you located the injury?" she asked calmly.

She felt a slight movement that indicated that he had either nodded or shaken his head.

"You need to talk to me, Vern. I have my eyes closed and can't see what you are doing with your head."

"Yes," he croaked, "I have found it."

"Good. Do you see the activity around the site? The blood flowing out, the way my body is responding to it?"

He nodded again, then remembered that she couldn't see him and added, "Yes."

"Look at the little alien elements around the wound. They are not supposed to be there, but will get into the wound, there is no avoiding that."

"How?"

"They cling to every surface in great numbers. Some of them are harmless, others not so. But the ones on the bit of pottery are no problem for my body because I am healthy and can deal with them."

"So if you are not healthy they might be a problem?" he enquired.

"Yes. Their nature and the state of the body determine whether this is the case or not. So in some cases the patient might need help to get rid of them." She wondered if he would be interesting in learning how to do that or would rather progress to the actual repair of tissue. But his next question took care of that.

"How do I do this?"

"By carefully redirecting the flow of the small amounts of blood with the little parts in it so it doesn't circulate through the whole body for now."

"How? I don't know how," his voice was high with nervousness.

"Imagine the path you would like the blood to take around the wound. Then gently send an impulse there to coax it along that path. Yes, that's very good. But go easy on the amount of energy you use. Different from fighting, the accomplishment is not the application of great strength once but how to dose and measure it in a way that it can be used like a fine instrument. This is not about brute force, but about skill, knowledge and inner strength."

She waited until he had created small vortices that had the effect of containing the tiny intruders around the wound before she continued. "Well done. Now push them out through the wound and then apply a very small amount of heat to eliminate them. Be very careful here or you will burn me. I will show you how to do it and then you take care of the remaining ones."

She felt the warmth on the wound when he repeated what he had seen her do. "Very good for the first time, you didn't hurt me at all. Next time you can use even less energy so I won't feel any warmth."

"How does this normally work? I mean, if you don't happen to be a healer?"

The surprise and joy at his interest made her smile. "Within the first few days the body purifies the wound with a clear liquid to wash out the dirt. We have just saved my body a lot of time. Are you ready for taking care of the wound?"

"Yes."

"Let's first have a look at the damage. Do you see how the skin is built?"

"Yes, it doesn't look anything like the smooth surface it seems to be from the outside. So many little blocks, like the bricks of a building."

"Exactly. And you have several layers of them. Some of the blocks I damaged with the cut. They can't be repaired and have to die and be taken away."

She felt the jolt of shock through his fingers. "Die?"

"Don't worry, my body can replace them easily. In fact, that's what our bodies do all the time, removing old blocks and replacing them with new ones. We just help to make this happen faster. Now we use a very small amount of magic to separate the damaged from the whole ones, like a very small, thin knife. I will show you first, then I'll let you try it."

This took him a little longer to master. He winced when he repeatedly damaged healthy blocks in the process.

"Don't worry, this is no problem. Really. Go on and try to breathe more evenly and deeply. This helps you to relax."

When the edges of the wound were smooth, she asked, "How are you doing? Would you like to take a short break before we continue?"

"No, no! Show me what's next."

"Now we tell the surrounding healthy blocks to make new ones and fill the gap. If you look at them more closely, you see that many of them look different on the inside. They are in different states of reproduction."

"Reproduction?"

She could hear the awkwardness in his voice.

"Yes. They can make copies of themselves. One copy takes them about one hour. As they are so small, a lot of copies are needed and that's why natural healing takes a while. We, however, can send them the energy to speed the whole thing up. Doing this faster also means that more building material is needed in a shorter time. The body can compensate for this for a short while, but after being healed a patient should eat well enough to replenish that stock."

"So I am now feeding them with energy? And they know what to do with it?"

"Yes. They know their job well enough, at least when it comes to less complicated repairs where you only need one type of tissue. Providing energy for each and every one of these blocks would take much too long, so you will lay it over the damaged area like a blanket that sends out a constant stream of energy. Like this."

When he imitated what she had just shown him, she heard his sharp intake of breath when her skin started to regenerate.

"You can stop now, I am whole again." She opened her eyes and watched the awed expression on his face. "That was very good work, I must say."

"That was…" He shook his head, looking for words that could describe what wonders he had just experienced. He gave up and smiled. "I would like to do more of this."

Eryn exhaled extensively. "Do you have any idea what your father will do to me if I turn you into a healer?"

"He doesn't care whether I want to become a warrior, either," Vern shot back defiantly. "And since when have you been afraid of my father? Nobody but you would dare to address him without his title."

"This has nothing to do with being afraid. It is a matter of his being able to make my life a misery. You remember the time after Gara's healing? He was mad at me for more than a week. He gave me more bruises to heal in just a few days than I had managed to acquire in the previous twenty years."

"So why did you show me this, why did you let me try it if you don't want me to learn more? This is all a bit cruel of you." He shot her a resentful look.

Eryn leaned back. He was right, and that made it worse. She had not really thought this through before offering him a chance to try magical healing himself. It had been egoistic of her to grasp the chance of sharing with somebody else what was important to her for the sheer joy of it without considering the consequences for him.

"I'm sorry."

Vern didn't respond, but just avoided looking at her.

* * *

They had been walking back towards the warriors' quarters in silence for several minutes before Vern stopped and pulled her aside. Eryn was unprepared for the unexpected movement and almost stumbled, being surprised by his sudden renewed attention after he had ignored her for more than an hour, making a point to talk only to Junar.

"So you refuse to teach me because you don't want to upset my father. You know, I do find that rather ridiculous, considering the circumstances of your stay here in the city, but let's leave that aside for now," he spoke under his breath.

"Why exactly are we whispering?"

"Because I am about to make you an offer that should not be overheard."

"Stop it, Vern. I am not going to teach you any more healing without your father's assent." She was about to turn around to continue her walk, but he grabbed her sleeve and held her.

"You could at least do me the courtesy of listening to me before you reject my idea! I will make you a deal."

Eryn sighed, feeling impatient and exasperated. "What could you possibly offer me that would make me change my mind? Unless you propose removing my shackles."

He smiled, sure of his victory. "No, for that my father really would kill me. I was thinking of teaching you the offensive side of magical fighting. Throwing bolts," he clarified. "That's one skill my father has neglected to teach you so far and he will most likely continue to deny it to you."

That claimed her attention as he was sure it would. She narrowed her eyes. "You would defy your father like that? If you think he would kill you for removing my manacles, why would your teaching me something like that be any better, especially in exchange for healing?"

"Oh, but that is the beauty of it: he won't have to know about either. Teaching me healing is something you can do anywhere. To learn throwing bolts we would need to find a secluded location, though."

"You are serious about this, aren't you?" She eyed him suspiciously.

"Sure I am." He smiled. "Was that a *Yes*?"

She had to admit that he had hit the mark with his proposition. That particular skill he was offering to teach her was one she was highly interested in, one that could be very helpful in getting away from here. But what of him? If they found out that Vern had taught her, the consequences would not be pleasant.

"What if they learn about it?"

"They won't. Don't be such a coward, Eryn! For a prisoner you are surprisingly uncooperative when it comes to gaining fighting skills that might get you out of here."

"If you really want to get me out of here, take off my shackles!"

"I would prefer to help you in a way that doesn't get me kicked out of the Order, if that's alright with you!"

"What is the difference? If I escape because you taught me how to throw bolts, there won't be much of a difference if you have taken the damned things off me or not."

"Wrong. The one taking the manacles off you will be the one with the problem, not me. After all, you won't be able to use the skill to your full advantage as long as most of your power is blocked."

"You really have thought this through, haven't you?" She tried to think of any other reasons against accepting his offer, but none came up.

Her lips slowly spread into a smile. "Alright, then. You have yourself a bargain. You will have to come up with a safe location for practising with me, though. I am not exactly knowledgeable when it comes to hidden places in the city."

"I will find something."

"When would you like to start?"

"Tomorrow. You gave me my first healing lesson already. I owe you one in return."

Eryn sighed. "I wonder if we are getting ourselves into serious trouble."

Vern shrugged and grinned brightly. "I am harmless, and not even old enough for sex yet. When they find out about this I will tell them how you forced me."

She snorted. "You devious little brat."

CHAPTER 15

Caught in the Act

Tyront looked up from the report in his hands and pursed his lips.

"What's the matter?" Enric asked, stifling a yawn. They had been sitting in Tyront's study for the last two hours, going through the Order's financial and administrative matters. "Another unjustified expense?"

"No. An interesting detail about Vern. His fighting skills seem to have improved recently."

"That is nice for him, and I dare say Orrin will appreciate it. Why are you receiving information about the boy?"

"I like to keep my eyes on the people Eryn spends time with. And from what I am told she spends *a lot of* time with him."

"We did consider this a good thing, didn't we?"

"Yes." Tyront drummed his fingers on the desk. "But why would he suddenly improve in an area he has never before shown any interest in?"

"He is a growing boy, he might have found out for himself that combat training is not so bad after all." Enric shrugged.

"With Orrin, the chief warrior trainer as a father? No. I dare say that if he'd had any inclination towards fighting he would have discovered it a long time ago. Why now?"

"Well, Orrin has made him train with Eryn several times a week. Improvement would only be natural, wouldn't it?"

Tyront smiled without humour. "With the sword, yes. But we are talking about magical skills for offensive use here."

Enric straightened. "I see. Now that *is* interesting indeed. But your informants would have found out about any exercises of that kind between them, I assume?"

"That I will have to find out about. Would Vern teach her how to shoot bolts? Surely not! His father would skin him alive."

The younger man gave a wry grin. "We *are* talking about the boy decorating ancient city maps with nude drawings, aren't we?"

"What if we find out that he really *is* teaching her?"

Enric shrugged. "Let him. Orrin teaches her indirect magical fighting by improving speed and strength in sword fighting, his son takes care of the more direct application. I don't see any problem in that. As long as the boy doesn't remove her shackles, we should be safe enough."

"You have put the finger on the problem. What is to keep him from doing that?"

"I think if he had intended to free her he would have done so already. But the problem is rather that he would be doing something he thinks is against the Order's wishes, and that might require a lesson in obedience."

Tyront lifted a brow. "You can't let him go on with it *and* punish him for it."

"Not at the same time, at least. Have your spy tell you as many details as he can if he observes them doing anything of that nature. We will step in as soon as she has mastered the skill sufficiently and *then* punish the boy."

* * *

Vern lit a candle in the dark root cellar, which was half filled with vegetables. They had been using it for the last two weeks to train shooting bolts as it was secluded and dark, and nobody but the servants - who had no other choice ever so often - came down here.

"You have learned the basic use of both types of strikes so far," he started lecturing, feeling very grown up and important. "One with the ability to stun your opponent with so much energy that his body can't deal with it and is overwhelmed, and the second with the more active capability to actually destroy objects, make them burst into flames or collapse them if they are not flammable. The second one we do not use on people as it will cause serious damage to the body or, if too strong, might even kill. The first one is permitted in friendly magical battles, the second one is not, and its use is severely punished."

"So that's it? I could now blast another magician away in a magical battle?" She grinned when he rolled his eyes impatiently. He looked so cute when he took on the role as her teacher.

"No, I seriously doubt that you could, as you like to put it, *blast* anybody away. At least not with the block on your powers. And even then you would hardly have a chance against a skilled, more experienced fighter if he manages to unleash the first bolt before you."

"Why not? I could shield."

"But your opponent will know how to guide the direction of his attack. Sending them straight ahead as we have done so far is not the only possible way of doing it. Today we will have a look at how to make them curve. Resisting those curved ones takes more energy because it is hard to predict where they are going to hit and thus a more elaborate shield needs to be formed and maintained. I will show you. Shield yourself, but not only in front but all the way to your back."

He waited until she had followed his instruction and then sent a bolt at her that indeed did not go straight for her centre as it usually did but followed a more complicated flight path and finally hit her left side.

When the sizzling of the bolt hitting her shield had faded, they both froze at sounds that seemed to be drawing nearer to their closed door.

Before she could do anything, Vern had silently moved to the candle and extinguished it quickly. It was utterly dark in the cellar with no windows to let in daylight. The noises drew closer and seemed to stop in front of their door.

Eryn felt her heartbeat increase and frantically tried to remember if there was anything in here that would provide sufficient cover, but they had chosen this room for its lack of combustible content. There were not even enough vegetables left to hide under or behind. Damn!

The door flew open and two middle-aged magicians stood there, holding lamps and eyeing Eryn and Vern coolly.

"What are you two doing down here?" one of them asked.

"Stealing food?" Vern said as if testing the credibility of his lie.

"Yes, of course. Raw vegetables when your servants bring you whatever you like," one of them snorted, clearly not fooled.

"Come on, the both of you. This has to be reported," the other one said.

"Who to?" Vern asked nervously.

"It's not your place to ask questions here," was all the reply he got and they both were nudged on to climb the stairs up into the corridors of the building that housed the warriors.

Eryn had expected them to escort them to Orrin's quarters, but it became clear quickly that this was not their destination.

They left the building and turned towards the King's palace. She saw the colour drain from Vern's face and swallowed. The palace?

There were only two possibilities, either they were being delivered to the King himself or to the Order's high command, Lord Tyront. She had no idea which option was worse. But considering that they were being escorted by two magicians, the King seemed the less likely alternative.

They entered the palace and turned left after the entrance hall.

"Lord Tyront," Vern murmured under his breath and shot her an agonised look.

"Don't worry," she whispered back, "I forced you, remember?"

"Quiet, the two of you!" The command was accompanied by a threatening look from both magicians.

The knock at Lord Tyront's door was answered immediately and a servant bowed and led them to what Eryn supposed was his study or torture chamber or wherever he took care of delinquents.

She checked her steps for a moment when she entered what turned out to be an ordinary study, very much like Orrin's. She had expected Lord Tyront, but not *him*.

Enric leaned against the windowsill, arms folded. He smiled with satisfied, cool detachment at Eryn and her reaction to his sight, the reaction he saw each time they met.

Lord Tyront sat behind his massive desk and didn't rise when they entered. He shot them both withering looks and nodded to the two magicians who had brought them here. "Thank you. Send Lord Orrin to me now."

Both of them bowed and left, closing the door behind them and leaving the four alone.

For a few seconds nobody spoke. Lord Tyront eyed Eryn and Vern from under half-closed eyelids, fingers steepled in front of him.

Eryn stood rigid next to the boy and forced herself to focus on the older man, trying to ignore the disturbing presence of the other.

His voice was deceptively soft when he started speaking, "It has been brought to my attention that there seems to have been some proscribed teaching going on between the two of you. Namely, the art of magical fighting. What do you have to say to that, young man?"

Vern opened and closed his mouth for a few times, but no sound came out.

Eryn gave the older man her best defiant look. "I forced him to do it."

Lord Tyront's brows rose and he shifted his attention to her. "Did you now." His tone made it absolutely clear that he didn't believe a word of it. "How?"

"Why would I tell you?"

"Because, young lady, there is some rather harsh punishment awaiting him if you don't." He stared into her eyes coldly, waiting.

She breathed out slowly as if reaching the conclusion that giving in was the only logical choice. "Alright then, if you must know. I found out that he stole a bottle of old and pricy wine from his father and drank it all. He wanted to keep it hidden and thus gave in to my threat of revealing his little secret to Orrin."

She could hear Enric's quiet chuckle and watched Tyront's smirk as he slowly shook his head. "You could at least have devised a more credible lie. A little effort, at least, is that too much to ask? I am not a complete idiot, you know. Something less obvious but more entertaining would have been nice. People hardly ever dare lie to me and if they do I appreciate a little creativity."

She frowned at him. Her lie was too uncreative for him? This was absurd. And the subtle warning that people were not normally brave enough to lie to him was not at all reassuring, either.

Play it cool, she instructed herself. Deciding on impudence, she asked, "Would you like me to try again?"

"By all means."

She thought for few moments, then said, "I have secret mind-controlling powers that only work on the very young. He is my mindless slave and does whatever I tell him. This is why I surround myself with children and adolescents, they are to become my minions in my quest to gain control over the city."

Lord Tyront waggled his head slowly in consideration, then nodded. "Better. But not quite good enough, unfortunately. There will still have to be punishment, of course. Not for you, Eryn, that hardly makes sense. And you didn't really defy the Order as such, as our keeping you captive rather anticipates your unwillingness to cooperate. But as for Vern... The thing is, he obviously knew it to be wrong and intentionally defied the Order, otherwise he wouldn't have taught you in a dark, hidden place."

"Not dark and hidden enough, it seems," she retorted.

"No. Hardly any place is." He smiled indulgently. "I do have very thorough sources of information."

Obviously, she thought.

At that moment a sharp knock sounded at the door and Orrin stepped inside without waiting for an invitation. He took in the scene and frowned at Vern before bowing to his superiors.

"Lord Orrin," Tyront said jovially, "so glad you could join us. I was just thinking about an appropriate punishment for your son here."

Orrin visibly fought for calm. "Punishment for what?"

"Teaching our guest here the art of magical combat, I'm afraid."

The scorching look that earned him made Vern cringe slightly.

"I see," Orrin said, his posture straight, his hands clenched into fists. "Has he confessed to it?"

"No, not yet. But you see, he was caught in the act and he has failed to defend himself so far."

"What punishment did you have in mind for my son?"

"I am not entirely sure. I was hoping for your assistance here, Lord Orrin. As far as I know, Vern enjoys books and intellectual challenges. So it will definitely be nothing like sorting books in the archives or the library. I was thinking about something involving hard manual labour."

Orrin nodded slowly. "I agree. There is some maintenance work being done at the eastern bridge currently. Several weeks of assisting the men for a few hours after his lessons every day will surely make him think twice before he does something like that again." Another devastating look at Vern made the boy swallow.

Tyront's brows rose. "Several weeks seems rather excessive in addition to his lessons. We don't want his intellectual progress to suffer, after all. I propose ten days. That should be a sufficient lesson."

"As you wish, Lord Tyront." Orrin bowed stiffly and his son followed suit.

"And, of course, you might want to be more careful around your charge here now that she knows how to attack you from greater distances," Tyront said with a thin smile. "Thank you, that was all."

Vern and Orrin bowed once more before they left. Eryn, as ever, didn't bow and just walked out.

She tried to convince herself that Vern had known what he was getting himself into and had still been willing to do it. And that it had been his idea, she had never asked him to do this.

The fact that they had not done anything to her made it all the worse. She had lied to their faces, after all, and very obviously so. But of course that's why they had done it. They wanted to demonstrate that Vern was the one who had to pay.

It was a punishment for her, though one she caused to herself, as if her conscience wanted to cooperate with them. She had got Vern into trouble. Stupid thing, conscience.

At least the Freedom Night now did have its use for her: it would serve as a distraction.

CHAPTER 16

The Freedom Night

She let her gaze wander and took in the lanterns made of linen and wood hanging from the trees around her swinging gently in the soft breeze. It was not quite dark yet, but she enjoyed the twilight, when lamp light still seemed rather superfluous but it was already too gloomy without it.

The mask covering the upper half of her face felt rather odd and she let out a long breath thinking about the absurdity of obscuring her face when the colour of her hair gave away her identity only too clearly.

But for whatever reason, Junar had insisted. It was custom, she had said. Not wearing a mask was like kicking the traditions in the face instead of respecting them. Right, she thought, no matter how stupid a custom was, if it was called a *tradition* it suddenly seemed perfectly sane.

As if the justification that it had always been done like that was a mystic protection against it being a bloody idiotic rule generations had followed without thinking. Maybe being modern and using one's brain was less appealing as it was lonelier than being on the same wrong track as one's ancestors.

The things people did to fit in, she thought and snarled at the thought that fitting in was exactly what she didn't do.

She tried to keep to the edges of the decorated area, assuming the role of an observer. Quite a number of people had turned up already, the women dressed in bright, airy linen dresses made to follow their every move, just like the one she herself had donned. The men were dressed in tight trousers of the same cloth and some wore sleeveless vests while others had opted for keeping their chests completely bare.

Everyone who passed her gave an unmistakeable flicker of recognition in their mask-rimmed eyes. In her turn, she tried to figure out some their identities, but the masks were well-designed and concealed just enough of their facial features to make anything but guessing very hard. The fact that there was hardly any variation in the colouring of their hair didn't make it any easier, either. And it was not as if she knew that many people in the city.

She sank onto one of two empty benches and felt the smooth bark of a tree at her back.

The sky turned a little darker with every minute and a small mixed crowd had started to gather in front of the refreshment tables laid out with numerous wooden cups. First encounters between men and women took place and she watched the ensuing flirtation with a half-smile.

Previous Freedom Nights she had attended in the countryside a few times came to her mind while she watched a woman's bold finger perkily following the outlined muscles of her conversation partner's arm.

It was a night of folly, of carefree pleasure, flirtation and more often than not the thrill of anonymous coupling with a stranger. The moments afterwards could go either way, be it the consensual unmasking of both or the unspoken agreement to remain strangers and never to learn about the other's identity.

This moment of truth, however, sometimes lead to frustration when only one partner wanted to shed the mask while the other did not. In such situations the wish to preserve anonymity had to be respected.

Many a couple had first found each other on one of these nights. Yet the concept seemed so out of place in a society with such rigid rules on etiquette, manners and rank. But, she now thought, watching the musicians preparing their instruments, maybe it was meant as some kind of compensation for the strictness of everyday life.

And, after all, people had the chance to fall in love or share a bed with members of other social classes who they would probably never have met otherwise.

She looked away from the musicians when she had the distinctive feeling of being watched by someone. It was several someones, in fact.

A small group of five masked men were standing together and discussing agitatedly while frequently darting looks at her. Two of them grinned sheepishly when she caught them out, two hurriedly averted their gazes and one winked at her unabashedly.

She forced herself to refrain from rolling her eyes, looked away and hoped that by ignoring them so obviously she would communicate her lack of interest sufficiently.

Then a woman in a stunning dark-red dress, the more salient among the off-white clothes and without a mask strolled self-confidently through the lingering crowd and positioned herself right in front of the small orchestra. A quick glance at the now completely dark night sky seemed to satisfy her and upon a slight nod of her head, music began to fill the night air.

It felt like liquid silk entering her body through her ears and coursing through her blood, warm and smooth. This was the most beautiful thing she had ever heard. Looking around, the other guests seemed to be enjoying it very much as well, even if they were obviously familiar with it, as their faces were free of the surprise she was sure was showing on her own all too clearly.

The first couples hesitantly entered the cleanly swept area in the centre and slowly began to move. Eryn watched them with interest and envied them the knowledge of the steps that allowed them to actively participate in this rich buffet of sounds.

The Freedom Nights she had been to had been less well organised, less formal, and the music had been more of the rustic kind craftsmen and farmers made.

A slight cough to her side startled her, and when she looked up, a man of indistinct age but impressive build shyly looked at her and silently stretched out his hand palm up in an invitation to dance.

Her smile polite, she shook her head apologetically, wondering if he was one from the group of before.

The almost uniform-like similarity of the clothes and masks in combination with blond hair that looked pretty much the same shade in the lamp light made it hard to distinguish the men unless they had any particular distinguishing features like visible scars or moles. The women at least had a greater variety of different hairstyles.

"I'm sorry, I don't know the steps."

His smile became a little more self-confident when he answered, "I can show you if you like."

His voice sounded young, probably no more than a few years older than Vern. Little brothers could sound like that, she thought, amused at herself. This one was no danger, one could have an innocent dance with a little brother, even though she suspected that he would not appreciate her thoughts and might be hurt in his manful pride if he knew them.

Eryn hoped he wouldn't hit on her, or she would feel like a dirty old crone leading children astray.

Her answering smile was quick, "That would be fabulous, thank you. I hope for your own sake and mine that you are patient and your feet are not too sensitive."

His grin was now relaxed and obviously relieved at not having been rejected when he took her hand. She saw him send a quick triumphant glance to a group of men.

She gave a silent chuckle and mused that he would have scored some points with his friends by having managed to persuade the famous stranger to dance with him.

He was sweet, taking her hands and explaining the steps to her while at the same time moving his own feet to show her. The steps were not hard to learn and the slow, dreamy melody did not require any acrobatic moves.

* * *

Enric was surprised at seeing her here. It was impossible not to notice her brown hair amidst all the fair-headed people around him.

At first she sat under the tree, observing the scene and would very likely have continued to do so had not the boy asked her to dance with him.

The weapon smith's youngest son, he had the muscles of a man having been an apprentice in one of the hardest professions for several years, but had still modestly put on a vest that displayed no more than his impressive arms. Enric had recognised him easily.

He had grinned when young Landon had, teased by his friends, set off valiantly to try his luck and was more than half surprised to watch her take his practically trembling hand and follow him into the dance circle.

The dress clung nicely to her form, he couldn't help but notice. It reminded him of his surprise when he had seen her in the blue tunic her seamstress friend must have made for her. Compared to the fighting attire he usually saw her in this was quite a contrast and he found his eyes following her moves.

She had learned the few steps easily and he wondered if she was asking herself why. Supposedly not. She would probably attribute her skill in acquiring new ways of moving to the increased dexterity that months of combat training had given her. This particular song had only very little magic in it, but he felt the whisper in his blood answering the gentle call.

Being more powerful than anybody but himself and Tyront, she would most certainly feel the tug of the song like every other magician above category D.

Looking around, he could easily distinguish them among the non-magicians. They were much more focused on the music and the ones who were not dancing usually had trouble keeping their feet still.

If one knew what to look for, one could easily recognise the magic at work when watching a man imbued with the calling dance to a song induced with power. He would move with an exactitude that at times tended to irritate his partners unless they were one of a few females who were so determined to bed a magician that they would spend all year training until they were proficient enough to impress their target sufficiently and be swept off to a night of charmed eroticism, or even a long-term relationship.

These women were not only skilled at dancing but also at recognising the slightest hint of magic in a guest. He himself was very careful to mask all the careless little giveaways that might mark him as a desirable target.

While being wooed was at times nice, it was not at all flattering to be pursued just because of the magicians' general reputation of being apt bed mates. Even unskilled lovers could please a partner with the aid of a little magic.

When he returned his attention to her, the song had ended and the young smith bowed to her. He seemed to be considering asking her for another dance, but he was nudged aside by another suitor and sauntered off with a frown, angry either at his own hesitation or his successor's well-timed forwardness.

Enric ignored the flirtatious glances several women aimed at him and kept watching Eryn from a distance moving to the low-level magic songs, considering.

She certainly seemed to enjoy dancing, but every overt or subtle attempt by her partners to get closer was quickly rebuffed by a dexterous move out of reach, a slight increase in distance at the next twirl or a faked misstep that broke any unwanted contact. Her design in attending the Freedom Night was clearly neither being made somebody's conquest nor making one herself.

He waited patiently for quite some time until the musicians took their break to approach Valcredy. She was a glamorous creature, enjoying immensely the contrast of being the only person unmasked and clad in bold colours.

Her mouth broke into a slightly crooked smile when she spotted him strolling casually towards her. "Well, well - look who left his solitary stone tower to mingle with us mere mortals," she teased him under her breath just loud enough for him to hear her without endangering his anonymity.

One corner of his mouth twitched in acknowledgement of her words. "How do you always know it's me?"

She snorted quietly. "How could I not know? You walk around like you own everything here. That's the kind of overconfidence a man shows when he knows his fingers can throw fire when he is angry. It's something that's hard to overlook."

He smiled, well knowing that it was not true. If he gave off such clear signals, the magician-hunting dancers would have already been all over him. She just had a talent, a knack. The general belief was that she was a direct descendant of the last female magician many generations ago.

"What would you say, how many magicians are left here tonight?"

She considered the question, letting her gaze wander. "Three. Four already went off to the huts." She shot him a curious look. "Why? You are not normally that interested in your men's love life."

"I need you to play a song for me, and I don't think they should be around for it," he said quietly.

His tone made her pause and stare at him with raised eyebrows. "Yes?" she asked carefully, her eyes on his.

He leaned forward and whispered into her ear. She drew back, surprised. This song, among a few others, was never played at the Freedom Nights as it did something to the magicians, made them restless, especially the more powerful ones.

It seemed the magic in the song called to them in a way that dancing alone could not settle and left them full of a nervous energy. Nobody wanted an unbalanced, irritated magician nearby with nervous energy radiating off him.

Her eyes followed his to the brown-haired woman who seemed desperate to get away from her admirers and enjoy a few peaceful moments alone. Understanding dawned.

It was a well-known fact that magicians reacted to magical songs differently. They instinctively knew the steps, could follow the melody with their eyes closed. The degree of magic in the songs varied, and strong magicians such as Enric reacted even to very low levels of magic.

Asking her for this song meant that he had to be very eager to learn about the effect the music had on their magical captive, as he might have to suffer quite some discomfort.

"Are you sure? The other three present are not particularly strong, but you might feel a bit… edgy."

He raised his eyebrows in amusement. "Edgy? That's a very diplomatic way of putting it."

"This might not be the best time to try this. Maybe you could bring her to me some other time without all these people around," she offered, frowning.

His eyes stayed fixed on Eryn. "No. There is no way she would dance with me if I took off the mask and she saw who I was. It must be tonight."

"I see." She nodded slowly. "One of your colleagues has just left and you might want to send the other two away, just in case."

"Yes." He watched the musicians return to their instruments. "Give me a few moments. Don't start playing until I am on my way to her."

* * *

Eryn sat under the same tree where she had started the evening, glad that her bench had remained unoccupied for the moment, and enjoyed a few minutes of peace. She didn't mind the dancing, she quite liked it. Amazingly enough, she seemed to have a gift for it.

It was strange, though, being the only one without the cloak of anonymity. It seemed to her that the men seemed to consider it either a triumph or a dare to dance with her. Small wonder, with her being the only female magician in these parts and so conveniently recognisable.

The first notes of the next song hit her like a gush of warm water, making all her nerve endings, from her toes upwards, vibrate. She still stared at the red-clad woman, who seemed to observe her with narrowed eyes, when she sensed somebody approaching her and looked up at a bare-chested man smiling down at her, about to extend his hand.

But then another man approached with determined steps and stepped between her and the first man. This later arrival was tall, his hair tied in a short ponytail at the nape of his neck, his stance unusually confident. When the bare-chested man seemed about to complain, the newcomer stood with his back to

Eryn and just lifted his mask for a second whereupon any resistance of the man seemed to drain away at once and he hurriedly stepped back.

Ponytail then turned around to face her after replacing his mask. He neither smiled nor offered his hand, but just took hers, seeming to take her consent for granted as he led her into the centre of the circle. And indeed, resistance was the last thing on her mind.

It was unthinkable not to dance to this song - it was like a demand, one she couldn't have resisted even if she had tried.

Not her dance partner's demand, though. It was as if the music itself was commanding her. Her mind fought for control of coherent thought, desperately trying to figure out what had caused this reaction in her. Why did none of the others seem so affected by it?

Then the music took control, and conscious thought gave way to something else.

He felt the tension building up inside him, just as he had expected. He felt his heart pounding in his ears, and where his fingers touched hers pulses of energy seemed to originate, which spread through him in waves. His whole body knew what to do, was born with that knowledge.

The insight that this song was meant to be danced with a female partner of magical ability came to him in a rush and was no surprise to him. It was as if this knowledge, too, had been lying dormant deep within him and was merely being awakened. The almost unbearable tension lessened with the first step of the dance he took together with her.

It was like being reduced to no more than an observer in her own body. She felt the sensations the music and the dancing unleashed inside her, the tension and relief that went through her muscles in alternating waves, the energy that shot through her body when after so much dancing she should instead have been exhausted.

Her senses were heightened and seemed to be aiming in all directions, inside and all around her. The assertive rhythm of the instruments melded with her heartbeat, the dark night sky, the twinkling stars, the gentle whispering of the leaves above her, the crumbs of soil crunching underneath her soles, the tingling of her skin where he was touching her.

Two melodies seemed to rise, intertwine, melt and separate again, one stronger, one weaker, and her body willing and eager to obey the stronger one's commands, while being completed by her partner's moves, which seemed to follow the other melody that seemed to her in the background, but obviously guiding him.

She let herself fall, not wasting a single thought on the possibility that she might not be caught, and she was not in the least surprised that hands indeed caught her, exactly as the music commanded it.

When the notes slowly drained away, it was like waking from a dream without the drowsiness of sleep clinging to her mind. Energy still coursed through her, but like a pleasant reminder, not like the frenzy before. Only now did she take in the man opposite her who still held her fingers in his and held her gaze with intense blue eyes.

She couldn't read his expression, the mask prevented it. But she had a feeling that it was not a particularly joyful one, more thoughtful and ponderous. He had shared this dazzling reel with her. Or had he? Had it been a mutual experience or were all these strange impressions Eryn's alone? He didn't look relaxed, but she might just have unsettled him with her vigorous dancing.

When she took a step backwards, one of his sinewy arms shot out and grabbed her hand. She swallowed hard and looked around for anyone to help her in case it was necessary to use force to free herself from the grasp. But people around them just stood still and regarded them with various degrees of surprise, shock and amazement visible on their faces. The first ones to recover fell into a frantic whispering with their neighbours.

When she felt a tug on her captured hand, she looked back to the man in front of her, whose serious expression had not changed, but who gently pulled her with him when he approached the woman in the red dress.

She tried to free her hand, but he just held on more tightly and turned his head to her to shoot her a quick warning glance that promised an even firmer grip if she continued her struggle.

The woman in red, too, was obviously affected by whatever spell the others were under, but she had recovered quickly and just nodded wordlessly when he whispered something to her.

Only moments later slow chimes reached her ears and she felt herself pulled back into the centre of the circle with him.

Before she could think of rebuking him for his rude behaviour, the music once more caught her, this time soft and mellow instead of the powerful blaze from before. The male voice that started singing to accompany the single instrument struck a different, but hardly less compelling chord inside her.

Fighting the sensations and trying to keep a grip on at least an ounce of willpower, she still all but melted into the arms that encircled her body and pressed her close to his muscled frame. She was slowly twirled away from him only to be pulled back into the same possessive embrace, again and again, the only anchor point his serious, piercing blue eyes.

Seduction, it shot through his head. That was the purpose of this song, no more and no less. No wonder these songs made magicians crazy when they heard them without the opportunity to lose themselves in them with a magical partner. He was the first one after more than three hundred years to be granted this privilege.

The music seduced him as much as it did her, or rather overwhelmed her. He could see the struggle for control in her eyes as they slid in and out of focus, but she kept losing the battle every time and returned to his arms just as the music intended it.

When the music died away, he didn't give her time to recover, but strengthened his grip around her middle and bent her head back to kiss her, swallowing her shocked cry and keeping both her arms pinned between their bodies to keep her from pushing him away.

She tried to turn her head away, but he simply cupped her neck firmly with his hand and deepened the kiss further. He recklessly invaded her mouth, plundering, until he felt her resistance cease, then his lips moved from hers to her throat, tasting, savouring her skin.

When she moaned quietly in response, he lifted her into his arms and carried her away from the gaping crowd towards the little huts that had been put up for that very purpose.

* * *

Eryn opened her eyes and sat bolt upright. How long had she slept for? It was still dark outside and the candles around her had not burned down so much. It could hardly have been more than an hour - two at the utmost.

Her anonymous bed partner's arm was lying limply in her lap on the sheet that she had used to cover herself.

There was no use in asking herself if it had been a wise idea, or regretting it. It had been a joyous experience, one she would not hesitate repeating. He had been generous, skilled and considerate in his lovemaking.

She looked at his sleeping form. He, too, was covered by a sheet that was draped over his lower body and only left his upper torso bare. She had not really taken the time to look at him before and took the opportunity to do so now.

Who might he be? His build was not the one of a man with a profession that required heavy lifting - no bulging, strongly defined muscles that stood out, but lean, well-toned and strong enough to lift her as if she weighed hardly anything and carry her for a distance without showing any sign of exhaustion. She recalled the man who had tried to dance with her before him. He had retreated quickly after he had glimpsed the face of the man lying next to her, so her lover was probably somebody of higher status, a rich man's son, an aristocrat, maybe even a magician.

Staring at the mask that still covered his face, she felt temptation tingle in her fingertips to lift it only a fraction to peep at the features it concealed. But that was not allowed and could get her into serious trouble. That thought made her almost laugh out loud. It was not as if her situation was not troubled already, so what exactly did she have to lose? Slowly stretching her hand towards his face, she stared at his eyelids to make sure they were still closed.

Her fingers had just brushed the rim of his mask, when his low, amused voice made her jolt back and almost knock over a candle.

"You are aware that this is against the rules." It was not a question.

She stared at the smirk that curved his mouth. Only then did he open his eyes and look at her, amusement clear in them and, to her relief, no trace of anger.

The flood of embarrassment flushed her face red and she swallowed. "I think we are not really on equal terms here. I dare say you are very well aware of who I am, so I thought it was only fair to see your face in turn."

"But you knew that before, when you decided to attend. I would assume that you were willing to accept that disadvantage."

She sighed. "I know. But I had not expected this to matter. I didn't plan on going to bed with anybody tonight."

"You didn't?" The amusement was still there. "What made you come here, then?"

"I was bullied into it, I think. A friend thought I could use a little distraction."

He pushed himself up on his elbow. "And? Did I manage that?"

That made her smile. There was no cockiness in the question, nor any trace of insecurity as if he worried about her evaluation of him, just a serious, genuine interest.

"Oh yes, there can be no doubt about that. I am most exceedingly obliged to you for your efforts and your commendable engagement," she said.

He chuckled and bowed his head. "Your humble servant."

Being so close to her without seeing contempt or fear flashing in her eyes was an immense pleasure, he noted. He had never really been around her when she had been in a good mood. Sure, he had seen her laughing when he had watched her at the training grounds from his window, but up close it was something completely different.

When he lifted a hand to wrap a strand of her hair around his fingers, she blinked several times. Not very used to intimate contact, he thought, but obviously not without experience when it came to bedding a man.

She leaned back and wrapped her sheet around herself, and as she moved away her hair slid through his fingers. When she made to get up, he quickly grabbed her hand to check her retreat, not yet willing to let her go. He pulled the hand to his lips and pressed a soft kiss on her knuckles.

"Where are you going? Stay with me a little longer." His voice was gentle, non-threatening. Yet the request seemed to make her nervous.

"I'd better get going. My day starts in a few hours and tardiness is not looked upon kindly."

"That is a pity. I enjoy your company very much."

She smiled at that. "Even though I tried to uncover your identity?"

"What can I say? I like a woman with a rebellious touch about her."

"Well, I am well known for that quality," she grinned.

"That you are," he smiled back and watched as she pulled her hand from his and rose to collect her dress. The candle light shimmered softly on her skin, shadowed alluringly along her curves and he watched her, engrossed, determined to lock this sight into his memory.

"Is there a chance of a last kiss?" she heard him ask and hesitated before she nodded.

He shook his head just as she was about to pull the dress over her head. "No, without the dress, if you please."

She chided herself not to be stupid. He had already seen everything there was to see, so why was she feeling shy all of a sudden? Probably because the heat of the moment was gone.

"Alright," she said with only a hint of reluctance and lowered it again, holding the dress in one hand to let it hang down her side.

He came closer on his knees until he had reached the edge of the bed. He sat down in front of her and pulled her closer until she stood between his legs. When she made to bend down to his lips, he shook his head again and smiled.

"No. That's not where I want to kiss you."

* * *

Less than two hours of sleep. That was definitely too little. She would make it through the day somehow. At least she could push away the weariness with the aid of a little magic every now and then, but that was a bad substitute for a restful night.

Not that she thought the loss of sleep had not been worth her while, quite the opposite. He had kept her there for another hour when she had first started to leave. Last kiss alright, she thought and shook her head silently. That had been cheating. He had claimed quite a number of kisses after that allegedly last one, and she had yielded to them more than willingly. Well, eventually: it had taken him no more than a few seconds to overcome her initial anger at feeling tricked.

She shook her head to free it from the images and return to the here and now. It would be nice to have had one of her free days today. But asking Orrin for that had not been an option after learning about *his* last Freedom Night. It was not a topic she wanted to bring up with him right now.

Vern would be starting his first day of compulsory manual labour today. She felt bad for the boy, but the thought of his lifting heavy stones and tools made her grin. The punishment was indeed a very good one, she had to admit. Lord Tyront knew enough about Vern to sentence him to the fitting punishment.

That brought up the thought of how much information Lord Tyront would have collected about her in the time she had been here already. His network of spies or whatever he used had to be very good. How else could he have found out about Vern's secretly teaching her magical fighting?

She looked around her suspiciously as she strolled over to the training grounds. He probably had somebody watching her at this very moment. Well, apart from Orrin who was very obviously watching her right now.

The warrior was leaning against the wall with folded arms, looking relaxed and well-rested. That alone irritated her. His tell-tale haughty grin made it worse.

"Had a short night, eh?"

"Oh, just shut up and let's get this over with for today. I need a few hours of sleep." She had planned to meet Vern after his work for the day was done, whenever that was.

"Don't snap at me because your night time activities kept you from getting a proper night's rest."

Rolling her eyes, she grabbed one of the swords that leaned against the wall next to him. Did people in the city know no personal boundaries at all?

"I would very much like to say I'm sorry, but it would be a blatant lie and you would very probably know it." She smiled sweetly.

Orrin chuckled in evident glee.

Why was he so cheerful today? Or did it just seem to her like that because the contrast to her own bad mood was so striking?

"Sleep deprivation is nothing that will make me go easy on you in case you have been cherishing any hopes in that direction."

"Hopes for mercy? I know you better than that."

"Good. I would have hated to smash them."

She shook her head in complete certainty. "No, you wouldn't. Can we start? I feel the overwhelming urge to attack you with something pointed and I happen to be holding an item for exactly that purpose in my hand."

He gave a thin grin. If lack of sleep could make her eager to fight he should probably fix the start much earlier in the morning from now on.

"I would be very interested in seeing what Vern has taught you," he said, dodging her attack easily.

"I imagine you would," she retorted dryly. "What a pity I have no intention of showing you. Yet. Maybe I can find a convenient opportunity to take you down while you show me your back, and then escape from this place."

"I see. Thank you for the warning. I will make sure to protect my back at all times, then."

He parried another blow and continued the conversation without even breathing any more heavily, as if they were doing nothing more strenuous than sitting together in his parlour with a cheery drink. "Vern will start his work today. I am sure this will do him good."

"Yes, right it will," she snorted. "That's why your punishment would have been much stricter than the one your puppet master has decided on."

"My puppet master? I thought the King was my puppet master according to you?" He almost managed to disarm her, but she turned to her left at the last moment.

"No. Your puppet master is the top magician. *His* puppet master is the King."

"Nice," he murmured and pushed her a few steps back. Relegated to a puppet's puppet. "Why did he do it? Why would he teach you this when he knew that he would be punished if it ever came out? What did he get in return?"

So he hadn't told his father about the healing lessons. Well, as Vern was the one bearing the consequences alone, he had earned the right to keep it a secret as far as she was concerned.

"Nothing. I begged him, he obliged. What can I say? He is a very considerate young man who can't resist a damsel in distress. Something he would hardly have learned from you, from what I have experienced so far."

Orrin eyed her indulgently. "You are telling me that you begged him to do something in your favour that would place him in considerable difficulties without your offering anything in return? That does not seem very much like the person running through the city and healing random people without compensation whenever she stumbles across them."

"Then you have a false impression of me, you know. The publican's companion was not healed for free. He has to feed my little orphan friend whenever she is hungry."

"Yes, quite right. And I am sure he considers this a great strain on his business."

"And I keep getting clothes from Junar as she feels the need to keep on showing me her gratitude. So you can hardly say I did it without compensation." Stay with me on this topic, let's just forget the other one, she thought.

"You are not trying to change the subject, are you?"

Damn. "No. Why would I do that?" She took great care not to seem too innocent but instead a little careless. Lying was a difficult skill, though she had spent almost all her life practising it. Or rather, concealment in place of lying.

He shook his head, obviously not convinced, but he decided to let it go for now. "It seems you will have to spend your afternoons alone for a while. I imagine Vern will be too tired for walking through the city after working on his tasks."

"Your concern about how I spend my free time is very touching."

A swift strike knocked the sword out of her grip and it landed on the ground a few paces to her side.

"I imagine you will spend the evening today sleeping," he said conversationally with a smug half-smile.

She went to retrieve her weapon and shot him an annoyed look. "You don't have to sound so damned pleased about that. I hope *you* will have a sleepless night, one day not too far away, and I can tease you about it."

When she stood ready for another bout, Orrin sighed, walked closer and gave her shoulder a push that almost sent her to the ground.

"Broader stance! I can't count how often I have told you this."

"What can I say? I just can't get enough of hearing you scold me."

* * *

Enric stood watching her from his usual window. The drink in his hand had gone cold, but he didn't notice. Only a few hours ago he had been holding her in his arms, her skin warm and radiant in the candle light, soft to the touch, and now she was again as far away as ever. When had he started caring about that?

She seemed a tad clumsier today, very likely a result of only a few hours of sleep. He couldn't help but smile at the memory of how he had stolen another precious hour of sleep from her before he had finally watched her slip away to her cell.

He would very much have preferred to keep her with him longer, but Orrin had always been a stickler for punctuality and he might have made her pay for being late.

Enric had been careful not to reveal his identity, avoiding any dead giveaways. Even though probably half the city already knew about it after he had lifted his mask for that one moment.

If only Tyront had been the one they had fetched to take her down when she had first revealed her magical abilities. Then it wouldn't have been necessary for him to more or less introduce himself with a bolt to her chest and she might have not have hated him quite so wholeheartedly.

He saw Orrin laugh occasionally and wondered what amused him. It was probably remarks from his grumpy, reluctant student.

He looked back at his desk and the pile of papers he was supposed to go through. The thought was anything but appealing.

He didn't feel tired, felt perhaps even a little invigorated, but paperwork was not at all the kind of activity he felt like using his energy on.

What would really do him good, he decided, was physical exercise, such as a sword fight. Unfortunately, there were not many able swordsmen around who could match his skill nor many who were able to match his strength.

A smile crept across his face. It was clear he had the one closest to meeting his requirements right there in his field of vision right now. And wouldn't it do Eryn good to see a little demonstration of what fighting really could look like?

* * *

Orrin frowned when he saw the tall figure approaching. Instead of his usual blue robes he was wearing leather armour and carrying a sheathed sword in his left hand. He walked straight towards them with determination. That did not bode well. Eryn did not usually react well to his presence and would probably refuse to continue training as long as he was nearby.

She noticed Orrin's puzzlement and turned to see where his gaze had wandered. Her breath caught in her throat and she cursed herself for the fearful reflex his mere sight caused in her. He was not in the usual attire that bespoke his high rank but was obviously dressed for fighting.

Orrin bowed when his superior was within earshot. "Lord Enric."

"Lord Orrin." Enric nodded his head and then darted a quick look at Eryn, who had taken a few steps away and was standing straight with her arms crossed, staring at him coldly. Only her chest, which was moving with her more rapid breathing, betrayed any anxiety.

"I was hoping for a little of your time to devote to some exercise."

"Yes… of course," Orrin replied with hesitation and then turned to his charge. "Eryn, you may return to your room for now. I will collect you as soon as we are done here."

"No," Enric spoke. "It will be a good demonstration for her." He turned to her and motioned to a nearby bench. "Stay there and pay attention."

The impulse to defy Enric on principle came to her almost as automatically as breathing, and resisting it was a matter of reminding herself of the likely consequence - namely a force field that would stop her from leaving and thus provide another convenient chance for him to humiliate her.

She walked to the bench stiffly and sat. Only then did Enric turn away from her and back to the warrior trainer, and unsheathed his sword with his right hand, throwing aside the scabbard with his left.

She only realised that they had started when she heard the clang of their weapons. The first blow came too quickly for her to see.

Despite herself, she watched in fascination. The speed of their movements was almost too fast for her eyes to follow, and sometimes even that was impossible. At times their forms seemed more of a blur than solid outlines.

She had occasionally seen the students at swordplay, but this here was something completely different. The two men in front of her had mastered not only their fighting but also the magical control over their bodies at a level that seemed to her had to be very close to perfection. They pushed their muscles, sinews and reflexes to what in her opinion was certainly close to the limit of what a human physique could accomplish.

When Orrin's weapon finally landed on the ground and the other one's tip pointed at his throat, she couldn't say how much time had passed. It had been an impressive spectacle but she had no idea why she had been made to watch it. The intention had surely not been to provide entertainment for her. A warning maybe? To impress on her that this was the kind of skill she would have to deal with if she tried to get away from here?

Enric let his sword sink and then bowed to Orrin. He retrieved his scabbard and sheathed the weapon again. Eryn pointedly avoided meeting his gaze when he strode towards her.

He stopped in front of her, waiting some moments for her to lift her eyes up to his. When she eventually did he nodded towards the centre of the training circle.

"I could remove your shackles and we could have a look at how fast you are with your full power at your disposal," he said casually.

Eryn's imagination furnished an unpleasant picture of her beaten and unconscious lying at his feet, Enric standing over her with a contemptuous sneer.

"No."

"There is no need to be afraid of me. I will not be cruel. I promise you."

She shook her head, looking away from him to signal that this conversation was over as far as she was concerned.

He shrugged. "As you wish."

My fingers shouldn't be itching to touch her, he thought. He had satisfied that need only a few hours ago. And yet resisting the urge to cup her cheeks and kiss her was more demanding than fighting Orrin had been just now. What in the world was happening?

Turning away abruptly he returned from where he had come, nodding to Orrin in passing. He had not really counted on her accepting his invitation, but it was time she got used to talking to Enric and being in his presence.

And he himself also had to get comfortable with inconvenient if pleasant snippets of memory emerging when he looked at her.

* * *

She was leaning against a house wall and watching him inexpertly use what she imagined had to be some kind of hammer even if it had a shape slightly different from that she knew. Maybe it was a specialised tool of some sort for working on stone. Vern looked nothing like the privileged young man he was with his dirty, and in places torn, clothes and sweat running down his face and arms.

He looked up in relief when a short, sturdily built man clapped his hands three times to signal the end of the working day. Waving a hesitant good bye to his fellow workers, he turned and caught sight of Eryn watching him.

The smile that spread across his face lifted a heavy burden from her heart. She wouldn't spend much time with him, only as long as the brief walk back to his quarters took because he appeared too tired to do anything else. His smile told her that he wasn't angry at her for not having been able to save him from his current predicament.

"Hello, my lad. How are you doing? Are the others treating you well or do I need to use my newly acquired ability to stun them?"

He shrugged. "It's not any worse than expected. I am the rich boy, after all. Some of them are afraid of me, others delight in seeing me struggle and make it as hard as possible for me. But at least I can lift as much as any of them. Magical strength has its merits every now and then." The last words he said with a tired half-smile.

"I am sorry about this, Vern."

He waved his hand. "No, don't say that. I knew the risk and I was willing to take it. And after all, I have managed to acquire new knowledge as well. They can't take that away from me."

"No, especially as you have managed to keep that little detail a secret so far. Your father, however, is not convinced. He asked me today what I did for you in return."

"That's no great surprise," he snorted. "He has been asking me that same question time and again in different variations."

"What will you do if the high lord or his Lordling ask you that question?"

He looked at her in shock at the complete lack of respect she showed when referring to the very powerful men who were in importance not far below the King himself. Then he chuckled. "Lordling. I like it."

She smiled. "Just make sure you don't repeat it. But you haven't answered my question."

He shrugged. "Lie, of course."

"Of course," she repeated dryly. "What else? Have I really been that bad an influence on you, dear boy?"

"Yes, that's what my father keeps saying whenever I contradict him lately. He seems to forget that I was not always a well-behaved and obedient son before your arrival. But maybe he just enjoys having somebody else than himself to blame for how I turned out," he shrugged.

"Whatever keeps him happy," she quipped. "If the thought of me corrupting you is a greater comfort to him than your just being a nuisance by nature, who are we to shatter his cheery yet flawed view of the world?"

Vern snorted. "He proposed this punishment, so I am not particularly keen on keeping him happy right at the moment. Is there any chance you would continue to teach me? We haven't been rumbled in this so far."

"Why don't we talk about it when your ten days of manual labour are over? You might change your mind."

"I doubt that very much. And I have finished another few drawings, if you'd like to see them. I have tried to capture the healing process of the skin, the different phases."

Sighing, she turned to him. "You didn't cut yourself on purpose for that, did you?"

He looked at her, surprised. "Of course I did. Do you think I remember every single detail from back at Junar's place? And look," he presented the back of his hand, "there is not a trace of it left! I am getting really good at this."

"Yes, it seems you are," she confirmed after examining the patch of skin he had indicated. "What am I going to do with you?"

"Indulge me because you are a compassionate person and hate to see me suffer for nothing?" he offered, brightly.

That made her laugh. "You know, not everybody would say it is you are suffering for nothing. But we can at least continue with studying the human body. Should there be occasions to use this knowledge for healing, then that's great, and if not it should not get you into any difficulties."

He looked at her with eyes that shone with contained calculated sorrow. "Does that mean there will be no more healing at all for now?"

Fully aware that she was being manipulated in a rather clumsy way she rolled her eyes and nevertheless relented. "Well, let's see what we can do without inflicting injuries on each other on a regular basis, shall we?"

"I take that as a *yes*," Vern said happily.

"It wasn't. It was more like a definite maybe."

"There is no such thing as a definite maybe!"

"How would you know?" she smirked. "It might be a popular expression in healers' circles."

That made him laugh. "How would you know about it, then? Wasn't your father the only healer you ever met?"

They had reached the warriors' quarters. "This conversation is over if you start using logic on me. You'd better accept the great sublimity of my superior knowledge unquestioningly if you want to learn something from me."

"Your modesty does you credit. Father is right, you are a bad influence. I have never before met anybody who treated self-importance as a virtue."

She just raised her brow and shrugged. "I never said I wasn't a bad influence."

She watched him disappear into the building, glad that his mood had not been embittered by the toils they had burdened him with.

In all honesty, she was glad that Vern was determined to continue his work on healing. In any case, Eryn would wait and see if he still thought so after ten days of hard, grubby labour.

She hoped he would continue, even though she knew it was selfish of her to hope for it. It would get him into trouble if they found out that he was defying the Order again. Yet after more than a decade it had been a gift to meet a kindred spirit. A gift she was not willing to give up. He would have no further chance to learn more once she had found a way out of the city, so they could at least benefit from each other as long as she was still confined here.

CHAPTER 17

Saving Vern

Eryn swallowed when she spotted Orrin on the training grounds. He was not alone this time but surrounded by a small group of four adolescent men. Vern had not been free for any training with her in the afternoons for the last week owing to his punishment, and Rolan had requested to be released from working with her after she had kicked him where it hurt him the most. Again.

She smiled at the memory of him almost collapsing to his knees, both hands gripping his crotch.

It seemed Orrin had gathered a new selection of training partners for her. However, she could not simply give these new youngsters a well-aimed kick if she found them annoying. It just wouldn't be right, they were basically still immature. Orrin was very likely counting on her restraint for that reason.

The young men looked at her curiously.

"What's that? The fresh meat I asked you for?" She let loose a dark cackle and eyed them as if determining who was to be her first victim. Three of them stepped one pace back together while one froze in place, staring in what looked like horror, judging from his widened eyes and hunched shoulders.

Orrin rolled his eyes. "Stop that - you are scaring them. Relax, boys. She is just messing with you."

She saw the young men exchange doubtful looks and gave them a wolfish grin that showed too many teeth, just for good measure.

"These are second year students. I want to see how long you can stand against them," Orrin explained.

"Wait - they have been training sword fighting for more than a year, and you want me to *fight* them? Is this some kind of revenge for my getting Vern into trouble?" She folded her arms and glared at him.

"No, this is to see how far along you are. They may have trained that much longer than you, but the fact that you had greater numbers of daily lessons should counterbalance that."

"Yes, I see now," she murmured. "I forgot how privileged I am."

He motioned for one of the young men to grab a sword and approach her. "Make sure to bring one for Eryn as well."

The young man made an audible gulp, nodded reluctantly and returned a resigned look to his mates before doing as he had been told.

She was surprised at how easy it was to avoid or block his attacks without even using magic to improve her speed. Even though she could have ended the fight any time by using a little magic and disarming him, she decided against it. Why make Orrin happy when she could avoid it?

"Alright, that's enough," Orrin called after watching her play around for a while. "Next."

Only the last of them posed slightly more of a challenge than the others had, and there was an occasion or two when she had to use some magic to escape a blow. Orrin soon ended that fight as well, thanked the young men and sent them on their way.

"Not bad, but also not overwhelming. I didn't bring them here as playthings for you."

She pouted her lips in mock hurt. "You didn't? And there I was, thinking you finally wanted to make a sweet gesture towards me."

"We will try the third-years next time. They should be more of a challenge for you."

"Great," she said without enthusiasm. But maybe she could have a little fun with them. The second years were easy enough to frighten. She would have to think of something a little more dramatic for the older ones.

* * *

Vern looked exhausted, dirty, scratched and bloody in places; but he was so relieved that this had been his last day that Eryn couldn't help but smile when she saw him trudging towards the house wall where she sat waiting for him as usual.

"You did it, my friend. You - soft, rich, city boy - have survived the torture of hard, manual labour. Congratulations!"

"Even your mocking words cannot push away my good mood, wench," he retorted with a weary smile.

She shook her head. "Wench? I bet you get beaten up a lot by the boys your age. No fifteen-year-old talks like that."

He shrugged. "They probably would if I weren't the only son of the great and powerful Lord Orrin. Nobody wants to get on the wrong side of him."

They started walking back to the warriors' quarters. "How convenient for you. Though I imagine your father would prefer if people were less careful around you as it might motivate you to improve your fighting skills."

"What can I say? It's his burden to bear. Have you eaten yet? You could join father and me for dinner, I feel like celebrating."

"I would love to, but I'm afraid your father is none too pleased with me right now."

Vern lifted his brows. "When was he ever? Why? What have you done this time that's worse than usual?"

"I might have spoiled his training plan for today a bit," she said, remembering earlier.

"He is used to that. You have not exactly been overly cooperative in the past. Come on, make me laugh."

"I told you about him bringing second year students to the training sessions a few days ago, if you remember. Today he brought some third-year students and, well, they ran off screaming."

"They did? Why?" His voice was full of delight.

"I might have used a bit of soap to make them think I had some kind of violent, contagious illness that made me walk towards them with outstretched arms and foam dripping from my mouth."

Vern started laughing until tears formed at the corners of his eyes. "I would have loved to see that!"

"You can always ask your father for more details. I am sure he will appreciate your sense of humour immensely."

"Sure," he snorted. "If he is in a really foul mood that might just earn me another ten joyful days of bridge renovation."

"It was his own fault. He told me that he would bring them, so I had enough time to prepare something."

"Yes, I am sure he would love to hear that. You should really come for dinner."

"No, thanks. I am not in a particularly suicidal mood today. Maybe some other time."

"You know, now that my ten days are behind me, my afternoons are free again and we could continue where we left off?" He looked at her appealingly, his eyes big and round with hope.

Of course he had remembered her words when she told him that they could talk about further healing lessons when his punishment was over. After serving his punishment without complaining, she didn't have the heart to disappoint him by trying to protect him from himself. He was willing to proceed, and she was grateful for it, glad that hard manual labour had not seemed to blunt his willingness to defy the Order by learning healing.

She smiled. "Yes, we could."

He rubbed his palms together. "Excellent!"

"You can start when you are back home by taking care of these cuts and scratches on your arms. Make sure your father doesn't see them when you come home or you will have some explaining to do when you emerge without them a few minutes later."

He shot her a pitying look. "You don't really think I am that stupid, do you?"

"Forgive me for questioning the unerring judgement that all your actions are based on."

He gave a twisted smile. "If you are referring to my punishment, I have to tell you that I would do it again without even thinking."

"Then your father was right. A *few weeks* would have been better for teaching you the error of your ways."

"Yes, he does know me well. Good thing for me then that Lord Tyront didn't listen to him."

"Yes, but I dare say he won't repeat that mistake next time they catch you."

He sighed theatrically and stared up at the sky as if addressing it, "But, alas, it is the price rebels like us have to pay."

"Oh dear," she said, shaking her head, "I have created a monster."

* * *

"Feet further apart. You will never find a stable stance otherwise," Orrin instructed and emphasised his words by using his own foot to push one of hers aside and broaden her posture. She cursed and fought for balance.

He shook his head in mock disapproval. "Such bad words from such a pretty girl. Is that how your father taught you to speak to your elders?"

She looked at him, her eyelids half closed. "Oh yes, that's exactly how he used to express himself when we discussed magic and fighting."

"What a pity I got my hands on you that late. Ten years earlier and I might have been able to rectify that nasty attitude before it stuck."

"Right. Because it's *my* attitude that needs rectifying."

"Well, it might be too late for your attitude, but we can at least do something about your clumsiness." He jostled her from the side, satisfied that she remained standing upright. "See? More balance already."

Before she could think of a reply, they heard the words "Lord Orrin! Lord Orrin!" shouted by a boy not much older than Vern. He ran towards them and then had to bend with his hands braced on his knees, panting. It seemed he had quite a sprint behind him.

"What's the matter, boy?" Orrin demanded, impatient that he had to wait for the boy to recover his breath enough to speak coherently.

"It's Vern," he gasped out between gulps of air. "He is hurt badly."

Orrin's posture grew rigid, his face a stony mask.

"Where?" he just barked, and started running when the boy wordlessly pointed his outstretched finger towards the smaller building next to the warriors' quarters where the trainee magicians had their lessons. Eryn followed unbidden, dropping back rapidly when she couldn't keep up with the older man's speed.

When Orrin entered the building and rounded the first corner, she had to rely on the sound of his footsteps to be able follow him. It didn't take long to find Vern.

When she entered what looked like a classroom with the tables shoved against the walls, she saw a group of students and two adult magicians standing in a circle around a recumbent figure. Fortunately, he appeared to be conscious. There was a pool of blood under him. His face was pale and panic shone in his wide open eyes. Orrin was already on his knees, frantically searching for the wound.

Eryn knelt next to him and pushed his hand away, blocking the coppery smell of the blood in her nostrils. Orrin resisted at first, but she caught one of his sleeves and looked him sternly in the eyes, pointing at herself, "I am a healer," then at him. "You are not. Get out of my way. Now." The last word was hardly more than a growl.

He stared at her uncomprehendingly for a moment, then moved away, fixing his eyes on his son.

She smiled down reassuringly at Vern's face, pale and twisted in pain, and laid a palm on the back of his hand to send in searching pulses of energy to find out what damage his body had suffered.

Closing her eyes, she swallowed hard when the picture of a wound in his back formed before her inner eye. Something sharp and long was buried in there, right in his muscle, dangerously close to the middle of his spine. It was not in there deep enough to have pierced any organs yet, but only barely. Moving him would be quite a challenge.

Without opening her eyes, she spoke, her words eerily reverberating in the room that was utterly silent despite the large number of people in it.

"Three of you should turn him onto his left side, away from me. One at his shoulders, one at his hips and one taking his legs. You will do this slowly and very, very carefully." Her tone was calm and steady. Letting her inner turmoil be seen by those around her would make the situation worse.

"Not you, Orrin," she added when she more felt than heard him move closer to help. She needed stable hands for this, not wanting to risk any jerky movements that might make things worse.

She kept her hand on Vern's to monitor the damage and the position of the intruding object while he was moved.

"Slowly," she instructed quietly when the object threatened to move.

When they had changed him into the position she had described after several ponderous seconds, she opened her eyes and saw a large, wooden fragment protruding from his back, more a chunk than a splinter, blood oozing around it.

"Hold his arms and legs, don't let him move," she instructed. He mustn't thrash around while she worked, no matter how much it hurt.

Closing her eyes and again letting magic replace them, she carefully grabbed the chunk of wood with one hand and placed the other on the bare skin next to it. When she started to move it very, very slowly only a little way, she felt him first tense and then release a shrill cry of pain.

Forcing herself to ignore it and maintain her concentration, she started mending the torn tissue and blood vessels inside him where the wood had been. It was too dangerous to remove it all at once, she had to do it little by little. The six hands were hardly able to contain him when he wailed in agony.

"Orrin," she commanded with her eyes still closed, "remove my shackles. Now!" she added more loudly when he didn't comply immediately. "I need more power or I can't take care of the pain *and* heal him at the same time!" She couldn't bear listening to Vern's pained whimpering that was interspersed by gut-wrenching screams any longer.

She felt ice cold hands at her skin for a moment before the metal dropped from her wrists to the floor with a gentle clunk.

Without giving herself time to enjoy the rush of energy with which her power returned to her in its entirety, she immediately redirected it to flow into the nerves around the damage and felt him relax at once when he no longer felt any pain.

With more magic at her disposal now she could expand her activities from merely assisting his body in the healing process to taking complete control over it and fuelling it with her magic. She was now able to remove more of the huge wooden splinter at once and repair the exposed damage. She repeated this twice more until the object had been dislodged completely, then she finally mended the outer muscle fibres and made the skin knit itself back together.

When he was completely whole again, she opened her eyes and sank back on her heels exhausted, her knees red and slippery from the blood on the floor.

Enric skidded to a halt in front of the open door, taking in the scene of Orrin's arms enfolding her from behind, fixing the bangles back on her wrists and then staying there to envelop her in a firm embrace, pulling her back against his chest. His cheek rested on her hair, his breath was laboured.

Enric watched them, kneeling on the bloody floor that had turned their legs red, with a dark expression, Orrin's arms wrapped around her, Eryn looking drained and pale and the boy on the floor slowly sitting up, looking confused but unharmed despite his torn and blood-soaked shirt.

* * *

"What happened? What kind of lesson was this?" Eryn looked over to Vern who had been brought a large tray of food to replenish the substance she had used to heal him. He was as an exception allowed to eat in bed. Orrin was relieved and behaving leniently at the moment.

"History," he threw out between two bites.

"History? Not usually the kind of lesson to get speared in one's back, I would imagine."

Vern shook his head, took another generous bite of his cake and swallowed it almost without chewing.

"That is not healthy - at least chew it! That's why you have teeth, you know? Maybe our next lesson should be the path food takes through your body." She took a quick look towards the study door to make sure it was still closed and that Orrin couldn't hear them.

"Do you want to scold me because of my eating habits or would you like to know how I got hurt?"

She motioned for him to go on.

"We moved the desks and chairs to the side to put together a large map of the kingdom and a chair broke in the process. So a few of us just took off the chair's legs and pretended they were swords."

"Wait, wait, wait. You have no interest whatsoever in combat skills training, but in your history lesson you discover your fascination for sword fighting?" She rubbed at her forehead and then grabbed one of the small cakes on his tray.

"Hey! That's mine!" he protested. "I am the one meant to be recovering."

"Spoiled only child. It's time you learned to share."

"With the sister I never wanted?"

"Brat. I told them to feed you whatever you liked and that's how you thank me. Better tell me why there was no teacher present to take the pointed wooden sticks out of your hands and hit you on the head with them instead."

"He had forgotten the border to the eastern sea on his desk and went to fetch it."

"Leaving a bunch of adolescent boys with too much energy and too little brain unsupervised? That shows a great deal of foresight." She sighed. "What happened then? Somebody just stabbed you in the back?"

"No, not as such." His words were hesitant. "It's more that somehow I staggered backwards and the boy behind me wanted to catch me, but he forgot that he was still holding the chair leg…"

She couldn't hide her grin completely. "So you fell onto it? You basically staked yourself by being a clumsy fighter, regardless of the weapon in your hand being real or not? That is warrior material if ever I saw it."

His expression grew dark. "I am very glad this amuses you. I bet father is reading the teacher's report right at this moment, and he will not be very happy about it."

That she believed. People would talk about the warrior trainer's son who couldn't dodge a sword made out of a broken chair, even when he was not actually being attacked with it.

She shoved the last morsel of cake into her mouth and then rose.

"Then I would say I will leave you alone now so you and Orrin can have a nice heart-to-heart when he emerges from his cave."

"Right. So much for my being a spoiled only child. When it comes to stealing my food you are willing to stay, but if it is about standing by me when I am facing trouble, you run away."

She smiled brightly. "You see, Vern, the trouble is that I am a spoiled only child as well. The trick with sharing is that you do it with other people's things, not with your own."

Winking, she closed the door to his room behind her and waved goodbye to Orrin, who had just opened the door to his study with a sheet of paper in his hand and a less than happy expression on his face. It looked as if the fun was about to start for Vern. Time to leave.

* * *

Tyront looked up when Enric entered his study. "Good, you are here. Orrin should arrive soon. I am not looking forward to this conversation, I have to admit."

"There is no avoiding it. I don't think the old fool can be trusted with her training any longer. He has made himself vulnerable to her." His voice was tight with anger.

As any father would have, Tyront thought, but didn't say it out loud. What he said instead was, "That might be a little premature. He is the best warrior trainer we have, after all."

"The most skilled one he may be, but clearly not the most far-sighted one. He has given her the perfect weapon to make him remove her shackles: his wish to see his son whole. What if her next idea is to harm Vern to make him do it again?"

"Let's consider one minor detail here: she let him put them back on afterwards without resistance."

"Yes, but only because she was completely exhausted from healing. In her state she could hardly have avoided being shackled again."

"Which she was obviously willing to accept." He leaned forward, staring at Enric. "She gave up her chance to run off for the boy's wellbeing. Let's not forget that. Your reaction to this seems rather excessive, considering that this has ended well."

At that moment a knock sounded at the door and the servant led Orrin in.

He looked weary and resigned to the reprimand that, without a doubt, awaited him. Or even the loss of his rank. He wasn't asking himself if his actions had been worth the trouble. When the choice was between his son and the Order, he didn't have to ponder an answer to that even for a second. In a similar situation he would act like this again and he was willing to bear the consequences whatever they were.

"My Lords," he said stiffly.

He saw Enric shooting an angry look at him, while Tyront, ever the gracious host, rose and offered him a seat.

"Lord Orrin, sit with me."

Enric remained standing, his arms folded, and kept glaring at the fighter.

"I assume you are aware why we summoned you," Tyront began.

"Because I removed Eryn's shackles without your authorisation, I assume." His tone was as stiff as his bearing. He kept staring straight ahead, avoiding eye contact, waiting.

"Indeed. I appreciate that you may have had valid reasons, but it was nevertheless a violation of direct orders given to you and thus it cannot remain unmentioned. Why did you do it?"

"She told me to," he said and regretted it instantly. This was not something a man in his position said to justify disobeying a direct order. It was not an answer he himself would have accepted from anybody else.

"Did she now?" Enric smiled sardonically. "Well, if that isn't a valid justification…"

Orrin rose, fury suddenly burning in his eyes. "You come back and discuss this with me after *you* have seen your own child lying on the ground, bleeding and howling in pain, you self-righteous…"

"That's enough, both of you!" Tyront's voice boomed through the room, silencing them both. "You two better remember your manners or I will have to teach you some."

That kept them quiet. Tyront was not known for making idle threats.

"Good," he said finally.

Orrin turned back to Tyront and said stiffly, "I resign my position."

Tyront sighed. "No, Lord Orrin, you don't," he explained patiently. "What you seem to deem a noble, self-sacrificing gesture to prove that your son is more important than your rank in the Order is in truth no more than defiance of Lord Enric, and what I consider a guilty conscience regarding Eryn. Your resignation is, therefore, for your own good and the Order's, rejected. What you *will* do is to continue to train Eryn and refrain from removing her manacles again."

Orrin swallowed. "Lord Tyront, I request to be released from any duty to train her."

"I see." His voice had lost some of its edge. "You feel you are in her debt and feel guilty, all the more if you have to keep on making her fight against her will." Tyront shook his head. "I can't let such considerations influence my decision. You will have to come to terms with this. As long as she has not joined us we cannot make exceptions for her or the King might challenge our compliance with the Order's regulations. Your training will make sure that this will not be an issue."

"I don't like doing it," Orrin replied, eyes on the floor.

"I am not asking you to. What I am asking you is to follow your orders, Lord Orrin." The reprimand was voiced calmly but nevertheless didn't fail to be recognisable as such.

Orrin looked up, now angry. "I was there, on the floor, kneeling in my own son's blood, watching her exhaust herself to save him. And when she was done, the first thing I did was to put those damn shackles back on." He sounded disgusted with himself. "She didn't try to run when I'd taken them off," he repeated what Tyront had pointed out to Enric before his arrival. "She stayed and gave away the chance to free herself so as to save my son. And then, once more, I blocked what little was left of her powers, so we can keep her helpless and unable to flee because we simply can't manage to convince her to join the Order or that we are worthy of her talent and her knowledge. And today, for the first time in many decades, I am not sure myself that we are." His voice had turned bitter.

"Who then would you entrust with her?" Tyront asked calmly. "Who then, in your opinion, among your colleagues can be charged with training her without torturing, hurting or breaking her to deal with her resistance? Give me a name and I will release you as you requested."

The silence stretched on for a time. Then Orrin sighed, defeated. "You win. I will continue to work with her."

He left, for the first time without waiting to be dismissed by his superiors.

"And now to you." Tyront lifted a brow and turned to Enric after the door had closed again. "Your behaviour was foolish, I am surprised at you. What is the matter?"

"The matter?" Enric exclaimed. "I thought that was obvious! Orrin doesn't have the required distance from her any more. It was a fatuous thing to let his son befriend her, and now he owes her a lot. And when I came to that classroom today, they were…" He stopped.

"Yes?" Tyront enquired calmly. "What were they?"

"They were kneeling on the floor and he was holding her in his arms." Enric's voice was steady again.

The older man sighed. That explained a lot, of course. Jealousy was hardly ever a good advisor. It was, however, inconvenient to have both Enric and Orrin on edge at the same time, especially as it was due to the same woman, if for different reasons. That was bound to result in more tension.

At least Tyront hoped very much that it was for different reasons. He somehow couldn't picture Orrin falling for a woman who was closer in age to his son than himself, even though an age difference of twenty-five years was not as such an insurmountable problem. Even so, he had not once seen any sign in Orrin's behaviour towards Eryn that would point to anything other than fatherly friendliness.

Enric, however, was clearly more sensitive to this possibility. This emotional reaction of an otherwise cool-headed man (and, at times, a man even considered cold-hearted) spoke volumes. Taking her to bed during the Freedom Night might not have been the best idea in hindsight. His judgement was obviously being affected, or he wouldn't have suggested replacing Orrin, who had never in all these decades given the Order any reason to doubt his loyalty or abilities, merely due to an embrace he had witnessed.

He wondered if Enric was falling in love with her. That would probably complicate things, even if his increase in effort to keep her here would benefit the Order. But for himself that might be a painful path to follow.

Eryn seemed to be in no danger of reciprocating such feelings, if indeed they even existed. Whenever she caught a glimpse of Enric, however great the distance, her expression showed plainly enough that there were no tender inclinations from her side whatsoever. Tyront wondered how she would react when she found out who the mysterious stranger who had swept her off her feet that night really was. He had no doubt that she would learn of it in time. Though she would probably be the last one who did.

* * *

Enric yawned and looked down at the breakfast tray. A small, light brown envelope embossed with a red crest was lying on his empty plate. Another summons from the King. He broke open the wax seal and unfolded the message.

Damn, he thought, and rose without touching the food. They had wanted to keep this matter within the Order without royal interference. No such luck, as it seemed. As it concerned what was officially still *his* captive, he had the right to intervene.

He was expected in less than half an hour and needed to get prepared quickly.

* * *

Enric was the first to arrive and waited in front of the double doors to the throne room. Orrin turned up shortly after him, giving him a curt nod and then staring silently at the door handles.

When the doors were opened for them to enter, Orrin waited a moment to let Enric as the higher-ranking magician go in first. King Folrin sat on his throne, following their approach through narrowed eyes, Marrin and Loft on each side.

Both magicians bowed and waited for the King to speak. That he did, after staring at them for an uncomfortable length of time.

"Lord Orrin. I have been informed of a rather serious matter concerning you and the incident with your son two days ago. It seems you have failed to comply with the Order's express instructions not to remove the golden manacles that bind the captive Eryn. These instructions were given, as I understand, to avoid the danger her powers pose to anyone but the two magicians stronger than her and thus to prevent convenient opportunities for another attempt at flight."

"Your Majesty, may I speak?" Enric came in before Orrin had had a chance to answer the accusations.

"By all means, Lord Enric. I am very interested in hearing why I was not informed of this matter immediately. From what I understand you were there to witness it. You may think that this is an internal issue concerning the Order alone, but as this action has endangered the safe custody of my captive, it constitutes an act of disobedience against *me*."

"It seems there has been a, what shall I say, misunderstanding, Your Majesty. We have no reason to doubt Lord Orrin's commitment to the task he has been assigned and his willingness to follow his instructions. Otherwise we would hardly choose to let him continue training her. The removal of the manacles that day was sanctioned by myself personally. I was, as you have correctly pointed out, present."

Marrin spoke as the King remained silent. "From what we have learned, Lord Enric, you arrived only *after* the healing of young Vern was completed."

"This is not quite true, I'm afraid to say. I arrived there shortly after Lord Orrin and Eryn. As she holds a deep aversion to me - as I believe is well known - I avoided entering the room as it might have disturbed her concentration on what appeared to me very exacting work. So when she demanded of Lord Orrin that he remove the shackles, I was there to avoid any unnecessary risk which restoring her full powers might have presented."

Marrin's eyes narrowed. "And Lord Orrin was aware of your presence?"

"Of course. When he hesitated to remove them and Eryn demanded it a second time, he looked to me for permission and I gave it to him with a nod."

"Why, then," Loft spoke this time, "did none of the other people in the room recall seeing you there before it was over?"

Enric lifted his brows as if surprised that the answer wasn't obvious enough for everyone to see. "I assume the excitement and horror that day might have pulled their attention away from the corridor to the boy bleeding on the floor and the unique chance to see actual healing performed right in front of their eyes."

The King looked him in the eyes. "So what you are saying, Lord Enric, is that Lord Orrin obtained your permission *before* he removed the manacles?"

"Exactly, Your Majesty."

"Can you confirm this, Lord Orrin?" King Folrin turned his gaze to the other magician who stood rigid, staring straight ahead, hands behind his back.

"I can, Your Majesty," he replied quietly after a short pause.

Silence followed this statement and the King leaned back and stared at both magicians, Enric returning the gaze steadily, Orrin still avoiding any eye contact.

"I see," the King said finally. "It seems we were misinformed. Thank you for coming here to clarify this matter. You may both leave now."

Each magician bowed and turned away to leave the throne room, Enric again walking one step ahead of his colleague.

When the doors had closed behind them, they stared at each other for a prolonged moment before Orrin bowed low and Enric accepted the gesture of gratitude with a nod.

Inside the throne room, Marrin pursed his lips. "Lord Orrin is a terrible liar."

The King's smile was wan and joyless. "Yes, indeed. Unfortunately, Lord Enric seems to have developed quite a talent for it. He has got so much better at it these days."

CHAPTER 18

Making Money

Another free day. The gap between each one always felt like an eternity, and then they were over in what seemed like hours.

She was walking through the streets with Vern. They would visit Plia at the orphanage. It had been quite some time since Eryn had seen the girl and she wanted to make sure everything was alright and the matron had kept her word that the girl wouldn't be harmed any more.

"It's getting colder. I need to talk to father about new warm clothes. The ones from last year are a bit too short. Maybe your friend Junar wants to take care of that matter? I don't particularly like the tailor we normally use."

Eryn lifted an eyebrow. "I wasn't aware that it is necessary to like a craftsman to buy from him."

He shrugged. "It isn't. But as I can choose who I want to give the chance to earn some money, I may as well make it somebody I like. And there is always the fact that it is so much pleasurable to be measured by a nice-looking woman instead of an old prune."

"That nice-looking woman is old enough to be your mother, if I may remind you."

"So what? I am not planning to subdue her and carry her over my shoulder to my dark lair but have her make clothes for me."

She shook her head at him. "Sometimes you worry me a little."

"That is completely alright, or so I am told. Growing boys are kind of expected to be a nuisance and unnerve those around them."

"Who tells you things like that? It's not as if you needed any further encouragement to be a nuisance."

"I find that a little offensive. Compared to other boys my age I am really uncomplicated to handle."

She thought for a moment, then said, "You know, I think that doesn't actually count if you say it yourself. I wonder what your father would answer if asked how easy you are to handle."

"That wouldn't count very much, either. Fathers tend to complain, no matter how good or bad their children are. There is always this little something lacking that would fulfil their expectations completely."

Sending him an impressed look, she replied, "Now I have to admit that is a fair point."

She looked down when she felt something tug at her sleeve. A small boy of about six or seven years with dirty cheeks looked up at her with big blue eyes and kept hanging on to her shirt.

"What is the matter, little one?" she asked and bent down so she was on eye-level with him.

"My father is ill," he squeaked, clearly not too comfortable talking to her.

She thought for a moment. It wouldn't really make sense to ask the child what the problem was, the reply would hardly be very enlightening.

Vern spoke instead. "Where is your father? Can you take us there?"

The boy pointed towards a house entrance at the other side of the street where a nervous-looking woman in an apron stood, kneading her fingers and watching them tensely.

Eryn rose and started walking towards her, Vern directly behind her. She felt anticipation emanating from him; he was clearly eager to watch another healing.

When she was within earshot the woman swallowed audibly and gave a summary bow.

"Good day to you. Is this your son?"

The woman nodded, "Yes, my Lady."

"Please call me Eryn. He said his father is ill."

"Yes. He hurt himself working with rocks and now he has fever which isn't going down." Her voice was full of foreboding.

"Why don't you bring us to him and then I'll have a look at him?"

"Would you really?" Rough hands grasped her own in gratitude, urging her into the house and through a dark corridor, then up the staircase at the far end and into a room with a large bed, upon which a heavily built man lay, facing the ceiling.

Eryn walked towards the man and started noticing details even before she reached him. Sweat, laboured breathing, pale skin, a blood-soaked bandage around one shoulder.

"I know him," Vern whispered into her ear. "He is the overseer for the bridge renovation. He must have had an accident."

She nodded and then bent down to the man to see if he was conscious.

"Hello? I am a healer, I am here to have a look at your wound. Can you hear me?"

Eyelids fluttered open and eyes as blue as his son's stared up at her without focus.

"Get the door up higher," he exclaimed.

"He has been like this since last night," the woman behind her said, "talking nonsense, not understanding anything we say to him."

"I see," Eryn replied. "What is his name?"

"Pran," the woman answered, never taking her eyes off him.

"Alright. I want you to get me a bowl of hot water, a clean towel and then you should prepare a hearty meal for your companion."

The woman nodded and left the room.

"What do you need the water and towel for?" Vern asked frowning.

"I don't. I need her to be busy so she doesn't feel useless and helpless. Now put your hand on his arm and look inside. If anybody comes in, remove your hand immediately. Understood?"

He nodded, glancing at the closed door and then laying his hand on the overly warm arm of the recumbent man.

"There is a lot of activity in his body. It is working very hard," he said quietly. "His heart is strained and so are the other organs. The wound at his shoulder is not clean. He is too hot." He opened his eyes. "Is that the reason for all this?"

Eryn kept her eyes closed and nodded. "Yes. The dirt in the wound has given a lot of germs the chance to grow in there and travel to all other parts of his body through his blood. His body reacts to this by increasing the temperature to try to kill them. The problem is, the body is not made for enduring such heat for too long."

"So you will heal the wound now?"

She nodded again.

"And then he will be well again?"

"It is not as easy as that. There is still the matter of the things in his blood. We need to get them out as well, and as this has obviously been going on for quite a while already, they have spread far and wide. We must heal his wound so that the source is taken care of. And then his body temperature must be lowered or it will suffer damage. But not too much, because it still needs to fight the intruders." She held out her hand for Vern's. "Come. Show me what you have learned. I will remove the bandage and you will start with cleaning the wound."

"Me? But I have only practised with small cuts! What if I am doing something wrong?"

She opened her eyes at the panic in his voice. "Don't worry. I will be watching everything you do. I won't let you harm him."

He stood frozen, looking down at the man he had seen not too long ago, when he waited for him to signal, with a triple clap of his hands, that he could go home after a long day of hard work.

"You don't have to, if you don't feel secure enough," she said gently. "I will take care of it. I am sorry, I didn't want to push you."

He straightened. "No. I can do this."

"Yes, I know. I wouldn't have asked you otherwise. The important thing is for *you* to know it as well."

She watched him take a steadying breath before he closed his eyes again and made contact with the suffering man. The first thing they did was sending him to a deep and relaxing sleep.

Both opened their eyes as soon as a hesitant knock interrupted the scene.

Eryn walked towards the door and opened it a crack to take the water, towel and plate with food from the woman. The woman tried to catch sight of the man on the bed and Eryn said soothingly, "Everything is going to be fine, don't worry. We need some more time, then you can come in."

When she had closed the door again, she returned to Vern and Pran. Vern had cleaned the man's wound and his work had removed the damaged tissue almost completely. He had done it very neatly, using infinitesimally small doses of magic for exacting actions. Eryn felt pride rising inside her and wondered if her father had ever felt like that when he had been teaching her. She hoped very much that he had done.

"Good. Now we can close the wound," she murmured softly. "I know you could do it alone, but it would take a lot of time. I will assist you by starting at the upper end and we meet in the middle. I will be able to work faster than you, but do not let that unsettle you. I have been doing this since before you were born and with the time comes speed."

When the wound was closed, both of them opened their eyes and smiled at each other. "You did well, Vern. I feel so proud I could burst. My father would have lamented the injustice of your talent being wasted here in the Order, you know."

She took his hand and pressed it tight as he swallowed self-consciously. Even though Vern's talents were so extraordinary, the Order such as it was didn't see them as anything to be valued. So he didn't really receive much praise when he excelled at something the Order did not consider useful. The rottenness of this lay heavily in her belly.

"Now let's see what we can do to lower his temperature a little," she said and put their joined hands back on the man's arm. "Let's have a look into his head. There is a tiny area where the temperature is controlled from. We need to convince it that it should cool down his body. The area I am talking about is right in the centre of his head, at about the level of his eyes but slightly further back. Yes! Here is the little spot we need to work on. This is very delicate work, as we cannot simply feed it with energy to increase its activity. We need to influence the nature of the activity we want. If we do it wrong then it might start increasing the temperature even further. We also don't want to cool him down too much, just a little."

"How?" Vern's voice was hardly more than a whisper.

"We need to change the information it receives."

"What information?"

"This little place here has a lot of… very small spies everywhere in the body that let it know about the temperature and other things."

"So we manipulate the spies?"

"Yes. We lie to them and they will pass on the lie. We will watch to see if we can cause the reaction we want."

"How do we lie to them?"

"By making them believe the body is hotter than it really is. This should start a cooling reaction. I will send a low energy impulse through his body, like a wave of warmth. It can't be too strong or I will harm him. Then we need to check the area in his head here. If there is no reaction, or it's not the one we want, we will have to try again with slightly more energy. Try to get an impression of how much energy I use. Ready?"

"Yes."

She felt the magical warmth flowing through her fingers into Pran's body. When she returned her attention to his head, she said after a while, "That was a good start, it is active. But it is not enough. I will send another impulse to increase the activity. Can you see the difference?" she asked.

"Yes. But I am not sure what I am seeing," Vern whispered in confusion.

"Streams of information. They are commands. If you follow them, you can see where they lead. Ultimately, they are received by areas of the body that will help decreasing the temperature. Our work here is done for the moment."

When she opened her eyes again, she saw him thoughtfully looking down at the sleeping man.

"Is everything alright?"

"I…" He shook his head. "It is just that healing seemed so clear, like cleaning a cut, removing the damaged blocks and repairing things. But this here… Something we did in one part of the body triggered a reaction in completely different areas. It's like biting my hand and feeling the pain in my knee."

"That was a little more complex, granted. It is not normally the kind of thing a beginner would learn; it is more advanced. So don't worry, we will get to that. But it was a nice opportunity to show you what else there is besides healing cuts. And you did exceptionally well with the wound. You have never before worked on something that big, after all. You used your energy well and you pay great attention to details."

He smiled at the compliment. "And now? Do we let him sleep?"

"No, not right now. We should see if his delusions have gone. He can sleep after he has eaten something, he needs to replenish the reserves we have used to heal his wound."

She touched him again and sent an impulse to his head. A few moments later his eyes fluttered open and he looked up, clearly puzzled by the two strangers in his bedroom. It took him a few moments to recognise Vern.

"You are the boy they sent us to punish him... what are you doing here?" His voice was a hoarse whisper.

"My friend Eryn has just healed you. Your companion was very worried about you."

"Healed me?" Only then he seemed to notice the colour of her hair in the gloomy room. "Yes, I have seen you waiting for the boy. You healed me? I am well again?"

"Almost. You need to give yourself another one or two days to get over it completely, but then you should be alright again. Now you need to eat, you need the energy."

She put the plate in front of him and then opened the door to let the woman in. His companion didn't seem to trust her own eyes when she saw bloody bandages lying to the side of the bed and the man's bare shoulder completely restored, without even a trace of what had been there only an hour ago.

She started weeping quietly, her face buried in both her hands. Pran smiled weakly and seemed a little embarrassed by this display of emotion.

"Stop weeping, you silly woman," he said gently. "Better get my pouch and pay her."

Eryn shook her head. "That is alright. Just do as I say and rest for the next two days, however strong you may feel."

His bearing became stiff and he sat up in his bed. "No. I can't have that. I pay my debts; I am not a pauper, whatever you may think."

Oh dear, now she had insulted him. "That was not what I meant," she said calmly. "I am not my own master, so there is no use for money for me here."

"Then you had better find one. You found a way to let the publican compensate you."

Ah yes, she thought unnerved, word had certainly travelled.

"Not by paying me, as you surely know."

"No. But as I can't offer you much in the way of providing for orphans, you will have to make do with gold."

His companion came in with a small leather pouch and took out three gold pieces. There couldn't be many more left in there, Eryn thought.

"This is what we paid the apothecary," she said and pressed them into her hand. "Only this time the expense is worth the fee."

Eryn sighed, letting two of the gold pieces drop back into the pouch. Another case of the apothecaries promising a lot and delivering nothing.

"I will take one, then. Don't bargain with me." She lifted her hand when Pran was about to disagree. "And if you insist on comparing me with the apothecaries I will start being infuriated."

He nodded and let himself sink back. "I need to pay for it. I couldn't look myself in the mirror otherwise - accepting charity with no way to pay you back."

That she could accept.

* * *

They sat together on the riverbank, watching the sun set. After several minutes of silence, Vern spoke.

"You know, people feel the need to pay for what you do for them. It is just what you do, what's right. They don't feel good when they think they are taking advantage of you."

She sighed. "Yes, I have understood that today. But what can I do? I don't think the King and the Order let me start a business here and earn money. And what would I do with the money, anyway?"

"There is nothing you could use it for?" He smiled. "You would be the only woman in the city with that problem, I think." Then he got serious again. "How about buying things that would make healing easier?"

She thought for a few moments. "Herbs," she then said slowly. "Is it possible to buy them here somewhere?"

"Only from the apothecaries, I think. They hire herb gatherers and buy the plants from them."

"Could I buy from them as well?"

Vern shrugged. "I don't see why not."

She looked down at the gold piece in her hand thoughtfully. "Where would I keep the money? My cell is not a good place. I'll bet it would be gone in no time at all."

"How about my room?" Vern offered.

She shook her head immediately. "No. Enough potential trouble lies in wait for you already over acquiring these healing skills without the Order's permission and for smuggling candles in to me. And they might also have an eye on you due to our little illicit combat lessons. I need a neutral place. Where do you keep your money? Is there a place for safekeeping valuables around?"

He nodded. "Sure. You could take it to the money lenders. They keep it safe for you until you need it."

"Money lenders? Why would they take my money if it is their business to lend it to people?"

Vern gave her a doubtful look, then shook his head and sighed. "I see there was not much civilisation going on where you have lived."

"Can you quit being a pain and just tell me what I want to know for a change?"

"They hold your money safely to have enough lying around whenever somebody wants to borrow a sum."

"So they give my money to other people? What if I need it back?" This idea didn't seem very safe.

"They hold money from more people, not only your own," he explained patiently. "So there usually is enough money available when you want yours back. But you can also tell them that you don't want them to lend your money to other people, only then you have to pay a fee for them guarding it for you."

"And they would give it back to me if I asked them to?"

"They'd better. If word got out that they hadn't given back money people left with them, it would ruin their business."

"I see," she said slowly. "And they wouldn't return it to anyone but me?"

"No, they wouldn't."

That didn't sound too bad, then. However often they searched her place, they wouldn't find the gold.

"Alright then. Let's do this." She rose. "Where is this place?"

"It's not far from the city centre. But there is one thing you need first if you don't want them to use your money for their business: a box. There is a carpenter who makes them in just the right size for their storage shelves. They put a piece of paper inside with the secret code word you have to repeat so the lenders know you are entitled to reclaim the money inside the box."

That sounded sensible. "Well, then let's go there first."

"Sure. It's not as if I should be home by nightfall or anything," he sighed.

"Now you start obeying the rules? Really?"

He shrugged. "Father tends to confine me to our quarters after I have arrived late, so it's less a need to obey than to protect my freedom."

"Then just tell me the way and I'll see to it alone. I think I know the city pretty well by now and should be able to follow directions."

"Why don't we wait until tomorrow? Then we can do this without haste."

She shook her head and lifted the fist with the gold piece. "No. I need to get rid of this money. They shouldn't be able to find it anywhere near me."

Sighing in defeat, Vern started walking. "Come on, then. But you tell my father that I am late because we were held up by another healing event and I am too much of a gentleman to let you return alone in the dark."

"He would believe that?" she enquired doubtingly.

"Absolutely. He is a strong believer in protecting the weaker sex and would not punish me when I follow his lead."

She followed him, chuckling. The question was if Orrin would consider somebody with the ability to shield and now throw magical bolts in her defence still a member of the *weaker sex* in any classical meaning. But that was for Vern to find out.

* * *

Plia was smiling when Eryn saw her come down the stairwell.

The girl looked much better now, she thought. The regular food the publican provided had taken away most of the hollowness in her cheeks and her complexion was less pallid. It was amazing what a difference a hot meal every day could make.

Also, there had been no more bruises since the agreement with Mistress Walchan.

She tried to make time to visit Plia at least every few days. The girl didn't have friends as such; life in the orphanage was more like a fight for survival among competitors. Friends were a weakness one tried one's best to avoid. There were enemies on the one hand and people who had a fragile, temporary detente with each other on the other.

What a sad environment to be growing up in, Eryn thought, and decided she would try to be a friend to the girl. Somebody Plia could turn to in time of need, who didn't expect to be paid or given any other compensation for a crumb of kindness.

"How are you, little flower?" Eryn ruffled the blond mane.

"Great, now that you are here!" she beamed. "What will we do today?"

"How about a nice stroll down to the river? We could take some bread and feed the birds." Only then did it occur to her that the thought of buying bread to feed it to animals might be seen as a terrible waste and an insult to a girl who had known times where food was scarce.

But to her relief the girl just smiled happily and took Eryn's hand.

"And on our way back I would like to stop at an apothecary's shop to buy a few things."

She had been quite busy with healing over these last few days. Several gold pieces had already found their way into her newly acquired savings box. Only today a man with a broken finger had approached her. She had charged him three silver pieces as it was not really a complicated piece of healing and had cost her no more than a few minutes of her time. That should be enough to pay for a few herbs she could use for concoctions against headaches and sore throats. They tended to be more frequent when it got colder and people went in and out of warm places frequently.

"But you can do so much more than them," she asked in puzzlement, "Why would you buy anything from them?"

"So I can make medicines that help people without using magic. The problem is that normally there are more people needing help than I have magic in me to use on them, especially with these on." She jingled her manacles. "And, of course, time is another factor. I can only heal in the evenings as they make me train my fighting during the day."

She shook her head. "That is so stupid. There are so many fighters and only one healer. Why don't they let you heal all the time?"

Eryn sighed. Even a twelve-year-old girl could see the sense in that idea, but not the omnipotent Order.

"I am not sure. I suppose they think they can turn me into one of them."

"Do you want to be one of them?"

"No, not at all."

"Why not? They are very powerful and have so much money. You would never again have to worry about food or clothes."

That would, of course, be a weighty argument for a girl who had nothing.

"I didn't have to worry about that before, either. I was not rich as such, but unlike a rewarding profession, loads of money does not necessarily contribute to happiness. They want to take that away from me. My father always said that they only squander magic using it for fighting instead of to help people."

"What will they do if you don't join them?"

Yes, she thought, that was the big question. "I don't know."

"They won't kill you, will they?" Sudden panic had crept into her voice.

"No, of course not." Probably, she thought.

Eryn felt the small hand she was holding relax. "And what will you do if they don't let you go when you don't become one of them?"

"I will try to find a way to get away from here without them letting me go, I suppose."

The girl's face fell and Eryn felt a stab of guilt. Of course the prospect of losing the only friendly adult in her life was not a joyful one. That was the trouble with forging bonds in a situation like hers. She thought of leaving Vern behind and pushed the thought aside immediately as it only made her sad.

But what was the alternative? Avoiding all contact with the people around her? She had been raised to be compassionate as according to her father that was one of the most important characteristics of a healer. That, and possessing sufficient healing skills, of course. As well as the constant wish to increase one's knowledge and pass it on. Increasing knowledge without anybody else to guide her had naturally been hard work. She had had books, but merely reading about things without actually seeing them done required a lot more time and caused a lot more frustration. As for passing the skills on, she had now for the first time in her life found a willing person to be on the receiving end, and for her this felt like finally closing the circle of what it really meant to be a healer.

"Why doesn't the Order have any healers?" Plia asked.

Eryn opened her mouth to answer, but found to her own astonishment that she didn't know. She had resented the Order for having none, but never really bothered to find out why.

"That is a very good question, and I have to admit that I don't know. I think we should ask Vern. He might have learned something about that in his history lessons."

The girl smiled shyly. "Vern is very clever, isn't he?"

Eryn looked down at her. An older boy who had a habit of using big words would of course impress a girl who wasn't used to it.

"Yes, that he is."

"But his father is the one who makes you fight," she added, with a frown.

"Yes, but I am beginning to think that there are worse men around for that task."

"So you don't mind?"

"I do mind. A lot. If I could, I would stop this at once. But when there is job to do that is none too gentle, it sometimes is a good thing to have a gentle person doing it."

Plia frowned. "I don't understand."

"Orrin has never treated me badly. Nobody would have blamed him if he had done - I am no more than a captive, after all. Somebody else might have used more force on me, or brutality or even worse."

"So Lord Orrin is not so bad after all?"

"Well," she smirked, "I wouldn't go that far. At least not as long as he makes me fight every damn day."

They had reached the river and Eryn took out the bread she had purchased earlier. "You won't feel bad if we give that to the birds?"

The girl shook her head. "No. Birds also need to eat, just like everybody else."

Eryn marvelled at the simple logic of the statement. It was amazing how poverty affected people differently. Some were greedy and willing to take what they could by whatever means necessary while others, like Plia, remembered kindness when it was shown to them and were eager to pass it on.

She gave the loaf to Plia and watched contentedly when she tore off morsels and threw them to the birds, always taking care that it wasn't only the strong and fast ones which had a share.

Eryn stretched out and began watching the people around them. A young man and a woman about the same age, just out of earshot, talked to each other in an agitated way, their hands moving to emphasise their words.

Plia followed Eryn's gaze.

"I bet they are companions and are fighting about money," the girl ventured. "Couples fight a lot about money," she added knowingly.

"Not them." Eryn shook her head and kept watching them. "They are siblings. She is trying to impress on her brother that his companion has to take care of their sick mother for a few days as she has to work. He doesn't seem to be very happy about that. She accuses him of being soft in the head and too much of a coward to ask his companion to do it. It seems she doesn't have a very favourable opinion of her brother's mate."

Plia stared at her. "How can you know that? They are too far away to hear them! Can you see that with your magic?"

Eryn chuckled. "No, with my eyes. I don't see him very well because he is sideways to me, but my view of his sister's mouth is clear. You see the way her lips move? This is how I can tell what she is saying."

"What?" the girl exclaimed in disbelief and stared intently at the woman's mouth. "I can't see what she is saying. Her mouth just opens and closes."

"It's a skill you have to practice. My father taught me. He was very good at it, much better than I am. The speakers need to be facing me so I can see their lips. And I have trouble if they speak too fast or mumble."

"How do you do it?" Plia enquired, still staring at the animated pair.

"It's the way the lips form letters and words. For an A you open your mouth a little more while your lips are slightly pursed when they form an O, for example. If you are interested and have enough patience, you can try watching yourself speak in front of a mirror and see what different words look like when you say them."

She saw the girl swallow and nod noncommittally.

"What is it?" she wanted to know.

"It's nothing. Really."

Eryn rolled her eyes. "Tell me, come on."

"I don't have a mirror," Plia said sheepishly. "They cost a lot of money..."

Of course she didn't. The children at the orphanage had trouble figuring out where to get their next meal from, so possessing a mirror would have been a stroke of luck as selling it would have secured them a few bites to eat. They wouldn't use it for something as frivolous as looking at themselves.

Eryn chided herself for her own lack of sensitivity. Being able to eavesdrop on other people was a fine skill to boast of when instead she should be more careful what was coming out of her own mouth.

When the bread was finished, they both rose. It was getting late.

"Do you know where the nearest apothecary's shop is from here?"

The girl nodded. "Yes, it's really close. Come, I'll show you."

Only a few minutes later they were standing in front of a medium-sized shop with a large window displaying glass vials containing different coloured powders, dried plants hanging from hooks and a large board informing that *your apothecary was the one to turn to when in need.*

Eryn took a closer look at the plants on display and frowned. Some of them did not have any medicinal properties at all as far as she knew. It seemed that they were there for mere decoration, which somewhat diminished her trust of the selection before she had even entered the shop.

"Would you wait for me here, little flower? This should only take a minute."

When she entered, the pungent smell of alcohol and the more subdued one of herbs almost made her eyes water. What did they do here? Just drown the herbs in liquor instead of distil the essences?

A man in his late forties with almost completely white hair was about to break into a smile at the sight of a customer, when his eyes alighted on her hair and a frown appeared instead.

"You are that healer who everybody has been talking about," he said instead of a greeting. "Come to utilise the services of a true professional, have you?"

Struck by the unfriendliness and the audacity of denying her the status of a professional, her first reaction was utter surprise. "What?"

"You heard me, I am sure."

"I haven't come to consult you in healing matters but to see what herbs you have on stock and buy some if they come up to my quality standards." Her voice had grown cold.

"We don't sell herbs just like that to anyone who claims to have knowledge of their use," he said with a disdainful look at her. "We feel responsible for their correct use and can't have just anybody trying a bit of mixing and then doing who knows what damage to whatever gullible fool can be persuaded to buy them."

"I see." She forced herself to remain calm. This jerk would not succeed in making her lose control. "Well, from what I could see from the decoration in your window and the smell in here I dare say your merchandise would not have been up to my requirements anyway. A good day to you." With that she turned and walked out.

Her father had told her to always say farewell gently even if she was very angry as it demonstrated to herself that she still was in control and to the other one that had he was not important enough to make her forget her good manners.

"That was very quick. Did you get your plants?" Plia asked.

Eryn shook her head, still not fully understanding what had just happened. "No, I didn't. He didn't want to sell me anything. How many apothecaries have shops in the city?"

"Five or six, I think. Would you like to go to the next one?"

"Yes, let's try." Would they treat her the same way or was this just the attitude of one single man?

At the second shop she was ordered to leave immediately and was instructed to stop her charlatan practices at once or the King would deal with her. The League of Apothecaries had already sent a complaint to him, she was told.

The League of Apothecaries? She shook her head. They had formed an alliance, it seemed.

She decided to try one more shop before giving up.

When she entered the small locale, a middle-aged man in simple clothes was leaning against a wall and eyed her with interest. He didn't seem to belong here, probably a customer, she thought. Another man came in through a curtain that hid a back room. He froze when he saw her.

"The healer," he spat.

Great, she thought. There it started again. "Yes, the healer. And I am willing to buy from you, spend my money here, as it were."

"The famous healer wants to buy from *me*?" he sneered.

"Yes, your herbs."

"We don't sell just herbs. We sell medication after taking the time and seeing what a patient needs."

"Of course. And my being just a non-professional who walks around healing carelessly, I do not qualify for your precious products." She gave him a saccharine smile.

"Exactly." His smile was just as insincere.

"I see. Good day to you."

She grabbed Plia's hand and forced herself to walk away in a relaxed way as if she was just taking a leisurely stroll along the street.

"No herbs here, either?" Plia asked in a tone that showed that she didn't really expect a positive answer.

"No. They just won't sell to me."

"And what can you do now?"

She shrugged. "I suppose I need to try getting in contact with a herb gatherer. I can't leave the city to gather them myself as I did at home, so that's the only other option I can think of right now. Come, let's get you back to the orphanage. It's getting dark."

When Eryn left the orphanage to return to her cell, she had the distinct feeling of being watched. She was used to drawing attention to herself when she was walking through the streets. Even if her presence here was not exactly new anymore, people still turned their heads at the unfamiliar sight of her hair.

Even though she was sure that there were not many people around that she couldn't stand against, she felt uneasy and raised a shield around her.

She walked on and stopped when she heard a hissing sound from a narrow alley to her left. Staring into it, she wondered what to do. A woman alone in the dusk walking into a dark alley was not usually the beginning of a story that ended well. But she was a powerful magician able to protect herself with a shield, right? Sure, common sense piped in, at least as powerful as the manacles allowed. And there was always the chance of another magician attacking her. With her shackles in place there would be many who could easily penetrate her barrier.

"Psssst," the sound came again while she was still considering her options. When she still didn't enter the alley, she heard an urging whisper. "I have an offer for you. I am a herb gatherer."

That made her ears prick up. She cautiously took a few steps into the dark lane from where she needed a few moments to adjust her eyes to the gloom.

"You are the man from the apothecary's shop!" she called out.

The man silenced her with a frightened gesture. "Would you just keep it down? Why do you think I am asking you into a dark alley? Clearly not because I am keen to be seen or heard!" he whispered.

"Sorry," she whispered back, cursing herself for her thoughtlessness. "Though lurking in dark side streets and luring women is not the usual way to inspire confidence."

"I wouldn't be doing this if I had the liberty to do it out in the open, would I? I have heard that you want to buy herbs."

"Yes. And are you willing to sell to me?"

"That would depend on the price."

"What is your price, then?" she asked.

"That depends on what you need."

"I don't know if you use the same names for the herbs here. I only know the ones from books that are not from here. I would need to show you pictures. But they should be available in this area."

"If they are easy to find, I take a silver piece for a standard bushel."

"What is a standard bushel?"

He looked at her in surprise. "Oh my, you are new in this business, for sure."

"New in the herb buying business, maybe. But not in the healing business. I gathered my own herbs back home, I never had to bother with such things as a standard bushel or what to pay for such a thing."

He pulled out a bundle of dried herbs that fitted roughly between her joined thumb and index finger.

"One silver piece? But not for easily obtainable herbs I hope?"

"It depends on how many bushels you buy," he shrugged.

Her head started to spin. These were a lot of variations for determining a price.

"I need five different herbs for a start," she whispered. "One of your standard bushels each."

"If they are fairly easy to get, let's say four silver pieces in total. If you buy more often we can negotiate again."

She nodded. That didn't sound too bad. "When can I meet you again to give you the pictures of the plants I need?"

"When do you visit the girl next time?" So he had been watching her long enough to figure that out. How handy…

"In about three days."

"Good. I will wait for you then. Not at this exact spot, though. You never know who is watching."

"Watching? You mean the apothecaries?"

"Who else?" His tone was impatient again.

"If it is so dangerous to anger them, why do you risk it?"

"Because the greedy sods keep lowering the price they pay. And there is nobody else to sell to if the League doesn't buy from you. Or there wasn't before." He flashed her a smile before vanishing into the darkness.

Well, the day had not ended so badly after all, she mused. The apothecaries had turned out to be a real hindrance and she had yet to see if there would be an intervention from the King so as to keep the League happy.

* * *

Orrin stood with legs astride and regarded her with his arms folded. In other men that stance might have seemed threatening, but he found it comfortable and was relaxed. He was pleased with her, immensely so. She would never be an exceptional fighter, but could still be a formidable opponent thanks to her magical powers and her precision in using them to make herself faster and stronger. He strongly suspected that her healing knowledge was a considerable advantage.

Currently she was fighting his son, and it was plain to see that she was playing around more than really tackling him in combat. She could already have disarmed him many times, but hadn't. Whether it was to spare Vern's delicate feelings or to keep her teacher from making her work harder with another opponent he wasn't sure. Probably a mix of both.

"Can you just end this, please?" Vern pleaded. "I have no chance of beating you and you just won't finish it!"

Orrin looked smug. It seemed he wasn't the only one who had noticed it.

Eryn shrugged then knocked the sword flying from his hand with one well-aimed thrust.

"That was embarrassing. You don't have to make your superiority that plain," he complained.

She rolled her eyes. "There is just no pleasing you, is there?"

Orrin addressed his son, "You can leave now. We will work for another two hours, then you can pick her up to rove about the city."

Eryn shot Orrin a mildly annoyed glance. Rove about. It was not like she had very much time to relax in her late afternoons and evenings. Word had spread that her healing services were available for a reasonable price, and more and more people approached her when they saw her walking through the city. She made sure to frequent the same streets so she was easy enough to find.

She had another meeting with her backstreet herb supplier today. If everything had gone well, she would finally get the plants she had ordered a week ago. They were a bit harder to find, as they grew higher up in colder regions, so the price was higher than for standard ones. Naturally.

But that was no great problem for the moment as the money kept flowing in. She didn't even have to take money from the savings box to pay her herb collector as usually there was a healing session or two that tended to come up when she was on her way to pick up the herbs, and so she could pay him with what she had earned that same day and deposit the rest on her way back.

In addition to using the money she earned for buying medical supplies she had started thinking about some purchases she could make that might enable her to leave this place somehow. Maybe she could acquire a cart and horse, cover her hair with a scarf and pretend to be a merchant on a buying trip? But that was usually a task no single woman would do. Or she could just pay somebody who passed in and out of the city without any trouble to hide her somewhere? Or…

"Stop staring into empty space!" Orrin rebuked her. "This is not an appropriate attitude when you are facing somebody holding a drawn sword."

She looked up hastily, feeling guilty. She hadn't even noticed that he was standing there, let alone the weapon he brandished. But pointing that out would not earn her anything but more reproof.

The two hours seemed to drag on endlessly and she was relieved when he finally shook his head and told her to go away on account of her dreaming making her completely useless today.

Vern was punctual, as usual, and she remembered the question Plia had asked her not long ago. "You are a smart kid, right?"

He tried to smile modestly, but failed completely. "I have been called that on occasion, yes."

"Why is it that the Order doesn't have any healers? I mean, wouldn't it be an enormous asset for warriors to have healers around when they are off to battle to patch them back together again?"

Vern stood for a few moments, frowning while pondering the question. "I have no idea. We just don't have any. Maybe we never managed to figure out how it's done."

She sighed. "These are quite a few things you don't have around here. Female magicians, different hair colours, healing skills…"

"Different hair colours?" he asked in puzzlement. "But we do have that. Look around."

"No, these are just different nuances of the same fair colour. I have a different hair colour. I mean, isn't it strange that this is the only different thing about me? My skin has pretty much the same tone as yours, my facial features are not in any way noticeably different…"

"Why would they be?"

"Because a different hair colour is normally not the only thing different when you are from a faraway place."

She remembered, through the eyes of a child, people with different skin tones from pale to very dark from a long time ago in another world. Of course he wouldn't understand that. He had grown up in a world of fair-haired people, knew nothing else and it was so natural for him that he didn't wonder about it. It was just the way the world was here.

And then there was Eryn - different hair colour, magical abilities despite her gender, unusual knowledge of healing, turning people's world upside down. She should probably be glad of just being held captive instead of having been executed on sight.

But then there was still her value as a female magician, even if not for her healing skills that nobody but Vern seemed to be interested in, but for using her as breeding stock. Although the Lordling had pretty much put a stop to that by lying to the King. Except for himself and his superior, that is.

She wasn't sure which one of them would be worse to endure. Probably the younger one. The mere thought of being touched by him in this way sent shivers down her back, and not in any pleasant way.

"I could ask my history teacher, if you are really interested in that," Vern offered. "And if he doesn't know maybe he can point out some books."

"Don't worry about it, it's just curiosity. Nothing to waste your hard-earned free evenings on."

He smiled. "Oh, but you know me; I am the bookish type. I don't mind looking into it. And since your arrival questions like that have crossed my mind now and then."

"Why have you never looked it up, then?" she enquired.

He shrugged. "I always think about those things when I am supposed to be paying attention in my classes or before I fall asleep. So when I am free to do it, I have usually already forgotten about it."

They walked on silently for a while.

"Do you need to do anything special today or do we just wait for somebody to come running, desperate for your services?" he asked.

"I need to pick up some herbs."

"Another back-alley deal?" Vern asked, rather pointedly.

She shrugged. "What can I do if my seller is too afraid of the apothecaries to deal it out in the open? I am glad I have finally found somebody to sell to me, no matter how shady the dealing location is."

"You know, in that one respect it would be an advantage to be in the Order. The apothecaries wouldn't dare threaten somebody who sells to an Order magician. They would have to be afraid themselves otherwise."

She stopped and frowned at him. "You know the way I think about the Order. And joining them would very likely not result in me increasing my healing opportunities but in being lucky if they let me do it at all."

"You don't know that for sure. Or have you discussed it with them?"

"Of course I haven't discussed it with them! As if the great and powerful Order would welcome it if a lowly prisoner proposed joining them. And even if they did, I wouldn't want such a thing."

"*Prisoner* is a rather strong term for your situation. You are not exactly behind bars," he pointed out.

"But that's not really the thing here, is it? Sure, I am not behind bars, but then I am not exactly free, either. And I have no respect for your Order and its priorities. Or its methods," she added darkly.

"Why are you so sure they wouldn't support your plans to perform healing? They haven't stopped you so far, and I am sure they know about your activities."

"I dare say they don't mind as long as it keeps me busy and out of their way. Yet they haven't showed any interest in it. You would think that an institution such as they would appreciate new and useful knowledge. I mean, they keep forcing me to train my fighting skills but haven't even once tried to make me tell them about healing. That is very clear sign of disinterest, if you ask me."

"Yes, you are probably right," he admitted reluctantly. "Would you have shown them if they had asked?"

"Of course. My father has taught me that healing knowledge is not a privilege but something every person has a right to. In case of magicians it should even be a duty. I wouldn't send anybody away who wants to learn it."

"A noble sentiment. And yet you didn't want to teach me at first."

"Don't make me seem selfish; I just didn't want to teach you because I wanted to keep you out of trouble. But it seems there is no keeping you away from it now," she quipped.

"So, if Lord Enric came to you and asked you for lessons in healing you would not hesitate to comply?" he asked.

She scowled at him. "That is a heartless question. You know I can't stand being anywhere near the man."

"So you mean *No*?"

"I refuse to answer your question."

"That is the same as saying *No*," Vern stated, satisfied.

"Why am I even talking to you about this? You are a being a pest."

"You are just saying that because I am right and you don't want to admit it. But let's change the topic. You get cranky when you are in the wrong. How much money do you have in your secret store now?"

She shot him another bellicose look and decided to let the topic go. "About twenty gold pieces so far."

"Will you spend all of that on herbs?"

"I have been thinking about what to do with the money. I have an idea or two."

"Which idea or two?"

"That I can't tell you right now. If word got out that you had known about this before you would be in serious trouble."

He turned to her, frowning. "You are planning an escape!"

She quickly pressed a hand over his mouth. "Shut up!" she hissed.

"How?" he whispered when she had released his mouth again.

"Didn't you just hear me? I am not going to tell you!"

He sighed, defeated. "You know, I would miss you very much if you somehow managed to get away from here. There is nobody around but you who sees anything remotely positive in my drawing skills and my interest in healing."

She ruffled his hair, gulping back her sadness. "Don't say things like that to me. It is hard enough for me as it is."

Relief flooded through her when she heard the familiar sound the herb gatherer used to make to gain her attention.

"Can you lend me five silver pieces? I haven't been to the money lenders yet. You will get them back later," she whispered to Vern, who nodded and reached into his belt pouch to take out the coins for her.

Another alley, full of discarded wooden planks and boards hid them from sight despite the broad daylight.

"Have you got everything I wanted?" she asked quietly.

A curt nod was all the reply she got.

"Good. Here are your five silver pieces." She handed over the money when he gave her the cloth in which he had wrapped the plants. She opened it, checked its contents and nodded in approval. When she looked up again, he was already gone.

The quality was fine. She had asked him to keep the herbs from drying as this needed to be done correctly. Just leaving herbs lying in the sun was a typical beginner's mistake.

She carefully took the cloth under her arm and returned to Vern who had been waiting patiently around the corner.

"You've got everything you need?"

"Yes. Let's pick up your money and then return. I need to start working on a few things."

* * *

Tyront handed over the sheet of paper he had been reading and waited patiently for Enric to do so as well.

"So finally they have reacted to the threat she poses. I was wondering what had taken them so long," the younger man said quietly.

"It wasn't that long. They already sent the complaint to the King several days ago and as he has not yet done anything, I suppose he will not comply with their request to stop her. I am worried about what they have done to the herb gatherer who has been selling to her."

"At least he is still alive."

"Barely so, from what the report says. I expect he will no longer do business with Eryn and neither will anybody else who has a sentimental attachment to their body parts," Tyront said sardonically.

"You are not afraid they will do something stupid and attack *her* the next time, are you?"

"I do not rule it out. She may be able to protect herself when she sees an attack coming, but I bet they are more cunning than she is. We need to keep an extra careful eye on her."

Enric sighed. "That we should do anyway." He pointed to the sheet of paper still in his hands. "She seems to be looking for a merchant who can get her out of the city unseen. We might have to put out a warning that everybody who is caught helping her will suffer dire consequences. How much money does she have in her savings box? It is possible that given enough money, a desperate or greedy cart owner might agree to help her."

"Seventy gold pieces. She is a capable little money maker. With a sum like that a man could live comfortably for quite some time in the city and even buy or build a house in the country," Tyront said.

"Then I think it's time to take it away from her. Better sooner than later before she puts it to bad use. Now that the herb gatherer can no longer sell to her she doesn't have much to spend it on anyway, besides bribery."

"Yes, I will send somebody over there tonight and have the box brought here." He sighed. "It is a shame. There seems to be quite a demand for her services here and the League doesn't make it easy for her. But as long as she is not in the Order we can't intervene. It is the King's problem right now and he would not look kindly upon our interference."

Enric nodded. "True. And I would venture that pointing this out to her will not be much use, either. She would think it was a ploy to lure her into our evil halls."

"Yes," Tyront said thoughtfully, "that father of hers seems to have had a fairly bad opinion of us. A pity we didn't get to him while he was still alive. What an asset he would have been. Eryn has expressed an interest in our history, by the way. Vern has asked his history teacher for information about why the Order has no healers and why no female magicians have been around for such a long time."

"Well, these questions were bound to come up sooner or later," Enric sighed. "What do you propose? Share with her the answers we have? They are few enough."

"Yes, I think we should. That might make her a little more well-disposed towards us and will help her understand her own situation here better. And I hope ours, for that matter. I will have his teacher provide him with a book or two from the palace library to pass them on to her."

"Or we could arrange a meeting between her and Lord Poron. He knows almost everything from the books and then some. And introducing her to what will strike her as a harmless, bookish old man wouldn't hurt, either, I feel. It might help to correct her image of the Order only comprising of battle-crazed savages."

Tyront nodded slowly. "Yes, good point. It just needs to be arranged in a way that doesn't look like something we did because we spied on her."

Enric grinned lopsidedly. "Which is in fact the case."

"Yes, but we don't have to make it that obvious."

"She will be aware enough of our attention when she next tries to take money out of her savings box," the younger man said.

"True enough. Let's hope she thinks it was the King and not us."

"We could mention the box to him and he might take this out of our hands and save us the trouble."

Tyront shook his head. "No, then she would never see it again."

"So we should return it?"

"Yes. I thought it might be a nice welcome gift for when she finally joins the Order."

Enric snorted. "A gift that consists of something we'd stolen from her might not have the effect you're aiming at."

"A demonstration of goodwill, nevertheless."

"Yes, after demonstrating the impudence of stealing it from her previously."

"You are not suggesting we should leave the money with her, are you?" Tyront frowned.

"No, that would be foolish. Money is power, and in her situation we can't let her have too much of either. Maybe we could just take away most of it and leave her a few gold pieces for whatever minor purchases she wants to make. She wouldn't find out that the greater part was missing so very quickly."

"True," the older magician mused. "Up until now she has never withdrawn more than two gold pieces at a time. It seems that she usually manages to collect the money she wants to spend on her way. And now that she won't be able to buy herbs any more she will need even less of it."

"Good, then let's take care of it. That, and the warning that she is not to be assisted in any way whatsoever with escape attempts. A few written notices and a town crier for those who can't read should be sufficient. Anything else?"

"Yes, how about her training progress? Orrin is rather reserved when it comes to reporting. You have a direct view from your window. What do you say?"

Enric took a few moments to think before he answered. "I would say that her progress has been very good. Orrin had her fight against fourth year trainees this week and she managed beautifully." He chuckled. "He always selects the most annoying ones for her to fight."

"Vern is a fourth year. Has she managed to defeat him yet?"

"Easily. I imagine Orrin will soon set her against fully trained non-magician warriors. Her command of physical enhancement by magic may be good enough to equal their superior skills already. And I am not even sure if she isn't holding back on purpose."

"Then we need to observe her more closely. As soon as her skills are developed enough to defeat Orrin, she is ready to join the Order."

Enric sighed. "Theoretically. But her fighting skills are not the main obstacle to overcome here. She still detests us and we can't force her into the Order." He shook his head. "That is a problem I never thought we would have to face. Whenever somebody detects what might be even a morsel of magic, they try to become accepted into the Order. We never have had to nudge anybody to do it."

"There is always a first time. Can you talk to Lord Poron about his meeting with her to satisfy her curiosity?"

"Of course. Maybe he can approach Vern and suggest he brings her with him because he has heard that she is interested in the topic. What about the apothecaries? Do we just keep an extra keen eye on them or should we talk to the King about this?"

"Not yet. He is surely aware of the incident with the herb gatherer and will have them under observation as well."

"Alright," Enric said and rose to return to his own quarters. "I will send word if there are any new developments. But you will probably be informed long before I."

Tyront shrugged. "It's your own decision not to use spies. They do have their merits."

Yes, Enric thought, and by now there were so many of them in the city that they could easily form their own league if anonymity wasn't their greatest virtue. It was a small wonder they didn't end up treading on each other's toes all the time. The King had almost certainly set one to follow Eryn and so had Tyront. If Enric himself sent another one, she would be trailing a line of men behind her wherever she went. And why bother with the expense of sending spies where Tyront had his own already? It was much more rewarding to have his superior being watched by an informant instead.

CHAPTER 19

Learning about History

She grimaced as her steps brought her closer and closer to the warriors' quarters and yet she still was not contacted by the herb gatherer. Even after more than two hours of meandering through the streets, passing spots that he had preferred in the past for their little discreet meetings, and even carrying out two minor healings along the way, she had neither seen nor heard from him. Today would be their usual time for exchanging orders and products.

Her herbs were almost completely used up and the colder the weather got the more quickly the demand for medicine rose. And it seemed that her reputation and surely also her prices had caused many people to turn to her instead of the apothecaries.

She watched a stocky, bald man in blue and red palace livery clumsily fish around in his bag for a hammer, keeping two large nails clamped between his fingers and a bundle of rolled-up papers under his arm. It seemed as if he was about to nail an announcement up on one of the wooden beams of a pub. He first fixed the rolled-up paper on top, then unrolled it to nail up the bottom end.

Her eyes bulged when what had started as a casual glance turned into frantic scrutiny. How was this possible?

The note clearly stated that whoever was caught helping the captive Eryn to flee the city or was overheard even considering it would be brought to justice. *Signed by the Order.*

Her mind raced. She had asked only four carters about the chances of hiding her amongst their possessions when they left the city next time. It seemed word had spread and had attracted the wrong kind of attention.

The palace servant turned at the sound of her gasp, his eyes widening when he recognised her. Then he quickly picked up the bag he'd left at his feet and hurried on to distribute the warning posters.

So much for that plan. Such rotten luck. And now that they were aware of what she had been considering, finding a willing helper wouldn't even be enough to carry out the plan. Doubtlessly the guards at the gates had already been instructed to search thoroughly every single cart intending to leave the city.

She continued her way back to her cell. Her time would have been better employed by visiting Plia instead of seeking out that unreliable herb supplier, she thought.

When she was about to open the door to her gloomy little room, she noticed a small slip of paper stuck between the door and the frame. Her heartbeat quickened. Maybe the herb gatherer had been here at her place.

But when she opened it she easily recognised Vern's almost illegible hand and immediately felt guilty in her disappointment. She frowned at the two lines before her. How was it possible that a person with such amazing drawing skills couldn't even write down a few words in a way that didn't make one's eyes water when trying to decipher them?

The note seemed to contain the words *history* and *information* and everything before, after and in-between was a blurry mess of inky scribbles and whorls. Refolding the paper, she decided to pay him a visit. Usually her mood improved in his presence and after two major setbacks in one day she could use a bit of cheering up.

At her knock, Orrin opened the door himself and nodded towards his son's room. "He is in there, drawing again from what I can tell." His brows rose at her tensed demeanour. "Not a relaxing walk, then, I gather?"

"No." She studied him for a few moments. How much did he know? Was he aware of her greatly increased healing activities and that she was taking money for them? Did he begin to suspect that Vern was more than a mere observer when she was healing somebody in his presence?

"What?" he said, unnerved by her scrutiny. "Is there something on my face?" He let an exploring hand glide over his features to remove potential remainders of his last meal.

"No, it's nothing. I am just having a rough evening."

"Seen the proclamations, have you?" he said with one raised brow. "So you were planning something and the Order has found out about it."

She stared at him blankly, not willing to talk about it right now. "Can I see Vern now?"

He went on as if she hadn't spoken. "The Order is very well informed, you know. You might want to consider that in your actions and when you talk about things with people."

She looked at him, puzzled. Was he warning her to be more careful when looking for ways out of the city?

"Pardon?"

He turned abruptly, moving towards his open study door. "Vern is in his room. Just go right in. He probably won't hear you knocking anyway."

Shaking her head in confusion, she nevertheless tried knocking and waited for a few moments. When, as Orrin had predicted, no reaction came, she walked in and found him sitting in front of the window with his pen and drawing pad to make use of the dwindling daylight.

He looked up when she stood next to him; his eyes needed a second or two until they were fully focused on her.

"You should light the lamps," she said in a friendly way.

He looked around as if surprised that the evening had drawn so near. "Yes, I suppose."

When he got up from his chair to do just that, she picked up the drawing he was working on. It took her a few moments to identify it and she quietly whistled through her teeth.

"That is the inside of a hair root. Well done. What made you think of that?"

He shrugged. "When I came home today I plucked a hair from my shirt and then…"

"Inspiration struck you?" She smiled. He had already drawn pictures that showed the entire muscular system of the human body, its bones, layers of internal and external tissue, organs and now he seemed to have moved on to other details.

She sat down on his bed. "You should think about having your drawings put together in a book. I would imagine that non-magicians especially would be very interested in what a living body looks like from the inside as they have no way of exploring it as we have."

Vern considered the suggestion, then began slowly, "I like the idea. But you know, many of the pictures are not exactly easy to understand without supplementary explanations if you don't already know something about the human body. It would be much more informative if there were texts to go with every picture." He looked at her pointedly.

"I suppose it would," she replied. It felt like she was dancing on something flimsy. He had just expressed the wish – or was it a conviction? – that she would stay longer. And she had to answer honestly so he wouldn't get his hopes up. "But I might not be around long enough to complete it."

"What would be the problem with staying here? I have lived here all my life, and believe me, it is not so bad. I mean, where would you go? Back to the village that just handed you over to the King as though they hadn't known you almost all your life?" He got up from his chair and started pacing. "Or back to the Western Territories where you don't even know why your father left and how they would receive you?"

"Look, Vern, it's not that easy…" she began but was interrupted.

"What is easier out there than here in the city? You would have to find a new place to live, hide from the Order and the King and fearing that at any moment somebody will betray you again. I mean, if it is about healing, you can do that here! There are many more people in the city to heal than wherever else you might go."

Letting out a long breath, she forced herself to remain calm, to remember that the reason he was upset was because he didn't want to lose her.

"They wouldn't just let me heal as much as I liked, the Order is a bunch of warriors with no regard for my craft. If I joined them I would have to let them tell me what to do, even if they forbade healing completely."

He shook his head as if he was losing his patience with her. "Why ever would they let you do it now and then forbid it when you join them? That makes no sense! Isn't the fact that they haven't stopped you by now a sign that they have no objection?"

She didn't want to talk about it, nor even think. "That's not all there is! They have brought me here and make me use magic in a way I despise each day. How can I join people who treat me like that, with no respect at all?"

Vern stared at her in what looked like utter disbelief. "Really? So this is all about your pride? Not about the chance to use your healing skills to help a lot of people instead of only a few? Where are these ideals you keep telling me about right now? Are they just empty words as soon as your pride gets in the way?"

Eryn jumped up and held her index in front of his face to silence him. "You stop right there, you have no right to talk to me like that!"

"I don't?" His laugh sounded bitter. "Then tell me who has. Father? Lord Tyront? The King? Or none of them, because your precious ideals lift you so high above them that the only thing that is important is what is best for yourself?"

"I don't have to listen to any of this," she spat and whirled around to march out of his room and slam the heavy door behind her. She almost bumped into Orrin who was just about to offer a seat to somebody who was pretty much the last person she wanted to see now, or ever. The Lordling.

Both of them looked at her in surprise and before either of them could speak, the door was wrenched open by Vern, who shouted, "That's it, just run and hide when you don't like what you hear! It's what you do best!"

Only when the words were out of his mouth did he notice the audience, then he swallowed. Blood started to rush to his cheeks when he recognised Lord Enric who began to study him with interest.

Eryn made her voice turn cold. "Then I'd better leave now so I don't dash your expectations again. That seems to be what I do next best." Then she nodded to Orrin, completely ignoring Enric and stalked out with her head held high, into the corridor, careful to close the door gently.

Enric pursed his lips and let his eyes wander from the door back to the boy who just stood there, frozen. He turned to Orrin. "I would like to have a word with your son if you don't mind."

Orrin frowned, but nodded. There was not much he could say, even though he would have preferred to have a few words with Vern himself first. What unfortunate timing for this outburst to be witnessed by Lord Enric.

Enric waited for a few moments, and when Orrin remained standing there added, "Alone."

The older man ground his teeth and then reluctantly retreated to his study.

"Come here, Vern. Sit with me," Enric said mildly and pointed to a chair next to him.

It took the boy a few moments to unfreeze and then stiffly walk over and do what he was told.

"What was that about?" the man asked calmly, and when no answer came, continued in the same non-threatening tone, "You might think that this is none of my business, but you would be mistaken. From what I have just heard I deduce that you were fighting about her intention to leave the city." It was a guess, but from Vern's reaction he saw that it had hit the mark. "The Order is as eager to make her stay as you are. And making her angry at you is not going to help our efforts."

Vern looked up in sudden defiance. "What *I* did isn't going to help your efforts? Really? What about what *you* are doing?"

Good, Enric thought and hid a satisfied smile. The boy's attachment to her was considerable, it fuelled his agitation enough to make him forget how awed and afraid he was of the Order's second in command. The trick would be to redirect this energy onto a more useful path. At the same time, however, there was some corrective effort in order to avoid letting him think that this was an appropriate way to talk to somebody of Enric's status.

He sent the boy a cold look and let him squirm under it for a few moments before he spoke. "You may leave that to us, young Vern. If I had wished to hear your judgement on this, I would have asked for it." The last words had a discernible caution in them.

That seemed to work - the boy lowered his head. But not well enough to make him apologise, which was fine for Enric at this point. Now it was time for kind words, confidentiality, trust, acknowledgement of the boy's importance and encouraging his self-confidence by including him.

"You are the most important positive factor binding her to the city," he said matter-of-factly. "We don't want to endanger this advantage. We need you to continue to be that person for her, Vern. Being angry at you will weaken this bond and therefore from now on you need to learn to express your feelings in a way that doesn't drive her away from you. Judging from your exams you are a smart lad. You will figure something out."

He could almost see the thoughts forming behind the boy's forehead. He was first surprised, then pleased that he was considered important enough that mighty Lord Enric kept himself informed about his learning progress. And he failed miserably when it came to hiding it.

"So you want me to go apologise to her?" Vern asked, the anger gone from his voice.

"Is that what you would have done without our conversation?"

He slowly shook his head. "No."

"Then don't. At least not yet. Let her think about it for some time. Give her a day. If she hasn't come to you by tomorrow afternoon, I would recommend approaching her."

The boy nodded.

"And I advise you not to mention our little talk. She might… misinterpret its significance," he said casually.

Vern's eyes turned cold. "I am not spying on her for you or anything of that kind!"

Enric allowed himself a faint smile. "You may safely rely on the Order to somehow manage being informed well enough even without your joining its network of informants." He fixed the boy with a cool gaze. Time for a little reminder how well deserved the Order's reputation was. "Or did you think it was a coincidence that you were caught practising magical combat in that root cellar? We held off our intervention for some time until we considered her mastery of the technique sufficient."

Vern stared at him, mouth half open. "You knew? Why didn't you stop us earlier?"

"Because you made her want to learn something voluntarily that will make it possible for us to accept her into the Order sooner. Maybe not even your father would have managed to get her to learn it otherwise."

"What?" His hands moved in agitation. "Then I did you a favour? Why did you punish me, then?" He shook his head in disbelief.

"Because," Enric steepled his fingers, "you thought the Order wouldn't approve. And then went ahead nevertheless. It was not the deed we punished, it was your willingness to defy the Order."

The boy's frown remained in place. This little piece of information clearly didn't sit well with him. But there was another piece that would let him forget his notion of having been treated unfairly.

"One more thing," Enric said while he was rising. "The herb gatherer she was buying her plants from has been found badly beaten up. We assume that he was punished for selling to her."

"The apothecaries did this?" Vern's eyes had widened, he was worried.

"That we cannot tell for sure. But it is of course a reasonable possibility. Eryn doesn't know yet. It might be of interest to her but I don't think she would appreciate hearing it from me. She might think the Order did it as a warning in order to stop her healing efforts."

Vern swallowed. Yes, that would very probably be her first thought. "Alright, I will tell her." He rose as well. "She isn't in any danger, is she? I mean, working without herbs will make her work harder, but not impossible. She will not stop because of it. And if they see that…"

"Let us be the ones to worry about that. We are keeping an eye on her. And now you will excuse me. I need to see your father."

The boy bowed and watched the Lord cross the room and enter Orrin's study. Damn, he thought. He had left the note at her door to tell her about the chance to talk about the answers to her questions with a magician, and now instead he had not only angered her but also had to worry about her safety.

He decided he would go to her after his classes tomorrow, before she left for her healing excursions. He wouldn't let her roam the streets alone any more. With her powers reduced to less than a third of their unfettered strength she was still a danger to most people, but she was not exactly trained in protecting herself without a sword.

A stab in the back was as lethal to an unsuspecting magician as it was to anybody else.

* * *

Vern sat in the parlour, watching the entrance door impatiently. His father should have been back already, it seemed he was making her train longer today. He didn't really need his father for anything urgent, just as an indicator of when Eryn would be free for the evening. It usually took her about fifteen minutes to get herself cleaned and dressed after her lessons, so his father's arrival should give him enough time to go down and wait for her in front of the building before she set out for her usual round through the city.

When the door finally opened and Orrin walked in, Vern jumped up. "You took your time today!"

"What?" That was not usually the welcome he received, especially as his son was lately normally either walking the city with Eryn or holed up in his room with pen and paper.

"The training. It has taken longer today."

Orrin frowned. "No, it hasn't."

"What do you mean, it hasn't? Why are you so late, then?"

He sighed. Eryn had been in a foul mood today, very probably due to the fight yesterday. And now it seemed that having endured her temper for several hours he had escaped to his home to more of the same.

"I wasn't aware that I was subject to a curfew. I was talking to a colleague for a few minutes."

"How many minutes?" His son's demeanour suddenly became more frenzied.

"Fifteen, maybe twenty."

"You keep lecturing me about the importance of punctuality! Is it too much to ask you to comply with your own rules for a change?" The boy lifted both arms in exasperation and shook his head.

Orrin watched his son race through the parlour and out the door, wondering why today he was everybody's prime target for throwing a hissy fit.

Vern dashed down the stairs and turned several corners until he reached the corridor where Eryn's cell was. He knocked at her door but got no reply. Cursing, he resumed his run and considered the most likely route she would have chosen.

She didn't know what had happened to the herb gatherer, so she would very probably take one that let her pass by the spots where he had waited for her in the past.

After leaving the building he turned right into Kingsway that just like every day at this time was filled with people. Bumping into several of them, he tried to move along as quickly as possible, earning a lot of unfriendly stares but nothing more, as people tended to be very careful when the source of their discontent was a magician.

It took him several minutes until to his great relief he spotted the unique head of hair amidst the stream of bodies that for the most part seemed to move into the opposite direction as if to purposely make reaching her as tedious as possible.

She was about to leave the busy main road and turn into a quieter one to her left, when she felt the hand on her arm. This did not cause the alarm it used to any more. She now knew that it was far more likely for a person to stop her because somebody needed her healing services than to rob her.

Turning, her polite smile vanished slowly and was replaced by a blank expression.

"Vern. What are you doing here?" Her tone was not unfriendly, but rather more formal than usually.

"I wanted to apologise. I shouldn't have said those things yesterday."

She nodded slowly. "No, you shouldn't. But I see why you did. The thought of leaving you behind here is not easy for me to bear, either. And yet I can't spend my life here so as to make you happy. That is a burden you shouldn't have to labour under. And trust me, a burden it would be. You would know that you were the reason I gave up my freedom." She tousled his hair when he just looked at her sadly. "I am on my way to see how Plia is doing. Want to join me?"

"Sure." He looked around to see if anybody was paying undue attention to them and then lowered his voice. "There is something you should know first."

"Yes?" She frowned when he scanned their surroundings once more before pulling her behind a cart.

"The herb gatherer who sold to you. He was found badly beaten up." He watched realisation dawn on her. She leaned against the nearest house wall and bent forward, bracing her hands against her knees.

"The apothecaries," she hissed. "I dare say it was not the Order, they would have more effective ways of stopping me. And this won't stop me. It just makes healing a bit harder." Straightening, she looked at Vern.

"Do you know where the man is? Is he hurt badly? The least I can do is offer to heal him."

"No, but I suppose I could find out."

She nodded, feeling a little awkward asking him for a favour when they had made up again just a minute ago. They continued their way towards the orphanage silently, absorbed in their own thoughts.

When the building had come into sight, she put a hand on Vern's shoulder.

"Wait. I have been thinking. They have beaten up a man because he sold his products to me. When they see that this hasn't stopped me they will probably consider other measures." She looked at him pointedly. "Like harming people closer to me. I think we should not be seen walking through the city together anymore."

The look this earned her was a combination of annoyance and disbelief. "Sure. Because harming you directly would never cross their mind. Don't you think they would rather hurt a prisoner without protection than me, an Order magician?"

That did sound halfway plausible, she had to admit. Then her gaze wandered over to the orphanage, and back to Vern. "Do you think...?"

He nodded darkly. "She would be the perfect target. No-one to protect her, no close associates who might take offence. And if anything happened to her, who else but you, a prisoner, would suspect them?"

Eryn abruptly turned on her heels and went back the way they had come from. Her tense posture and clenched fists bespoke the anger and frustration she felt.

"Where can I find this damned League of Apothecaries?"

"What?" Vern caught her arm and stopped her. "You can't just go over there! You have no proof that it was they who attacked the herb seller, and they won't be careless enough to admit it openly! And even if they did, the word of a prisoner would hardly be more credible than theirs should you try to involve the King or the Order."

"So you are saying I should just stand by, be a danger to others who are somehow involved with me and wait for them to have another handy idea about stopping me from healing?"

"No," he said reasonably, "that is not what I am saying. I suggest that you take some time and think before you do something impetuous. That's advice my father never tires of giving me, and watching you makes me see that he is right about it. Something that's rather unnerving for a boy to realise," he added as an afterthought.

She stared at him, glowering. "Why do I sometimes have the feeling that you are the grown up and I am the adolescent one amongst us?"

"Because I am uncommonly smart and sensible for my age. Having established that, you had better come back home with me and we can think this matter through."

Without waiting for her consent, he started walking, keeping his hand firmly held around her fingers to make sure she came along.

* * *

Enric watched Vern all but dragging her behind him towards his quarters. Eryn didn't seem particularly happy and the boy looked determined in a rather grim way. But they had obviously made up and were spending time together again, even if this didn't seem to be something putting either of them in a good mood at that moment.

He was relieved to see that Vern was so protective of her. He doubted that Eryn would have any further chance to walk through the city without him at her side. A boy of fifteen might not be much of a protection, but he hoped the apothecaries would think twice before trying anything when there were two magicians instead of one to be considered.

It was high time to move along the process of encouraging her to join the Order. At least then he wouldn't have to worry about her safety any more once that was taken care of.

Her skills had improved considerably, especially since she had taken up healing. It seemed that being able to spend her free time doing something she considered useful made her more compliant when it came to her training. Yet judging from her efforts with the carters she still had not accepted being stuck here in the city. That would making her agree to join the Order quite a challenge, he imagined.

But seeing how far exactly she was along would be interesting, nevertheless. He would discuss arranging a competition with Orrin. The warrior would have to find a way not only to make her participate but also to fight with everything she had. They would have to remove her shackles for that, he mused. But as he himself would be there to watch, this was not too much of a risk in case she decided to try and flee once again.

For now, however, the problem with the apothecaries was still to be considered. Unfortunately, he couldn't do anything as long as they didn't make any stupid mistakes.

The herb gatherer had been questioned but had claimed that he had no idea who his attackers were and why they had beaten him. Considering his injuries he had received a thorough warning not only to cease selling to Eryn but also to keep his mouth shut tightly.

Enric had discussed with Tyront whether or not to interrogate the man again, this time with a truth block in place. But his superior had opted against it. They would not learn anything they didn't know or at least hadn't strongly suspected before, and it would also get the herb seller into even more difficulties when it came out that he had, though probably not voluntarily, given away information that hinted at his attackers' identity. They could always do that later when they needed proof.

Enric felt restless. Every time he laid eyes on her he felt the urge to do something, even though he wasn't entirely sure what. But action surely had to be preferable to stagnation, didn't it?

He sometimes imagined how she would react if he revealed to her that it had been he who spent this one night with her three months ago. In his more optimistic imaginings she suddenly realised that he was not such a bad sort after all and started seeing him in a very different light. When he was more realistically inclined, however, he saw her hating him even more than she already did.

It was probably better to wait for approaching her until she had joined the Order. First, she needed to get to know him better, to get used to seeing him not as one of her warders but a colleague, a reasonable superior and, after a while as a lot more than that, he hoped.

* * *

"Who is this Lord Poron?" Eryn enquired as she followed Vern through the corridors of the palace towards the library. The Order did not really have its own, but only a few rooms in the royal one. It seemed that the collection and preservation of knowledge was not one of the Order's priorities. At least it was clearly not important enough to maintain their own library. Well, another surprise there, she thought.

"He is in charge of the books and keeping track of history, adding to it and so on. He also creates the teaching plans for history teachers. Several years ago he was the second in command before Lord Enric was assessed for the position."

"How old are you when you are assessed? Have you been tested yet?"

He shook his head. "No, I haven't and won't be for a while yet. They do it after we finish our training, which normally is at 21 years of age. Lord Enric was tested when he was one year older, as they said he was a very lazy student." He grinned. "That is something the teachers try to hide from us, but everyone knows anyway. It is not exactly the best motivation if you know that good grades are not exactly necessary when you have the power or that very good grades will not on their own enable you to rise high in the hierarchy without having power."

Eryn shook her head in surprise. "Wait, what? The Lordling was a lazy student?" That did not at all fit her picture of him. She would have bet that ambition was one of his driving forces.

Vern nodded. "Yes. It was a nasty shock for him when they assessed him and he was categorised as an A, which is the highest standard we have. I heard that they made him repeat all tests where he had scored average or lower. In addition he had to start extra training for his new position. I heard that people hardly saw anything of him for more than two years, and after that he had changed so much that they barely recognised him anymore. No more fun and games but instead responsibility, discipline and the need to be taken seriously by people much older than himself."

She frowned, suppressing the feeling of sympathy with relentless determination. She reminded herself that it didn't matter what he had been before he had become a bastard, only what and who he was now. Sometimes the empathy that was so necessary for being a good healer turned out to be a real nuisance when it came to everyday matters. Like when she just wanted to maintain her bad opinion about somebody without having to ignore facts that didn't quite fit the picture.

"So I imagine Lord Poron was not too pleased with being relegated to third place?" she asked.

"I don't know. He doesn't seem to hold any visible grudge against Lord Enric, but I may of course be mistaken. It's not like I have a lot of insight, and father doesn't talk about such things to me."

"So he has kind of taken refuge among the books?"

"Maybe. I mean, people normally have some plan of what they want to do once their training is finished. Hardly anybody really counts on being strong enough to land one of the top positions. It is common belief that Lord Poron had planned a life as scholar and maybe that being released from his position as second in command was not that much of a disappointment for him. Well, after the initial shock of losing it to a lazy young wastrel, that is," he added after a moment's thought.

They turned another corner and finally stood in front of elaborate double doors.

"Are we finally there? I hope you won't leave me alone here, I would never find my way back out. I would be doomed to wander these corridors until the end of my natural life."

Vern lifted a brow. "In a gloomy mood today, are we?"

Then he opened the doors with a determined shove and heard Eryn suck in a breath when she laid eyes on the shelves that stretched on from the shiny floor up to the high ceiling around all the four walls surrounding her. She could see open doors that led to more rooms just like the one she had just entered.

"Incredible! I have never in my life seen anything like this!" She let her eyes roam about the room, not knowing what to look at first. Stepping in front of a random shelf, she started reading the titles of books about etiquette and genealogy.

She turned when she heard a voice behind her that was definitely not Vern's.

"It is nice to see young people appreciate the sight of books. It doesn't happen often enough if you ask me."

The man had to be in his early seventies, grey hair bound in a neat ponytail, brown robes and green eyes that studied her with obvious interest.

"Lord Poron?" she asked and bowed when he nodded.

Vern stared at her dumbfounded. "This is the first time ever I've seen you bow or heard you call any magician *Lord*! You don't even bow to Lord Tyront!"

She smiled. "A man who dedicates his life to books and knowledge deserves to be bowed to."

Lord Poron smiled. "An interesting sentiment. Would you like to have a look around or rather talk about the topics young Vern has brought you here to learn about?"

Her smile broadened even further. "If your time allows it, I would very much appreciate a closer look at this place first."

"Then allow me to be your guide. I don't get many visitors with that request."

Eryn walked along rows of books in different colours, shapes, sizes and even languages. Lord Poron seemed to understand most of them and of the books he had not read himself, had at least a basic idea what they contained. There were three large halls filled with books that belonged to the Order and five more that were part of the royal library.

"What about books on healing, on medicine? Do you have anything here?" she asked an hour later.

"We do, but from what I have heard they will hardly meet your standards," he replied in a good-natured way and led her to a shelf at the far end of the second room. He bent down and retrieved three books which he then laid out on one of three tables that were placed at the centre of every room.

She opened the first one with curiosity and then frowned in dismay. "It says that the best cure for a broken nose is bathing in the river under a full moon. Seriously?"

Taking another one and opening it a random page, she rolled her eyes. "*The colour of the blood enables a well-trained physician to draw from it conclusions about the patient's character,*" she read aloud. "Oh dear." She pinched the bridge of her nose and closed her eyes. "That is probably the crassest thing I have ever read. I think it should be a crime to create books like this. Books are meant to spread knowledge, not stupid fallacy. Do I even want to look at the third one?" she asked without much expectation.

Lord Poron sighed and took all of them away to shelve them again. "Judging from your reaction to the first two, probably not."

"That brings me to one thing that really interests me and also surprises me: why are there no magicians who heal in this kingdom? Do you know anything about that?" she asked when he had returned.

The old man sighed and motioned for her to take a seat before he turned to Vern. "Young Vern, please fetch us another chair from the table over there so we can all have a seat."

The boy nodded and joined them a few moments later.

"Healing, you see," Lord Poron started, "has from a long time ago been considered more of a curse than a benefit. Records talk about great fights between warriors and healers in the Order. They each considered their craft the more valuable one for the kingdom and failed to understand that neither one nor the other could bring the benefit which both of them together would."

"Are we talking about actual fighting or heated philosophical discussions?" Eryn enquired.

"It started with fiery words and resulted in battles inside and outside the city. Many buildings were destroyed, magicians and other citizens were hurt and many of them killed."

"As there are no more healers around I assume they lost the fight?"

"Indeed. Many were killed, as of course in battle the combat skills of the warriors were far superior. The ones who finally realised their cause was lost and capitulated were banned from the kingdom." He smiled and nodded at her brown hair. "It is said that they went west. And how apt that after such a long time healing seems to return to us from the west."

"Why has there never been any attempt at rediscovering that knowledge?"

Lord Poron shrugged. "Refusing to acknowledge that the defeated and banned magicians might have possessed or known anything of value was for a long time a matter of pride. It would have made it necessary to pose the question whether banning them was such a smart move after all. If there is one thing you may safely say about the Order, then it is that we were always very good at not doubting ourselves," he said, without any irony in his voice. "And once enough time had passed the memory of magical healing dwindled away. You see the kind of books on healing we have left here. The foolish king back then permitted them to take all their books with them and burned the ones they left behind when they couldn't carry more."

Eryn nodded. "I see. What is the attitude towards healing nowadays? The Order has not stopped me from healing people but neither has it encouraged me exactly."

The librarian smiled faintly. "Dear child, when the Order doesn't stop you from doing something, you may consider this in itself as encouragement. It may be they are watching you just to see how it turns out and may stop you yet if they are not satisfied with what they see."

She pursed her lips. That didn't sound too bad for now. "What about female magicians? I have heard it mentioned that you used to have them here a few hundred years ago. Where did they go?"

"That is something I have been asked quite a few times since your arrival, and I am afraid I do not have an answer. I have looked in many of the books to see if anything is mentioned. Some of the older books talk about female magicians, but not of the reason behind their disappearance. They just have not been mentioned in the books for three hundred years now."

Eryn sighed, disappointedly. "That is a pity. I was really hoping to learn something about that. There is one last thing. The hair colour. It seems rather odd to me that everybody I have seen in this kingdom is fair-haired. I remember people from my childhood with different colours, so I know I am not an anomaly as such, but only here."

Lord Poron shook his head apologetically. "To that I have no answer, either. I am sorry to disappoint you yet again."

Eryn smiled and rose. "No, there is no need for that. I am grateful for the time you have taken to show me around and tell me about the healers from the past. It cautions me not to show any undue thirsting for power that might make people nervous in a healer," she added as a quip.

"You speak very lightly of considerations that will doubtlessly matter to the King, even if the Order seems to have got over the past remarkably well," the man said, his tone now a serious one.

"Are you saying that he might be afraid of me trying to take over the Order and turning his most valued and powerful line of defence into a bunch of good-for-nothing healers?" She chuckled and saw that neither Vern nor Lord Poron found anything amusing in her statement. "Really? Oh, come on now!" she exclaimed.

"The truth may not be as exaggerated as you phrased it, but I might venture that avoiding the mistakes of the past will and must be a consideration for both the King and the Order. Many lives and a lot of knowledge were lost back then. The Order would want to avoid a repetition of this at all costs."

Eryn sighed and shook her head. "I have no ambitions whatsoever to gain power of any sort."

Lord Poron smiled. "Power is a devious thing, young lady. When you had a taste of it, it is hard not to struggle to retain it or strive for more."

She looked at him thoughtfully, wondering if he was referring to his own situation.

CHAPTER 20

Fighting Them All

Orrin sighed and watched Eryn listlessly poking at her breakfast at the other side of the hall filled with noisy fighters. Lord Enric had told him to make sure she would participate in the competition, something which had not been a request.

She would of course not give a hoot about this order. Whenever the second in command of the Order had wanted her to do something, it had been necessary to coerce her as she always resisted doing anything that might please her captors. Which was, of course, hardly something anyone could blame her for, least of all the warrior himself.

Orrin himself was not a friend of using force and never had been despite his profession. He had learned to respect and even come to like her in these past months of training together, and that made his task even harder. Her progress in this short time had been outstanding, especially considering that she had a deep aversion to fighting. He was torn between sympathy because of the situation she was in and excitement.

The first female magician in more than three hundred years, and he had the rare chance to work with her, train her, watch her develop new abilities. It was a shame that she was a captive, but he knew of course that she was too important to be let out of their sight to wander the kingdom unsupervised. Well, at least from the Order's and the King's point of view.

He himself found it hard to imagine her roaming the lands in search of opportunities to cause harm and destruction. It was certainly not what she had been doing these last two decades. But the danger was very likely rather that she might leave here without sharing her knowledge with them.

They would maybe even try to, for want of a more suitable expression, breed with her, he assumed, and try to produce offspring from her, especially female ones, with great magical potential. He supposed there was not much of a question of who would be chosen to sire the young ones. The only two men in the kingdom strong enough to subdue her were Lords Tyront and Enric. Lord Tyront was old enough to be her father and happily conjoined. The King would not ask him to do it since it was likely that this would cost him the cooperation of a very useful ally.

Lord Enric, however, was unencumbered and much closer to her in age. He would be the logical choice, even if the demand would not please him at all and he would probably even refuse to obey it. It was a matter of principle not to be told who to have children with.

Or they could chain her with enchanted gold manacles that blocked her powers entirely, then anybody who had more physical strength than Eryn would be able to take her to bed. The thought of such degrading abuse was deeply troubling, and something he hoped was beneath them.

But hadn't he heard something about a protective field inside her that prevented unwanted intrusion? That would at least rule out the second – and in his eyes more despicable – option, even though she would hardly appreciate Lord Enric as designated father of her offspring as an alternative.

Lord Enric, he mused, might actually be willing to do it, but would want to be given the choice instead of a decree. Rumour had it he had already taken her to bed at the Freedom Night, and seeing how Enric's interest in her had increased since then, Orrin was inclined to believe it.

He had heard the story of the two dancers several times, and although the versions naturally deviated slightly depending on the teller and the number of repetitions, the basic facts of a man dancing with her in a way that left everybody speechless and wondering and then carrying her off was hugely revealing. The mask had been lifted for a single, brief moment and the few who had seen Lord Enric's face had spread the news.

He very seriously doubted that she herself had been aware of her lover's identity and questioned if that had been a good thing. She would learn of it sooner or later - too many people were in on the news of the couple to avoid that in the long run. But then hardly anybody would want to be the one to tell her about it.

Her magical skills had grown with her fighting skills and there was not a single one of his students she couldn't defeat if she set her mind to it. It was only a matter of time until he himself would have to succumb to her magically aided speed and agility, especially if they took off her shackles.

He had told Lord Enric about her growing strength and that he would not much longer be able to train her as her powers would soon exceed his own and she would be too much for his fighting skills to defeat if she had all her power at her disposal. As the primary target was to make her fit for joining the Order, it made sense to check how far along she already was without the manacles and if any further fast track improvement was even required now.

His guess was that the whole competition was aimed at determining her strength without raising her suspicions. But for it to work she obviously needed to participate, and *that* was the challenge.

At that moment Eryn looked up and caught him studying her with a pensive expression. She frowned. People looking at her with a thoughtful expression had in these last few months usually preceded a decision with less than pleasant consequences for herself.

She grabbed her bowl of grain gruel and walked over to Orrin who didn't seem very thrilled by her approach.

She stopped directly in front of him, never taking her eyes of his when she ate a spoonful and then said, "You are considering a new torment for me, I can see it from your face. It's the way you were watching me. I was wondering when the next one was due. Let's get it over with, then. Tell me about it so that I can tell *you* to inflict nasty, painful things on yourself."

He shook his head and sighed in exasperation. "Yes, because your suffering is my only pleasure in life." Patting the seat next to his, he motioned for her to sit. She remained standing, staring at him.

"The competition today. I was thinking about how to get you to participate." He watched her expression go from grim to indulgent.

"Then I can save you quite some mental effort: I won't participate in your little game. Did the Lordling command you to make me fight today?"

He stifled a groan. Mentioning that Lord Enric insisted on her participation would just increase her determination to refuse. He opted for diversion.

"I wish you would stop referring to him like that."

She snorted. "I'll call him what I like as long as he keeps me caged here. Even though it pains me greatly to hurt your delicate feelings by showing disrespect for one of your highly-esteemed masters."

"Your consideration for my delicate feelings honours me," he said. "And now tell me what you want in return for fighting so that I don't get my hide tanned."

Her eyebrows rose in genuine surprise. "What? You are trying to negotiate instead of threatening, forcing, blackmailing or tricking me? I must be fast asleep and dreaming," she concluded.

"Are you done or do you need to unload any more jibes on me?"

"Just give me a moment, my wildly beating heart might otherwise burst with the unexpected sensation of my being treated like an actual human being."

He rolled his eyes. "Why am I even talking to you? I should just shackle you in gold and promise the first lad who draws blood from you a night in your bed."

With satisfaction he watched her eyes narrow. "Right. What a pleasant image. Not that it would work, mind you. I carry a nice little protection inside my body to avoid incidents like that. So, what are you offering?"

So he had heard correctly, there was a field inside her. Good. He was relieved about that, even though he was aware he shouldn't be. It was not exactly loyal considering that this circumstance had thwarted the Order's and probably the King's plans.

He smiled when an idea hit him. "That little friend of yours, the orphan girl you saved from bullies…"

She remained silent and waited for him to go on.

"You have been meeting her on and off, haven't you?" He saw her swallow.

"What of it? I wasn't aware that I had to ask for permission to see her." She fought down the anger. If they used Plia to blackmail her, she would launch herself at him right here and now and throttle him; or fail bravely in attempting it. Well, it would get her message across, in any case.

"Calm yourself, there is no problem. I was just thinking of an opening in the palace kitchen for an apprentice." He let his words sink in.

She stilled. An apprenticeship in the palace kitchen was an almost unrepeatable chance for an orphan girl with no connections. She would be able to work in the warm kitchen, take home leftovers and get her own little warm room as part of the payment. Having learned her trade in the palace, every major household would be thrilled to hire her should she decide to leave the palace following her training. This would guarantee her a life in relative comfort and security, especially compared to what she had known until now.

Once her eyes shifted back to his and she began to clear her throat, Orrin knew he had won even before she began to speak.

"And you could make sure she gets this apprenticeship?"

He just nodded.

"In exchange for me fighting in your competition."

"In exchange for you fighting *really well* in my competition," he amended.

"Really well?"

"Well enough either to win it or convince me that you didn't lose on purpose."

She pursed her lips. "Alright, I can do that. And Orrin…"

"What?"

"I will not fight *him*. That is not part of the deal."

He didn't have to ask who *he* was. And fortunately, Lord Enric had not instructed him to be sure she would fight him, too. The magician was not officially part of the competition and as the whole thing was only being arranged to test Eryn's abilities and not to provide the framework for a fight between her and Lord Enric, he had no problem with her little limitation.

"Well, I can live with that."

"Good. One more thing: Why does he want me to fight today? He keeps watching me in the arena from his damned window, so he knows well enough how far along I am."

That surprised him. So she had figured out that Lord Enric had been watching her fight.

"He wants to see how many you really can defeat. How much you have been holding back." And if I can still stand up to you and thus continue training you, he added silently. "And he will probably try to fight you if you win."

That was not much of a surprise. She nodded at him and left to change for the fighting without uttering another word.

* * *

She let her gaze wander and took in the combatants. There were 127 of them, not including herself. Seven rounds would decide the winner, and all of them would be fought today. It was late morning, so she hoped the whole thing would be over by early evening.

She knew her first opponent by sight only, but from his stance she could see that he would not be much of a challenge. She wondered if Orrin had paired her with him first to remind her that she would have to be very convincing if she lost – and that would hardly be possible with this one here. And true enough, it took her less than two minutes to rid him of his weapon.

* * *

Enric had discarded his robe of office and donned the simple clothing of a soldier to better blend in and remain anonymous for now. And indeed, the participants and spectators were too busy to spare more than a fleeting glance at yet another black-clad fighter. Eryn tended to freeze on the spot whenever she beheld him, and that would just distract her and thus defeat the purpose of this whole event.

It was noon and the third round was still in progress for some participants, while those who had won their bout had already sat down and were eating a hasty lunch. Eryn was among them, of course.

Enric was pleased with Orrin for coaxing Eryn into fighting and wondered how he had accomplished it. Knowing Orrin, it would probably have been a bribe of some sort.

* * *

Eryn surreptitiously scanned her surroundings. She was surprised that *he* was not present to watch as observing her fighting skills seemed to be the only reason for this whole commotion, especially now that they had removed her shackles. She looked up at his window, but it was closed and there was no movement discernible behind it.

She rubbed her unshackled wrists absent-mindedly. Why was he so sure that she wouldn't try to run now that she had her magic at her disposal again? Did he know about Orrin's offer? But even if he did, would he be that confident that Plia's future was more important to her than making use of a convenient chance to escape?

At her table sat the other twenty-nine victors from the third round. Two more fights were still going on and some of the men around her speculated who would join them. A few others eyed their fellow winners calculatingly, probably gauging who might be their adversary in the next fight.

When the last bout of the round was over, Orrin came to their table and unrolled some paper to announce the pairings for the next one. Her former training partner, who had been told to cut her tunic back then, was one of the last two winners joining the table and sneered at her when he heard that they were to face each other next.

She sighed. He was a skilled fighter, she had to admit, even if in her opinion he was useless in any other regard. No holding back today - she would wipe that arrogant sneer off his face before he knew what had hit him.

* * *

Rolan marched out of the arena with long angry strides. Enric indulged in a barely noticeable smile. He had watched him training with Eryn and remembered that the young man had requested to be released from that duty.

Their fight just now had been remarkably short. He had clearly underestimated her considerable advantage thanks to her superior powers. He had only ever trained with her with Eryn wearing shackles.

She had not resorted to any of the less *honourable* attacks she had used in her sparring with him before. It had been a clean and swift defeat, as if she had mobilised all her magic to aid her in getting him out of her way as quickly as possible.

He had clearly intended to caper about with her a bit, but that had been a stupid and arrogant mistake, as he had seen only a few moments later, when she had suddenly been behind him and held the edge of her blade to his throat.

She had made it intimate, defeating him while being very close to him, intruding into his personal space.

Enric had been amused about that. He remembered Tyront's words when they had observed the training session from his study window. The day they had been looking forward to, when she would finally be in a position to teach him a lesson, was today.

Right now Rolan looked so furious at having so unexpectedly and, more than anything, so quickly lost against her that none of his friends dared approach him. Eryn herself looked remarkably calm and collected, hardly any outward sign of triumph visible, just a half-smile curving across her lips.

* * *

Round five presented her with another magician as an opponent, and she strongly suspected that each of the six other remaining fighters had magical abilities as well. The increase in speed and precision was immediately noticeable and she made sure to end the round quickly before one moment of inattention might cost Plia her chance of a worthwhile job.

The magician acknowledged her victory without great surprise or enthusiasm and walked off with his mouth set grimly.

The closer the competition got to its end, the longer the bouts took. Small wonder, she thought, now the ones with accomplished fighting *and* magical skills were at work, and they would not be defeated that easily any more.

She noticed all at once that she was one of four remaining fighters. That should basically be enough to keep Orrin happy even if she lost the next one, shouldn't it? She walked towards the winner's table where he already awaited her.

"A good start, but you are not done yet." His voice had a warning undertone as if he had read her mind.

Eryn just took a gulp from the jug of water he offered her and once more scanned the rapidly growing crowd for the blue robe and the face she disliked so much. On the one hand there was relief that she was being spared his sight, and on the other incredulity that he would miss the spectacle he himself had insisted on arranging.

"Who will I fight in round six?" she asked.

"Moris, most likely. He will be a bit more of a challenge than the ones before. But nothing you can't handle."

So, she thought, he had given her to understand very clearly that losing the next round would be considered an act of deliberate choice on her part. That was inconvenient. She spotted Plia's flushed face in the front row, waving her arms at her and radiating excitement. When she turned her head, she saw Orrin smiling at the orphan girl.

"You did not by any chance make sure she had a place at the front so I would see her?"

He lifted his hands in mock innocence, "Dear me, why ever would I do that?"

* * *

He had been right, round six was the first *real* challenge. She was under no illusion about the fact that she would have lost without her superior magical strength. But Moris' fighting skills eventually had to relent before her magic.

And then, finally, the last round. The sun had begun to set and men and women started to light torches both in and around the arena.

Her last rival appeared to be in a kind of trance as he moved slowly towards her, his eyes half closed. But of course this would be a trick as he would never have progressed this far otherwise. Even though she was aware of this,

his first blow was surprisingly swift and seemed to come out of nowhere. It almost disarmed her.

She immediately regained her balance and fought off a series of attacks that each seemed to strike from different directions. This defensive position was not sound, she knew. She had to interrupt this somehow, or one of his strikes would soon hit her. She concentrated hard and for a second, time seemed to slow down. She more sensed than saw the blade coming closer from her right side. In a move that seemed no more than normal speed to herself but like a mere flash of motion to the watchers she dodged the approaching weapon and spun around to place her own at her opponent's neck.

Orrin lifted his arm to signal that the fight was over. She had won and the audience erupted in applause and shrill whistling. She saw Plia jumping up and down, her eyes shining in the torch light, her joy obvious in her flushed face.

She turned around as Orrin approached her in the centre of the arena. The sun had almost completely set now. His face determined, he stopped several strides away from her, facing her.

"I held up my end of the deal, Orrin. I won in this damned farcical event. Will you honour your side?"

"That I will. But the fight is not yet over for you, girl."

She looked around frowning in confusion. "This was round seven and I told you I will not fight the Lordling." Then it dawned on her as she took in his stance and the hand resting on the hilt of his sword.

"You?" she whispered, "He wants me to fight *you*?"

He nodded.

"The deal," she said quietly, "does not include defeating *you*."

"No. But it does include winning or convincing me that you didn't let yourself be defeated deliberately." Something in his eyes flickered, and it seemed to her that this was not only due to the torch lights reflected in them.

"You mongrel," she spat at him softly enough so that only he could hear her. "You could have warned me. What happens if I somehow manage to defeat you?"

"Then it will obviously not make sense for me to continue teaching you."

She narrowed her eyes at him. "No more fighting lessons for me, then?"

He very much doubted it. Lord Enric would very likely take over her training - nothing less would explain his considerable interest in her progress. But telling her this now would push her to decide between deliberately losing and thus crushing the little girl's hope for her future, or trying to win, which would result in her having to endure her nemesis' presence and even more intense attention from him. He had sworn allegiance to the Order and thus obedience to Lord Enric, so it was his duty to avoid endangering his plans, even if she hated him for it afterwards. But he promised himself that he would keep his promise regarding the girl, even if she did lose this fight on purpose. He exhaled slowly and kept his voice steady.

"So it would seem." It was not a lie, technically.

She nodded slowly. "Alright then, Orrin. Let's give the Lordling a good show. We wouldn't want to disappoint him," she added bitterly.

* * *

Enric felt the bafflement of the crowd around quickly turn into delight. Everywhere around him excited whispering and heated discussions about the likely outcome of this showdown erupted. He watched Orrin and Eryn exchange words in the arena that were too quiet to be heard by the crowd. He himself had no problem following the conversation as he just manipulated airstreams so that they would carry the sounds to him. He smiled at her use of the derogative nickname she had picked for him and approved of Orrin's lie, appreciating what it had cost him. And he had learned how Orrin had coaxed her into entering the competition. A promise of a favour, just as he had thought.

He was looking forward to this fight. This was the only one where the result was truly uncertain.

He saw both of them slowly drawing the swords from their sheaths but making no other move, as if each of them was reluctant to start the battle and waited for the other to attack first. After a while they started to circle each other and the crowd cheered when their swords first met with a loud clang of fierce metal.

* * *

Orrin had no misguidedly modest notions about his fighting skills. He knew he was the best, even if his magical strength would never allow him to triumph over Lords Tyront or Enric. Lord Tyront was simply too strong, and Lord Enric had in addition to his immense magical abilities almost unparalleled fighting skills that came very close to Orrin's own abilities. He had, however, in the past defeated magicians whose strength had been superior to his own thanks to his considerable skills.

Eryn's skills were far from being as developed as Orrin's, but her magical potential was enormous and he truly wondered if she would win tonight. Skills honed over decades pitted against speed and agility enhanced by superior magical strength. He wondered if his standing would suffer if the young woman was able to beat him and scolded himself for such thoughts. They only lead to defeat.

She had been holding back in the last months, he knew, and this made gauging her real strength impossible. And this was the first time they ever let her fight without the blockade on her powers. Some of her moves today had shown him that he had to be careful not to underestimate her.

He blocked the swift stab she aimed at his left side and retaliated with several quick blows that drove her back a few steps.

* * *

Enric pursed his lips when both fighters started to move more swiftly in what non-magicians would perceive as no more than blurs. The shake of his head was almost imperceptible when he considered Orrin's foolishness. He had very likely just given away his chance to win. He made the wrong choice to engage in a battle of speed with her. This he could never reasonably win. So it seemed she had held back enough these last weeks to lull her trainer into a false sense of security. That had been quite a feat with a man like Orrin.

* * *

Their swords met with frightful blows that rang out through the arena in such quick succession that the ear had trouble distinguishing between them.

The audience seemed to draw in their collective breath when Orrin struck hard enough to cause both their swords to deform and become jammed together. The fighters both stared at the mangled messes before them for a second, then at each other.

"And now?" Eryn growled. "I didn't even know that could happen. Maybe you should employ weapons of a better quality, at least for your competitions."

Orrin exhaled and motioned for two new swords to be brought for them.

"This is not a matter of quality," he explained patiently. "Do you have any idea how much energy swords in a magically enhanced fight need to withstand?"

"That hasn't been my primary area of interest so far, so I'd have to say no," she shrugged. "But from this it seems quite a lot."

A leather-clad fighter approached them and handed each of them a new sword, eyeing the entangled weapons with interest while carefully picking them up and removing them from the fighting area.

Eryn weighed the new weapon in her hand. It was a little heavier than the first one, but it was not as if balancing it using a little extra strength in her muscles was much of a problem.

Orrin resumed his attacks, and she pushed herself magically to keep up with their speed and force. She wondered if he was holding back, testing her, trying to make her push harder or if that truly was the limit of what he could do. How much stronger than him was she really? Was it wise to find out now?

She dodged a hit and whirled quickly so that she came to stand behind him, ready to touch him with the flat of her blade to end the fight, but he reacted quickly and dove to one side.

So that was how trained reactions, instincts and reflexes could overcome mere superior magical strength, she mused. But there had to be a certain difference in magic that made even honed fighting skills obsolete. Obviously, or she would not have been able to defeat the other, more experienced fighters in the last rounds.

Time to see if Orrin measured up to nothing more than brutal strength.

She waited for him to lift his weapon for another blow, caught it with her own sword and then pushed him backwards several steps. She could see his worried frown and followed him carefully, never taking her eyes off his. That had been promising, but she couldn't defeat him with skill. And he couldn't overcome her strength. That meant he would hardly be able to deal with speed increased by the same amount. Time for some offensive combat.

Her first thrusts were careful, but they increased in speed and boldness with every additional one she dealt. Orrin made to retreat, but there was little space left behind him. Two more steps, and he would find himself with a stone wall against his back. He tried to swerve first to one side, then to the other, but Eryn managed to keep him in one place. She drew in a deep breath and pushed the last bit of magic she could muster into her muscles for a hit that was so fast the keen steel edge seemed to sing as it cut through the air.

Moments later Orrin's sword lay in the sand out of his reach, while Eryn's weapon pointed at his chest. The fight was over.

* * *

The applause around her was like an explosion, so sudden and unexpected that it all but made her flinch. It was such a stark contrast to her own feelings which were not triumphant, but strangely benumbed.

She let her sword sink slowly and replaced it into the sheath at her side. The sun was completely gone by now and the flickering torches were the only light.

She looked back at Orrin, who had already reclaimed his sword from the ground and was putting it away.

"Well done." His voice sounded tired. His gaze darted over her shoulder to the entrance of the arena and back to her. "I will take care of the girl as we agreed."

She furrowed her brows and turned around. And froze.

There he was, dressed in the simple soldier's uniform all fighters including herself had worn today. No wonder she had not been able to spot him in the crowd - she had been looking for his usual blue robes while he had opted for anonymity instead. Why had she been so convinced that he would wear them? Probably because the idea of him voluntarily giving up the most easily recognisable badge of his power had seemed ridiculous. So much for her assumptions.

She wondered how anyone could mistake him for no more than a mere soldier; the aura of power around him was almost tangible. But then only magicians would be able to sense it.

He held a drawn sword in his right hand and walked confidently towards her with his face set determinedly. His cool blue eyes bore into hers, the light of the fires around them bathing his skin in liquid gold. He stopped several steps away from her and gave the confusedly whispering audience the opportunity to identify him in his unfamiliar clothes. The last whisper that ran from one astonished mouth to the next was his name, then they fell silent and followed his every move with rapt attention.

Only then he spoke, loud enough for all to hear, "Your skills have improved very much. Your training with Lord Orrin is finished." He paused for a few seconds before he added, "From now on you will train with *me*."

Eryn tried to swallow but her mouth was dry. She took one step back, away from him and started shaking her head.

She frantically searched for Orrin, but he was absent from the arena now. That had not been the deal. She turned around to leave the arena through the exit behind her, but the pale blue shimmering force field directly in front of her brought her up short. Whirling back to face him, she saw that he had taken the two steps towards her that she had managed to take away from him before.

"This is not a request," he said calmly but with steel in his voice, "It is an order."

"No. I don't take orders from *you*." It was barely more than a whisper. She edged away from the magical field behind her to hurry to the other exit through which he had entered the arena.

Suddenly the careful distance she had kept to him was gone and in a movement too fast even for her eyes, he had grabbed her from behind and held her back firmly pressed against his chest. His arm lay along her collarbone and she felt on her skin beneath her shirt the tingling of the magic he used on her muscles to keep her immobile against him. In a feeble attempt that seemed to amuse him she tried to push against him with her own power. In vain.

"Your lack of enthusiasm wounds me deeply," he said with a low chuckle close to her ear, fighting the unbidden memories that the scent of her skin brought back and that threatened to distract him.

She could feel his warm breath on her skin when he spoke. "But as you seem rather upset by my order I will give you the opportunity to prove that you would not benefit from my expertise. I am a reasonable man, after all."

Too close, much too close, was all that whirled through her head. Raging anger started to blossom hot in her chest… at herself for trusting Orrin, at Orrin for betraying her and at Enric for so many reasons, anger unfurling like a flower of melted stone.

She felt him gently push the cold steel tip of his sword across her cheek without drawing blood or otherwise marking her.

"If you fight me and win, you get to choose your trainer or not to train at all. If I defeat you, however, you will stop your resistance and finally start following my orders."

When he then loosened the magical vice and she could move again, she turned to face him and drew her sword in one swift movement. The anger and the helplessness from only moments before made her breath escape her lungs in gasps.

Enric considered the sword in her hands and waited, watching with fascination the battle taking place behind her eyes. Then, in a sudden movement, she lifted her sword and tossed it right in front of his feet.

"No, Lordling. I'm tired of your games," she spat and marched out of the arena, through the crowd and into the darkness, hoping desperately that he would let her leave this time. The chance never came.

Another barrier shimmered before her and she angrily raised her palm to send out a blast, watching with little surprise when it was stopped and dispersed with a crackle.

"One more thing before you rush off," Enric's amused voice said behind her.

When she turned back to him, clenching both her teeth and fists, she saw something golden shine in his palm. She groaned quietly. The shackles. Of course. They would hardly let her run around without them.

He quickly stepped closer, fixed the manacles around her wrists while she stood stiffly, waiting for him to finish. When he did only a few moments later and then collapsed the barrier behind her, she turned away.

He watched her all but running away from him, a thin smile on his lips. It was the first time she had used her derogatory nickname for him face to face, and in public, too, for everyone to hear. He would have to punish her for it, of course. Publicly.

* * *

She exhaled when the knock at her door came. She had been expecting it. Very likely a summons to join the Lordling for the training.

She rose slowly from her bed and opened the door a crack, spotting a liveried palace messenger.

"Lord Tyront asks you to see him in his study," the young man informed her. "I am to escort you there."

Lord Tyront? That was unexpected. She opened the door wider and slipped out.

"Alright then, lead on," she said with mock cheerfulness. "Can't let such an important man wait, can I?"

The messenger gave her a slightly fazed look, but nodded and preceded her out the warriors' quarters and across the square to the palace.

She remembered the way from the last time she had been brought there about three months ago when she and Vern had been caught at their little training exercises. Three months. Time was flying by.

They climbed the two flights of stairs and the messenger knocked at the respective door, which was opened almost immediately. A servant nodded and asked her to follow him to what was the study door.

"Come in," she heard Lord Tyront's voice from inside after the servant had knocked.

She entered and looked around, relieved when she didn't see Enric.

"Good morning, Eryn," he smiled and was about to step towards her to take her arm and guide her to a chair when he thought better of it. "Take a seat, please."

"I would rather stand if it's all the same to you," she replied politely. "Why am I here?"

Tyront acknowledged her wish to come to the point immediately without wasting time with social pleasantries. Thus he refrained from offering her something to drink.

"Because I want to show you a gesture of goodwill, so to say. But let me first congratulate you on your very impressive performance yesterday. We were wondering when you would be able to defeat Lord Orrin, and it seems you have been holding back quite a bit in the last few weeks." He didn't appear angry or displeased, but simply stated a fact.

She just raised her brows at him as if impatiently waiting for him to come to the point.

"As a token of our appreciation and also a credit of trust I have decided to take off your manacles for the time being." He chuckled when her eyes went wide. "I see this comes as a surprise. Though I have to warn you that this privilege is only in effect as long as you are not seen approaching either the city wall or the gates. And trust me when I promise you that any attempt on your part to do so will be observed and reported to me immediately. As will any attempt at escape."

"Why?" she asked, bewilderment clear on her face.

"As a sign of goodwill, as I mentioned before. We want you to look on this city not as a prison, a place of containment, but an area where you can move around freely and without limitations."

"Apart from the city walls and gates," she amended.

"Exactly," he confirmed. "Though of course you are free to decline my little offer. I wouldn't want to force this upon you."

Very funny, she thought and barely managed to stop herself from rolling her eyes at him. As if she really would have used that particular situation to make use of the freedom of choice he saw fit to grant her. Not even to defy him on principle. She lifted her arms for him to take off the shackles.

No more block on her powers, not even a partial one. Well, well, if that wasn't a sign to start looking for a way out of here.

"Please, don't try anything stupid," Tyront warned her while he took the manacles off her wrists and placed them on his desk. "Or they will be back on quickly enough, this time with the full block again."

"Of course not," she promised with honesty, giving him a slightly wounded look that he might make such an insinuation, before turning to leave his study, a faint smile on her lips.

CHAPTER 21

The Trap

Enric stood at the window of his study, hot drink in hand, and looked down to the soldiers' training area. Eryn had just arrived there, standing outside rather forlornly. Orrin was not allowed to teach her any longer, but the routine of several months now had still made her come here, he mused.

Tyront, standing behind him, cleared his throat. Of course he had heard about yesterday's occurrences. It seemed everything had gone according to Enric's plans. Her refusal to either fight or accept him as her new trainer was hardly a surprise, and yet he seemed to be in a ponderous mood.

Tyront considered the younger man for a while.

Enric was neither cruel nor hungry for power, whatever some people might claim to the contrary. He had been pushed into a position of great power and forced to take on great responsibility barely after reaching adulthood. The mischievous boy had had no other choice than quickly to make his peers and elders accept him as their superior. People had been surprised by the changes they saw in him as he grew fully up to attain the rank of the second-most powerful magician, a rank occupied by one usually much older. Tyront himself had been more than satisfied, even delighted, by how Enric had managed to adapt to the new office.

But of course there had been a price to pay, and still was, as he himself knew only too well. Friendships hardly ever survived the enormous chasm of rank when one was on top, especially when it was more a leap than a climb. Former friends now bowed to him and reverently fell silent when he entered the room. And, of course, they had to follow his orders. In addition, there were the rumours about the extent of his abilities - many of them gross exaggerations - some true, others not even suspected.

He was in his mid-thirties now and so used to being shown obedience. Maybe Eryn would be a good lesson for him. A magician who did not bow to him for a change, who resisted, was a challenge that couldn't simply be dealt with by applying overwhelming magical strength. In addition, he strongly suspected that Enric found her defiance entertaining, at least at the moment.

"What are your plans for her now?" he said into Enric's thoughts. The younger magician turned and returned to his mentor and superior with measured paces.

"I am not entirely sure how to proceed. I need to get her to fight me in order to train her, but she keeps refusing."

"Well, you can hardly blame her. The last two times you fought her she spent the next few hours unconscious. You haven't exactly used the kid gloves in your treatment of her. At least not in the encounters with you she is aware of."

Enric shot him a sideways glance. Of course he would have heard about the last Freedom Night. He sometimes thought Eryn herself had to be the only one in the city who wasn't yet aware of her lover's identity.

"She will learn about it sooner or later. Unfortunately, I am sure this will not be enough to provoke her into a fight with me or I would reveal that secret myself."

Tyront chuckled. "Are you sure you don't underestimate the depths of her aversion to you?" He regretted his words instantly when he saw Enric tighten his lips and look away. "I'm sorry," he conceded, "that was in poor taste." After a short pause he went on, "I heard that her young charge, the orphan girl has started work in the palace kitchen today thanks to Orrin's intervention. That wouldn't have anything to do with how he persuaded her to fight yesterday?"

Enric smiled. It was hard to keep anything from the wily old man - he seemed to have informants everywhere. "Yes, as a matter of fact, it would."

"Well then, if nothing else works you could always use the threat of the girl's losing her job if Eryn doesn't comply."

He shook his head. "No. I need to do this without threatening people dear to her. She is so cowered by me already." His voice was full of regret. "I'm afraid our little encounter in the arena yesterday has not really helped matters along." He stepped back to the window and watched her wandering around aimlessly. "I need to trick her somehow," he mused. "Something that drives her really mad and provokes her into fighting me. Something public."

"Ah yes, of course. There would still be an open score to settle. I heard she called you *Lordling* for everyone to hear. You have to admire her pluck."

Enric smiled. "I do. But you are right, that doesn't mean she will get away with it. I can't be seen letting such disrespectful behaviour pass. It might set a bad precedent." A scheme started to form in his head. Maybe he could use the orphan girl after all.

* * *

Eryn felt unbalanced and tense in more than one way. One week after the competition she had neither seen Enric nor had she received any orders from him. That was unexpected. And there was the matter of her calling him a

Lordling to his face in public. Somehow, in hindsight this didn't seem to have been such a smart move; it could not have gone down well. Yet so far he had left her alone, although this did not make her feel any less apprehensive.

The second problem was that despite suddenly having a lot more time on her hands, her plans to break away from this place had not really progressed very far. After the Order had warned people from helping her escape in any manner, seeking assistance through bribing somebody was more or less out of the question.

She raked her fingers through her hair in frustration, eager for something to do instead of spending hours trying to think of a brilliant plan. She considered exploring the city. One never knew if a spontaneous chance for an escape might present itself. That thought was at least more appealing than standing around uselessly and watching the warriors train.

The mornings were busy in the city, but that was not so much different from the village where she had lived before.

She used a head scarf to hide her brown hair to avoid drawing too many eyes. People had been pretty much used to seeing her wandering the streets, but the competition had changed that and she was a sensation once again.

When she passed a blacksmith's workshop she heard angry shouts and metal clanging to the floor. From what she could see the smith had specialised in crafting weapons, something which would make sense so close to the warriors.

Not far down the plastered street the buildings opened into a crossroads and she strolled towards it. So far her disguise had worked nicely - no unwanted attention as yet.

She grimaced when she heard a muffled cry and stopped walking. It had sounded like a girl. The shout came again, this time more agitated and greater in volume.

Wasn't that Plia's voice? Her heart hammering in her chest, she started running towards the commotion around which a small crowd had already gathered. Her eyes went wide at the scene that presented itself to her when she rounded a corner.

Plia was kneeling on the ground, a thin trickle of blood down the corner of her mouth, sobbing softly and protecting her tear-streaked face with both hands. Towering above her stood a man Eryn didn't recognise. He was large and muscular, scowling angrily at the girl and shouting words Eryn couldn't make out.

Without thinking she ran over to him, swept past him in an agile move and grabbed the knife he was wearing in a sheath on his belt before he could react.

Her thoughts raced and her eyes darted back and forth between him and the girl. Something was lying on the ground between them. It looked like a rather heavy money pouch. Her eyes darted to the girl's widened ones. Had she stolen it? Her Plia? Was this a punishment for theft? That couldn't be the way they dealt with a misdemeanour like that in the city, could it?

Eryn had had so much anger inside her already, but the anguish of seeing a defenceless child physically harmed threatened to bring her to her knees.

The man now turned fully to Eryn and focused his attention away from the girl on her and his knife she was holding pointed at him. Plia just sat there, eyes tearful, but made no move to get away.

"Plia, get out of here. Now."

But the girl didn't move and only stared at her. Still frozen in fear, Eryn assumed.

She returned her icy gaze to the brutal stranger. "I hope you are very proud of yourself. Beating a girl certainly is a feat that proves how manly and strong you are."

"A thief, however old or small, is still a thief who needs to be punished," the man said unimpressed.

"Get away from the girl or I swear I will make you pay for this here and now." Her voice was quiet and betrayed nothing of the storm inside her.

"Eryn, drop the knife," Orrin's voice suddenly said behind her. "Now."

She half turned to him and squinted at him. "What? Don't you see what is going on here? He has attacked Plia!"

"I asked you to drop the knife. A prisoner cannot threaten one of the King's citizens."

Staring at him, she wondered if she was somehow trapped in a nightmare. The situation felt unreal, like a badly written theatre script.

"Orrin," she said slowly. "The man lifted his hand against a child. Are you telling me to stand here and watch instead of intervening?"

"What I am telling you now for the third time is to drop the knife. Otherwise I will have to take it from you."

This was unforgiveable, she would never in a million years have thought him capable of it. He was a father, after all! Would he have acted so mercilessly if Vern had been the one on the ground, hurt and bleeding? Certainly not! Was stealing in his eyes an offence of such gravity that it justified a reaction like this? Or was a mere orphan girl not worthy of a magician's protection in this sad city? The thought made Eryn clench her fists, her fingernails gnawing painfully into her palms.

"If this is what you feel you must do, I can hardly stop you, can I?" she said with a forced calm she by no means felt.

He slowly drew one of two swords from his belt and walked closer.

They stood in the middle of the road, drawing more and more spectators around them, even though they kept what they considered a safe distance from what looked to be an imminent sword fight. To her relief, the man who had beaten Plia had decided to retreat as well.

"What is the matter with you, Orrin?" she tried one last time. "Have you gone completely crazy?"

She watched the sword. It was obviously very well made and the knife she held would hardly survive more than one blow if even that. If he really intended to fight her. And at the moment the evidence seemed to point in that direction.

Maybe she could use the knife to distract him enough to grab his other sword from his belt.

Then he attacked. She sacrificed the knife just as she had intended and then managed, through more luck than skill, to get her hands on his other sword, drawing it in a swift move from its sheath.

Now holding a matching weapon, she easily parried his blows and let him push her back a few steps.

It seemed much easier to fight him, now that she knew for real that she could defeat him. His superior fighting skills wouldn't help him against her superior magical strength. She caught another chop aimed at her side and then started to strike back several times in quick succession, increasing her speed enough to make him struggle.

Whenever she caught a glimpse of Plia still sitting on the cobbles helplessly, her anger and strength seemed to increase a little. Concentrating her wrath into a single blow, she hit his weapon hard enough to force him to his knees. She looked down at him. The short fight had cost him a lot of energy, pearls of sweat stood on his forehead.

Even as she watched, he drew back his sword for another attack, this time aimed right at her throat. There was what felt like an eternity compressed into just one split second in the course of which an icy hand seemed to clutch her heart and squeeze. He truly had made to deliver a lethal blow to her!

The thought all but choked her breath. Almost as if in a trance she moved her hand to drive her weapon into his chest instead, her eyes swimming in unshed tears.

Only when her arm had started the unstoppable thrust, she saw the image of Plia over Orrin's shoulder flicker and disappear. She barely had enough time to look back into his eyes, the horror blank in her own. The tip of her sword was about to touch his chest, when it burst into a blizzard of brightly shimmering fine metal dust.

Her thoughts whirled and couldn't seem to break free from the vortex of impossibilities that had just occurred around her. Something had shattered inside her in this one instant when she had known that she would kill him without justification and that there was no chance to divert the blade from its course. She had not yet progressed to the question of who would play such a cruel trick on her.

Still locked in Orrin's shocked gaze she sank to her knees and felt the first tear run down her cheek. Orrin looked as miserable as she felt and pulled her into a hard embrace. She buried her face in his shoulder and found comfort in the warmth that enveloped her.

She could hear the murmuring of the crowd around them like through a fog. They had obviously appreciated the spectacle.

When she lifted her head again she saw that the crowd had shifted, leaving an opening large enough to make the tall man with his sword pointing downwards in a relaxed grip stand out in stark contrast to the emptiness around him. The sun just rising above a low roof painted a dark figure silhouetted against blazing light from behind. She didn't have to see his face. His presence was like a punch to her perception, almost as if he somehow occupied all the space around her, his magical senses brushing against her own, creating a sensation of intrusion, raw and annoying. She had not felt this in his presence before, so it was probably something he did on purpose just to irritate her.

She slowly released her arms from around Orrin, reading in his eyes the knowledge of what was about to follow. She knew he had participated in Enric's plan but she couldn't deal with that right now. Anger at him would cost energy – energy she needed for the man patiently standing there and waiting for her. His stance was as confident as ever, as if he had no doubt that this time she would not turn away from his challenge.

And why should he? She saw vividly in her mind - oddly detached from her churning mass of racing emotions - that he had chosen his manoeuvre well and it was unthinkable not to respond to it. He had gone just far enough to seize her undivided attention without affecting anybody but herself. Yet who knew what he would resort to if this failed?

But this was nothing she needed to worry about now, it wouldn't be necessary for him to take any other measures. For the first time she *wanted* to fight him, hurt him, however remote the chance of her accomplishing this feat might be.

She slowly rose to her feet without taking her eyes off him and wordlessly stretched out her hand into which Orrin quietly placed the hilt of his remaining sword, the one that had not been shattered into dust by magical force. Her fingers closed around it, feeling the lingering warmth of where Orrin had clasped it in the frenzied fight before.

A strange calmness settled over her, one she knew would not last long. It was mere quiet before a storm. The last motes of metallic dust were still twirling through the air around her when she started walking towards him.

He had expected to feel satisfaction when he finally managed to induce her to fight him, but instead there was only relief mixed with sympathy and eager anticipation. Apart from Tyront, all his training partners needed to be treated with special care when it came to fighting. His average strikes tended to penetrate their shields like a knife cutting through butter. She would be able to manage a lot more. Hardly a real challenge, but still more exercise than he'd had in a while.

The scarf Eryn had worn to cover her hair was hanging down her back in a limp knot after her fight with Orrin had loosened it. The specks of sunlight glinting off tiny metal particles clinging to her skin and floating on airstreams around her gave her an ethereal, surreal aura that made him swallow. It conjured up memories from a certain night many weeks ago when her naked skin had been bathed instead in candle light. Back then under much more delightful circumstances the tension in her muscles had not been caused so much by anger and hatred but more by pleasurable sensations of the flesh.

He noted the thin layer of restraint that didn't reach her eyes. They resembled twin fires of utter fury. The rest of her body betrayed no sign of agitation. He very much looked forward to changing that.

He would leave the choice to her whether to keep the fight practically non-magical by only enhancing physical capabilities or to turn it into an unrestrained magic battle. He knew she hadn't been training to fight with magic since her few sessions with Vern, but he strongly suspected her to have tried a few things on her own, as magicians tended to do.

He would defeat her, but not brutally. First she needed to get an idea of the unused and unsuspected potential still lying inside her, and that he alone could help her tap.

She halted several paces away from him, the sword hanging from her hand, mirroring his stance. Without warning she swiftly jerked up her unarmed palm and hurled a blue bolt of energy at him. He neither moved a single muscle nor broke eye contact with her while he raised a shield that absorbed the attack.

Shaking his head in mock admonishment, he raised his voice, "It is customary to warn your opponent in a friendly fight before unleashing your first magical attack. Just imagine if I had failed to raise my shield in time. I might have been hurt."

"Oh yes, and that would be the very last thing I wanted..." she retorted. She would show him exactly how *friendly* she considered this fight.

Not too bad, he thought. The strike had been charged with enough energy to breach a weaker barrier, but there was still quite some room for improvement.

"Too much light and heat, more focus on the main purpose of your strike," he instructed.

She frowned in disbelief and stared at him. Had he in actual fact just said that? He really had the nerve to lecture her on fighting techniques when she had just made a very genuine and unmistakable attempt to throw him violently to the ground. Nothing that would have killed him without a shield, but still something that would have sent him tumbling helplessly had he not been prepared for it. Her anger seethed even more. He was not taking her seriously, he ridiculed her by treating her with the indulgence he might grant a child playing with something it had no understanding of.

She released another streak, this time not at him, but at the cobbles very near a horse cart. The animal shrieked in panic and turned away from the smoking spot on the stones, sending onlookers scattering away in fear as it galloped in the opposite direction and thus, just as she had hoped, directly towards Enric.

He waited until the very last moment before jumping aside, grabbing the horse's bridle in one hand with unnatural and undoubtedly magically aided strength and speed before he briefly touched his flat palm to its throat. The panicked tension instantly drained from the equine body and it snorted placidly when he patted the side of its head. Then he sent it off in a carefree trot and raised his brows at her.

"Creative, but risky."

Honestly, more evaluation? She snarled, "You can keep your pathetic little lectures!"

Completely unperturbed by her hostility he nodded thoughtfully. "Well, I aim to please. And anyway, I have always felt that practical demonstrations are so much more valuable."

Immediately after his final words he sent an almost transparent blue ball in her direction that didn't hit her barrier but instead the sword in her hand. She jumped back, dropping it hastily and watching as it flew into nothing more than a gust of hot air and a few flecks of silver dust before it had come even close to hitting the cobbles.

"How do you like my practical lesson?" he enquired with a conversational tone. "It's definitely a more vivid illustration, I would say. But for the sake of completeness I feel I should add that you could have avoided this easily if you had extended your shield enough to also protect your weapon instead of only your body." His eyes didn't leave hers for an instant when he called out, "Lord Orrin, the lady needs another sword. It seems I owe you two new ones now."

Bastard! Bastard! Bastard! went through her head in circles. The violent urge to go for his throat with her bare hands grew stronger and stronger, but she fought it. Doing so with a sharp-edged weapon promised to be so much more satisfying.

Moments later a sword was sent hovering towards her on a magical field. Orrin was not so foolish as to come anywhere near them. She plucked it out of the air and held it ready in front of her when she approached him.

He nodded approvingly. "A wise move. Never try to engage a magician much stronger than yourself in a direct purely magical battle when there is another choice."

"Why can't you just keep quiet?" Her outburst had a slightly shrill undertone that made her take a calming breath.

"Why don't you come here and make me. You aren't still terrified of me, are you?"

It was the contented grin that did it. The over-confident, arrogant little smile that implied that he knew everything about her.

Yet the reason why his words stung so hard, she knew, was that they were so very true. And he was aware of that.

There was no other choice, she could no longer let her fear of him paralyse her.

Finally, and to his great satisfaction, she raised her sword and attacked him, both of them knowing fully well that she didn't have the ghost of a chance of prevailing against him.

He met her frantic strokes evenly and without any apparent effort. When she magically enhanced her speed he followed suit and adapted the velocity of his purely defensive blocks to that of her attacks.

After several minutes he sensed her beginning frustration over his passive stance and dealt his first blow, sending her several paces backwards. She remained upright and her free hand dashed forward and threw a barely visible but compact bolt of magic at him. He just raised the side of his left hand and the magic she had hurled at him seemed to split in two and curved away from him along two wide arcs before hitting the cobblestones at a safe distance.

She staggered back, open-mouthed. There had not even been a shield, he had just… just blocked and diverted it with his bare hand! From the reaction of the watching crowd she could gather that she was not the only one seeing this trick for the first time.

Her thoughts raced. They would be used to seeing fighting magicians as the training sessions were out in the open, and yet they had reacted very much like her – as if they had never seen it before. Was he the only magician who was capable of this? Her eyes sought out Orrin, who looked equally shocked. This had been new even for him, the chief warrior trainer!

Enric smiled faintly. This was quite the impression he had hoped to make on her. "I could teach you. This and many other things."

Despite her inability to form coherent words she managed to shake her head and retreat backwards when he started walking towards her.

His blows grew stronger and she felt her strength diminishing rapidly when she kept infusing her muscles with enough power to parry his strokes. Her steps were becoming clumsier, she noted with rising panic. And he of course was showing no sign of exhaustion whatsoever.

She caught her foot in a gap between two cobble stones and fell on her side, still staring at him and barely noticing when he put his foot on the weapon that had fallen out of her hand. He placed the tip of his sword at her throat.

"Do you acknowledge my victory?" he asked calmly, looking down at her with raised brows.

She slowly woke from her stupor. "What if I don't?"

"Then we will continue fighting until you either capitulate or collapse from exhaustion."

She suddenly felt infinitely weary, her reserves of strength all but depleted by the fight. She would not last another one, didn't even feel strong enough to pick up that damned sword again.

Slowly she closed her eyes and let her head sink to her chest in a gesture of surrender.

He sheathed his weapon and looked down at her. "Good. And now to the little matter of you calling me *Lordling*. A public affront requires public retribution, however much I would have preferred a private one. But surely you appreciate that I have a standing, my reputation, to protect."

She lifted her head again and stared up at him blankly. How much more retribution than having her lying on the ground at his feet did he need? Whatever he had in mind he would have to do while she was down on the street, she didn't have enough strength left to get back to her feet.

A sudden prickling in her back made her flinch and she turned her head in puzzlement. He had conjured a force field behind her that gently pushed her up until her position was upright again.

Stepping very close to her, he pulled her against him with one arm around her centre before he let the field disperse.

She tried to use what little remained of her strength to push him away but failed miserably. While she had trouble merely standing on her own two feet, he wasn't showing even the slightest sign of weariness.

"What are you doing? Let go of me," she hissed, cursing herself and him for the stab of fear he still caused in her, the more at this close proximity.

"Taking what victorious men have claimed since the beginning of time," he explained matter-of-factly. "Or at least hinting at it."

"Barbarian," she spat, enraged even further by the amusement in his eyes.

When he then put his second hand behind her neck to stop her from turning her head away, she froze and stared up into his now very close face, mouth open in astonishment.

That was exactly the way she had been held one particular night by a tall, blue-eyed man with a mask before he had carried her off... Her vision began to blur, her breath caught in her throat.

Oh no, please not that. This could be a coincidence, couldn't it? Her eyes frantically wandered along his lips, then up to his eyes, begging fate that she would not find anything familiar in his features. But it was unavoidable - she recognised those contours, those keen eyes. She stifled a sob. How could she have let this happen with him of all men in this detestable city?

"No, this can't be true..." Her voice almost broke.

He raised his brows questioningly, then the phantom of a smile began to play around the corners of his mouth. "You have finally figured it out, then. It is the way I hold you, I assume. I am very pleased you remember." His voice was soft, almost purring with satisfaction.

New desperation returned some of her energy and she tried to push him away once more. He just tightened his grip slightly.

"No fighting," he whispered close to her face, "You must be seen to offer this tribute reluctantly, but in acceptance of your defeat."

"Reluctance you can have, Bastard! But I am afraid I am out of compliance right now."

Insulting him felt good, it kept the anger alive. It wouldn't do to show him that all she really wanted to do was run and hide from him somewhere.

The renewed strain of resisting him drained even the strength to stand from her and her knees began to yield. She felt a sudden boost of his energy surge into her leg muscles to keep her upright.

"Witty," he acknowledged. "But no slipping down yet. We wouldn't want people to think you enjoyed this so much you are melting away in my arms. This is meant for *my* pleasure, after all."

With this he lowered his mouth onto hers and took possession, forcing her lips open and invading without hesitation.

Sucking in a shocked breath, she then bit down hard, but only managed to graze his tongue slightly with her teeth before he retreated swiftly. His blue eyes narrowed and he continued to hold her neck firmly to keep her head in place. He was still close enough for their noses to touch and his voice was no more than a low growl when his lips moved to warn her.

"Do not try that again or I will paralyse you."

"What difference would…" she started, but his lips cut her off.

When she once more attempted to hurt him with her teeth, she felt warmth from his palm seep into her neck and the muscles in her jaws resisted her command and instead kept her mouth open for him to access as he pleased.

She had nothing left to throw at him and cursed herself for her weakness, as the only thing she could do now was to endure this intimate assault. Her heart was beating so rapidly it caused a rush in her ears that drowned out all other sounds. Where did it take the energy from when the rest of her body wouldn't even stay upright on its own?

He kept on kissing her, his persistent tongue relentlessly exploring and tasting as if he had every right to. And to make an unbearable situation worse, neither her fear of him nor the humiliation he made her suffer was able completely to subdue her body's reaction to him.

Her nerve endings started to vibrate and she felt a treacherous tug. It took all her resolve to keep her arms from wrapping themselves around his neck and to clench them into fists against his shoulders instead. Giving in to a good kiss was one thing, but not to one that was meant as a punishment. And not with this man.

Kissing him back would be nothing more than assisting him in abasing her. But feeling an urge to participate in doing so was embarrassing. Demeaning. Painful.

Shame for reacting like this to what was the final, wretched detail in a deliberate, public humiliation caused hot tears to start running down her cheeks. It was as if after Orrin's betrayal she couldn't even trust herself any more.

He had imagined kissing her again for months, dreamed of it at night and during the day when he had watched her from his window. Keeping his hands from re-discovering the familiar shape of her body was almost physically painful and he used the tension in his arms to press her even harder against him.

But he realised that this made restraining himself even more arduous, as the outline of her form, warm and tight against him, was definitely no way to calm the longing he had urging him on, clawing against the layer of self-discipline he kept in place with iron resolve.

When he released her jaws again and withdrew, much too soon for his own liking but necessary if he didn't want to lose control, he saw the wet streaks of tears and caught her chin as she tried to avert her face.

Blue eyes bore into her brown ones and she could hardly bear the sympathy she read in them.

His thumb swept tenderly over her damp cheek and he let his lips brush hers again, this time in a gentle touch that seemed almost worse, more daunting than the submission he had forced her into before.

"Orrin will help you back to your quarters," he said quietly. "We will talk tomorrow, when you've had time to recover."

He motioned for Orrin to approach and stepped back as the older man gently lifted her into his arms to carry her back, its being impossible for her to walk unsupported. She slung her arms around his neck and pressed her face to his throat to shut out the world around her and silently let tears of humiliation, defeat and exhaustion trail down her cheeks.

Enric ignored the inflamed look the warrior sent him. Orrin had not been pleased about having to contribute something to this farce, and found it equally distasteful seeing her like this now. But that was Orrin's problem alone right now.

He had enjoyed it, there was no sense in denying it. Watching Eryn fight through her fear of him to prove his words wrong when she knew them to be true. The relief and wild triumph that had surged through him when she had finally realised that it had been him that night. The glory of conquest when he had held her, defenceless in his arms, the joy of domination.

And, of course, the kiss. Her taste, that he remembered so well and that had brought him very close to the edge of recklessly claiming what he had mentioned to her. It might have been seeing her tears that had dampened his animal urges, he pondered. A good sign, he thought, one that showed that, despite this primitive side of him, he had the discipline to control it and thus avoid letting it wreak damage beyond recall.

Enric watched her being carried away, defeated and humiliated. She would recover and emerge from it stronger than before. But the sight of her clinging to Orrin gave way to another stirring of emotion: regret.

CHAPTER 22

Experimenting

She paced up and down in her small room and had been doing so for almost an hour now. Upon waking, a multitude of thoughts, memories and impressions from the fight with the Lordling had jostled for her attention, but she had sorted through them as if through a stack of books, deciding which ones to consider right now and which ones to save for later.

The realisation of having spent this one night with him was something that definitely had to be kept aside for now. Or maybe rather forever be buried deep down in the vaults of her consciousness. Orrin and what he had done was also a matter for later perusal. What was worth focussing on right now was what she had seen during her fight yesterday, especially one particular skill that had taken her breath away.

How was it possible to stop a bolt of energy without a shield? How could he have caused a change of direction with no visible use of magic? It seemed impossible for him to be resistant to magical attacks without protection. Had he used an invisible, non-magical one? Did something like that even exist or was that a contradiction in itself?

She tugged at her hair in frustration.

She had slept for almost a full day after her encounter with the Lordling. She remembered Orrin taking her to her room, not saying anything but tucking her in and staying with her until exhaustion had won and taken her into a deep, dreamless sleep. When she had awoken, a tray with fresh bread, meat, cheese and wine had been placed next to her bed on a small table.

Since waking about one hour before she had not let anybody know that she was awake yet. *He* had said that he wanted to talk to her, which was something she wanted to avoid as long as possible.

Forcing her thoughts back to the matter of his shield-less block, she remembered her father telling her that like every other living thing, magic needed air. It rode on airstreams, which was why no magic could work where air couldn't flow. Healing through a wall for example was not possible as the wall would block the stream of air between healer and patient.

But there had been nothing, absolutely nothing to block the stream of air and thus magic between her hand and him. How could he have stopped it? She stopped dead in her tracks. But the magic hadn't stopped, had it? It had merely changed direction. Could it be so simple? Would magically changing the flow of air not also change the direction of a magical strike? She knew that redirecting air was a useful skill, especially when one had to deal with sick people who were averse to opening windows for fresh air. One couldn't force them to do it, but instead discreetly change the air quality in the room by slowly circulating it towards cracks in the wall, a purposely unclosed door. Or redirect a stench away to be able to concentrate on the work.

Well, *simple* might not really be the right word here. The underlying idea was elementary, but the execution was hardly comprehensible. The change in the air currents would have to be very quick and precise not only to deflect a high-speed attack but also spit it in two. Splitting it was only for showing off, she first thought. But then it occurred to her that the split would have the advantage of turning one strong strike into two with half the original power – and thus danger – in each.

She sat down on her narrow bed when the potential of mastering such a defence dawned on her. It could easily be used against stronger magicians as it would simply halve the destructive force! Even if she didn't manage to turn the strike away completely she could surely hold a shield against a bolt reduced in force by half.

She shot up. That was her chance! Learning alone how to do it would not be easy. She started pacing again, but the hope and impatience put new energy in her steps.

* * *

Two hours later she collapsed onto her bed and covered her eyes with her forearm. This was not the way to accomplish it. She had for quite some time been shooting weak bolts into the air and trying to change their paths.

But they went off too quickly and the further away they were, the harder the air was to manipulate, as air currents from further away, differences in temperature, disturbances, air draughts, and all manner of variables, influenced the result.

She assumed that it had to be a lot easier when the bolt was coming directly towards her, provided she was able to react in time. Air immediately in front of her was the easiest to manipulate.

This was why the Lordling had let her bolt come really close before he had diverted it. The closer they were, the safer it was to turn them away – if one was fast enough and knew what one was doing. And the added benefit was of course that it appeared immensely impressive to the watcher, just like the magic was being averted with a bare, unprotected hand.

She had tried diverting airstreams with a candle and seen from the way the smoke curled that it was not too hard. But smoke was easier to redirect than a strike with enough force to knock out an adult.

The problem was now how to make the bolts come towards her instead of shooting them away from her. That didn't seem possible without another magician assisting her. And this was not an option; it was completely out of the question. Her attempts at figuring this out had to remain a secret.

If her next attempt to escape should again put the Lordling in her way, she needed him to be unprepared for this trick to work in her favour. It might be the one shot he would count on to defeat her that made the difference.

Suddenly a loud pounding shook the wooden door. Before she could even consider whether to answer, it was pushed open and there he was, just the man she wanted to see least of all.

He had to duck his head slightly to avoid bumping his forehead against the low door frame.

"Good," he nodded. "You are awake. I was told that strange noises were coming from your room, so I assumed you were back among the living." He looked around at the darkened spots at the stone walls her experimental bolts had left. "Been letting off some steam, have you?"

She swallowed and just stared at him. Convenient, he had saved her from having to think of a plausible lie.

"Come." He stepped closer and held out a hand to help her up from her bed. A gesture she studiously ignored. When she didn't make any move to get up he let his arm sink again.

"Alright then. We can talk here. It's rather more intimate. Not exactly cosy after your... attempts at redecorating, but soldiers' quarters hardly ever are. If you move aside a bit, I can take a seat on your bed."

She jumped up quickly. In here with him was not a good idea. The room was crowded enough with one person in it, let alone two. And especially with him.

"Changed your mind?" he quipped.

She waited for him to leave first, but he just stood and looked at her. "After you."

Taking a steadying breath, she forced herself to squeeze past him, taking care to contact him as little as possible in the process, all the time aware of his eyes never leaving her.

He followed her out of the small room and the building and when she turned around to see where he wanted to go, he indicated the way to the palace with his hand.

"The palace?" She didn't like that one bit.

"Yes, the palace. That's where my quarters are."

"I'm not going to your quarters!" She took a step back.

"No need to be afraid. We will just talk in my study."

She looked around, taking in the training grounds and the people around them hurrying about.

Folding her arms, she shook her head. "We can talk here. What do you want?"

"No. This is not a matter to discuss here out in the open. You either come with me on your own two feet or over my shoulder. Make your choice."

She could see his patience beginning to wear thin. "Well, how could I possibly turn down such a charming invitation?"

* * *

After what had been quite a long journey through the palace passages, they had come to stand in front of a large wooden door which he pushed open and motioned for her to enter before him. She did and looked around. They were in a large, comfortably furnished parlour with dark wooden tables, chairs and settees. It was large enough to entertain at least twenty-five people without any problem. Funny, she hadn't pegged him as the social type.

He moved on through the parlour into a smaller room that was obviously meant for working. It was dominated by a ridiculously large black desk on a brightly coloured carpet which was probably quite a nuisance to clean. The walls were lined with shelves filled with thick, leather-bound books. In front of one of two large windows was another settee with a small round table and two chairs. For more casual meetings, obviously.

She was relieved to see him walk behind his desk and sit down in his chair instead of in the cosy meeting corner. The large, heavy desk between them helped her to let go of some of her tension.

"Have a seat," he offered, and she sat down on one of two chairs in front of the desk.

"What do you want?" She folded her arms in front of her chest and stared at him.

"Right to the point, I see."

At that moment the door opened and a middle aged maid brought in a tray with tea and fresh bread buns, butter and small slices of cake. Enric nodded at her and noted Eryn's eyes dart towards the food for an instant before she had her greed under control again.

When the maid had left, he rose to pour two cups and handed her one. "The food is for you. It must be quite some time since you last ate."

She sipped at the tea and resisted for a few long moments before she gave in and reached for the first bread bun.

"What I want is to talk to you about is the chance of your joining the Order."

Barely avoiding spitting out her mouthful of bread, she forced herself to swallow first. "No," she just said before taking another bite.

"This was," he continued as if she hadn't spoken at all, "the reason why we started to train you in fighting. The Order is the protective institution of magic in this kingdom, and its primary task is military defence. You are a magician, and a powerful one, too. That makes you a candidate."

"Oh dear, be still my heart," she twittered. "And there was I, thinking that I would never be good enough to be accepted into the sacred halls of your Order. I was absolutely sure that being a spy from enemy lands and a danger to your entire population here would have reduced my chances to nothing."

"We do not consider the Western Territories as enemy lands as such. Neither did Tyront and I ever think you were a spy, if that gives you any consolation."

"No, not really," she shrugged. "I couldn't care less what either of you is thinking."

"What do you think about joining us?" he asked, bracing himself for the unfavourable reply he was about to receive.

She huffed. "Your precious Order has taken me from my home town and kept me prisoner. Yet even without this I would not join an organisation that can see no better use for magic than fighting and killing."

"I don't think you really appreciate the chance you are spurning here. And it was not the Order that had you brought here, but the King."

Rolling her eyes, she said, "Very well, let's focus on that detail, shall we? Are you really expecting me to be enthusiastic about the chance of joining you? You forced your training programme on me and treated me like an experiment! And you – were you told to start breeding for gifted offspring with me? If the answer to that is Yes, let me save you the trouble of continuing your efforts; they are futile. I can influence my fertility with magic. You may be stronger than me, but you have no idea how to counteract my measures."

His eyes glinted dangerously, even though his voice remained calm. "There are limits to what I am willing to do for my King, even if you do seem to see me as no more than a mindless minion." He laid both hands palm down on his desk. "So, what you are saying is that you don't approve of how the Order uses magic. I was told you made a living as a healer back in your town. I assume this is what you consider a worthy use of magic?"

She leaned back and folded her arms. "Yes. If you put half the effort of your preparations for war into doing something your people might actually benefit from, many of them wouldn't have to suffer unnecessarily from illness and injury."

"Something people might actually benefit from? So you are saying that keeping them safe from attackers is nothing they benefit from?"

"Attackers? Where from? Hasn't the kingdom been isolated for who knows how long? And even if there were any danger from outside, it's not as if the people really care who sits on that golden throne," she huffed. "Most of them never even lay eyes on the King in their entire life. Kings are exchangeable.

People have everyday problems such as if the crops will turn out alright, if they can afford to have warm winter clothes made for their growing children, if their boots will make it through another season and domestic matters like that. What do they care that their mighty and all-important sovereign keeps a small army of pet magicians to protect him or his claim to power that arises from nothing more than being born as a son to the man who claimed it before him?"

Enric closed his eyes and pressed his thumb and index finger to the bridge of his nose. She surely had a point. Or two. But *pet magicians*? She made the Order sound like a bunch of misled idiots.

"So, instead of protection, what exactly is it you think magicians should do? Should all of us be healing people?"

She shot him a defiant look. "Of course that would hardly seem as noble a task to you, would it? You don't have any magical healing knowledge from what I have seen, not the tiniest particle. Because in these last couple of centuries you have focussed on only one thing: fighting. And at the same time you can't even heal a broken leg. Magic is not meant to serve the ambition of only a few powerful people - it should be used to serve everyone." She swallowed hard. It was like hearing her father talking inside her head.

"So you would turn us all into healers?"

"That's not what I'm saying!" She jumped up from her chair and started pacing up and down, the agitation too great to remain seated. "And apart from you, I don't think that there can be only one single purpose for magic. And limiting all magical efforts to training warriors? What I am saying is, shouldn't you at least be able to do things that have nothing to do with fighting? Like healing a bleeding child or making it rain when the crops threaten to wilt?"

He followed her restless movements. "And you can do those things?" he asked carefully, intrigued despite himself. Influencing the weather sounded fascinating.

"What?" She stopped distractedly to look at him. "Sure, it's not that hard. But there is so much more, things my father could do that I will never have a chance to learn, especially if you are trying to chain me into this narrow-minded, power-hungry, ignorant Order of yours." She collapsed back into her chair and looked at him with raised eyebrows. "The answer was No, in case I was being too subtle."

He smirked. "There might be quite a number of faults people attribute to you. Subtlety is definitely not among them. Let's leave the topic alone for now." He needed to talk to Tyront first.

When he slowly rose from his chair and sat on the corner of his desk that positioned him near to her without touching, her eyes became fixed on his every movement. He noted how her hands now gripped the armrests tightly. Of course, he could hardly blame her for being nervous in his presence after what had happened yesterday, especially if he came that close. He leaned back slightly to increase the distance a little and give her some more space.

"About yesterday," he began and stopped when she jumped up again.

"I don't want to talk about it," she said curtly. Memory flashes of his lips on hers and older ones of his lips in many other places made blood flush to her cheeks. "Just don't dare to touch me anymore. Stay away from me."

She turned abruptly, and when she was about to grab the door handle she noted the slight blue shimmering of a force field. She took a deep breath and turned back to him.

He was still sitting on the edge of his large desk, watching her and thinking how appealing her blush was.

"What?" She lifted her arms in exasperation and let them fall back to her sides again.

"Staying away from you might prove rather difficult. I will take over your training, after all."

"My training?" Her arms akimbo, she stared at him. "I thought I had made it clear that..."

He interrupted her. "Yes, and now let *me* make something clear to you: The training will take place. And who knows, even somebody with your noble disposition may learn something useful from a barbarian such as myself. You might be dead set against joining us for now, but you might change your mind, and then you may as well be ready for it. And we can't have you join the Order when every first-year warrior trainee could beat your fighting skills, if not your power."

He lifted a hand when she was about to speak. "And as for the other - not touching you - I have to say that I am not happy with that, either, though for more personal reasons. I have enjoyed touching you very much, both times, and intend to do so again." He fought his impulse to approach her when he saw the panic in her eyes. He removed the force field with a sigh.

"Meet me in front of the palace tomorrow at sunrise. Bring a sword. Oh, and, Eryn..." he added when she was already halfway out the door, and saw her freeze in mid-step. "Don't make me come and get you, will you. Believe me, you wouldn't like it."

* * *

Enric leaned back comfortably in Tyront's parlour. The invitation to dinner had arrived barely an hour after Eryn had left his quarters. The food had been excellent as always and Vyril, Tyront's companion, had retreated to her study to give the men privacy.

Tyront placed two glasses half filled with a dark brown liquid that smelled richly of smoked wood and malt on a small round table between them and sat down as well. Enric had been thoughtful during dinner. He had made polite conversation with Vyril, answering her questions, asking a few in return, but something had clearly been on his mind and still was.

"How did it go, then?" he asked, knowing he didn't have to specify what he meant.

"It was... interesting. Of course it is hardly surprising that she is fairly unenthusiastic about joining us."

"No," Tyront mused, thinking of how Enric had tricked her into fighting the other day. That wouldn't have helped. He waited for the younger man to go on. There was more, obviously.

"You remember that her father was a healer?" Upon Tyront's nod, he continued, "and that he had started to teach her the craft?" Another nod. This, too, was not new.

"She thinks we waste our magic by using it for no more than defence and combat. In her opinion we do nothing more than serve the King's wish to remain on the throne and revel in the power he grants us instead of doing something useful for the people."

"So she has started you thinking?" Tyront chuckled.

Enric looked at his mentor. "Tyront, she can do things. She mentioned healing and influencing the weather as if it was nothing. How can a simple country healer have knowledge we can't find in any of our books? Are those on the other side of that accursed water so much more advanced than us?"

"Well, there are things she didn't know. She hadn't even heard of shielding when we tested her. So I might say there is a thing or two she could learn from us, too."

"Nothing she cares to learn, I'm sure. But I'm beginning to think that we should learn a few things from *her*."

"Do you think she would be willing to teach us?"

"Why would she? Would you, in her place? I'm sure she won't as long as we keep her here against her will. She doesn't trust us."

"As long as she refuses to join the Order, the King decides whether she stays or may leave. And he won't let her leave."

"But as soon as she joins the Order she magically binds herself to us and is barred more expressly from leaving here without the intention to return. She has not much of a choice here - either she stays voluntarily or she is made to. You know, we will need very good arguments for this."

Tyront took a sip from the strong drink. "Exactly. So, how can we convince her to join us?"

"If it were up to me, I would say: Let her spend her time and efforts on whatever she wants to do. We can only profit from it."

"I see. Unfortunately this does not meet with the regulations of the Order. Combat training is compulsory, whether she likes it or not." He shook his head when Enric seemed about to argue. "And yes, maybe it is time to adapt the rules. But we can't be seen to be adapting them for *her* sake before she has even joined us."

"It wouldn't be only for her. We would profit from it as well."

"Be that as it may, that's not what the King and the people will see. It would make her seem too powerful, too important on her own terms. And if she continues to treat the King with as little respect as she does right now, he will be forced to do something about her, whether she is under the Order's protection or not."

"So you are saying we need her to join us on our terms as long as she is still our captive, and only then we can make the changes that would make it attractive for her to join us in the first place?" He snarled at the contradiction.

Tyront nodded. "Yes, we must. It will strengthen our standing. We can't be seen to be giving in to her. That would give a message we don't intend. Once she has joined us, however, the matter is a completely different one."

Enric's expression was thoughtful. "I see. If she is part of the Order, she can make changes with our approval instead of forcing us to meet her demands. Even if she is seen as the one causing the changes, it would be down to an Order magician and not a mere captive. It will be quite a challenge to convince her to join us under these circumstances. She won't believe me if I promise her changes, but only after she has committed herself to us. She doesn't exactly trust me."

"That is putting it rather mildly," Tyront chuckled. "But you won't be the one to have to convince her. I will." At Enric's frown he added, "I imagine it's hard for the two of you to hold on to a coherent line of thought when you are in each other's presence. You have not exactly been shy about your intentions and you need to keep your hands to yourself; she will be busy enough keeping her distance from you. Whatever you say will be met with resistance as a matter of principle."

"And you think as the big, bad Order's leader your chances are better?" Enric sounded doubtful.

"Well," Tyront leaned back confidently, "I'm not a threat to her, physically speaking. I am no more than an old man trying to do what's best."

The younger man smiled and shook his head. A man with enough power singlehandedly to fight a minor army of magicians without even sweating, a master in the game of politics and the one with access to what was probably the most efficient network of spies in the kingdom aimed to pass as a harmless old man who was no threat. Very convincing.

CHAPTER 23

Training with Enric

Eryn leaned against the palace wall and watched the sun slowly rising above the roofs of the city. The mornings had started being chillier of late, a clear sign of the approaching winter. And she hadn't had breakfast yet. This was not a good combination.

She had considered not showing up but had seen herself being dragged out of bed and across the yard. Then she had reconsidered.

Enric stepped out into the cold morning air and was pleased to see her waiting. When she looked up it was plain enough to see that she was not all too thrilled about the sight of him.

"Come along." He motioned for her to follow him back into the palace. He led her through a dizzying maze of corridors until after several minutes they had reached a small garden surrounded by high walls. That is, if anyone could call it a garden rather than a courtyard, she thought. Apart from a patch of grass and a stone bench there was nothing much to suggest to her a garden. When she took a closer look at the bench, she saw a sword lying on it.

She took a step back when he turned to her.

"Take off your armour," he instructed.

"What?" Only now did she notice that he wasn't wearing any himself, just a pair of trousers and a loose linen shirt.

"We will start with shielding. You don't need your armour for that."

Shielding? But she had already learned how to shield herself.

As if reading her thoughts, he said, "Knowing how to raise a shield is not all there is to it. If your shield is too large, it consumes more energy than necessary. If it's too small - well, you saw what happened to your sword two days ago."

She swallowed an acerbic remark and remained silent when he went on, "Up to now it wasn't really necessary for you to be careful with how much of your strength you used. That is the disadvantage of being stronger than your training partners and even than your former teacher." He smiled grimly. "This will no longer be a problem. And I distinctly remember that I told you to take off your armour for now."

She hesitantly loosened the clasps and took off the leather breast protector under his waiting gaze. When she stood before him in her bright linen shirt, his eyes wandered down to her breasts and remained there. She looked down and saw her nipples stiff from the cold, pressed against the revealingly thin cloth. Hurriedly folding her arms across her chest she gave him an annoyed look that he acknowledged with a half-smile.

"Protect yourself," he said and launched a weak strike at her a moment later. Eryn staggered back a few steps and barely remained upright as it hit her right in the chest. She looked up and sent him a murderous look.

"It seems the next thing we need to work on is your reaction time," he commented without sympathy.

"Bastard," she muttered, barely audible in reply, and stood straight again, only this time a raised barrier shimmering in the air before her.

He started attacking it with a number of strikes, each a little stronger than its predecessor, but not powerful enough to break her shield.

"Everything alright so far?" he asked.

"Sure," she replied coolly. "I could do this all day long."

He smiled superciliously. "I doubt that very much."

After another two minutes of battering her protection, he stopped. "I can see the first signs of weariness in you. Let's try this again, this time reduce the size of your shield to fit your body more closely."

He watched as the area of shimmering air around her shrank. "More. Make it follow the outline of your body," he instructed. When she had reduced the size to his satisfaction he shot another salve of bolts at her.

"Do you see how the amount of strength necessary to maintain the shield has decreased?"

She had, but was reluctant to admit it. "Will it help me to stand against you?"

He raised his brows. "Obviously not. Otherwise it would have been rather foolish of me to show you."

"How does this help me then? All other magicians here are too weak to penetrate my shield, however much energy I expend on it."

Inwardly sighing, he began to explain patiently. "Maybe, but if several weaker magicians attacked you together, saving energy might be the one thing between standing up and lying on the floor after a while."

He then went to the bench and bent down to retrieve a small dark leather pouch to take out something thin and golden. She gasped when she recognised two slim bangles and immediately balled her hands into fists.

He saw her reaction and tried to placate her. "There is no need to be afraid."

She grunted. What an idiotic thing to say to her. "Really? Well, silly me. There was I, thinking for a moment that these are the bloody manacles meant to block my magical power. But obviously they are just jewellery to lend this celebratory occasion more elegance."

"They are just for demonstration purposes. I need to show you the level of your fighting skills without your being able to push your physical limits."

"You want me to fight you while I am blocked?" The incredulity in her voice was very close to panic.

"I will not use any magic, either."

She folded her arms. "Fine. Where are *your* manacles, then?"

"I don't need them. I can be trusted not to use magic."

"Ha! You can be trusted? Not from where I am standing. You put on those things, then I will follow your example."

He fought the urge to roll his eyes. "I see. So, what you are suggesting is that I block my own magic in your presence while yours stays intact. Did you have any real hope of my agreeing to that or are you just trying to be difficult?"

"I'm trying to be difficult," she snapped at him.

"I had a feeling that you were. Now, hold still and let me put them on you."

"You are joking!" She hastily put her arms behind her back and out of his reach.

He quickly stepped closer and his arms followed hers so that she found herself in something that felt dangerously close to an embrace.

Before she could think of moving away, she felt cool metal at her wrists and heard the quiet snap of clasps. A slight tingling sensation told her that he had just sealed the manacles.

When she expected him to step away again he remained close to her for another moment and said quietly into her ear, "I will remove them again when our training is finished for today, I promise."

Breathing was difficult when he was close, not being able to avoid smelling him and feeling the warmth his body gave off. She drew in a deep breath when he had stepped back again. She automatically tried to draw magic and felt the void, the terrible emptiness she remembered so well.

"I hate this," she whispered.

"I know. Magicians generally do. But there is something you need to understand. Your magic can be taken away from you for a time, quite easily as you can see. Yet you should still be able to defend yourself." He picked up his sword and motioned for her to draw the one at her hip.

She let her arms hang down in a relaxed manner and shot him a withering look.

He sighed at her determination to be uncooperative and lifted the tip of his sword to her throat. "Draw your weapon."

Her eyes narrowed at the blade pointing at her. Bullying only worked if the victim gave in.

"Try and make me," she spat at him. She was almost positive that he wouldn't hurt her. Much.

She didn't like the slow smile that spread on his face. "Alright."

She drew in a sharp breath when she felt the cold steel on her skin, moving downwards to the collar of her shirt before he sheathed his sword. Then he stepped close to her.

Staring straight ahead at his shoulder she forced herself not to retreat but stand her ground. There was a light tug on her shirt and then she heard the sound of fabric slowly being ripped apart.

When she looked down at the bottom seam of the shirt, she saw a perpendicular rip growing gradually between his fingers and already exposing her navel. She tried to peel away the linen from his hands, but her endeavour didn't even seem to slow him down. He just kept tearing the fabric, bit by bit. Her efforts became more frantic when the rip was on the verge of exposing her breasts.

"You know," he whispered into her ear, his warm breath sliding across her skin, "right now I really hope you won't draw that weapon…"

Cursing him silently, she quickly put her hand on the sword hilt at her hip and hastily slid it out of its sheath far enough to let him see that he had won. So much for her plan to stand up to him and withstand whatever means of persuasion he would use on her. She could have resisted pain to a certain degree, she was sure. But not him getting too close.

He stepped back, sighing disappointedly when she drew the weapon completely.

"What a pity. This time I would have enjoyed your defiance more than your cooperation."

She shot him a dark look, took a step back and lowered her sword. "I'm putting my armour back on if his Lordship has no objections."

He waved his hand in a generous and at the same time dismissive gesture. When she stood again sword at the ready, he drew his own and started demonstrating to her how inadequate a swordswoman she was without her powers, even after training with a master swordsman for several months.

When she stood panting, her palms resting on her knees, he looked down at her, not even breathing faster himself. "You are slow, you lack stamina and you fail to raise your cover in time."

"Thank you for your words of praise, kind Sir. It is an honour to be tortured by you," she gasped without looking up.

"You want praise? Then earn it. And most of our fellow magicians would consider it a great privilege to be trained by me."

She straightened slowly, stretching her tired limbs. "At least you don't suffer from undue modesty. I think I will go on being ungrateful for the unwanted privilege of your attention you bestow upon me so generously."

She turned around when she heard a quiet cough behind her and her face lit up. There, between the wooden door and the small stone bench stood Plia, holding a large breakfast tray in her small hands. The girl returned the smile shyly, casting nervous glances in Enric's direction.

Eryn stepped closer to the girl and took the heavy tray from her hands to put it on the bench. She remembered the image of the girl lying on the ground that had been conjured by Enric only two days ago and fought the urge to run her hands over Plia's limbs to make sure everything was alright with her. Even though she knew the vision had been no more than a trick, she felt relief and gratitude at seeing her up and well.

"How are you, little flower?" she asked the girl, taking her hands and looking her over. She looked neat and tidy in her new kitchen uniform, her cheeks rosy from the still fresh morning air. Eryn felt sweaty and dirty in contrast.

"I'm fine, thank you," she replied politely, clearly eager to act in accordance with her new position as servant.

Enric turned away and walked a few steps. The girl was obviously anything but relaxed in his presence and he wanted Eryn to enjoy the moment. This, however, did not stop him from following their conversation from a distance by redirecting airstreams that carried the sounds of their conversation towards him.

"I heard you fought Lord Enric and Lord Orrin when they made you think I was hurt and injured," Plia whispered. "I'm so sorry, I never wanted..."

"Stop. It was neither your doing nor your fault. They just used what they knew to be precious to me to manipulate me."

The girl's eyes were brimming with tears now. "And that's me?"

Eryn's heart broke a little at the thought of that pretty young girl who never had been given the feeling of being loved by anyone. She seemed to have a hard time really believing that somebody cared for her.

"Of course that's you. That conceited brute over there knew well enough what would work on me," she whispered while indicating Enric with her a nod of her head in his direction.

Plia clasped small hands in front of her mouth in a mixture of shock and dark delight at such disrespectful words in connection with the powerful lord. Her eyes fell on the gold glinting at Eryn' wrist.

"Oh," she said with big round eyes and a slightly pained expression, "you have your jewellery back on. They are stopping your magic again."

Her eyes followed Plia's and she snorted. "Yes. These things are not exactly a token of his appreciation."

"He just took away your magic again? And you let him?" The girl's shock and indignation and her conviction that she could have stopped him just like that felt good.

"He didn't ask me. And it's not as if resistance from my side makes much of a difference for him."

"Cook says you are strong and independent. And that it does Lord Enric good that you don't throw yourself at his feet like all these women without any self-respect. Or let yourself be ordered around like the other Order members.

She says he is so rough with you because he fancies you and is lonely and frustrated because he can't get you to go to bed with him again after the Freedom Night…"

Eryn clasped a hand over the girl's mouth. What? How did everybody know about this when she herself had learned about it only two days ago?

Eryn took a deep breath and looked around to make sure that Enric was still far enough away not to hear them.

"Why does Cook think I went to bed with him that night?" Eryn whispered, ill at ease about talking about this to a girl, but eager to find out how far the tidings had spread.

"Because he lifted his mask for a short time to scare away a man who wanted to dance with you. The man was the son of the man where Cook's nephew works."

And, of course, he had told his dear aunt and who knew how many other people all about it. Eryn let her head sink into her hands, covering her face.

"Cook also says that you would do good to take Lord Enric as your companion, because he is very powerful and can protect you from all the other idiots. And that his being very attractive should really make putting up with his bossy ways easier for you. Is everything alright?" Plia asked concernedly.

Eryn sighed and rubbed her face. "I think I need to have a word with your cook. Her plans for my future are not exactly what I want for myself, so I'd thank her for keeping her matchmaking plans to herself."

The girl's eyes widened in panic. "Oh no, please don't! She is so nice to me and I don't want her to think that I have been gossiping…"

Which was exactly what she had done, Eryn thought.

She heard steps behind her as Enric returned and joined them. He took her wrists into his hands and she felt the armlets fall away. Magic coursed through her body in a soothing wave and was welcomed like a long-lost friend. She exhaled in relief, making him smile. He knew the feeling well.

"How do you like your work here in the palace?" Plia froze in shock when Enric addressed her.

"Very well, My Lord," she replied timidly.

"You know, not everything they say about me is true."

"My Lord?" Eryn could hear the puzzlement in the girl's voice.

"I'm not that horrible."

"I know," the girl replied with a shy smile. "Cook told me about that one time when you were a boy and you stole a whole cake that was meant for a ball. She said she quickly made another one without telling on you and next day she found a new black cloak in her room with a note of apology." She looked up at Eryn, who stared at him in surprise.

"What?" he chuckled. "Surprised that I have some human traits after all?"

From Plia's expression, Eryn guessed that seeing Enric laugh was not something people were generally used to.

"Plainly speaking – yes. My guess was that you were born an arrogant bastard."

Plia drew in a sharp breath. Even after hearing Eryn call him a Lordling when everybody could hear her, it was still a shock to her how anybody dared to speak that way to a man as imposing and frightening as Lord Enric. Eryn had to be the most courageous person in the world.

She curtsied quickly. "I must return to the kitchen. Enjoy your breakfast, Eryn. Lord Enric." A moment later she was gone.

Eryn rubbed her wrists as if she could still feel a distant echo of the manacles. "So are we finished for today?"

"Almost. There is one more thing you must endure: breakfast with me."

He selected a bread roll and poured himself a cup of the sweet, strong brew city people seemed to prefer. Sugar was used a lot more generously here than in her little town.

He sat down on the stone bench, shifting the tray so that there was space for Eryn to sit as well without being too close to him. She did so carefully. The chance to talk to Plia had mellowed her enough to indulge him, even if what she had heard from the girl didn't exactly contribute to her peace of mind.

"So," Enric said into her thoughts, "Cook thinks I am attractive. Funny, she always treated me like something that has crawled in from a back-alley."

Eryn almost chocked on the piece of bread she was chewing.

"How could you possibly have heard that?" she exclaimed, looking back to the place where he had stood all the time while she had been talking to Plia. She thought of what else they had been talking about and felt her stomach churning in embarrassment.

"Just one of a few useful skills I have acquired over the years," he said lightly and shrugged.

"Eavesdropping from faraway distances is a skill you picked up on the way?"

"Yes. And a very useful one, too. Especially as not many of us know how to do it."

"How many?" she enquired suspiciously.

"I can't say for sure. I have my suspicions, but let's say it probably pays to have some conversations in really private places."

She looked around at the high walls, wondering how many of her seemingly private conversations had already been overheard. "Would this qualify as a private place?"

He looked at her and suppressed a smile. "Are you trying to make me reveal how it's done?"

"What? No! Surely not." She was all innocence, apparently appalled by his suspicions.

"What about you? Do you share Cook's excellent taste in men? Do *you* think I'm attractive? My being a conceited brute doesn't diminish my looks, I hope."

He immensely enjoyed her obvious discomfort at hearing the unflattering words she had used to refer to him repeated.

She avoided his amused gaze. "No, I really don't. Attraction is more to me than a matter of appearance - it is very closely connected with someone's character."

"I see. So you *do* find me good-looking," he grinned.

"That's not what I said! But of course it's what you would choose to hear. What else could a woman say about the all-powerful prince of magic, the glorious second in command of the magnificent Order?"

He laughed quietly. "I like that description better than your last one. Maybe I will have it engraved on a sign to put it up on my door. You need to think of another one for Tyront or his feelings will be hurt."

"I doubt that very much."

"Why? He has a great sense of humour."

"Does he now? I just remember his great voice for yelling."

Enric looked blank for a moment, then he nodded once, remembering. "Ah yes, the little matter of your removing your shield when you had fifteen magicians plus myself shooting bolts at you. Yes, that really got to him, but mostly because he wasn't prepared for it. He takes great pride in his abilities when it comes to judging people. And his error in judgement almost cost you your life."

"But oh, wasn't there valiant Lord Enric around to save the day? I imagine he was very pleased with you."

His expression had grown irate at her words. "I was so angry I could have bound you in gold for the rest of your life. You were lucky I decided to hold back to let Tyront rant instead. What drove you to do a thing like that?"

She looked at him directly. "A very distinct aversion to being abducted, kept prisoner and used for what seemed like target practice. This might be news for a passionate warrior like yourself, but we non-combatants without nerves of steel tend to feel a touch desperate in situations like that. At that time the option of not being your plaything but ending it quickly was the more appealing one," she said tartly.

And her fear had hampered her ability to think clearly just enough to be actually willing to give her life for a mere demonstration of defiance. In hindsight that had been immensely stupid. But at that time she had been counting on them to either enslave her, torture her or lock her up. Her confinement had then turned out to be completely different from what she had expected. But that was none of his business.

Then she narrowed her eyes. "What gave you the idea to raise a shield in front of me, anyway?"

"You looked grim, as if you had made a decision. I just had to think about the most stupid thing that a person in your situation could do and prepare for it. And alas, you complied beautifully," he growled. "When you plan your next act of rebellion, make sure you have a chance of surviving it. At least if I'm not around to protect you from yourself."

She ground her teeth and stood up stiffly. "I assume our training session is finished?"

"Yes, for today. Same time and place in two days. You are done eating already? You have hardly touched a thing."

"Somehow my appetite has gone. I couldn't say why."

"Make sure you eat enough. You will need your strength for the training."

"A neat transition from saviour through prison guard to father."

He looked at her thoughtfully. "I wonder if one day we will manage to have a peaceable conversation between us."

"Possibly. It will probably be the day you set me free," she replied curtly and left the garden.

CHAPTER 24

Escape

She felt her stomach rumble. It was past lunchtime and she had not eaten anything since the few bites in the morning after the training with Enric.

She had spent another two hours trying to figure out how to manipulate airstreams effectively to divert streaks of magic. And had failed abominably time and again. She looked at herself in the small mirror on the wall and saw her frustrated expression and the tousled hair reflected. Suddenly, disgusted by her own appearance, she shot a bolt of energy at the mirror intending to smash it into pieces and take scant comfort in destroying something other than her own patience.

She had to duck down quickly when the streak of energy was sent back towards her. The mirror was not, as she'd expected, a sorry heap of shards, but little more than cracked in several places. Staring at it, she slowly traced her fingers along the cracks. How interesting, how very interesting. So mirrors could be used to reflect magical attacks. Not completely, obviously, or the glass would not have been damaged at all, but a good part of it had been returned to her.

If she used the mirror to shoot weak bolts towards herself instead of away from her, this might be the edge she needed. The streaks needed to be calibrated carefully. If they were too strong she would not only destroy the mirror very quickly but also harm herself. Shielding, striking and diverting air at the same time needed a little too much effort.

The first try almost ended in setting her already ripped shirt on fire, but the second attempt showed the first signs of success. She had not managed to divert it as far as she would have wished, but for the first time after countless strikes she had deflected its path slightly. New energy coursed through her and she increased her control over the bolt's trajectory a little more with each try.

When she finally managed to divert four out of five bolts successfully, she sat down and rubbed her face. The light in the room had grown dim and it would soon be getting too dark to continue. A candle was definitely too dangerous for her kind of pastime.

She guessed that there was still half an hour of good light left and decided to go for the next challenge: splitting the bolt while diverting it.

That turned out to be easier than anticipated after her many hours of experimenting with air currents. It was no more than a matter of adding another air stream to the one the bolt was already riding on and then dividing them into a curve that arced away from her shortly before impact.

She fell down on her bed, grateful for the day's success and hardly able to keep herself awake long enough to pull off her boots. Amazing, she thought, already dropping off to sleep, how powerful magic was influenced so easily by something as plain as air.

Her dreams were confusing and unfocussed and she once jolted out of sleep some time at night after dreaming about a world without air where no magic was possible and people had to wear bubbles around their heads to survive.

* * *

She still had breakfast with the warriors, even though she no longer trained with them. Her head rested on her palm, too heavy to remain upright without help. The other palm covered her mouth through more yawns than she could count.

"You look like you've had a long night. Or rather a short one," Orrin's voice came from behind her. He held a bowl of porridge and a piece of bread in one hand and sat down next to her.

"What?" Her eyes focused on his far too wakeful and alert features. "Not really. I have slept long enough, but not very peacefully."

His face radiated sympathy. "The training with him has not been very pleasant, then?"

She blinked. Well, if that wasn't a convenient explanation... The second one in as many days. "Well, I hardly expected it to be," she sighed and had to admit that she had in fact pictured it worse than it had actually been, even if he had shackled her for a time.

"No training sessions today, I assume?"

"No, he wants to continue them tomorrow." She played with her bread and then looked up into his face. "You know that I would have killed you that day, don't you?"

He nodded gravely. "Yes, I know. But I don't blame you for it. At least not too much," he amended. "He employed a very powerful image to incite you."

She nodded slowly. Yes, that was true. And yet she felt foolish and embarrassed for falling for the incitement. Looking back, it had been inept and absurd and she should have been able to see right through the illusion. Orrin wouldn't have been protecting a man who had hurt a child. And neither would he ever have attacked to kill in a situation like that.

Her first impulse was to ask Orrin for forgiveness not only for the killing blow she had been about to deliver, but also for misjudging him so completely. Yet considering the circumstances of his tricking her, apologising to him felt wrong somehow. He had participated in the Lordling's scheme, no matter if he had been under orders or not. And he was with the Order, which acted more or less as her prison warder as long as the King thought that keeping her in the city was a good idea.

She looked back at him. He, too, regarded her thoughtfully.

"I am not going to apologise for how I acted," he stated defensively.

Eryn blinked, then gave a weak smile. It seemed he was dealing with similar guilt issues and was feeling bad about tricking her.

"Very well. That makes two of us."

A faint smile played around his mouth when he nodded once to tacitly acknowledge that neither of them would apologise but each was aware that such a thing would be justified.

"If he had intervened only a moment later..." She shook her head. "Do you really trust him that unconditionally? Had he been only a moment late or unfocused or distracted, I really would have killed you."

"Very true. But if you are in the Order you need to be able to rely on your fellow warriors. If he had let me die in a situation like that, he wouldn't have been a reliable ally in war, either."

She sighed. One probably had to be a man to really understand that line of thinking.

"If it is any consolation I would have found a way to make him suffer for it one day if he had allowed me to kill you," she said quietly.

He smiled and took her hand in his. "You know something, that does console me." He looked over at a table of young warriors. "I need to leave you now. My class is about to start and if I don't come in time these young fellows tend to disappear into thin air and claim there was no trace of me."

He got up and squeezed her shoulder as he left. He didn't wait to see the expression on her face.

Disappear into thin air... She felt how a strange thrill ran through her body. She slowly put down her spoon and forced her brain to keep up. There was something, only a thought away, just out of reach. Something important, disappearing into thin air.

She sucked in air deeply. Yes, there it was. From a mix of images from her dreams and Orrin's words one thought emerged: Where there was air, magic could exist. Where there was none, it would simply disappear into the ether, into nothing. Rising slowly and calmly making her way back to her room, her thoughts raced: no air. Was it possible?

She closed her door quietly and leaned against it to collect her thoughts. Could magic contain air? Or would it just drift through a magical field? How could she find out? Her eyes fell on a half-burned candle and she stared at it for a while before she could muster the courage to try the idea that had formed in her head. It had to work, it simply had to.

She lit the candle and built a small but strong circular force field around the wick after blowing it out again. Curls of smoke floated around inside the shimmering shield, restricted by the barrier around them.

She let go of the breath she had been holding and a smile grew slowly on her lips. The smoke couldn't leave the field. It was contained, captured. She watched the curls diffuse into an even light grey haze before she dropped the shield again.

So it was possible to lock air inside a magical field. Then it had to be possible to lock it *outside* as well. The challenge was now to create a barrier with no air inside. It would have to be a growing barrier, one that was so small to begin with that there was hardly any space for air inside it. After several tries she had managed to create a barely visible speck of shimmering light and fed it with more and more energy. When the globe had reached the size of her head she stopped and let it float in the air. It didn't look any different, she mused. But it had taken more power than usual to create it.

She stepped away and shot a bolt right through the hovering ball. It passed the front of the ball and then vanished completely. Eryn stared at where the streak had disappeared and fell to her knees.

That was it – her chance to get out of here! These were two shots which could make all the difference – two shots she could counter without him being prepared for it! This was the ultimate defence against stronger magicians. She almost burst out laughing when she imagined the Lordling's face.

She forced herself to breathe slowly and evenly. It wouldn't do to rush things now. She had managed to achieve it with a small globe, but that wouldn't be enough to keep herself safe. Very likely she would have to face several attackers and would therefore need a large shield to protect her from as many sides as possible. Or, she mused, looking out of the window at the inner portal embedded in the city wall, a very large one that sealed the opening of an entire gateway.

She spent the rest of the morning altering size and form of the shield, until she had managed to create a large, flat, double barrier containing no air inside it. Creating such a barrier demanded a lot from her. As she experimented, she saw how reducing the energy of the shield and thus leaving a little air inside decreased the effectiveness when it came to stopping bolts. Then she switched to varying the diameter of the barriers – would a thinner airtight layer be enough? Would it save more energy to create two thin layers instead of a thicker one? Were they equally effective?

She discovered a great many things that afternoon: For strong bolts it was better to have a really air*tight* layer ready, while weaker bolts would also disappear in an air-reduced barrier. One thicker layer required less energy than two slimmer ones. The barriers could at the same time be weaker; they needed to be flexible enough to let a bolt pass through the outside of the barrier without disrupting it, or air would get in and render it useless. There would then be no more than an ordinary barrier left that could easily be penetrated by an opponent superior in strength. The strength of the barrier had to be exactly right to achieve a balance that allowed both their being airtight and having enough flexibility to let a bolt pass into the air-free space where it would dissolve.

That evening she forced herself to wash quickly before she fell into bed. Two successive days of using up nearly all her energy couldn't be healthy. She needed one day of rest to replenish her reserves before she could carry out her plan. Even if she fired hardly any bolts herself and used her newly mastered splitting-method, she would definitely need a lot of magic to keep the shield in place *and* protect herself from the non-magician guards at the gates.

Should she try to steal a horse? She yawned and decided against it. It would be hard enough to do this without drawing attention to herself prematurely, a horse would probably give her away too soon. And she just needed enough of a head start to reach the nearby woods. There, they would find it very hard to track her down.

* * *

This time Enric was the one waiting for her. He frowned visibly as Eryn approached, sluggishly fastening her armour at her side and hardly managing not to yawn every few steps. Her eyes were half closed and bloodshot and she looked pale.

"What have you been doing? You look terrible, like you haven't slept in days," he commented and wondered if she was even able to hold a sword, not to mention use it.

"Right, and a very good morning to yourself," she managed between yawns.

"Now really, what have you been doing?" he insisted.

"None of your business," she replied with no real force to it.

"Of course it's my business. I can hardly train you effectively if I need to worry about your tripping over your own weapon and slicing off parts of yourself."

She giggled lightheadedly. "I can promise you seriously to try to avoid that, if that makes you happy."

"You haven't been drinking, have you?" He stepped closer and tried to discern any tell-tale smells.

"If I have, it was way too much, because I don't remember any of it."

He considered her thoughtfully. "What am I going to do with you, Eryn? You seem in no shape to fight. Or to concentrate on anything for that matter."

She stifled another yawn. "Then you should probably send me off to bed and tell me to meet you tomorrow morning instead." When she hoped to be already gone from here.

"Yes, it seems I don't have much choice here, do I?"

"I'm so sorry."

"Now, if that had sounded halfway sincere, you might have got away with it. But we don't want to set any precedents here."

"We don't?" she replied flatly.

He shook his head. "No. You will instead spend your morning cleaning rooms. I'm sure the maids will be thrilled to get some extra help. It might teach you modesty if not fighting."

"As if you need to teach modesty to somebody who has spent several months in that poor excuse of a room you put me in."

He just lifted an eyebrow.

"Alright then. Let's get it over with. Which rooms will I be cleaning?"

"Mine, of course."

He smiled at her groan of displeasure.

More than three hours later she dragged herself back to the warriors' quarters. He had been true to his word and had let her clean his quarters. Not all of them, obviously, but enough to exhaust her even further – a feat she hadn't thought possible. He had been standing behind her, instructing her, checking the results and had enjoyed his role of taskmaster far too much for her liking.

Back in her room she literally fell on her bed and was asleep almost before her head had touched the pillow. She didn't even bother with her boots this time.

* * *

"Something is not right," Enric announced when he entered Tyront's study unannounced and without knocking.

Tyront looked up from the papers he was reading, but didn't comment on the lack of manners. People did not normally interrupt him like that, not even Enric. So it was without a doubt important.

"What's the matter?" he simply asked.

"She was completely exhausted today. I suspect she had no more magic left in her than your parlour maid."

"Interesting. From what I hear she has spent the last days since your, er, encounter in her room. Alone."

"When I was in her room the other day there were quite a number of black spots on the walls."

"Strike impacts, I assume?"

"Yes. She must have thrown quite some magic against the walls. I talked to Orrin. He said when he saw her yesterday during breakfast she could hardly keep her eyes open. That's two days in a row where she must have used up most of her power."

"Could she have been practising something you have taught her?"

Enric snorted. "Not very likely. Orrin said she has never shown any interest in her training, she just manages to keep an upper hand in fights by profiting from her superior powers. I can confirm that fairly well. The idea that she might have been practising her fighting skills voluntarily seems more than strange. And then I am not teaching her magical fighting presently."

Tyront leaned back and considered. "Is it possible that she is planning to flee and is preparing for that somehow?"

"She hasn't made any attempts in these last months. Why would she try now?"

"Has anything happened between the two of you?"

Enric lifted his eyebrows. "Why don't *you* tell me?"

"Because the location you chose for your first training lesson was rather remote and there was no way to find out what you did with her in your quarters this morning," Tyront admitted unabashedly.

"There was nothing particular. During the training I shackled her in gold for a short while, but that is standard procedure for trainings. She was not too happy about it, but didn't seem too disturbed by it, either. And today… she was too exhausted to do any fighting so I made her clean my quarters."

Tyront's brows shot up and his eyes seemed to bulge in astonishment. "You did what?"

"I could hardly allow her to use a weapon in her state. But I didn't want her to think that this was a good way of avoiding training sessions, so I made her do something a little unpleasant instead."

"And she did it?"

"Yes. Amazingly enough, she didn't even put up her usual resistance. That alone is disturbing."

"I see," Tyront mused. "So, what do you propose?"

Enric raked his fingers through his hair. "I'm not sure. How many pairs of eyes do you have on her right now?"

"One. I'll make that two for the next time."

"If she tries anything I would imagine she will do it at night. Not so many of us around, even though the gates are guarded more heavily."

"I agree. For the present we can't do much more than wait and see."

* * *

When she next opened her eyes the sun was about to sink. She got to her feet quickly; there were still a few things to prepare before she could commence on the dangerous part of her plan. She took the few things she had in her possession and wrapped them in a small bundle. She really needed to eat sufficiently tonight. Not huge quantities that would slow her down, but enough to be able to bear some time without food. Who knew when her next chance to eat would present itself.

She thought about Vern and gulped. She had avoided him for the past week since she had been planning her departure. The temptation to go and see him to say goodbye was great, but she knew this was not an option. They would very likely find out about it and punish him for being aware of her escape plans in advance. It would be easier for both of them that way.

Her eyes fell on the cracked mirror. What a pity that she couldn't use it for emergencies to reflect unexpected bolts. She frowned. Or could she? Magic strikes were normally directed at the chest as this was most effective. If she covered hers with pieces of mirror that might be one more attack she could withstand. However, this mirror was rather small. But she had sufficient funds in her savings box to buy several of them.

She would buy needle and thread to mend the tunic Enric had ripped and then sew on the pieces of broken mirror.

* * *

"What do you mean, there are no more than two gold pieces in my box? This is quite impossible! There must be about seventy at least!" She stared at the bald man in horror.

He shook his head. "No, I'm afraid this is all there is."

Lifting the box and opening the lid for her he let her look at the two coins rolling around the emptiness. The bottom of the chest should not even have been visible for all the gold that she had expected to be in there.

"You either give me my money back right now," she threatened with a raised finger, "or I will spread the word that you are no more than a damned thief unworthy of anyone's trust. That wouldn't be good for your business, would it?"

"Look, I didn't take your money!" The clerk gestured desperately with both hands.

"Then it must have dissolved or been eaten by vermin, I suppose," she hissed. "You better give me back my money or I will forget that I am someone who never uses magic to hurt people!" Her narrowed eyes all but shot bolts of fire towards him.

He took an involuntary step back and raised his hands before him. "No, I swear - I don't have your money! It was taken away to the palace!"

She exhaled and closed her eyes. Stupid! she scolded herself. This should not have come as such a surprise to her. Of course they had not only heard about her healing activities but also that she had been taking money for it. And the conclusion to look in the one place half the city stored its money did not require anything but connected thinking.

"Then give me the two coins that are still in there," she ordered sharply.

He complied hastily and she strode with a grim expression back to the warriors' quarters.

Then she needed to get the mirror from somewhere else. Two gold pieces were not enough to purchase one - they were rather expensive luxuries.

Would they give her another one if she asked because she had accidentally broken hers? Well, it had been an accident, hadn't it? She had intended to smash it, after all.

* * *

"She has asked for a new mirror. And sewing equipment for mending a tunic that she claims you have ripped." Tyront looked up from the written report. "Have you? Really now, what have you been doing to her?"

Enric cast his eyes up at the ceiling, avoiding his superior's gaze. "I ripped open her tunic when she refused to draw her weapon." Somehow, it didn't sound especially convincing when said like that.

The older man exhaled slowly. "Aren't you supposed to present us in a more favourable light so she will consider joining us, instead of harassing her?"

"I didn't harass her. Well, not very much. She drew her sword before it got interesting." He paused. "I wonder why she wants to mend the shirt herself. There are servants to do it for her."

"Maybe she has a liking for needlework. I will have the items sent to her unless you have any objections? They seem harmless enough."

"Sure, do that. I don't see what devious things she could do with them."

* * *

She had not only eaten well but also managed to take an extra loaf of bread with her. It went straight into the bundle. The small fragments of the mirror she had broken and partly sewn onto the crudely repaired tunic reflected the light of the half-burned candle in front of her, giving a mosaic pattern on one wall. Only a few more, then she was finished.

When she had cut the thread and looked at her creation, she decided that she needed to wear another shirt on top of it to avoid reflecting the torch light outside.

She knotted the bundle with a piece of rope and fastened it around her waist like a belt so as to keep her hands free. Then she blew out the candle and gave her eyes time to adapt to the darkness. It had to be started around midnight, she decided.

Slowly she felt her way to the door when silhouettes first began to take shape around her. The wooden door creaked only slightly as she opened it carefully and then she stepped into the hallway, listening for any sounds of activity. When everything was quiet, she closed the door behind her and followed the corridor towards the exit of the building.

When she opened the entrance door a crack, the only light she saw came from the starlit night sky above. Nobody seemed to be around; the court was empty and seemed oddly deserted. Slowly pulling the heavy door shut after her, she continued to let her eyes wander and decided on the safest route towards the gate that was sited furthest away from the palace. When they found her out, she wanted the powerful lords to arrive as late in the process as possible.

Moving silently in shadows, taking back-alleys and ducking behind carts, it took her almost an hour to get to the western gate. She found a hidden spot and observed the guards. She knew there to be four men on guard duty here - two at the inner gate, two at the outer one a few paces beyond.

The pair she could view from her hiding place looked bored and weary. Good!

Getting close enough to them to overwhelm the first two without being noticed wouldn't work. Their comrades on the outer gate would hear the commotion. Magical strikes were not a silent means of attack, especially when there were no other sounds around to provide a handy masking background. She moved closer, taking great care to remain in the shadows at all times. There were two torches affixed to the wall, one on each side of the gate. She would extinguish them as soon as the guards were down.

Taking a deep breath, she aimed the flats of her palms each at one guard and let loose a pair of strikes powerful enough to knock them out for several hours. The noise of the two trails of energy hissing through the air seemed so much louder in the dead of night and she half expected the men to dive out of their path in time. But instead, they froze in shock at the sight of the bolts, doubled over when each hit, then fell quietly to the ground. Convenient. She expected the second pair of guards to rush forward to find out what had happened and lifted her hands to unleash another brace of bolts as soon as they were visible.

Nothing happened for some long seconds, then she heard the loud clear sound of a horn sounding an alarm. Cursing under her breath, she started running towards the gate, already hearing footsteps quite some distance behind her. What was this? How could they be so fast?

She had almost reached the gate and now saw the remaining guards hiding in an alcove. Two quick bolts took care of them before she turned around and gasped. Enric, Tyront and two other magicians were running towards her, stopping when they were close enough to aim. Enric barked a command and then a blue strike cut through the night air towards her.

She took a deep breath, concentrated hard and changed the direction of the airstreams underneath the bolt, splitting in two and making both of them curve away from her in wide semi-circles. She saw Enric's lips press into a thin line and his look of worry deepen. She had troubled him. That, at least, was good.

Stepping between the two gates, she quickly raised a double barrier large enough to cover the opening between her and the magicians. Only moments after she was done she saw the first bolts being swallowed by it, disappearing completely without doing any damage. A surge of triumph rushed through her body, and she allowed herself a small smile at the magicians who were staring at her open-mouthed in disbelief.

Tyront raised both his palms to send twin blasts of highly concentrated energy at her barrier. She froze in apprehension, not knowing if the protective field could take that much. This was the final test. If it withstood the intense attack from the most powerful magician in the kingdom, the barrier truly was unbreakable.

The airtight space took care of it, and her fears collapsed like the last fritters of blue light. Now she could see outright panic on all four faces. Tyront and Enric had entered into a frantic discussion while the other two warriors kept firing what were useless strikes at her.

She whirled around to the last obstacle between herself and freedom: the outer gate. Unfortunately, she had not had any opportunity to study it before now. It looked sturdy enough; it would take quite a powerful strike to break down that door. She would very likely not have enough power left to maintain the barrier behind her, so that was not really an option now. Her eyes fell on the huge metal hinges and she dismissed the idea of breaking the gate down completely.

She spied the stairs that led to the top of the outer wall. Checking the angle, she decided that she would still be protected by the inner wall from her pursuer's bolts if she dared to climb. She would have to find a way down from there without getting hurt. Or at least not getting hurt badly so that she could heal herself quickly and run.

When she was halfway up the stairs she heard an explosion and saw part of the inner stone wall collapse and reveal Tyront and Enric with their raised hands aimed at the destruction. Before she had a chance to build another double barrier in front of her she saw Enric loosing another bolt at her. There was not enough time for the special shield, she was not able to build it quickly enough yet. So she would have to split it again.

Concentrating on the approaching ball of energy she redirected two air currents and knocked a bolt off course. She had only a moment in her panic as another one hit her hard in the chest and made her stagger backwards against the outer wall, almost losing her footing on the stairs. The mirror shards deflected the greater part of the magic, which would have knocked her out otherwise.

Why hadn't it worked this time?

Looking down, she saw the front of her second tunic that she wore on top burned away to reveal the pieces of mirror that were now broken into even smaller parts with some of them having fallen away completely. They wouldn't protect her from another attack. This had been the last one of her surprises, and now she was defenceless.

The magicians were hastily climbing the heap of rubble in front of the hole and she attempted to turn around and dash up the remaining stairs when another strike hit her, dislodging the remaining shards from her tunic that had still protected her enough not to lose consciousness but instead caused her to feel dizzy and disoriented. Enric caught her before she could fall down the stairs and held her while Tyront was the one to send her off to sleep this time.

Enric lifted her up into his arms as her knees buckled under her. Tyront took out the golden manacles from the inside pocket of his robe and fastened them around her limp wrists.

Then he turned around to one of the magicians and said grimly, "Wake the King. We have a problem."

CHAPTER 25

The Offer

The first signs of dawn were visible on the horizon when the two magicians returned to Enric's quarters. He had left Eryn lying on his bed, guarded by two strong magicians. She was unconscious and shackled in gold, but after tonight he wanted to avoid even the slightest risk. Dismissing both men with a nod, he strode into his bedroom, closely followed by Tyront.

She lay there exactly as he had put her down several hours ago, her head still inclined to one side, one arm across her abdomen, the other one angled away from her body. More than half of her brown and now dusty hair had escaped the knot into which she had tied it.

Both men stared down at her. Then Enric sighed and bent down to take off her boots.

"You know," he said, "we have to act quickly now. We were no more than lucky that she didn't get away completely. The King will keep her in manacles and lock her in a dungeon cell if she doesn't join us soon. He will hardly want to risk another escape attempt."

Tyront nodded. "He is worried. And he should be. But not stupid enough to agree to Loft's suggestion of executing her now while she is helpless." He shook his head. "What a mess this all is."

"Should *we* be scared as well? However did she manage that? Is she stronger than we thought? Has she managed to delude us all these months?"

"No, I don't think so. I think she is as strong as we assumed and we saw the impressive result of two days of her experimentation in solitude."

"She taught herself how to redirect bolts after she saw it done only once before. I have no idea whether to be proud or seriously troubled by that." Enric sat down on the bed next to Eryn and brushed few strands of hair out of her now peaceful face. "And that barrier of hers..." He whistled through his teeth. "I have never seen anything like it. Has she discovered that, too, only in these last few days? She wasn't even able to willingly raise a simple force field when we first took her here about half a year back."

"It is the ultimate defence against a stronger opponent. Nothing we want our prisoner to be able to use against us," Tyront mused. "And then there is the matter of using mirrors to reflect magical attacks. Underestimating her inventiveness was clearly a mistake. But then who could have foreseen that she would figure out a thing like that?"

"We even sent her the items to put the shirt together." Enric laughed quietly. "And she discovered all this even though she has nothing but contempt for the discipline of fighting."

"With the basic training of a country healer," the older man added, deep in thought. "What an immense potential. Imagine what else she could do."

"Well," Enric retorted, "she might not have discovered those things had she not tried to get away from here. That was very probably the motivation behind her feats."

"So you are saying she will sink into sloth if we don't keep her as our captive? I doubt that very much. We need to resolve this situation. Maybe it was just as well that she has forced our hand. She will find a way to leave sooner or later if we coerce instead of convince her to stay here. We need to avoid that likelihood." He laid a hand on the younger man's shoulder. "Come. Let's work on an offer we can make to her when she awakens. Something that won't drive the Council or the King to desperation, if possible."

* * *

The King frowned, his bright, grey-blue eyes calculating when he lowered the piece of paper Tyront had handed him. He passed it on to Marrin who held it low enough for Loft to read as well.

"So now we are rewarding her for her disobedience?" Loft huffed angrily.

"Technically, she was not disobedient," Tyront observed patiently. "First, she was not born in this country and is thus not really one of his majesty's subjects and second, she is being held captive. We can't really fault her for trying to escape."

Marrin cleared his throat. "Be that as it may, this offer of joining the Order is not in complete accordance with your rules, is it?"

"We have been extraordinarily careful not to violate the regulations of the Order. The offer meets them, strictly speaking, by making the minimum requirements - such as honing fighting skills - obligatory. We have, however, added a few terms suited to this situation without contradicting the rules, such that the Order and subsequently the kingdom may benefit from her abilities as much as possible," Enric replied smoothly.

"Indeed," Marrin commented wryly, "and, of course, this has nothing to do with making it hard for her to refuse you. It's all purely for the Order's benefit."

"We aim to make being in the Order an arrangement with benefits to both the organisation *and* the members," Enric replied with a smile.

Marrin rolled his eyes. "Dear me, we really have turned you into one of us. When have you found your diplomatic side now?"

Enric didn't comment on that uncharacteristically prickly remark and simply smiled. Marrin hardly ever showed anything but serenity, but today was one of these rare occasions when he demonstrated a modicum of humour.

"What if she doesn't accept the offer?" Loft asked. "What do you propose we do with her?"

"We would have to keep her magic blocked," Tyront replied. "At least for the time being. I recommend we do that anyway as long as she hasn't taken the oath."

"So you really are afraid of her," Loft commented, hardly able to hide his delight.

"*Afraid* is not the right term. Let us say we are reluctant to risk losing her and have developed a healthy respect for her abilities. Very impressive abilities, as she has demonstrated tonight. And I suspect that is only the beginning of what she can do."

"The primary purpose of the Order is defending the kingdom. You are our most important line of defence. I don't think it is a wise move to concentrate on other matters too much," Loft said dismissively.

"She has proven that even non-combative tactics and methods can be used in defence most effectively. I would think it rather unwise to dismiss all the opportunities her knowledge as well as her talent would open up," Enric countered. This remark earned a hardly discernible nod of approval from Tyront.

Marrin pursed his lips. "Will you be able to control her, Lord Tyront? For the first time in centuries it seems that strength alone doesn't seem to be enough to prevail over weaker magicians. This might change the nature of the command structure in the Order."

Tyront met his gaze steadily. "That is possible, of course. But I like to think that magical strength alone is not what keeps the leaders at the top of the Order. After all, we still have the Magic Council that consists of men who have distinguished themselves outside the field of magic by being level-headed, reliable and intelligent regardless of their powers. And when she has joined the Order I hope we will learn everything about her extraordinary discoveries."

Marrin smirked. "If she really shares the secret of this barrier of hers with you, watching warrior training sessions will certainly be enlivened in the future." He turned to the King. "Your Majesty, my recommendation would be to let the Order make the offer before you. All Council members have agreed and signed it."

Loft's face fell. "This will be an enormous mistake! Your Majesty, she is too dangerous! Even though she is weaker in powers than Lords Tyront and Enric, they were barely able to retard her last night. You have seen what measures we had to take to stop her – it will take weeks to repair the damage to the inner wall! What would hold her back from taking control of the Order once she has been admitted? She might even try to usurp the throne!"

Four pairs of eyes rested doubtfully on Loft.

"I would like to point out here," Enric explained carefully, "that she has used her considerable advantage last night not to attack the palace but to try and free herself from captivity. She has not killed anyone in the process or resorted to any violence other than stunning four guards. From our conversations with her we have gained the impression that her main interest consists in employing magic in a non-aggressive way to help people."

The King lifted his hand to stop the discussion. "Make the offer. Bring her here when she has woken. I would like her to see that the King supports it. And, of course, I am very interested in seeing how she will react."

* * *

Eryn woke with a slight headache and a gritty feeling on her skin whenever she moved. The bed was unusually comfortable and when she opened her eyes, she instantly recognised Enric's bedroom. After all, she had spent over one hour cleaning it the other day.

The room was empty but for her and she looked down and was relieved to find herself wearing the clothes she had donned before trying to leave the city.

Sitting up slowly she discovered a glass of water on the bedside table and gulped it down gratefully. Only then, and without much surprise, did she notice the bangles encircling her wrists.

The room was dimly lit by a sparse daylight that passed through the window. Was this dusk or dawn? She set her feet upon the soft carpet, wondering what they had done with her boots. Walking to the bedroom door that led to the parlour she listened for any sounds of activity. Nothing.

The door opened noiselessly and she saw Enric fully dressed in black on a settee, book in his hand. He looked up and put his book aside, looking her over.

Without a comment, he got up from his seat, walked to the entrance door, opened it briefly and gave what sounded like a short command.

"Welcome back among the living. A bath is prepared for you, and then we will have breakfast," he said.

Breakfast? So it was morning. The situation seemed oddly absurd. After all that had happened he wanted to sit down and have breakfast with her?

She cleared her throat. "I would have expected to wake up in a dungeon cell. Why am I in your quarters?"

"Because we decided that you should from now on be under constant surveillance from a magician more powerful than yourself. Although you have challenged our perception of power yesterday night," he added dryly. "Tyront lives in a companionship, so your staying with him was not an option. That leaves me. Not that I mind," he said.

He motioned to another door next to his bedroom that turned out to be a wash room with a metal tub at one end, filled with water. Next to it was a small square table, marble-topped, upon which towels, clean clothes, soap and a hairbrush were piled. Enric walked in first and dipped the tips of his fingers into the water. Seconds later it started to steam.

"Go on. I will wait outside for you." He closed the door behind him, leaving her alone.

She quickly stripped and let herself sink into the water, which, although slightly too warm, eased her skin of its uncomfortable sensation.

* * *

When she was clean and clothed in the pants and tunic made of a soft dark green fabric, she brushed her wet hair and went back outside where Enric was waiting, seated exactly as before. He rose when she appeared and indicated a larger wooden table in front of the window where quite an opulent breakfast had been prepared.

When she hesitated he took her arm and led her to a chair.

"You said *yesterday* night, didn't you?"

"Yes. You slept for quite some time. No wonder, after these last few days."

No anger in his voice, she noted. She hesitated only briefly before she started eating. It had been about one and half days ago since she had last eaten, and she was ravenous.

"Why are you so relaxed?" Eryn enquired, having decided to take the direct route.

"Well, as you are wearing gold, you are no imminent danger to us," he smirked.

"What? No, that's not what I meant."

"I know what you meant. You are wondering why this massive act of resistance made us bestow increased hospitality on you when minor acts earned you punishment."

"Yes, something along those lines."

"Let's say you have opened our eyes to your situation and we are now rather anxious to find a solution to the impasse. Now, we depend on your cooperation for that - at least, if we want to achieve a solution that both sides can live with."

She raised her eyebrows in genuine astonishment before it dawned on her and she smiled broadly. "Oh, I see. You are eager to learn how that little barrier I created works. And you are aware that I am not very likely to share that with you as long as I am a captive."

He smiled back. "Yes, that's one thing. And we are very eager to see what else you can come up with. I was more than a bit surprised that you managed to teach yourself how to split a strike in half in such a short time. I am impressed," he admitted with what sounded to Eryn like forced generosity.

She thought back to the night of the escape. "When I did it the second time, it didn't work."

"It worked all right. Only I adjusted my strike to make sure it wouldn't help you much."

"How?"

"My, my! I never thought I would live to see the day that you ask me for combat instructions. It's an easy trick: instead of one powerful strike you send a bundle of weaker bolts. A maximum of two of them may be diverted but the rest will hit the target."

"I see. Why were people so surprised to see you do it when you... you know... tricked me into fighting?"

"It's not common knowledge among magicians that manipulating airstreams can have that effect. I stumbled across it when I was a boy and kept it to myself, afraid to admit to my teachers that I had been playing around with magic unsupervised."

"But quite some time has passed since then. Why have you never shared it so far?"

He regarded her thoughtfully. "You know, I had hardly left adolescence behind me when I took on an immensely important position in the Order. I figured out that superior power might not always be sufficient when it came to defending it. And then there are one or two very useful things that can be accomplished through the basic principles of air current manipulation."

"So you are keeping the useful things to yourself to have an advantage? Oh dear. If every single one of you in the Order does this it is no wonder that you are stuck in ancient battle techniques." Then her eyes widened. "Ah! That's how you manage to overhear distant conversations – you let the air carry the sounds towards you!"

He shook his head in amazement. "Your mind really is a marvellous thing. You are right. That's exactly how it's done." He leaned forward. "Is there any chance of your telling me about your barrier?"

"No. It's the only thing I have in my favour. It would be foolish of me to give it away like this. And I am cuffed in gold. That tends to make me rather uncooperative." She jingled the bangles.

She was right, of course. But he had to try.

"Are you done with eating? The King and Tyront are expecting us."

She swallowed nervously. "Is this concerning the solution you want to find?"

"Exactly. I think you will find our offer extremely reasonable. It is quite revolutionary from the Order's point of view."

She sniffed. Reasonable? That remained to be seen. She dabbed at her mouth with a napkin and rose. "Let's not keep all these important people waiting, then."

He shook his head at the sarcasm. "You might be advised to show some respect there, you know. They are not as forgiving as I am."

"You think you are forgiving? Really? I have experienced you as a rather vengeful and resentful sort."

"What a flattering appraisal. Thank you so much for that."

"Don't feign hurt. You have earned that assessment well enough. Or would you like a list of the many benevolent deeds in your dealings with me?"

He ushered her out the door. "No, thank you."

They reached the throne room after a few minutes and Enric motioned for the two guards at the heavy double doors to let them in.

When they entered the room, Eryn saw Tyront and the King with his two advisors standing in front of a huge table at the opposite end of the dais. So the big man wouldn't just be watching from his golden throne but instead would take a seat with the mere mortals. She must have ratchetted up her importance through her attempt at flight.

"Lady Eryn," Marrin welcomed her and indicated a slight bow. "It's good to see you up and well. Please take a seat."

Lady? When had that happened? Well, well. Somebody was obviously trying hard to make her happy. The King and Loft both gave her a curt nod and Tyront approached her like a long-lost daughter, smiling and taking her arm to lead her to the stone table.

"Your behaviour is really unnerving," she murmured. Enric coughed to hide a laugh and Tyront shot him a warning look.

When they had all sat down, Tyront cleared his throat. "The reason why we are here is that we would like to extend an offer to you which we hope that you will consider and not discard out of hand due to any resentment you might be harbouring."

"You think I *might* be harbouring resentment?" She lifted her golden manacles for all of them to see. "Whatever would give you such a notion?"

The muscles in Loft's cheeks clenched at her sarcastic tone, while the others seemed to take it reasonably well as far as she could tell.

Tyront continued, ignoring her comment. "We feel that it is high time to resolve the position you are in. As we are convinced that you are not a spy, we would like to make you an offer."

"No," she said with determination, "you want to make me an offer because you want to know how I managed to keep two stronger magicians at bay, and you are afraid I might finally manage to slip out of your grip before you have learned all about that."

Silence. The King looked concerned, his steadfast gaze fixed on her, while his advisors eyed him nervously.

When nobody spoke, she sighed. "Make your offer, then. That your motives are not as pure as you like to pretend doesn't mean I'm not interested in hearing it."

The atmosphere seemed slightly more relaxed after that, even if she could see that Lord Tyront was not exactly delighted with her lack of respect. Pity for him that she wasn't here to cheer him or anyone else with what she said.

"We are offering you a place amongst us in the Order," he said stiffly, "with the rank that you are entitled to due to your considerable level of power."

"The rank of third in command? Subordinated to you and the Lordl... Lord Enric?" She raised her brow.

"Eventually, yes."

"Eventually?"

"A position like this requires knowledge and insights that must be obtained by training. You need to be able to think strategically, assess situations, evaluate them and make informed decisions. We can't entrust you with this rank unless we are sure that you can master the responsibility and everything it entails to our complete satisfaction."

"How long do you propose training me for it?"

"A year of intense tutoring at least, not to mention honing your fighting skills. But Lord Enric is working on that already. And from what we have seen two nights ago I think we needn't really worry about that," he added.

"I think I have made it more than clear that I consider it a great waste using magic solely for fighting."

Tyront nodded indulgently. "Yes. But we hope that you will consider meeting with the requirement of dedicating at least a part of your time to honing those skills."

"And what would I be doing with the rest of my time?" she asked.

"What you seem to rate highest: healing."

She straightened abruptly, not sure if she had heard correctly. "Healing?" Then she narrowed her eyes. "Like providing healing services to the nobility to make sure that this highly deserving class of people have no more ailments?"

"We would leave the nature and clientele of your craft to your discretion. Of course, it might be seen as rather strange to discriminate against the upper classes by denying them medical treatment. Especially as they would be in a position to pay handsomely for your services." Tyront hid his smile at the sudden interest that last remark had sparked in her eyes.

She pursed her lips. "What resources would be provided for my craft, as you call it?"

"Resources?" Marrin frowned.

"Yes." She turned to him. "Healing is not what your local apothecaries do, it's a matter of collecting and stocking herbs and other ingredients, preparing medication, treating people and instructing them accordingly. I only have experience in healing in the setting of a small town, but I imagine that tending to the medical needs of such a great number of people as you have here in this city is rather more than one person would be able to handle."

"What exactly are you asking for?" It was the first time the King had spoken since she had arrived.

"Space, at least six rooms. The more space, the better. Some people who want to learn the craft. Adequate funds to obtain the materials that are needed on a daily basis, such as medicine, bandages and so on."

"Why would you need funding for this? I would expect your services to be self-funding," Marrin asked.

"Because," she was almost looking forward to that one, "I intend to base the rate for my services on the patients' income. My services will be affordable by everyone, whether that person can pay in gold or with a bunch of carrots."

"So you expect the Crown to pay for the healing expenses of the people," Loft commented acidly. "What a preposterous idea!"

Enric admired her cool reaction to Loft when he would have expected her to throw something at his head in reply.

"I propose a scheme that would enable your people to remain healthy and able to work in order to pay their taxes," she replied. "And the funding might as well be undertaken by the Order as they are the ones laying claim to me."

"The Order will consider your request," Tyront replied, clearly not all too happy about the unexpected draw on financial resources which accepting her into the Order would involve.

"Do that," she smiled. "And you would of course have to let me leave the city occasionally in order to gather herbs."

Tyront dismissed her remark with a hand gesture. "That wouldn't be a problem. You would give a magical oath that would bind you here so that leaving without the intention to return wouldn't be something to even consider."

"What?"

Her startled expression made Enric close his eyes. That had not been a good thing to say to her at this stage. Tyront should have known better than to let this slip in front of the King.

"You want me to give *what*?" Could she have misunderstood what he had just said?

Loft was eager enough to specify. "Well, *Lady* Eryn, all magicians joining the Order swear fealty to the King. And so would you, of course. It is more than a mere promise, it contains a magical binding as well."

She stared at him. A magically binding oath? She looked down at her golden bangles. She would be exchanging one bond for another. She was not at all sure which one would be worse. She looked up, exhaling slowly.

"I am not swearing an oath to the King."

Enric put a hand on her arm in warning. "Eryn."

"No." She shook free of him. "I am neither swearing to the King, nor to the Order. An oath requires trust and respect, and you could never expect me to bestow one of those upon either of you in my present position."

She looked at the disturbed expressions on the magicians' and Marrin's face. The King was considering her coldly and Loft seemed triumphant, as if Eryn's words had only confirmed his opinion of her.

Tyront rose from the table, eager to halt this meeting before even more damage could be done. "I think we all need some time to consider what has been said today."

Loft stood up with Enric and turned to Eryn, "I assume we can trust you not to undertake any more attempts to flee as long as you are considering our offer?"

She gave him an ironic smile. "Totally. You just go on and assume that…"

The King raised one eyebrow at her, so did Marrin. Loft's face flushed red with fury.

Enric, she saw, was pursing his lips and had pressed his fingers in diplomatic consideration while Tyront had fixed his eyes to the ceiling and was releasing a long breath.

* * *

The King watched the three magicians leave hurriedly. Each of the men had taken one of Eryn's arms and all but dragged her out the throne room.

"Her behaviour was perfectly outrageous, Your Majesty. A blatant demonstration of disrespect," Loft said when the doors had closed behind them.

Marrin sighed. "She didn't show any particular disrespect for you, Your Majesty. And after all, she remains our prisoner."

"You know," the King said slowly, "I rather think we should fund her pet project. And let people know it's *us* doing it and not the Order. They have been gaining more and more influence these past years. It will help the Crown to appear as a benefactor. If we play this right it will look like the subversive female magician is working for me, as if I had tamed the one who dealt such tribulation to the Order."

Loft nodded. "Very good, Your Majesty."

"So you think we should accept all her demands? She refuses to swear the oath," Marrin pointed out.

"The Order will come up with a solution for that, I am sure of it. The one thing I will not accept is her swearing an oath to the Order instead of the Crown, and I am sure Lord Tyront is very well aware of this." The King leaned back. "The only thing that needs to be done now is making her stay willingly and for her to start her work." He thought for a moment. "How about Lord Enric? He is obviously interested in her. Has he taken her to bed yet – apart from that one night, of course?"

Marrin shook his head. "No, I venture he has not. The way she tries to avoid every physical contact with him would suggest this."

"Yes, that's what I thought. He is rather proprietorial, is he not? It is time for measures that will induce him to act on it with rather more assertion."

"Jealousy tends to do the trick most of the time, Your Majesty," Loft suggested.

"He would surely eliminate any adversaries for her favours. His position allows him to do so quite unchallenged," Marrin pointed out.

"True. But there still is somebody he cannot intimidate with his position, somebody who could approach her and who would hardly be told by him to stay away". The King smiled a confident, yet thin smile. "Myself."

* * *

Eryn had tried to storm off to her old cell at the warriors' quarters only to be restrained by the guards and reminded that she was now under constant surveillance and was thus to stay in Lord Enric's quarters. She had then taken occupancy of his bedroom, slamming the door as hard as she could.

Enric and Tyront had remained in the parlour in unspoken accordance that following her would not be a very wise move at the moment. Instead, they settled down comfortably.

Enric shook his head. "I thought I would burst out laughing when Loft told her not to try running away while we are waiting on her answer. Keeping a straight face was quite a challenge…"

Tyront shook his head in mild disapproval, "Yes, that was plain enough to see. You have this expression, when you pucker your lips and press your fingertips together. I hope for your sake that nobody else has figured out that you do this to keep yourself from laughing."

"Me?" He affected innocence. "Look who's talking - your way of looking up as if to beg the stars for guidance and strength and exhaling longer than should be possible for any human being is not too subtle, either."

"Well, my covering mechanism at least gives off an impression of sympathy."

"Pure pretence," Enric countered. "You don't have an honest bone in your body."

Tyront shrugged. "I do feel some sympathy with Loft at times. The poor fool is just too easy to catch out."

Enric snorted. "It's not Loft I feel sympathy with."

"I see. So the rebel has softened you." He shook his head in mock surprise. "Dear me, and people say you don't have a heart."

Enric lifted his brows. "Nonsense, people never say that."

"Trust me, they do," Tyront assured him. "Heartless, relentless, unshakeable, but absolutely gorgeous. There doesn't seem to be a single woman who wouldn't let you be intimate with her."

"Envious, are you, old boy?" Enric sneered, then turned serious again. "And I know at least one who wouldn't let me."

"I've had my fair share, thank you. As for the other: you have managed it once already."

"Yes, wearing a mask and with the aid of some serious old magic."

Tyront studied him. "You know that it may depend on you to give her a good reason to stay and join the Order, don't you?"

"I'm not happy with the way you put it. It makes me feel cheap. I have my own reasons for making approaches to her, and pleasing the Order or the King are not among them." His anger began to show in his voice.

"I am quite aware of this. I am not asking you to do something you wouldn't do anyway. It might just be wise to move things along a bit more quickly. It is, as you have pointed out, in your own personal interests to make her stay."

Enric sighed. "I just don't think pressing her right now is a good idea."

"And yet you insis... ahem... *recommended* having her in your quarters," Tyront pointed out.

"That's a matter of getting her used to seeing me as a human being instead of some monster. And, of course, she needs to be supervised by a strong magician."

"Of course," Tyront replied, carefully refraining from mentioning the fact that she was hardly a danger to anyone as long as she was wearing the manacles.

"What are we to do about her refusal to accept the oath to the King?" Enric changed the topic.

"It was to be expected that she would not be too happy about it," the older man said. "The question is now if we should try to change her mind or the oath."

"I suppose there is no chance the King would accept her swearing an oath to the Order?"

"You may safely count on that, dear chap," he replied grimly. "And it's as well he wouldn't. The Order should not serve its own purposes; we are too powerful for that and might become corrupted by it."

"But serving the King's purposes is alright for us?"

"That is a dangerous question to ask, Enric. One bordering on treason, you know. Whose purposes do *you* propose we serve?"

"Eryn says that the people should be the beneficiaries, that magic should be used to serve *them*."

"Eryn says that, eh? And what is it you say?"

Enric paused a few moments to think. "That it has been quite some time since we were last attacked and somehow it seems that we magicians have not really been using our powers for anything other than readying ourselves for war." He continued when Tyront cocked his head. "How can I not begin wondering when she talks about healing and I walk down the streets, seeing people who suffer from illness and injury, asking myself if I could harness my power that can break stones into one that offers relief and cures? How can we all not be caused to start wondering?"

"The King would hardly be very enthusiastic about us all turning into healers," Tyront added.

"Ah, and there we are again: the King wouldn't like it. And we have to oblige him, because we have bound ourselves to him. Or rather sold ourselves?" Enric lifted his arms in frustration and let them drop again. "I was raised in the belief that the Order is what secures peace in the kingdom, because that is what we keep telling people. And also telling our own young magicians, because what else can we tell them? That the kings in these past few centuries have kept spending huge amounts of money to keep us content and in luxury so we don't get any dangerous ideas that might endanger their claim to the throne? That we are so complacent with that effortless importance we are granted that laziness and dependence is but a small price to pay for being lifted high above everybody else? We at the top let ourselves be addressed with *Lord* to distinguish our noble status that is justified by nothing other than being born with the ability to use magic. No tangible, conscious accomplishments, only magic! We were granted this eminence, the privilege of having others look at us like some sort of elite for no other reason than to cajole us. And to our own great shame it worked splendidly. And it still does." He took a deep breath and went on in a more serene tone, "I grant you that putting resources into being prepared for the chance of a military attack is a reasonable course of action for a country, but limiting all our efforts to that one thing? We have effectively pawned our potential and free will, and have been doing so for an eternity. And what we get is pleasant quarters, status and money! We are essentially without function as long as there is no war!" He took a deep breath, surprised that all this frustration had been inside him somewhere to come out like that. Had it always been in him or was there something of Eryn's doing in there?

Tyront watched him calmly without any visible sign of disapproval or surprise at Enric's outburst. When nothing more came, he shook his head indulgently. "You never were one for being idle and useless, dear boy. I wonder if you are aware why you started your first business several years ago. And why you have kept continuously adding to it in the time since then."

Enric closed his eyes when the answer emerged as if it was the most self-evident explanation in the world: because he had been bored and under challenged, stuck with mental capacities that were not needed for anything more remarkable than dealing with chores. His unconscious escape had been putting to use what his father had taught him as a boy so as to earn some feeling of accomplishment. And Tyront had obviously been aware of that for some time.

"We really need Eryn in the Order," Enric murmured. "That rebellious woman will shake us all awake, challenge us, question our current way of doing things and increase our knowledge for the first time after all these years. *She* will just not fall prey to the passiveness we have adopted. We have doomed magicians to ineffectiveness by limitations we impose on ourselves. And through the accursed oath that binds us to the King with magic to ensure our obedience," he continued in a less agitated tone. "May I ask what you find so amusing?" he added when he saw Tyront smiling.

"You know, maybe the time has come to let you in on a secret. As you are to take over my responsibilities if something happens to me, you should know of it anyway."

Enric felt a magic barrier build around them, closing them in and making the transfer of air and thus sound impossible. This of course limited the time they could spend inside it.

"Some of our predecessors have shared your concerns. For this reason they have started to work on a spell to counter the oath's effect." Tyront leaned forward. "It was about a hundred years ago that they succeeded."

Enric's eyes glinted dangerously. "Are you saying that we are able to release ourselves at any time from our obligation to the King?"

"That is exactly what I am saying. But this does not necessarily mean such a thing is a good idea. You remember the history lessons about the times before the oath and why it was created?"

"Yes. Powerful magicians terrorising the population, being responsible to no one, fighting among themselves and against anybody who tried to stand in their way."

"Exactly. We should be responsible to somebody. The temptation is too great otherwise. Especially for those who are powerful enough easily to dominate others."

"Like us two?"

"Yes. Imagining a better world and then being convinced that you could achieve it if only you were dominant over everybody else. The oath is meant to prevent that."

"Provided the ruler is not corrupted by it himself."

"That, too. But as long as he makes no attempts at invading other countries without provocation or terrorises his people, there is no justification for us to break the bond."

"The people..." Enric mused and then looked up sharply. "Could we get away with letting her swear an oath to the people instead?"

"What do you mean, the *people*?" Tyront frowned. "The King is supposed to represent the people. It would be like an oath to him, anyway."

"I hope very much that this is the way he will see it. But the phrasing would be different. It would be about serving the people and acting in their best interest." He became more agitated. "The effect of the oath itself always depends on how the magicians interpret the wording. As she has a rather bad opinion of the King and considers him indifferent to the needs of the population, this would not really bind her to him that tightly."

Tyront nodded slowly. "True enough. Yes, we will consider that. If the King refuses we can always put it to public attention. An Order magician willing to swear an oath not to a powerful institution, but to the population instead might work in our favour. Unfortunately, the King will almost certainly realise this, too. He is very careful about not letting us become too powerful."

"We just need to be careful of the wording and include phrases along the lines of *in the best interest of the people which is represented by the King...* That should satisfy him as he doesn't know enough about the way magical oaths work to see that words that have a certain meaning for him but are empty or interpreted differently by the one who swears, don't really bind anyone that tightly. The Order has in the past been very eager to assist the King with the wording to a more or less watertight oath. I suppose it is time for a new one, anyway."

"Careful," Tyront warned. "We have a way to counter the existing oath, but not any new ones. So don't be too hasty in discarding the dungeon we have the key for in favour of one we can't get out of. And then there is the minor matter of avoiding overzealous or overambitious magicians getting to the top without being responsible to anyone."

Enric swallowed and shook his head as if to clear it. "It's feeling a little stuffy. I think it's time for some fresh air."

Tyront nodded and removed the barrier, allowing them both to take a deep breath of the fresh air outside their shield.

"What have you two been doing?" Eryn's deeply suspicious voice startled them and they turned to see her leaning against the wall, her arms folded, her brows furrowed.

Enric rose to approach her and stopped, when she tensed and her eyes narrowed.

"We were discussing confidential matters," he told her.

She nodded slowly. "Under a barrier that prevents sound from escaping..." She had been watching them for a short while, their lips moving inaudibly. Enric had seemed rather displeased judging from his body language. "Must be a bit hard to breathe in there after a while."

Tyront smiled. "That's very perceptive of you."

She shrugged. "Hardly. As sound travels on air just like magic, blocking the flow of air stops whatever you want to remain unheard. Or at least some of it," she added with a sly smile.

The two men exchanged a worried look.

"What exactly do you mean by that?" Tyront enquired. "Don't tell me you have heard what we were talking about."

"No, of course not." She smiled indulgently. "However would that have been possible?" A little shock would do them good, she decided. "But learning about your ability to counter that one magical oath *was* rather interesting."

That had them staring at her, momentarily speechless. She was about to go back into the bedroom, when she saw a familiar shimmering in the air in front of her. She sighed: a pity, it would have been a good moment for flouncing out without another word, leaving them wondering. Well, she hadn't really expected to escape without their pressing her for an explanation.

"Would you care to elaborate how you managed to gather those details? It seems that we have yet to assess the limits of your magical abilities." Tyront had found his voice again.

"Magical abilities?" She chuckled. "Of course. What else could it be?"

"You are saying you did it without magic?" Enric said.

She raised her wrists and once again jingled the manacles. "How could I have used magic? Really now, so little confidence in your tools of restraint?"

"With you I am not really sure what we can still rely on," he murmured. "So you overcame a strong magical barrier without any magic." Now he appeared really perturbed.

"Yes. And so could everybody else, whether or not he or she is magically gifted," she said nonchalantly. She noticed their alarmed expressions with delight. She could literally see their thoughts racing how to make her tell them. "You said I have to stay in your quarters. I assume you are aware that I will not be sharing the bed with you."

"What?" Enric looked at her, clearly thrown off track by the sudden change of subject.

"Where will I sleep?"

"You can choose between my room or the guest room over there." He pointed at a door next to his study.

"Then I'll take the guest room," she decided immediately.

"What can we offer you in exchange for the information about how you penetrated our shield just now?" Tyront asked, refusing to be side-tracked from that topic.

"That's easy. Remove these damn golden things."

"That is not possible, I'm afraid. Unless you are also willing to talk about how your special barrier works."

"No." She folded her arms.

"What about if I remove the bangles when you take an oath not to use the barrier against us?" Enric suggested.

"A magical oath?" That sounded rather dangerous. "I can't do that! The barrier is only for defence! If one of you decided to attack me I would be completely helpless."

"We will only attack if you attempt to escape again. But if you prefer swearing a little oath that you will no longer try to flee from here…"

"Hardly," she said, adding after a few moments, "How long would an oath not to use the barrier against you remain effective?" She really did miss her magic.

"Until we release you from it. Which we will do as soon as you have joined the Order."

"That might never even happen!" she protested.

Tyront smiled. "We will do our best to ensure it happens. You would be a great benefit to the Order."

"Of course I would," she huffed. "But I don't see you fully grasping it. You see me as a tool to improve your fighting skills and would merely indulge me in allowing me to do a little healing as long as it does not interfere too much with what you want from me."

"Well, that is what it takes for now to make healing possible for you," the older man answered, "You can't really expect the centuries-old institution of the Order to change its views overnight."

"From my past experience with the Order I have learned not to expect anything from it," she retorted.

Enric suddenly smiled. "There might be something we can offer you in exchange. After we learned about your magical abilities, we had your books and papers brought here." He was pleased when he noted her tense interest. "We still have them locked up. I'm assuming you would value having them back?"

She had not really counted on ever getting these things back. Most of them were from her father, a few he had written himself. She had over the course of the years since his death added her own notes and even made a few corrections.

"So I tell you how I managed to get through your barrier and you return all my books and documents to me?"

"Yes," Enric nodded.

"Alright," she agreed without hesitation. Both men leaned forward. "I didn't penetrate your shield. And, of course, I couldn't hear you. But my view was unblocked. I *saw* what you were talking about."

"Saw?" Tyront shook his head uncomprehendingly. "How can you possibly see what people talk about?"

"By reading your lip," she explained patiently. "The movements of your lips let me see what you said."

When both men regarded her doubtingly, she sighed and then said, by way of an offer, "Why don't you go back under your barrier, say something and I tell you what it was."

They immediately recreated a barrier and each said a few sentences before removing it, looking at her expectantly.

She nodded at Tyront. "You said that the harvest was rather meagre this year and you hope the one next year would be better." Then she turned to Enric. "You said something about Orrin and how you used to play tricks on him when you were a boy and he was your teacher, such as hiding his swords."

Enric quietly whistled through his teeth in appreciation. "How can I learn this?"

"By observing people and practising."

Tyront nodded. "I will have your books sent to you as soon as I am back in my office," he promised. "How did you acquire this skill?"

"Out of necessity. My father and I often tended to old and very infirm people who had great difficulties speaking in more than a whisper and could often no more than move their lips."

"Amazing." He looked at Enric. "I'm afraid I need to leave you now. There are quite a few things I need to discuss with the Council. Good bye, Lady Eryn. Enric."

When Tyront had closed the door behind him, they just stood there for a while, looking at each other.

Finally, Enric spoke, "I think we need to talk and clear the air between us."

"I don't see what there is to talk about," she replied coolly.

"There is the fact that you are angry at me for spending this one night with you."

"Is that a fact?" she asked, mocking.

"I'd say it is. Are you denying it?"

"I won't deny being angry, but there is a little more to it than that. You represent the institution that has been keeping me here and wants to do so in the future by binding me with a magical oath. Even though you seem to have managed to find a way to circumvent it, I would suggest you are hardly likely to share that knowledge with me any time soon."

"Alright, then, why don't we start with the matter that affects the two of us directly." He went to the settee he had occupied when he had talked to Tyront before and indicated with a hand gesture for her to take the seat opposite.

She considered refusing him, but maybe dealing with this was not such a bad idea. The way it looked right now she would have to spend a lot of time with him, at least over the next few days. It didn't need to be more unpleasant than necessary. She slowly went to the chair and sat while he took out a fresh cup and poured her a drink.

The distance was comfortable and the little table between them at least served as an illusion of a barrier. Of course it would be utterly useless in keeping him at a distance. He could make it go up in flames with a flick of his wrist if he wanted.

"What is the great problem with the fact that *I* was the one you spent the night with?" he started without any detours.

She swallowed. That was direct. "I would assume that this is self-explanatory," she replied stiffly.

"Me, the big bad prison warder taking shameless advantage of you, the poor and helpless prisoner?"

Her scornful look reminded him that his aim was not to provoke her. "I apologise. For the remark, that is. Not for the Freedom Night."

"However ridiculously you phrase this, it is hardly proof of manliness if you needed to use magic to seduce a woman."

He narrowed his eyes. "Pardon?" Sitting up straight and leaning forward, he spoke slowly and deliberately. "I have never in my life needed to enchant somebody to have sex with me. You may believe this or not. As for the seduction…" He leaned back again and smiled thinly. "Seduction is considered as making somebody sexually compliant, thus I might as well accuse *you* of the same."

She shot him an angry look back. "You are not saying *I* seduced *you*, are you?"

"You might not have started it, but neither did you stop it. My plan when I first started dancing with you was not to take you to bed. And I don't remember any desperate attempts at escaping while we were dancing."

Eryn folded her arms and raised her brow at him. "You don't? I recall an occasion when I made my discomfort known to you, sometime after the second dance, when I tried to free myself. When you… you…" She faltered and averted her gaze, feeling awkward at not even being able to say the words out loud.

"When I first kissed you?" he said softly and found her discomfort oddly becoming, fighting the temptation to let the deed itself follow his words.

She swallowed. "Yes, that."

"I admit I might have been rather… assertive on this occasion. But do not put any blame for spending the night with me on me alone. I would not have taken an unwilling woman to bed. And Eryn," his voice grew deeper, softer, rougher when he leaned forward over the little table, cupping her cheek before she could lean out of his reach and let his thumb brush over her lips, "you were *very* willing, delightfully so."

She abruptly got to her feet to escape his touch, turning away to hide the flush of heat that had risen to her face. "Enough. I don't want to talk about this anymore."

He remained seated and gave her the space she seemed to need. "I think we must. This should not remain between us, especially as we will be spending some time together here. And you can hardly expect me to simply let you walk away after accusing me of magically subduing you so that I could have my way."

She remained standing, her face averted. "You said your plan was not to take me to bed when you danced with me. Then, pray, what was your plan?"

"An experiment. As you are the first female magician we have had here after a very long time, there are numerous things that we might now have a chance to fathom. We have old songs that have been passed down for several hundred years now, some of them imbued with magic to varying degrees."

She turned back to him, intrigued. "Magic, in music? How is this possible?"

He hid a smile. Her curiosity seemed to be stronger than her embarrassment. "I am not completely sure myself. But it works. The weaker, obviously considerably less influential, songs are played at different occasions. Non-magicians don't feel anything and we, depending on our powers, feel an itch to dance. But some of the songs…" He paused.

"They contain more magic, like the two you had the musicians play that night?"

He nodded. "Yes. They practice the songs as they are part of our cultural heritage, but they are usually not played when magicians are around. It makes us feel restless and uneasy. And I think the reason for this is that there are no more women with magical abilities around to dance them with. It does not work with non-magical partners."

She frowned, then looked up in sudden realisation. "The magic… that's why I knew how to dance the last two songs, instinctively knew the steps, why the other songs were so easy for me to learn."

"Exactly. I watched you dancing, following the steps so easily, sometimes adding a movement here, a step there that was different from what our young women learn. That's when I started wondering what other lost old knowledge you might be carrying around inside you."

"So this second song…" She looked at him, a distasteful thought forming.

"…was one of seduction." He smiled. "I was rather surprised myself when first I realised it. There had only ever been guesses as to why listening to it made us so restless."

"Then we were both victims of an ancient, magical fertility rite?" Her nose wrinkled at the repellent image.

He stared at her for a moment, then burst out laughing - a full, rich sound from deep within. He fought manfully to get a grip on himself when he saw her scowling at him in reproach.

"May I ask what's so funny?" She narrowed her eyes, not thrilled at having her words turned to ridicule for his amusement.

"The magic in the music does not control us like this. It can't make you act against your own urges. It can't overpower you or violate your nature - it only helps along what is present already. It certainly does *not* turn us into helpless victims." He rose, reached out, seized both her hands and pulled her closer to kiss her fingers. She was too confused to fight his touch. "This may hurt your delicate notions of decency, but I'm afraid I would have got you into bed with me sooner or later anyway. My wearing a mask was a convenient way to hurry it along because your fear of me was not in the way."

He could see that this didn't sit well with her. She tried to tug her hands free, but he held on to them. "You don't really prefer seeing yourself as a victim of either me or a magical song instead of accepting that you are attracted to me, do you?" His voice was calm.

Had his question contained even a hint of the mockery he tended to use with her, she would have turned away and disregarded it as impossible nonsense, as an insult. But his tone was serious, urging her to consider it honestly.

When she remained silent, he stepped closer and slipped his arms around her in a smooth move. Her eyes filled with alarm and her hands made to push him away. He didn't press her closer, but neither did he free her.

"There is no music here," he spoke softly. "We could find out right now. Whatever reaction there will be comes from you, not from any magical influence. Let's consider it a test, shall we?" He could see the thoughts racing behind her forehead. She turned her face away when he started to lower his own to it.

Sighing disappointedly, he regarded her. "Coward."

The flicker in her eyes that was triggered by this one word intrigued him. He gently held her chin and turned it back to him. "What did you feel when I kissed you after our fight in the street?"

She tried to pry his hand away from her face. "That is a stupid question."

"Is it? Indulge me." He could clearly see the uneasiness and discomfort his question had caused. Maybe he could make it easier for her by confessing first. "When I kissed you that day, I wanted to lift you up and take you to my chambers. The reasons why I had dragged you in front of these people - retribution, protecting my reputation - were suddenly meaningless, forgotten. I would rather have let them see me as a weak fool defeated by a situation I had brought upon myself than take my hands off you."

She blinked at him. "What stopped you, then?"

He brushed a thumb across her cheek like he had done that very day. "Your tears."

Feeling pressure rise inside her chest, she swallowed hard and looked away. She didn't want this. The distance to him had been safe, this was not. He shouldn't hold her in his arms like that, making this so intimate when he was the enemy.

He was simply ignoring her hands that tried to push him back. "What did *you* feel when I kissed you?" he repeated his question softly.

"I can't talk about this. Please..." She struggled to escape his embrace but stilled when he spoke.

"I just told you that I was about to embarrass myself in front of people that have for the last ten years seen me as a dangerous, all powerful warrior. What are you afraid of?"

He kissed her forehead, breaking her resolve with gentleness. "Tell me, Eryn. Tell me that there was something inside you that day that was stronger than all the hate, desperation and anger you felt."

Pressing her palms against her face to hide it, she nodded, the shame she still felt making it impossible for her to meet his gaze.

She felt his chest expand and fall in a long breath. He then tenderly removed her hands from her face and lifted her chin to kiss her.

He had been right. No magical music was necessary to make her react to it.

When he opened her lips to deepen the kiss, she tensed, desperately trying to remember all those reasons why it was wrong to do this, to let him get that close. Her thoughts frantically kept running over how he had stopped her from getting away from here as his warm, delicious taste threatened to prevail over her resistance.

Feeling the tightening of her muscles, he withdrew a little, not breaking the contact with her mouth but using no more than his lips and thus keeping the kiss less urgent, almost playful. Her attempts to free herself from his embrace, however, he thwarted by holding her firmly but not tightly against him.

Her vision swam. The shield, how he manipulated it, she managed to remember. She turned her head away and thus freed her mouth from his. Her breathing was heavy and still he didn't release her from his embrace.

She felt his hand in her hair at the back of her head turn her face back to him, close again.

"Eryn," he murmured urgently, forcing her to meet his blue, impatient eyes, "Stop fighting me!"

He lowered his mouth onto hers, this time claiming it completely and making her gasp in surprise. Taking her arms, he lifted them to put them around his neck and held them there for a moment when she made to pull them back.

"Damn you, kiss me back!" he demanded in a hoarse whisper and crushed his lips against hers once more.

Her thoughts then dispersed into nothingness, and caught between the demands his words, hands and mouth were making, the last remainder of her resolve vanished, she surrendered to what her body was compelling. She gave up fighting the urge to kiss him back, and leaned into his touch.

She could taste, feel his relief when her arms finally did tighten around his neck and her lips and tongue started to move in response to his.

When she felt his bare hands on her back under her tunic, she opened her eyes and pulled back.

"Wait," she gasped. "We can't, we're not going to…"

His mouth claimed hers once more.

"Oh yes, that is exactly what we are going to do." His gaze was intense and fierce and his breathing laboured. "I have been thinking of little else in these last few months," he said under his heaving breath.

Her thoughts began racing again. Kissing him was maybe not smart, but it was a forgivable thing, a minor thing - indulging in a weakness for that man that shouldn't be there. But she couldn't let him take her to bed. Not as long as he kept her locked in his quarters. And shackled in gold. It just wasn't right. It was like acquiescing to being treated that way.

She gripped his shoulders when she felt his lips moving over her throat and his hand exploring her breast.

He chuckled when she moaned softly. It was not a sound of pure pleasure but clearly conveyed some impatience with herself, her frustration with her own body that had its own idea of what it desired to do. It was definitely not following the mind's lead to restraint and caution.

"I can't think," she whispered and tried to clear her head by shaking it.

"Good. That should make things easier." He then wrapped both arms around her and lifted her slightly so that her legs no longer touched the floor.

"Wait," she breathed at his lips.

"Why?" he replied distractedly and kept kissing the side of her face.

"This doesn't change anything. I mean, that we…" She stopped to search for an appropriate expression. Why was it so hard to think properly? Where did the haze in her head come from?

"That we are very much attracted to each other?" he suggested.

"Yes, that. It doesn't mean that I accept being held captive, respect the way you use magic or from now do whatever you think you can demand of me."

"I wouldn't dream of assuming anything else."

"I am just mentioning it so you don't feel hurt or betrayed when… if I try to get away from here again."

He pursed his lips. "I thank you very much for taking my feelings into consideration. And you, in turn, will of course not be angry at me should I happen to be the one to foil your attempts." He kept her lifted off the floor and carried her with him to the bedroom.

She swallowed and frowned. Had she just increased his motivation to keep her from escaping by welcoming his attentions?

He set her down in his bedroom right in front of the large bed and kissed her again, freeing her head of these and any other thoughts.

* * *

Lying beside him on his decadently oversized, soft bed, pleasantly exhausted, she covered herself with a blanket and looked at the bangles. They were the only thing she was still wearing.

"You know," she said in a moment of reproach, "you could at least have taken those off me."

His smile didn't reach his eyes. "No. We wouldn't want to give you any ideas how to use me to get rid of them so you can try to run away again."

"Your lack of trust wounds me," she sighed.

"You know, you will get over it somehow," he replied and pulled her closer towards him until she lay in his arms again. He tugged at her blanket for his own pleasure, revealing what she had just covered and intertwined his fingers with hers when she made to pull it back up again. He remembered her reluctance at intimate touches afterwards from the last time and wouldn't make avoiding them as easy for her this time.

"That would depend on you."

His brows rose. "Why would it?"

"Well, does sleeping with you bring any benefits?" she asked sweetly.

"Other than the benefit of enjoying my considerable skills as lover? What a romantic woman you are." His tone was brittle.

"You talk about romance? Really? The first time you took me to bed was anonymous and the second time you keep me shackled in gold." Her voice was less ironic than coldly factual.

"Alright, I concede that these are not ideal circumstances. Let me make a concession, then. I will remove the manacles for a short while - say, two hours. But before that you take an oath not to use your barrier against me or try and flee. The oath would bind you only until the two hours are over and you have your jewellery back on."

She was about to turn him down, but then thought better of it. To feel the familiar store of energy, the subtle power coursing through her body... that would definitely be worth an oath that would cease to bind her after a mere two hours. And she had no idea for another escape attempt anyway.

"Alright." She lifted her wrists. "I agree."

He chuckled and shook his head. "The oath first, if you please."

"How do I do it? Make an honest promise? I promise not to run away or use my special barrier against you for the next two hours. Good enough?"

"Nice try. I will phrase it for you, you repeat after me and we join our hands like this." He took her hand so that he could press his palm firmly against hers. "I herewith swear that for the next hours as long as I am released from my binding," he spoke, waiting for her to repeat it and then continued, "I will neither use the special barrier that stops stronger bolts nor make any attempts to escape from you."

"...from you," she ended and felt a warm surge of power through their connected hands. Then he let go and put his fingers on the golden manacles. They fell away, and she sighed with relief when she felt the familiar presence of magic return. She created a small round barrier around her fingertip just because she could.

"That would be a neat way to keep your fingernails clean," he smiled and caused the tiny shield to crackle when he touched it lightly.

"Yes, depend on the Order to put magic to sensible use," she snorted.

He leaned forward and over her. "I could show you what else magic can be used for. There is a reason why even less... creative magicians are in high demand as lovers. Only if you are up to it, of course."

When she just grinned he peeled away her blanket completely to demonstrate.

* * *

Enric studied her asleep on her side, facing him. Her breathing was deep and even, her hair tangled in a wild brown halo around her head. She had buried one arm under her pillow, the other one lay limply beside her.

It was close to evening, they had spent almost the entire day in bed. He had used magic before during sex, to stimulate, give pleasure. But with another magician, where he was both on the giving and the receiving end, it was something completely different. She had been pleasantly surprised and eager to learn and was – as she had already proven – quick on the uptake.

No wonder she was exhausted. So was he, but he couldn't afford the luxury of sleeping when there was work waiting for him which he had so far neglected today. He looked at her again, regretting that he had to leave the warm bed and the sight of her and got up to put on a robe.

* * *

Eryn opened her eyes and found herself alone in his bed. There was no disorientation, she knew instantly why she was there. It was getting dark outside, she had been sleeping for quite some time. She was grateful that he was not there right now. A little solitude would help her to figure out how she felt about ending up in bed with him again, consciously this time.

It had been unbelievable, there was no denying it. It seemed there was at least one use of magic they had worked out that was not connected with fighting.

But there was the question of his motivation behind all this. Keeping her happy and content would surely increase their chances of convincing her to stay in the city, join the Order. How much of it was mere calculation and how much was real?

And how important was that question, really? She had enjoyed the passionate lovemaking, whatever his reasons were. And in the end, she would do what was right for herself, whatever his and the Order's plans and intentions were.

She swung her legs out of the bed and looked for her clothes. Sleeping in his bed during the night was not something she wanted. Somehow sharing a bed with him, lying beside him, naked and vulnerable, seemed overly intimate, even after the things they had done with and to each other a few hours ago. She would move to his guest room, just as he had proposed. It would let him know clearly that she was open for pleasure but that this was all the change there was.

Carefully looking out into the parlour and finding it empty, she scurried across it to the door of the guest room he had indicated earlier that day. She opened it as quietly as she was able to and then closed it again after her.

The room was comfortable and bare of anything that reflected the quarters' inhabitant. Perfect.

The water jug was filled and using the bowl next to it she quickly washed her face and slipped into bed. She was not exactly tired, but lying in a warm, soft bed after the months she had spent on the bunk bed in her cell was a luxury she intended to enjoy as long as she could.

And there was a thing or two to consider. The Order's offer. Enric.

The offer was interesting, she had to admit. The chance to return to healing after so many months was compelling. It was true, she had been healing people on a minor scale after they had removed the manacles with the total block. But that was like a few drops of water to a thirsty man.

Training other healers. That thought was exciting and intimidating at the same time. To work with people who knew her secret, exchanging knowledge and experience, not having to hide her magical abilities any more... But how did the process of training healers work? Where to start on it? Her father had introduced her to the profession gradually by taking her with him whenever he was called somewhere, and then had let her watch, explaining what he was doing. She was a child then, but training adult healers needed another approach, a less time consuming one. She could hardly afford to wait for ten years until they were able to work alone.

Teaching was new terrain. She had given instructions to patients, explaining to them how to manage an illness or injury and avoid it returning in the future, but she imagined that teaching was something completely different. Showing Vern a thing or two which she thought would interest him was hardly a structured enough approach to training professionals efficiently.

But the real problem was the oath. Binding herself in fealty to a man who had wanted to have the shield inside her removed so he could have children with magical abilities by dragging her into his bed was unthinkable. There was personal pride and also the lack of trust and respect. These should definitely not be missing when it came to such a commitment. Who knew what imperatives he might come up with in the future that she would then be magically bound to obey. It was impossible.

She would have to continue the combat training, but if this was the price for healing, she would pay it willingly, although, grudgingly. Provided they found a way around the oath, that is.

And then there was Enric. He could not be trusted, of course, acting as he did on behalf and in the interests of the Order. And undoubtedly his own interests were meshed in there somewhere.

She sat up with a jolt when the door to her room suddenly burst open and the dark silhouette of a person stood in the doorway, illuminated from behind by light spilling in from the parlour.

Enric sighed in relief when he spotted her in bed, shielding her eyes against the light he let into the room. "Here you are. You had me worried for a moment."

"Would you prefer me to leave a message on your pillow next time?" she smiled.

"No." He would prefer her to stay in his bed next time. He came closer until he stood right in front of the bed. She saw now that he had not dressed and was wearing no more than a robe.

"Why have you come here?" he enquired calmly.

She had the impression that it wouldn't hurt to be very careful in answering that question. His voice was not accusing, but there was *something*.

"I distinctly remember your offering me this guest room today. I assumed the offer was still valid," she replied levelly.

"That was in the morning. I hoped that in the meantime you would consider *my* bed a more attractive option."

Tricky one, she thought. To anger him now in what seemed to be his rather vulnerable mood was not a good idea. He would probably make her pay for that somehow. But then she had no intention of returning to his room for the night, either.

"I found your bed a little uncomfortable, to be completely honest," she said.

She could hear the amusement in his voice. "Indeed? I am sorry to hear that. After the bed in your room at the warriors' quarters I would never have guessed such a thing. And the one in here is more to your liking?" he enquired, only a hint of sarcasm discernible.

"It is fine, yes," she answered.

"That is interesting. It seems that of the two beds in my quarters I have somehow managed to select the less comfortable one."

"Oh, I wouldn't say that. I mean, preferences depend on personal inclinations, after all." Too cheerful, she thought. She tended to sound much too happy when she wasn't and tried to hide it.

"So are you saying you prefer the guest room to my bed?" The lightness was gone from his voice and it was clear that they were no longer talking about pretences of discomfort.

"I have lived alone all my life. I find it rather hard to share something as personal as sleeping space," she confessed, deciding that honesty was probably the least troublesome path here.

He raised his brows in surprise, which she couldn't see in the dark. Sleeping space was more personal to her than what had happened between them before? But then she had lived almost all her life in a place where she had had to hide the person she was. Even if she didn't have to conceal her magical abilities any more, privacy was probably still something very precious to her and protecting it must have become an ingrained habit after all these years.

"And then there is the little matter of whether this was one-time thing," she added. She wouldn't want to find somebody for just one night in her bed again.

He leaned down to her, seeing her fight her reflexive reaction of recoil at his proximity. He didn't blame her. Whenever he had been close to her in the past, something unpleasant had happened to her. The testing, when he had knocked her out so she couldn't provoke Tyront anymore; her first attempt at flight when he had cornered her in the turret; the audience with the King where he had strengthened the shield inside her; the fight a few days ago at the end of which she had learned about the Freedom Night, and, of course, the most recent one: her second bash at escaping.

"Trust me: It was not," he said with a smile. "I intend to repeat this frequently, so you are welcome to sleep in my bed. Very much so, in fact." His lips touched hers lightly. "We will work on that. You know where to find me if you change your mind." He kissed her again, more assertively this time to let the taste of what she was missing by staying here alone linger on her lips.

Then he straightened. "Good night, Eryn. I will wake you in time for the training session tomorrow."

Smiling to himself when she groaned, he closed the door on his way out of the room.

* * *

"What do I call you?" She put the cup back on the table and leaned back in her chair, finished with her breakfast and comfortably replete.

True to his word, he had woken her much too early so as to drag her over to a little garden somewhere in the bowels of the palace. After mercilessly pummelling her for nearly two hours in the training he had finally taken pity on her and led her back to his quarters to feed her.

"Pardon?" he frowned at her, not comprehending.

"How do I address you?" she rephrased her question patiently.

"Well, as long as you don't keep referring to me as Lordling or Bastard... That would seem rather inappropriate considering the circumstances," he replied crisply. "I like the ring of *Lord and Master*. Or *Mighty and Powerful One*."

"I think I will stick with *Bastard*, actually. You keep reminding me how well it fits," she sneered.

He just smiled at that. The banter was not exactly his notion of tenderness, but it definitely helped her relax when she was around him. Good.

"Call me a traditionalist, but I would think my name would be a good way of addressing me."

"Enric?" It seemed strange to say it out loud like that. She had only ever heard him referred to as *Lord* Enric. Omitting the title felt somehow incomplete.

"That's the one I meant, full marks," he smirked.

"And in public?" she enquired with a meaningful look. "With your title?"

"I was not aware that we needed a particular way of addressing each other in public."

She rolled her eyes at him and wondered if he was being slow on purpose because he enjoyed trying her patience. "For public address this seems rather pally, don't you think? People will immediately conclude we are sleeping together."

The left corner of his mouth curved up. "Which would be an outrageously wrong impression to make, as you insist on staying in the guest room."

She breathed in and out slowly. He is surely doing this on purpose, so don't accommodate him by getting angry, she reminded herself. "You know exactly what I mean."

"That I do." He leaned forward, his tone serious now. "I do not intend to keep it a secret."

She swallowed and frowned. "This does seem a little indiscreet of you. I am surprised. I wouldn't have pegged you as a man who shares close private details with the public to provide entertainment. Quite the opposite."

He chuckled. "I am not doing it to brag. I want to make it clear to everyone that you are not available anymore."

"Oh, I'm not, am I?" She raised her brows and looked at him from under half closed eyes, smiling faintly.

His eyes narrowed. "As long as you are sharing my bed…" He rephrased it quickly. "As long as you frequent my bed with occasional visits, you will stay away from other men's beds."

"Frequent your bed with occasional visits…" she repeated thoughtfully. "Would I term twice in almost seven months occasional? I'm not sure. And the first time was not even in *your* bed." She saw the pique spark in his eyes and gave a smirk. Oh yes - two could play that little game.

"Don't try me, Eryn. I don't share." The warning in his tone was mild, but clearly there.

She thought for a few moments about this display of rather premature possessiveness, then decided to leave it alone for now and return to the matter of address.

"What if we stop sleeping together? Will we let the public know by calling each other *Lord* and *Lady*?"

He sighed and got up from his chair, bending down to take her hand and pull her up as well. "You talk too much. Really."

"What are you doing?" she asked when he pulled her towards his bedroom, although a pretty good idea was forming in her mind already.

"Increasing the frequency of your visits. You are right, one is clearly not enough for them to be occasional. And whenever I see an imbalance of some kind, I feel the urge to correct it."

She grabbed the door frame. "You could just rephrase your statement instead, that would correct the imbalance, you know."

He laughed, prying her fingers loose to pull her along with him the last few steps to his bed. "Surely not."

CHAPTER 26

The Apothecaries

She wandered around in Enric's parlour, bored. She had spent the last three hours in his guest room going through the books Tyront had sent to her. She had welcomed the promised books like long-lost friends, touching their bindings, sniffing the pages which evoked her earlier life. Leafing through them had made her smile at how crude the pictures seemed to her, now that she had seen what Vern could create with a pen and a piece of paper.

Vern. She had not seen him for several days and wondered if they would allow him to come here and visit her. Would he even want to do that? He didn't exactly seem relaxed in Enric's presence. But then, who really did?

She wasn't allowed to leave Enric's quarters without him along, and he usually locked the entrance door to make sure she didn't break that command. She had tried being angry at him for it, for his lack of trust, but if she was honest she had to admit that she would have left already otherwise. He spent hours at a stretch in his study and she could be back before he even noticed she was gone.

She went to the door and examined the lock carefully. Even without any particular expertise in lock picking, this didn't look as if just inserting any pointed object and moving it around a bit would open it. She pressed down the door handle, hoping against hope that he might have forgotten to lock it today. Or that he had even decided to show a little trust, however unjustified that would obviously have been.

"Going somewhere?"

She started, jumped back and knocked over a candelabra, sending it to the floor with a clutter, the candles rolling in all directions. Enric stood in the door frame to his study, leaning against it with one shoulder, his arms folded, an expectant look on his face.

How did he manage to show up just when she needed him least? He had locked himself in there more than seven hours ago and then he chose this exact moment to make an appearance. It really was excellent timing.

Shaking his head slowly and deliberately at her, he said. "I knew you couldn't be trusted."

She snorted. "Yes, quite. As if that were a great surprise."

He unfolded his arms and strolled through the room until he stood in front of her. "Trying to run from me again? I was hoping we were done with that."

"With the shackles back on I wouldn't get very far, would I?" she sighed and bent down to tidy up the disorder she had just made. He watched her crouch down on the floor to pick up one candle that had rolled under the chest of drawers next to the door.

When she got back on her feet and made to stick them back onto the candelabra, he took them out of her hands and laid them down, taking her hands in his. He enjoyed that he could just touch her now whenever he felt like it without her freezing in fear or disdain. Having her stay in his quarters was immensely convenient.

"Where did you want to go?" he asked softly, pulling her closer.

"Nowhere in particular. I just wanted to see whether you had locked the door." She didn't object when his arms circled her, though she had to fight the reflex of panic his closeness still induced the first moment.

He pursed his lips. "And what would you have done if you had found the door unlocked?" Her reaction had not been lost on him and he wondered how much time it would take for her to relax without actively reminding herself that he was no longer a threat to her. Well, not an imminent one at least. It was amazing how she was this unfaltering rebel, this resolute revolutionary, only to be so vulnerable in her other aspects. He bet there were not many people she had allowed to see any weaknesses in all her life and was almost sure she was not aware she was showing him this one.

"Knocked at your door to inform you about your lapse, naturally."

He marvelled at how she could maintain a straight face while lying with such bare-faced cheek. "I see. That is very considerate of you. And now the truth, if you don't mind."

She looked up at him and studied his eyes. They were not unfriendly, but there was a hint of steel, even if it had not been audible in his voice yet. The transition, once again, from casual to serious from one sentence to the next was unnerving. Within moments she again felt exactly like the prisoner she was. She knew that stepping out of his embrace right now would be impossible. He wouldn't let her without answering him first.

He was so very used to being obeyed, she thought. And she had been used to following no will but her own since she was fifteen years old. Sooner or later, the friction between the two would cause something to burn. But not right now.

"I would have visited Vern. It has been a while since I saw him. I wanted to show him one or two of my father's books that might interest him."

"You could have asked me."

The ever-gracious warden, she thought and swallowed a sigh. "I am not good at asking for favours."

His lips brushed hers. "Then this is your lucky day. I feel generous today and I am very good at bestowing them."

He took her hand and pulled her with him into his study, where he opened a drawer to take out an expensive looking piece of paper with the Order's emblem and a pen. He started writing with elegant and energetic moves, then he folded the message into what resembled a crude bird and opened the window.

She stepped next to him, looking down directly onto the training grounds where she had for so many months been training with Orrin. The view was really superb from up here.

Today he was there with a group of young boys who surreptitiously were trying to stab each other with their wooden sticks when they should have been listening to their teacher instead.

Enric placed the artfully folded paper on his palm and she felt the rush of air he employed to send the angular bird off towards Orrin. One of the boys spotted it first and pointed his finger upwards. Orrin plucked it out of the air and unfolded it. When he had finished reading it, he lifted his head to where they stood and nodded once to Enric for confirmation, smiling when he recognised Eryn next to him.

"That is an interesting way of sending a message," she remarked.

"Yes, but it only works if the recipient is close by. In this case it was faster than calling for a messenger." He closed the window again. "Vern will come here after dinner. I have some more work to do in the evening, so I don't have to worry about you roaming my quarters to find an escape route."

"So you just wanted somebody to watch me? Why would Vern stop me from escaping?" she smirked. "He likes me better than you."

He smiled back. "Yes, but he is afraid of me, unless I am very much mistaken. And liking you will not make him help you escape when it would mean losing you." He kissed her forehead. "A sentiment we share."

She looked up at him. This sounded suspiciously affectionate. Weren't they enjoying each other's company mostly for carnal reasons? An uneasy feeling began creeping over her.

Taking a careful step back, slowly, not to make it seem like the escape it was, she smiled casually. "I seem to have collected two devoted admirers. Something quite flattering for a simple country girl."

She saw in his eyes that he understood the message of her putting his attachment to her on the same level as Vern's purely friendly one.

He sighed and accompanied her to the study door. "Can you occupy yourself for another hour until dinner? There is something I need to finish."

"I will probably manage it somehow," she said in mock torment.

He leaned against the door after closing it behind her. Of course he was aware that she had had a mere two days to get used to the differing nature of their relationship. He himself had been interested in her for more than three months now, but that didn't make her holding him at a distance any less unpleasant to endure. There was nothing more he could do about that at the moment, however. And after how quickly things between them had developed in these last days, the least he could do was to give her some time to get accommodated to the situation and get over her concerns about being used for his own or the Order's purposes.

* * *

Enric accepted Vern's bow when he had opened the door and stepped aside to let the boy enter.

"Good evening, Lord Enric."

"Vern. I appreciate that you accepted my invitation."

Eryn stood behind Enric and rolled her eyes mockingly. As if there were many people who would dare refuse his invitation in this city or even the kingdom. She smiled and stepped forward to take Vern's hand and lead him to the guest room she occupied.

"Come, there is something I need to show you!"

The boy looked back at the magician, making apologetic expressions for not being in a position to make the usual polite remarks before he retreated with Eryn and saw with relief that he seemed more amused than irritated.

She closed the door behind them.

"It is so good to see you once more! I really miss our walks through the city. I have been locked in these stuffy rooms for more than two days now."

Vern gave her a half-smile. "I heard about the stunt you pulled at the western gate and had a look at the hole in the wall they made to stop you." Then he turned serious, his eyes piercing hers. "You were going to leave without saying goodbye. Just like that. I would have got up next morning and learned you were gone and that I might never see you again. Damn it, Eryn, how could you?"

She gulped. She wasn't really sure why she wasn't prepared for his anger. After their last and so far only squabble she should have known that he wouldn't be pleased about her attempt at getting away.

"I am sorry, Vern. But saying goodbye to you would have placed you in great danger. Imagine they had used magic to make you speak the truth and had found out that you knew all about it before without telling anybody."

He folded his arms. "Father says the Order has offered you a chance to join them. Will you do it?"

Oh dear. How was she supposed to answer that question if she didn't even know herself? "That would depend on a thing or two."

"Like what?"

"There's an oath to the King. I couldn't do that. It just doesn't feel right."

"What exactly does that mean? That you don't accept the offer?" His eyes narrowed.

"I was told that they would be thinking about that, so I'll bet they come up with one further option at least."

"And if this option was alright, you would join us?" he persisted.

She let out a long breath. "Yes. No. I... probably." The words tumbled out quickly. She threw her arms into the air. "I don't know! Don't hurry me!"

The small chance of her staying in the city seemed to mollify him somewhat and he unfolded his arms again, his stance becoming more relaxed. "Alright, then let's wait. What was it you wanted to show me?"

She looked at him, grateful that he had changed the topic and went over to one of two large chests at the foot of the bed.

"They brought all of my books from my old cottage."

Vern stepped closer when she opened the lid of the left chest and took out two books. She handed one to him.

"This is about the workings of muscles and how they are composed. I thought this would interest you as you have drawn so many pictures of them."

She watched him turn the pages, clearly intrigued. He looked up with an elfish grin. "The pictures are not very good."

Smiling herself, she shook her head. "No, they are not. I was wondering if you would be interested in replacing them with your own. The texts are all there, so really good drawings are the only thing that's missing."

He bit his lip while he considered her proposal.

"We would have to have the book copied, of course. With spaces free for your illustrations to go. And, of course, your name would have to be next to the author's." She'd hooked him with that last one, it was plain to see even before he spoke.

"My name? For everyone to see?" Awe resonated in his voice while he stared at the cover, as if he could see the letters spelling out his name there already.

"Of course. The drawings are as important as the texts for understanding the content."

"Can we really do that? I mean, the writer wouldn't object?"

"I don't see how he could, even if he should ever enter this kingdom or were even alive today. He just needs to look at his drawings and then at yours to see that his work benefits very much from your talent."

The flattery worked well on Vern and he didn't seem to be in control of his broad grin any longer. "Then I should probably consider it. I mean, just to help the author. And the future readers."

Eryn nodded solemnly. "That is very noble of you. And the prospect of seeing your name on the cover of a book makes no difference to you in any way, does it? You would be much too modest for such vanity."

He laughed. "That is not very flattering, but I have to admit it's true. So, how does this work? We give the book to one of the scribes in the library to copy the texts into a new one?"

She thought for a moment. "I think we should ask Lord Poron. He might be interested in helping us and I suppose there is a thing or two that might be useful to know when trying to rewrite a book. Can you talk to him? I am not free to move around presently."

"Sure, I will go to the library tomorrow after my lessons. So he doesn't let you out of his quarters? Not at all?"

She sighed. "No, he keeps me locked up in here. He is afraid I might make more trouble."

"Which is an absolutely preposterous presumption," Vern quipped.

"Oh, just stop goading me. And it's not as if I would be of any use, even if I could walk through the city. They changed the enchantment on these manacles. My powers are now completely blocked. I can't heal even minor things."

"Didn't you tell me about a healer's real strength not being his magical powers but what is up here?" He pressed a finger to his forehead.

"Yes, and I am sure people will value that fact very much when they come running for help." She rolled her eyes. "And it is of no importance anyway as long as I am stuck here."

Vern considered her for a few moments. "And if somebody was watching you when you left his quarters?"

Her brows rose. "Like who? You? I doubt he would entrust me into your care. You can't be trusted with anything after teaching me magical fighting."

The boy smiled and went out of the guest room, moving swiftly towards Enric's study before she even thought of asking him what he was up to. He knocked and opened it when the permission to enter came.

Before she could follow him he closed the door in her face. When she tried to grab the door handle, she felt the discharge of a force field against her skin. Damn it! Now even Vern was using them against her!

She took a seat on one of the parlour chairs and stared at the door, waiting. He wouldn't be daft enough really to ask Enric for permission to act as her guardian, would he? Yet he had seemed confident. Why?

When the door opened several minutes later, Enric stepped out, closely followed by the boy.

"Young Vern here will accompany you and keep an eye on you in case you want to leave and I have no time to do so myself," he announced.

Her eyes bulged. There might have been quite a few statements she would have expected. This was not among them.

"Wait a minute, what?" She shook her head in confusion. "You are keeping me here under your special care that no other magician can provide according to you, and then you let me walk around guarded by a fifteen-year-old boy? It's not that I want to question your powers of judgement, but I am rather surprised by it all."

Enric inclined his head. "Vern's powers far exceed yours at the moment. And I have impressed on him the dire consequences of assisting you in anything I wouldn't approve of."

"And what about my outwitting him?"

Vern snorted. "I will be extra careful. And you wouldn't want to ruin my future in the Order by making me seem unreliable and easy to trick, would you? I am rather surprised about your complaint, though. Shouldn't you be glad about any chance to get out of here now and then?"

"Of course I am glad," she conceded, "but also confused." And she found it hard to trust what she couldn't understand.

"That's settled, then," Enric concluded their discussion. "You can pick her up after your lessons. Make sure to bring her back in time for dinner."

Eryn was still frowning at Vern, when Enric suddenly leaned down to her. She realised that he was about to kiss her in front of the boy and made to retreat, when she felt the touch of his hand on hers and the warm energy that seeped from his skin through hers, taking away her command over her muscles.

He leaned close to her ear, whispering, "Don't fight me. You wouldn't want Vern to see me force myself on you, would you?"

When he then released his hold over her body, she barely managed to remain in place when he lifted her chin with his finger and kissed her on her lips, his slightly open and lingering on hers gently, yet possessively. A demonstration, she thought angrily, and one carried off well enough not to embarrass Vern unduly but still make him see that there definitely was physical intimacy between them.

He ended the kiss after a few seconds and straightened, the look on his face obviously pleased with her compliance. She controlled her expression to mask her annoyance when she looked back to her visitor. The boy had not yet mastered the skill of hiding his feelings as effectively, and his wide eyes and rigid posture showed his shock all too clearly.

"I think I'd better leave now…" he stammered.

"Alright, then let me show you to the door. I need to unlock it first," Enric said and went to the entrance door to open it for the boy.

"Lord Enric," Vern said and bowed stiffly, shooting a last confused look back at Eryn before he left.

She waited until he had closed and locked the door again, before she said coldly, "That's just perfect; you have put him on the back foot now. That was completely unnecessary."

He turned, walked back to her calmly and looked down at her. He decided against sitting with her - standing would demonstrate his position of superior authority more effectively, especially as she would not appreciate what he was about to say.

"On the contrary. I told you before that I have no intention of keeping this a secret. And I assumed that you had not informed the boy yourself. Correctly so, judging from his reaction. Consider this a little foretaste of what is to come when we are out in public."

She got up from her chair to reduce the daunting effect of his towering over her and folded her arms. "I find parading this affair in front of everybody somewhat tasteless."

His eyes narrowed. "I see. Then I should probably rectify your perception. I concede that you haven't had very much time to get used to the new situation between us, but let me make one thing clear: this is not an affair." He quickly grabbed her by the wrists when she made to turn and leave. "No, not yet."

She fought the impulse to kick him and glared at him instead. "It certainly is. As long as I am locked in here it is surely nothing more!"

He held on tightly when she kept trying to wriggle her wrists free from his grip. "Locked in my quarters or the city?"

"Are you provoking me on purpose?" she hissed and aimed a kick at his shin to make him let go of her.

Sidestepping her attack easily, he pulled her against him with a sudden move.

"Maybe," he smirked. "I do admit that I find our little tussles... quite stimulating."

She stilled at that, staring at him coldly. "So whenever I am angry you find it satisfying because you can live out your savage urge to subdue me? Is showing the world how you are having your way with the stubborn prisoner part of that?"

He laughed, enraging her even further. "No, that is a matter of satisfying a completely different savage urge: marking my territory. But if you prefer to show the world that *you* are the one having your way with a powerful, mighty lord of the Order, I would be perfectly alright with that, too." More so, in fact, he added silently.

She huffed, indignant. "I have no intention of laying public claim to you."

"Then you will have to endure my doing it. And I would like you to show to everyone who is watching that this is mutual and not because I subdued you."

"But you did! Everybody has either seen or been told about how you fought me in the streets! You will show them a compliant prisoner, tamed even into accepting you into her bed!"

He shook his head and chuckled. "No, trust me when I tell you this: whoever watches you for more than a minute can see there is nothing tame about you."

She tried a different approach, looking up at him pleadingly. "Can't we just keep this between us? I don't like making private matters known publicly."

"No, I'm afraid that is not a good idea," he said. "Even though you had to guard your privacy very well in the past to protect yourself, this time it is the other way round: public knowledge is what will keep you safe. People need to know that causing you trouble means challenging *me*." Especially if there was resistance to her joining the Order in the not too distant future, he added to himself, with more than a particle of hope.

"Why?" She frowned. "Are you expecting any particular trouble?"

"Nothing particular. I just like being one step ahead."

She sighed. "Protection. A less savage if hardly less ancient impulse. But I really don't look forward to explaining this to Vern tomorrow. That one you left to me, of course," she added reproachfully.

Chuckling, he finally released her. "Absolutely. There is no impulse I sense in myself, savage, ancient or recent, that makes me wish to lay claim to that task." He felt her mood mellowing. "Is there a chance that you will spend the entire night with me this time?"

She smiled sweetly, glad to be able to repay him at least on a minor scale. "No, none whatsoever."

* * *

She looked up from her book and took a deep breath when the knock sounded at the door. That had to be Vern. Enric came out of his study and took the key from his pocket to unlock the door.

As expected, Vern stood in front of it, bowing to the older magician and flashing her a look that told her that she had some explaining to do.

Eryn got up from the settee and grabbed Enric's hooded cape that would not only keep her warm but also hide her hair and keep people's attention off her.

She was about to pass Enric on her way out, when she felt him take her hand and stopped. He lifted it and turned her palm so he could press his lips into it.

"Keep her safe for me, Vern," he said and closed the door when the boy nodded and bowed.

They walked through the corridors in silence and when they had left the palace, they turned right into the street that led to the city centre.

"Well?" Vern finally said.

"Well what?" she replied, buying time.

"Are you together with Lord Enric or what was it yesterday and just now?" He sounded impatient.

"No, we are not together."

"Then you are just sleeping with him?" Accusation had replaced impatience.

She stopped and turned to him, scowling. "Yes, as a matter of fact, I am. And as I am a grown woman this is entirely within my rights, even if you don't approve."

"I thought you hated him!"

"I did." How to explain this to him when she herself wasn't sure what exactly had happened to change that?

"But not anymore, as it seems."

"Obviously."

"What happened? He didn't force you, did he?" Vern's eyes had gone wide in repugnance at the thought.

She lifted her head in a dismissive air. "Don't be an idiot, Vern. Wouldn't that make me hate him more than before?"

"Yes, I suppose," he said, relieved. Then he paused. "You are sure you are not together?" he then asked carefully. "He does seem rather... determined to convey that impression."

She swallowed. Oh dear, did he have a talent for putting his finger on the sore spot. "Of course I am sure. He probably has his own devious reasons for wanting to make you think otherwise."

"Yes, he must have," Vern retorted with a pitying look. "Making a wrong impression on me is undoubtedly a major concern of his. Surely *I* am the one who misunderstands what's going on..."

They had reached the crossroads where Enric had tricked her into fighting. Had that really been only a few days ago?

"I am not together with him!" she said, in a more insistent voice.

He lifted his hands palms facing away from him, "It's alright, whatever you say."

She rolled her eyes and walked on determinedly, forcing him to run a few steps to keep up with her.

"Where are we going?" he asked.

"Nowhere in particular," she answered. And where could she go, anyway? Plia was no longer open to visit; it made her a target for the apothecaries. Buying herbs was no longer possible and neither was healing. Sitting by the river was definitely too cold at this time of the year.

"How about visiting Junar?" he suggested. "Maybe she could shorten that cloak. You are dragging it in the dirt - it's much too long for you."

"I can't just have it shortened. It's not mine. Returning it dirty is better than giving it back too short and thus rendering it useless for him."

"Ah yes, I forgot that you're just sharing a bed and nothing else," he snorted.

"Could you just stop it? I am starting to think about how to get rid of you, regardless of whether this endangers your career in the Order or not."

A girl about Vern's age came running towards them and Eryn automatically stepped back to get out of her way, but she stopped directly in front of them. Looking up at Eryn, she grabbed her apron and twisted it between her hands.

"You are the healer, aren't you?" she asked pleadingly.

Oh no, Eryn thought, not today when she had no powers for healing at her disposal. "I'm afraid I can't help you right now. They took my powers away as punishment." She jangled her wrists, wondering too late if the girl was even aware of the practice of blocking magical powers with golden bangles.

"Couldn't you still have a look at my brother? Please? Just to see if it is serious? Please!" Her words became more and more desperate as she spoke.

Eryn sighed. "Alright, then. But I can't do much more than have a look at him."

Without herbs or her powers she was rather useless, and it was too dangerous to ask Vern to at least do the analysing. Word of his developing healing abilities might get around.

The girl nodded gratefully and led them to a narrow house at the end of an alley to their left. She was greeted by the usual dimness in these kind of houses as she entered ahead of Vern, who followed closely behind. The girl climbed a narrow, creaking staircase and opened one of four doors on the first floor a crack, then beckoned for them to enter.

Eryn felt a sharp pain at the back of her head and a commotion behind her before she hit the floor and darkness enveloped her.

* * *

Enric's heart almost stopped when he stormed, closely followed by Tyront, into the room the spy downstairs had indicated. Eryn lay on the dusty wooden floor, motionless. A man was bent over her to determine if she was still breathing.

Without taking notice of anything else in the room, he immediately kneeled next to her and placed a hand on her side, checking for the shield inside her abdomen. He let out a long sigh of relief when he detected it. So there was still enough life force in her to power it.

Only then did he look around. Not far away from her Vern lay on the floor as well, not unconscious but clearly not too far away from it. He had an injury on his forehead, which bled slightly, and from his eyes he seemed rather dazed. In one corner of the room three men stood huddled together, kept at bay by four of the King's soldiers with drawn weapons.

The man who had been checking on Eryn before bowed to the magicians and then left the room hurriedly.

Enric's gaze returned to her. He carefully turned her so she lay on her back and saw a scratch on her cheek she had probably gained when she had fallen to the floor.

Fallen to the floor. He started seeing pictures of her being attacked from behind while trying to help, her yelling out in pain, knees buckling under her, and her limp body hitting the hard floor.

Tyront could literally see the wrath inside the younger magician grow into something almost tangible, something that changed the quality of air in the room. He felt his hair stand on end and laid a warning hand on Enric's shoulder. A powerful magician on the verge of losing control was a very dangerous thing indeed and had to be dealt with before it was too late.

"Stop this right now or I have to take you down," he growled and saw with relief how the focus returned into Enric's eyes. He had not yet been gone far enough to snap out of it on his own. The dancing flames burning in Enric's eyes turned into ice and he looked at the men in the corner. They stared at him, fixated in horror.

"Take them to the dungeons," Enric barked and the soldiers obeyed instantly, eager to get as much distance between themselves and what seemed like a magician about to lose control.

Tyront crouched next to Vern and examined the wound. "That looks like a nasty blow. How do you feel, my boy?"

The young man squeezed his eyes tight for a moment, then opened them again, obviously dizzy. His gaze fell on Eryn and his eyes widened with panic.

"No!" he croaked hoarsely, "she isn't..."

"She is alive," Enric said in a voice oddly free of emotion without taking his eyes off her. At that moment Eryn stirred. She groaned quietly and her hand moved towards her forehead, eyes still closed.

Enric carefully lifted her shoulders slightly off the ground so he could gently pull her into his arms, leaning her head against his chest. He stared at her, wishing fervently for the first time that he had the ability to heal. The mark on her cheek seemed to deride his helplessness. He touched the back of her head, feeling for signs of an injury, for the warm, sticky touch of blood. His breathing slowed a little when he found nothing.

Her eyes fluttered open and she looked up at him, not seeming to comprehend. Her gaze wandered along the ceiling and walls of the room for a few seconds before he felt her muscles tense. He grasped her firmly before she could make any sudden movements.

"Vern!" she exclaimed and pushed against the restraining arms that kept her from jumping up.

"I am here."

She sighed in relief when she heard his voice. He moved into her line of sight and she stared at the mess on his forehead. When she stretched out her hand and he took it, she pulled his to her cheek and closed her eyes.

"How badly are you hurt?" she said quietly, a lump forming in her throat.

"It looks worse than it is," he replied soothingly.

"Can you take the manacles off for a moment?" she pleaded weakly and opened her eyes to look up into Enric's strained face. He nodded curtly and removed them at once as she had hoped. With the two strong magicians present and herself dizzy after a blow to the head there was not much danger of her overpowering them, even with her barrier.

She closed her eyes again for a moment and felt Vern's hand in hers tense before he ripped it out of her grip when he felt the warm tingle of magic flow from her body to his.

"Stop that! You are in no state to heal others! Take care of yourself first! I am not the one who was unconscious," he scolded her and scowled at her angrily.

Enric frowned down at her. "He is right. Heal yourself first."

She began shaking her head but stopped when the room tilted. "I can't heal myself right now. The damage is inside my head and shouldn't be healed by somebody with concentration problems. I might make a mistake and increase the damage."

"But *me* you can heal?" Vern's voice sounded accusing.

"Your damage is external only. This is routine work, even if my concentration has suffered a bit," she replied tiredly.

"The boy is right." Enric snapped the armlets back onto her wrists. He shifted from under her and stood, bending down to lift her up into his arms.

"I am just a little dizzy, I can walk," she protested, trying to lower her feet to the ground but felt Enric's hold on her knees strengthen instead of loosen.

"No."

She took a closer look at his face. There was tension. Jaw muscles tight, brows furrowed, eyes not merely cold but filled with ice. Was he angry at her? What for?

Only then did she think of asking, "What happened?"

"You were attacked." His voice came out from between clenched teeth.

"Why?" She tried to think back. "A girl came to ask me to have a look at somebody…"

"She was paid to do so," Tyront offered. He followed them down the stairs, keeping his hand around Vern's arm to steady him.

Enric had been dangerously close to snapping only minutes ago. He had been about to violate one of the most sacred laws in the Order: never to attack a non-magician with magic. The consequences for that would have been dire, even – or especially – for somebody of his rank.

The tension was still there, clearly visible in the set of his shoulders, the barely contained anger in his imperious strides.

She waited patiently until pieces of memory slotted back into place. Everything inside her head seemed so slow and fuzzy, as if moving through mud.

"So her brother is alright?"

Tyront looked at her, concerned. It had to have taken quite a blow to slow down that quick mind. "There is no brother, dear girl. She was paid to lead you in here."

"Me? What for? Who?"

"The apothecaries. At least one of them. We can only assume what their intentions might have been."

Her eyes opened wide and her hand at Enric's chest balled into a fist. She writhed, trying to make him set her down. "Them? But…"

"That's enough! Stop it, both of you," Enric ordered sharply.

Vern stared at the three of them. Lord Tyront was not usually seen to being ordered about, especially not by subordinates or in such a tone of voice. He waited if some kind of explosion, reprimand or some such was about to follow, but Tyront just studied him worriedly.

"Stop it? I can't just…" She tried to push herself away from his chest, in vain.

Vern watched as all tension left her body in an instant and her head and limps fell back.

Tyront sighed and shook his head. "How many times have you knocked her out now?"

Enric stared straight ahead while moving. "I have lost count."

*　*　*

Oddly, her first thoughts when she opened her eyes were about the cloak she had borrowed from him for her stroll through the city with Vern.

She looked around and found that she had been brought to Enric's bedroom and was wearing a dark red night gown. And the shackles, of course.

Enric sat in a chair next to the bed, reading a book. But he didn't appear particularly relaxed. He looked up when he felt her gaze on him and smiled. It didn't reach his eyes.

"Your cloak," she said before he could speak, "It's muddy. It is too long for me."

His brow rose in mild surprise at her peculiar priorities. "I admit I didn't pay any particular attention to that little detail. But we will have it shortened for you, unless you would like to order a new one instead."

She remembered Vern's suggestion when they had walked along Kingsway and how he had jibed that he had forgotten that they shared nothing more than a bed. Was for Enric giving her his cloak and having it altered mere generosity that didn't require any further explanation, or did it imply something else? And when did a cloak turn into something representing their… well, whatever it was they had together?

He rose from his chair and sat down next to her on the bed, stroking her hair cautiously as if afraid that she might shatter into a thousand pieces otherwise.

"How are you feeling?"

She considered the question for a moment, taking time to answer it from a medically satisfying point of view. "My head is aching a little at the back, but it's nothing major. The dizziness is mostly gone and my ability for coherent thought has come back, in the main. At least I think it has; I wonder if I would notice if it hadn't, as noticing it probably requires the ability to think coherently. Which would mean that if I noticed its absence, thinking clearly would have to be there in the first place..." She stopped when he placed his index finger to her lips, smiling faintly, but this time for real.

"Confused, but clearly yourself again. That's good enough for me. Well, for now."

Her eyes went wide when the memory of her last waking moments returned to her. She pushed away his hand.

"You did it again! You just put me to sleep!" she cried out accusingly. "We really need to discuss that tendency of yours!"

"Whatever you say." He leaned forward and kissed her on the forehead. "Come. Let's get you something to eat. Do you want me to remove the shackles before that so you can heal yourself?"

"What? Without any oaths that keep me from escaping? You are oddly forthcoming at the moment," she said, eyeing him suspiciously.

"Interesting. Usually you complain about how I am never obliging. You are hard to please." Without waiting for her answer, he removed the bangles and watched when she closed her eyes, took several long, relaxing breaths and remained still for a few minutes.

When she opened them again, she smiled and he leaned forward to kiss her mouth while he replaced the manacles. She wondered if he had added the kiss to take the sting out of the gesture of shackling her.

"Will you tell me what happened? All of it?" she asked.

"Of course. Just let me get you something to eat first." He rose from the bed and went out into the parlour where a tray with a hearty breakfast was waiting for her. He put it on the bed beside her and stretched out on the other side.

It felt odd being cared for by him - actually, being cared for by anyone. That had not really ever been necessary before in her life. Illnesses and injuries had been healed away in a matter of minutes and the only head injury she had had before was the one she incurred several months ago, the one that had led to her being brought here.

"When you and Vern left yesterday for your walk, Tyront had a watcher follow you. And so did the King, as it turned out."

"By *watcher* you mean a spy, I assume?" she interrupted him.

"Whatever term you prefer. *Spy* does seem rather offensive to them, for future reference. They prefer to be referred to as *agents*. But whatever you want to call them, two of them were following you and thus witnessed your being lured into the house. One of them followed you inside and saw Vern being hit on the head when he entered the room right behind you. He then ran back to get the King's guards to intervene and the other sp..., erm, agent followed you up the stairs and kept them at bay. That's all there is to be told."

"You said it was the apothecaries, didn't you?"

"We don't know if the entire League was involved, but at least three members were, for sure. They are being questioned as we speak. Tyront should be here soon with some news."

She looked at him thoughtfully. "From your reaction yesterday I would have expected *you* to be doing the questioning."

Enric smiled grimly at that. "I wanted to. Tyront forbade it. He was worried about me being a little too... enthusiastic."

"I had the impression you were angry at me. Were you?"

"Not at you. At myself for letting you out of my sight. In hindsight that shows very bad judgement on my part. The apothecaries took the first chance to get to you when they observed that you were relatively unprotected. They even risked attacking an Order magician. They must have been pretty desperate."

She shrugged. "There would have been other situations sooner or later where you would have had to let me out of your sight. If it had not happened yesterday, it would have at some other time."

He slowly shook his head. "No, it wouldn't. As soon as it became public knowledge that you are involved with me, they wouldn't have dared to lay a hand on you." He looked at her intently. "This is why I don't want to keep us a secret. This way I can give you the protection of my status in the Order even though technically you still are the King's captive."

"Politics." She wrinkled up her nose in disgust. "So you can practically protect me from everyone except the King and your own superior?"

"Practically, yes. For my protection from those two you would have to enter into a companionship with me." He hadn't thought she would react very favourably to that piece of information, but almost choking on a mouthful bread bun did seem rather unexpected and he raised an eyebrow at her. "You can relax. That was not a proposal, just an explanation of my limits."

"What? No! A crumb just went down the wrong way," she said casually.

Yes, that's it, he thought.

At that moment a knock sounded at the door and Enric got to his feet. "That is probably Tyront. Why don't you get dressed and join us in the parlour? I will ask him to wait with his news until then."

"Dressed in what?" she asked and looked around for something to wear. In vain.

He pointed to a chest next to the window. "First drawer." And he was gone.

She frowned at the door he had just left through. He had put clothes for her to wear in a drawer in his bedroom? Swallowing, she pushed the breakfast tray aside and went over to the chest of drawers, opening the one he had indicated.

As she had dreaded, there were not only a pair of trousers and a tunic placed among Enric's things, but the whole drawer had been emptied to make space for three shirts and pairs of trousers in her size. Was he sneakily trying to move her from the guest room into his bedroom? She wondered where he had slept last night. Very probably not in the guest room.

She needed to put a stop to this somehow. Gently, of course: she had no wish to hurt him, but rather protect him from a rude awakening later. It was for his own good. Right now it was hardly a good idea for him to form too close an attachment to her. If they somehow gave her a chance to leave, she would still take it. Maybe the King would reconsider the options. Chance would be a fine thing, and all that.

Sniffing at her own delusions, she grabbed a dark brown tunic. It matched her eyes. She stared at it for a while, wondering if he had picked the colour for that reason or if it was just a coincidence. She hoped the latter.

When she entered the parlour, both men rose from their seats. The older men nodded to her. "Lady Eryn."

She nodded back. "Lord Tyront."

Enric stepped towards her and took her hand to lead her to a settee and pull her down right next to him when he sat, draping an arm over the back rest behind her.

Oh no, she thought uneasily. It seemed this was now becoming the demonstration for Lord Tyront.

Tyront watched them with well disguised interest. Enric had apparently been successful in changing her opinion of him, even though she was obviously still not as relaxed in his close proximity as he was in hers. He enjoyed touching her casually, while Eryn tried with little success to keep him at a distance and didn't seem as ready for this kind of intimacy. Probably the more so when it was not entirely private, as now.

Seeing Enric with a woman at his side was odd, especially one as unsure of her own regard for him as Eryn. But after ten years of all obeying him unconditionally a little challenge was very likely a side benefit for him.

"I assume Enric has filled you in on the incident yesterday, at least as much as was known to us at that time?"

She nodded.

"Good. Then I can start right away with the interrogation. They all confessed to their plan of luring you into the house and attacking you, because they said you pose a danger to their business. When they figured out that beating up the herb seller was not enough of a warning to make you stop, they decided that more drastic measures were in order. Agents had informed them of the offer the Order made you and this has put them under considerable pressure. They correctly assumed that as we didn't stop you from healing before, we would very probably not be doing so after you joined us."

"And our putting a complete block on your powers after your attempt at escape was a stroke of luck for them," Enric added ominously.

"Indeed," Tyront agreed. "And as they had been watching the palace for quite some time after you were locked in here, they acted quickly when they saw you leaving here escorted by a young man possessing no more than average magical strength. Attacking you after you were accepted into the Order would have been too dangerous, of course. Firstly, you would have had your considerable powers at your disposal again and secondly, the Order's retribution would have been something for them to fear."

She frowned. "But hasn't attacking Vern opened that door anyway? I mean, he is an Order magician and yet they hurt him."

"True. But they intended just to knock him out before he could identify anybody, then leave him outside somewhere to be found."

Eryn swallowed. "And me? What had they intended to do with me?"

Enric narrowed his eyes at Tyront and shook his head almost imperceptibly.

Tyront sighed. "She needs to know, Enric. She is not a child, however much you might want to spare her."

"They wanted to kill me, then," she said quietly and shivered. Enric moved his arm from the backrest to her shoulders and pulled her against him.

"Yes," Tyront confirmed. "And they will very probably be sentenced to death for this intention."

Her head jerked up, staring at him. "What? Why would you do that?" Twelve-year-old memories arose in her mind, of the baker who had taken her father's life and then was executed by the townspeople in turn.

"It's not us doing it," he replied. "It's the King."

"But I am no more than a prisoner to him! Why would he kill people for hurting a prisoner?"

"A prisoner he is very eager to keep alive, mind you. Attacking you is an act of defiance against the sovereign. He cannot let that pass. And there is also the matter of pleasing the Order."

"Pleasing the Order? That means you could intervene by telling him that it wouldn't please you! The attack on the Order magician was not with an intention of killing and I am not a member!"

She looked at each man in turn. Their expressions were indulgent.

"I will do no such thing," Tyront said mildly. "When the King announces the verdict, I will demonstrate our appreciation."

She freed herself from Enric's arm and jumped up. "Why? You can't just have them despatched! You wouldn't even have lost anything if they had succeeded! I am not one of your members and I probably will never be!"

Both men exchanged a glance at her desperate attempts of saving the lives of people who had shown no qualms about taking hers.

Enric followed her agitated movements with his eyes. He resented her comment about their not losing anything with her death, but decided to let it go for now as she seemed, for whatever reason, to be outraged by the news.

"What is it that troubles you so much about their impending execution? I would think that the King's demonstration of how much he values your life is quite a compliment," Tyront said, observing her closely.

"I can't be responsible for somebody's death!" she exclaimed and then covered her face with her hands before adding more quietly, "Not again."

Enric rose slowly and stepped close to her, though refrained from touching her, when she glanced up at him as if ready to bolt should he make a wrong move.

"What do you mean by *not again*?" he asked softly. There seemed to be something in her past causing her this considerable pain that was being stirred up again by the recent incidents.

"That's none of your business," she snarled, knowing that it was not fair of her to direct her anger at him when in truth it was aimed at herself. But neither was she able to talk about that right here and now.

Her thoughts started revolving around how she might have prevented this whole mess. She should have forced Vern to take her to the location of the League of Apothecaries. Maybe they would somehow have found an agreement if she had just stormed in there that day. She probably should have tried harder to cooperate with them.

"Whatever your personal reasons may be, the Order will not object to a death sentence being handed down to the miscreants," Tyront said calmly but left no doubt whatsoever that there was no changing his mind. "And we will have to work on how to behave properly towards me as soon as you have joined the Order."

Her smile was cold. "Then I should probably refrain from joining you the more. It would give me the freedom to continue treating you with honesty instead of pretence. I was taught that the former is the *true* sign of respect. But of course you would need the courage and aplomb to face it. Pretence is so much nicer for the ego, after all."

Tyront's answering smile was equally glacial. "I fancy that this would be almost the only freedom you could be sure of retaining."

"I think," Enric cut in decidedly, "that we should probably continue this conversation at some other time." He looked to Tyront intently.

The older man nodded slowly. Enric's need to protect her was strong indeed, he thought. Even, and probably foremost, from herself.

"That is fine with me," Eryn said stiffly. "There is nothing much I have to say right now. Lord Tyront. *Lord* Enric." She gave both of them a formal nod and turned to return to the room she had only several minutes ago emerged from. Then she hesitated and went to the guest room instead, hearing Enric sigh before she carefully closed the door behind her.

"With her joining us, the Order will not be facing very peaceful times." Tyront shook his head and sighed. "I really hope she will master her temper. Otherwise I will have to spend a good deal of my time punishing her on a regular basis."

"I am just glad to see that I am not the only one who loses his composure when dealing with her," Enric replied in a matter-of-fact way. "At least, if it keeps happening even to you, I don't have to blame myself for it."

"I wouldn't say that it keeps happening," the older man frowned.

"I dimly recall an incident in the throne room when she made you shout at her quite impressively."

Tyront massaged his temples with two fingers. "I am really glad that you reminded me of that."

Enric gave a smirk. He was rather looking forward to seeing what the Order would turn into after Eryn joined it. Tyront in his current mood would probably murder him for putting that into words, so Enric decided to keep that sentiment to himself.

CHAPTER 27

Moving

Eryn looked up when the guest room door was opened without knocking and Enric strolled in.

"You should knock when you enter a lady's room. It's considered polite, you know. I could have been naked."

He smiled. "That's alright. I have been moving in high circles for quite some time and my response to something like that would have been adequate."

"Yes, I can just imagine your response." She chuckled, finding it hard to stay angry at him because of their conversation yesterday evening.

"Of course you can. There is only one thing to do for a true gentleman, after all - taking off all his clothes as well to make the lady feel less awkward." He strolled closer to the bed on which she was sitting cross-legged with what he assumed was one of her father's books. "What are you reading?"

"Something about the correct treatment of herbs. My father was very much into herbs, which is understandable, considering that he had to be very careful when using magic for healing."

"Indeed." He sighed. "I wanted to let you know that Tyront and I have been summoned by the King. I assume he wants to announce his verdict on the apothecaries."

She stiffened. "I see. And you really think he will have them executed?"

"That's what I expect, yes." He bent down to her. "And even though I can see that you don't approve of a death sentence, I have to tell you that any other punishment would upset me very much." When she remained silent and just looked at him reproachfully, he straightened again. "I need to leave now. Don't do anything I wouldn't appreciate while I'm gone."

"What could I do, locked in and without magic? Hide your robes?"

He smiled and bent down to kiss her cheek. "I am sure you could come up with something if you put your mind to it. Not that I am encouraging you to."

She stared at the door after he had left. Damn him. She had started to get used to his constant little touches and kisses here and there.

* * *

"Lord Tyront. Lord Enric." The King watched both men bow to him and then continued, "I assume you are aware why I have sent for you. I have made my decision about the apothecaries. As you surely had expected, they are sentenced to death. By decapitation. Is this verdict to the Order's satisfaction?"

"Yes, Your Majesty, very much so," Tyront replied and bowed.

"Good. How is your guest doing, Lord Enric? I assume she has been able to make good whatever harm was inflicted on her?"

"Yes, Your Majesty. She is up and well again."

"Excellent. Then nothing will keep her from attending the execution in ten days."

Oh no, Enric thought, that was not good, not good at all. "If I may implore Your Majesty to reconsider this order?"

The King raised his brows. "In what way, Lord Enric?"

"I am afraid Lady Eryn will be very upset about anyone being executed publicly. She feels a very strong obligation to protect and preserve human life. And she feels personally responsible for what has happened."

"I see," the King said quietly. "I appreciate your concerns. Unfortunately, I need the intended victim to be present or the occasion will lack the required credibility. And if she is to join the Order, she will have to learn to obey orders even if they are not to her personal liking. Let this be an occasion for her to demonstrate this impressive aptitude for learning I have heard so much about."

Enric bowed in resignation. "As you wish, Your Majesty."

"And there is one more thing I wish you to convey to her. She is from now on no longer subject to the curfew order and thus is free to leave your quarters as she pleases. This, of course, also includes the permission to choose her own accommodation." He watched the magician closely for any visible sign of dismay and seemed almost disappointed when none came.

"I will inform her of this, too, Your Majesty."

"Good. You are dismissed, My Lords."

Both of them bowed and the King watched them leaving. When the heavy doors had closed behind them, Loft frowned.

"Forgive me, Your Majesty, but I am afraid I am at a loss as to why you have decided to allow her to leave his rooms. I had the impression that you agreed to confine her to his quarters to give Lord Enric a chance to form a closer attachment to her."

"Indeed. And that he has. He is, however, rather more patient than I can afford at the moment. I need him to make a move, a bold one at that. And as long as she is so conveniently close to him, he might decide to take the route of patience instead and just enjoy her company for now."

"Which would no longer be the case if she moved out of his quarters?"

"Exactly."

"Why would she return to the warriors' quarters when her current accommodation is so much more pleasant?"

"Because," the King said with a quiet smile, "she still insists on sleeping in his guest room."

"Is it possible, Your Majesty," Marrin spoke for the first time, "that he is not yet as attached to her as you are hoping?"

"No. He almost attacked the apothecaries with magic, endangering everything he has been working for in this last decade. He *is* attached to her - I am convinced of that." The King interlaced his fingers and smiled. "We need to organise a ball."

"A ball, Your Majesty?" Loft asked in confusion.

"Indeed. One week from now should be enough time to frustrate Lord Enric sufficiently to be susceptible to my little challenge. And for Lady Eryn to arrange for a ball gown."

* * *

Junar opened the door and exclaimed, "Eryn! What a surprise! I thought they had locked you up for good after what you did to the city wall!" She laughed and pulled her into the small sewing shop she ran.

Eryn was not exactly in a good mood, but Junar's bubbly spirit was contagious and she smiled back. "Well, it was not exactly *me* who did the damage."

"You were the cause for it, so that's pretty much the same. Tell me everything – is it true that you are together with Lord Enric now? And that the apothecaries tried to kill you?"

Eryn sighed. "Well, I wouldn't call it being together. Let's say we have a grown-up, mutually satisfying arrangement. As for that other matter..." She grimaced and shook her head. "That is true, unfortunately. They are posting announcements of the death sentence around the city just now. At least the King seems to feel badly about his subjects luring me into death traps because he has lifted my curfew order. I have been able to move out of Enric's quarters again."

Junar shot her a doubtful look. "Don't tell me you have voluntarily returned to that tiny hole at the warriors' quarters? He can't be that hard to endure."

"It is not about enduring him, it is about independence and not being more of a prisoner than I have to be."

"And he treats you like a prisoner?"

"At times he can be a bit overbearing, no matter whether I am an actual prisoner or not." She stopped when she saw Junar's teasing smile. "You think I am completely crazy, don't you? All everyone sees is a nice face and a lot of money united in one man."

She shook her head earnestly. "No, dear. That is not all we see. We see a very attractive man and wouldn't stop looking at his face when the rest is hardly any less appealing. And then there is of course a position of immense power and a lot of money to go with it. Whatever his faults may be, they can only be minor in comparison."

"What can I say?" Eryn shook her head in mock self-loathing. "I am an ungrateful creature and should be ashamed of myself."

Junar laughed and patted her shoulder. "Oh, you really should be. Quite ashamed."

"Well, at least I can visit Plia again and don't need to be afraid of making her a target for the apothecaries."

"Dear me, your life really is exciting, eh?"

"Believe me, I would gladly exchange it for a quieter one."

Junar grinned. "If I get Lord Enric, I will swap mine with you any time. My most exciting change in schedule is an order for the upcoming ball the King is giving."

"Then I will cause you even more excitement. I need a ball gown as well. I have been ordered to go there," she said darkly.

"Ordered? By who? Lord Enric?" Junar frowned.

"No. By the King himself. He calls it an invitation but if you read between the lines nothing apart from an earthquake or a flood is an acceptable excuse for my staying away." She narrowed her eyes. "He is ordering me about a lot these days. I am also expected to attend the public execution of the apothecaries."

"And so you should! It is you they tried to kill, after all! I will be there, and if it is only to make sure they really get what they deserve." Junar's expression had become incredulous. "Why would you even have to be ordered to go there?"

"Because killing doesn't become any less deplorable if the King is the one doing it. Quite the opposite, I think!"

"So you would just let them live? As if nothing had happened?" She shook her head in confusion.

Eryn gestured helplessly. "No, not really. But locking them away is punishment enough. Why take their lives away? I mean, they have families, after all." And being left behind was not a nice thing to happen to a child, she thought. It was hard. And painful.

"They should have thought of that before they tried such a despicable thing!" Junar exclaimed. "And leaving aside the fact that they knew well enough what the likely consequences of being caught would be, what might be the alternative? Locking them up for the rest of their lives?"

"That's surely one option, yes."

"That would just be a way of prolonging their suffering and thus hardly an option if we are talking about the inhuman aspect of killing," Junar reasoned. "As you may imagine the living conditions in the dungeons are not the most bucolic or... even friendly. Keeping prisoners strong and healthy is clearly no priority there. And rightly so."

"So we are talking of killing them off quickly with an axe instead of slowly with bad living conditions?" Eryn huffed. "I am also not in favour of treating those in one's care badly!"

The seamstress sighed. "What is it you would want for them, then? A nice, comfortable cell with all comforts they need to have a happy, carefree life behind heavy, cast-iron doors? Have occasional visits from their family members, read a few books to pass the long months and years? You know, the crime rate in the city would explode if it meant such a step up in living circumstances, especially among the poor. It would be like rewarding criminals instead of discouraging them."

Eryn gave in. This was a useless discussion. She wouldn't convince Junar, there seemed real conviction behind the words Eryn heard. And what would it change, anyway? The King would be the one who needed to change his mind, and there was little chance of that.

"Anyway, be that as it may, I need you to make me a ball gown. The King has included a little slip which will pay your costs if you take it to the palace." She handed the card with the gilded edges to Junar, who whistled between her teeth when she took it and examined it closely.

"I have heard about these, but never actually seen one. This one is worth ten gold pieces." She looked up at Eryn again. "We can turn you into a queen with that much gold," she said, beaming a wide smile.

* * *

Tyront suppressed a yawn. It had been a long day. He poured himself another cup, then leaned back on the settee in his parlour.

"Why don't you make her move in with you? It's not as if people don't know about the two of you. You made sure of that. And she seems to spend most nights in your bed anyway."

Enric just snorted. "Firstly, she doesn't spend the nights with me. She always returns to the confined, dark cell she has been complaining about since she got here and which nevertheless still seems more appealing than staying with *me*. And secondly - in case you haven't noticed - she doesn't really take well to being *made* to do anything. I first hinted at moving in with me over dinner and she tipped over a bottle of wine. I swear to you this had nothing to do with clumsiness - she did it on purpose to distract me. And, well, half a bottle of wine over your trousers tends to do the trick."

Tyront smirked. "That was not your only try, I assume, as you said it was your *first* attempt?"

"No. I thought it safer without any food or drinks around." He shrugged. "So I brought it up again during our training session."

Tyront flinched. "You thought it was *safer* to do this when she was wielding a weapon?"

"Now in hindsight, it doesn't seem so brilliant after all," he admitted. "She almost took my head off. She really is faster and fiercer when she is tense."

"Well, there is always the option of just moving her things to your quarters while she is out. If you have the nerve for it, that is," the older man chuckled.

That was actually an option Enric was already considering. He was still in the process of weighing the trouble this would cause against the benefits he might get, though the longer it was since she had been permitted her own place again, the more the scale tipped towards the latter.

"It's only a matter of time until she gives in. I am very persistent. And as you say, I can always give her a little push in the right direction," Enric smiled.

Tyront looked at him. "Very confident. So you wouldn't mind a little bet? Six gold pieces say she does not give up her room in the next month."

"Betting against me? I am sorely disappointed in your lack of trust in me."

"What can I say in my defence? I think you are about to learn a lesson, and as I won't be the one giving it to you I should at least be allowed to profit from it."

* * *

She sighed and rubbed her shoulder where she had caught another strike today. Enric was not exactly squeamish when it came to using his advantage of superior strength. Although only to improve her skills, for her own good, as he didn't tire of pointing out.

Pushing open the heavy door to the warriors' quarters, she thought longingly of the refreshing bowl of water that usually awaited her for washing. After that she would pick up Vern for another nice stroll through the city. They still had a few hours of daylight left.

She reached her door and was about to push it open when she noticed the folded piece of paper affixed at eye height. She carefully plucked it from the pin that had been used to secure it and unfolded it.

First she felt the blood drain from her face only to have it rush back again as anger took over. Standing frozen, she stared at the words, reading them again and then once more. It was from Enric, telling her that he had had her possessions moved to his quarters and was looking forward to seeing her there for dinner.

She let the message sink slowly and then grabbed the door handle to push it open. It didn't budge. So the bastard had also locked her room and forced her to come to him for a place to sleep.

He had tried to convince, cajole and pester her into moving in with him, but she had refused time and again, and he had seemingly become tired of waiting. He had decided that her consent was a nice bonus, but no absolute requirement. Bastard!

She crumpled the paper in her fist and was about to throw it on the floor, then reconsidered. It would be so much nicer to throw it in his face. Or make him swallow it, though there was not much chance for her being able to accomplish that.

What to do now? She was basically without accommodation. Going to *him* was not an option. She would rather sleep on the street or in the horse stables.

She started moving slowly, putting one leg in front of the other, thinking of how to get back at him for this insolence, this affront.

When she next looked up, she found herself standing outside Orrin's door. Yes, she decided, that was a good place to go for thinking. The door opened at her knock and the servant informed her that Lord Orrin was in his study.

He looked up when she knocked and entered his study without waiting for him to call her in. She didn't look like good news, he decided instantly. Exhausted and sweaty, probably because she had just returned from her training. Her expression was a mixture of disbelief and indignation.

He waited until she had taken a seat before he asked her, "What's happened?"

Shaking her head, she just handed him the crumpled paper and waited for him to read it.

He raised his brow and sighed. Now, that had been an ill-judged action if ever there was one. He felt anger rise inside him and fought to contain it. What she needed now was sympathy.

"I assume he will be taking his dinner alone today. And probably quite a large number of other meals as well if I judge your mood correctly."

She shook her head. "Can you believe that? I mean, moving in together is not something just one person decides. And I've told him several times that I have no intention to move in any time soon. I am sure there was no room for misunderstandings. This is not the usual way in the big city, is it? I am not just a country girl with no idea of how the real world works, am I?"

Orrin shook his head. "No, that is not usually how it goes." But it probably would happen more frequently if the average city man had Lord Enric's resources at his disposal, he thought. It was a reassuring thought that the mighty ones used their power so responsibly.

"Why can't he be content with what we have? We have come quite a long way in a very short time, after all. Why is this not enough?" She shook her head in incomprehension.

Orrin smiled. "Why don't you use that capable brain of yours to find the rather obvious answer to that?"

"That he is insane and should be locked up, shackled in gold? Or that he is a bastard who needs to control everything in his own and other people's spaces and should therefore be shackled in gold and locked up?"

He rolled his eyes. "What is it with you and locking people away with golden manacles? How about that he is very attached to you and is worried because you are keeping him at a distance?"

"What? That doesn't make any sense at all! All he manages with this," she pointed at his message, "is to increase that distance."

He sighed. "Sense is not normally what people act on when emotions are involved. What are you going to do now? It seems you don't have much choice in the matter with no place to stay."

No place to stay. Yes, somehow they kept taking those away from her, first her little house, and now even that poor excuse for an accommodation they had put her in. But it had been *her* poor excuse! She looked up. He had a guest room, didn't he?

"Orrin, I know this might land you in difficulties, but would you let me stay in your guest room for now? I would rather cut off my arm than go to that bastard."

"Of course. Just make sure he knows that I didn't offer it first. I dare say he would interpret it as my encouraging you to defy him."

She snorted. "Oh yes, as if I needed encouragement for that."

Very well - tell me about it once more, he thought.

"And I would appreciate if you stopped referring to him as *bastard* in my presence. I have to follow his orders after all, and the word popping up in my head whenever I see him doesn't really help."

She frowned. "His orders... Can he order you to throw me out of your quarters?"

"Theoretically, yes. But it would not put him in a good light and Lord Tyront would probably take him aside to have a nice, long talk with him." He rose. "Welcome to your temporary new home, then. Is there anything you need?"

"Yes, practically everything. The only clothes I have are the ones I am currently wearing, and they are in need of a wash after the training, as am I. And I can't even brush my hair with anything other than my fingers - he has removed everything."

"This shouldn't be a problem. You can wear some of Vern's clothes, he won't mind and they should fit you well enough until we have new ones made for you. As for the rest, you just take what you need. And now get out of here, I need to get some work done before *he* comes storming in here."

She smiled gratefully and took both his hands in hers. "Thank you, Orrin. This is really a great favour."

And she earnestly hoped that it wouldn't get him into a lot of trouble.

* * *

It didn't take Enric long to figure out where she was.

She recognised the sharp knock immediately and gulped. The servant came out of the guest room which she was just then preparing for Eryn and opened the door.

He walked in looking unapproachable and powerful in his blue robes. This was official Enric, the Order magician. She had become used to seeing him in his training outfit or casual clothes at his home, and his robes brought back memories of their encounters when he had worn them in the past. Most of which had been decidedly unpleasant.

He looked calm, not in a relaxed manner but rather as if he was working hard at keeping something bottled inside.

Eryn carefully put down the book she had been reading and was surprised when he bent down to greet her with a light kiss on the mouth.

"I was expecting you for dinner."

She gave him a chilly look. "Yes, I gathered as much from your message. But somehow I felt disinclined to join you."

"I see. Why don't you come with me and we can talk about this at home?"

"If you want to talk, we'll do it here. This is my home for the moment."

She watched sudden realisation dawn on him.

"You have moved in here? Into Orrin's..." His gaze flickered to the door of the master bedroom.

"Into Orrin's *guest room*," she said emphatically. "Really now, what do you take me for? Some lewd strumpet who jumps from one bed to the next?"

He was trying to hide his agitation, but she could see how his jaw muscles clenched. "So it seems that living with me is less desirable than moving in with Orrin."

She rose from her seat and glared up at him. "At least he didn't want to coerce me into doing it. He merely granted me shelter when I asked him for a place to stay as some complete bastard has locked up the one I had."

"You still have one," he said quietly.

Anger returned to her in a fiery rush. "No, what I have is a nicely furnished prison with my own personal warder! You try to push me into staying there even though I keep telling you that I don't want to."

"No - you prefer to stay alone in a tiny, uncomfortable cell instead of a roomy place featuring all imaginable comforts and including *me*. How am I supposed to feel about this?" he retorted.

"Right now I don't care at all how *you* feel about anything. I am so mad at you, I could..." She looked for something that would aptly describe her frustration and failed. "I don't know exactly what I could do, but it would be unendurable for you."

He reached out for her and grabbed both her shoulders to pull her closer. "Come home with me. You can yell and throw breakable things at me. Let's take care of this together."

She wriggled out from his hands and took a step back. "No. This is not how it works. You don't make a decision alone and coax me into accepting it. You will include me in the process and respect it if my answer is No, instead of having your way regardless of the consequences. I will stay here for now. You will see me at our training sessions."

His gaze became intent. "Are these the only occasions where I will be seeing you?"

She lifted her chin. "For now, they are."

"Good day to you, Lord Enric. I thought I heard your voice."

They both turned to the study door where Orrin was leaning against the door frame, his arms folded. His demeanour was not exactly friendly.

Enric straightened. "Lord Orrin. May I have a word with you?" He flashed Eryn a glance. "Alone."

Orrin nodded curtly and beckoned for him to enter his study. He caught Eryn's frown of disapproval before he closed the door.

This did not happen often, he thought when he sat down behind his desk. Usually the situation was reversed, Enric on the chair behind the desk and he the visitor who had to wait until he was offered a seat.

He motioned for the younger man to sit.

"What is it you wish to talk about, Lord Enric?" As if he didn't have a pretty good idea about that.

"Your willingness to provide shelter for her is admirable, Lord Orrin. My intention, however, was to induce her to consider *my* quarters an alternative to her cell, not yours."

"I see." Orrin leaned back in his chair. "Unfortunately, Eryn does not seem to be very taken with this idea from what I have learned."

Enric shot him a look. "Yes, indeed. I dare say this has a lot to do with the alternative that presented itself to her."

Poor fool, Orrin thought. Did he really think that she would have come to his quarters anyway if she had not found another convenient place so quickly? He felt a mischievous pleasure in seeing this man, who was his junior by about twenty years and yet held such a high position, falter in the face of a woman. Especially as he had in the past managed to handle matters of whatever nature in a way that had earned him a reputation of somebody not to be trifled with.

"What is it you wish me to do now, Lord Enric?" Let's see how far you are willing to go, my boy, he thought.

"I wish for you to rescind your invitation."

Orrin's gaze grew cool. "Is that an order?"

Yes, Enric wanted to shout, it bloody well is! But they both knew that he couldn't say it out loud. The cunning old fellow had outmanoeuvred him. He could point out that he would consider it a favour, but he was well aware that Orrin was more inclined to grant *her* a favour than him. And the fact that Orrin was basically impossible to bribe had in the past been reassuring but was in this case a major setback.

"No," he finally said, sighing, "of course not."

Good, Orrin thought with satisfaction, there were remnants of sense left, then.

"Then I suppose there is nothing more for me to say but thank you. I am sure it is a great comfort for her to have in you a friend she can turn to." However much he himself wanted to be that person.

Orrin raised his brows. Now, that was a surprise.

"I would like to compensate you for the expenses her stay causes you."

"This will not be necessary. Next to a growing boy the little extra food she needs will hardly matter. But I imagine she would appreciate some of her clothes. Vern's are roughly the same size, but only just."

"I will have them sent over." Enric wearily rubbed both hands over his face and then rose. "You are aware that her moving into your quarters will very likely give rise to speculations about the nature of your relationship, I assume?"

"Like it did when she had to stay in your quarters?"

"No, nothing like that, I would hope for your own sake." He smiled thinly. "In my case the speculations were true."

Orrin slowly rose from his chair. Was that supposed to be a warning? "I take it you are not assuming that I would behave in any untoward manner?"

"I am not assuming anything, Lord Orrin. I am just preparing you for what people might say. And how it might affect your son."

That's good. Back to being manipulative, arrogant and superior. Bastard. He cursed when the word came to his mind and cursed Eryn for putting it there.

Orrin returned the insincere smile. "Thank you so much for your concern, Lord Enric. Fortunately, my son is a smart boy and well able to distinguish between rumours and what he sees with his own eyes." Unlike you yourself.

The words hung between them, unspoken.

"Well, then I suggest everything seems settled for now. Eryn is due for her training session after sunrise, in case you wish to instruct your servant. She does not require breakfast; we usually have that together afterwards."

Yes - usually, Orrin thought. Usually, though probably not after what you tried today.

He just nodded and followed Enric back into the parlour, where Eryn stood with her arms folded, waiting.

She studied them both, trying to discern from their posture and body language how their conversation had gone. Enric seemed displeased, as if not everything had been to his liking. Orrin, his stance defiant, his expression determined, looked as if he was the reason for this.

Enric walked over to her and without further ado lifted his hand to the back of her neck, pulling her close for a less than chaste kiss that felt more like a demonstration for Orrin and a way to release frustration than a show of affection.

"I see you in two days at the training ground. Don't be late."

With this he turned, gave Orrin a curt nod and left.

CHAPTER 28

The Ball

She waited for him in the little yard used for their training sessions, pondering if he were still angry. He was tough enough to work with when he was in a good mood. Anger hardly changed that for the better. Her own annoyance would scarcely make much of a difference to him thanks to the block on her powers.

The door opened and he smiled when he stepped outside, placed his sword on the small stone bench out of the way and pulled her into a kiss that made her forget her own anger at him for a few moments. She leaned her head further back so he could deepen the kiss.

When he pulled away, she blinked and needed some time before remembering that she was angry at him. And why. Locked cell, message, attempt to force her to move in with him. All of that.

"Good morning to you. It's nice to see that you'd been missing me, too," he chanced.

She returned a staid glance. "Kissing a man is nothing that requires missing him. I have done so quite a few times before."

He pursed his lips. Of course - it was obvious that she was provoking him and keeping him at a distance at the same time. Unfortunately, his being aware of it didn't stop it from working well enough anyway.

"So you are saying you didn't miss me at all? That's not what it felt like just now."

"Some behaviour can be deceptive," she said loftily. "Shall we begin? There are a few things I need to do today and I mustn't be late."

"I see." So she was determined to remain aloof. Alright then, he thought. Fighting him would help her get rid of some of her frustration and tension. "Then I will not take up more of your precious time than absolutely necessary," he said mildly and drew his sword.

"That's unexpectedly considerate of you, I must say," she said sweetly.

He knocked the sword out of her hand in a single blow and hid a smile when she frowned in dismay.

"More fighting, less talking, my love." He smiled when he saw the flash of annoyance in her eyes at the endearment.

Without speaking, she picked up her weapon and managed to retain it a little longer in her hand this time. When he next sent it flying through the air, she narrowed her eyes at him.

"You are doing this on purpose," she said. "You are using much more strength than usually, which I find rather unfair, considering that I am still wearing shackles that block my entire magic."

"What can I say? Life is unfair. For each of us, it seems."

How she wanted to wipe that smug smile off his face!

"Do you have everything ready for the ball tomorrow, my love?"

"Stop calling me that!"

He pretended to think for a moment. "I will, if you come here. Let me kiss you a second time and then tell me again that you didn't miss me."

"Not very likely," she said coolly.

"Then you will have to endure my little term of endearment, my love." He drove her back a few steps towards a corner with a few well aimed strikes.

When she realised what he was trying to do it was almost too late, but a desperate manoeuvre that let her duck under his sword freed her from the trap. She was about to laugh out in triumph when she bumped straight into a shield.

Cursing, she turned back to him. "That has nothing to do with fighting skills! Now you are just being a show-off bastard! Again!"

He smiled thinly. "I can't help it. According to you this is my main character trait." He stepped closer, pushing her into the corner he had created with the wall and his force field.

"Stop right there," she warned, lifting the tip of her sword to his chest. He just lifted his hand and used a little magic to pluck it right out of her hand and throw it behind him. It landed on the stone floor with a loud clang.

When she tried to break out to the only opening to her left, he caught her easily with his arm around her waist and pulled her back, trapping her between his body and the wall at her back.

She looked up into his face and saw that his mischievous mood had changed into something different. He looked down at her, his expression serious.

"Come back to my quarters, Eryn. You can stay in the guest room and I will not try to coerce you into sleeping in my bed until you are ready."

She closed her eyes when he bent down to press his lips against the side of her neck and let them wander south to her collarbone. Collecting every ounce of willpower, she pushed against his shoulder to make him stop, but he only broke the contact long enough to straighten and press his mouth on hers instead.

She gasped when she felt his hands under her tunic. "Stop this!" she hissed.

"Come to my quarters with me," he whispered into her ear.

"No!"

"Then this here will have to do," he said grimly and almost ripped her shirt in two when he pulled it over her head and let it drop to the ground.

She quickly lowered her arms that had been lifted over her head in the process and tried to cover herself, frantically looking around, an unnecessary action as they were the only ones in the small court. Even though the stone wall pressed against her back coldly, she felt the heat of embarrassment warm her from within.

He got rid of his own shirt and pulled her close again, his naked skin warm against hers.

She quickly turned away her face when he leaned down again. "Please, don't."

"Then come to my quarters and spend the evening with me," he coaxed.

She looked up at him, suspiciously. "Are you blackmailing me?"

"Yes."

"So if I refuse..."

"If you refuse I will get rid of your pants next. But I would prefer to take my time later instead of this here. If this is all I am to get, though, I will take it. Make your choice. And quickly. The longer you wait, the more likely the second option becomes."

"Evening," she blurted out.

He smiled and stepped back to pick up her tunic and help her into it.

"Good. I am not willing to accept your staying away from me any longer."

"Any longer? Two days is not what I call a time span that justifies complaining."

"I have waited far longer than that. And I don't complain - I make demands."

"You blackmail helpless women after unfairly disarming them in a loaded fight," she corrected him testily.

He chuckled. "That was redundant. I don't think fairly disarming you in a loaded fight would work."

"I am just trying to make a point here," she snorted.

"Lost on me, I'm afraid."

"Yes, I can see that."

He slipped his own shirt back on before picking up her sword and handing it to her. "What things do you have to take care of today?"

"Junar needs to see if the dress fits and make last changes if necessary."

He smiled at the thought. "I remember the only time I saw you in a dress before."

"Yes. Though I had the impression that getting me out of it was more important to you than admiring it on the outside," she retorted.

"I spent some time looking at you while you were wearing it, so I did actually appreciate that dress. What does the one for tomorrow look like?"

She shrugged. "I don't know exactly. Something in purple, I think."

"I thought women paid more attention to their attire in general and for festive occasions in particular?"

"That shows how much *you* know," she sneered.

"So after the fitting of the dress you are free for the evening?" he enquired.

"I think so, yes."

"Good. Then let's get on with our training. I wouldn't want to detain you unnecessarily."

* * *

It had been dark for several hours when Eryn returned to Orrin's quarters and carefully opened the door. She smiled when she saw him sitting in an armchair, pretending he was reading a book.

"Don't tell me you have been waiting up for me?"

Orrin looked at her wide grin. "Can't a man have a quiet evening in his own parlour with a good book without any suspicions about hidden motives?"

"No." She shook her head good-humouredly. "I think you have been waiting up to see if he would keep me locked in his chambers and you had to come to my rescue."

"Delusions. He is much stronger than me and he is my superior. If I came storming into his bed chamber, I'd imagine he would kick me out of the window. If I were lucky, that is."

She laughed. "His quarters are on the second floor and you are a magician. I doubt that you would suffer a lot of damage."

"Judging from your mood I assume you two have made up again? Does this mean that I will be deprived of the pleasure of your company anytime soon?" he asked.

She smiled at his irony. "No. Lucky for you, I will continue to stay with you for a bit. Don't tell me you are tired of having me as a guest already? I thought you could use a little diversion. And Vern loves having me here."

Orrin gave her a quick look. "Yes. So much, in fact, that one of his teachers has asked me today if he gets enough sleep because he can hardly keep his eyes open during his lessons. Have you two been talking again all night long?"

She swallowed guiltily. "Well, I don't think *all night long* would be an accurate statement..." More like the greater part of the night, she amended silently.

"Eryn," he sighed. "This was the second night in a row. I can't blame the boy for it, but you ought to know better. And it's not like you had a chance to sleep in yourself. Do me a favour and make sure he goes to bed before midnight. Otherwise I have to send you both off to bed after dinner. Which will be quite a challenge if you are visiting Lord Enric regularly now. Which is what I am assuming you will do?"

"Are you trying to sound me out, Orrin?" she queried.

"For details of whatever you two are doing? Oh, spare me." He rose from his chair and stretched. "It's time for me to retire to bed. And you should follow my example. It is going to be quite a long day for you tomorrow. Ball days generally are for women."

She frowned at him. "Wait a minute, what was that? Why?" How long could it take to slip on a bloody dress, after all?

He looked at her in surprise. "Well, there is the hair, the dressing up, all the face painting and whatever else you do to make yourself presentable when moving among high society."

"Face painting?" She frowned and wrinkled her nose. "Do I need to do that?"

"Oh dear. You don't know about these things?"

"How would I? We didn't really have royal balls in my village, you know! The highest society I used to move among consisted of the mayor, the blacksmith and the publican!" she exclaimed. "Can't I just braid my hair and go unpainted?"

"No," he said slowly, "I don't think that would be received very favourably." He shook his head, sighing heavily. "You better take care of all this in the morning. Your friend Junar should be able to help you here."

"But I have nothing left to pay any face-painters or hair-people! They took all my money away!" she wailed.

"Didn't the King send you a payment slip for ten gold pieces along with the invitation? That should take care of a dress and whatever other decorative measures are necessary to make you presentable."

"I have given it to Junar. She might have used it all up for the dress."

Orrin smiled lopsidedly. "Must be quite a dress, then." He walked over to his study door and entered the room, returning only a minute later. He pressed five gold pieces into her hand and then frowned when her words from before came back to him.

"What do you mean, they took all your money away? What money?"

"I had saved about seventy gold pieces in a box at the money lenders. When I wanted to take something out, he said it had been taken to the palace."

He stared at her. "You had earned seventy gold pieces? Through *healing*?"

"Well, what did you think I had earned it with?" She looked at him with her brows raised in annoyance.

He just shook his head in puzzlement, not hearing her question. "Seventy gold pieces. That is quite an impressive horde."

"Was," she corrected. "It's gone. I don't even know who has taken it, the King or the Order. Enric won't tell me, of course, even if he knew anything about it."

Depend on that - he does know, Orrin thought, but didn't say anything aloud. Chances were that he himself had arranged the confiscation.

"Probably not," he said instead. "Well, these five gold pieces should get you through the day tomorrow."

She smiled. "Thank you, Orrin. You are not such a bad sort, after all." She bent over and kissed him on the cheek.

He scowled. "Don't spread it about. It might harm the bad reputation I have so carefully been garnering these last thirty years."

He couldn't help but smile as she walked towards the guest room to retire, laughing heartily at his humour.

* * *

"I still feel this is a little too revealing," Eryn said, staring critically at the low neckline that revealed rather too well to the world what until now only a few favoured men had been able to lay eyes on.

Junar chuckled. "This is the current fashion. I can see that you are not really used to this, but it is only for one evening, after all."

To Eryn's great surprise and relief, Junar had brought a hairdresser with her who had taken care of Eryn's hair and face for the ball.

"So people won't keep staring at my breasts throughout the evening?" she asked uneasily.

"I seriously doubt that," the seamstress stated with a laugh. "I took great care to present them favourably. It would be a shame if they didn't receive the attention they are owed."

"Really, now! You are impossible. I think I will cover my chest with a table cloth!"

"That would make quite an impression, I fancy," Junar quipped and kept arranging the folds of the dress. "Now you are ready. You look absolutely beautiful," she sighed.

"Good. I don't want to look like Orrin's poor country cousin."

"I don't even have any country cousins," Orrin's voice came from his bedroom door. She turned and raised her brows at the sight of him. He wore a dark brown waistcoat with black trousers and black boots that reached his knees.

"Look at you!" Eryn exclaimed, "I had no idea you were handsome somewhere under all that leather armour!"

He snorted. "Nice. And who would have thought that there is enough fabric in this city to make you look like a lady. Unfortunately, though, you won't have to worry about looking like *my* poor cousin. Lord Enric will be your escort to the ball."

"I have an escort?" She lifted a brow. "That is a pity. I would have preferred going there unencumbered, wild and untamed and just picking the first good looking chap as my companion for the evening." She smiled at him. "That would very likely have been you, Orrin."

Vern strolled into the room, rolling his eyes. "I take offence at that."

She looked the boy over and whistled through her teeth. "Don't. I have two arms, one for each of you. Walking between you two might even take people's eyes off my cleavage."

Vern took a casual look at her and shook his head with an adolescent smile. "Not very likely."

A knock sounded at the door and when Vern opened it, a servant announced that their coach had arrived.

"You are joking, aren't you?" Eryn laughed. "The palace is only across the square – why would you order a coach?"

"Do you have any idea what we would look like after walking there, even if it is only a short distance? We would be covered in dust from head to toe," Vern laughed.

Orrin nodded to Junar and led his son and his guest out the door to their first ball.

* * *

Enric waited in front of the ball room for Orrin to arrive. He had promised to deliver her here in time. Just when he was starting to wonder if he should better have picked her up directly instead of waiting for her here, he turned his head and a delighted smile spread slowly on his face.

She looked stunning. Her dress was a dark purple, hugging her figure and cut low to present an inviting glimpse of cleavage. Her shoulders and arms were free of fabric, showing the soft curves of her bare neck as her hair had been pinned up artfully. At hip level the fabric changed to a lighter shade and started billowing into a wide skirt at an angle that made her slim waist seem almost fragile.

The only jewellery she wore were the golden manacles that had once been the property of Tyront's companion Vyril. They looked like elegant ornaments and nothing about them betrayed their true function.

Enric walked towards her, lifting her hand to his lips and delicately kissing her fingers. She seemed uncomfortable and rather nervous.

"You look absolutely breath-taking."

Her answering smile was strained. "Thank you. Though I am more afraid of my own breath. It might make the dress explode if I take a very deep one."

He nodded to Orrin and his son and put Eryn's hand on his arm. "That would surely make the evening unforgettable for many people here. Come! We are due to enter soon. The magicians are usually announced last of all. We do so appreciate an audience."

When they arrived at the line that had formed in front of the door which was assigned for entry, people moved aside to let them pass and take their place in the second row right behind Lord Tyront, standing beside someone who Eryn assumed had to be his companion. The woman would be in her late forties, Eryn guessed, and her bearing and the confidence with which she wore the bright blue dress implied that she was used to attending these kinds of occasions.

They turned around and Tyront lifted his brows. "Lady Eryn. I hardly recognised you."

The woman beside him gave him a look of mild annoyance at such a blatant lack of manners and then turned to smile at Eryn. "I am Vyril, my dear. Tyront's companion. You must be Lady Eryn. I have heard so much about you."

Eryn inclined her head. Before she had a chance to say something in return, the large doors in front of them drew open slowly and a liveried servant announced the names of Lord Tyront and Vyril, who then entered the ball room.

She let out a slow breath and put her hand on her stomach. A little magic to sooth her nerves would have been nice right now.

"Don't worry," Enric said softly, "there is nothing to be nervous about. We will walk in towards the King, bow before him and then take our place among the crowd to wait until all other magicians have entered."

She only nodded.

A few moments later their names were announced, Lord Enric and Lady Eryn. Lady. So they officially used the title even though she had not agreed to join the Order as yet. That was either a show of confidence or a concession to her current standing.

Adapting her pace to Enric's, she entered the ball room with him and blinked. Several huge chandeliers hung from the ceiling, bathing the gigantic room in dazzling light, the effect multiplied by the numerous mirrors on the walls.

People looked at her with curiosity, whispering as she passed them. The two stopped in front of the King and bowed. When she straightened again, she could see him smile at the sight of her, clearly pleased about something. It was a calculated smile that made her stomach churn.

"Lady Eryn. I am very pleased to see you."

"Your Majesty," she said simply. As if his invitation had left room for any other option than attending.

They stepped aside and she all but hid behind Enric when the other magicians were being announced. Too many eyes on her. People on the streets were used to seeing her due to her many walks, but to the aristocrats here she was still a novelty.

Junar had been right, though. Revealing dresses were indeed in fashion tonight, so it seemed.

Enric could feel tension in her hand on his arm and let his gaze wander over the crowd in the ballroom. Most eyes were on her, either openly curious or more surreptitious. Some averted their eyes when he caught them staring at her, others bowed their heads in respect.

When the last of the magicians had been admitted, the heavy wooden doors were closed and the King rose from his throne to address his guests. He welcomed them and expressed his delight at their acceptance of his invitation for this little social gathering that was meant to lend a more jovial air to the beginning of the colder months that were about to follow.

At his nod the musicians at his left side began to play and the King looked around to choose a partner for the opening dance. He glanced at Eryn for a moment and she closed her eyes in relief when he moved on and lifted his hand to a woman seemingly in her early forties who graciously accepted.

When after a minute more couples had joined the king and his partner and the noise level had risen due to conversations around them, Eryn leaned closer to Enric's ear and whispered, "What if somebody asks me to dance? I don't know any dances." Strange, why hadn't this occurred to her before?

"I will make sure nobody asks you," he responded quietly. "That shouldn't be too hard. People generally try not to annoy me, especially when I stare at them."

A faint smile played around his lips when she looked up at him.

"Let's find a seat. It might look strange if we are standing around without dancing." He took her hand and led her towards one of several unoccupied couches.

"How long do I have to stay before I can leave again?" she murmured.

"Two hours at least, I would say."

She nodded. "Very well. I can live through that, I think. Don't leave me alone at any time, not even for a second," she implored him.

He smiled. Words he wouldn't have expected to hear from her so soon. Maybe the ball was not such a great waste of his time after all.

Tyront returned from the dance floor with his companion and Enric rose to make space on the couch for Vyril to sit down.

"You are not dancing, Lady Eryn? Don't tell me your young man hasn't asked you to?" she enquired with a questioning look at Enric.

"I don't dance," Eryn replied with a smile. "I don't know the steps."

Vyril laughed. "Oh, but with a magician this is not really a problem, my dear."

"Probably not," she agreed and added, "But it might give non-magicians the notion to ask me as well, as it would seem as if I know what I am doing."

"That is a shame," the woman sighed. "You are a pretty sight and I dare say some gentlemen would be very eager to dance with you. You are our local sensation, after all."

"That she is," Enric smiled and kissed her hand again, not at all regretting that he didn't have to watch her dance with other men.

"I am?" Her smile looked a little tensed. "Unfortunately, I have no intention of doing anything sensational tonight. I'm afraid looking at me will have to suffice for His Majesty's guests for now." She hoped that would reduce her entertainment value enough not to make the King summon her to future occasions like this.

"I have offended you," Vyril sighed. "That was not my intention, my dear."

"No, please. I am just a bit unnerved and would rather sit in a quiet room with a good book instead of being in all this."

"Of course you would. Why don't you two get Lady Eryn and me something to drink?" She looked up at the men.

Eryn quickly grabbed Enric's hand and smiled apologetically. "I am very much depending on him to keep away unwanted attention, if it's all the same to you. And I am not thirsty, anyway."

They looked up when Marrin made his way towards them and nodded at them politely. "Lady Eryn, His Majesty asks you to join him."

She frowned. "Can you tell me why?"

"No, I am afraid not."

"We will come at once," Enric cut in and pulled her to her feet.

Marrin shook his head. "No, Lord Enric. He has asked only for Lady Eryn."

"Alright," she said with a calm she didn't feel. "If you would show me the way, please."

The King's advisor led her through the crowd and up the dais to the throne where the King was standing and watching her approach. When she stood in front of him, he dismissed Marrin with a nod and took hold of her hand to kiss it.

"Lady Eryn," he said with a smile. "Let me tell you how immensely beautiful you look tonight."

"Thank you, Your Majesty," she replied politely and waited for him to go on. He still hadn't released her hand and she wondered how he would react if she just pulled it from his grip. It was probably not very wise to find out.

"You are wondering why I asked you to come here, I assume."

"I have to admit, I do," she said with a thin smile.

"I would like to invite you to my chambers for tonight, Lady Eryn."

She closed her eyes, swallowed, took a deep breath and opened them again. "Pardon me, Your Majesty?"

"I think you understood me." He watched her carefully and held on to her hand when she tried to pull it away.

"With all due respect, Your Majesty, but I am afraid this would be to no avail." She felt her heart beat in her throat. Didn't he remember what she had told him several months ago? That the shield would prevent unwanted intrusion? What game was he playing?

"Only if you resist, I seem to remember. And I am confident that we can avoid that." His smile was cool and disquieting.

Words she had exchanged with Enric came to her mind and she remembered herself asking, *So you can practically protect me from everyone except the King and your own superior?*

And, of course, it now had to be one of those two she really needed protection from.

She started shaking her head, fighting the panic that had started to rise. "I... I am involved with Lord Enric, as you surely know."

The King watched her breathing getting heavier and doing interesting things to her cleavage.

"There is no official arrangement between the two of you, as I seem to recall. So he has no claim to you from where I stand."

He took a step closer to her, still holding her hand in his and looking into her wide eyes, pressing her hand against his chest. "I will send for you when I retire. Be ready."

"Your Majesty."

The King released Eryn and turned to look at the man he had been waiting for. He had arrived right on time. "Ah, Lord Enric."

He noted with amusement the well-hidden, but to keen eyes still discernible, signs of agitation in the magician. Finally a crack in that marble shell.

"What is it you wish?"

Enric turned to Eryn and lifted his hand for her to take. She did so with visible gratitude and let him pull her to his side, for once accepting with relief the possessive arm around her waist in public.

"I wish to ask your permission for my commitment to Lady Eryn, as she still remains in your custody for now."

Eryn stiffened but remained silent.

"An official commitment. How interesting." The King seemed to consider this for a moment before asking with his brows raised, "I assume the Lady has given her consent?"

Enric paused for a few long seconds before speaking. "I have asked her but I have yet to receive the answer."

"Then I would suggest you take a few minutes and then inform me of her answer, Lord Enric." With this he turned away, dismissing them.

Enric didn't hesitate and pulled her with him, his arm still around her waist, out the next door and into the first unlocked, unoccupied room.

Only then did she let out her frustration by grabbing the first breakable looking object, a vase of some sort, and hurling it against a full-length mirror, both items shattering loudly. She breathed heavily and leaned against the wall.

"Enric, what are you doing?" she then wailed. "A *commitment*?"

He looked down at her, willing himself to be patient. Emotions would not make her comply. He needed to reason with her, keep the situation under his control.

She took a few calming breaths, then crossed her arms and stared up at him defiantly. "This is hardly an appropriate reason to enter into a companionship!"

He shook his head, his faint smile not reaching his eyes. "You're right, it isn't. And if it were the only one I wouldn't be proposing it to you. I would have liked to wait a little longer, but the King has left me no choice."

She swallowed, her throat suddenly tight, her heart beating faster again, but not from joy. "Wait a bit longer? What? You were planning to do this anyway? With hardly more than ten days since I let you touch me? You can't be serious!"

Feeling the need to move, to express her agitation somehow, she commenced pacing the room restlessly, careful to remain out of his immediate reach.

Forcing himself to remain standing where he was instead of reaching out for her, Enric folded his arms. "Yes, that was my plan. I had no illusions that you would agree to it at this time, so I wanted to give you the time you needed. That, however, is no longer an option."

Turning to him, she lifted her arms and let them drop again helplessly. "We don't even live together!"

His glance was slightly exasperated. "Yes. But not due to a lack of effort on my side, may I remind you."

"Your *effort* was what made me move in with Orrin, if I may remind *you*! That was what happened when you tried to rush me last time. Why do you think it will work better this time?"

"Because," he replied in a calm voice, marvelling at his own level-headedness, "I very much hope that taking the oath with me is the more attractive option, when you consider what the alternative is now."

She scrubbed at her eyes, wishing this was all just an annoying dream she would wake up from any moment. "Don't you see that he is manipulating you?"

There had to be another way to do this, and she suspected that he didn't even want to look at it. Maybe he would reconsider if he understood that she had no intention of agreeing to this.

"Of course I see it!" His hand came down on a small table with a whack and made her jump. "Knowing it doesn't make it any better. And it doesn't change anything. He doesn't make empty threats, it would undermine his credibility. Whatever his reason is, he has chosen his leverage well." His voice had lost its calm, despite his concentrating to maintain it.

"But there is still the shield inside me," she reasoned, forcing her voice to remain calm when she wanted to shout instead. "He can't just have sex with me like that. I wasn't lying when I told you that it will not be a pleasant experience for anyone who tries to without my cooperation. So there is no reason for such extreme measures as a commitment."

Enric pinched the bridge of his nose. "Eryn. You don't know about any ways to overcome that obstacle. He could use drugs to make you compliant or drowsy. Do you have any idea how the functionality of your shield is influenced by drugs that induce relaxation?" Despite his more than strained patience his voice was calm and reasonable again.

She shook her head in defeat. "No. No, I don't. But taking an oath and binding myself to you can't be the only way to avoid his physical attentions!" she exclaimed. "This is ridiculous. I am sure he doesn't even want to go to bed with me!"

"You know, I think he will risk that ordeal," Enric retorted sarcastically. "Otherwise he wouldn't have made that move."

"This is all nonsense. I will go to him immediately and clear this matter up. He will hardly want to make me do it against my will."

When she started for the door, she felt his fingers on her upper arm, pulling her back.

"You will do no such thing! If you go out there now without telling him that you have agreed to become my companion, he will not let you leave again." He grabbed her other arm to make it impossible for her to turn away, willing her to see his point. "Listen to me very carefully: he is the King. He will do whatever he deems useful, and there is nobody to hold him accountable for it. Especially if he doesn't violate any rules. There is only one way out for you, for us, and that is accepting my protection. My official protection that will only be acknowledged if you take this oath with me as soon as possible."

"Protection," she murmured. "That is quite a reason for such a decision."

Enric looked down at her, frowning. "No, it isn't." His voice was harsh. "And I have better ones which you would not even listen to as you are so wary of closeness that you won't even sleep in the same bed with me over night. I could tell you about my going insane at the mere thought of another man touching you, about how I want to bind you to my bed every time you rise instead of staying with me. But the only reason I know that has the potential of changing your mind is the protection I can give." Bitterness had crept into his voice, when he added, "However much I would want the others to matter more to you."

She lifted both hands to cover her face. There was no room inside her at this moment to face his hurt feelings, she was too tied up with her own troubles. His pride was obviously injured, but that was his problem right now - her own were so much more serious.

Her voice sounded muffled and desperate when she spoke, "This would keep me from leaving here. Forever. An even more secure prison than before."

Pulling her closer into an embrace, he whispered against her temple, "Yes, I am aware of that."

This was the only positive thing about the whole mess - that she wouldn't be able to leave him so easily anymore, even if an opportunity presented itself. But he knew better than to put words to that.

She would honour the commitment if she made it, she had little choice of doing anything other. Violating it would land her in serious trouble, wherever she might try to hide.

"And I promise I will do my best not to make you feel like a prisoner ever again or give you any other reason to regret binding yourself to me."

He waited for her to say something, but she remained silent. There was not much time, he needed her answer.

"Eryn." She lifted her face and her crushed expression almost broke his heart. He had imagined asking her this question under entirely different circumstances, in happier moments than these. There should have been candles, good wine and romance. Not tension, an imminent threat of being forced to another man's bed and what sounded like a business proposal.

"Will you take the oath with me so I can protect you?"

She nodded, not looking at him. It was as if she had just given up any and all rights to determine her own life ever again. They had made her train for fighting all these months she had been here, but she had resisted. And now they had made her give in and merely given her the chance to choose her preferred means of acquiescence.

*　*　*

Enric crossed the ballroom, holding her hand firmly in his, and stopped before the throne.

The King raised his brow at Eryn, questioning. "Your decision, if you please, Lady Eryn. Have you accepted Lord Enric's proposal to a commitment?"

She lifted her head and stared at him coldly. "I have accepted it, yes."

"Then I congratulate you both very much." He smiled down at them. "This is a very nice setting tonight, wouldn't you agree, Lord Enric?"

Enric closed his eyes for a moment when the implication of the King's words dawned on him. "I wouldn't want to trespass on your hospitality for this," he replied stiffly.

"It would be my pleasure. In fact, I insist." The threat in his voice was no more than a hint.

"As you wish, Your Majesty," Enric replied calmly, and bowed.

"Insist? On what?" Eryn whispered to him frantically when the King turned to the crowd which fell silent immediately.

He started addressing the ball guests before Enric had a chance to warn her.

"Dear Lords and Ladies, it is my pleasure to announce that Lord Enric has asked me for my consent to bind himself to Lady Eryn. I have granted the wish."

Eryn's gaze fell on Tyront, who had been about to take a sip from his glass and had frozen with the glass halfway to his mouth. Vyril next to him covered her mouth in surprise and then clapped her hands delightedly. This started a wave of clapping that just made her want to crouch behind that hideous throne and never come out again.

The King let them express their excitement for a few moments, before he once more lifted his arms for silence and continued, "Now let me further announce that I have decided to administer the oaths myself this very evening and thus offer you the privilege to watch an occasion that has last occurred centuries ago: the commitment of two magicians."

What had before been an expression of mere excitement and surprise now turned into something resembling a riot. She stared at the people who just unquestioningly rejoiced at their King's words. She knew they didn't deserve her resentment, that it wasn't their fault, but still.

She located Orrin and Vern amidst cheering people like an island of calm, both wearing twin expressions of disbelief. Odd, she mused with a strange detachment from the situation around her, she had never really noticed the similarity in their facial features before. Maybe it only showed when they were both dumbstruck.

She felt a giggle that wanted to rise in her throat and clasped both hands over her mouth. This was not a good time for hysteria, she tried to impress on herself. But when, if not now? People would attribute her laughter to her happiness at being joined to such an eligible bachelor instead of a desperate coping mechanism.

Enric pulled her into his arms in what he made to appear to those around them like a joyful embrace instead of an attempt at keeping her from falling apart.

"You have to get through this with me, Eryn," he whispered urgently at her ear. "This will take no more than a few minutes, then we can leave here. I promise."

She swallowed hard a few times and then nodded. He released her and made himself smile for the audience's benefit before they turned and faced the King, who seemed immensely pleased with himself.

*   *   *

"Lord Tyront," an urgent voice said behind him. He turned and found himself face to face with Orrin, whose expression mirrored Tyront's own fury. Though Orrin did not yet seem to have reached the state he himself was in after realising his own impotence here: resignation.

"May I have a word with you? Now?" Orrin's voice almost matched the barely-contained hot anger in his eyes. Tyront nodded curtly and pulled him aside into an alcove, away from the crowd that had focussed its rapt attention on the three people on the dais, not noticing that only the King's smile was genuine while Eryn looked to be in a state of shock and Enric kept his arms firmly around her as if to keep her from bolting.

349

"Why don't you stop this?" Orrin whispered urgently.

"I can't," Tyront replied grimly. "He requested the commitment and she has agreed to it. There is nothing I can do to intervene."

"Then I will do something. I will make a claim to her myself! This should at least delay that nonsense," he snarled and made to march towards the dais.

"You will do no such thing, Lord Orrin. You will stay and watch quietly, nothing more. You will not interrupt the ceremony or openly demonstrate your condemnation of this whole matter by leaving the ball. This is a direct order." His voice was like a quiet hammer, force that didn't need volume.

When Orrin's gaze went back to the dais, Tyront grabbed his arm for emphasis. "I am warning you, Lord Orrin, if you disobey me in this matter, I will contain you right here in this alcove with a force field or even knock you out before you do something foolish. And this time you will face charges."

Orrin shut his eyes and balled his hands into fists. "Yes, My Lord."

"Yes you will obey or yes you will face the charges?" Tyront asked to make sure he hadn't left any doors open for semantic games.

"I will refrain from interfering," the warrior forced himself to say.

"Good." He let his hand sink from Orrin's arm. "Trust me, I understand your sentiments very well. But the King is no fool. He has created a situation where our interference would harm no-one but ourselves and the Order, and would at the same time achieve nothing."

They saw servants carrying several items up to the dais. The ceremony would start in a matter of minutes.

"Come," Tyront said. "The least we can do is to be there when they are forced into this."

They returned to Vyril, and Tyront made sure to have the warrior right next to him, just as a precaution.

Vern joined them shortly afterwards, still shaking his head in incomprehension. "I just don't understand this. I mean, she practically ran away from him and moved in with us! She never mentioned anything about planning something like that!"

Orrin just stared ahead grimly, remaining silent. Tyront looked at the boy and frowned to silence him. Vern swallowed and ducked his head before turning back to the throne to watch.

* * *

The King motioned to a servant to step closer. All eyes followed the man, who was carrying a black velvet cushion with a curved knife lying in its centre. Then he turned towards the pair next to him and waited for Enric to step behind his companion-to-be and lift his own and her hands, palms up.

He saw Eryn close her eyes and noticed that her arms were shaking slightly. After enduring fighting lessons for so many months she would hardly be afraid of two small cuts, so it had to be the situation as a whole that put such a strain on her, he mused. The King took her unnaturally cold hands into his, one after the other, to make the quick cuts across the centre first of her right, then of her left palm. Then he did the same with Enric and watched as the magician joined both his hands with hers so that the slightly bleeding cuts were resting against each other to symbolise the unity they were about to become.

Eryn opened her eyes again and looked at the now bloody edge of the knife the King placed back on its cushion. She felt the sting of the cut and the slowly oozing liquid that was trapped between their tightly joined hands. Enric's felt unbelievably warm. Or was it just that her body was as icy on the outside as she felt inside?

"Lord Enric," the King spoke loudly enough for all to hear, "your vow."

The crowd had fallen silent, only the occasional rustle of a dress or shuffling of feet was audible.

Enric cleared his throat, his heart pounding. The commitment vow that every child knew and that one only started to fully grasp in its entirety when standing there about to give it in truth.

His voice was clear and calm when he started to speak, betraying nothing of the anger at his sovereign, the regret for the woman he held against him or the stirring of joy that he felt was unwarranted and could yet not be suppressed completely.

"I give you my blood and yours I take in return to bind us, unite us and make us as One. My love, too, I give you and all that is mine, my body, my spirit and all that I own. This bond shall prevail in the darkest of times, giving strength and protection until the end of our lives."

Sound carried well in the room, even though the words were not spoken loudly, and numerous sighs could be heard, inspired by a handsome man speaking the words with sincerity.

"Lady Eryn. Your vow, if you please."

She had to swallow. And then a second time. Her throat was dry, tight. After taking a deep breath, she spoke - her voice almost as shaky as her hands had been, "I give you my blood and yours I take in return to bind us, unite us and make us as One. My..."

The next word seemed to be stuck in her throat, even though she knew that it was no more than another empty shell in this farce.

"Love," the King offered quietly.

"My... love... too, I give you and all that is mine, my body, my spirit and all that I own." It seemed to get easier after that one barrier. "This bond shall prevail in the darkest of times, giving strength and protection until the end of... the end of..."

"Our lives," Enric ended the sentence in her place and dared the King to object to his finishing the vow for her. But then, why would he? He was the last one to put any obstacles in their way when he himself had obviously planned this so carefully. Even the knife had been ready.

Another servant stepped forward with a bowl of soapy water while a third carried a white cloth. Their bloody hands were washed and dried, and thin strips of bandage were wrapped around the cuts. They would wear them for the next few days as a visible sign of their conjoining.

The King waited for the servants to step away again before he raised his voice once more, "I place this bond on you and advise you to honour it the way it is meant to be."

Eryn almost laughed at the absurdity of his words. The way it was meant to be? As if it was *given* the way it was meant to be?

No cheers, as she would have expected at the completion of the ceremony. Then she felt Enric lift her chin and only then remembered that there was still one element missing to seal it completely: the kiss.

She heard even the last sounds from around them vanish when he built a barrier around them. It was so quiet and as she couldn't see either the crowd or the King from the angle her head was tilted up and back, they might as well have been alone. It felt oddly private, even though she was still aware of their presence and their eyes on the two of them.

"Forget them, Eryn," he said softly. "There is only you and I right now." Then he lowered his face to kiss her softly, and to his surprise found her lips opening in invitation as if she desperately wanted to embrace something life-affirming and positive. He wanted to be that for her and kept on kissing her until he found it very hard to stop his hands from wandering where they ought not in public, then released her lips again.

When he removed the shield, the sudden noise of the cheering crowd made her flinch.

The King's mouth broke into a smile, then he called for another servant, this one carrying a compact, dark wooden chest in his hands. King Folrin opened it and took out a rolled-up piece of heavy paper, unfastening the cord around it and unrolled it. He stepped towards Eryn, noting how she would automatically have taken a step back had Enric not been right behind her.

"Congratulations to the both of you. I have a present for you, Lady Eryn." His next words were softly spoken, only to be heard by them, "One I trust you will consider well and not refuse unwisely because you feel an urge to make a point." He looked at her pointedly.

When she made no move to take the document from his hands, he narrowed his eyes and said, "It is the deed to a building. One you might find suitable for the healing services you wish to provide."

He noted with satisfaction when her eyes flickered to the document for a moment. Then she took it hesitantly out of his hands and started reading. When she reached the part where her name was written down as owner, she frowned and looked up. It said *Lady Eryn, member of the Order of Magicians.* So his little gift came with a hefty price tag attached: It was only valid after she had joined the Order.

"Yes," he smiled thinly, "there are obligations attached to it, my dear."

She boiled, wanted to throw it back at him, right at his face, but then Enric's hand took the deed out of hers and he said loudly enough for everyone to hear, "Thank you, Your Majesty, for your generosity."

"It was my pleasure," the King replied. "Now I am sure the two of you are eager to retire to your quarters for the night."

Glad about the quick dismissal, Enric took her hand and led her down the dais and straight towards the tall double doors, smiling and nodding to the cheering and clapping crowd around them.

Tyront watched them leave through the double doors and looked at Orrin. "Come. That we couldn't stop this doesn't mean we aren't due some answers."

Both men left the ballroom unnoticed and followed the couple that had hurried out only moments before.

* * *

Enric had just closed the door to his quarters and was about to turn around, when he heard an insistent knocking and frowned. Whoever this might be, he was in no mood to receive any visitors right now. When he opened the door, he faced Tyront and Orrin, both looking grim and determined.

Enric sighed. "This is not a good time right now. We will talk tomorrow." He had been about to shut the door, when Orrin pushed it open again, placing a foot within in complete disregard of the younger man's words.

"And a good evening to you, too. Of course we would like to come in, thank you so much for asking," Orrin growled and sat down on one of the chairs ostentatiously, arms folded.

"I think you are forgetting your position, Lord Orrin. Once again. I am beginning to feel really annoyed with your impertinence," Enric scowled but stopped when he saw Eryn worry at the scene unfolding itself before her eyes.

Orrin just stared at him in silence, utterly unimpressed, waiting.

Tyront had also entered and closed the door behind him. He, too, walked towards the table Orrin had taken a seat at and made himself comfortable, conveying the very clear message that there would be a discussion right now, whether this was to Enric's liking or not.

"What happened down there?" Tyront asked and then turned to Eryn. "Why was Marrin sent to bring you to the King?"

Eryn sighed and took a seat with them. Talking about this right now was the last thing she wanted to do. But for Orrin's sake she decided to comply. At least *he* deserved some kind of explanation. He looked so angry, but not with her, but Enric. And Enric was not to blame this time. For once.

"The King instructed me to be ready to be summoned to his chambers after the ball," she said and felt the chill she had felt then again at the memory.

"What?" Orrin frowned in confusion. "I thought there was this field inside you?"

"Yes," Enric answered, "but I think he might have tried to drug her to lower her resistance. We have no idea if the field can be influenced this way, but…"

"But you didn't want to take the chance," Tyront offered.

Enric nodded. "Exactly. He said that as there was no commitment, I had no formal claim on her. And when I told him that I had already asked her, he demanded an answer."

Orrin closed his eyes in sympathy for a few moments. So she had been given the choice between very probably being drugged and taken advantage of by the King or commencing upon a commitment with Enric, whom admittedly she was already involved with, but had purposely avoided getting too close to in the past. He felt no particular compassion when it came to Enric. He was undoubtedly pleased enough with the situation, even if he was not happy about having been pushed into it instead of being the one doing the pushing.

"I am surprised at the King," Enric continued. "This manoeuvre was uncharacteristically blunt instead of the subtler manipulation he usually favours."

"He obviously didn't want to waste any time on subtlety for whatever reason in this case," Orrin mused. "Not only making you agree to a commitment, but carrying it out right then and there is a rather extreme course of action. He had everything prepared beforehand, from the knife to the gift at the finish. And doing it himself makes sure that you have next to no chance of dissolution any time soon."

"What?" Eryn stared at him, and he was sorry he had to deal her another blow.

"The oath, girl. Only the institution which takes it from you can dissolve the connection again. He has ensured that neither threatening nor bribing anybody can end it, which would definitely have been an option if the clerks had done it as usual."

He doubted very much that Enric would have had any interest in pursuing that line of action anyway. And thanks to his position it wouldn't have been very hard for him to make sure *she* would not have been successful had she tried. He had got what he wanted, even if he had not obtained it the way he first desired.

She groaned in torment and leaned back, covering her face with her hands. Lately, shutting out the world was turning into a more and more frequent need, it seemed. When she dropped her hands again, she saw all three of them regarding her with various degrees of sympathy and regret.

"I am tired," she said. "Can we leave, Orrin? I just want to lie down and sleep and forget all this for a few hours."

"I am afraid this is not possible," Tyront said very carefully after a very pointed silence. "The King would not respond well to your continuing your lodging with Lord Orrin. He expects you to *live* this commitment, not only use it as an empty cover to protect yourself from him. He has made you do this to bind you to the city by binding you to Enric. He would not tolerate your living anywhere else."

Enric nodded. "He is right. And he said as much when he sent us to retire to *our* quarters."

"He said *your* quarters," she contradicted him weakly. "He could have meant..."

"No," Tyront interrupted her, "he didn't mean *Enric's* quarters. Otherwise he wouldn't have mentioned it so explicitly."

Of course, she thought. If she really thought about it, it was logical, wasn't it? It would hardly look good to the public if a commitment the King himself had forged was so obviously not a genuine one. It would undermine his credibility.

She looked around. So there she was again, only this time staying with Enric would not be a mere temporary matter. It was no more than eleven days since she had woken up in his quarters for the first time. Eleven days in the course of which she had become intimate with him, been attacked by the apothecaries, moved in with Orrin and finally committed herself to a man who kept knocking her out when her behaviour was not to his liking. However had she managed before, for more than a decade since her father's death, to live a fairly uneventful life?

She sighed and rose, turned towards the guest room and then stopped, looking at Enric with uncertainty. Freshly joined companions were supposed to sleep in the same bed, weren't they? How far did the King's influence go? Did it stop at the entrance door of what she would from now on have to consider *their* instead of *his* quarters? Would Enric accept it if she slept in the guest room instead of in his bed? Would she comply if he didn't?

As he walked over to her she tensed, so he kept his hands to himself instead of letting them run down her arms as he had intended. Even if she didn't blame him, he was still the one she had been tied to.

"Go on," he said calmly. "You can sleep in there. I will give you all the time you need."

She nodded and entered the room, closing the door behind her without bidding good bye to any of the magicians.

Orrin watched his superior stand there, oddly perplexed and looking at the door his new companion had just closed behind her to spend the night without him. Sadness radiated off him; an undercurrent of angry grievance clear in his tense posture. Maybe the King's actions had not been that much of a favour for Enric after all, Orrin mused and felt some of his own fury drain away.

Enric turned his face into a neutral mask before sitting down with them. "You don't happen to know why the King is in such a hurry to make her stay here, do you? Is it because of her escape attempt?"

Tyront shrugged. "Probably. That was pretty close, after all. And, of course, she is far enough along with her fighting skills to be accepted into the Order."

Enric narrowed his eyes. There was more he wasn't telling, but if he wanted to keep whatever it was to himself, there was no use pestering him. Especially in Orrin's presence.

"The Council has accepted the rephrased oath for Eryn," Tyront continued. "It has been sent to the King and as soon as he approves we can see if she agrees as well."

"She will probably not be too keen on joining us right now. It is, after all, the reason the King has blackmailed her into accepting me as her companion. She might consider refusing a last line of defence."

"Then it is on you to change her mind. As she has to stay here now anyway, she might as well enjoy the privileges that being a member of the Order entails."

Enric raised a brow at his superior. "There are a few duties as well, if I may remind you. She will have to do the training lessons voluntarily and has to answer to the two of us and, as we have to, to the King. I imagine the last prospect is the one that will repel her the most. She still is his prisoner, after all."

Orrin frowned. "How can she still be a prisoner after she is joined with an Order magician? This doesn't make any sense."

"And yet he has not released her from this status so far. But I prefer her to be *his* prisoner for now, I wouldn't want her to be the Order's captive. That would be worse, considering our plans with her," Tyront spoke. "There is not much we can do for now. We need to wait for the King to approve the oath, and then the real task of persuasion will start." He looked at Enric. "That's where you come in. So you'd better make sure she enjoys her new role in your life."

Enric gave him a cool look in answer. "Whatever I do or do not attempt with my companion is not primarily intended for the Order's or the King's benefit, even though both seem to believe that."

Orrin followed the exchange with interest. So there was palpable tension between the two mighty Order leaders. That earned the younger man another few points in Orrin's book. It seemed his loyalty to the Order already came second to Eryn. How very interesting.

CHAPTER 29

Membership Negotiations

She woke up after an uneasy and restless night. It was early, and the first glimmers of dawn were visible when she looked out the window. She had spent the few hours of sleep tossing and turning. Her bed looked like a battlefield with crumpled sheets, one blanket on the floor and the other lying in a heap at the foot of the bed.

She wondered how restful Enric's night had been. He had looked unhappy when she had left him alone with Orrin and Lord Tyront yesterday night. She felt a stab of remorse. He was in this with her, after all. The act of commitment might not have been as undesirable for him as it was for her, but he was now stuck with a companion who had made it very clear that she didn't wish to be joined to him, who didn't share his bed and who hadn't even considered in hindsight the very logical consequence of living with him after their commitment ceremony. Well, the King had at least solved the last little dilemma, hadn't he? Enric had been imploring her only the day before yesterday to move in with him. He had offered her the very guest room she was staying in now, she recalled.

It was very early in the morning and he was probably still asleep, she mused. She would surprise him by slipping into his bed. The thought made her smile.

It was dark and quiet in the parlour and she cautiously navigated between the chairs and small tables to the other end, holding her hands out in front of her. She carefully opened the bedroom door and slipped in, only to find the large bed empty. Standing there and frowning, she wondered whether to return to her own bed to spend one or two hours reading or knock at his study door where he had very likely retreated to, when she felt warm hands on her shoulders and jumped.

He turned her and looked down at the dark silhouette that panted now from the scare he had just given her.

"Seriously, how do you do that? One of these days I will drop dead when you keep sneaking up on me like that," she exclaimed.

He chuckled. Seeing her standing in his bedroom had cheered his spirits considerably. He had heard her opening the guestroom door while he had been working in his study, reasoning that sleepless time could be spent much more sensibly working than just lying in bed and staring into the dark.

"Forgive me. I will be more careful with that fragile life of yours," he said with a smile and then had to think of the apothecaries who had only days ago tried to take it away. He forced the thought aside for now. They would get what they deserved soon enough. "Is there anything you need?" he asked gently.

She sighed. Explaining the gesture was so much less effective than just snuggling up to him while he was still in bed, but that was obviously not an option any more.

"No, not exactly *need*," she said awkwardly. "I thought we could just... lie together for a bit before getting up?"

She sensed his smile rather than saw it in the dark when he took her hand and led her to the bed, pulling up the blanket for her to slip underneath and then joining her, pressing her back against him and wrapping both arms around her.

It felt good - being held like that, warm and safe - after the hours of doubt, anger and exhaustion alone in the darkness of her room across the parlour. She felt him press his face against her neck and heard him inhale deeply.

"You are not checking my body hygiene, are you?" she asked lightly.

"Shut up, you," he retorted softly and nibbled where her neck joined her shoulder. "You are destroying the moment."

"Sorry," she giggled. "My capabilities for romance are rather limited, I think."

"I have noticed," he remarked dryly.

She remained silent for a moment, enjoying his warmth enveloping her, before she enquired, "What happens now?"

He didn't have to ask what she meant. "Tyront has sent a new version for an oath to the King for his approval. If he approves, you will be asked to have a look at it. If you agree to join the Order, we will work on taking care of it as quickly as we can."

"Have you seen the new version?"

He nodded. "Yes. I am a member of the Magic Council. I had to approve it as well."

"Did you work on the wording?"

"No. Tyront himself did. He wanted to keep me out of it. I am too much involved with you to work on it objectively."

"What does it say?" she asked, half turning to him.

"That you will see as soon as the King has approved it. There is one thing we need to learn to deal with, Eryn." His tone had turned serious. "I will become your superior when you have joined the Order. That means we need to find a way to separate our functions in the Order from our relationship. These two aspects of our life will keep intertwining whether we like it or not, but we can at least try to make room for us two where the Order has no influence. Like the bed, for example. I would ask you not to talk of anything that concerns the Order or the King while we are in bed together. Best thing would be to use the study for this."

She thought for a moment, then nodded. That did sound sensible. "Always assuming I am willing to join the Order."

He mumbled into her hair, "Of course, always assuming that."

* * *

They were eating breakfast when a knock at the door made them look at each other.

Enric rose and opened the door to a royal messenger who handed him a sealed envelope and then bowed before he left again.

Eryn watched him standing there, reading the message.

"Is it about the oath?" she wanted to know.

He shook his head. "No. But it is about you. You are now officially no longer a captive of King Folrin. Your status is the one of a free citizen with all and any duties and rights this entails. Your shackles, however, are to remain in place until you have joined the Order by swearing a magically binding oath."

She frowned at him. "A free citizen? How can I be free as long as I am wearing the manacles? They are what keeps me from leaving here, after all!"

He gave a stern look. "No, my darling, your commitment to *me* is what from now on keeps you from leaving here. The shackles are no more than a reminder that the last step towards your being a completely free member of society, namely joining the Order, has yet to be undertaken."

She swallowed. She had chosen her words poorly and managed to annoy him. "Yes, of course."

Enric frowned when another knock sounded at the door. This time there were two men carrying a chest and telling them that the King had sent them to collect her belongings from Lord Orrin's quarters to bring them here.

"Oh my, isn't he obliging," Enric said sardonically. "Now imagine you had left with Orrin last night - they would probably have stuffed you in the chest together with your things and brought you here as well."

"That is not funny," she grimaced and thought back to the conversation from the night before when she had actually intended to return to Orrin's guest room instead of the one here. So the King's parting remark in the ball room really had been a warning. One she had not been in a set of mind to duly register. But Enric would of course be more attuned to subtleties like that.

He eyed the small chest with her belongings and turned to her. "Do you mind if I have a look?"

She shrugged. "No, go ahead. I don't have any secrets." None they hadn't found out about anyway, she thought and remembered the box of gold somebody in the palace had taken from her.

Enric went through the few pieces of clothing, a hairbrush, two of her father's books and a rectangular parcel wrapped in sturdy brown paper. A note was attached to it.

He rose from his crouch in front of the chest and brought the package to the table.

"It seems there is also some sort of gift for you."

He pushed aside the breakfast tray so there was enough space for her to open it.

She plucked the note from the string that held the wrapping together and immediately recognised the wild hand of her favourite fifteen-year old.

"It's from Vern," she said smiling. "It says something about being sorry, a gift and honour. Seriously, they need to teach him how to write properly."

Enric held out his hand. "Can I try?"

"Sure, be my guest."

"*Dear Eryn, I congratulate you on your commitment, though I have to say that I am sorry you have moved out from our quarters again. I enjoyed having you here,*" he read without hesitation, making Eryn's eyes bulge with surprise. "*Here's a gift for you. I hope you like it and will do me the honour of accepting the very first copy. Your friend always, Vern.*"

"You can read this? Or have you just made that up?" She eyed him suspiciously.

He chuckled and handed back the note, using his other hand to flick a strand of brown hair behind her ear. "No, my love. But I have to read regular written reports from his father, and it looks like very bad handwriting runs in the family."

"First copy..." she murmured and then sucked in a breath. "Could he really have..."

She grabbed the string, impatiently pulled it off the parcel and unfolded the paper hastily. Her joyful laugh at the sight of the newly-bound book with Vern's name next to another one embossed on the sturdy red leather binding made him smile. She let her fingers glide over the cover and then opened it, looking at the intricate drawings that were so very superior to the ones in the old version she had given to Vern.

"Can you believe that?" She quickly brushed away a treacherous tear from the corner of one eye. "He did all this alone! We just talked about this once, and he took care of everything! I'd had completely forgotten about it after these last few days... And he gives the first copy to *me*!"

Enric bent down to kiss the top of her head. "A precious gift indeed. We will have to find a good place for it. And for your father's books in the guest room." He meticulously avoided calling it *her* room, not wanting her to get used to it too much. "A chest is not a good place to keep them in, especially if you are going to use them for your work." He squatted down next to her. "How about we have a look at the building you are going to own? You could see if there is enough space for a small medical library."

She narrowed her eyes at him. "You are baiting me, aren't you?"

He smiled. "Maybe. Does it work?"

"No comment at this point. But I will have a look at the building. You don't have to come."

"I want to." No locking me out of that part of your life, my dearest, he thought grimly and looked up in surprise when another knock sounded. "Three times in one morning? That is certainly above average," he sighed and walked to the door to open it and find himself facing another royal messenger. My, my, he thought, the King had been busy this morning.

He brought the message back to the table and sat to open it. Eryn saw his lips curving. He looked up at her, the satisfaction on his face evident.

"The King has approved the new oath for you. Get dressed quickly now. I bet the next knock at our door will be Tyront."

Our door, she thought as she rose. He was adapting to this shared quarters thing really quickly.

Picking up the book to take it with her, she returned to the guest room and started to dress.

Enric had been right. Just when she had finished washing and braiding her hair, the fourth knock of the morning resonated through the parlour - this time a confident, powerful one she definitely did not associate with any messenger.

And true enough, it was Tyront who strolled in holding a folded sheet of paper in his hand.

"Finally!" He seemed to be in a good mood when he walked over to Enric and slapped him on the back. When he saw Eryn coming out of the guest room, he smiled and nodded. "Good morning to you, Lady Eryn. Come, we need to talk." He went straight into Enric's study, and Eryn followed him, wondering if Tyront would take his place in Enric's chair behind the desk.

But he went towards the small table and chairs before the window and motioned for her to take a seat next to him. She turned to make sure Enric would be with them and relaxed when he entered and closed the door behind them. The thought of being alone with Lord Tyront made her uneasy. There was still quite some tension between them.

"Enric has probably told you about the revised wording of the oath we sent to the King, seeing that you refused to swear to our usual one?"

She nodded. "Yes. And it seems he has agreed to it."

"Indeed. It has taken us a few attempts and altered versions to get him to agree, but now it is settled. The last thing that remains to be done is for you to give consent as well." He handed her the paper and leaned back to watch when she unfolded it and started reading.

She read it through once, then a second time. She was rather surprised at the text appearing reasonable enough. Which was exactly why she read through it a third time, trying to find the catch that had to be hidden in there somewhere.

It spoke about the duty to defend the kingdom against unwanted intruders, protect the people and the King, obey her superiors, hone her fighting skills for that purpose and addressed the people instead of the King. She would swear fealty to the people and never to leave the city without the intention of returning unless granted the freedom to do so by the King himself. So the monarch was still the one to decide, but this oath bound her less tightly to him than all other Order magicians. She remembered the conversation Enric and Lord Tyront had had behind their soundproof barrier, where Enric had learned about the chances of nullifying the magically binding oath. Neither of the magicians was very likely to share the knowledge of how to do it with her, but at least it was a last resort. She had shown herself good at figuring things out on her own, after all.

"It does look alright," she said carefully.

She wished she could talk to somebody about this, but Enric would hardly be interested in pointing out dangerous phrases to her as he himself had been one of the magicians to approve it and also had the added personal interest in keeping her here.

So what choice did she really have? The commitment to Enric kept her in the city anyway. Abandoning a commitment was not looked upon kindly, and if the one left behind was a man with considerable resources at his disposal such as for example a magician with a very high status in the Order, hiding would be almost impossible, especially as she didn't even have the protection of the local hair colour any more to lend her anonymity.

She returned her attention to the two men, who were watching her patiently. "But the oath alone is not enough to make me join you. Let us talk about the things you were willing to grant me when we last talked about this. And I want this written down and confirmed both by the Order and the King with your official seals."

"Of course," Tyront said, pleased with her acceptance of the oath and care in pursuing the matter. Enric got up from his seat and took out several sheets of paper and the pen he had used for writing the message to Orrin several days ago, the one he had sent as a paper bird instead of by messenger. She had to suppress an amused smile at the memory of this playfulness.

"The King has already given you the premises you can use for your healing services, unless I am very much mistaken," Tyront said and looked to her for confirmation.

"Yes, but I would have to look at them first to see if they really are suitable. If he has given me a tiny, narrow, dark hut that was intended for demolition anyway, I would not consider it an appropriate location."

"Alright. When can you verify the building's suitability for your purposes?"

"We will do this today. I had already proposed it before you came," Enric cut in.

"Good. And we should have a list of requirements drawn up beforehand so as to compare them with what you find there," the older magician said.

Eryn sighed. Where was the trust? So he wanted to avoid her rejecting the building out of principle and insisted on valid reasons if she did. Well, that was something she was willing to concede.

She nodded. "I am fine with that. How about the details of my healing services? I need the chance to teach people healing instead of doing it alone. So there must be funding for that as well."

"The King has agreed to fund everything in connection with the training of medical staff and the expenses of the daily healing business." Tyront leaned forward. "Though I have to tell you that this is not in your or the Order's best interest in the long run. I would strongly suggest securing funds that are not provided by the Crown."

She raised her brows. "Because it might seem as if the King was doing something useful for the people when you want it to seem like the Order is the great benefactor?"

"I am not particularly happy with the way you phrase it," Tyront said coolly. "Let us just say that this arrangement makes it seem like an Order magician is employed by the King, which would very likely contribute to weakening our influence as an institution. And as for yourself, you might want to consider what financial dependence from the King would mean for you. If he decided for whatever reason that healing is not worth the funds it requires, you would from one day to the next no longer be in a position to offer your services. Which, of course, will make you more susceptible to blackmail."

That last part sounded like a valid reason, she thought with an uneasy feeling. The King had proved only yesterday that he had no scruples in following that path when it came to convincing people to do his bidding.

"How do you propose I accomplish this, if I may ask? I am not willing to charge the prices the apothecaries asked. The main purpose of all this is still to provide affordable medical services to everyone who needs them."

"After joining the Order, you will have our considerable resources at your disposal. Among those there are also treasurers who can help you when it comes to matters of calculation and planning," he replied.

That didn't sound too bad, either, she decided. Then she narrowed her eyes. "How about magicians choosing to enter the profession of healing? Will this be something the Order encourages or sanctions?" She thought of Vern and the chance this could be for him.

"We have discussed this matter in the Council meeting," Enric spoke. "And the magicians are sceptical. They fear that we will not be able to concentrate on our primary purpose any more when healing is another option to take."

She thought for a moment. "I see. So magicians are banned from entering the profession, if I understand you correctly?" This was not good news.

"No," Tyront cut in. "They are not. We decided that a certain ratio between warriors and healers must be maintained. And healers would of course have to be trained and kept fit in fighting as well."

"So healers have to train fighting, but fighters are not bound to learn even the most basic healing skills? That doesn't really seem balanced."

Tyront sighed. "No, it doesn't, and I am fully aware of this. But you need to consider the changes we are going through right now. This is a completely new concept - a change of the Order's structures, something unfamiliar. You can't change the whole system from one day to the next but have to prove first that the changes we are making work to our satisfaction before you suggest even bigger ones."

That did seem reasonable, she had to admit. "So, should there be any magicians who wanted to learn healing you wouldn't stop them?" She wanted to be absolutely certain about this.

"There will be a maximum of five healers who would be able to join you in the beginning. But I have to warn you, the willingness of members of an institution dedicated to fighting and defence to learn healing might not be what you hoped for," Tyront remarked.

She nodded. "Yes, I am aware of that. But in case some of them do become interested I want to be sure I don't have to turn them away."

"Every magician who wants to be trained as a healer will have to obtain the Order's permission first anyway," Tyront stated.

"The Order's permission being...?"

"Mine," he said simply.

She gave him a cold look. "So this is your way of ensuring my cooperation by simply denying the permissions? It would be a pity if only the King had a hold on me and not yourself, wouldn't it?"

"I don't like your tone," Tyront warned her. "And neither do I like your implication."

"As long as we are negotiating the terms of my joining the Order, I am afraid you will have to put up with both. When I have joined you and I am yours to command, you are free to discipline me as you see fit. But not yet." She forced herself to calm down again and get rid of the hostile undertone in her voice before continuing, "I don't like *you* being the one to grant this permission. And how would you know who was suitable for the profession anyway without any training to give you an idea what prerequisites a candidate should bring?"

He snorted. "I see. That would of course make you the only one fit to make that decision."

"Yes, it would. Basically. Which doesn't mean that I insist on deciding this alone. I just want the chance to participate actively."

"So the two of you would decide together?" Enric said doubtfully. "Seeing how well you two are getting on I could imagine we are bound for mayhem, then," he concluded.

"True enough," she agreed. "Thus a third person should be involved. Somebody to tip the scale."

"I hope you are not suggesting your companion."

She smiled thinly. "No. I wouldn't want to do this to him. He would find himself caught between the two of us all the time. No, it has to be somebody who has no close personal connection to me or to you and can thus make a valid decision. My suggestion would be Lord Poron."

Tyront pursed his lips. Lord Poron was an excellent choice; he himself couldn't have come up with a better suggestion. And it would restore to him some of the importance that losing his rank twice to younger and stronger magicians had cost him.

"I agree," he said slowly. "I will contact Lord Poron and offer him this responsibility." He wrote on the paper Enric had given him. "Now that this is cleared, we need to get to the matter of your own rank in the Order. Your strength entitles you to quite some influence, you know. This, however, is also connected to a lot of responsibility and requires certain knowledge."

She raised her hands to stop him. "I have no intention whatsoever to get involved in your power games, your intrigues, spying, manipulation or blackmailing. I feel I have had my share of that, thank you very much."

"This is not an option for now, I am afraid. Third in command is a very important role and you will have to adapt to it as Enric had to more than ten years ago. You will, of course be mostly involved with healing, but for major decisions you will have to be available and ready to make them."

She exhaled heavily in defeat. "So, you have mentioned the need to indoctrin... erm... school me for a year to make me fit for the position. How intense would this schooling have to be and would it even leave me enough time to pursue healing? I mean, you also insist on my continuing the combat training, so it doesn't seem to me like there is a lot of time left for me to do much else."

Tyront raised his brow for her use of indoctrinate, but decided to let it pass. She was right, after all. He didn't have the authority to discipline her. Yet.

"You will of course have to divide your time and attention between these three areas, whereas the combat training will very likely be the one taking up the smallest part of your time. Enric trains with you every second day for two or three hours, as far as I am aware. It is to his discretion to increase or reduce this amount of time. That is not within my ambit. As regards your other education, you'd need to reckon on at least three to five hours a day for this. The rest is yours to fill with whatever you deem necessary or useful. Should you feel that establishing your healing services takes more time than you have at your disposal, you may of course ask for help. I will, however, not force anybody into this - the magicians have to undertake this voluntarily."

She nodded. "That is only fair. *I* wouldn't want to force anybody to work with me, anyway."

He wrote again on his paper and then looked up. "About your barrier. As a member of the Order you will be required to share this and other knowledge relevant to defence."

She shrugged. "Sure. No objections there." Then she leaned forward. "And, of course, as soon as I have joined I hope you will remove these damn manacles for good."

Tyront smiled. "Of course. You are so much more useful to us without them. Is there anything else you wish to discuss at this point?" She shook her head and he rose, pointing to the paper with the oath. "Good. Then we are done here and I can take care of finalising this. You will need to learn the oath by heart - it can't be read out. I am not sure when exactly the ceremony will be, but you may be sure that it will only be a matter of days." He smiled. "We are very eager to have you with us finally. We have been awaiting this for many months now."

She didn't smile back. Being bound to follow his commands was nothing she was looking forward to. She really would have to work on phrasing her objections more diplomatically or whatever they did here to punish impertinence and/or disobedience would become her main experience.

When Lord Tyront stepped closer to her, she fought the impulse to retreat and watched him warily. He reached out and touched her manacles for a moment.

Breathing in, she felt a tiny trickle of magic flowing through her body. He had weakened the restraints a little. Not enough to return more than a very low level of magic to her, but it was a gesture.

"To make the waiting more bearable," he smiled thinly. "Please don't make me regret my generosity again."

CHAPTER 30

The Execution

Enric opened the door to the guest room quietly. The day was beginning to dawn and he could already see enough to find the way to her bed without bumping against anything. He had considered his move to slip into her bed and decided that they both had to be entitled to equal rights. She had come to his bed yesterday, he was joining her in hers today.

He lifted her blankets and slid close to her, carefully pushing his arm under her neck so she would lie on it and hugging her close with the other one, swallowing when he felt her body press against his, and willing down the very masculine urge he felt awaken. That was not what he had come for. He was doing this to get her used to having him in her bed with her, and as he had managed to insinuate himself into her bed without waking her, she would even see that it was possible to sleep comfortably in his presence. As for the other urge, he might still be able to take care of that when she was awake sometime later...

Holding her felt right. Mine, he thought and felt the truth of it inside him, however long it would take *her* to reach that conclusion. He closed his eyes and felt himself for the first time in many days fall asleep without any problem.

* * *

He woke slowly when he felt her stir next to him. Bright daylight shone through his eyelids and told him that he had spent quite some time with her.

When he opened his eyes to smile at her, he found her staring at him in surprise and was about to wish her a good morning when his gaze was drawn to her hair. Her dark red hair.

They stared at each other for a few moments, before both of them started speaking at the same time.

"What are you...?"

"Your hair! It's..."

Both stopped and Enric lifted his hand to touch her tangled strands. They felt the same like before.

"What happened to your hair? It's red! Did you do that?" Stupid question, he scolded himself immediately. Of course she had done it, who else? "I mean, did you do it on purpose?"

"Yes. And no. And what are you doing here? When did you come in here? Why didn't I wake up?" She frowned.

"Because it seems I am finally wearing you down and you're starting to get used to having me around, I would assume," he quipped and found his attention still drawn to the novel sight of her hair. "What do you mean, yes and no?"

"I was experimenting a little when I couldn't sleep last night. My father has somehow managed to change the colour to blond, but I have not been able to do it. I had an idea how it might work, but somehow…"

"It went a little wrong," he finished her sentence and shook his head in dismay. He had really, *really* liked her brown hair. It went nicely with her eyes. This shade, however, made her look pale and unnatural. "Is this permanent? Will it take another head injury to get rid of it?"

She chuckled. "Don't tell me you hate it so much you'd consider bashing me over the head to get my old colour back? No, it shouldn't be permanent. It was much deeper last night and is starting to fade already."

He swallowed. "This is what it looks like when it has started fading? Dear me." But the prospect of its being only temporary cheered him up. "So, how did you do it? Anything a barbaric non-medic like me would understand?"

She smiled. "I can try explaining it. The colour of our hair is determined by small points of colour inside it. I have tried to change the nature of these little dots by using other colours we have inside us."

"And you have used the colour of blood, so it seems," he remarked.

"Yes, it was the easiest one available. Though I have to eat something soon, because the colour in the blood is what makes it transport oxygen and I do feel a little dizzy. I think I have used a bit too much of it and need to replenish that."

"If this is the way your father did it, why does it keep fading? And do you even have anything with the right colour inside you that would help you to become blond?"

She shrugged. "Well, currently nothing I would like to use after seeing what consequences using the blood's colour has brought with it. I was wondering if eating something coloured would provide me with the right substances. But I would have to keep track of where it is going in the body or my skin will turn that colour instead. If you think that red hair is strange, wait until you see the rest of me turn the same shade."

He leaned over and kissed her mouth, observing that she didn't flinch, even though her eyes had a cautious flicker in them for a moment. Good enough, he decided. Definitely progress.

"You are good at experimenting and figuring out new things. I thought my heart would stop when you first split the bolt I shot at you. And then that barrier. If you are that good with the warrior practices you despise so much, I wonder what you can do with your healing skills."

"That was easy," she shrugged. "I just had to use basic principles from healing, such as redirecting airstreams. But with healing it's harder. I have not even managed to recreate the field my father has placed inside me." She shook her head, impatient with herself.

"What is the problem with that? The strength or any other hard to comprehend medical characteristics?" he enquired.

She looked at him sheepishly. "No. The first obstacle is the shape."

He stared at her for a few moments before he began laughing. When she made to get up angrily, he grabbed her hand and said, still smiling. "No, please don't go. I apologise. I was surprised, my love, that you seem to have no qualms using medical knowledge to experiment on fighting, but that it has never occurred to you to use the bad, useless, evil techniques you have learned here for improving your healing skills. We really need to work on this attitude."

"What is that supposed to mean?" she frowned in incomprehension.

"That what you have inside you is no more than a shield. And we have taught you shielding, haven't we?"

"But this is much more complicated! You can't just wrap an organ in a round shield, it needs to follow the exact outline instead of including parts of other organs. Because the characteristics that are right for one particular organ are harmful for the one next to it."

Enric sighed and got up. "Wait here. I will be back in a moment." With this he went outside into the parlour and returned a few seconds later with the candelabra she had knocked to the ground that one day.

He brought it back to bed with him and held it upright, removing the candles.

"I instructed you one time to adapt your shield to follow the outlines of your body, if you remember. It saves energy."

"I remember. But the outline of the human body is far less complicated than the one of an organ."

"I assumed as much. But with a bit of practice you can adapt the shape of a shield to whatever form you wish. Watch."

She saw the shield he created around the candelabra shrink until it followed the exact outlines of the complicated ornamentation and the spikes on top. Carefully lifting a finger, she waved it through the small empty spaces to see if he really had followed the exact outlines or had cheated somewhere. No tingling sensation anywhere. He really had created within seconds a shield that was highly irregular and closely enveloped a complicated structure.

Her expression was incredulous when she turned to him. "How did you do this?"

His delight in being asked by her, the great wielder of secret knowledge, made him laugh. "Just as you did when you made it follow the outline of your body, only adding many more details." An idea struck him. "Why don't we use the training session today to practice shielding? We could do it here in bed."

She smiled broadly. "I like the idea."

That was one thing she had never thought possible: a fighter teaching her skills she could use in healing. But he was right, this was a very clear sign that a change of attitude was in order. It seemed it was not so much about which skills one learned but what they were used for, whatever the one teaching them to her intended. So obviously her father had not planned for her to use her healing knowledge to invent a barrier that could keep stronger magicians at bay, and Lord Tyront had surely not thought of her using shielding for medical purposes when he had first showed her how to do it. Oh dear, that required a lot of thinking. Cataloguing all her skills and knowledge, re-evaluating the use they could be put to, experimenting on how else they could be used...

"Eryn? Where are you with your thoughts? Are you even listening to me?"

She returned to him and smiled apologetically. "Sorry. I was caught in a crisis of values for a moment."

"Was? For a moment? That means you have solved it already? That was quick - or it wasn't a very fundamental one," he said.

"You know, I think it was rather fundamental." She leaned forward and kissed him, registering his mild surprise. "And I think you are the one who solved it for me."

* * *

Eryn watched as Enric opened one of the two notes a messenger had just brought. Somehow they always seemed to arrive while they were eating. This time it was during their evening meal.

He took a deep breath and looked up at her. Now it was time to tell her, he couldn't put it off any longer.

"What? You look like you have bad news." She let her fork sink back to the plate and waited. "Out with it, then."

"The apothecaries. I told you that they would very likely be executed."

"Yes?"

"This is the official announcement of it. And the two of us are expected to attend."

She closed her eyes and sighed. "Yes, I know. Why doesn't he spare me?"

"Because they are to be executed for what they wanted to do to you. If you are not present when their punishment is enforced, it would appear as though you did not support the King's verdict."

"But I *do* not support his verdict!" she protested.

"Which is something the King wouldn't wish to be public knowledge. It is an order, Eryn. Sorry, we don't really have a choice," he said softly.

"How will they be killed?" she asked with resignation and defeat in her voice. "Will it at least be quick?"

"Very quick. And painless," Enric said. "Decapitation."

"When?"

"Tomorrow noon. On the square in front of the palace."

"Nice. Remind me not to eat anything beforehand," she said irritably.

Enric picked up the second message. It was sealed with the Order's emblem in dark red, which meant that it came from Tyront. Enric himself sealed messages with dark blue sealing wax.

A smile spread across his face while he was reading and Eryn waited for him to tell her. She could really use some good news now.

"Your requests have been granted and a date has been set for the ceremony." He took her hand and kissed her knuckles. "You will join the Order in four days. Four more days, then your shackles will be gone. You will again be mistress over your powers and I will have to be a lot more careful around you." He smiled at her and noted that the red in her hair had almost completely faded by now.

She acknowledged his attempt at cheering her up with a chuckle. "Yes, you probably should be."

"This ought to give you enough time to take care of a nice dress for the occasion. I liked the one you wore to the ball," he said and regretted his words instantly, as the memory of what had happened there was not something he had wanted to evoke at this time.

But Eryn just frowned and asked, "A dress? I wasn't aware that special attire was required for that."

"This is a very festive occasion. Joining the Order generally is, all the more in your case. You were really hard to get, after all. And it is not exactly every day that we have to chance to accept a woman - an immensely powerful magician and one with such a unique set of skills - into our illustrious circle."

"I thought you would probably want me to wear robes or some such?"

"They will be given to you in the course of the ceremony."

"Then a dress would be rather superfluous, wouldn't it?"

He sighed. "We've never really had to worry about that before. I know you would prefer to turn up there in something more practical like a vest and pants instead, but as you will don the robes only at the end of the ceremony, people will still see what you are wearing."

"I would like to wear something simple that doesn't contradict the purpose that makes me want to offer healing in this city. How can I promise affordable medical treatment when I spend the annual income of a small family on one set of clothes?" she frowned.

Sighing, he leaned back. "Why don't you invite your friend Junar over tomorrow? She might have an idea or two how to solve this problem. No, don't tell me there is no problem," he added quickly when he saw that she was about to contradict him. "The Order wants you to look festive and distinguished and you'd like to go there in your everyday clothes. That is a problem, believe me. And while she is at it she can take care of the rest of your clothes. You are conjoined with a very wealthy man, my love. And to a certain degree you need to dress accordingly."

"Why? You yourself only wear black or your robes most of the time."

"My clothes are elegant and of very high quality. And I don't need to wear colours. I am known to be dark and dangerous and too much adornment would just not match my reputation," he grinned. "But if you keep on wearing the clothes you were given as a captive, people will begin thinking I don't provide for you properly."

"You are aiming for dark, dangerous and *generous*, then? So this is all about what people think about you, if I understand you correctly?" she asked with an insincere smile. "How about what *I* think about you? Because dressing me up like one of the many useless, rich pretty faces in this city will not really improve *my* opinion of you, in case you cared."

"I am not planning anything of that sort." He shook his head in mock desperation. "How did I end up with probably the only woman in this kingdom who needs to be forced into buying clothes?"

"Why can't I run around in robes all day long like most of you magicians do?"

"Because they are not really practical, if you must know. They are more for being recognisable as the magicians we are. We usually wear something underneath them so we can take them off anytime. Which requires that we are not ashamed of what we wear underneath."

"I am not ashamed."

"But what you wear shames *me*. And I wish to buy new clothes for you. Why is this so hard for you to accept?"

She stared at him and thought for a moment, not entirely sure of the answer herself. "I suppose because I have always had to work for everything I had. Just being given expensive things seems... wrong, no matter how much money you have."

He smiled at that. "Well, that at least reassures me that you haven't taken me for my money, my love."

"No," she sniffed. "I fell for your gentle ways of persuasion, *my love*."

"Good. Then what I have to say next should not surprise you too much: If you don't cooperate in this matter, I will have the servants exchange your clothes against a new set every time they take them away to be cleaned. You then either wear the good things or go and buy a new set of cheap ones, which will after a while be a lot more expensive than just accepting the ones I want to give you."

"Why do you always have to threaten, intimidate or simply overrule me?" she complained.

He sighed. "Because persuasion and convincing don't work very well with you."

"That's because you don't have any valid arguments!"

"There is one argument I can give you besides not wanting to appear like a neglectful companion: the wish to do something for you, to give you something useful and to know that you let me take care of you at least a little."

Eryn looked at him for a while and then sighed. "See? That was not so hard, was it? I will send for Junar tomorrow. I dare say you will want to be there to have a say in what I choose?"

He rose and said with a smile, "Yes. Letting you do this alone is too risky."

Two good things had come from this, he mused. He had got her to accept him as somebody who took care of her, and he had successfully taken her mind off the upcoming execution.

* * *

She looked down from the parlour window that showed the square that would be the venue for the cruel spectacle that was about to unfold in no more than a few minutes. People had started gathering more than two hours before around the fenced-off area, which had three wooden blocks on which the convicts would place their heads.

Always eager to get a good spot for gruesome entertainment, she thought with disgust. There was no doubt that she herself would not have to worry about that. *Her* line of sight would not be blocked by anybody else. But then this was more about nothing blocking peoples' view of her, she was there to *be seen* and not so much to *watch*.

Enric stepped behind her and pulled her against him. "This will soon be over."

She turned around to him. He was wearing his blue robes and looked official, tall and powerful. And so attractive. Something she had not noted for quite some time and wondered now how she could have missed it. Well, fear and hatred were rather strong blindfolds, she mused.

"Are you ready? We need to leave. We can't be late for this."

"Yes," she said gravely. "It would be a pity if it were over before we got there."

He didn't answer. He himself had no objection whatsoever to watching the men die, the men who had intended to take her from him. It would be safer for her to walk the streets when they were gone. He was willing to support the King in this one matter as it coincided with his own wishes. But of course she would not at all appreciate hearing that right now.

They both turned towards the door when they heard a knock. Enric opened it and saw a messenger in the royal colours, bowing and stating that he had been sent by the King to accompany them to the execution.

How neat, he thought. The King was apparently not willing to take the risk of their missing it and even made sure to have them escorted there. The messenger had obviously been instructed not to leave without them.

Enric sighed and picked up the two cloaks which his servants had prepared for them, fastening one around Eryn's shoulders and then putting on his own. Then he took her chilled hand in his and nodded to the messenger to walk ahead.

The messenger escorted them to an area right next to the wooden dais that had been erected the night before. Tyront, Orrin and several other important magicians were standing there already. Lord Poron gave her a smile and nodded at her. She nodded back, managing a frail smile in return.

Vern looked over and motioned for her to stand next to him. Enric obliged her by leading her to a free spot next to the boy.

"Thank you for the book, Vern," she said. "It is incredible. And you took care of everything without me. I am so proud of you."

He smiled. "Thank you, but I can't take all the credit. Lord Poron was a great help. He told me how to instruct the scribes, reorder the text, what size the drawings should be and stuff like that."

Lord Poron, she thought. She had a good feeling about him and hoped he had willingly accepted his new role as third member in their little council without needing to be pushed by Lord Tyront so her joining wouldn't be threatened.

"Well, you might not deserve all the thanks in creating it alone, but I am honoured that you gave me the very first copy. I can't tell you what a great pleasure it was to see your name printed on it. And you managed this with that amazing talent of yours." She pulled him close and kissed him on the cheek, making several magicians turn towards them. When they had seen Enric watching the scene calmly without any alarm or annoyance while keeping her hand in his, they returned to their conversations.

Then the fanfare sounded and the King entered the square, closely followed by Marrin and Loft on his right and left respectively. He climbed the temporary dais and turned to face the crowd who bowed as one. When he sat down, they straightened again.

At King Folrin's nod the three apothecaries were brought outside, each of them with their wrists bound and held on their upper arms by one guard apiece. One of them was limping badly and had to be half carried. They were brought before the King, and Eryn stared at them, seeing their faces for the first time.

So these were the men who had resorted to such drastic measures. They didn't look threatening or evil, but cowered with wide eyes and were all pale and unshaven. Nothing like how she would have imagined the powerful League members to appear. But of course, they would have looked different only a few days ago. Well dressed, immaculately groomed, probably sporting golden jewellery.

The King rose again and turned towards the area where the magicians stood.

"Lady Eryn." He waited until she had lifted her pale face to look at him. Only after Enric nudged her did she utter, "Your Majesty?"

"One of the men who has attacked you is injured. A man should at least be in a position to face his own death walking straight. Therefore, you will heal him." He kept staring into her eyes, while she fought for calm.

Her gaze wandered to the limping man, who stared right back at her. She slowly started shaking her head. Healing a man who was to be killed in a few moments? Why? To make the execution seem more justified because killing an injured man just didn't look that impressive?

"Lady Eryn. This was an order," the King clarified patiently and didn't take his eyes off her for even a moment. When she still didn't react, he said, "Step before me."

The apothecaries were led back a few paces to make space for her. Enric took her elbow, his face set in a grim mask and accompanied her before the dais. When they stood in front of the King, he released her elbow and put his hand to the small of her back under her cloak as if to keep her from stepping back.

"Lady Eryn, I command you to heal the man. If you refuse me once more, you will face the consequences," he said quietly, but she had no doubt that he meant every word.

She looked up at him. Staring into his eyes, she drew in a breath to tell him that today she wouldn't be his puppet on a string, when she suddenly felt all tension drain from her muscles. She felt herself go down on one knee, lowering her head in a gesture of humility, none of it her own doing. She saw from the corners of her eyes that Enric was doing the exact same thing. Enric. With his hand on her back.

She tried to fight the grip of his magic, but even without the shackles that would have been useless. Anger and the feeling of betrayal coursed through her without any vent to let it out. And now? She wanted to scream at Enric. What is the next step in this brilliant plan - forcing me to heal when you have no idea how it works?

Then her heart almost stopped when she heard a familiar voice speak out. Vern.

"Your Majesty?"

She imagined that all eyes would now have turned towards them, but all she was able to see was the pattern of the cobblestones on which she knelt.

"You are Lord Orrin's son, are you not?" she heard the King say calmly.

"Yes, Your Majesty," the boy replied.

"What is it you have to say?"

"I beg Your Majesty to permit me to take over the healing that Lady Eryn feels she is not up to."

Eryn's eyes filled with tears. He had given up his secret not only to his father, but to the Order and the King to step in for her.

She heard the magicians start murmuring - first quietly, then more loudly. They ceased their conversations at once when the King started speaking.

"You are in a position to carry out such healing?" the sovereign asked, somehow managing to sound not in the least surprised. She wondered if he truly was so hard to astound, if he had been aware of Vern's secret or if he was just a very convincing actor.

"Yes, Your Majesty," the boy replied in a loud and clear voice.

The King must have made a permissive gesture, because she heard the shuffling of feet and heard Vern's steps move towards where the apothecaries were standing with their guards.

"You may rise again," the King said in their direction and Enric moved together with her to stand up straight again, not for an instant releasing his grip on her. Simultaneously, he made them turn towards the boy to allow Eryn to watch.

Vern stood in front of the limping man and took his hand, closing his eyes in the way she had shown him, to shut out the external world and be better able to concentrate on the inside of his patient's body. She could see the man gasp in surprise when he felt something happening inside his leg. Vern stepped back after only a few minutes. It seemed the injury had not been a very complicated one, probably a broken bone.

The King nodded to the two guards to each side of the apothecary to let him walk for a few steps and smiled when there was no more limp discernible.

"Well done, young man. I will definitely be keeping an eye on you."

Vern bowed and returned to his place next to his father.

Enric turned towards the King and waited. King Folrin studied him for a few moments and then motioned for them to step back among the other magicians.

Being extra careful not to lose the physical contact with her, he made her step back with him next to Vern, who gulped back his feelings when he saw tears drying on her face.

The magicians around them were quiet. Most of them were probably staring at Vern. She wondered how many of them were aware that her body movement was currently not under her own but Enric's control.

The charges were read out loud and she heard one of the men sobbing. Then she was turned towards the centre of the space to watch the execution. She could not even avert her eyes as Enric made sure she made no move that would enrage the King any further.

The three men were led towards the wooden blocks that had been prepared for them. Two of them went quietly, resigned to their fate. But one fought, cried out, tearfully begging for mercy. He shook violently from his sobs, dusty cheeks now tear-stained, and there was a rapidly growing damp patch visible down one dark green trouser leg. He was the first they made to kneel.

A burly man holding a massive axe in front of him waited for them to be fixed to the blocks with ropes.

With one single chop, the man's head neatly separated from his body with a ghastly, wet sound and it land in the basket that had been placed there for this exact purpose. Then the next blow only seconds later, and finally, the third.

There was the taste of bile in her mouth when she watched the decapitated corpses twitching a few times before they went still and lifeless.

The crowd started murmuring, breaking the eerie silence and thus the spell of the gruesome spectacle.

She felt herself being steered back towards their quarters, only noting the details in passing as she did not have any chance of intervening with what was done with her. To her.

The steps right behind them suggested that they were not going back alone. Lord Tyront would be among them, and, of course, Vern, and thus also Orrin.

Enric opened the door into the parlour and led her inside, making sure the door was closed behind the last one of their entourage before releasing his hold on her.

She stumbled a few steps forward and held on to the nearest available stable object, a chair, to keep herself from crumpling. Slowly regaining full control over her muscles, she straightened and turned. Lord Tyront, Orrin, Vern and Lord Poron looked at her with worried expressions. Enric's own was a mixture of his personal fury and grim anticipation of her reaction to what had just occurred.

She stared at him, then slowly walked towards him and swallowed before she lifted her hand and slapped him hard across the face. As she withdrew her hand, breathing heavily, she saw the red mark her palm had left. Another tear ran down her cheek.

He merely looked down at her with narrowed eyes and waited for a few moments before asking quietly, "Are you finished?"

When she just gave a frown in confusion, he grabbed her hand and pulled her close with a jerk. And once more he caught her swiftly after he had sent her to sleep.

"Seriously now? How was that necessary?" Vern burst out, enraged. Orrin clapped his palm over his son's mouth that had just formed the words to that which he had forced himself not to say aloud.

Enric's gaze locked onto Vern, making him take an involuntary step back. "You'd better watch your words, boy," he said sharply. "Or we will continue our little discussion about defiance."

He then lifted his unconscious companion into his arms and carried her into his bedroom.

When he returned after laying Eryn down on his bed, the magicians - each one with their arms folded - were standing around Vern, who did not look so much afraid as wearily resigned.

Tyront spoke first. "Vern. This was quite a surprise you sprang on us out there. How long have you been acquiring healing skills?"

He thought for a moment before answering, "For about five months."

"Why?" Orrin asked, not managing to hide completely how offended he was.

Vern looked at him pleadingly. "I was never good at fighting. You know that. I was never stronger or more capable than the others. But healing... this is about knowledge, about thinking, not about strength... I knew you would be disappointed, but after seeing what I could do, I..."

"You know not a thing, son," Orrin said stiffly. "What disappoints me is not that you learned healing, but that I had to learn about it in such a way as this."

The boy stared at him in confusion for a few seconds as if to gauge the truth of the words before asking incredulously, "You wouldn't have minded?"

"Not as much as your lying to me," Orrin replied curtly. "But this is neither the time nor the place to discuss this."

"How did you get her to teach you?" Tyront asked next.

Vern frowned. "Well, quite easily. I just asked her. At first she didn't want to because she thought I would get into trouble, but then..." He fell silent.

"But then you offered to teach her magical combat skills?" Tyront suggested.

Lord Poron cleared his throat. "You say she didn't want to teach you at first because she wanted to protect you from getting into trouble? Why would she assume that you would be punished for it?"

"Because she said that it was obvious that the Order had nothing but disdain for the art of healing. She said that you... that the Order was forcing her to learn fighting but never even once tried to make her teach healing."

"She thought we were not interested because we didn't try to force her into sharing her skills with us?" Tyront asked with raised brows.

Vern shrugged. "She was pretty much forced into everything else here, so she thought *not* being coerced equalled a lack of interest."

"And how would she have reacted to our interest in healing?" Lord Poron enquired.

"She would have showed you, same as she showed me. She says that healing is not a privilege, but something that should be part of every magician's set of skills." Vern watched the magicians around him exchange baffled looks.

Tyront cleared his throat before asking, "So the only reason why she has never shared this knowledge with the Order is *that nobody has asked her to?*"

They all turned when they heard a chuckle behind them. Enric was standing next to the drink cabinet, pouring himself a generous glass full of something clear and dark brown that smelled rather potent. He shook his head at the world around him and drowned the glass in one go with several great gulps.

Tyront raised a brow. That promised to become interesting. Enric hardly ever drank. He had to be really tense.

"I wonder why this even surprises me anymore," Enric said, shaking his head. Empty glass in hand, he strolled to a sofa and took a seat. He still had all eyes in the room on him. "I never even asked her why she is so averse to fighting. It's true, she keeps saying it is a waste of time, but I wonder if there is more."

"There is," Vern said calmly.

Enric looked at him and nodded. "Go on."

"She told me that healing and fighting are exact opposites in her opinion - one to restore, one to destroy. That she has been taught all her childhood that healing is the only right path and the other is despicable and wrong. She said being made to fight every day is a violation of everything she believes, it causes damage instead of repairs it." He saw his father close his eyes and turned to him. "She also said that she doesn't blame you any more than anyone else, as you were not alone in doing it to her."

"I see," Enric said quietly after a while. Then he slowly got up from his seat and walked towards Vern, whose eyes widened in alarm.

"You have saved Eryn today, Vern, and I repaid you with scorn when you objected to my rough treatment of somebody who has been a friend to you. And whose friendship you have today proven to be more than worthy of. Not only did you lift the burden of the King's order from her shoulders, but you also provided a public explanation that will very likely enable the King to refrain from dealing out severe punishment without losing his face. I owe you greatly." And then, to everyone's amazement, the second most powerful magician in the kingdom bowed to a fifteen-year old boy.

CHAPTER 31

Confrontations

It was evening and Enric was sitting on the edge of his bed, watching her. He remembered the last two times he had been sitting like that. The first was after her escape attempt, when Tyront had sent her to sleep, and the other was when he himself had knocked her out after the attack by the apothecaries. This had been hardly more than two weeks ago, yet he wondered how so much could have happened in the meantime.

Today they were companions, while back then she hadn't even let him take her hand in his. Though the chances that she would be keen on being touched by him were not likely to be much greater after her waking now, he mused.

He thought about the execution and pondered in hindsight if he would have reacted any differently. Not stopping her from publicly wording her disobedience was unthinkable. Making her bow had at least signalled some degree of submissiveness to the watchers, even if the King himself had probably not been fooled by it.

The King, he thought and shook his head in anger. The bloody fool had misjudged her completely, almost endangering his own plans of getting her into the Order and thus indirectly under his control. Had he really been that sure of her unconditional compliance after what he had put her through at the ball only three days ago?

He remembered kneeling on the square with Eryn, wondering what to do next after taking away her control over her muscles. Vern's intervention had been more than he might have dared to dream of. That boy had saved quite a lot of plans from ruin, Enric mused. The Order's, the King's and Enric's own, which pretty much consisted in keeping her alive and happy. Alive he had managed so far, but happy was another matter entirely.

He watched as the rhythm of her breathing changed and became less deep. Her lids opened slowly and she looked at him for several seconds before her eyes widened and she sat up abruptly. She rolled to the other side of the bed, then jumped up to run out of his bedroom

That was not good, he decided immediately and improved his speed magically to swing the bedroom door shut and lean against it before she had any chance to slip out. Locking her in here with a shield seemed... wrong. Impersonal somehow. He would have accepted her shouting at him, attacking him with hands or throwing at him whatever items around the place she managed to grab, but just running off was not an option. They needed to take care of this.

"Eryn," he implored, "no running. Talk to me."

"Talk to you," she whispered. "And if you don't like what you hear you will just put me back to sleep for a few hours?"

"I am sorry about that. I was not exactly in a frame of mind to judge my actions sensibly." He knew better than to touch her now, even though it would have taken no more than reaching out.

She looked up at him. "No. Sensible it wasn't."

He waited for her to go on, but she didn't. "And neither was the King's order. He should never have placed you in that position and I am sorry you had to endure it. But acting the way I did down there was the only thing I could think of, and still can."

Shaking her head, she went back to the bed to sit. Good, he thought - at least she was willing to talk. Not that he intended to give her much of a choice. She had no chance to get out of the room.

"You can't treat me like this when we are supposed to be living together. I am an adult, a grown woman - not a child you can steer as you please. This is not how you treat another person in a relationship!"

Enric's face turned serious. It seemed she had not really grasped the possible consequences of her public refusal to obey the King.

"Eryn, what do you think the King would have done to you?"

"Done to me?"

"Yes. You refused to follow his order twice. In public. The third time would probably have cost you your life. Or at least your life with me when he shackled you and never let you out of the dungeons again. My understanding of a relationship includes protecting each other from a fate like that." He sighed and raked his fingers through his hair. "And in three days I will also be your superior. Which means protecting you not only as your companion, but also in that capacity. Especially if you disobey your King. I may not like what he did to you, to the both of us, but for now we need to find a way to deal with that in a way that doesn't cause him to harm us."

"Like letting him do whatever he wants to me?" she shot at him coldly.

"If I hadn't intervened then, Tyront would have, you can depend on it. He, too, takes his responsibilities towards his magicians very seriously. And seeing how tense your relationship with him is already, I think it was better I was the one to act. This at least gives you a chance to express your anger without consequence."

She closed her eyes and leaned back on the bed, feeling tired and exhausted. These magically-induced sleeping periods were not exactly restful. "Yes, I know."

They each remained silent for several seconds before Enric spoke, looking up. "Vern said a few things today that made me think. He told us that you would have showed us how to heal if only we had asked you." He looked out the window and chuckled at the memory. "That took us all aback, believe me." He became serious again. "And then he talked about why you hate fighting so much. About your beliefs and what you were taught. I don't know about the others, but it made me feel like a monster." He shook his head. "Yet you had it in you to let me get closer to you after all these months basically of torturing you, to consider joining the Order. You went out there and healed strangers, believing it was against our wishes. All that without ever losing that spirit, that power inside you that drives you on."

She was now sitting upright on the bed, staring at him.

He looked back at her. "You even managed to convert Orrin into a friend. Did you know that he wanted to give up his position so he wouldn't be asked to force you into training with him any longer?"

Eryn shook her head. "He did?"

"Yes," he smiled faintly. "Tyront had quite a hard time making him stay. And he only did after deciding that he wouldn't entrust you to anybody else but himself. This was when the jealousy I had started feeling after seeing you in his arms really started driving me crazy."

"What? When was I in his arms?" She frowned, thinking back.

"The day you healed Vern after that stupid accident with the broken furniture. I came in when you had finished and Orrin was holding you in his arms." He omitted the detail of Orrin being questioned by the Order and the King for removing her shackles.

"And you were jealous? Of Orrin? But that was months ago!"

"Yes," he smiled lopsidedly. "I have had my eye on you for quite some time. This is why I can't move on fast enough. I sometimes forget that for me this is what I have been waiting for, but for you it is still new. You have only just ceased hating me."

She drew in a deep breath, then exhaled slowly. "That was a lot. I am not really sure how to feel right now or what to do."

He came closer to the bed, very carefully, and crouched down in front of her when he saw no more alarm in her eyes. "I can't tell you what to feel, but I have an idea or two what you, what *we* can do. Firstly, I would like you to forgive me for what I did in the parlour today." He waited for her reaction.

She studied him for a while, then nodded slowly. "Alright. I forgive you for knocking me out. Again."

He smiled at the little sting at the end of her statement. "Thank you. I will not apologise for what happened during the execution. And I want you to understand and accept that I did this to protect you."

A sigh, then another nod.

A powerful wave of relief went through him. "What we need to do next is face the King. He will summon us, I have no doubt about that. I want you to stand before him and follow my lead, to trust me to do what is best for you, best for us two. I will tell him that the strain of the whole setting was too great for you, and that the mere thought of touching a man who wanted you dead almost paralysed you. Vern has helped us to a very good start here by saying that you didn't feel up to it."

"Alright," she said. "Anything else?"

"Yes, one more thing." He took her hand into his and pressed it against his cheek. "I would like to wake up with you tomorrow. So either I can come to your room, or you can come to mine if you wake up before me. This is my last bold demand for tonight."

A hesitant smile spread across her face. "Yes, I think I can live with that."

* * *

She smiled when she felt his arm slip around her from behind and opened her eyes. It was still dark outside. "Enric?"

"Yes. Or were you expecting anyone else?" he whispered.

"Orrin maybe. He does so like to drop by at night," she murmured.

"Nice. I shouldn't have told you about my jealousy."

"No, probably not. But now it's too late," she grinned and turned around to snuggle against his bare chest.

"I was going to apologise for waking you, but I have changed my mind and will take advantage of your alertness instead."

"As long as I don't have to clean your quarters again," she yawned.

"*Our* quarters," he corrected her with just a hint of reprimand in his voice.

"Our quarters, then." He felt her head shake. "What made you even think of a thing like that?"

"Well, it was a way of getting you into my bedroom. And watching you while you were kneeling on the floor and bending over things was quite a test to my resolve, I should say."

She snorted. "I hope you don't expect any compassion from *me*. I was so tired back then, hardly managing to keep my eyes open, and yet you made me clean this place for three hours. I didn't even have enough energy left to curse you for it."

"That says something," he said. "I haven't seen you too tired to abuse me before or since."

She sighed. "What can I say? Most of the time it is well deserved."

"Only most of the time?" he chuckled.

"Yes." Her tone had become serious. Maybe it was a good thing they were in the dark. Having him look at her wouldn't make this easier. "The way I acted yesterday, that was... unfair, especially after what you did for me. I hit you right in front of the other magicians. I shouldn't have done that. I suppose I can hardly be mad at you for reacting the way you did. A lesser man would have hit me right back."

She felt him bury his face in her hair, so that his voice sounded muffled. "I could never hit you."

"Thank you. That makes me feel even worse."

His breath felt warm on her scalp when he laughed. "Don't worry, however hard you hit me, I can take it. At least as long as you do it without magic. I am a big, strong warrior, after all."

She felt relieved at his playful tone and gratitude that he made it so easy for her. She let her hands wander over his naked skin until they met his trousers.

"Didn't you want to take advantage of me? I distinctly remember you mentioning it," she purred and lifted her head so he could access her mouth.

He smiled in the dark. Another victory. It was the first time *she* had been the one to suggest sleeping together.

* * *

She lifted her hand to stop the sun from blinding her through closed eyelids and then turned her head before opening her eyes. Enric sat beside her, reading what looked like a royal summons, judging from the seal. She managed to identify them easily enough now and had come to dread them.

"A summons from his Royal Bastardness?" she mumbled.

He raised a brow at her. "I do take offence at my personal sobriquet being used for another man. And at the implication that we are on the same level in your esteem."

She shrugged. "Don't. I will find another unflattering one for you, if you like. And I can always return to *Lordling*. It has earned me my first unmasked kiss from you, after all," she added with a grin.

He looked down at her in surprise. It seemed she was starting to look back over the very particular chain of incidents that day with a certain humour. If it had not been for the summons, although he had been expecting it, this would have been a perfect start to the day.

"So, when am I due?"

"We," he corrected her. "He wants me there as well. Which is just as well. I would have come anyway."

"He might have sent you away," she pointed out.

He smiled without humour. "No. He has forced you into a commitment with me, but we are entitled to certain rights as well. Standing with my companion when she is facing difficulties is one of them."

It would be good to have him there, she thought. She remembered his words from the evening before about finding a way of dealing with the issue that would cause them no harm. Her temper was the problem, she knew. Somehow there was always a new situation that exceeded the limits of what she could handle.

"What are you thinking about?" Enric said, interrupting her thoughts.

She looked up. "I was thinking how talented the King is when it comes to making me lose control. Almost as effective as you were. And still are at times."

"Then it is time to work on how to maintain control. This will be a useful skill for you, for facing both the King and Tyront."

She sighed and bit her lip. "Any suggestions here?"

He thought for a moment. "You are the healer. What happens inside you when you are about to lose control?"

"I am not really relaxed enough to focus on my body functions when I am agitated. So no great insights there, I'm afraid," she frowned.

A slow smile spread across his face. "How fortunate, then, that we have another healer at our disposal to help you there, isn't it?"

"What, Vern?"

"Yes, unless you have been training any others secretly," he retorted and swung his legs out of the bed.

"Where are you going?" she called after him when he walked out the door and into the parlour.

"I am going to summon our young friend to assist you," he replied and moved towards his study.

She quickly grabbed a blanket to wrap it around her before following him. "But he has lessons right now!"

"No, not anymore after the note I will write," he chuckled and bent his head over a piece of paper. "You better get dressed, my love. He will be here shortly and we wouldn't want him to see you like that. This is my privilege."

* * *

She looked up when she heard the knock. Enric had been right, it had been quick. Binding her hair together with a piece of string, she walked out of her room and saw Vern step into the parlour and bow to Enric when he closed the door behind the boy.

"Am I in trouble?" he asked Eryn nervously when he spotted her.

She smiled and went towards him to ruffle his hair. "No, dear lad, *I* am. And we need your help."

His posture changed immediately and he seemed to grow a little.

"How?" he asked in a business-like manner that was very likely meant to impress Enric.

"Enric thinks that you can help me figure out and control my physical reactions to stress so I can keep myself calm when I need to."

The boy looked at her in surprise. "But even I can tell you how the body reacts to stress." He used his fingers and started listing. "Increased heartbeat and thus breathing, increased sweating…"

"Yes, I am aware of the general symptoms, actually," she stopped him. "But people react to stress differently and I need you to have a good look at what happens with me *specifically*."

"Alright. And how am I supposed to trigger such a reaction in you here and now?" Vern asked in puzzlement.

Enric joined them and smiled roguishly. "I think I can assist. Is there any special part of her body you need to touch?"

"No, a hand will do," the boy replied.

"Good. Then get ready."

Before she could ask what he intended to do, she felt his fingers close around her wrists and then her arms being pushed behind her back. He took both her hands in one of his and used his free one to hold her head immobile.

"Oh, come on! You can't be serious!" she cried out when his face came closer and she tried to free herself. He just smiled and stopped a hair's breadth away from her lips to say, "Vern, do your thing."

Then he touched her lips, opened them and felt her squirm against him. Doing this in front of the boy didn't bother him much, but she was clearly uncomfortable. Good. It was the idea of all this, after all.

When after a few seconds she seemed to be resigned, he moved his hand down to her left breast and felt her gasp at the touch and then renew the attempts at freeing herself. When she managed to turn her head away, he lowered his lips to her exposed throat and nibbled at the sensitive skin there.

"You can stop now," Vern said in a voice that had somewhat of an awkward edge.

Enric released her hands and let her push him back a little. Her face was scarlet and he grinned broadly. "You are blushing. I find that endearing."

She slapped his hand away when he lifted it to her cheek.

"That was…" she started angrily and was interrupted by Vern.

"Useful. Even if I feel the need to cut out my eyes right now," he said reproachfully. "You could have warned me at least!"

"It worked, didn't it?" Enric just said, obviously pleased with himself.

"Should you look so satisfied after making me uncomfortable by *kissing* me?" She shot him an evil look that clearly failed to hit its mark.

"Me kissing you was not the problem, my love. The audience was," he said, still smiling.

She heard Vern snort beside her. "Yes, and the audience is not too thrilled, either."

"Oh, shut up the two of you," she rolled her eyes and then turned to the boy. "So, what are your findings?"

"Increased heartbeat, as was to be expected," he said expertly. "More blood in your muscles, less in your intestinal system."

She raised one brow at him. "You have been reading that other book I gave you, haven't you?"

He smiled modestly or at least tried to. "Well, I try to keep up." Then he frowned. "And then there is a lot of stuff that has been released into your blood. A lot of different substances from different parts of your body. That was confusing."

"They are a mix of messengers and nutrients to trigger reactions. But let's leave that aside, this is too complicated to influence spontaneously. What other reactions have you seen apart from the heartbeat and thus the increased level of blood in my muscles?"

"Only that your body temperature has increased a little, which activated the sweat glands."

"Yes, that is necessary or the body would overheat," she explained absently. "So there was no great surprise there. That means the main thing to do for me is to control my heartbeat by slowing it down with magic as soon as it starts to increase." She swallowed. "I am not very comfortable with that. The heart is always a tricky thing to meddle with."

"And you need to do this with magic?" Enric enquired. "There are other ways of relaxing your body. You don't need to influence your heart directly, especially if you don't feel up to it. How about breathing exercises? It's what warriors do."

"I don't really think breathing exercises will work when I am under great pressure," she replied. "I need something a little more potent."

Enric shook his head indulgently. "It seems you have lost the connection to your own body and what it can do without being constantly healed, maintained and influenced by healing magic. You will probably not believe it, but there are ways of dealing with agitation without using magic."

"Such as breathing." Her voice was flat.

"Yes. And now we will try this again, only this time you concentrate on breathing slowly and regularly, no matter what I do."

Vern sighed. "Alright, let's get this over with. If anybody asks why I was summoned to your quarters, I will just cover my ears and start singing to drown out the memory. Most of my peers think I am strange, anyway."

"Wait!" She lifted her hands when Enric pulled her close again. "Maybe we can find another way to do this. I am uncomfortable with heights, so maybe…"

"Right, I will just hang you out the window, head down and Vern will hold on to your leg to see if your breathing exercises work," Enric quipped. "No - this is quicker and works just as well."

"Yes, right," Vern mumbled, but touched her hand as it was again held in her companion's grip behind her back.

"Don't forget to breathe, or Vern has to suffer for nothing," Enric grinned, clearly enjoying himself more than the situation warranted from her point of view.

This time he didn't kiss her, but watched her face as he slipped his free hand under her tunic. She drew in a sharp breath and closed her eyes for a moment, forcing herself to ignore what he did with her in Vern's presence. At least the boy couldn't see anything from where he stood, even if he probably had a pretty realistic idea of what was happening.

His fingers had reached her breast and teased around it, while his mouth neared hers and he took her lower lip between his teeth, tugging gently.

She swallowed and repeated the simple rhythm of in and out, in and out to herself to regulate her breathing, pushing aside whatever other images were trying to stalk her.

"It works better this time," she heard Vern say and exhale in relief.

"Wait a moment," Enric instructed the boy. "Keep monitoring her heartbeat. And close your eyes."

He crushed her mouth, grasping her buttocks and pressing her close to make her aware of the effect she was having on him.

"Heartbeat increasing again," Vern commented, his eyes clenched shut with determination. "Very much so, in fact. Whatever you are doing, I don't think I should be in the same room with you if you don't stop right here."

Enric released her and quickly stayed her when she was about to stumble. "Good. I just wanted to see how much you can really breathe away. I would hate to think that you can tune me out just like that."

"From your broad grin I assume that you have been able to dispel your concerns," she remarked dryly and took a seat to keep enough distance to him to recover her composure.

"Yes, that I have," he said smugly. "You have another two hours to practice your breathing, then we need to leave." He turned to Vern. "Thank you for your help, Vern. You may return to your lessons now."

"Yes, right," he murmured when he quickly walked to the door, "like I will be able to think of anything but hiding in a dark place with a blanket over my head."

* * *

Enric took her hand and gave it a reassuring squeeze when the guards opened the door to the throne room for them to enter.

The King wasn't sitting on his throne as Eryn had assumed he would be, but standing by of one of five magnificent tall windows at the other end of the room, with his back to them. She noted that only one of his advisors was with him today, the one she remembered taking her to the King at the night of the ball. Marrin.

The thought at what had happened that night and the sight of the man who had only the day before tried to coerce her into something yet again made her jaw clench and she forced herself to breathe, just as she had been practising.

King Folrin turned when they stepped closer and watched them bow to him.

"Lady Eryn. Lord Enric," he said and studied them, noting their joined hands with a thin smile. "So nice to see that you are getting along so well. I was rather worried about the two of you after yesterday."

Breathe, she ordered herself and stared straight ahead.

"How so, Your Majesty?" Enric enquired with polite interest.

"Because judging from the impression I had from your companion, Lord Enric, I would have assumed that she doesn't usually take kindly to being released from the control over her own body - which is what you did, obviously." The King paused for a few moments, his meek smile never ceasing. "I wonder what you would have done next if Lord Orrin's son had not spoken out. Were you even aware that he had started to learn healing?"

"No, Your Majesty," Enric replied calmly. "This came as quite a surprise to us."

"I see. Though in hindsight it doesn't seem so unforeseeable, does it? A young fellow, bookish type as I am told, with no great interest in combat lessons, spending a lot of time with a woman with a unique set of skills that require a more intellectual approach, something that has appeal to him. And Lady Eryn," he stepped into the line of her stare to get her full attention, "so eager to perform her craft that she wanders the streets to proffer her help to whomever seeks it, and has negotiated with the Order so valiantly to make healing possible after her joining. Why had we ever thought that you would not share this knowledge willingly, I wonder?" He narrowed his eyes at her rigid posture and spoke without looking away from her, "Lord Enric, I would ask you to let go of your companion's hand. I would like to make sure she is in control of her own body right now."

She felt cool air where only a moment ago his warm touch had been.

"Lady Eryn," King Folrin said quietly and stepped closer than she felt was comfortable. "There is the matter of your disobedience. I do not look favourably upon such behaviour. I was wondering what the right way to deal with you is. I admit I am not entirely sure about that. Leniency, as you are not yet bound to me via the Order and still need to get used to the recent and admittedly very considerable changes in your life? Or severe punishment to teach you a lesson you are not likely to forget in a hurry? I find myself torn between the wish to be clement and the need to demonstrate a point."

Breathing in, breathing out. In and out.

"Fortunately for you, your young friend made quite an impression yesterday, and his words indicating that you didn't feel up to the healing have made it possible for me to let you out of this without punishment. You are in his debt - greatly so, I feel I should point out."

"Your Majesty, if I may speak?"

"Lord Enric. By all means. Your companion does seem unusually silent today, considering everything."

"Lady Eryn did indeed not feel up to the challenge of facing and touching a man that has only days ago tried to end her life. I would beg Your Majesty to take this into consideration."

King Folrin chuckled. "Ah, dear Lord Enric, I do find watching you in your role of protector so very entertaining. How unfortunate that it seems to require rather a lot of reconstruction of the truth of late. Although I really appreciate how well you have mastered the skill. Even now at being accused of possessing and using it, you seem all confusion and innocence. No, there is no need to reply to that," he added when Enric opened his mouth to speak. "There is nothing you can say, after all. Denying it would be pointless and admitting it would be very imprudent."

He returned his attention to Eryn and walked around her in a semi-circle until he came to stand behind her.

She closed her eyes for a moment, concentrating on her breathing more than ever, pushing aside the thought that Enric had just been accused of having lied repeatedly to the King.

"Lady Eryn," she heard the King's voice close by her side, "There is one more thing I wish to let you know. Should you again feel unable to comply with my orders, I may in turn feel that funding your healing services is a drain on the Crown's resources that needs to be stopped. Have I made myself clear?"

She nodded and only after a few seconds realised that this was not enough for him and he was waiting for something.

"Yes, Your Majesty," she said obediently.

"Excellent, so you still are in command of your voice," he commented dryly. "I was rather worried, to be completely honest. One can never be quite sure what a powerful magician really is able to do, even without touching you. There are rumours, but they are a questionable source of information. I venture to say we have just started to find out about *your* abilities, my dear Lady." He then stepped in front of her again, smiling coldly. "I very much look forward to having you in the Order. Finally." He took her cool hand and lifted it to his lips to kiss it. His smile warmed when he noticed the flicker in her eyes and how her breathing became deeper, if not faster. "You are learning to master your temper, I see. You are lucky to have such a resourceful companion by your side who can teach you such a variety of different skills in addition to the ones you already possess." He released her hand and took a step back. "You may leave now."

She felt Enric's warm hand wrap around hers again and pull her down into a bow before leaving. Breathing in and out again for one last time, she left the throne room with him and the doors closed firmly behind them.

She stopped and leaned against a cool pillar, waiting for her vision to clear again.

"Oh dear, I am dizzy. Who would think that you could breathe too much?"

* * *

The King watched them leave and then turned to Marrin, looking thoughtful.

"My father told me how very annoying he found it not to have any leverage on Lord Enric. He has always been very careful not to make himself vulnerable. His friendships have not survived his rise to his position of power, and he has had no more than casual affairs."

"Until now," Marrin remarked.

"Very true. Until now. But it seems that where Lady Eryn is concerned, particular care is needed. The degree of his attachment to her surprises me, and there is no saying how he will react to any threat to her."

"She does seem to have warmed to him as well, though she does seem nowhere near to his own regard for her yet."

The King nodded and smiled. "This is no more than a matter of time. Only a few weeks ago she loathed him, and look at them now. I strongly suspect she has started falling in love with him already, and he *is* very persistent. Though keeping *her* under control is less of a problem. She has quickly made friends here. But if everything works out, there is no need for such measures. They are a very powerful couple and I would prefer to keep them happy instead of merely under control."

"She will not react well to the news, I assume," Marrin said carefully.

"She most likely won't. But Lord Enric will start appreciating what he might still consider a very harsh course of action from my side as soon as he sees how close he came to losing her."

CHAPTER 32

Joining the Order

Enric opened his eyes slowly and looked over her recumbent form. She was sprawled across half the bed, clearly not used to sharing her sleeping space with anyone else. The thought pleased him; he was the first one to be granted that privilege. Luckily enough, his bed was large enough for this not to be a problem. It could easily accommodate two more. Not that his inclinations ran that way.

He had taken his time with her last night. A lot of it. Hours. And exhausting her so much that she didn't even manage to return to the guest room was obviously one way to get her to spend the night with him. He smiled. With that he could start to work. And would.

He quickly closed his eyes when she began to stir. From the shift of her weight on the bed he assumed that she had just turned and realised where she had unintentionally been sleeping. Her sudden intake of breath confirmed his suspicion. He let her climb out of the bed slowly and cautiously to avoid waking him, not moving a limb himself. It wouldn't make sense to stop her now, even though he would have preferred to keep her close for a little longer. The main thing was that she had realised that she had spent an entire night with him without a need to return to the guest room - voluntarily. More or less.

That would be food for thought for her. And it was a great incentive for him. If he could do it once, he could do it again and thus bring her around so she got used to sleeping in his bed such that returning to the other would at some point no longer make sense.

When she had left his bedroom, he opened his eyes once more. So she didn't want him to see that he had succeeded this time. Games, he thought with a sigh. It seemed they were going to continue playing them for a while yet.

He waited for another few minutes before he rose and got dressed. When he stepped into the parlour, she was already sitting on of the chairs, holding a steaming cup in her hands.

"Good morning," he said and strolled over to her to kiss her forehead.

"And to you," she replied, taking a sip. "I just remembered that we haven't taken care of my attire for tomorrow yet. I suspect it is a little late now."

Enric shook his head and drew up a chair next to her to sit. "No. I had sent for Junar two days ago, but as you were rather... incapacitated that afternoon I ordered a few things and asked her to bring them over as soon as she has finished them. She has your measurements, after all."

"*You* ordered something for me?" she asked doubtfully.

"Yes. But you don't need to look so worried. I asked her to make whatever she thought you would like without making me seem like a miser. And she said she had an idea of what you would probably be willing to wear tomorrow for the ceremony."

She raised a brow. "Quite the organiser, aren't you?"

He shrugged. "It comes with the position, I suppose. How about your preparations for tomorrow? Have you memorised the oath yet?"

"Yes, *father*. I have." She rolled her eyes.

"I would thank you if you didn't call me that."

"Then I suggest you stop behaving like one," she retorted. "I want to be treated like a grown person. It will be nice for a change."

"Demands, demands," he sighed theatrically and smiled. "You will get rid of your shackles tomorrow. I was considering inviting a few people here to celebrate after the official festivities are over, if you don't mind. There are a few people who would like to raise their glasses in your honour, I am sure, and a few selected others you might want to meet officially."

"A social dinner? Here?"

"Yes. It will be our first time hosting a social get-together as a couple. We were expected to have done so already after the commitment, but as we have another occasion for celebrating only days later, we will be forgiven that lapse if we make up for it tomorrow."

"I am meant to host this with you?" She swallowed nervously. "I have no idea what to do! Will standing in one corner and holding on to a glass be sufficient?"

"No, I am afraid that will not do," he said. "You will look radiant with happiness after two marvellous things happened in your life in such quick succession. Furthermore, you will allow me to introduce you to people you don't know and talk to people you do know."

"I don't go around refilling empty glasses or some such?"

"No, my love, we have servants for that. And you will be much too busy for it, anyway. Everyone will be eager to talk to you."

"Great," she murmured. "Who will be on this illustrious guest list, then?"

"Tyront, Lord Poron and Orrin, obviously," he began.

"How about Vern?"

"I wouldn't dare leave him out of this," he replied good-naturedly. "Your friend Junar. And the orphan girl, Plia, if you like. The rest will be a few key people from treasury and teaching, members of the Magic Council and their companions, of course."

"Forging useful contacts, then?" she smiled.

"I certainly hope so. And as I am now no longer a bachelor, I am expected to host these things together with you occasionally. That will make it easier for you to maintain and increase these contacts."

"Are you turning me into some kind of society trophy?" she frowned. "This sounds like a time-consuming task."

"It's not so bad. You will be able to meet many of them on those occasions we have been invited to in return."

Another thing to do in addition to building up a structure for healing services, learn whatever they deemed useful knowledge and train her combat skills: socialising. How nice. What else would she be doing with all that extra time?

"It seems like being the companion of an important man such as yourself is quite demanding," she remarked.

"Oh, absolutely." He smiled. "And this is just what the *others* expect from you."

"The others? What is it *you* expect from me, then?" No, she decided, that had not been a good question. Asking a question one might not be prepared to hear the answer to was not a smart move. "Don't answer that," she added quickly, "I take it back."

He shook his head slowly. "No, I think I should answer that one." He thought for a few moments, his face serious. "I expect you to work on this relationship with me and to honour the promise we made to each other, however reluctantly it was done from your side. I further expect you to stop running from me when there are difficulties. However else you feel you need to express anger, frustration or fear, running away is the one thing I will not accept." There was more, but for now all that she needed to hear.

She sighed. As if running from him had worked even once in the past. And as regarded honouring the oath… the passage about love and being with him until the end of their lives was a lot to ask.

"I see," was all she said, and was relieved when he no more than smiled at her instead of demanding some affirmation.

He then rose when they heard a knock at the door.

"Junar, probably," he said and his assumption turned out to be correct.

He greeted Junar politely and asked her in after she had bowed to him, careful not to drop the large bundle of clothes she was bearing in her arms.

"I have brought the things you asked for, Lord Enric," she said and smiled gratefully when he released her of the load to put it on one of the sofas.

"That was incredibly fast. I would have expected no more than the clothes needed for tomorrow by today." He eyed the stack of clothing, clearly impressed.

"I had some help," she smiled, and thought of the two girls she had been able to hire for this with the generous down-payment he had given her. "Lady

Eryn," she continued and bowed, "if you would undress, we can see if any changes are necessary."

Eryn frowned in displeasure and was about to object to having her title used by someone she knew well, but Enric was the one to speak first, his tone assuring. "Junar, I don't think this formality is required. Eryn has been your friend before, and I am sure she would appreciate it very much if you omitted the title and refrained from treating her differently now."

"Of course, Lord Enric," she replied and smiled at Eryn. "I was not really sure how to handle this. I would have understood if your new… situation would have made continuing our friendship impossible."

Eryn lifted her brow and looked at Junar coolly. "That is very generous of you. Though I am not so flattered at how easily you would have given that friendship up."

"I am sorry if I have displeased you," the seamstress replied stiffly.

"Please, stop behaving like a servant towards me!" Eryn lifted her arms helplessly.

Now Junar became irritated. "What do you expect from me? I can hardly treat you like the prisoner you were when suddenly you are not only joined to an immensely important man, but are about to become a high-ranking magician!"

"You never treated me like a prisoner. So I trust you have it in you not to treat me like a stranger now."

She watched the seamstress gulp and lower her gaze. Then Junar shook her head and sighed. "You are right. I am sorry, very much so. I just didn't want to assume I had any undue privileges."

Eryn smiled. "You didn't. All the privileges I grant are just and fair."

Junar then straightened, clearly a little ill at ease. "Then don't stand around like that! Get naked so we can see if the things I brought are to your liking."

"Oh my," Enric sighed and made himself comfortable on a sofa. "I never thought I would hear words like these spoken from one woman to another. This could be my lucky day."

Eryn shook her head at him. "That statement just made it impossible for me to undress in front of the two of you." She grabbed several garments from the stack and he noted with satisfaction that she chose the bedroom and not the guest room to go and change into them.

When she returned to the parlour, he raised his brow and nodded in approval. She looked well-dressed in a simple, dark blue tunic and black pants, but not overly adorned. The high quality of the cloth was easily discernible and the expert cut made it flow around her and cling in all the right places. Subtly embroidered designs lent it a certain elegance.

He whistled through his teeth. "Well done, Junar."

Junar smiled and blushed slightly at the simple praise. Now they both looked at Eryn expectantly. She was the one who ultimately had to approve, after all.

Eryn looked down at herself and shrugged. "A little too ladylike, if you ask me. But then I am about to be turned into a lady tomorrow, so I guess it is alright. I do appreciate that you are not trying to make me wear dresses every day."

"Ah yes," Junar noted, "talking of dresses. I think we should have a look at the one I made you for the ceremony tomorrow."

She grimaced. So it would be a dress instead of the more practical attire she had hoped for. "Why can't I wear this one here for tomorrow? It is elegant, after all. It looks much too fancy to wear it every day, anyway. And I suppose the robes will look really strange if I wear a dress underneath, all rucked and crumpled."

"No, they won't. As there aren't really any robes available for female magicians, I was asked to make you some." Junar smiled. "And you can depend on it: they won't look crumpled or whatever other poor excuses you have yet to come up with." She pulled out a long brown dress from the centre of the pile and handed it to Eryn. "Be a good girl and put this on."

"Good girl?" she muttered and rolled her eyes, but took the dress and vanished back into the bedroom.

When she came out this time, Enric straightened. The dress looked simple enough, but seemed to take all its elegance from the body that wore it. He imagined that creating a dress this way would require quite some skill. It did not follow the current fashion, but was tailored to her own taste, reflected her personality: straight, unembellished and yet soft. The colour was a dark brown that matched her eyes and hair most agreeably.

"I have to admit, I like it very much," Eryn said with a surprised undertone. She looked over to Enric. "Your reaction just now suggests that it will be acceptable for the ceremony?"

"Yes, very much so. From what I have seen so far I'd say I wouldn't have to worry about the other garments you have brought. The only thing I would like to have a peek at before I leave you two to your fitting are the robes."

Junar nodded and pulled something long and heavy looking in dark purple shades out of the stack, which still held quite a few more garments.

"Interesting," Eryn commented. "This is to be the healers' colour?"

Enric nodded. "Yes, that it is. Can you live with that?"

"Well, if I couldn't, asking me now would be a little late unless you want to make Junar sit up all night making a new one, don't you think?"

He looked at her. "It was more of a token question. I didn't really think that the colour of your robes would be a major concern for you right now. Now put them on - I want to see what the Order version of you looks like in comparison to the poor sack-clad captive."

Junar helped Eryn slipping the robe over her head and pulling it down so that it fell down to her ankles, just like the dress underneath.

"I changed the cut a little, obviously," Junar explained.

"Obviously," Enric confirmed with raised brows. It was clearly a female version of their official attire, not only reduced in size. The waist was set off, and so was her bust. The arms were shorter, so as to ensure that she could wear them for work without being hindered by sleeves trailing. That would please her, he mused. A mere garment for showing off her rank but which was useless in every other respect was definitely nothing she would wear regularly. And that would of course cause problems with the Order, as they liked to advertise. It was amazing what a few skilled stitches could help avoid. Not that there wouldn't be enough other occasions for her and Tyront to quarrel, though.

"I think I will have you take a look at my own robes. I think there might be a few improvements possible," Enric mused.

"And alter the traditional cut that lends you so much dignity, if so little shape?" Eryn chuckled. "You are in a revolutionary mood today, aren't you?"

"I don't think it's a revolution if your rank is high enough," he smiled. "Then it's called progress." He rose and lifted one of her hands over her head to twirl her once. "I like it. Very shapely. And the robes are nice, too."

Junar smiled when Eryn pulled her hand from his and pushed him towards his study, clearly embarrassed at the compliment and the affectionate voice that had delivered it.

"Go. There must be a lot of work waiting for you. Enough to keep you in your study until we are done here at least."

He sighed. "Alright. I will take that very subtle hint and leave you to your own devices." He quickly turned to grab her hand again to press a quick kiss into her palm before he left to take care of his paperwork.

"Watching you two is really strange," Junar commented. "This is not exactly the impression he has made over the last few years, at least as far as I am able judge from a distance."

"You mean aloof, demanding and relentless? That he still is."

"Not with you, it seems."

"Well, aloof maybe not, but the other two character traits are still there, he just tries to conceal them with sweet words and kisses."

Junar watched her and just smiled. Sweet words and kisses from Lord Enric. And Eryn didn't even seem to appreciate that, but instead considered it something to be endured. She tried to be sympathetic but somehow found that very hard. Just as almost every other woman in the city would.

"I see how much you have to endure, you poor soul," Junar sighed.

Eryn gave her a look. Of course she would only have seen him from a distance, never having been knocked out or overpowered by him another way and then forced to comply with his demands. She would thus have a more glorified picture of a noble, powerful and good-looking man. Eryn herself had no illusions of that sort. To her he was still a man who had yet to learn to respect certain boundaries, no matter how influential or dashing he was. And there was still that feeling that Enric equalled imprisonment of some kind, though she was determined to work on that. But somehow, something new always seemed to turn up to throw them back again when they had made some little progress with each other. Her being in the Order would not make that any easier either, she supposed.

"Speaking of endurance," she said. "There is a little social thing tomorrow evening Enric insists we need to hold. Can I persuade you to come? It may be a bit boring, though. Which is exactly why your presence would be very welcome to me."

Junar cleared her throat. "You want me to come to a social gathering after your joining the Order? You are aware that my position doesn't really warrant this kind of invitation and people may be rather... surprised at seeing me there," she said carefully.

Eryn folded her arms. "This is my celebration and whoever has a problem with seeing my friends there can take a jump out of the window for all I care. Furthermore, I will have you know, that my dear companion was the one to first mention that he intended you to come. So if the high and mighty Lord - who is very aware of social rules even if he doesn't seem to care much for them - thinks you should come, I don't see how you could object. Unless you really don't want to come. Which I would of course respect. Not that I would appreciate your refusal," she added with one raised eyebrow. "But respect it I would."

Junar grinned. "Well, I am but a humble seamstress. I can't afford to anger the newest and powerful addition to the Order, can I?"

"Excellent." Eryn nodded with satisfaction and made to take off the dress. "Can you give me a hand here? I don't want to rip anything. And he ordered you to make all this? This is more than I owned in my entire life! Who needs so many clothes?" She managed to free herself from the dress and picked up the tunic that lay on top of the heap. Silver-grey.

"He ordered a small selection of everyday clothes for a start. The next order he asked me to discuss with you directly. Oh, Eryn," Junar sighed impatiently. "A woman of your status needs proper clothing. You can't run around like a pauper, it wouldn't look proper. You need a new dress for every major occasion, you can't be seen wearing a ball gown twice, for instance."

"What?" Eryn's eyes bulged. "I wear a ball gown once, and then what? Give it to the servants to use it for rags? Really now, this is the most idiotic thing I have heard yet. What are you doing?" she asked when Junar closed her eyes and breathed in and out slowly.

"I am thinking of the downright indecent amount of gold your companion pays me to dress you properly and remind myself that it is worth putting up with your antics."

"My *antics*? Because I don't see any worth in that unnecessary expense?"

"Well, I am not saying your antics are of the usual kind. But, fortunately, Lord Enric is pleased with my work, and your cooperation is not required because I have your measurements anyway. This was just an attempt at accommodating you, but as you are determined to be difficult, I will put together what I think you will need."

"What *you* think I need?"

"Yes. This will be a selection of simple everyday dresses like the one you have just tried on, a few more tunics, trousers, one or two cloaks and, of course, a few nicer dresses for semi-public occasions. Ball-gowns we will take care of when the next ball is announced."

"This is not a good start! I don't even have a say in what I am going to wear!"

"That's because you don't make any attempts at adapting to your new life accordingly. And I am sure there will be a lot of occasions where you can make others do what you say, *Lady* Eryn."

"I am trying to make *you* do what I say, but I keep failing miserably!"

"That's because your companion already told me what to do first, and even if you were in the Order already, he would still outrank you," Junar retorted gleefully.

* * *

Eryn waited in front of the throne room, staring at the heavy double doors. She cast her thoughts back to other occasions when she had waited to be permitted to enter this same room. The first time had been at her testing so many months ago. Then there was the matter with her shield that Enric had manipulated and then lied to the King about. The next time had been the offer to join the Order, and the most memorable one was the ball that had ended so unexpectedly with the commitment ceremony.

She hoped there would not be any unpleasant surprises this time. This ceremony was not usually held in the throne room, she had been told, but as a larger than usual number of people were interested in this event, and the King himself had decided to grace them with his presence, the throne room was the logical setting.

Of course he wanted to witness the whole thing, she thought angrily. He had taken quite extreme measures to make sure she would join and wanted finally to make sure she did.

She went through the oath one last time to make sure she hadn't forgotten anything. Then the doors were opened for her and she lifted her chin and took one last calming breath before she entered the room.

Red ropes separated her from the audience and marked the path she was supposed to walk along towards the dais on the steps of which the oath would be given. She saw the King on his throne, watching her approach. Lord Tyront in his dark crimson robes stood on the third step of the dais, Enric in his dark blue ones a step below. All three of them seemed pleased with what they saw.

Eryn stopped in front of the dais as she had been instructed. Lord Tyront offered her his hand and gently pulled her up to the step he stood on. She was almost on eye level with Enric now, the step was nearly as high as their difference in height. She was amused at herself for noting such minor details when she should instead be focussing on the significance of what was happening.

"The occasion for which we have gathered here today is one that will go down in history: this is the first time after three hundred years that a female magician joins the Order." Tyront's voice boomed through the room, enhanced by a little magic. "You are all aware of how this ceremony is usually carried out. Due to the unique circumstances we will deviate from this course today. Generally, a magician joins the Order at a young age, commits to it and then starts his training. Today, instead of a child, we have a grown-up woman who is going to join us. She brings with her valuable knowledge which she will share with us, but is also in need of training that will enable her to take the position her magical strength entitles her to."

Then he turned to her and lifted his hand for her to take. "Now the oath, please, when you are ready."

Eryn nodded, grabbed his hand as she had done with Enric when she had promised him not to flee that one time, and immediately felt the warmth of the magic Lord Tyront released in a slow and steady stream. Then she took a deep breath before she faced the crowd and intoned in a loud, clear voice, "I swear to you, the people of this kingdom, here in these halls before the King, that I will protect you against all and any threats with my life," whether they come from outside or from within, she added silently. "I will not leave this place or you without orders or the intention of returning. I will bring honour upon the kingdom by serving the King and the Order in all that is right. I will obey my superiors in good faith and without deceit. I will, as per the statutes of the Order of Magicians, hone my skills in fighting to be ready to use them in your defence at all times."

She felt the warmth increase slightly and then begin to cool after she had spoken her final words. She turned back to face Lord Tyront and saw his broad smile of satisfaction. Enric looked relieved as if he had feared that something might have prevented this from happening at the last moment. Probably a change of heart from her side or an unsanctioned changing in the phrasing, she thought, feeling amused to consider his worries.

Tyront released her hand and motioned for Enric to step between them. She frowned in confusion and looked up at him.

"Your manacles," he said quietly. "I have asked for the privilege of returning your freedom to you."

A symbolic gesture, she thought and couldn't help being moved by it. She watched his long fingers touch the shackles and took a deep breath when she felt them open and her full power returned to her in a soothing wave.

"Welcome to the Order, my love," he whispered and lifted her chin to press a gentle kiss onto her lips. In front of several hundred people. It lasted only a moment but her cheeks felt hot. How could he be so comfortable when it came to public caresses? It seemed like he did not care at all about the crowd.

When he stepped back again, Tyront presented the purple robe to her and she accepted his assistance in slipping into it. When she stood straight again and dressed in her new official attire, she saw that the King had risen from his throne and stepped closer.

"Lady Eryn," he spoke and took both her hands in his. "These last few days have bestowed on me the great honour of first committing you to Lord Enric," he began, smiling at the glare he received for that, then continued unperturbed, "and now witnessing how you have committed yourself to a kingdom you were not born to, but which nevertheless is now your home."

She drew in a sharp breath and forced herself not to shy back when he leaned closer to kiss her first on the left, then on the right cheek. That was hardly something he usually did, was it? It was too friendly, too close. He did this only to tease her, she was quite sure, and judging from the glint in his eyes he could guess her thoughts well enough. How boring and uneventful did his life have to be if he needed little deeds like this to spice it up for him?

Now that the King had spoken, the crowd started applauding, and he didn't object when she withdrew her hands from his with a forced smile.

"I am sure we are about to face interesting times while you are adapting to the Order," he said almost inaudibly with a faint smile.

She was about to retort that she was happy to provide some dissipation for him, when Enric stepped towards them, bowed to the King and then to her.

"Lady Eryn," he said in a playful tone, "there are quite a number of people here who want to congratulate you."

"Then you should not keep them waiting, dear Lady," the King smirked and turned to leave the throne room.

"I don't like it when he touches me," she whispered.

Enric nodded. "Neither do I. But he doesn't overstep any boundaries, he only plays with you."

"Nice," she muttered and smiled when she saw Orrin and Vern approaching. The official ceremony was over, and with the King gone, the atmosphere had lost most of its formality.

"Lady Eryn," Orrin said solemnly and bowed.

A slow grin spread across her face. "Now, isn't it funny how things have changed? It seems I am your superior now."

Vern laughed at Orrin's audible gulp and patted his back.

Eryn took the warrior's hands and smiled. "You don't bow to me, Orrin. And I don't want to hear you call me *Lady*, either." She chuckled. "I, at least, have no intention of addressing you with *Lord* from now on. Looking back, it would make all my efforts at defying you by ignoring the title useless, I feel."

Orrin shook his head slowly. "And *you* are to be a person of authority in the Order."

"I think wielding authority will be more to my liking than being subjected to it," she shrugged and winked at him.

Then people started to approach them from all sides, faces known and unknown, to offer their congratulations.

CHAPTER 33

An Unpleasant Surprise

Enric slipped the note Tyront had sent him surreptitiously under the breakfast tray when he saw her entering the parlour, naked under a blanket, and with half-open eyes and ruffled hair. One corner of his mouth curved upwards in an appreciative smile. A sight that no sophisticated hairstyle and ball gown could compete with.

He leaned back in his chair and motioned for her to sit on his lap. She shrugged and complied, snuggling up to him.

"How long have you been up?" she yawned without bothering to cover her mouth.

"For a while," he replied and kissed her head.

"You are not sleepless from worry because I am free and unshackled and so am able to attack you viciously from behind any time now, are you?"

He laughed quietly. "Unshackled you may be, free you are not. And trust me when I say that the magical oath that binds you here is not the greatest obstacle you would have to overcome to leave here. I would find you, wherever you went."

She looked up at him, shaking her head. "That is very possessive. You wouldn't hold me here against my will any more, would you?"

He caught her chin between his thumb and index finger and his smile was gone when he said quietly, "Don't try me."

She couldn't hold the stare with his now deadly serious eyes, so she looked away and thought about how she could restore the relaxed mood she had just killed with her words.

"I was surprised at how well everything went yesterday," she said airily and slipped off his lap to sit on a chair instead and grab a warm bread bun.

"What difficulties did you expect?"

"Well, not exactly difficulties, but I was amazed at how short and simple the ceremony was."

"Not disappointed, are you? Would you have liked a bit more pomp and festivity?" Enric smiled and she was relieved that the seriousness seemed gone from his voice.

"No, not at all. It was a positive surprise." She smiled. "Though I had the impression that you were relieved when I had finished the oath."

"I was. I have been waiting for that moment for quite some time. *Of course* I was relieved when everything worked out."

"I see. So you were worried about my causing any last minute trouble?"

"Constantly," he sighed with a somewhat playful expression. "You are hard to control, and I have a feeling that giving you a position of power will not make this any easier, whatever Tyront and the King may think."

She dunked the bread bun into her cup and made Enric grimace.

"I thought only old people without teeth did that."

"What?" She looked down and shrugged. "A habit my father tried to break me loose from, but somehow I like it and I refused to give it up then. At least I have managed not do it in polite company."

"Are you telling me I don't count as polite company?"

"Your category is more the confusing, disconcerting kind," she remarked. "And as you have chosen me yourself and have thus no one to blame for that but yourself, you'll also have to put up with my more annoying habits."

He smiled at that and decided that he wouldn't comment on her habit of dipping her bread in her drinks any more as it was obviously something she only did when she felt safe from judgement. This was exactly how he wanted his presence to be for her.

"The evening was very nice, you did well at your first official appearance as my companion," he said.

"As your companion?" she snorted. "People didn't even notice *you* were there! Everybody was so keen on talking to me that I had to ask Orrin to talk to Junar a bit so she didn't feel completely lost without me."

"I didn't have the impression that she did," Enric commented. "From what I heard she had quite a few compliments for the robes she made you and a number of requests for her services. Orrin has ordered some garments for Vern and himself already. It seems that being close to you does wonders for her business."

"What can I say?" She smiled broadly. "I am a good luck charm."

He bent over to kiss her on the mouth, lingering for a few moments. "You are for me."

She looked away and heard him sigh.

"Why does it worry you when I say such things?" he asked softly.

"Because I don't know what to say in return. Because I can't say anything of that kind back."

He took her hand and pressed it against his lips. "Then don't. I told you that I have had a lot more time to fall for you. But you will get there in time."

She looked back at him, her brow raised at the natural confidence and what seemed to be a promise in his voice. And looking into his blue eyes, which could turn cold in an instant but were warm and gentle right now, she realised that he was right. With him she would get there.

* * *

Enric took the note hidden under the tray with him to his study when she had returned to the guest room to get dressed. He opened it to read it again.

This was not good news, especially considering the timing. But it explained a lot. The King's actions had been a clear sign of how urgent the matter was. He had put aside all subtlety, which was uncharacteristic for him. And for good reason.

Enric wondered what King Folrin would have done if things had not developed like this between himself and Eryn, if she hadn't tried to escape and landed in his quarters and subsequently in his bed. Maybe he had had other plans but changed them when he heard about the development between them? Or he had very likely been aware of them spending the Freedom Night together and was confident that more would come of it eventually. In this case he had waited very patiently considering how little time was left now.

Enric shook his head. Young Folrin had learned quite a lot from his father, the cunning old man, before he had died. Undoubtedly, he had, apart from the throne, inherited a few useful sources of information and also the flexibility to be both unobtrusively manipulative and convincingly forthright, whatever the occasion called for. That was something to be admired at in a man of no more than twenty-five years.

Twenty-five, he mused. Hardly younger than Eryn. He remembered the night of the ball, when Eryn had stared at the monarch after he had informed her he intended to take her to bed. Enric had listened to the entire conversation from a distance and had been ready to intervene, just as the King had doubtlessly expected. The fact that not getting her into his bed had served the King's plans far better than the alternative was a relief, but he still resented the ways he found to touch her. Such as kissing her on the hands the day after the execution, and on her cheeks yesterday at the ceremony. Unusual gestures of intimacy between King and subject, even though he probably only did it to amuse himself by watching her discomfort. And the fact that she was a beautiful woman would by no means make it any less of a pleasure for him.

But he could hardly stay angry at the King when he had managed in a few days what the Order had been pondering over for months. And only just in time, too. Only a few more days, and she would never have joined them willingly.

That, of course, would make her unbelievably angry, there was no doubt about that. He wondered who would be the one to tell her. He himself had no intention of doing so, and he doubted that Tyront would volunteer either. But she needed to be informed, and soon.

He pursed his lips. The Council would be informed of the situation today in the afternoon. And Orrin was a member. Maybe he could take over the role of messenger delivering the difficult news to her.

He felt like a coward, but was determined not to endanger the few blissful moments they managed to have by informing her about this himself. Especially as he was not even remotely blameable for it.

* * *

"Come, they are already waiting for us," Enric said and held out his hand for her to take.

"Am I supposed to wear my robes? You are wearing yours, after all."

"Yes, that might be advisable. You will freeze if you wear no more than shirt and trousers."

"I wasn't really worried about freezing but of the impression I am supposed to be making," she frowned.

He chuckled. "Worried about complying with the Order's rules already? You are adapting really fast."

"Well, I should show some goodwill, at least," she shrugged and took the robes from a hook next to the door to slip into them.

He then took her hand and pulled her with him out the door. He was really looking forward to this. Now he would finally learn about her special barrier.

They hurried through the palace, through corridors she had never before been along and would probably never find her way out of if left to herself. She saw Lord Tyront and Orrin standing in front of great double doors almost as grand as those to the throne room. They turned their heads when they heard the approaching steps.

"Lady Eryn," Tyront said and nodded.

"Lord Tyront," she nodded back and then smiled at Orrin. "Hello. It seems I will finally be able to teach *you* something."

"You have already taught me patience, my dear girl. More than I ever thought I would need," he replied dryly but with an amused undertone.

Tyront motioned for them to enter the hall and Eryn looked around curiously. An enormous oval table stood at the centre of the spacious room, surrounded by about fifteen uncomfortable-looking chairs with wooden backrests. The high windows at one side let in the daylight, affording a view of the meadows outside the city wall.

She stepped closer, staring mesmerised at the green hills. It had been a while since she'd had any chance to feel earth under her feet. Months... She felt Enric's gaze on her and turned away from the window, uncomfortable at being observed in her private moment.

"So this is where the Magic Council meets? Impressive," she commented. "The chairs don't exactly look cosy, though."

"This is to remind us that we are not here to play around but work," Orrin said.

"Why does the Council meet in the palace? I noticed that there are no buildings that belong to the Order, apart from the warriors' quarters and the building where you teach the young ones."

"Kings like to keep us close," Enric explained. "We are trained defenders, after all. Maybe they sleep better knowing that we are not far away. But there are parts of the palace designated for the Order to use, such as our quarters, meeting halls like this, archives, part of the library and so on."

She looked up at the high, vaulted ceiling and let loose a piercing whistle, grinning when it was reflected back at her from different directions.

She saw the three men watching her with amused expressions, happy to allow her a little time for playfulness. She cleared her throat, slightly embarrassed and clapped her hands.

"Well, gentlemen, ready for a lesson in effective defensive fighting skills?"

"As opposed to the ineffective ones you have been taught all these months?" Orrin smirked.

She grinned back. "If that is how you want to put it, I won't object." She walked towards him, stopped, folded her arms and adopted the broad stance he usually took, trying to imitate his stern voice, "Now, Orrin, what is the great prerequisite for using magic?"

He raised his brow at her. "Magical abilities."

"Well, that is self-evident. What else?"

"Control," he then said.

"No. Not necessarily. Otherwise I would never have been able to shield accidentally when you first questioned me. Control is just what you need to use magic consciously. And what you are expected to have in order to use it sensibly." She took pity on him. "It's air. You need air to do magic. Where the flow of air is blocked, magic can't work either."

"So what you do is block the flow of air?" Enric frowned. "How? Stronger bolts should be able to remove that blockage."

"My barrier was not meant to hold your attacks, but swallow them up and make them dissolve. It consists of not only one field, but two of them. They are flexible enough to let your strikes through, but tight enough to keep the air out."

"Keep the air *out*?" Tyront asked, confused. "How can you create a barrier with no air inside?"

"Easily," she smirked, enjoying herself immensely teaching them in a discipline they thought they were as good as undefeatable. "I create a very small, round barrier first, a small ball." A shimmering dot appeared in the air before them at eye-height. "Hardly any air fits inside. And then I feed it more power to make it grow."

When the barrier was about the size of her head, she stopped. "Orrin, a bolt please. No need for restraint."

Orrin's palm released a strike so quickly that she hardly saw it coming even though she was prepared for it. It went through the shield and vanished almost immediately. Orrin stared. He was the only one of them who had not been there when Lord Tyront and Enric had witnessed the effectiveness of her barrier on the night of her escape attempt. He had only been told about it.

"Incredible," he whispered.

"The trick is to find the right consistency of the shield," she explained. "It needs to let the bolts through, but not the air. For this you have to change the nature of the shield accordingly. *Your* defensive barriers are meant to let nothing through, but *my* protection is not about fighting strength with more strength. Otherwise I would not have been able to keep two magicians more powerful than myself at bay. I should have thought about those bloody city walls, though," she added, more to herself.

"Yes. And that's why you will be having lessons in strategy, amongst other things," Enric remarked, thanking his lucky stars that she had not possessed any of that knowledge when it would have helped her to get away from here.

"How do I do it?" Orrin was clearly intrigued.

"First create the shield. Start as small as you can, then make it grow without letting any air in."

They watched a shimmering sphere growing in front of them.

"Now stop." She lifted her palm and shot a strong bolt at it. The shield disappeared instantly and the magic hit the opposite wall, burning a smoking black hole into a painting of the young King, right through his left shoulder.

"Ahem, are you sure this is a good location to do this?" she asked and grimaced, looking at Tyront, who drew in a long breath and looked up at the ceiling.

"Probably not, now you mention it," he replied and shook his head. "This will doubtlessly make a nice impression when we arrange for the painting to be repaired."

Enric grinned broadly. "He will never believe that it was an accident. But he likes Eryn, so he will probably see the humour in it."

"He doesn't *like* me. He likes to threaten, blackmail and annoy me. That is a difference," she retorted angrily.

"He likes you well enough," Tyront said mildly. "I have seen how he treats people he doesn't like."

"So, do you want to continue in here and endanger your interior or shall we go somewhere else?" she asked testily, eager to change the topic.

"We should stay," Enric said. "This is not something we wish to be witnessed in for now. Even if we have to have a few things repaired afterwards."

Tyront nodded. "I agree. So, what was wrong with Lord Orrin's shield? Why didn't it hold your bolt?"

"Because it was inflexible. Superior strength disrupted it enough to allow air in. The air is supposed to stay outside. The lack of it is what starves the bolt and shrinks it to nothing."

"Let me try," Tyront said and created a small orb that quickly grew bigger.

Eryn shot a bolt at it and it dispersed, unable to penetrate the powerful shield. She sighed. "This is much too strong. No one in here is able to break through one of your barriers, anyway, Lord Tyront. You need to use less strength or we will never find out if you have mastered the skill."

The older man looked sheepish for a moment and then nodded. "Try again."

The next bolt she shot passed through the barrier, was reduced in speed and size and came out at the other side hitting a chair. The remaining power was too low to damage it, though, and it just rocked and fell over with a loud crash.

"A good start, but there was some air inside still. You took most of the strength away, but there was still enough left to do a little harm," she explained and pointed to the overturned chair. Then she turned to all three of them. "This is not a matter of strength. A stronger barrier is not more effective than a weaker one. Weaker magicians can create such a barrier without any problem, they are just limited as to the size of it. Think of the nature of air. It consists of very small and elusive parts, so the structure of your barrier needs to be tight. But magical strikes are destructive and will shatter everything that resists. So your shield must not resist them, but instead welcome them. You need a tightly woven, but flexible structure. This may take some time to practice, but this is basically all it needs." She lifted her hands. "Congratulations, My Lords. You have uncovered the great secret of my barrier. Now it's up to you to practise."

"May I?" Enric took a step back and raised a round shield between himself and Eryn. "I am ready."

She raised her brow at him. "If I attack while you are standing directly behind it, I will hit you. Are you really that confident?" She knew the answer to that question even before the last word had left her mouth. "Have it your way, then. But don't complain when I send you to the floor." She smiled. "Taking you down with a single bolt has been my favourite daydream for many months. Maybe this is my lucky day."

She heard both older magicians snicker and looked at Enric's fake wounded grin before sending a bolt towards him. It entered his shield without resistance and almost immediately dissolved into nothing. Eryn pursed her lips in slight disappointment. Well, what had she expected? It would have been too good to be true. Of course he had figured out how to do it, otherwise he hardly would have risked standing behind the shield.

"You know, I think this is how it's done," he said smugly and collapsed the barrier again. Tyront nodded appreciatively.

"Well done, my boy. It seems Lord Orrin and myself will have to practise this a little."

"Will you teach the others?" Eryn asked.

"Not yet. We need to consider what impact this will have. Our hierarchy is based on magical strength, and this may cause quite a few changes."

She smiled without humour. "Then maybe it is time to base it on skill instead, when power can now be resisted more easily."

"My, my," Orrin said. "You only joined us one day ago and already are trying to start a revolution."

"I am told that it's known as *progress* if your rank is high enough," she grinned, then turned serious again and added impatiently, "This is a defensive skill. How bad can teaching it to your students really be? Don't tell me the stronger students don't torment the weaker ones just because they can. I dare say children are the same everywhere - even the rich ones. The barrier would be a fabulous equaliser."

"Lord Orrin?" Tyront turned to him.

"Yes, of course they do. Strength has always been a means of exercising power, especially for young boys. Magicians are no exception, only they don't have to use their fists. But we need to put this before the Council. I agree with Eryn. This would be a valid defensive skill for any magician. And as it can't really be used for attack, there should not be any danger in teaching it."

"Then we will discuss this at the next Council meeting," Tyront agreed and added only half-jokingly, "But not today. Only after the two of us have mastered it as well. I don't want to make a fool of myself."

"Nice," Enric whispered to her when they left the Council hall, "it seems you made your first major change in the Order. Not bad after only one day."

She smiled and took his hand. This was only a minor thing. If she had any say in it, there would be quite a few more to come.

* * *

"What are your plans for the afternoon while I am at the Council meeting?" Enric enquired.

"I will visit Vern, I think. We haven't really had much time together with everything that has happened in these last few days. He surely is in desperate need of another few books. I have never seen such hunger for knowledge in anyone."

"Lucky for him that he has you to still it, then," he smiled.

"For the moment, yes. But I dread the day when he is completely through with both chests. I hope he will by then be far enough along in his training to start writing his own books." A thought occurred to her. "If he is permitted to start the training, that is. Orrin has not mentioned anything or given me the impression that he is angry at me for teaching Vern, but neither did he say that he approves."

"I wouldn't worry about Orrin. From what I have seen after the execution, Orrin was angrier at being kept in the dark about it and not so much about Vern's learning healing as such."

"That leaves Lord Poron and Lord Tyront. I suppose Lord Poron might agree. And Lord Tyront's approval would then not be necessary."

Enric pursed his lips. "You are right from a mathematical point of view. Two votes defeat one. But trying to find a consensus and listening to find whether he has any objection will serve you better in the long run. Diplomacy, my love, that is the key."

"Yes, so you keep telling me. But somehow it seems to be little more than a fancy word for *lying*."

Enric rose at the knock at the door. "That must be Tyront to pick me up for the meeting. Enjoy your afternoon with Vern."

He left his quarters, nodding in greeting to Tyront.

"Have you told her about the delegation yet?" Tyront asked after the door had closed.

Enric shook his head. "No. I will leave that little task to Orrin. There is still the matter of his letting her move in with him when I locked her cell."

"Revenge?" Tyront smirked. "Isn't this rather petty here?"

"Maybe. But I have a reputation to protect. And I do like to keep him on his toes."

"You might want to be careful about annoying him too much. Eryn might make you suffer for it. They have become quite good friends from what I can see. He was determined to interrupt the commitment ceremony and make a claim to her himself. I almost had to overpower him to prevent it."

Enric stopped abruptly and gaped at his superior. "He wanted to do *what*?" He shook his head and gnashed his teeth. "I am going to kill him. Slowly. Painfully."

Tyront looked stern. "Still jealous? Calm down. He wanted to cause a delay, not take her away from you. She was living in his guest room at the time, so he was well enough aware that she was hardly joining you of her own free will. Don't embarrass yourself," he warned. "Orrin treats her like a daughter, and anybody can see that. Apart from you, that is."

"You are right, of course," Enric sighed. "It is difficult for me to see another man close to her, but I will have to work on that."

"You do that," Tyront nodded satisfied. "She is the only woman in an Order consisting only of male magicians, after all. It's not as if you could stop her from interacting with her male colleagues."

They had reached the meeting hall that had only a few hours ago been used to teach them the new barrier. The damaged picture had been taken off the wall to be repaired, so no more than a blank white spot betrayed what had happened.

"Let's spread the news then," Enric said and entered first.

Tyront waited until all of the other eleven Council members had taken their seats, remaining standing himself. It was better to address them from an elated position as this would very likely cause some agitation. It would be easier to call for order when he was looking down on them.

"Good afternoon to all of you, My Lords," he began. "The reason for this meeting is a very important one, and I am glad that each of you has managed to attend, even though it was at short notice. Two months ago the King received a request from the Western Territories." He paused to let the murmuring die down before he continued. "They have requested permission to send a diplomatic delegation to us, and the King has granted it. It will arrive in four days."

He left them some time to talk among themselves, catching snippets like "after centuries", "crossing the sea" and "dangerous".

Then Orrin spoke up. "This is hardly a coincidence. They must have heard about Lady Eryn. Why else would they choose to contact us now?"

Tyront nodded. "Yes, we believe they have heard."

"How is this possible?" Orrin shook his head and frowned. "How would they have managed to learn about this?"

"Lady Eryn's father obviously possessed knowledge of how to cross the sea unharmed", Lord Tyront replied, not surprised that Orrin was the one asking. "I would imagine he was not the only one amongst his people with that ability. Especially as the messenger that was sent here also managed to brave this ordeal."

"Are you saying that more of them may have come here?" Lord Poron exclaimed, taken aback. "That they may be spying on us?"

"Considering the recent developments, that is a valid assumption, yes", Tyront answered, careful to appear calm and unperturbed. He needed to avoid causing a panic. The Council needed to be level-headed and able to think clearly in order to handle this situation properly. "But rest assured that we will address this matter when the delegation has arrived."

"Is it possible they want her back? Is this why she was made to join Lord Enric, and subsequently the Order, so quickly? To bind her here magically and keep them from taking her with them?" another Council member asked. "I didn't have the impression that she did it completely voluntarily. No offence to Lord Enric, but at times I had the impression that she was about to bolt from the ball room during the ceremony."

Look at old Lord Woldarn, Enric thought, still quite the observer.

"So Lord Enric was ordered to make her his companion?" Lord Seagon, the treasurer asked.

Enric decided to answer this question himself. "No, Lord Seagon, let me assure you that this was not the case." His voice was calm. The question was hardly an unexpected one. "I might have been persuaded to move a little faster than I would have otherwise, but in time I would have made her mine anyway."

The general relief after Enric's reply was evident. If powerful Lord Enric could have been ordered to bow to a scheme like this, nobody in the Order would be safe.

"How did Lady Eryn react to the news?" Orrin said next.

Tyront looked at Enric. "Lord Enric?" If he wanted to lie to the Council to make Orrin deliver the bad news for him, he had to do it himself.

"Surprised and not very enthusiastic, as was to be expected," Enric shrugged.

This brought on a flood of questions that could not be answered, such as if the delegate would be a magician, if diplomatic relationships were intended, if it was possible that they just wanted to see how belligerent the kingdom was at this point, if they would insist on taking Lady Eryn with them despite her strong if rather new connections to the kingdom and Lord Enric and so on.

Tyront spent about half an hour repeatedly assuring them that he had no idea, rephrasing the sentence itself about a dozen times to lend some variety to his lack of information.

* * *

Both men looked up in surprise when the door to Tyront's study was shoved open brutally and banged loudly against the book shelves directly behind it. Eryn stomped in, and even without the less than finessed entry it would have been obvious from the mere sight of her narrowed eyes, flushed face and tightly-balled fists that she was anything but happy. Her eyes locked onto Lord Tyront and she marched towards him to stand, her arms akimbo, staring at him.

„This is a cruel joke, isn't it? I haven't just learned that a delegation from my home country will be arriving only a few days after my commitment to this forsaken place, have I?" Her voice had become rather raised towards the end of the sentence.

"I'm afraid not. It is true," Tyront answered calmly.

She whirled around to face Enric. "Were you involved in this? I can't help but wonder why this eagerness to make me your companion was so precisely timed."

Enric gave a look of mild annoyance towards Tyront. "Not intentionally, just manipulated into providing the desired results. It seems that due to my fragile emotional state since my involvement with you I have lost my reputation of trustworthiness with my King and my Order."

"That is not true, and you are very well aware of it," Tyront sighed.

Eryn breathed in deeply and exhaled slowly to make sure she had herself under control and wouldn't start shouting any moment. "Let me make you aware of something. If this is a taste of what will await me as a member of your elite institution - namely being manipulated and having my own personal interests trodden into the ground for what you and your King seem to consider the greater good with no concern whatsoever for my wishes - you will not enjoy having me in the Order. I can promise you that."

"I can see that you are upset," Tyront spoke calmly, "but let me assure you..."

"I am so glad this hasn't escaped your notice. How very perceptive of you. And whatever you are trying to assure me of, you can save your words. Why would I believe anything you say any more?"

Tyront's eyes narrowed. "You are aware that I am your superior, aren't you? Thus I would ask you to reconsider your tone when talking to me."

"Really?" she frowned at him in disbelief. "You choose this moment to remind me of what a poor leader you are?"

Enric closed his eyes, forcing himself not to intervene. She would hardly thank him for it, and she needed to get used to facing the consequences of angering Tyront anyway.

Tyront rose slowly, his expression making her take a step back. "I do understand that you are upset. But you have just overstepped a boundary, and I can and will not ignore this anymore. If you behave like an insubordinate child, then you shall be treated like one. Three days of stable duty for you."

"Stable duty? Like shovelling manure?"

"Yes, exactly like that. This is of course in addition to your lessons starting tomorrow. You will need to get up a few hours early to handle all of it. And don't even think of disobeying, or I will make you pay for that, too," he warned her with narrowed eyes.

She turned slowly and left, not yet knowing where she would go, but preferably somewhere she could let off steam.

Both men looked at the door she had just left open.

"That did not go well. And it is not a good start to show hate towards her superior only after joining us," Tyront said sourly.

"Well, that is hardly a surprise, is it? I myself am not too happy, and I am not the one primarily concerned here. You have kept this information from me, too, for quite some time, I imagine." His tone was curt.

"How would you have acted, had you known?"

"The same way I did. It wouldn't have changed anything. And in this you should have trusted me enough to tell me."

"*Not* telling you before has saved you some trouble with your new companion. Why make her mad at both of us? She needs a friend in the Order, somebody she can trust."

"You can't reduce me to the role of her friend. I am still her superior, and sooner or later I will have to do something or make a decision that will anger her. That's something we will have to learn how to deal with, and keeping important bits of information that concern her from me is not the way to do that. Quite the opposite, in fact. If there is something going on that poses a danger to her staying here, I want to know about it immediately. I don't want to depend on anybody else to work something out."

"Very well. But rest assured that it was not lack of trust that has made me withhold that particular information from you. I didn't want to make the start of your new life together any harder than necessary."

Enric sighed. "I appreciate the sentiment. Though I don't really see how that start could have been much harder than it already was."

CHAPTER 34

The Delegation

Eryn turned away when she felt hands trying to shake her awake.

"Go away," she growled, burying her face in her pillow to escape the lamp light.

"Come, get up now. You brought this upon yourself by provoking Tyront. No compassion here." Enric pulled away the thick blanket, to which she reacted by pulling her legs up into a foetal position. He sighed and slipped one arm under her knees and the other under her shoulders and lifted her off the mattress.

"Hey!" she protested and hung on to her pillow, hugging it close to her chest as if trying to preserve some remnant of the warmth and cosiness she had just been pried from.

He put her down on a chair in the parlour in front of a ready breakfast tray.

"Here, get something into your stomach before you go. I imagine you will need your strength for the task."

She could see an amused gleam in his eyes. "You are laughing at me! Which I find completely out of place, as you are not without blame in this yourself!"

"Me? What did I do?"

"If Orrin knew about the delegation from the Western Territories, you must have known before him. And you didn't tell me yourself, you used him to inform me. Poor Orrin! Do you have any idea how shocked he was from my reaction yesterday when one moment I was sitting with Vern over a book and the next I started cursing violently?"

Enric shrugged. "I admit, I did use him. It was a little payback for letting you move in with him."

"I can't have you punish Orrin every time he does something nice for me," she scolded him. "From where I stand this is a gross misuse of your position."

"Is it?" He smiled, unperturbed.

"Yes," she snapped at him. "And I object to it. As I do to the Order's manner of distributing information." She leaned back and shook her head in frustration. "A delegation from my birthplace. Do you have any idea what a chance that could have been for me? Judging from the things my father knew, there doubtlessly is a lot I could have learned!"

"Probably," Enric replied calmly but with unmistakeable coldness, "but whatever they can teach you will have to happen here. I may not have been informed about this delegation, but I would have done whatever is necessary to keep you here."

She stared at him angrily. "It's a shame then that Lord Tyront didn't have more trust in you. It seems you would have acted in the Order's best interest no matter what. I'd say he underestimated you."

Enric got up so fast his chair fell to the floor behind him. He grabbed her upper arm and pulled her up from the chair so that her face was right in front of his.

"Not in the *Order's* interest, in my *own*! How blind are you, damn it?" He forced himself to let go of her and took a step back. "You should get dressed now; don't give Tyront any further reason to be displeased with you."

Eryn turned stiffly and went back to the guest room to get dressed for her morning ordeal.

Enric leaned his forehead against the cool glass of the nearest window and sighed. He had impressed on her how important keeping her temper was, but lately his own ability to remain in control also left a lot wanting.

He dreaded the arrival of the delegation. It would undoubtedly make her want to leave here even more and increase her frustration at not being able to. And his own frustration at seeing her this way.

He raised his head from the window and walked into the guest room, startling her as she was about to bind her hair with a piece of cord. He had to get some proper ribbons for her hair, he noted.

Pulling her towards him, more gently this time, he kissed her, holding her tight and savouring the warmth of her mouth.

"I can't lose you," he whispered roughly, kissing her again. "I am not going to let you leave me."

She swallowed and shook her head, slightly dazed by his mood swing. "I won't."

"Good." He smiled, relieved. "Now run and serve your sentence in dignity."

"Shovelling manure with dignity?"

"True dignity comes from within. No task, however demeaning, can take it from you," he said wisely and grinned when he heard her mutter.

"Words of inspiration from the man who will return to his warm bed. How nice."

* * *

The first subject she would be taught was history. Though she did have a basic understanding of which major things had happened at approximately what time, the Order's requirements were higher, naturally. She had the knowledge of a country girl raised by a father who himself had not been much of an expert on the history of the country he had fled to. But she was now in a position where they expected her to protect the future of their kingdom and thus know about its past.

The teacher was in his mid-fifties and she had seen his face before, even though she couldn't remember where. But after so many months in the city she expected there were not many people in the Order she had not yet seen somewhere.

He provided her with a reading list and a deadline and offered her assistance whenever she needed it. There would be a test, of course, when she was through.

Lord Poron was very helpful when it came to finding the books in the library and offered her a desk to work at as she was not supposed to take them away.

It seemed that the kingdom's records did not go back much further than three hundred years. Which was interesting, wasn't it? This was when they had had their last female magicians here. It could hardly be a coincidence, she mused. Something must have happened then. There were hints of a war with a land from the west and she wondered if it was her home country they were referring to. Was this the reason why there had been no contact with it for such a long time? This would be helpful to know, especially as the delegation would be arriving in three days. Would the Western Territories have more information stored away somewhere? If so, would they be willing to share?

At noon she closed her books and returned to her quarters, where Enric was already waiting for her so they could have lunch together.

"How was your morning?" he asked. "History, wasn't it?"

"Yes. But there isn't anything available about the things that would really interest me," she sighed.

"And they would be what?"

"Why there are no female magicians remaining here, for example. What happened to your historical records? Hardly any of them are older than three hundred years."

Enric smiled. "Ah, yes. The big questions. Historians have been pondering those for quite some time now. There are theories, of course. Many think that there was a great war with the Western Territories. Some say we won it gloriously and that's why they keep out of our way; others think we were defeated and thus better not try to provoke them."

"What do you think?"

He shrugged. "I am careful with what I think when there is no real evidence. But I suppose the second option is more realistic, that we were defeated. If there really ever was a war. There are hints at ancient knowledge that was lost, such as imbuing music with magic, for example. It might have been taken away from us. As this must have been done rather effectively by destroying or stealing all and any historical records connected with it, I would assume that only a victorious force could have done it."

"But even if they had taken away your records, wouldn't people have started writing things down again afterwards? At least about the war?"

"That's a valid assumption, yes. Many before you have wondered about that already. This is the most powerful argument against a war happening between the countries."

"Why have there never been any efforts to contact the Western Territories? Three hundred years are a very long time, after all."

"There is the little matter of certain geographical disadvantages in the kingdom. In the north there are the mountains that keep us separated from whatever lies beyond. Many expeditions were undertaken to find a way to penetrate them, but to no avail. And then there is the sea around us in most directions. Expeditions were sent there, too. But the ocean currents seem to be so vicious that all we ever saw of our ships was debris washed ashore."

She thought for a moment, then frowned. "But if it is practically impossible to leave or enter the kingdom, how did my father manage?"

Enric smiled. "Ah, there we have another big question. And one that shows you why we are not willing to give you up just like that. When you were brought here, we had great hopes of your being able to answer that very question. But you have no idea yourself, having been brought here at such a young age. It is a great shame your father never made contact with the Order. I dare say he would have been an immensely valuable source of information for us."

Eryn shook her head sadly. "He wouldn't have done that, ever. His disdain for you… us, I should say now, was too great. I wonder if it had anything to do with why he ran away from his home in the first place."

"Maybe we will find out soon. The delegate will know quite a few things, I imagine. The question is how much of it he is willing or permitted to share with us. But since they have managed to communicate with us via messenger, your father was obviously not the only one knowing how to brave the stormy seas. Maybe we can at least learn about that."

"Do you think they made contact because of me?" she asked.

"Yes. We have no doubt about that."

"They might want to take me back with them, then."

"We have considered that question," he said with a determined expression. "They will not at all find that easy. This was the reason the King was so eager to bind you here and at the same time demonstrate to the delegate that you are not here as a prisoner, but of your own free will, voluntarily bound by a magical oath you decided to take without being coerced in any way."

She suppressed a cutting remark about the redundancy he seemed to deem necessary. Free will, voluntarily and without being coerced in any way? How apt.

"What would happen to me if they took me without my consent?" she asked instead. "Would the oath trigger something inside me that would make me suffer or kill myself?" The thought was not very pleasant. Not at all.

"No. Nothing of that kind. The magic would just make you want to return so badly that you would do anything to manage this somehow."

"I am not really sure if that is much consolation. Being taken away with no chance of returning and feeling the urge to do so anyway wouldn't be good for a person's sanity."

He leaned forward and took her hand. "If they took you from here, I would find a way to get you back. Depend on that."

With any other man it might have been no more than grandstanding, but the calm and serious way he said it was not for show. It was no more or less than a promise.

She smiled at him. "Brave Lord Enric, the noble warrior."

"Indeed," he smiled back. "Ready to save his mate from the clasping claws of the foreign intruders."

She laughed. "That is not a very positive attitude towards our visitors. If you forget the diplomacy you keep trying to impress on me, you will never hear the end of it."

"I won't. But I will be cautious. I have no intention of leaving you alone with the delegation. I am not willing to take any risks here." He looked into her eyes. "And I expect you to fully cooperate with me in this matter."

So he really was nervous about the visitors. Three hundred years of isolation would probably do that to a population, she imagined. At least it didn't stop them from welcoming the delegation. Or were they afraid of another war, if there had ever been one?

* * *

On her last day of cleaning the stables, she sighed with relief and put aside the fork. The work itself was not the problem; she had her full magic powers back and could enhance her strength accordingly. But needing to rise so early that daylight was still several hours away combined with the reek of manure were the really unpleasant aspects.

She wouldn't have expected Lord Tyront to come up with a punishment like this. It was not cruel as such - there were people who earned their living doing this, after all. But it was a reminder that life would be a lot less comfortable for her if she didn't have her position in the Order.

Would Enric have stayed with her if she had not joined the Order, she wondered. He had taken that risk by committing to her before she had even agreed to the proposal they had made her. So he probably would have, especially if his feelings for her really were as strong as he obviously wanted to make her believe. Or was that a clever way of ensuring her willingness to stay in the kingdom? A little extra motivation to keep her here in case the visitors had a way of countering the magical oath?

She fervently hoped not. Even though she had not yet brought herself to trust him fully and unconditionally, finding out that all this had been no more than a very convincing act on his part would very likely devastate her. So she really had started falling in love with him. How very inconvenient.

* * *

Eryn looked up from her history books when a royal messenger entered the library, breathing heavily. "Lady Eryn, the delegation has been sighted. You are requested to make yourself ready."

She felt her heartbeat quicken and nodded. "I will. Thank you."

"So they are about to arrive." Lord Poron had stepped next to her, studying her. "This must be quite an exciting situation for you, I imagine. And a difficult one. Divided loyalty is never an easy matter to deal with."

She shook her head sadly. "I'm afraid quite the opposite is the case at the moment, Lord Poron. It seems that I don't feel particular loyalty towards any country right now. There is the one I was born in, although apart from that I have no particular connection to, and the other one that has only very recently stopped treating me like a prisoner."

"But then there is Lord Enric," he said with a soft smile.

"Yes, and then there is him," she sighed. "Whatever that will turn out to mean."

"You don't know him as well as we do here, Lady Eryn," he said in a reassuring tone. "And seeing him so changed in your presence is a very clear sign of his regard for you, my dear. This is not a matter of political consideration for him."

She looked at him thoughtfully. "You don't have any secret mind-reading powers, do you?"

He chuckled. "No, luckily not. And observing people is a skill that very often makes them unnecessary, anyway. Now get going, dress yourself nicely. I dare say the delegate will want to see you there when he enters the city so he knows he has come to the right place."

* * *

She picked a dark tunic and trousers. It wouldn't really matter what she wore, she thought, as the robes would cover her clothes anyway.

Enric strolled into the guest room while she was braiding her hair in front of a mirror. He seemed casual and relaxed, but the sharp and alert expression in his eyes betrayed a certain tension.

"Are you ready?" he asked calmly. "They should arrive at the gate in no more than ten minutes."

"I think I am, yes."

He watched her use a piece of cord to bind her hair. "Wait a moment. I ordered something for you." He left the room and carried a small wooden box in one hand when he returned.

She opened it curiously and smiled when she saw the content. It was a collection of about fifty delicate looking hair ribbons in different colours, picked to fit the different colours of her tunics and about a third of them in the colour of her robes. He really did have a mind for details.

"That is very thoughtful of you, thank you." She picked a dark purple band and removed the string to tie it on instead. "Well, then with this last little improvement I hope I shall not disgrace you in the eyes of the foreign visitors."

He smirked. "If you do, it will not be because of your appearance."

"A compliment wrapped in an insult. Charming."

"I had the impression that compliments made you uneasy. So I try to deliver them in combination with something you seem to respect: an honest insult."

"Delightful," she said dryly. "Have you ever considered that your way of delivering compliments is the reason why I feel uneasy about them?"

He seemed to be considering her words for a moment, and then shook his head. "No." Then he took her hands into his and kissed them both. "You look beautiful, as always. I am a very lucky man."

"Good," she grinned. "And don't you forget that."

He wouldn't, he thought and pulled her with him towards the door. It was high time for them to leave.

*　*　*

"You took your time," Tyront scolded her when they took their places behind him.

"Why? The delegation has not yet reached the gates, has it?" Eryn retorted with a seemingly unperturbed shrug, looking around. The large square in front of the palace was once again filled with people, and this time for a more appealing spectacle than an execution. The King was waiting in the throne room for the visitors to be brought to him. The Order would officially welcome them.

It seemed that half the city had decided to attend so as to catch the first glimpse of the people from foreign parts, and Eryn couldn't blame them for it. She herself was getting more and more excited by the minute and Enric squeezed her hand reassuringly.

Then they arrived at the gates and were without much pomp led into the city.

The delegation consisted of a group of five people, two of whom were obviously servants judging from their positions at the back of their group and their less elaborate garments. All of them were dressed colourfully in flowing materials and looked exotic and strange.

The one in charge seemed to be a man of about thirty years with dark, almost black, hair, tanned skin and an appealing, friendly face. He smiled when he saw the large number of people welcoming them. When his gaze fell on Eryn, his smile seemed to grow even wider.

The two riders right behind him were older men, both of them clad in rich attire that bespoke wealth. One had completely grey hair, the other one strands of grey in a mane of dark red.

The servants, both male, were dressed less flamboyantly in simple red tunics that reached their knees combined with trousers of the same colour.

All five of them got off their mounts and walked the last few steps towards Tyront. Then they stopped and bowed as one.

Tyront did the same and then spoke first, "It is a great honour for us to welcome you to our city. It has been a long time since there has been any contact between our countries. I am Lord Tyront, the Leader of the Order of Magicians, the institution that governs the use of magic here. We hope that you will have a pleasant stay in our city."

The young dark-haired man smiled and when he spoke, his voice had an exotic lilt and he rolled the letter r over the tip of his tongue.

"Lord Tyront, thank you for your warm words. My name is Ram'an, I am the ambassador for this mission. These here are my attachés Belgon and Margil."

"Welcome," Tyront repeated to the two who had just been introduced. Then he turned to indicate for Enric to step forward.

"This here is my second in command, Lord Enric." They bowed again.

"And Lady Eryn, whom you are undoubtedly eager to meet," Tyront then continued and watched the attaches exchange a glance. It seemed they were surprised to have her introduced with a title.

"Lady Eryn," Ram'an said softly and stepped towards her to take her hands and keep her upright as she was about to bow. "It is a great pleasure to meet you again."

She stared up at the slightly taller figure in surprise.

"Again?" she asked and frowned.

"Yes," the man smiled and his eyes seemed to take in every detail of her face. "It has been quite some time, but I remember you from my childhood. Our families had social connections. You were but five years old when last I saw you."

Eryn swallowed, aware that all attention of people around was focussed on them, and took a step back to break both the physical contact of their hands and the hardly less intense one of his brown eyes. She felt Enric's hand take hers to put it on his arm while giving a cool look towards the newcomer.

Ram'an followed the gesture with interest and then returned his attention to Tyront, who felt it wise to intervene at this point and offered, "I would imagine you have an exhausting journey behind you. We have quarters prepared for you if you wish to refresh yourselves before meeting King Folrin."

The ambassador nodded and smiled. "That would be most welcome, Lord Tyront. We do not wish to stand before His Majesty covered in dust. Maybe Lady Eryn would care to show us the way?"

"Lady Eryn has unfortunately not been involved in the preparations for your arrival," Enric spoke before his superior had a chance to answer. "But I would of course be delighted to take you there myself." And make a few things clear on the way, he thought grimly.

"Of course," Ram'an replied, hiding his disappointment well. "Thank you so much, Lord Enric."

Enric caught Tyront's warning look before he led the group inside the palace, leaving Eryn behind and increasing the distance between her and the newcomers with every step.

They walked through the corridors for several minutes in silence, before Ram'an cleared his throat.

"Lord Enric," he asked with a nonchalance that appeared rather forced, "what is Lady Eryn's status here, if you do not find it too bold of me to ask?"

Enric smiled. He had been looking forward to that question and stopped to observe the reaction his answer would cause in the other man.

"Not at all. Lady Eryn is a full member of the Order of Magicians and as such bound to the kingdom by a magical oath. She will take over her rank of third in command as soon as her training for this position is finished."

The frown on Ram'an's face was gone quickly and Enric hid a smile.

"And then there is her status as my companion," he went on, "which is of course more of a private matter but of utmost importance to myself."

"I see," the ambassador said quietly and gave Enric a forced smile. "How very fortunate for you to have managed to secure her hand for yourself."

"Indeed," Enric admitted generously and resumed walking. That would, he hoped, put the man in his place and make him think twice before touching her again.

When they had arrived at the quarters that had been assigned to the delegation, Enric lifted his hand and three servants stepped towards them.

"These servants have been assigned to you for the duration of your stay here. They will take care of all your wishes as best they can and provide assistance if required. Should you need anything, do not hesitate to let them know and they will take care of it. They will also lead you to the throne room as soon as you are ready to meet King Folrin."

"Thank you so much, Lord Enric," Ram'an replied, and seemed glad to be alone with his escort. Doubtlessly to discuss the news about Eryn, Enric suspected. If they had any plans to take her with them, they would now know that this would certainly be a lot harder than they might have thought. And he himself had decided that the ambassador was not to be left alone with her at any time.

CHAPTER 35

Being Diplomatic

Eryn got up from the chair when the door opened and Enric walked in.

"I think you were a little bad-mannered down there," she said and folded her arms. "Is that your idea of diplomatic behaviour?"

Enric just lifted his brows. "I found I was very civilised. I do not take well to strangers touching you that way."

"Touching me that way? He just took my hands, which might be a cultural thing. Maybe this is how they greet each other in my home country, and he thought that it was appropriate in my case as I happen to be a fellow countrywoman."

"I don't care what kind of address he is used to. If he wishes for his appendages to remain unharmed, he will adapt to our ways as long as he is here. This was a friendly warning. The next one will be less amiable."

She sighed. "Jealous? Really? From your reaction one might think that half the kingdom is after taking me away from you."

He looked down at her. "*This* kingdom is not the one I am currently worried about."

"Well, I would think you managed to inform the delegation in passing about my having joined the Order, wouldn't you?" she enquired.

Smiling, he took a seat and stretched his legs out. "Indeed. And about your being my companion. Though I wouldn't say it was in passing. The ambassador distinctly enquired about you."

"Of course he did," Eryn said mildly, "wouldn't you in his place?"

"Probably," Enric admitted reluctantly.

"Why do I have the feeling that you are going to be difficult about this?" She eyed him suspiciously.

"Me? I have no intention whatsoever of complicating things."

"So you wouldn't object to my paying the ambassador a visit?"

"No, absolutely not. I understand that you must have many questions for him. We can make an appointment with him any time."

She rolled her eyes. "We? I am not even allowed to be alone with him? What does Lord Tyront think about this?"

"I have no idea. This is what *I* think. And anything Tyront as your superior permits I don't have to agree with as your companion provided he doesn't explicitly order me to leave you two alone. Which he won't - trust me on that."

Patience, she reminded herself. You can't beat him if you lose control. Breathing in and out. "But there is also no order for me *not* to meet him alone, is there?"

"I give it to you just now if you insist: you are not to meet him alone."

"Is this an official command from Lord Enric of the Order of Magicians or from my companion?"

He narrowed his eyes at her. So she had started learning how to play this little game. "What is the difference?"

"The difference is that if you give it to me as my companion, I am under no obligation to comply as this is not a function in which you are entitled to give me any commands. If you are ordering me as my superior, I will at once consult Lord Tyront to confirm it. Which I suspect he will not do, as he is hardly willing to risk the Order's reputation to accommodate your jealousy." She watched the flash of annoyance in his eyes with satisfaction.

"So you need an official command because me asking this of you is not enough?"

"Don't make me sound reckless and selfish if I don't follow your completely inappropriate command. You may even prevent me from gaining information that he would probably not share with me in your presence."

Yes, he thought - this kind of confidentiality was exactly what he wanted to avoid occurring between them.

"So you will try to be alone with him? Is this what you are telling me?"

She sighed. "I am sure he will want to spend some time with me alone sooner or later. And I can hardly tell the ambassador that I am being treated like a child by my companion and may thus only be with him when we are supervised. What impression would that make, I ask you?"

"Do what you think best, then," he sighed and rose.

"Where are you going?" she exclaimed. "We are in the middle of a discussion here!"

"No, we aren't. You have made up your mind and there is not a thing I can do about it," he replied curtly and went into his study. Apart from finally hiring a few spies himself, that is.

* * *

Eryn jumped up and ran out of the guest room when the knock at the door sounded to pull it open before Enric had a chance to react.

"Junar!" she exclaimed in relief. "I need your help! I am supposed to be at this formal dinner the King throws for the delegation and have no idea what to wear!"

The seamstress smiled and held up three dresses she had slung over her left arm. "Luckily, your companion is rather more far-sighted than yourself. If you had asked me to make you something now, a mere two hours before you are meant to be there, the result would not have pleased you very much."

Eryn leaned against the wall and exhaled in relief. "I know I should be angry at having again been excluded from everyday matters that concern me by the two of you, but right now I am just grateful."

"Good," Junar grinned, "this should make you more cooperative."

They disappeared into Enric's bedroom and when they reappeared, Enric nodded in approval. Junar was worth every gold piece he left with her.

He had been blocking all of Eryn's attempts to talk about the delegates for the last three hours and she had finally given in and retired to the guest room to sulk. She had once dashed outside with a piece of paper she had shoved into a servant's hand, obviously to summon Junar.

"So, let's talk about why you need formal dresses, shall we?" Junar asked sweetly.

"Oh, shut up, you. Gloating is not attractive in anybody," Eryn rolled her eyes.

"Maybe not. But it does wonders for my soul."

"You brought two more. Which one will I wear?"

"That will depend on your companion's attire."

Two pairs of expectant eyes made Enric look up from the book in his lap. "Pardon?"

"What are you going to wear tonight?" Eryn asked with a testy undertone. "It seems I have to adapt to your choice so I can be the perfect accessory for you."

Enric sighed. So she was still angry at him. "I am going to wear dark blue."

Junar nodded. "Good, then the white dress should go very well with it."

"White," Eryn said dismayed. "Do you have any idea how long this will stay clean if they give me something to eat? Which will be what they intend to do at a formal dinner, as I understand. You have just condemned me to an evening of strategically hiding stains behind my napkin! Why do you hate me?"

"No, you bloody fool," Junar explained in exasperation, "this is why they serve food fit for ladies at these occasions. You will stick to things that don't spill, dribble, splash, stain or make any other kind of mess. That means dry things without sauce or cream that don't have to be cut or eaten with a spoon."

"So I will basically eat only cold, dry things? Bloody brilliant!" She threw up her hands. "Seriously, who makes these rules? I will starve!"

"You are not supposed to binge on the food there and stuff yourself to the brim, you glutton! That would not look very ladylike, would it? That's why you eat something *before* you go there. Why don't they give you any books on etiquette to read?" Junar cried out in desperation.

Eryn looked at her in astonishment. "You know," she said slowly, "I thought that I was the one of us given to sudden outbursts of frustration, but I feel I am being outdone today. What is the matter?"

Junar sighed and closed her eyes for a moment. "Nothing, I am sorry. I just had a very demanding customer today and am still a little edgy."

"Well, well," Eryn smirked. "It seems I have finally managed to break through that annoying calm of yours."

"Oh, Eryn," she sighed, "you really are a pain. Now go and try on the other two dresses so we can see if I need to alter anything. You will need them soon, I think. The King will very likely want to entertain his guests more often than this once."

Eryn nodded and retreated to the bedroom once again, wondering at the kind of customer that had managed to upset her composed, serene friend in such a way.

* * *

Eryn looked around curiously when she walked into the banquet hall, arm in arm with Enric. The huge table in the centre was set for about forty people, so the King had kept it rather intimate.

"Ah, Lady Eryn," she heard the foreign sounding voice from her left side and felt the muscles in Enric's arm tense under her fingers. That did serve him right, she decided and turned with a bright smile on her face.

"Ambassador Ram'an, how nice to see you again so soon," she beamed.

"And you, Lady, for you are a sight to behold. No other woman in here can compare with you." He made to take her hand to kiss it, but reconsidered at Enric's cold stare.

Orrin entered and looked slightly concerned at the obviously tense situation between the three of them. A man making the mistake of showing more than a passing interest in Eryn was guaranteed to keep the evening interesting. Orrin smiled and approached them.

Eryn looked up, clearly relieved with the diversion. "Ambassador, please let me introduce you to my good friend Lord Orrin. He has been a beacon of stability to me in a time of insanity," she smiled and winked at Orrin.

"As you were a challenge for me in a time of mediocrity," Orrin replied in a charming mix of warmth and mischief that made her laugh.

More and more people entered the hall, many of whom she recognised as members of the Council, others she had not yet met officially even if there was a familiar face among them every now and then.

When a gong sounded, servants stepped forward to escort the guests to their designated seats. Eryn saw that she was lead to one side of the table and Enric to the other. They would face each other, but be too far apart to talk casually. Which was fine with her for now.

She smiled when she saw that she had been placed right next to Ambassador Ram'an, who was obviously equally delighted.

Then King Folrin entered the hall, closely followed by Loft and Marrin, and proceeded towards the head end of the table. The guests stopped their various conversations instantly.

"Ladies and Lords, I am very pleased to welcome you to our little gathering in honour of our guests from the Western Territories. I welcome you to our lands, Ambassador Ram'an. May your stay be a pleasant one and may many more follow."

All guests around the table turned to the Ambassador and he accepted their bows gracefully.

"Thank you so much, Your Majesty. It delights my heart to be welcomed so warmly after so many years, centuries even, without any contact between our lands. Your readiness to accept a stranger into your halls shows the generosity of your hearts, and I will be sure to spread the tidings of your friendliness among my people upon my return." He bowed to the King and the assembled guests in return.

They remained standing until the host took his seat, then followed his example, immediately resuming the myriad conversations interrupted by his arrival.

Ram'an turned to her immediately. "I am very grateful to His Majesty for this seating arrangement, I must admit. I have been hoping for a chance to converse with you, Lady Eryn. Will you tell me the tale of how you came to be here?"

She gave him a half smile. "I will. If you answer me that same question in return, Ambassador."

Ram'an smiled, clearly amused at her blunt enquiry about what he himself was doing here. "I see you do not waste your time with sugar-coating your words. How very refreshing."

"I apologise, I am rather new in this diplomacy business. Did I understand your answer to be affirmative?"

"And assertive, too. What a fascinating person you are, My Lady. And indeed, I would be glad to share this information with you. But not at this time and place. May I be so bold as to invite you to my quarters tomorrow? I am sure there is a lot you would like to ask, and I would be more than happy to satisfy your curiosity."

Eryn gulped and cast a quick glance over at Enric, who doubtlessly had been following the conversation with his neat little air trick. He narrowed his eyes at her in warning and shook his head almost imperceptibly.

"Ah," Ram'an smiled, "your companion, Lord Enric. He is very protective of you, is he not? I have the impression that he will not let you join me without a chaperone."

She smiled apologetically. "Yes, it would seem so."

"You have been companions for a long time?" the ambassador enquired.

"No. The commitment ceremony was exactly ten days ago." She smiled. "So we are still in the process of readapting our lives to include each other fully."

Ram'an's brow rose and he pursed his lips. "Only ten days ago? How very interesting." He gave Enric a calculating look. "And, if I may ask this of you as well, how long have you been a member of the Order of Magic?"

She looked into his dark eyes, wondering if she was supposed or even permitted to give away that information. After another look at Enric, who did not at all look relaxed, she decided that as she had not been told to keep it a secret, she would use her own discretion here.

"Four days exactly."

"I see," the ambassador said calmly. "What an amazing coincidence. Were you aware of the delegation's pending arrival at the time of your commitment to Lord Enric?"

"Ambassador Ram'an," Enric's voice rose and made them both look up, "I hope your quarters are to your liking?"

"Very much so, Lord Enric, thank you. They are very comfortable and spacious." A gleam entered the ambassador's eyes. "I was, in fact, just trying to invite your charming companion to visit me there tomorrow to tell her a little about her home country."

The tension between the two of them seemed almost palpable. Eryn watched the barely contained anger in Enric's blue eyes meet the fierce challenge in Ram'an's dark brown ones.

"What a commendable idea," the King's voice suddenly cut in, making both men break off their staring contest to look at him instead. "Though I would propose a delightful tour through the city instead. Lady Eryn will show you around. She has spent quite some time walking the streets here and will undoubtedly be a very able guide. Unless, of course, you feel the need for privacy for some reason?"

Ram'an smiled politely. "No, of course not. What an appealing idea, Your Majesty."

Eryn lifted her napkin to hide the smile she couldn't prevent from tugging at her lips. So the King had mastered this game of diplomacy well enough. He had avoided an open confrontation in front of his guests and given both men only part of what each of them wanted. The ambassador would be alone with her, or as alone as Enric could tolerate with whatever means of observation were at his disposal.

And she herself was more than satisfied. She would get to spend some time with the ambassador without Enric, and as the King had been the one to arrange it, her companion could hardly blame her.

Maybe the entire idea of diplomacy was not so useless after all. She wondered if Lord Poron had a book about it somewhere.

* * *

431

Eryn looked up from the last of her history books as Enric strolled into the library.

"You are late for your training session," he stated and closed the book, narrowly avoiding squeezing her fingers in the process.

"Training?" she frowned. "I wasn't aware we had a lesson scheduled for today."

"You weren't? I distinctly remember putting it on your training plan."

She groaned. "You are not serious, are you? I need to finish this book today and I have arranged to take my walk with the ambassador in less than three hours!"

He just smiled thinly. "Then you'd better hurry now and return in a timely fashion from your walk so you can finish it in the evening."

"You are doing this to make me return earlier! Isn't this rather petty?"

"I have no idea what you are talking about. Come. I have prepared everything at our usual spot. You can change there, I have brought a set of clothes and your training armour. I would hate to shred that nice new tunic."

She beamed an angry look over to him before she rose and neatly slid the book where it belonged. He was in charge of her combat training, so there was nothing she could do. This time he had the Order's authority behind him, whether she liked it or not.

She shivered when they went outside to the small courtyard and sighed when she saw the clothes she was supposed to change into lie on the stone bench next to the two swords they would use.

"Are you really going to make me undress out here in the cold?"

"Yes. If you had not forgotten our appointment, you could have done that inside." He leaned against the wall with folded arms, waiting. "Go on."

"Forgotten. Sure," she murmured grumpily under her breath. "Do you have to watch?" She looked at him testily.

"Nothing I haven't seen before, my love," he replied mildly.

"Bastard," she muttered and turned her back to him when she slipped out of her soft tunic and into a coarse linen one. Then she changed her trousers and finally slipped on the protective armour. "Let's get this over with, then," she growled and picked up one of the swords, the smaller one.

Enric started slowly by making her block a few low thrusts, then moved on to attacks that required magical enhancement of speed.

"Where will you take the ambassador?" he asked casually.

Ah yes, she thought, there we go. "I am not entirely sure yet. Along Kingsway, then maybe along the river for a while, it depends on what he is interested in."

Their swords met another five times before he said, "You are aware that some information better remains unshared, I assume?"

She smiled without humour. "Like the fact that I have been made to join the Order without knowing that a delegation from the Western Territories was due only a few days later? This kind of information?"

"Yes. This kind exactly," Enric replied and sent her sword flying out of her grasp to get her full attention. "You may be angry at the King and Tyront for withholding that from you, but think of the implications. The consequences of this getting back to the Western Territories might be severe."

"Really?" she asked coldly. "How come that nobody has considered this before? So the success of this manoeuvre depends on the cooperation of the one person you tricked into everything? Fools, all of you!" she snorted angrily. "What will you do if I tell him anyway? He certainly was very interested in that particular question yesterday, as you have no doubt overheard. I assume your timely interruption was no coincidence."

"No, it wasn't," he admitted. "Just think of the people who would be in danger if we do something that might cause a war. Orrin. Junar. Vern. Plia."

She put her hands on her hips, staring up at him with narrowed eyes. "Don't you dare place this burden on my shoulders! I am not the one responsible for all this, it is the work of the Order and the King, so don't make me the one who is meant to avoid any and all consequences of your actions. This is an unfair move, and you know it!"

He sighed. "Yes, it is. And one I have to make nevertheless. Eryn, I command you not to share the fact that you were not informed of the delegation prior to your commitment to me and thus your joining of the Order. This is an official order from a superior magician. The Order and the King are behind me on this one."

She nodded slowly. "Alright, then. This doesn't leave much room for me, does it?"

"None," he said simply.

"So I will tell a lie to the ambassador today. Excellent. My very first act of diplomacy; you must be so proud."

* * *

The ambassador watched Eryn leave the palace at a half-run towards the centre of the square where he was waiting for her. She was right on time. Adjusting her robes before she came to stand in front of him, she bowed and received his bow in return.

"Lady Eryn," Ram'an said with his usual smile at seeing her, "I am so glad you could make it. Is there a way I can offer you my arm without causing any breach of good manners or protocol? I can do this at home without any problems, but here I might overstep boundaries I am not aware of."

"Yes, you can offer me your arm. It would not constitute any violation I am aware of." Apart from Enric grinding his teeth, there was no problem at all, she thought. She was willing to bet everything she possessed that he was at this very moment watching them from his study window, and forced herself not to let her gaze wander up there to check.

The ambassador's expression grew serious after she had put her hand on the arm he had offered. "Before we start our little walk, Lady Eryn, I would be very interested in returning to the question I asked you yesterday evening and that has so far remained unanswered. I trust you know the one I am referring to?"

She nodded slowly. "I do, Ambassador. And the answer is Yes. I had been informed of your arrival prior to my commitment to both Lord Enric and the Order."

Ram'an studied her face for several seconds. "I see. How very regrettable for us that you would choose to bind yourself so tightly to this place without considering what your own country has to offer you."

She gulped and looked away from him. "You must understand, Ambassador, that I have no connections to your country. I have spent almost all my life here - I know nothing else."

They started walking down Kingsway towards the city centre.

"Of course. This seems to upset you, so let us say no more of it for now. And I would very much appreciate if you would address me not with my title, but my name instead. My friends call me Ram'an, and I hope to make you one of them."

She smiled. "I would be honoured. I am Eryn to my friends."

"So, Eryn, would you be interested in learning what your name was before you came here?"

"My name?"

"Of course. Your father changed it when he brought you here. Doubtlessly to make you less noticeable. To make you fit in more easily and harder to track."

That did sound logical, she thought. And yet she had never thought about the possibility that there might have been another name before.

"Yes, please. I would be very interested in hearing it."

"It was Maltheá, after a very beautiful flower that grows at great heights and has considerable healing powers. People would call you Theá for short."

"Maltheá," she murmured, trying to decide if she liked it. Then she looked up. "What did you mean by *harder to track*?"

Ram'an put his hand over hers. "Your father had taken you away to a forbidden land. Of course we were trying to bring you back. A group of men followed you and searched for you all over the land for quite some time. But your father was very clever at hiding and had moved around quite a lot before settling down with you. We managed to find the village he had chosen to stay in only several months ago. When we questioned the villagers, we learned that your father had been dead for a very long time, and that you had been taken away to the city only days before our arrival."

Eryn stopped and pulled her hand out of his, staring at him. "You are telling me that you have never stopped searching for me in all these years? And if I hadn't had the accident in the woods..."

"Then you would now be at home with us instead of here," he finished her sentence.

"You would have taken me with you? What if I hadn't agreed?" She fought her agitation, tried to apply the breathing exercises, but somehow they didn't work here.

"Why wouldn't you have agreed?" he asked in earnest puzzlement.

Because I had a home here, she thought, one you would have taken away from me just like the King had.

She closed her eyes and thought about the many nights in the chilly, tiny cell at the warriors' quarters when she had cursed herself for her clumsiness that day in the woods when she made the slip that landed her in captivity. Now it seemed that it wouldn't have made any difference; she would just have been a prisoner to another country.

"Eryn?" His worried voice cut through her thoughts. "I have upset you again. Forgive me."

She opened her eyes once more and forced herself to smile. "No. It was just a surprise. I am perfectly fine, I assure you." She took his arm again to prove it and walked on with him. "Why hadn't you given up the search after all that time? My father left your country more than twenty years ago. Why not accept that he was gone?"

"Because you were born as a member of a very influential family which was determined to get you back," he replied.

She raised her brows. "I was?"

"Indeed. A family, I have to add, which will not be very pleased to hear that even though you have been found, you cannot be returned to them."

Be returned to them, whether she would have agreed or not, she thought grimly, not return voluntarily. She felt the anger at Enric's command not to reveal her ignorance of the delegation's arrival fade.

"Tell me about yourself," she changed the topic. "You seem very young for such an important position, especially as your attachés seem so much older than you, if you don't mind my bluntness."

He smiled and squeezed her fingers lightly. "No, I do not mind at all. I find your openness very refreshing. I, too, was born into a very important family. This tends to open doors for young people with the right abilities."

"Such as ambition, a talent for diplomacy and the courage to brave strange countries?"

"Yes," he said and stopped to turn to her. "All of those. And this especially."

She felt the surge of warm energy flow from his hand into hers and gasped. "You are a magician!"

His dark eyes reflected his pleasure at her reaction. "Indeed, I am. And one that is considered rather powerful among my people, too."

Oh dear, she thought, Enric would not like this. Not at all.

CHAPTER 36

Foreign Magic

Enric turned when Eryn burst through the door. He had seen her stroll back, arm in arm with the ambassador in what had seemed a relaxed pace from his window and frowned at the unexpected urgency in her demeanour.

"What is the matter?" he asked and went to her to take her by the shoulders. "Has he done something to you? Upset you?"

She shook her head. "No, I am alright. Wait for a moment, please. Lord Tyront should be on his way, I have sent a messenger to him. You both need to hear this."

Enric's gaze narrowed. For her to voluntarily summon Tyront, who she usually tried her best to avoid, could hardly mean good news.

"Alright. Let's go to the study, then, and wait for him there."

He took a seat in one of the two chairs in front of the desk, instead of behind it. She nodded in appreciation at the sign that he left the position of power in the room to her, but she was reluctant to sit in his chair and instead leaned against the desk as a compromise.

Tyront arrived only a few minutes later and looked at both of them, taking in Eryn's serious expression. He closed the door and sat next to Enric, both of them looking up at her expectantly.

"Ambassador Ram'an is a magician. A strong one, by his own words," she said without introduction.

"Splendid," Enric forced out between clenched teeth. "Just perfect."

Tyront remained silent for a few more seconds, staring out the window thoughtfully before he spoke, "Well, this is rather inconvenient to put it mildly. It makes him even more unpredictable. We have no idea how strong or skilled he is." He looked up at Eryn. "What else did he tell you?"

She closed her eyes for a moment, trying to remember as many details as possible. "About their looking for me and my father for all these years. He said they had arrived at my village only days after I had been brought to the city."

Enric sucked in sharp breath. "You are saying they have been roaming the land unnoticed for more than two decades?" He felt almost dizzy at the thought that they would very likely have taken her away from here without his ever meeting her.

"So it seems," she nodded.

"What else?" Tyront enquired.

"He said that my family would not be pleased about my being bound here, that they are influential. Which is why the search was never stopped. And he told me that he, too, is from an important family."

Tyront watched her with pursed lips. "Why have you told us about this? You could easily have kept it to yourself and waited for a chance to leave with the ambassador. He might possess the knowledge of how to break the oath that binds you here."

Her gaze was cool and so was her voice. "Because he told me that I would have been taken away from here, whether I had agreed or not. This made me doubt that my own people would have been the lesser evil. And I have committed myself here, after all," she added, looking at Enric with a smile.

Tyront looked away to something on the nearest wall that must have caught his sudden interest, when Enric rose from his chair and took her face into both his hands to kiss her fervently with what she felt was a mix of immense relief, gratitude and affection.

* * *

Enric awoke earlier than usual and smiled when he felt the warm body his arm still held nuzzled against him. He had managed to keep her with him an entire night a second time. This time, though, he wouldn't let her pretend that it had not happened. No more sneaking about while he let her think that he was still asleep.

She twitched when he started kissing her shoulder in the dark and the tension in her body gave away the exact moment she was awake. She froze for a moment, then whispered, "Which bed am I in?"

"Mine," he said, then corrected himself, "Or rather: ours. And as I have now for the second time proven to you that you can sleep in the same bed with me, I expect you to take all your things, put them in here and make me no longer sneak about in the early morning hours into the guest room to steal an hour or two with you."

"Second time?" she asked weakly.

"Yes, the second time. I was well aware of the first one. Will you move in here voluntarily or do I have to make you? I am warning you, there will be no compromises whatsoever."

"Why are you even asking me, then?" she retorted testily.

"Because you insist on being treated like a grown woman, and I will thus give you the choice of making it very easy or hard for you. The result, however, will be the same."

"How about giving me all the time I need?" she protested. "That's what you promised me! I distinctly remember you using these exact words!"

"And I have kept my promise. As you have now for the second time slept in one bed with me without suffering from nightmares, sleeplessness or any other noticeable grievances, this clearly proves that you have had all the time you need. Now stop stalling and answer my question: the easy or the hard way?"

She tried in vain to make out his features in the dark, but didn't really have to see his face to know that he was serious. His voice had conveyed that message well enough. He was right - she had now spent the second night with him so far, and as nights went, both of them had been restful enough. Yet the thought of giving up her own sleeping space, the refuge her own bed had always been, even while she had been held captive, made her uneasy.

"How much time do I get to consider this?" she asked. "I think two more days of sneaking should be bearable for you."

She heard him sigh. "Is it possible that I have failed to make myself understood? You will not be spending even *one* more night in the guest room, let alone two. Am I to assume that you have decided in favour of option two? The hard way?"

"Now, wait a moment! What would the hard way entail?"

"A variation on throwing you over my shoulder and bringing you here, knocking you out and then bringing you here or the all-time favourite of locking you out of the guest room and then bringing you here."

She chuckled finally. "I do recognise a pattern in this."

"I am very glad you do," he replied, smiling. He could hear from her tone that he had won. "That means I have finally managed to make myself clear."

"So, if I am to move in here, can we get rid of that terrible carpet? And those curtains?"

"What? You have spent two nights in here and already plan to start redecorating? How about respecting my personal preferences?" he cried out in mock despair. She could repaper the bloody walls if she liked for all he cared.

"My dear Lord Enric, the easy way for me is not necessarily the easy way for you. Congratulations. You have just extorted yourself a roommate."

* * *

Vern looked thoughtful while sitting on his bed, slurping noisily from his cup. "A magician? Do you have any idea how strong he is? Stronger than you or Lord Enric? Lord Tyront even?"

She shrugged. "I have no idea. I am not even sure I am allowed to talk to you about this."

He grinned. "And yet you do. Lucky for me I am not the one who would get in trouble for this."

"Only if you don't keep your mouth shut." She narrowed her eyes at him. "Don't anger the mighty and powerful Lady magician."

"I wouldn't dare. Seriously - it would end my supply of healing books in no time."

She sighed and shook her head. "I am so glad you have the right priorities here. Books are definitely what you should be worrying about right now."

"Alright, let's get back to worrying about the ambassador, then. Is there a way for you to discover how strong he is?"

"I don't think so. Unless I challenge him to a fight, which I have no intention of doing. And for now I am not really that interested in his strength. I am rather more curious about his skills. My father could do a lot of things and if he knows only half of that… I wonder what I could learn from him."

Vern frowned. "Why would he teach you anything?"

"I think he wants to keep me happy for now. It seems he has come here with an agenda, and angering me or making me think badly of the Western Territories is not part of it."

"You hope he wants to keep you happy by teaching you some of their magic? Why would he want to keep you happy, anyway? He can't take you with him."

She nodded. "Yes, but he doesn't seem particularly happy about that. It appears that he was sent by my family. Or what's left of it."

Vern's eyes became wide. "Maybe you are heir to their throne or something similar, and they are willing to do anything to get their long-lost princess back!"

Eryn rolled her eyes. "Why haven't I thought of that? That is the only logical conclusion, isn't it? And my father, the former King, has been trained as a healer because that is such a jolly way of spending his free time."

He shrugged. "Could be. You don't know anything about the country, they could be completely different from us, and having healing kings might be absolutely normal for them. One more thing," he added with a shake of his head. "What happened to your hair? Is it only me or a trick of the light, or does it really look green?"

"It is just another failed experiment. I keep trying to change my hair colour the way my father used to, but the colours look nothing like your blond. I am doing something wrong here."

"Obviously," Vern nodded slowly. "Is this the first time you have tried this or have you just never managed to find out how it's done in all these years?"

"It's the second time. After my first attempt a few days ago I ended up with red hair. And no, I hadn't tried it before that. And it should be fairly clear why not. As long as I didn't know how to do it on my own it would have been too dangerous to risk losing my father's protection by playing around with it."

"Why didn't you play around with colouring your hair while you were still a prisoner?"

"Because only now I came up with a way I think it might work."

He grimaced. "Well, not exactly. But this colour would go nicely with that green tunic of yours. You wait until one of the court ladies sees you in matching hair and clothes and it will become the latest fashion in no time."

"Right. And I will specialise in dying hair instead of healing. What an appealing thought." She shivered.

"Speaking of healing - what about the building the King gave you? Is anything happening there yet?"

"I have contacted a builder to have a look at it with me tomorrow afternoon. I think we'd need to add a wall or two, enlarge one or two windows and some such. Possibly without having the whole thing collapse on top of me."

Vern looked thoughtful. "I suppose that would be an added side-bonus. Where do you keep the plans?"

She looked at him, dumbfounded. "Plans?"

"Oh, come on! Don't tell me you don't have any plans? How are you going to plan this properly without any drawings? If you don't give the builder any plan and he knocks down the wrong wall, you could never prove that it was not what you agreed on. Seriously, how have you managed without me for so long?"

"Through sheer, dumb luck, as it seems," she murmured. "So, how do I get these plans? Can I make them myself?"

"No, *you* can't make them. *I* can." He put his cup aside and got up from the bed, taking a notepad and a pen from his desk. "We need a measuring tape as well. I will send a servant to get one for us." He left his room and returned only a minute later to sit down again, pen and pad on his lap.

"Let's make a list of rooms you need there."

She closed her eyes for a moment and started listing, "A waiting room, then one for preparing medicines, another one for storing them, treatment rooms, a library would be good…"

"Wait," he said, scribbling frantically, "how many treatment rooms?"

"I have no idea. That would depend on how many people are willing to be trained as healers."

"You're aiming to charge money for your services, aren't you? Where would you keep that?"

"The money? At the money lenders, I think."

Vern pinched the bridge of his nose. "No, I mean before you take it there. There are a lot of criminals in the city, so you also need to protect it from thieves while it is in the building."

"You mean have an extra room for it? I don't think there will be so much it really warrants a whole room just for the money. We are not about to get filthy rich with this."

"I am not saying you need an extra room just for the money, but you should really think of a safe spot somewhere. As far away from the waiting room as possible is what I would recommend. A room with an extra strong lock on the door and maybe even a shield in place."

"Alright, a small secure room somewhere."

"What else?"

She thought for a moment. "A place for the healers to relax for a few minutes. A room where they can wash and change their clothes in case it gets bloody. A room or two for people who need to stay here for some time under supervision. A room where I can do the paperwork."

"That's eleven rooms so far, including only one treatment room for the moment. How big is that building?"

"Big enough," she assured him. "With all that we should have no more than half the building full. Wait – teaching rooms for healers! Make that two, one for theoretical knowledge, the other for practical exercises. And if we manage to interest enough healers in joining us to fulfil the Order's quota, another five treatment rooms. And one room for storage."

"Nineteen rooms," Vern commented and looked up when a servant knocked at his door to bring the measuring tape. "Come," he said and grabbed his writing accessories, "Let's make a plan of that building of yours."

* * *

When they returned several hours later, both of them looked dusty and tired and Orrin had a concerned look on his face when he saw them. "I hope you are not planning to sit down in my tidy parlour like this? Go and wash yourselves first, then we can eat something and then you can tell me what you have been up to."

"I don't think you can talk to me like that anymore, you know," Eryn frowned at him and faltered under his stare. "Right, wash and then tell you all about it," she murmured and slunk off to the sanitary room behind Vern. "Can I borrow a shirt and trousers from you?" she asked as she undressed in front of him, with Vern staring at her in alarm.

"What are you doing?" he whispered hoarsely.

She kicked her dirty clothes aside and rolled her eyes at him. "Seriously? You have seen every detail inside my body, and now you are squeamish when I undress in front of you? What are you going to do when a patient has to undress? Hold your eyes shut tight?"

He gestured helplessly, searching for words. "This is different! Lord Enric is going to kill me!"

"*I* am going to kill you if you don't stop being silly and instead turn on that brain of yours."

He closed his eyes and breathed in and out slowly. "I am good. This is completely normal. I am standing in our sanitary room with the naked companion of the second most powerful magician in the kingdom. But that is completely fine. As long as he doesn't find out and kill me with a bolt of energy that will make my intestines explode so quickly that no healer, however skilled they may be, can save me from bleeding to death."

"This is how you calm yourself? Interesting. We should probably work on the wording a bit," she cackled and took a jug of water, heated it with a little magic and poured it over her hair into a bowl. The water was grey and a number of dead spiders floated around.

She cringed. "I hate spiders! Crawly, long-legged little buggers. But I suppose they go well with the green hair." She applied soap to the wet, dirty mass on her head and then rinsed it until the water looked reasonably clean.

"Can you hand me a towel?" She stretched out her hand in his direction and looked up after a few seconds. "What are you doing, lad? Open your eyes or you will smash something. And you haven't even started to wash yourself!"

He opened his eyes reluctantly, staring up at the ceiling and shoving the towel in her general direction. "While you are in here?"

She sighed, aware that she needed to be patient. "Vern, when you work with a lot of ill, sick and injured people, you need to be ready to wash and change into clean clothes, even if you are in the presence of colleagues, male or female. Consider this a first test."

He groaned. "Just a word of warning: if you start picking healers by making them undress in front of you, this will not improve your reputation."

She laughed out loud at this. "Probably not. And Enric would tan my hide for it!"

Vern looked at her for a moment, then started laughing himself.

* * *

It was early evening when they left the warrior's quarters to take a stroll through the city together, the first after quite some time.

"Eryn," a now familiar voice said from behind them when they were about to leave the square to turn into Kingsway.

She turned and smiled. "Ram'an, what a pleasant coincidence. May I introduce my friend Vern to you? You may remember his father from the dinner at your first day here: Lord Orrin."

"Lord Orrin," he mused. "Serious looking man, muscular with a thin scar down one side of his face?"

"Yes, that's father, unmistakably him," Vern nodded and bowed. "You must be Ambassador Ram'an. I am honoured to meet you."

"It is always a pleasure to meet a friend of Eryn's," Ram'an replied smoothly. "I hope I am not keeping you two from an errand?"

"No, we were just about to take a walk. You are very welcome to join us, if you like," Eryn offered.

"I would like that very much, thank you." He cleared his throat. "I could not help noticing your very interesting hair colour today, Eryn. Is this a fashion in this place?"

She laughed and touched her hair self-consciously. "No, I am afraid it is not. It is another unsuccessful attempt at figuring out how my father managed to colour my hair blond all these years ago."

Ram'an smiled and raised his brows. "Would you allow me?" He waited for her to nod cautiously before lifting his fingers to her cheek. She felt warm energy enter her body through his fingers and heard Vern gasp beside her.

When the ambassador took a strand of her hair to hold it before her eyes, she stared at something fair and yellow.

She drew in a quick breath and looked up at him. "How did you do that? Can you show me?" She closed her eyes. "I am sorry, I don't want to push you into giving away knowledge like this without even knowing if you are inclined or permitted to do so. It is not very diplomatic of me."

"Eryn, it would be my pleasure to teach you this skill," Ram'an replied in his calm and musical voice and then looked at Vern. "And to the young man as well, if he is interested?"

Vern's eyes went wide. "Interested? That would be absolutely fabulous!"

"Then may I invite the two of you to my quarters and take this walk with you at some other time maybe?" He winked at Eryn. "As we have a chaperone with us tonight, your companion might be willing to let you join me."

"I should think so, yes," she smiled back.

When they entered the ambassador's quarters, Vern whistled through his teeth and Eryn looked around curiously. There had not been many changes, but the effect was stunning. Some of the settees in the parlour had been moved aside to make space for large, colourful cushions on the floor that reflected the style of the ambassador's clothing. Exotic scents hung in the air, seeming to emanate from a round, softly glowing ceramic bowl.

"I always try to bring a little bit of home with me wherever I travel," Ram'an said and motioned for them to sit on the cushions. "May I invite you to experience a little taste of my home?"

Vern waited for Eryn to take a seat first, then plopped himself down right next to her. "Very cosy," he commented and leaned back. "I could get used to this."

The ambassador smiled, but remained standing. "A young man open to new influences, I see."

Eryn looked at the boy warmly. "I have come to know him as a person open to everything new. He has been very insistent on learning how to heal and is also a very talented artist with a pen."

"Is he now? Artists are very highly valued in my country, especially in combination with a skill such as healing."

Vern stilled. "They are?"

The man chuckled. "Oh, yes, immensely so. The ladies especially are very keen on their services. They often specialise in healing practices that enhance beauty, as this requires both a keen sense of aesthetics and the medical skills to carry them out."

Eryn frowned. "Healing for reasons of beauty?" That did sound awfully decadent.

"Like you did with Plia, if I remember correctly," Vern pointed out as if reading her thoughts and reproaching her for them.

"Well... yes, I suppose," she admitted reluctantly.

"May I offer you a beverage? I have brought a few bottles of a very nice fermented drink we like to take in the evenings with friends."

"That would be very nice, thank you," Eryn accepted politely and watched the ambassador walk to a small intricately carved chest from which he took an elegantly curved bottle containing a dark purple liquid and three square glasses that were thin enough to fit inside the circle of her thumb and index finger.

He sat next to Eryn and handed them a glass each before pouring the drinks.

Eryn sniffed at hers and looked up in surprise. "It does smell familiar... how strange, after all these years..."

"This does not surprise me in the least, dear Eryn. The human sense of smell is a very important one and developed almost from birth. It is very susceptible to long-lasting impressions. I am pleased that it managed to trigger a distant, if not conscious memory of your home. The drink contains herbs we use for cooking, so this must be where you have encountered them as a child." He then lifted his glass. "I drink to new friendships, to embracing the new, sharing the old and to an interesting future."

Vern and Eryn both lifted their glasses and then carefully tasted their drinks. The velvety liquid seemed to develop its many tastes in waves. First a warm and heavy impression that turned into something fresh and flowery only to finally settle on the tongue with a spicy aftertaste.

"This is very good, I must say," she nodded appreciatively. "What is it made from?"

"Ripe fruit, fermented in a rather lengthy process. Each step requires adding different spices in the precise amount and then the mix needs to rest for some time. It is quite a science, I understand, and it takes a long time to reach the desired result. At least if you are willing to wait and pay for the high-quality product. There is a less sophisticated version as well, but it is mostly consumed by young people who like to get drunk quickly and without spending too much money," he added with a smile.

Eryn shot a quick look at Vern, who clearly enjoyed the drink as well. "I think this is enough for you, my lad," she said and took away his empty glass.

Vern frowned at her. "Back in big sister-mode, are you? Don't forget who the chaperone here is. And I have to say that I am very confused by the sight of you right now." He stared at her newly blond hair.

"Which brings us to my promise of instructing you how to do it," the ambassador said and lifted his hand palm upwards for Eryn to take. Warmth immediately coursed along her arm and up to her head.

"I see how you have gone about this," he said. "You replaced the little coloured pieces - we call them pigments - with colours that your body can provide. This may turn out to be rather dangerous, though. If you use the colour of the blood, for example, long hair such as yours might take away too much of the blood's capacity to provide your body with air."

She nodded. "I have to admit that I felt rather dizzy after I had tried that. So you are a trained healer as well? You seem to know a lot about the body and its mechanisms."

"No, not really. I possess no more than the basic healing knowledge every user of magic in my country has to acquire."

Every user of magic possessed basic healing skills, she thought, amazed. She wondered what it would take to make the Order adopt that idea.

"The problem was that you took the complicated route here when an easier one would have sufficed. Colour is something that is perceived with the eyes, and thus it is the eye that needs to be tricked. We do not change the colour or nature of your hair, we just change the way the eye sees it by influencing the path which light takes to make it visible."

"The path of light?"

"Yes. The angle at which your hair reflects the light is determined by its structure and the colour elements inside. If we change the angle of reflection, your hair appears in whatever colour you wish."

"How do I do this?"

"By applying a shield with a very low energy level."

Eryn frowned. "A shield? But wouldn't this be visible?"

Ram'an shook his head. "No, it would not. You adapt it very closely to the hair." He took a strand of her long hair to hold it before her eyes and made her watch as he turned it from blond to the same dark shade as his own.

"Amazing," she breathed. "But the shield can't be too strong, or it would keep away water, dirt and whatever else, wouldn't it?"

"It would indeed," he confirmed. "This is why it needs to have different characteristics. The inside of the shield must be made to manipulate the light while the outside must be flexible enough to let external influences, such as water, make an impact."

She frowned. A shield with different capacities, just like the barrier she had invented that was meant to keep air inside and be flexible to attacks from the outside.

"How do I influence the shield to make the colour appear lighter or darker?" she asked intrigued.

"If you want to make it lighter, the light reflected from your hair must be stronger than the original light. If you would like it to appear darker, it needs to swallow some light instead of reflecting it. Depending on the natural shade of your hair this is a matter of experimentation, I am afraid."

"May I try now?"

"Please do."

She let go of his hand and closed her eyes to focus on her head, the shape of it and the hair that surrounded it. She created a small shield and adapted it neatly to the outline of her hair the way Enric had taught her. Then she fed it a little more energy and opened her eyes again.

She started laughing happily when she held a strand of now almost white hair up to her eyes. "I did it!"

"Yes, you are a very perceptive student," Ram'an smiled. "A pleasure for any teacher."

Closing her eyes again, she changed the colour to green, black, white, blue and finally purple. "What do you think, Vern? That would go nicely with my new robes," she chuckled.

"Show me now," the boy demanded eagerly.

It took him no more than a few minutes to learn, though adapting his shield precisely was more of a challenge for him as he had not had, unlike herself, the advantage of Enric's tutoring for that. Practising on the candlestick had been a useful preparation for moulding a shield to complicated outlines. When he opened his eyes again, his hair had turned to a glowing orange.

Eryn snickered. "This is so *you*! You finally found your style!"

He snorted. "Says the women with the purple hair to match her robes."

"Try my colour," she suggested and watched his hair turn brown after a moment. She nodded appreciatively. "Not bad. I have to say it suits you."

She closed her eyes and turned her hair blond again. When she looked up at Ram'an, she saw the slight frown he was not able to hide in time.

"Are we trying your patience too much, Ram'an?" she asked and tried to keep the tone light.

"No, not at all. I have to admit that it does pain me a little to think that you would learn this skill to hide the only visible sign of your origins, though."

"This is nothing permanent, I assure you. It is just what I will use to play a little trick on my companion tonight," she smirked.

"Lord Enric will not approve of this?" he asked casually.

"Probably not at first. But he will get used to it as I intend playing around with it for some time yet." She turned to Vern, who had started drumming his fingers on his thighs and then said to the ambassador, "You would not by any chance have a piece of paper and a pen somewhere to hand? From what I can see Vern here is eager to get something out of his head by drawing it. If we don't oblige him, he will chafe a little, I am afraid."

"A true artist, then," Ram'an said and rose. "The call of that talent is not something you chose to follow but that you agree to obey, as we say in my country." He went to a chest of drawers and, taking out a note pad and pen, returned to hand it to Vern who thanked him with noticeable relief in his voice. He began drawing at once.

Eryn and the ambassador both watched with interest the image that took shape under his eager hand. It was a single hair surrounded by a shield that made it appear darker from one side than from the other.

"Astonishing," the ambassador marvelled.

"He is," Eryn nodded. "He has taken one of the books my father used to own and exchanged all the paintings for his own. He gave it to me as a gift; it is the most amazing thing I own." She put a strand of hair that had fallen into his line of sight back behind his ear with an affectionate gesture he didn't even notice in his trance of drawing.

"You are very fond of the boy," Ram'an commented.

She looked up at him. "I am. He was the very first friend I made here in the city and he probably even saved my life once."

He leaned forward, intrigued. "I would very much like to hear this story."

She shook her head in regret and gave him a lopsided smile. "I am afraid I can't tell you about this at this point, for diplomatic reasons."

"Then I will not press you for it," the ambassador replied gallantly.

She studied him for a while, then said, "You know, I am not very good at this game of diplomacy - knowing when to say something or conceal it, or which questions not to ask. There are things that interest me greatly, and I suspect that you might possess this knowledge. I would like to ask you a few things, and you should either answer me or tell me openly if you are not permitted or inclined to do so. Would this be acceptable for you?"

He watched her for some time before he finally nodded. "Yes, we can do that. But only if you are not angry at me when I am not able to provide the answers you hope. Promise me this," he said and took her hand for emphasis.

"I promise." She straightened then. "How did you manage to cross the sea when all ships that were sent out from here were either destroyed or lost?"

"I am afraid I am not at liberty to share this information with you as yet," he replied and she could hear the regret in his voice at already having to refuse the very first question.

"Alright, I understand. Can you tell me if there was a war between your country and this kingdom three hundred years ago?"

"Yes."

She waited for a moment, then frowned. "Yes, you can tell me?"

"Yes, there was a war. Which my country won."

So Enric had been right. She wondered if it wouldn't be a better idea to share this information with Lord Tyront, Enric and Lord Poron, and hoped that the ambassador would agree to that.

"Ram'an, I would very much like to invite you to our quarters tomorrow evening to dine with me and a few of my colleagues. Would you be willing to share some of the details that you can give with all of us instead of just me?" She swallowed. "This does not of course mean that you are not invited unless you agree to share that information." Shaking her head at herself, she leaned back against the large cushions. "I am not very good at this, I am afraid. Let me try this again: I would be honoured if you would agree to be my guest tomorrow evening. And if you felt in the course of the evening comfortable enough to fill some of the gaps in our knowledge, I would very much appreciate that."

The ambassador chuckled at her attempts and nodded. "I gladly accept your invitation."

She smiled in relief. "Good. Can you promise me one thing? Please don't let anything I say start a war. Now that I know that we lost the last one, I am rather nervous about opening my mouth."

Ram'an leaned back and she heard him for the first time let out a loud, honest laugh.

CHAPTER 37

More History

She opened the door to their quarters carefully and quietly slipped inside. It was a tad later than she had planned, but Ram'an had insisted on emptying the bottle, it being bad luck according to his culture not to do this once it had been opened.

And then she had had to get Vern back home. He had not been so steady on his feet any more after his third glass, but luckily Orrin had already retired or she would without a doubt have received a nice tirade for returning his son to him half drunk. Somehow their relationship hadn't really changed that much, she mused. He still scolded her, she still endured it.

The door to Enric's study was left ajar and she could see the light spilling out through the gap. So he had been waiting for her, otherwise the door would have been closed to avoid interruptions.

She cursed silently when she stubbed her toe in the dark against the chest of drawers behind the door. That bloody thing had to go, she decided then and there. Or be moved to another spot. Or burned to ashes.

Her moves were not as coordinated as they used to be, so it seemed that she, too, was feeling the effects of the potent liquor from her home country.

She heard the chair in his study being shoved back and only moments later his dark silhouette was visible against the bright light shining behind him.

"Good evening," he said calmly. "I was expecting you back earlier. I was about to go over to Orrin and fetch you. I trust you had an enjoyable evening?"

Oh dear, she thought. That would have been a nasty surprise for him not to find her there when he had expected her to spend the evening with Vern.

"What? Oh yes - very nice evening, very nice," she babbled and made her way to the bedroom. Maybe she could get to bed and tell him in the morning about where she had spent the evening, instead of now. Not that this would change a lot. He would still be furious. But dealing with him after a good night's sleep seemed more appealing than having to do it here and now, when both her mental and physical coordination was a little slow.

"Stop right there." His voice was sharp and he lit the lamp while she stood as if frozen in place.

Shielding her eyes with one hand against the sudden brightness, she sighed. No such luck as a peaceful night before the storm.

He came closer, arms folded in front of him and looked down at her with narrowed eyes. "I see you somehow managed to figure out how to change your hair colour," he remarked calmly. "Would you care to elaborate?"

Her hands flew up to her hair. Dash, she had forgotten about *that* little thing. So the plan of just slipping into bed wouldn't have worked anyway with her newly changed blond mane.

"That is a funny thing, you know," she said slowly. "It seems I have been going about this the wrong way. It is done with a shield instead of really changing the colour itself."

"And how did you manage to acquire this very helpful method of changing your approach?" he enquired in a voice that was much too friendly. Even when he really was friendly, his voice didn't sound like that. Not good.

"Why don't we talk about this tomorrow? I really am tired, you know." She yawned for good measure and made to turn away, but his next words stopped her.

"I have agents that follow the ambassador," he said calmly.

Damn - so he knew exactly where she had spent the evening and had just tested her with the little remark about picking her up from Orrin's quarters. And she had failed miserably, of course, as he now knew that she had had no intention of confessing where she had really been. Well, not right at this moment. Later. Tomorrow morning. Very probably tomorrow noon. Before dinner, at the latest.

"Vern was there with me," she said quickly as if mentioning this little detail would work like a miraculous screen against the displeasure he was hiding so well, but that was doubtlessly simmering underneath his smooth exterior. But thanks to his spies, or agents, as he liked to call them, he would have been aware of that little fact already.

"I see," he nodded in pretend contemplation, "and you would consider a fifteen-year-old boy sufficient protection against a magician about whose strength or abilities we are still unclear?" He leaned closer and sniffed once. "Especially as he seems to have given you something to drink that does smell rather more potent than your usual choice of beverage."

"I thought it would have been rather impolite to refuse, considering diplomacy and all..." she said weakly and wondered if she was imagining the fire in these blue eyes that normally seemed as clear as water.

"Diplomacy. It was very thoughtful of you to take this into consideration when entering a stranger's quarters against my express wishes."

She wondered how he managed to appear taller whenever he was angry. A neat trick. She doubted that he would teach her or even admit to using it, though. Why give up such a formidable advantage, especially as they seemed to stumble from one disagreement into the next and he could use it against her so often?

"Why are you staring at my legs, if I may ask? Am I boring you?" His voice had taken on a dangerous edge.

She looked up guiltily from checking if he was by any chance standing on his toes to make himself taller.

"What? No! I was just..." She stopped herself in time. Putting words to it sounded too crazy and she would admit to her straying thoughts, which would probably infuriate him even further. Why was it so hard to stay focussed?

"You were just what? Trying to follow my words through the haze of alcohol?"

She laughed too loudly. "How very absurd of you to say a thing like that!"

He rolled his eyes and smirked. "I find it impossible to remain mad with you right now. You are adorable when you are tipsy, but I would very much prefer you to be in my presence when achieving this state next time."

A grin started to spread across her face. "You can't be angry at me because I am too cute right now?"

"So much for trying to have a serious conversation with you," he sighed. "Can I at least impress on you that it would save me a lot of worrying if you didn't go to his quarters just like that? Meet him in public, if you must, but don't go into his quarters again. No more being alone with him where I can't have an eye on you. And no, I don't count Vern," he added when she opened her mouth to protest.

She smiled. "Oh, then I have something you will just love! It meets all your requirements." Using her fingers, she listed, "I won't be alone with him, you can observe me all the time and I won't be alone with him."

"You said that last one twice," he commented with a raised brow. "You either wanted to emphasise it desperately or you really need to lie down."

"Emphasis," she said quickly.

"So, what is it you wanted to tell me that I will love?" he enquired patiently.

"We will be having guests for dinner tomorrow! The ambassador has accepted my cordial invitation to dine with us, Lord Tyront and Lord Poron. Isn't that great?"

He covered his eyes for a moment. "Just splendid. I assume you haven't asked Tyront and Lord Poron yet?"

"No," she admitted, "I suppose you should invite them. Tomorrow. Seems a bit late for that right now. I hope they have time. Would be a shame if they didn't." Beaming up at him, she slung her arms around his waist. "I think I am getting good at this diplomacy business. Maybe I can be an ambassador one day. Or is it ambassadora? Ambassadress?"

"Yes," he commented, suppressing a cold shiver, "that would certainly provide for interesting times. Come to bed now, ambassadora, you need to get up early tomorrow. And as you are about to host your first dinner party without any time at all to prepare for it, it will be a long day for you. Very long. Trust me." He smiled at her slightly alarmed look and gently guided her towards the bedroom.

* * *

When Enric returned from his meeting and lunch invitation at Tyront's place, he entered what seemed like mayhem at first glance, but soon turned out to be the kind of organised chaos that preceded social gatherings. He had at times beheld it from a distance, but never really been involved at such close proximity.

Junar was standing at the centre of the room, sending servants running with a mix of spoken commands and pointed fingers that gave the impression as if she was conducting an odd kind of orchestra that produced rustlings of cloth and clatterings of tableware instead of music.

Eryn stormed out of his study, holding two envelopes in her hand and smiling triumphantly. "They both accepted and will bring their companions!" She grinned when she spotted Enric. "You'd better stay out of the way," she warned, "or Junar might send you on an errand. She really is good at this kind of stuff." Then she frowned. "Oh dear, is it so late already? I need to leave now for my appointment with the builder."

"I'll accompany you," Enric said quickly. If he had the choice of staying in the middle of this or fleeing without appearing cowardly, he knew which option to take. Junar, however, was obviously not fooled for a moment if he had to judge from her grin.

"You think I can't handle this alone?" Eryn asked suspiciously.

"No. I am just interested in what you are planning." And in getting out of here before somebody wrapped him in a length of fabric or made him polish something shiny, he added silently.

She shrugged. "As you wish." Then she slapped the flat of her hand against her forehead. "Ah! I almost forgot the plans. Wait a moment - I need to fetch them." After Eryn had disappeared into the guest room, where she still kept her books and other paper-work, Junar looked over to him and gave Enric a knowing smile.

He narrowed his eyes at her. "If you tell on me I will make you suffer for it."

"Oh, but you are already," she replied. "You are making me clothe her."

At that moment Eryn returned, waving a bundle of rolled-up papers triumphantly above her head. She stopped to look at each of them in puzzlement. "What did I miss?"

"Nothing," Enric said and put an arm around her shoulders to guide her out of the parlour into the corridor, grabbing their cloaks in passing and flashing a final warning glance at Junar. "Absolutely nothing." When they walked along the corridor towards the staircase leading them out of the palace, he said, "I am impressed you have plans ready for this appointment."

"Unlike my usual unorganised approach to things?" she asked with her brow raised, wincing only slightly at the memory that without Vern she wouldn't even have thought about bringing any plans, let alone drawing them.

"No," he said. "I just didn't think you had any expertise in this area. Good thing that Vern had some time yesterday afternoon, isn't it?"

She stopped to glare at him. "You have to stop following my every step, damn you! I am not a prisoner any more, I am a free woman and can do whatever I want and go wherever I want! You can whistle back your spies. If you don't, I will just do whatever crazy things come to my mind to make you pale when you read their reports."

"Relax, my love," he said and took her hand. He held on to it when she tried to pull it out of his grip. "I have no agents at your heels. For the moment. I met up with Orrin at Tyront's quarters in the morning. He told me about it."

"Oh," she said lamely, feeling foolish at throwing her unjustified insinuations at him. Assuming that he would receive information through the usual, socially accepted channels like a normal person hadn't even crossed her mind.

They reached the building and looked around for the builder she was supposed to be meeting here.

"He is late," Eryn commented and looked the façade up and down. "I was thinking of having the outside painted purple, in the new healers' colour."

"Well, that would make it instantly recognisable for a start," he replied guardedly.

"You don't like the idea?" she frowned in disappointment.

"Purple seems a little bold, if you ask me. I would think that quiet advertising is more suited to the profession of healing than shouting it out like that. How about painting it white and adding only a few touches or some writing in purple?"

She considered his words for a few moments, then smiled. "You know, maybe it was not such a bad idea to bring you. You have your useful moments."

"You didn't bring me. I brought myself."

"Yes, because you panicked in the face of decoration. Don't think I didn't notice," she grinned and then pointed to the stocky man who came bustling up the street towards them, clearly horrified at the thought of letting such important people wait. "Look who's finally turning up."

The man skidded to a halt in front of them and bowed. It took him several seconds, however, to straighten again while panting.

"My Lady, Lord Enric," he gasped out and Eryn watched in fascination how his shoulders extended and collapsed with every deep breath he took and released.

The magicians waited for him to regain his breath enough to talk about the project at hand, and Eryn went ahead inside the building. She used a little magic to clear an old wooden table of the thick layer of dust and made it settle on the floor instead. Then she spread the first of her rolled up sheets, pinning down the four corners with stones to keep it from curling up again.

The builder looked down and nodded. "Nice to see that you have come prepared. That will make it a lot easier. This is the ground floor, obviously."

She nodded. "Yes, exactly. This is a plan of what it currently looks like. And this," she said and pulled out another paper roll from under her arm and almost dropped several others, which were caught just in time by Enric, "is what it is supposed to look like afterwards."

The second plan had some of the walls removed and doors and windows where there were presently none.

"I see," the builder commented. "I need to have a look at some of the walls first. I am afraid that we can't remove the one in the centre, it is a load-bearing wall and without it the building would collapse."

Enric watched her change her plans several times and take a stroll through each floor with the builder, enjoying the way she discussed with, contradicted and learned from the man. At one point she pulled out a pen from somewhere inside her tunic and made notes and new lines on the plan.

He stayed in the background, not acknowledging the builder's initial attempts to include him in the conversation, letting her do all the talking.

When they left the building again a full two and a half hours later, she seemed exhausted and dusty, but happy and very pleased with herself.

"The whole thing should be ready in no more than two months! I can't wait finally to do something here!" she rejoiced once the builder had left them and they were back on their way to their quarters.

Yes, he thought, and he would make sure they were finished. Builders were not generally known for adhering to time schedules, but Eryn would probably have to encounter quite a few challenges and defeats along the way to her goal, and this would not become one of them if he had any say in it. His occasional visits to the construction site would undoubtedly increase the speed of the work a little.

"You handled this very well, I must say. I really look forward to seeing what it will look like when it's finished," he said and took her hand.

"So am I." She pursed her lips. "There is something I have been thinking about. How much is still left of the League of Apothecaries? Not all of them participated in the attempt at killing me, did they?"

"No. Three out of seven did. That leaves about half of the League intact, though their reputation has suffered drastically after what has happened. People are reluctant to be seen to associate with or buy from them; they don't want to anger the Order," he explained and observed her unhappy reaction.

"So the ones who didn't participate are paying the price now?"

"No, I would not put it like that. They have not been treating their patients very well for quite some time and are now more or less paying the price for that. You know what they did to the herb gatherer who sold to you in the backstreets."

She exhaled and closed her eyes. The herb gatherer. She had completely forgotten about him. She had intended at least to heal his injuries.

"Is everything alright?" Enric asked worriedly.

"Yes. It's just that I was thinking about the herb gatherer and that I had wanted to heal him after what he has been through. I'd completely forgotten about him until you mentioned him just now!"

He chuckled. "Don't feel bad about it. Young Vern has already taken care of that."

"He has?" Pride warmed her from within and made her smile. "He is a fabulous lad, isn't he? So unbelievably thoughtful, and at this young age. He will make a splendid healer."

"Yes," Enric nodded. "I think he will. I am glad for him and the people around him that he has the chance to do this instead of becoming a warrior or administrator. It would have been a great loss of talent and compassion."

Eryn looked up at him, touched by his sincere words of appreciation for both her closest friend and the healing profession.

"That means a lot to me, thank you," she said quietly.

He looked down at her and lifted her hand to kiss it. "I do enjoy it that something I said finally affects you in a positive way. It almost pains me to have to hurry you on to avoid being late to your own dinner party."

She shook her head in wonder. "My own dinner party. If you had told me this half a year ago I would have jabbed you with that wooden stick Orrin made me train with."

"You would have tried at least. At that time you hardly realised which end was supposed to go where," he quipped and earned himself the thrust of her elbow into his side.

"I do now. So you better take care."

"You wouldn't do it now. You have come to like me."

"Hardly," she snorted. "I barely tolerate you."

"Charming," he commented and picked a small wooden splinter out of her now dusty blond hair. "Is there a chance you can change your hair colour back to what it used to be? Oddly enough, I have come to realise that I am not into blond women."

She laughed and changed her hair back, smug that it didn't take her longer than a moment. "Then you are a very, very lucky man to have found me, considering how very unlikely it is to encounter women with any other hair colour in this Kingdom."

* * *

She stood in the bedroom, a large white towel wrapped around her body after her bath and looked doubtfully at the dress Junar was holding in front of her. The colour was a bold, distinctive dark red and the cut looked suspiciously scanty in the upper chest department.

"I can't help but thinking that this does seem a tad... flamboyant, don't you think?" Eryn said carefully.

"And why shouldn't it? You have the complexion for it, and you are entertaining a man from a land where bold colours are apparently very common. You just have to look at his own clothes," Junar said and pointedly kept holding out the dress for Eryn to take.

"Is there an alternative in case I can't stand wearing it because it makes me feel like a bottle of wine?"

The seamstress rolled her eyes. "Shut up and try it on. When have you ever not felt comfortable in any of my creations, you ungrateful thing?"

"When my breasts kept threatening to jump out on the evening of the ball," Eryn retorted dryly.

"Yes, and that particular evening earned you a very influential and attractive companion, unless I am mistaken. So I don't see any reason for complaints here. Now, will you take that towel off now or do I have to wrestle you for it?"

Eryn smiled. "This is the moment when I would have expected Enric to appear and make an inappropriate remark."

"I am far ahead of you," his amused voice came from the door, where he was leaning against the door frame, grinning unabashedly. "And I doubt that there even *is* an appropriate remark to a statement like that."

"She refuses to put on the dress," Junar complained to him. "Again," she added with a cutting glare at her friend. "Can't you knock her out for me so I can dress her recumbent, defenceless form? It really would save me a lot of trouble. And nerves. And time. Have I mentioned nerves?"

"I do understand your sentiment," Enric replied seriously, "but she does react rather badly every time I do it. I try to resort to knockings out only in emergencies. If she isn't dressed within the next ten minutes, I shall declare it an emergency and will comply with your request."

Eryn cursed and took the dress out of Junar's hands none too gently.

"Careful," her friend warned, "If you rip it, I will sew it back together while you are wearing it. And I will make sure to accidentally poke you with my needle as often as possible."

"Out, the two of you!"

"You will need my help - it needs to be laced up at the back," Junar replied.

"Then out with *you*, Enric. I don't need an audience. Make sure the wine is the right temperature, the plates are clean or whatever else could go wrong is fixed."

"Everything is perfect," he said. "The only thing not ready and a potential danger to the evening's success is yourself, my love." But he turned and closed the door behind him to leave the women to their last-minute preparations.

Looking around in his now very altered parlour he was at a loss what to do. On the rare occasions when he had invited other men to spend an evening with him, this had been a lot less formal. They arrived, a bottle of something tasty was opened and the evening was usually uncomplicated and relaxed. He had of course been invited to occasions where women had been involved in the past, but had never hosted one, as his prior adventures with the other sex had been nowhere serious enough for any undertaking such as that.

He sighed in relief when he heard the knock at the door he easily recognised as Tyront's: assertive and self-confident. He was a little too early, but that suited Enric just fine.

He opened the door and beckoned Tyront in, looking slightly inquisitive when he didn't spot Vyril.

"She will join us a bit later. She is still busy with makeup and otherwise decorating herself," Tyront explained. When he stepped inside and looked around, he clucked his tongue. His gaze wandered over the colourful fabrics that decorated the windows, the settees, chairs, dressers and even the large dinner table that had been set in the centre of the room instead of the usual assortment of smaller tables that were normally spread across the parlour.

"Eryn did all this?" he marvelled.

Enric laughed at the thought. "No, she can hardly be pressed into letting herself be dressed up nicely, let alone decorating an entire room. Let's say she has a lucky hand in choosing her friends."

At that moment the bedroom door opened and Eryn stepped out, desperately trying to pull up the front of the dress to cover more of her bulging cleavage, closely followed by Junar, frantically attempting to fix the last matching dark red ribbon in Eryn's braided hair.

"Will you stop for a moment if it's not too much to ask? I am trying to make you look like the lady we want the world to believe you are - despite all evidence to the contrary! And if you don't change that hair colour back this instant, I am going to wallop you until I finally manage to knock loose some sense…"

Both women looked up at the same time and right into Lord Tyront's completely astonished face. Junar's own face turned a bright scarlet, while Eryn was torn between instinctively hiding her front and bursting out laughing at her friend's reaction to so unexpectedly facing the Order's leader with what even a very liberal minded person would consider a more than inappropriate dialogue between a seamstress and her client.

"Lord Tyront," Eryn smiled and bowed, observing that it took him several seconds to recover enough to reciprocate the greeting.

"Eryn," Enric sighed. "Change your hair back, please. Orange is just not the colour to go with your dress. Trust me on this."

She grinned and watched Tyront's eyes go wide when she changed it back to her usual lush brown in an instant.

"My newest trick. Do you like it? Lucky for you I did not manage to figure out how to do it while you were holding me prisoner, or you would never have managed to stop me from getting away from here."

Tyront simply blinked several times, still absorbed in taking in the details of her attire. The cut of the dress was not elaborate, but covered just the right amount of skin to seem neither too revealing, nor overly prim. Simple lines accentuated her curves, revealing some and cleverly hinting at others that were concealed. The fabric shimmered slightly in the lamp light and lent her skin a warm radiant glow. Her eyes seemed a tad darker than usual, doubtlessly thanks to the efforts of the rather flushed looking woman at her side who seemed to be in charge of making her presentable.

When he looked over to Enric, he noted that the younger man's gaze had shifted to his companion's cleavage where it remained for a while, making him smile appreciatively. The ambassador would have a good grip on is eyes and wouldn't let them wander to where Enric would not tolerate them, he hoped.

"I am leaving now," Junar muttered to Eryn. "Everything is ready and even you won't make a mess of this if you let the servants do their work." She bowed to Tyront and Enric and left.

"Lady Eryn," Tyront smiled. "You look very beautiful tonight. I have to say that dressing up does agree with you, very much so."

She lifted a brow. "How unfortunate then that *I* do not agree with dressing up at all."

"Indeed? That is a rather unusual attitude for a woman in my experience."

"I am not used to wearing dresses like this. They are not made to make moving around comfortable for the wearer but rather to present a woman as nice to look at for others. I have never really considered myself as much of an ornament. I don't see *you* showing off any interesting attributes for *my* benefit with your vestments," she complained and then looked around. "Is it possible that you forgot your companion?"

"She will be with us shortly," Tyront replied, grateful for the change of topic. "I was very pleased to receive your invitation for today, Lady Eryn. Though it is customary to give your guests a little more than half a day's notice. It usually does increase the number of people who will be available," he added, a touch reproachfully.

She shrugged. "It worked out fine though, didn't it? You and Lord Poron are both free. And as this is an occasion that includes the Ambassador, you would probably have found a way to somehow reschedule any other prior engagements."

Tyront just replied by way of a certain look and turned to Enric. "Your companion is rather demanding of other people's time, so it seems."

"Don't look at me, I learned about this sometime last night when she came home intoxicated from another man's quarters. She is no more considerate of my time than of yours."

"Are you two done whining? Let's not forget why we are here, shall we? Surely not because I am in such great favour of dressing up. It's because we have the chance to learn about a few things of immense interest to you. So stop complaining about your precious time when for once can do something useful with it."

"Now, you wait a moment, *Lady* Eryn..." Tyront began with a lifted index finger and then stopped himself and breathed out to steady himself. "This is not the moment to teach you manners."

She smiled. "Good. Because there is another thing I would like to address now that I have both of you here. It is about the apothecaries."

"The ones the King had executed?" Tyront frowned.

"No, the ones who were not involved. I would like to negotiate some possible cooperation with them and I imagine I'd need the Order's approval for that."

"Yes, that you would," Enric nodded. "What kind of cooperation?"

"I want them to work for me, or rather for the healers. They could take care of preparing medicines. Only after they have been trained to meet the standards I expect, of course. I think it would make more sense to use the healers I have for healing instead of mixing herbs, provided others in addition to Vern are willing to join me."

"They might not be very thrilled about the prospect of working for you. The reason why their colleagues are dead is the threat your plans posed and still do pose to them," Tyront pointed out. "They would have to give up their independence in more than one way by following your orders and losing their main source of income, namely what they consider healing services."

Eryn folded her arms. "I know. I like to think that I am not normally cruelly inclined, but my opinion of their healing services is very low and I would like them to stop offering them rather sooner than later. They do more harm than good. I can't guarantee them riches, but a steady income, which is more than they can count on without cooperating with me. I will probably drive them out of business sooner or later anyway, especially as they will hardly dare to intimidate the herb gatherers any more now that I am in the Order. If they know what is good for them, that is."

"Then your willingness to include them in your plans shows a noble purpose. I don't have any objections from the Order's point of view. Enric?" Tyront turned to his second.

"None from my point of view, either. But I would like to be there when you talk to them. It should remind them that the Order supports you in this matter."

Eryn looked at him and frowned. "That should be self-evident when I ask them to meet me in the palace and wear my robes. You are aware that it is not necessary to protect me from them anymore, aren't you? I think it undermines my credibility when you turn up everywhere I am meant to do something. So I would ask you to let me do this alone."

Enric folded his arms. "You don't know how they will react to your offer. So no."

Tyront sighed. "Yes. You will let her do this alone, Enric. She is not a child and if she wants to be taken seriously you can't stand behind her glowering all the time. And she is not exactly completely defenceless. She is a strong magician and can shield herself against whatever they could throw at her." He looked away from a displeased Enric back to her. "Your trick with the hair colour is very impressive, by the way. Can I prevail upon you to share this knowledge with the Order as well?"

She smiled, clearly satisfied with her little victory over Enric. "Sure. It's really simple, especially as you already know the principle of my barrier. It's no more than a shield with different characteristics. The outside lets external influences penetrate, the inside changes the way the light is reflected..." Her voice trailed off and her eyes widened.

Both men watched her when she hit her forehead with her flat palm and exchanged a perplexed look when she started muttering with closed eyes. "A shield with two different characteristics! How stupid can I be? Really now! Stupid, stupid, stupid, stupid!" She opened her eyes again, taking Enric's hand and laying it on her abdomen. "Remove my internal shield."

He looked at her indulgently. "No."

"What do you mean, no?" she cried out in annoyance. "Come on! Hurry, before our guests arrive! I need to find out something."

"I will not remove the shield as long as our foreign guests are staying in the city."

She wrung her hands impatiently. "This is absolutely ridiculous! Ram'an is hardly interested in ravaging me!"

"Ram'an, is it?" Enric smiled coldly. "On very familiar terms with him, aren't you?"

"Enric!" She took a deep breath. "This is not about the ambassador, but about my trying to see if I have just understood how the shield inside me works. Would you just remove it now or do I have to find another way?"

"Another way?" The threat in his voice was unmistakeable. "What other way? Asking Ram'an and hoping that he is strong enough to remove it?"

"No, you bloody fool! Asking the man standing next to you who definitely *is* able to do it," she hissed back and dropped his hand. "Lord Tyront, I request the removal of the shield inside me. It was placed there by my father and was increased in strength by Lord Enric without my permission. He has thus violated my right to be in charge of my own body. This might have been acceptable while I was a prisoner, but as I am now free and a member of the Order, I can no longer tolerate this and ask you to rectify this matter."

"Tyront?" Enric asked calmly.

The older man sighed and shook his head. "Very well, then. I was wondering when I would first get perched between the two of you when you disagree on something. It was sooner than I had thought." He straightened. "Lady Eryn, I grant your request. Enric, your need to protect her is admirable and understandable, but not to the degree that limits her personal freedom." He held out his hand and Eryn took it gladly, soon after feeling the shield inside her diminish in strength and finally disappear. She stood still for a moment with closed eyes to take in the new sensation of having after so many years for the first time no quietly pulsating source of energy inside her.

"Thank you," she said and nodded to Tyront, avoiding looking at Enric.

Closing her eyes again, she concentrated on where the shield had been and carefully started building a new one, adapting its outline to the complicated structure of the organs it was meant to protect. She waited after it was finished, trying to determine if it felt right. A few minor corrections of the shape here and there, a slight change in the degree of permeability, then she opened her eyes again, a wide grin on her face.

"I did it! The shield is in place, the functionality of the organs is intact, and the flow of everything that is meant to get in and out works perfectly. I can't believe I've figured it out - after all these years!"

"So your shield is intact again the way it used to be?" Enric asked.

"Mostly. There is one little detail I have not been able to figure out, though: how to connect it to my life force. So in the case of my falling unconscious, it would disappear again as it would then no longer be under my active control."

"Great," Enric commented unnerved. "The one thing that made it reliable protection, and you just took that advantage away." He took her hand and held on to it when she tried to pull it away with an irritated look. She felt him send warm energy to her abdomen and felt the level of the shield rise again. And again it was out of her control.

"No, seriously?" she scolded him. "Again? I thought I had just pointed out that you doing this violates my rights as a free woman! And you don't even know how strong the Ambassador is! If he really has any intentions and he is stronger than you, it wouldn't even help! So you might be treating me like a helpless child for no reason at all!"

He just looked down at her coolly, not at all impressed by her tirade.

At this moment somebody knocked at the door, causing a look of immense relief on Tyront's face. A servant came out of the guest room where the utensils for the evening were stored and admitted Lord Poron, his companion and Vyril.

"Lady Eryn," Vyril smiled and stretched out both hands to take Eryn's. "What a beautiful dress! And the parlour looks fabulous! Very impressive!"

Eryn forced herself to smile and returned the compliment, saying how very nice Vyril looked in her pale green dress with the matching jewellery.

Then Lord Poron stepped forward, greeted her warmly and introduced her to his own companion, Aurna, a woman his own age whose wrinkles realigned appealingly when she smiled.

The servant returned to open the door again when another tapping was audible.

All eyes turned when Ambassador Ram'an entered, and Eryn smiled and walked towards him, letting him take her hands and holding them to her sides to take in the sight of her.

"Ah, Lady Eryn, the sight of you would heal a blind man," he sighed and his delighted smile lost some of its warmth when Enric stepped beside her to take her hand out of his and put it on his arm.

"Ambassador," he said politely. "It is a pleasure to welcome you to our place."

"The pleasure is mine, Lord Enric," Ram'an replied and bowed.

"May I introduce you to our other guests, Ram'an," Eryn said, eager to put some distance between the two of them.

She introduced first Vyril, then Lord Poron and Aurna, then nodded to a servant to serve drinks.

When they raised their glasses to toast, Eryn spoke, "To the sharing of knowledge - for it is one of the few things that is not diminished in size by so doing, but increased."

Enric took her hand and lead her to the table, motioning for the Ambassador to take a seat at the centre instead of next to the hostess at the head on the right side as Eryn had intended. She glowered at him and hissed so that only he could hear, "This is a blatant demonstration of distrust!"

"Good," Enric whispered back and pulled out her chair at the head of the table, "I had not intended for it to be a subtle one."

Clothing her face in smiles, she sank onto the chair and calmed her mind by imagining ways of paying him back for this later.

To Eryn's great relief the dinner conversation went smoothly. Ram'an praised the food, asking about ingredients he couldn't identify and talked about common herbs in his home country.

When they had finished the last course and leaned back, Eryn knew it was time to subtly direct the conversation towards the topic she had wanted to talk about all evening.

"Ambassador Ram'an, I would like to thank you very much for joining us tonight. Your presence is a great pleasure, and now we hope that you will also grant us the chance to learn from you about ourselves."

"Eryn," he said with his warm smile that seemed so familiar to her already, omitting the title to Enric's dismay. "It would be my honour to share with you what I can."

"Thank you very much, Ram'an," she said, returning his smile. "When I asked you yesterday if there had ever been a war between our countries, you told me that there was one indeed. One we lost, as it seems."

The others at the table remained motionless, eagerly waiting for the ambassador to speak.

"That is correct. It was three hundred years ago, a great war that diminished the population of both countries considerably. We did win, but oh, at what price! It was a narrow victory, and one that has made us very eager to avoid another confrontation with your kingdom any time soon."

"Then I assume you caused the destruction of our knowledge through our historic records to ensure this?" Enric asked mildly.

"Not destruction, Lord Enric. My ancestors took them to the other side of the sea and made use of them. There was a great century of progress in science and art that followed the war. People were eager to rebuild what had been destroyed and included a lot of what they learned from your books to achieve this. Even nowadays the influence of your architecture from that time is still visible. I realised this only when I arrived here, marvelling at some very recognisable structures in your older buildings."

"How is it possible that there are no records about the war left here in the kingdom?" Eryn enquired. "I mean, even if you took away most of the books and documents, wouldn't people back then somehow have preserved knowledge of the war for their descendants?"

Ram'an nodded. "You are right, this is exactly what they did. Or tried to do for quite a while. Magicians kept returning here to destroy whatever records had been made and blocked memories to keep people from passing on the knowledge orally. This was intended to prevent any acts of retaliation. When after several decades the knowledge of the war had more or less dwindled away among the population, we withdrew and have stayed away ever since. Until now."

Eryn nodded with satisfaction. Who would have thought that she would get an actual answer to that question only days after pondering it with Enric in this very room?

"We still have some remainders - hints of old knowledge, or parts of it, around us. Like magical music. We can play it still, but we have lost the understanding of how it is created. Would this be one of the things your ancestors learned from us and, by any chance, passed on?" Lord Poron asked.

"Oh yes. Music is a very important part of my own culture. Well, it is nowadays. It was practically a primitive collection of random sounds before the war compared to what we have now. We have developed the method further and found a lot of different uses for it apart from the very… rudimentary ones."

"Rudimentary?" Eryn asked.

"Such as seduction," Enric smiled and took her hand to kiss it, making her blush in embarrassment and silently curse him for bringing this up in front of their guests.

"Yes," Ram'an confirmed. "There is that. We have managed to change the nature of the spells and now use it to increase the growth of plants, for healing, teaching..."

"For healing?" Eryn interrupted him and leaned forward eagerly, making Enric frown at the insights she granted unthinkingly.

"Indeed. Music is one of two ways we use to heal or make healing more efficient without actually needing a magical healer present."

"What is the second way?"

"Herbs."

"I see," she nodded. "I, too, use them for medicines. But mostly after the actual treatment, not instead of it. Sometimes they take too long to take full effect."

The ambassador studied her. "Not if you imbue the medicines with magic."

Eryn straightened. "You imbue medicines with magic?" she whispered and stared unseeingly at the table cloth, imagining what possibilities that would open up. Those who were too ill to come to her could be sent medication that would nevertheless improve their state reliably without her being forced to leave the healing centre and thus neglect all other patients.

"I can see that the idea intrigues you," he chuckled. "I am not a professional healer myself, as you know, but I can show you the basic principle of how to go about it."

Eryn's rapid and deep intake of breath drew several pairs of eyes to her chest, and she let it out quickly, her face flushing red again. "I don't know what to say, Ram'an. I have no idea how to repay you for this, and yet I can't bring myself to reject your offer."

"Then do not reject it, my dear Eryn. Let me share this knowledge with you. The pleasure of seeing you appreciate this so much is compensation enough for me," the ambassador said gallantly.

"This is very generous of you," Tyront said, kicking Enric lightly under the table to remind him to keep his expression neutral when it threatened to show his disapproval all too clearly. "Lady Eryn has informed me that you are currently not in a position to share with us how you managed to cross the sea that presents an insurmountable obstacle for us in making contact to people beyond our natural borders. So I will not press you for it."

"I thank you very much for that, Lord Tyront." Ram'an inclined his head.

"Of course. Are you permitted to tell us more about the war? Do you know what started it back then?"

"I do have a version of the truth for you, but it does not make your kingdom appear in a very good light, I am afraid. Just consider that as the victors are the ones to write the history books, they are eager to make themselves appear as honourable as possible to generations to come, those who will one day look back and judge their actions."

"Please do go on."

"Lore has it that you attacked our country for mineral deposits in our southern mountains. You sent ships in great number, but the climate beyond the mountains was hard to cope with for your warriors. Their heavy armour was too much for the drastic difference in temperature, which nobody had anticipated. The mountains, you see, rise high enough to block the clouds, and thus the humidity, from the sea entering our country from the southeast. Thus temperatures on the other side are considerably higher than where your soldiers had landed with their fleet."

"And this unforeseen obstacle, the high temperature, was what ensured your victory?" Lord Poron asked and added, "Would you mind terribly if I took some notes? My memory is not what it used to be, and I would be devastated if I forgot anything you told us."

"By all means, please do so. I am happy to see that you take such great interest in our common past, even though it was not a friendly one." He waited for a servant to provide Lord Poron with a notepad and pen before he answered his first question. "The temperature was one of two factors that benefited us. The second was a great storm that destroyed more than half of your fleet laying at anchor behind the mountains."

"So you managed to defeat the attackers on your home soil," Enric said. "Then you came here, I assume, to make sure we wouldn't threaten you again anytime soon?"

"Yes, that is exactly what we think was done. It was decided that we needed to prepare for such attacks in the future to avoid falling prey to an ambitious conqueror. So we came here, not encountering much resistance as most of your warriors had already fallen on our land. We took most of your books with us, thus ensuring that passing on knowledge would not be so easy for you in the future, slowing down your progress considerably. We did two more things that do seem rather cruel in hindsight," he admitted reluctantly. "I am not sure it is a very good idea to tell you of those now, as I fear it might endanger our present friendly but fragile relationship. But I see that you are still searching for the pieces of your past we took away from you, and I hope you will see the revelation of these truths as the sign of goodwill they are meant as."

Tyront, Enric and Lord Poron exchanged a glance, then Tyront spoke, "We would be very interested in hearing what you have to say, Ambassador."

Ram'an thought for a few moments, clearly considering how to put words to it. "The reason why Lady Eryn is such a great asset to you, one you wish to protect from being taken away from here, is undoubtedly that she must be the very first female magician you have encountered in this country since the end of the war." He waited for Tyront's nod before he continued. "Your magical abilities, you see, were quite a shock to my people according to the diaries of that time. Our primary aim was thus to rob you of that advantage. One step was to take away your records, the other was to make sure that your magical abilities were not passed on to succeeding generations."

"How would you have been able to achieve a thing like that?" Enric asked with narrowed eyes.

"We tried to put a spell on your entire kingdom to make it impossible for new-born children to ever develop magical abilities. This, however, did not quite work out the way our ancestors had planned. They managed to block magical abilities only in the females. This is why you do not have female magicians in your kingdom. The effect of the incomplete spell still seems as potent today as it was then. An interesting side effect of this was that after a few generations all different colouring in your hair had disappeared. This is why shades of blond are all you have left now."

"What about the women who still had magical strength after the war? Did the spell take it away from them, too?" Vyril spoke for the first time.

"No," the ambassador replied. "That was why they were taken to our capital city."

"What happened to them there?" Eryn gulped, keeping her gaze pinned on her empty glass, dreading the answer.

"They were held as slaves mostly, I am afraid," Ram'an said quietly. "They were less civilised times then, you must understand. We long ago abolished this practice and have come to value our own freedom as well as respect other peoples'."

"So our number of magicians must have decreased considerably without any women to pass on the ability," Lord Poron said after several seconds of uncomfortable silence.

"Not as much as was to be expected, interestingly enough," the ambassador said. "It seems that your numbers have indeed decreased, but the general strength of the individual magicians appears to have increased."

"How would you be able to judge that, with all due respect?" Enric enquired with a raised brow.

"I watched a few training lessons your warriors had in the morning. As they have them out in the open I assumed that it was no violation for me to watch them?"

"No, not at all," Tyront confirmed. "Go on."

"The shields they use, the strength of their attacks and the speed I witnessed was rather surprising. I mentioned to Lady Eryn that I myself am considered one of the strongest magicians in my country. I have started wondering how I would compare here."

"But you must have very strong magicians yourself," Enric pointed out. "When we tested Eryn we were very surprised at her considerable powers."

Ram'an smiled at her. "I imagine you would. Lady Eryn is the progeny of not only one, but two very powerful magical blood lines. The fact that she is only third after Lord Tyront and yourself does say a lot."

Eryn swallowed. This sounded like she was the final result of a breeding programme. She felt uneasy, wondering if this was the reason why they had sent somebody to the kingdom: to return to them what was meant to secure the next generation of power in the families. But would the ambassador be sharing this information so willingly if this was his real agenda? Hardly. She hoped.

"When we first met, Ram'an," she said, desperate to change the topic, "you said you had met me before as a child. I assume that it was not just on a single occasion or you would hardly remember me after all this time."

"You assume correctly. Both our families are politically active and thus also in close social contact, have been ever since. So I do remember the rather serious healer who was so reluctant to sit with his companion's friends and talk about matters of state. And his little daughter, who was so eager to stay up late when she was supposed to go to bed instead. I am three years older than you, and I remember feeling very smug and grown up because I was allowed to stay up when your mother fought battles to make you stay in bed." He grinned at the memory.

All eyes were on her, Enric and Tyront both smiling, obviously having no trouble whatsoever imagining her as a rebellious child fighting the injustice of being sent to bed.

CHAPTER 38

Breaking the Barrier

Eryn closed the door after their guests had left and leaned against it. Enric stood right next to her and looked down at her with a thoughtful smile.

"You did well, my love. And I think Lord Poron will not be able to sleep for quite a few nights with all the things he has learned tonight," he chuckled. "I have to admit that some of them were quite a surprise for me as well. To think that if their spell had worked the way it had been meant to, none of us would have any magic today."

"You are lucky that they were a bit clumsy back then with their enchantments. The way it turned out, your lack of female magicians was compensated by increased strength in the rest of you. That is at least something." She bit her lip. "I wonder if there is a way to counter that spell. But I suppose it is a bit early to ask Ram'an for that little bit of information." She grinned. "I can't believe I am going to learn how to make magical medication!"

"Yes," Enric said slowly, "how very considerate of him to offer." And surely with no ulterior motives whatsoever, he thought, but found it wiser not to voice. The reaction would hardly be a favourable one as she would only accuse him of jealousy. Which would not be completely unwarranted, he had to admit. But the ambassador seemed to show rather more than a polite interest in her. As he didn't pay the same kind of attention to other females around him, it was surely not only a cultural trait.

"I found the information about your family very interesting. I was surprised you didn't ask him any further questions about them. It seems they are quite eager to learn about you."

She sighed. "It was the way he phrased it, I think, that put me off. *The progeny of two powerful bloodlines,*" she repeated Ram'an's words and shook her head at the repellent expression or rather the idea behind it. "It's as if they treat their magicians as breeding stock. Who knows what their plans for me were before I was taken away by my father. He might have done me a great favour bringing me here."

Enric smiled and pulled her closer. "He certainly did *me* a great favour bringing you here."

"So no plans to use me to start your own dynasty of powerful magical rulers?" she said, only half-jokingly.

"Not at the moment, no. But ask me again when the King annoys me the next time. Then, I might consider replacing him with my own invincible offspring."

She laughed and let him pull her towards their bedroom. "Poor unborn children! These are quite tough expectations for them to live up to. Imagine they decided to become healers instead of invincible tyrants."

"Not acceptable, of course. Yet we would have to figure out how to make them do our bidding. With each being invincible it might be quite a challenge. Especially if they take after their mother," he smirked.

"Yes, right," she murmured. "I am the hard to control one, oh smelter of other people's swords…"

"Ah yes. So you heard about that. Orrin still complains about it? It has been years. And he made me work at the smithy to replace every single one of them."

"As was well deserved. I dare say you learned your lesson?"

"I learned a lot of things in that one month, among them how to make my own sword. With the blacksmith's help, of course. I still use it occasionally. It is very good, even if I say so myself."

"You made that sword?" She looked him up and down. "I wouldn't have pegged you for a man working in a hot, sweaty, oily, dusty place forging his own weapon."

"No? What kind of man would you have pegged me for?"

"Suave, superior, commanding, demanding. And all that in a clean, tidy study."

He pursed his lips. "But you *have* noticed that I am considered quite an apt fighter, haven't you? How does this fit your tame office-type picture of me?"

"Fighting was more a necessity to learn due to being in the Order than any actual wish of yours, I would imagine. Even though you probably enjoy it to a certain degree. But being in your current position, I would think it has its uses for you. And as you are quite demanding of yourself as well as others, possessing average skills would not do, would it?"

He looked down at her, intrigued. "I am rather surprised at how well you have assessed me. I suppose I am so used to being the one doing it that I considered myself immune to being the object of somebody else's critical observation."

"You bet quite a lot of people observe you, your being quite an important man and all that."

"But I wouldn't have thought they did it to such a degree."

She shrugged. "I am the one living with you; why does it surprise you that I have managed to get a halfway realistic picture of you?"

"I am not surprised that you have managed it, but that you were interested enough to make the effort."

Inclining her head, she considered him thoughtfully. "I seems I don't really make you feel appreciated, do I?"

"No, that's not what I am saying. I know that you have come to like me, very probably more than you are aware of. Which is almost a miracle after all that has happened between us since you were brought here." He grinned. "I credit this to my dashing looks and charming ways of gentle persuasion."

She rolled her eyes. "And back to being cocky in an instant. Gentle persuasion, my goodness."

"I like that dress very much, by the way. Did I mention that?" His finger started to follow the seam of her neckline.

"Not with so many words. But your wandering eyes gave me a good idea of what you particularly appreciate about it," she quipped.

"Junar said that it needs an extra pair of hands to lace it at the back, didn't she? I assume this also applies for getting you out of it? I would like to offer my services for that. Completely unselfishly, of course."

"Of course. How very altruistic of you." She turned with a grin to let his long fingers unlace the delicate bands before he pushed the fabric aside far enough to allow it to glide off her shoulders to a heap around her ankles.

"If that pompous idiot does not keep his hands off you, I'll break them. Same goes for his eyes," he murmured, ignoring her irritated glare at this remark.

* * *

Eryn exhaled slowly, letting her gaze wander through the room they had placed at her disposal for the meeting with what was left of the League of Apothecaries. She had come half an hour early to get a feeling for the room and determine where best to position herself, testing the acoustics.

The sun was shining through the windows and gave the room a pleasant, warm glow. This was good - she didn't want to intimidate them. But she needed to impress them. The room was larger than would have been necessary for a meeting with the four men, but Enric had pointed out that a surplus of space was a nice edge if one understood how to use it to one's advantage.

When she had just stared at him in incomprehension, he gave her a few very relevant and surprisingly effective insights into the art of taking up space, securing territory just by placing herself strategically, turning her shoulders this way or that way, and always avoiding taking a step back as it signalled uncertainty. At the same time she needed to avoid getting too close to the apothecaries unless she wanted to use physical proximity to consciously warn or threaten them. And in addition to all that she was of course required to make sure her actual words made sense. Who would have thought that the simple act of talking to people could be so involved?

He had also told her that there was a lot more to learn if she was interested, such as reading people by the signals their bodies unconsciously gave out, but this was for a later time when all this information would not just serve to make her even more nervous than she was already. She had been pleasantly surprised at his willingness to support her. She would rather have expected him to be resentful, as he had initially planned to be there himself had it not been for Lord Tyront's order to stay out of it.

She had prepared a list of things she would offer them along with demands to go with them. Enric had advised her to present them in combination, as packages of one positive item that was attached to certain requirements. That should make it easier for them to swallow. She had rewritten the list accordingly, formed little clusters to put forward piece by piece.

The acoustics in the room were very good, and she would have to be careful not to speak too loudly unless she intended to intimidate them. Which would, hopefully, not be necessary.

Her hands felt sweaty. She needed to distract herself somehow and formed a barrier in front of the table, shooting small balls of energy at it in elegant patterns to amuse herself. Then she built a double barrier with air-free space inside and continued her playful attack. Absentmindedly she toyed with the strength of her bolts, their trajectory and numbers.

She built small round shields around her fingertips and smiled when she thought back at Enric's suggestion to use them to keep her fingernails clean. That had been after their first time in bed together, if she didn't count the anonymous encounter at the Freedom Night.

Lost in thought, she shot another weak bolt at her barrier and cringed when the backrest of the chair that stood behind it suddenly burst into a number of splinters and the remainder sported several small flames.

She stared at the burning wreck of the chair and then at the barrier that was, incredibly, still shimmering in front of her.

"I'll be damned, what have I done now?"

* * *

Her mind raced when she was on her way back to her quarters. Two matters battled for her attention, the meeting she had just finished and what had happened only minutes before it. She had managed to remove the debris just in time before the apothecaries had arrived. She imagined that a discreetly burning chair would not really have been a comfortable sight for them as they might have misinterpreted it as a warning of what their failure to accept her offer would result in.

She opened the door to the parlour and went straight to Enric's study, knocked impatiently and hoped that he was alone.

When he called for her to enter, she went in and flopped onto the settee at the side of his desk. She radiated agitation, restlessness and worry.

He looked at her, concerned. "You seem flustered. How did your meeting go?"

"Hard to tell. I managed not to openly insult, threaten or shout at them, so I would say I did reasonably well. I followed your advice about positioning myself in the room and all that. They were not, however, at all willing to commit themselves to anything. When they left I had no idea if the meeting had been successful or a complete waste of time."

"Wait for them to come to you. And they will soon enough. An offer from the Order is not something they can afford to turn down just like that. Agreeing to anything then and there would not have been very wise of them. They first need to talk among themselves."

"So I just wait?"

"Basically, yes. There is nothing more you can do at the moment."

She nodded and then leant forward to take the cup from his desk and drown it in one go.

"Help yourself," he quipped.

"You did say something about giving me all that is yours at the bloody ceremony, didn't you?" She replaced the empty cup and then rose again. "I broke a chair."

Enric shrugged. "So what? We will have another one made. There is no need for you to be upset about it."

"I broke a chair that was behind a barrier," she said slowly.

His eyes narrowed, the truth beginning to dawn on him. "What kind of barrier?" he asked carefully.

"The impenetrable one."

He stared at her for a few moments, then exhaled loudly. "Why am I even surprised at this anymore?"

* * *

Orrin took a seat in front of Enric's desk and waited for his superior to finish the report he was reading.

"I just received confirmation of Vern's acceptance as the first Order magician to be trained as a healer," Enric spoke and let the paper sink. "It seems Lord Tyront and Lord Poron have both agreed to it. Congratulations. I wasn't even aware that the official application had already been handed in. Eryn is still a little worried about your not being too happy about this."

Orrin smiled. "That is good news; Vern will be overjoyed. And I have seen what she can do with her hands and what Vern *can't* do with a sword. It's best for him, I think. Though I am a bit worried about his new responsibilities interfering with his current schedule."

"We can work around that," Enric promised. "He is the first one to brave this new challenge, so he is entitled to some special treatment, I would say."

Yes, Orrin thought, and it will please your companion immensely which will no doubt be beneficial for yourself. Seeing Enric with this new serenity, this mellow joy his relationship was giving him, was still unusual. Well, at least as long as they were not just in the middle of one of their frequent arguments. But they seemed to resolve them fairly quickly these days.

"I passed by the new healers' building this morning," Orrin said. "Looks pretty busy - lots of noise and dust flying through the air, which I would assume is a good sign at a construction site."

Enric hid a smile. He himself had been there this morning as well, and he imagined that two high-ranking magicians checking on the progress on the same day would keep the builder on his toes well enough. Maybe he could encourage other colleagues to drop by frequently as well. Lord Poron would be happy to comply, he obviously liked Eryn.

"Yes, it is. I have great hopes of their being able to finish their work ahead of schedule." His face gave a thin smile. "I try to drop by as frequently as possible. Seeing a magician somehow seems to motivate them for some reason."

Orrin grinned. "Does it now? That is good to know. I have been considering taking more walks anyway. Good for the health, I am told."

They beamed at each other. The tension, the coolness that had marked their relationship for the last few months, was gone, Orrin was interested to see. But then Enric's attention was now focussed on the newcomer from beyond the sea, who, he had to admit, seemed rather flagrant in his admiration for Eryn.

"I have been working on the barrier," Orrin said. "I think I have finally worked it out. A few more hours of practice and I should be able to conjure it quickly enough. Lord Tyront has also been eager to master it. I met him on my way up; he has summoned Eryn to the training grounds to have her test it out."

Enric suddenly froze, staring at Orrin, his face draining of colour. Then he jumped from his chair and whirled to face the window behind him that overlooked the palace square and training grounds behind it.

"No. No. Nononono," he muttered urgently when he spotted Tyront standing in the middle of the square and saw Eryn leaving the palace and walking towards him. He turned and started running.

Orrin looked after him, frowning. That was a very unusual reaction to such trivial news, he mused, especially from a man like Enric, whom hardly anything could throw off track. Usually. But something did seem to be wrong. And not just a little, judging from the force of his reaction. That surely warranted a closer look.

He rose quickly and followed the younger man.

He left the palace gate only moments after Enric and saw Lord Tyront standing several paces away from Eryn, holding a shimmering double barrier that covered his full height in front of him. The older man nodded towards Eryn and she lifted her hand.

Enric increased his speed magically to reach her in time, but her bolts had already left her hands when he reached her with a mighty jump, slung his arms around her to press her hands down and had the impact of his momentum throw them both to the ground.

Orrin just stared at them, standing with his arms akimbo. Then his gaze wandered to the bolts that had reached the barrier in front of Lord Tyront. And went right through it. A very short moment of utter astonishment and panic was visible on his face, then the magic hit his chest and he collapsed to the ground and lay still.

Without thinking, Orrin started running towards his leader, kneeling down next to him and taking his wrist to check for signs of life. He detected a strong, even pulse and looked over to the pair who were still prostrated on the ground of packed dirt, Enric with a defeated stare at the sky, Eryn with a smug smile so broad it threatened to split her face in two.

Around them warrior trainees and trainers stood frozen at the sight of powerful, invincible Lord Tyront lying on the ground, felled by the healer that was still wrapped in her companion's tight grip but seemed the only one neither surprised nor troubled by the very recent events.

"What just happened here?" Orrin said slowly, forcing himself to remain calm, collected and reasonable.

Eryn looked up at him, laughing. "I figured out a little trick today: I can now pierce through my barrier! It seems I neglected to mention it to Lord Tyront, though..."

* * *

She looked up from the settee in Enric's parlour where the two magicians had unceremoniously dropped her after literally dragging her here, each with one of their hands locked in a tight grip on her upper arm. She looked concerned when she saw them standing right in front of her, both of them having adopted a twin stance with broad legs, folded arms and a furious stare.

"What would make you do an idiotic thing like that, you damned fool?" Orrin growled at her.

"Do you have any idea what he might do with you?" Enric hissed, clearly fighting for countenance. "Damnit, Eryn, he is your superior! You can't just knock him out like that! And in front of all these people!"

"What were you thinking?" Orrin chimed in. "What did you hope to accomplish by this? Or is thinking a luxury you have given up altogether now?"

Eryn made to get up from her seat, but two hands, one from each magician, pushed her back and then returned to its respective chest to interlock again with its counterpart.

"What are you two doing? That weirdly coordinated force and body language you use here is really disconcerting me," she complained.

"Eryn." Enric's voice had dropped in volume and speed and he spoke to her as if facing a toddler. "You do not seem to be fully aware of the trouble you are in. You have just attacked a superior. And this really is an accomplishment, as there really are only two of us in that entire bloody kingdom. And of those two you have managed to pick the one who will be less inclined to show you any leniency."

"He knocked me out once, now I've knocked him out right back. From where I stand we are even," she said sullenly.

"Even?" The calm in Enric's voice seemed to be balancing on an even more dangerous level than before. "You think attacking him in public to get him back for when he knocked you out to keep you from fleeing while you were still our prisoner is an acceptable way of getting *even* with him?"

"I didn't pick the spot! He wanted to do it where everyone could see him! That was not my idea," she defended herself.

"No, you idiot," Orrin retorted, "but that is hardly an excuse. You childish, headstrong fool! This has not only made Lord Tyront look bad, but hardly helped along your own reputation. You are meant to be a role model! Third in command here!" He wrung his hands. "You are meant to take over great responsibilities and want to lead the healers! Is this your idea of responsible behaviour?" While Enric's voice had become lower and lower, his seemed to increase with every sentence.

"Alright, alright, I get it," she sulked. "I was wrong. So what now? Do I let him knock me out in public so he can save his face? Or do I fall on my knees out on Kingsway to beg his forgiveness? Do I go to him right now and sit at his bed to guard over him as he sleeps?"

"You will stay right here. Being close by when he awakens is the last thing you'd want. I will go to him and see what I can do. Don't leave. If I don't find you here when I return, I swear to you I will shackle you in gold for the rest of your life."

She just gulped and nodded silently. Each man shot her a last devastating look before leaving. She sighed when she heard Enric turn the key in the lock for good measure.

* * *

Vyril opened the door at Enric's knock and smiled when she permitted him. "Enric! Good morning to you. Tyront has been waiting for you. He woke up a few minutes ago."

Enric nodded. "Good morning, Vyril. How is he doing? Furious?"

She considered his question for a moment. "No, not particularly. He is not exactly happy about what your young companion did, but I am sure he will find a way to get back at her for it."

Yes, that was also what he himself feared.

"Don't look so worried, dear Enric. You know he will not be cruel or anything of that sort. Go on, he is in his study."

"Come in," was heard from inside when Enric knocked.

Vyril was right, he did not look as disgruntled as might be expected.

"Enric. Good. Come in." Tyront rose from his seat behind the desk and went to the less formal sitting arrangement, waiting for his visitor to join him there. "Listen. There is a bit of talking we need to do, my boy. I distinctly remember your running towards us and trying to stop her before her strikes hit me. This doesn't leave much room for interpretation, now, does it? You obviously knew about her new trick beforehand. Why wasn't I informed? That would have been immensely useful." His tone was mild but his gaze was not.

Enric exhaled slowly and nodded. "You are right, I did know. I am aware that it might seem now as if I had planned to withhold information from you, but I assure you I had planned to tell you at our meeting scheduled for the same afternoon." He shook his head tiredly. "I had not even dreamed about the chance of her getting a shot at using it before then. And really doing it. She discovered it only yesterday morning, while she was waiting for the apothecaries to meet her. A coincidence - just playing around and discovering a thing like that by accident…"

"So she didn't even try to figure it out? It just happened?" Tyront looked at him sharply.

"Yes, so it seems. She said she was playing around with her shield to distract herself because she was nervous about the apothecaries. And then she managed to smash a chair without disrupting her barrier that was in front of it."

"How?"

"By putting a small shield around her bolt that keeps a minute supply of air intact inside it, enough to avoid starving the magic. So it didn't disappear like unprotected bolts when entering the air-free barrier."

"And she says that was an accident? How can you discover a thing like that by accident?" Tyront asked suspiciously.

"She played around with shielding her fingers and when she next released a bolt, the shield seems to have stuck to it and enabled it to go through the barrier."

The older magician sighed. "Incredible. I wonder if she really is that smart or just damn lucky."

Enric smiled. "I am not too sure myself. Yesterday morning I would have said smart, but then she pulls a stunt like knocking you out and I start wondering."

"Yes," Tyront pursed his lips. "That was a rather... interesting demonstration of her new discovery. Do you know what prompted her to do it? I assume you have asked her."

"Petty, childish revenge. It seems she considered this a convenient way to repay you for knocking her out when she tried to run from here."

The older man rolled his eyes, then shook his head and sighed. "How very imprudent of her to take revenge only *after* joining the Order. She is aware that she is basically in my hands now, right? I could block each and every one of her requests, the healer applications and everything related."

"This is how you will punish her?" Enric frowned, not fond of where this was heading.

"No. But she should not have counted on that. That was a risky trick she decided to play on me. But this doesn't mean that I will not punish her. You are aware of this, I hope."

"Yes, I know. And you must. Just don't involve *me* in the punishment if you can help it."

"I won't. You just need to back me when it is time for it. No siding with your companion here."

"No, I am aware I can't. You need to teach her basic respect. And it's not like I won't profit from that myself. I am her superior as well. If she does a thing like this to you, I shiver at what she might do to *me*."

Tyront smiled. "So happy to be of service. You know, I am still stuck between admiration and anger with her. It is quite amazing what she is capable of. But I really, really wish that she wouldn't be the one finding out all of this on her own. I feel I have to protect myself every time she is displeased with me. There is no telling what she could come up with next. It would be nice to have you or Orrin figure out these things instead of her."

"I don't think there are any great chances for that. She has been forced to rely on her own devices since she was a mere fifteen years old. Whatever her father had not taught her she had to work out herself from his books and by experimenting. I suppose it is a way of thinking she has had to adopt."

"Have you tried it? Can you do it?"

"Yes. The principle is rather simple, if you think of it. It does demand more power, though. The shield around the bolt slows it down considerably, so you need to throw it with more force to have a visible impact after it has passed through the barrier."

"So it seems we are back to superior magical strength again," Tyront smirked. "The barrier may have been an equaliser, but this is no longer the case with her new discovery. This means she has inadvertently strengthened your and my claim to power again." He shook his head. "If she hadn't chosen to make this known by striking me down in public, I would be very pleased with her."

* * *

Vern cleared his throat to get her attention. Eryn turned and smiled when she recognised the figure leaning against the palace wall.

"I heard about your latest escapade yesterday," he said without a greeting.

She groaned and rolled her eyes. "Oh no, if you start scolding me as well, I will just stay inside and bury my head under a pillow for the next month!"

He shrugged. "I am not saying it was the smartest of moves on your side, but what really annoys me is that I haven't seen it myself. Can't you make sure I am present next time you try a stunt like that?"

"How very inconsiderate of me," she sighed in mock regret. "Next time I will make sure you have a place up at the front."

"Hey, don't be angry at me! It's only because people keep asking me questions, assuming that I am fully informed due to our being friends and all that. And I have to tell them that I don't know anything other than what is being talked about. That really is annoying. I feel like I don't meet people's expectations!"

She shook her head. "Poor Vern. And there I was, thinking I was in trouble for knocking out the big man when you have to face uttering the phrase *I don't know* again and again."

"Don't complain to me about being in trouble, you idiot," he said. "Nobody told you to do a stupid thing like that, that was your own idea."

"What is it with you and your father? Don't call me an idiot! I effectively am both your and his superior!"

"Yes, that's right. Considering how you treat your own superiors, I could say that expecting politeness from us is totally in line with your own approach to leadership," he retorted, then appeared content at her exasperated look.

"Oh, you just shut up. Why did you waylay me here? To vex me?"

He shook his head. "Not primarily, no. It's just an added side benefit. I am here because I received a formal notice of acceptance as the first healer to be trained by you."

She stared at him in surprise. "Really? I didn't even know you had applied already! Why wasn't I told about this?"

"Don't ask me. What do I know about how information is handled in the high echelons of power? Maybe they wanted to surprise you. Which would be quite funny, as that would mean that you knocked out a man who intended to do something nice for you."

She closed her eyes and shook her head. "Can't you just stop talking? I am considering locking you in an airtight shield until you faint just to make you shut up."

"I don't think this would be an appropriate use of your powers," he countered. "Not that you have impressed us mere underlings by using them very responsibly of late," he then added.

"This is enough! I am not talking to you anymore right now." She turned on her heels and returned to the palace gate.

"Hey! I came to talk to you about my training schedule!"

"You should have started with that part instead of teasing me," she called back over her shoulder.

"That is mean!" he called after her.

"Oh, please! The nuisance is calling *me* mean…" she snorted and turned the corner to flee to her quarters to avoid encountering anybody else today.

She hoped Enric was either not yet back from wherever he had gone in the morning or had locked himself in his study. She was in no mood to endure any snide remarks from him right now.

Naturally enough, he was there when she opened the parlour door. Steeling herself, she closed the door behind her and went straight towards the guest room. She paused when he spoke.

"Sit with me for a moment, will you?"

She turned slowly and walked towards him, sat on a chair and stared at him expectantly. "What?"

He studied her. "A little fractious today, aren't we?"

"You could say that, yes. What is it you want?"

"I haven't told you about my meeting with Tyront after he woke," he explained and noted with satisfaction that he could see no sign of yesterday's smugness. Good, he thought, at least they had managed to make her think. "He was not especially thrilled about what happened yesterday. Though I have to say he seemed remarkably calm."

"So?"

"So what?"

"So what's the verdict?"

Ah yes, getting nervous. Finally. He hid his smile. "He hasn't mentioned anything. Yet. Maybe he is still thinking about something nice."

"So I still am an Order magician?" she said stiffly.

Now Enric sighed. Being nervous was one thing, but he didn't want her to fear being banned. "Of course. You did play a nasty trick on him, but the only thing that got injured was his pride. He is no fool. He won't sacrifice a strong magician like yourself. And kicking you out of the Order would not only displease the King, but also deprive him of the chance of taking revenge on you."

She closed her eyes in relief for a moment. "Good. I was kind of getting used to you all."

"That's nice to hear. We are still getting used to you, though," he smirked. "Lucky for you, he is inclined to view this matter humorously. So whatever he does to punish you, he will pick for its entertainment value, I'd bet."

"So it will be dignity for dignity?" she asked with a rather defeated sigh.

"No, my love. His kind of humour is not as harmless."

CHAPTER 39

Talking to the Apothecaries

Eryn sat in Orrin's parlour and observed Vern's progress with shaping complicated shields.

She had sent him a message after her own lessons, this time strategy, were finished for the day, telling him that she was willing to teach him if he behaved. His response had been a promise to be a model student and an invitation to join him at his quarters, as Orrin was out for the afternoon.

They sat at the dining table, both staring intently into a glass bowl filled with water. Vern was shaping intricate forms with a shield which kept the water flowing in complicated patterns. She herself had only recently started playing around with small, elaborate shields when she thought of the use they might be put to for healing. It seemed like a handy enough skill to pass along to her trainee.

"That looks good. Try to make the diameter a bit smaller at the end. Nice. You did pick that up very quickly."

He grinned. "I practised a bit with shaping the shield over my hair." His current colour was a deep, lush green.

"Yes, I can see that. Your eyebrows are a dead giveaway that it is not your natural colour, though," she laughed.

He touched them with his index fingers. "Good point." A moment later they, too, changed their colour to green. "Better?"

"A lot. That's so you. I think you found your style."

"Thank you. I am rather taken with it myself. If only people didn't look so damn shocked," he complained. "But let's get back to this here. Why am I playing around with these fussy mini-shields?"

"Because they are a very useful way of staunching a bleed quickly if you need to deal with something else first or just need to assess the overall damage before you start."

"Why not just heal it and then move on?"

"It might be only one of several serious injuries, and bleeding wounds can be held in check with this rather easily so that you can take care of them later.

Other damage might require more immediate action and it would be nice for the patient not to lose too much blood in the interim."

"Alright. I think I can do that now. What's next?"

"I thought we might have a look at repairing different types of tissue. You have mastered skin, muscle and bone already, so we could move on to the internal organs now. Their tissues look a little different. Did you read any of the books about the intestinal system I gave you? They describe quite a few different types of tissue."

"I did, yes. But I admit I didn't understand everything. I think they were written for a more advanced healer than myself because they don't really deal with the more basic questions I have," he shrugged.

"Then fetch one and we can go through the things that were unclear. Afterwards we can have a look at your own intestinal system and see if you can identify what you see."

He sighed. "Then I should probably not have eaten all that sweet stuff today."

"That doesn't really matter. Eat a piece of cheese now and when we are through with the book we have a look at the reactions it triggers in your stomach and the other organs involved." She rubbed her hands. "Go on. I have an appointment with Ram'an in the evening and I want to finish this chapter today."

"What does Lord Enric say to your meeting with the ambassador?"

"Why do you ask?" Eryn said evasively.

"Because I think he fancies you a bit."

"Of course he does. He practically hit me over the head and dragged me into his lair," she quipped.

Vern looked serious. "Not Lord Enric, the ambassador!"

"Oh please! Not you, too!"

"I assume your companion shares my observations, then?"

"Go and get the book, Vern," she sighed, tired of discussing that topic and watched him walk to his room with a knowing look on his face.

The knock at the door made her turn, and without any scruples about not being in her own home she went to answer it. It was a palace messenger. He bowed and handed her a note, informing her that he had been instructed to wait for an answer.

She turned the envelope to see if the royal crest was on it somewhere and opened it when she didn't find anything.

"What is it?" Vern said behind her and looked over her shoulder to read the note.

She gave him an annoyed glare and turned away to block his sight. "I am not reading *your* messages, am I? What if it is something secret and important you are not supposed to see?"

"Then saying these exact words would just make me even more eager to read it. So. *Is* it super-secret and important?"

"No," she admitted, reading the note a second time. "It's from the League of Apothecaries, they request a meeting with me at my earliest convenience. It seems they want to talk about the offer I made them two days ago." She looked up. "I should go and see them now. Do you want to come?"

"Definitely. I don't trust them; you shouldn't be alone with them," he said, straightening.

"I do appreciate your wish to protect me, my lad. But I have already been alone with them once and they wouldn't dare trying anything stupid now that I am in the Order."

"Still," he insisted.

Eryn turned to the messenger. "Let them know that I will meet them in fifteen minutes in the same meeting room as last time." Then she closed the door again. "I need to get back to my quarters. I should wear my robes for the meeting. It's a pity you don't have your proper ones yet. I bet we would make an intimidating picture."

"I am not yet fully grown and much too lanky, and you are a woman. I hate to destroy your illusions, but compared to Lord Enric we hardly look at all impressive, I am afraid."

"It is not just about appearances! You need the right attitude to be impressive. Enric taught me a few nice things about that."

Vern looked at her doubtfully. "Yes, for sure he did. Like he needs some more tricks in that department."

She opened the door again and pulled him outside with her. "You are deeply awed by him, aren't you? Is this an admiration thing or are you still scared of him?"

He thought for a moment. "A mix of both, I suppose," he said honestly. "But the scared part has dwindled quite a bit since I healed the apothecary before the execution. He likes me because I saved you. He even bowed to me. My father almost fainted from the shock," he grinned.

"How sweet. So glad I could help you two bond," she huffed.

"You should. He helped me quite a lot by having my schedule changed. My fighting lessons were reduced by half to make room for healing lessons."

She stopped. "Really?" He personally took care of such details? "That was… thoughtful."

"Yes. Though I strongly suspect he was thinking more of you than me when he did it. But as long as I stand to benefit, I don't mind that at all," he grinned broadly.

"You know, he doesn't always think of *me* when he does something. Especially not after… you know. Two days ago."

He looked at her doubtfully. "No? Doesn't seem like that to me. But it's nice to know that even the big, strong and handsome guys have to do some work to keep their girl after getting her."

She rolled her eyes and continued walking. "That's not really how it worked, you know. I didn't sink into his waiting arms, bedazzled by his appearance. Quite the opposite, in fact."

"Really? Then on the Freedom Night it wasn't his looks that made you go with him but rather his outstanding character?" he sneered.

"No, smart boy, it was his choice of music, if you remember all the gossip."

"That alone? Really. So if, let's say, Lord Poron were to have danced with you there instead, the result would have been the same?"

"Oh, come on! What kind of a question is that?"

"One you seem to try to avoid answering because you don't want to admit that girls prefer the tall, muscular types to the bookish, lanky ones!"

"That is utterly untrue! I was always into the quieter, more studious kind of men."

"And yet the warrior type has snatched you up. So it seems they even get the girls that are not into them! This is so unfair!"

"Why exactly are we talking about this? Are you unhappily in love or something?"

He sighed. "No. Just pondering my future."

"Your father is the warrior type," she pointed out. "And he is without a companion. So it doesn't seem to be the main prerequisite. And Lord Poron definitely is the bookish type, and look at him, he has been in a relationship for decades."

That seemed to cheer Vern up a bit. So he was starting to think about girls, Eryn thought with wry amusement.

They reached the door to her quarters, and she opened it and grabbed her robe from the hook next to it. She fumbled for several seconds to locate the holes for her arms and head, when she heard Vern sigh and felt his hands adjusting the fabric for her finally to don it properly.

"Seriously, how hard can this be? How do you manage to dress yourself when you have to wear a dress?"

She shrugged. "Junar helps me. And don't smile like that! You try getting one of these torture garments on by yourself, then we can talk."

"But the robe is hardly a torture garment," he pointed out. "You have worn trousers for so long you have forgotten how to put on girls' clothes."

"I will remind you that you called the robes *girls' clothes* on the triumphant day when you are handed your official ones in a few years." Then she looked down at herself and smiled. "And as the healers' colour is purple, they will look especially fetching on a young man. Apart from that, you are already wearing your students' robes and I assume you don't consider them girls' clothes. Especially as there are no girls around to wear them."

"Thanks to Junar's efforts my robes look a lot different from yours," he snorted. "Yours are girls' clothes - mine are not."

She looked slightly taken aback, but didn't comment. In her opinion the robes all looked like plain dresses, but he wouldn't want to hear that.

They walked on towards the meeting room and stopped in front of the doors.

"Vern, could you please get rid of that hair colour. I need to be respectable and make a serious impression. This doesn't work with green hair and eyebrows."

"I thought it wasn't about external appearances?" he grinned with wicked delight but changed it back to blond.

"Not primarily, but you'd need a lot of charisma to counter the effect of dark green hair," she shrugged. "Come along, they should be here any minute. I am told that being there first and picking your position is an advantage."

She opened one of the doors and let Vern enter first. He looked around the room, taking in the ambience.

"There is an uneven number of chairs," he commented. "Is this another one of your fancy negotiation tricks?"

"No. That is because I made one burst into flames when I was... researching my new, mighty bolts. They haven't replaced it yet," she replied and caused him to raise his brows.

"That was in here? Nice. So, where do we sit? Or do we stand?"

"We can sit over here. The idea is to have a bit more space behind you than the others and avoid either of us having to sit with our backs to the door."

"Why?" he frowned.

"Because it makes people uncomfortable when they can't see the door. And we want them to be cooperative."

They heard the knock at the door and quickly walked to the chairs she had indicated before, stepping next to them before Eryn called, "Come in."

The door was opened by a liveried servant and one after the other the four apothecaries entered and bowed.

"Lady Eryn," they murmured.

"Gentlemen," she said calmly and indicated the chairs she had intended for them. "Take a seat."

After they were seated, she and Vern followed and Eryn leaned back and looked at them with composed expectation, as she had practised in front of the mirror. "I am listening."

The oldest one of them, the one she remembered asking her if she had come to consult a real healing professional when she had tried to buy herbs that first time, spoke, "We have considered your offer thoroughly, and there are a few suggestions we wish to make." He pulled a piece of paper from his pocket and smoothed it out in front of him. It was a list.

"First, the requirement of training is something we consider superfluous. We have been in the business of preparing medicines for decades and do not need instructions on how to do it."

Eryn smiled at him coldly. "I have been to your shop, as you surely remember. I saw things there that *still* make me shake my head when I think of them. Herbs that had been dried so long they lost almost all of their healing qualities, herbs on display that had no healing qualities in the first place, at least as far as I am aware, and plants that had been entirely stripped of the parts that contained the healing substances. And this was just from a casual glance around in about one minute. Don't tell me you are not in need of training."

The four apothecaries exchanged worried glances and then looked at their speaker, who lifted his chin defiantly.

"If our services are so inferior, why do you wish to cooperate with us at all?"

Vern cut in before she could answer. "Because she has a soft spot for idiots. She doesn't wish to cooperate with you, she wishes to keep you from completely losing your income, because she is compassionate and doesn't want to see your families suffer. Consider this," he suggested and leaned forward, using his fingers to list his arguments. "Your colleagues tried to kill her, your reputation is one of providing overpriced services that are most of the time worse than useless, and she needs to train you first because you seem to have no idea how to go about healing anybody. She doesn't need you. You need her. So when you next open your mouth you'd better have something sensible to say or this meeting will be over and the healers will do what most people in the city deem overdue anyway: squash you like bugs."

Eryn stared at the boy, just as the apothecaries were doing. Where had that come from? She wondered whether to stop him now before he made them either ridicule him or ran away screaming. He suddenly didn't seem like the young man of fifteen any more, young Vern with the disapproving expression she knew so well from his father, and now glaring at the men who were so much older than him, but seemed to think it wise to take him seriously for now.

Another man cleared his throat after a few moments. "About that training. What would it entail?"

Vern nodded to her to explain.

She suppressed a grin. "Botanical studies with a focus on medical use, treatment of plants such as properly harvesting and drying them, further processing with and without alcohol, production of salves, crèmes, potions and powders, determining the quality of the finished products, dosage, interdependencies and things like that. And at the end of each part there will be a test which you will have to pass before we work with you."

"Why would we have to learn how to harvest and dry them? The herb gatherers take care of this," the oldest one of them interjected.

"Because you should be able to see if it was done right," Vern said and rolled his eyes. "Seriously, have you never even heard of checking the quality of a product before you buy it? How have you been able to survive so long?" He paused, then added with a nasty smile, "Ah yes, I remember: misusing your unchallenged status as providers of medical services at extortionate prices."

Eryn swallowed, wondering how to rein him in a bit without criticising him.

"These are the training requirements and conditions, no less. Of course, you'd be more than welcome to take the test without prior training if you feel you possess apt knowledge in any particular field already?" he added with a cold smile.

Brilliant move, she thought and watched two of the men swallow in discomfort. Now they either had to agree to being trained or prove that they didn't need to be, and the second option was not even remotely likely from what she had seen in their shops.

"How about the herb gatherers?" the youngest of them, in his mid-thirties, asked.

"They will be trained by us as well, though hardly as extensively as their responsibility ends after drying the herbs," Vern said curtly. "But that is none of your concern, as they will no longer deliver to you, but to us."

Eryn blinked. She hadn't even thought about the herb gatherers yet. And here he was, planning their training and how they would be included in this new network she was trying to build. Maybe she should let *him* do all the talking, she thought. He seemed to be able spontaneously to come up with ideas she had not even considered after days of thinking the matter through. And very good ideas, too. There he was, only months ago worrying about not possessing the required magical strength or skill to be an exceptional warrior, when it now seemed that he had all the prerequisites to singlehandedly plan the organisational matters, negotiate contracts, draw up the teaching literature and treat the patients. And there was ambition. She could see it in the way he treated the apothecaries - corralling them into agreeing to his demands, and enjoying his small victories. But she would have to be careful or he would take over healing altogether and soon enough be commanding *her* instead of the other way round.

*　*　*

She bustled into Enric's study without bothering to knock and jumped onto his lap, laughing giddily and weaving a piece of paper in front of his nose.

"You will never, ever believe this! It was incredible!" She planted a firm kiss on his mouth.

He raised his brow. "What was? What have you got in your hand?"

"The contract! The apothecaries sent me a message and I met with them today together with Vern. It was unbelievable!"

"So I assume it went well?" he ventured and tried to snatch the paper out of her hand. She sniggered and quickly moved it away and out of his reach.

"No, wait until Lord Tyront is here. I have sent for him. You two need to look it over and approve it. And I have no doubt whatsoever that you will." She hugged her other arm around his neck and pulled him closer for another kiss.

He wrapped one arm around her to keep her from slipping off his lap. Spirited, overjoyed Eryn was a new experience, and a very nice one, too. She had to be really excited if she had sent for Tyront just like that. It would be the first time she met him after she had knocked him unconscious, and she wasn't even nervous, the triumph too great to make space for a petty thing like anxiety.

"You did manage to have them agree to your demands, I assume?"

"No! I didn't! Vern did! I was so shocked, I hardly recognised him in there! And he didn't only make them agree to my demands, he even added a few of his own!"

Now Enric looked incredulous as well. "He did *what*?"

"Who did what?" Tyront's voice said from the door, watching them. "I am not interrupting anything, I hope?"

"No, come in and sit," Eryn ordered and jumped up from Enric's lap. The two men exchanged an amused look at the combination of her not only having taken over Enric's study but also instructing her superior.

She waited until both of them sat in front of her and then flourished the paper with a grand gesture.

"My Lords, it is my great pleasure to present to you a work of art, a masterpiece of negotiation for your approval to be signed in the name and on behalf of the Order to enable healers to cooperate with apothecaries."

She gave the contract to Lord Tyront and watched Enric lean over to read it as well.

They alternately raised their brows, exchanged surprised looks with her or each other, and murmured incomprehensibly.

"You negotiated that?" Enric looked up in astonishment when he was done reading. "Along with Vern?"

She shook her head with a broad grin. "No. Vern did it; I was more of an onlooker. He just took over the negotiations."

"And you let him? He is only fifteen years old!"

"I did after I saw that he was doing it so much better than I ever could have. And you are holding the proof in your hands! How can you doubt that it was the right thing to do?"

"She has got a point there," Tyront said and looked up from the paper. "Young Vern did this? Orrin's Vern? Lanky, nervous fellow with wild looking, strangely coloured hair?"

She laughed out loudly. "Unbelievable, isn't it? They looked so scared every time he opened his mouth! I wish you could have seen it!"

"Yes," Tyront said, eyeing her curiously, "so do I." He looked back down at the contract. "They agreed to be trained and tested by the healers? And to a probation period of two months to see if their work is up to standard?"

"The second part was Vern's idea. I almost burst out laughing when he demanded it. And nobody dared saying anything! They were just exchanging these panicked glances and then they all nodded in agreement." She wiped a tear from the corner of one eye.

"And they accepted that rate? And the exclusivity? You don't really have the mind-controlling powers you claimed when I punished Vern for teaching you magical combat, do you?" Tyront asked, shaking his head in astonishment.

Enric pointed to another section with his index finger. "They even agreed to relinquish control of the herb supply to the healers. I am really impressed. I hope Vern never decides to negotiate for increased fees when he becomes a fully trained healer. He would bankrupt us in no time."

"Does this mean you approve? Will you sign it?" Eryn had to keep herself from jumping up and down in excitement.

The two men exchanged a look.

"How can we not?" Tyront said. "It's nothing short of brilliant." He took off his seal ring and waited for Enric to heat the wax before he pressed the Order's official emblem onto the document.

CHAPTER 40

Orrin's Secret

Eryn yawned and turned another page of the thick book on battle strategies. How had they managed to write books such as this when there had not been any wars for the last three hundred years? It would probably prove to be complete nonsense as it was no more than theory that had not been put to the test in centuries. And yet they insisted she learn about this. What which flank of the troops had to do when, while they hoped the opponent did nothing but stand around in confusion waiting to be ambushed.

"You look tired and displeased. The book is not to your liking?"

She looked up at Lord Poron, who had stepped next to her with a sympathetic smile on his face.

Sighing, she closed the book and shook her head. "Look weak when you are strong, look strong when you are weak. What tripe is this? I mean, if your opponent has read the same book they will very probably have a very good look at you anyway before they attack. And, of course, they will automatically distrust anyone appearing to be strong, as it might just be an attempt to avoid being attacked at this moment."

"I must admit I have never been a great admirer of warfare literature," Lord Poron said. "I feel that if it really comes to war then it is a failure of the greatest kind."

"And yet the Order prepares its trainees for war instead of how to avoid it. Brilliant." She shoved the book away in disgust.

"Well, the King is the one meant to prevent wars," the magician pointed out. "We need to be ready when this is no longer within his power."

Shaking her head, she sighed. "This might have been a cosy idea for the last three hundred years, but now that for the first time there is contact with another country again, I feel I should learn how to handle things. I mean, the King expects me to spend time with the ambassador, and yet he should be worried that I might say or do something that will make the man run home angrily because I have no idea that I shouldn't have said this or done that. You know me, don't you? I tend to be very direct."

"I don't see any imminent danger here," the old man smiled. "He seems to be very taken with you."

"For now," she snorted. "When I first insult him or his country inadvertently he might change his mind."

"Don't be so worried about this. It is technically also your country, so your insulting it should not be as grave as you fear."

"My country," she murmured. "Enric would not like to hear you say this. He is afraid the delegation will try to whisk me away from here back to the Western Territories."

Lord Poron nodded. "Of course he does. Most in the Order believe that your presence here is what made them seek contact with us after all this time. If their interest in you is that great, taking you with them might indeed be their plan. Lord Enric does well to consider this possibility seriously."

A flash of bright blue caught her eye and she turned to the door to see Vern strolling in, his hair in stark contrast to his dark grey trainee robes.

"What are you doing here? Aren't you supposed to have lessons? And blue is really *not* your colour," she added, with a sisterly smile.

The boy bowed to Lord Poron and then shrugged. "My afternoon lessons were cancelled. My teacher has fallen ill. And I look fabulous in blue."

"Whatever illusions you need to be happy," she said. "Good timing. I have just decided that I can't stand reading another page of this masterpiece of instructive literature today. I might as well go and check on the progress of the healers' building. Do you want to come?"

"Sure, why not? I have no other plans. Maybe we could then have a look at the intestinal system? Last time we were interrupted by the apothecaries and I still have a few questions there."

She nodded and rose to bow to Lord Poron. "Then I will see you tomorrow." She looked at the book and suppressed a shiver.

"Yes, I expect you will. A nice day to you, Lady Eryn. Vern."

The air was frosty when they left the palace and Eryn shivered. "I should have brought my cloak. It's getting really cold these days."

"Soft womenfolk," Vern teased. "Always freezing."

"You better be careful, or I will go and heal your teacher so you can have your lessons today after all."

"Now, there is no need for nasty threats like that," he said sulkily.

They reached the construction site in no more than a few minutes and Eryn nodded in appreciation. "They seem to be getting on quite well, I think. I don't know why builders have such a bad reputation when it comes to adhering to schedules. Let me have a quick look inside, then we can go to your quarters. You will have to order a huge pot of something warm for me."

The inside looked busy: workers hammering, sawing, discussing and carrying around heavy things. She had no idea what exactly they were doing, but it looked as if people were bustling around, and activity always had to be a sign of productivity and progress, didn't it?

When she emerged from the building again, she saw Vern amusing himself by shooting bolts at a stone and making it jump around.

"Good, let's go. Everything seems fine from what I can see, and I really need to get somewhere warm." She shivered.

"That should teach you to wear your robes more often."

Rolling her eyes, she accelerated her steps. "You sound like Enric. Why does everybody feel the need to lecture me?"

"Because we see the dire need for it?" he asked as if this was obvious.

"Why do I feel the need to tell you to shut up more and more often these days?"

"Because I am a brilliant negotiator and you are at a loss for words and don't want to admit it," he said with apparent self-satisfaction.

"Oh dear. That meeting with the apothecaries has boosted your self-confidence, hasn't it?" she said.

"Don't pretend it isn't justified. I did very well in there, otherwise you wouldn't have let me carry on." He smiled. "And the result was pretty awesome. Don't deny it, you had a hard time keeping your face straight when we went through each point with them at the end and they just kept nodding with sour expressions."

She laughed at the memory. "Yes, that steel-tipped tongue of yours finally turned out to be useful. I plan to see the herb gatherers next and would love to have you at my side again. Or rather be at *yours*, if it goes anything like last time. Though I have to ask you to be more civil to them than to the apothecaries. They have not been treated well themselves and I would like to impress on them that we are going to be different."

"Sure, no problem," he beamed and seemed to grow a bit. They had reached the warriors' quarters and Vern held the heavy door open for her to enter the corridors.

Eryn raced the boy to his quarters to get herself warmed up, arriving there first.

"That is cheating, you know," Vern scolded her. "It is considered common courtesy not to use more magical strength in a competition than your opponent has at his disposal."

"Really? Maybe you should impart this little pearl of wisdom to my companion. He doesn't seem to be encumbered by such concerns when I have to train with him."

Vern pushed open the door to the parlour and then froze. Eryn frowned and then tried to push past him to see what had shocked him.

"What's the matter? Move out of the way!" She gave him a good shove and made him stumble forwards.

She drew in a sharp breath when her view of the parlour was clear.

"Woah!" she exclaimed and stared at the two half-undressed figures on the sofa.

Junar and Orrin stared right back, wide-eyed and frozen.

Junar was the first to wake from her stupor, disentangling herself from her suitor, frantically tugged at the shirt that had obviously been on its way to being slipped off, pulling it back down. Then she pushed Orrin's shirt, which already had landed on the floor, into his hands and swallowed, turning to the newcomers with a broad forced smile of composure on her lips that did not match the horrified expression in her eyes.

Junar and Orrin, it shot through Eryn's head. How could this happen? Him, almost twenty years older than she was! She tried to look at him with a woman's eyes instead of whatever strange daughter-like role she had assumed. He was not unattractive as such. Good build, which was something of a must for a warrior, or rather a consequence of his frequent exercises, an aura of authority that emanated from him and facial features that were not chiselled like Vern's, but strong and manly - the effect enhanced by the thin scar down one cheek. She shook her head to get out of this frame of mind again. This was not how she preferred to think of him. He was still her grumpy, too demanding, inappropriately authoritative Orrin figure. And he had a girlfriend. And not just any girlfriend. Her friend. Would Eryn have to listen to intimate details about them now? She hoped not! Would Junar feel the need to take over a strange, misplaced mother role towards her or Vern now?

Now Orrin was moving as well, and hastily slipped on his shirt as if covering himself would erase any evidence of what had been going on. Then he cleared his throat and got up from his seat. He adopted his typical broad stance, folded his arms and scowled at them.

"What are you doing here? You are supposed to be having lessons right now," he barked at his son.

Vern's brow shot up in disbelief, but he remained silent, not yet able to voice his thoughts.

"Now, you wait a moment!" Eryn replied and lifted her index finger at him. "No diverting from this with angry words to your son! *You* are the one who has some explaining to do here! And now sit, both of you, and speak!"

Junar looked at Orrin, unsure what to do.

"I will not be told what to do in my own quarters!"

"Don't make me do something you will regret," she retorted with a warning that was received with narrowed eyes.

"Like what, pray tell?"

"Like my enveloping you in a shield and using a truth block on you."

"You wouldn't dare! This would be a gross misuse of your powers and the Order would make you pay for it."

She smiled thinly. "Only if you manage to remember enough to tell them about it."

That had him worried, she could see the lines on his frowning face deepen. After another few moments of tension, Junar lifted her hand to Orrin's arm and said calmly, "I think we should tell them. We knew this moment would come sooner or later."

His gaze turned to her and he considered her for a few moments before finally nodding and taking a seat again, but not on the sofa they had been discovered on just now.

"Junar and I are seeing each other," he declared grandly, challenging Eryn and Vern who had both decided to remain standing and had folded their arms.

"You don't say!" Vern replied dryly, having had enough time to find his words again. His accusatory tone of voice showed how much the situation disturbed him.

"How long has this been going on?" Eryn demanded.

"That is none of your business," Orrin snapped, but Junar gave him a somewhat pleading look and he took a deep breath and visibly forced himself to calm down. "For about two weeks now," he admitted reluctantly.

"Two weeks?" Vern called out. "And all this in secret! How long would you have continued sneaking about if we hadn't caught you?" He shook his head in disbelief. "I will never be able to look at that piece of furniture again without wincing!"

"Why didn't you say anything?" Eryn asked, looking at Junar.

She sighed and looked at Eryn pleadingly. "I had no idea how you would react to this. You are very close to him, after all. I didn't want to endanger your friendship with him, or ours."

"And my surprising you in the middle of what was obviously going to be copulation at some point is better?"

"Ow, don't say it like that!" Vern howled.

"The facts remain the same, however I put it," Eryn pointed out and turned back to Junar. "I am happy for the two of you, really, but I would have preferred learning about this a bit more gently, if you know what I mean. And as for Vern... I'd say that this has not been the best way for him to learn about it, either."

"Damn well it wasn't!" he confirmed angrily. "I am a growing lad, easily impressionable and at a critical stage of my adolescence. This is not a good time to scar me for life!"

"Scar you for life?" Eryn repeated. "If you think *that* has scarred you, you should have come in here a few minutes later."

Orrin covered his face with both hands. "Why me?"

"Yes," Eryn gasped in mock horror. "Poor you, bearing the cruel fate of having a considerably younger lover truly is something to make people pity you. It's your own fault. Had you been less of a coward and owned up to it you wouldn't be dealing with it like this now."

"This is why we had so many new clothes made recently!" Vern said in sudden, shocked comprehension. "I was wondering why I needed so much new stuff when I am not even fully grown yet and it will probably not even fit any more by this time next year! This was just a pretence for the two of you to keep meeting without raising suspicions!"

Eryn grinned. "Sneaky. I wouldn't have thought you had so much subtlety in you. What now? Are you going to make it official or will you keep playing your little hide and seek game?"

"Not much use anymore, is it?" Orrin sighed.

Junar smiled and squeezed his arm affectionately. "I have to admit, at least that is a relief. Worrying that you would visit me while Orrin was with me or, well, Vern bursting in on us one day…"

"If you were worrying about that, why didn't you take any precautions? I mean, what is wrong with the bedroom, I ask you?" Vern exclaimed, still agitated.

"Well, sometimes, if passion gets a bit out of hand…" Orrin began, but stopped, when Vern lifted both hands in a halting gesture, his face contorted in disgust.

"You know what? I have changed my mind. Don't answer that question. I'll be in my room now. Eryn, I am sorry, but I am in no mood for healing lessons right now. I was in contact with the functions of the human body as much as I would wish for now, thank you so much." And then he stomped off into his room, closing the door behind him noisily.

Eryn regarded Orrin's helpless stare at Vern's room door and said in a soothing voice, "You know, he will not be like this forever - give him some time. And he will likely get back at you for this by making you burst in on him with his first sweetheart when they are having fun."

Orrin groaned and looked up at her. "Why are you still here? What do I have to do to make *you* storm off in a huff?"

She smiled indulgently and pointedly took a seat opposite him. "You know, I don't think you could right now. I have to admit that I'm really enjoying your discomfort, immensely so in fact. I intend to stay a bit longer and revel in it. Junar, why don't you be a darling and offer me a drink? It seems like you are quite at home here already."

* * *

"You will not believe what I have just learned!" She stormed into his study, making him look up from what seemed to be some sort of report. He really had a lot of those to deal with, she thought. How dull.

Enric sighed and put the paper away. Being interrupted was not helpful, but when it came to interruptions, she was the one dealing with was a pleasure at least. Well, most of the time. If she wasn't angry or upset. Which clearly did not seem to be the case at the moment. She looked excited, her eyes gleaming.

"What have you learned?" Enric asked with a smile, thinking of how charming it was that she came running to him with her news to share them.

"Junar and Orrin - they are seeing each other! Have been for two weeks now!" She looked at him expectantly for some reaction. Shock, surprise, whatever.

Enric pursed his lips. "So he finally told you? I was wondering how much more time he would take."

She stared at him in dismay. "You knew? And you didn't tell me?" He caught her hand swiftly when she made to hit his shoulder with her fist.

"I can't just run around spreading other people's personal secrets. And as it has nothing to do with the Order, telling it to you would have been completely unjustified."

"There is a difference between spreading it and telling *me*!" She huffed and jerked her wrist out of his grip. "How do you know, anyway? Don't tell me he told you but not me? I am really going to make him pay for that!"

"No, he didn't tell me. But Tyront has his informants everywhere and he found out through them."

She raised a brow at him. "And Lord Tyront told you? So he isn't as concerned about not spreading personal details as you are."

Enric smiled. "He didn't tell me as such. One of my agents did."

She stared at him. "You spy on your superior? But he is also your friend! What if he finds out?"

"I'd bet everything I own that he is aware of it. He would be deeply offended if I didn't spy on him. It would mean that he hasn't taught me properly."

Eryn let herself flop onto one of the chairs in front of his desk and slowly shook her head in incomprehension. "I really don't get your little games here. You spy on him, but he welcomes it because it shows that you were a good student. Is there anybody I am supposed to spy on? Do I have spies on my heels already?"

He grinned. "Love, you had spies on you the moment it was known that you have magical powers. And I do, too. The nice thing for our observers is that we now live together and they can gather information on both of us at the same time."

"And you know all this and don't do anything against it?" she cried out in disbelief.

He shrugged. "That's the way it is. And knowing about it means that I don't live my life with a false sense of security. I have a better chance of keeping things secret than non-magicians, though. If a conversation needs to be kept private under any circumstances, there is always the sound-proof barrier."

"Which can be made redundant by anybody who manages to read lips," she countered.

"Yes, that was a nasty surprise," he admitted. "But I now make sure that there is no clear line of sight for any watcher when I use it."

"Do *you* spy on me?" she enquired suspiciously.

"Not anymore. Having you live with me is quite a useful way of gathering information about you," he said. "And no report, however detailed, could have conveyed the realistic image of you after waking up."

"Bastard," she said gently and got up to leave him to his paperwork.

CHAPTER 41

Magical Medicine

Enric knocked at the guest room door. It had been converted into a temporary study for her as long as the construction works at the future healers' building were still ongoing.

"Come," he heard her call and entered. She sat at the small desk in front of the window and made use of the last daylight to read something.

"It's too dark in here for reading," he scolded softly and went to the lamp next to her on the desk to light it.

She looked up and out of the window. "Oh, is it so late already?"

"Yes." He bent down to kiss her on the temple. It had turned into a ritual for him to greet her like this and while she had been obviously disconcerted by it at the beginning she was now used to it and no longer showed any signs of discomfort. He had noticed that when she was deep in thought or otherwise occupied and thus let her guard down, she even lifted her face to meet his lips. Showing affection was still an effort for her, the more if somebody else was present.

"How was the Council meeting? Have you made a decision about teaching the barrier to all magicians?" she enquired.

"Yes. The Council has decided against it for now. They want to have a closer look at how you overcame it and need some more time for thinking. You had your talk with the herb gatherers today, didn't you? I assume you had young Vern along with you?"

She smiled. "Yes to both. It seems he really likes negotiating. I had to keep him on a shorter leash today, or he would have made them agree to things they can't really afford, just to get him out of their hair."

"The herb gatherers are not organised like the apothecaries, are they? I assume you had a lot of people there today."

Sighing, she stood up and stretched. "Yes, about twenty. I suggested forming a league, association, guild or whatever else they want as a governing body for their services, but after dealing with the apothecaries they seemed rather reluctant to do this. They have always acted independently from each other and don't want to be tied down. But applying standards is of course much harder when they don't have to answer to a governing body for their profession."

"So you have to negotiate each and every contract with every single one of them?" he asked with a sympathetic look of concern.

"No, Vern took care of this. He called it a standard agreement and said that additional wishes would only be granted in exchange for additional services, such as obtaining especially valuable plants and those that are hard to find, and so on."

"Then you are satisfied with the result?" he asked and took her hand to pull her to the parlour with him.

"Yes, all in all everything was fine. What are you doing? I wanted to finish reading the draft so we can have it finalised for your approval." She tried to pull free, but he shook his head.

"Dinner time. I shouldn't have to tell you that regular meals are necessary to stay healthy. And I refuse to eat alone while you are in here, locked away. That's one of the benefits of living together: keeping each other company." He pulled out a chair for her and they both sat in front of their dinner trays.

"How is Vern doing? Has he got over the shock of finding his father locked in a passionate embrace with a lover yet?"

Eryn looked worried. "Why do I get the impression that you find this funny? It is hard for him. Never before in his life has he seen his father showing any interest in a woman - and suddenly this." She shook her head. "And I told him only a short while ago that he needn't worry about girls being more into warriors than scholars, as even his father, a typical warrior if ever there was one, was alone. Thanks to Junar that argument is now meaningless."

Enric smiled. "Interested in girls, is he?"

"Yes, I think. Though I don't know if there is a particular one he likes or if he worries in general that he will have to spend his life in solitude."

"So he thinks the chances for success with the ladies are better for warriors?"

"Yes. For whatever reason. I told him that I had always been more into the bookish type, but then he pointed out that I was snatched up by a warrior nevertheless. And what can you say to that?"

He leaned back, studying her. "You prefer the well-read, intellectual type?"

She quickly checked herself, realising that she had probably just insulted or hurt him. "It's not like I don't appreciate the added benefits of your continuous training. You have a very nice and fit body, for one thing. Well-muscled, lean, athletic. Professionally speaking, now."

"So my great physical attributes are sufficient compensation for my lack of intellectual capacity?" he said mildly and smiled when she looked up, slightly horrified.

"I never said that! I never thought you were stupid or uneducated! My problem with you in particular was that you were scary and seemed aloof, merciless and reckless!"

"Typical warrior attributes, then?" he asked and laughed when she desperately searched for a way out of the conversation. "I am just teasing you, my love. You are stuck with the *warrior type* label, whether you like it or not."

He tried to push away the thought that the ambassador did appear rather bookish to him. And that he had healing knowledge that would ensure him Eryn's undivided attention.

"You are a brute," she murmured and gave him a disapproving look before she resumed her eating. "You make it very easy for me to leave for my appointment later."

"Appointment?" he frowned. "Not with the ambassador, I hope?"

"The very same," she said, gleeful at the sight of his cool expression. "He will teach me to imbue medicines with magic to increase their effectiveness."

"In his quarters? Only you and him?" A heavy undertone had entered his voice.

She sighed. "Yes, because anywhere else would hardly be quiet enough, and having somebody there watching us would seem rather childish, don't you think? We need to work on that jealousy of yours. What will you do when I work together with other men at the healers' building?"

"That will be strictly professional, I would expect. And if I see any of your colleagues expressing undue interest in you, I will intervene. Unfortunately, I cannot do this with our visitor, as his status protects him. But I don't have to sit by idly while he creates circumstances where he can spend time alone with you."

Steel in his eyes, she thought. He would not give in on this - discussing it would lead nowhere.

"What do you propose, then? I am to turn down his offer to teach me something that is immensely valuable for my work because you feel you can't trust me to be alone with him?"

Enric kept his calm, but it was hard work. "It is not *you* I don't trust. It's *him*. I would not dream of asking you not to learn this, but I do insist on a different setting. You can send him a note to come to our quarters and do it here instead."

She huffed. "Yes, right. And you will sit behind us, staring at us all the while, making a fool of yourself and ridiculing me."

He folded his arms. "I will be in my study with the door open. Take it or leave it: either he comes here or you are not seeing him tonight."

She balled her fists. "I am no longer a prisoner. This is also *my* home now. You can't lock me in here!"

His smile was cold. "I can't? I managed it before, didn't I?"

When she was about to charge him with misusing his superior powers and that the Order wouldn't like it, she paused and then started laughing.

Enric looked at her with a confused expression, clearly none too happy about her unexpected burst of merriment while discussing a topic that caused him so much worry.

"I just remembered a similar situation with Orrin when I forced him to talk to me about him and Junar. I threatened to use a shield and truth block on him and it seems as if I am threatened in a similar way right now. Funny, when *I* did it, it didn't seem so unfair."

"Yes," he commented factually. "That's how perceptions change when you are on the receiving side."

She pursed her lips and studied him. "You know, this is not the right way to handle situations where we disagree. If you keep subduing me like this I will find a way to make you pay for it. But in this particular case I will comply, as I appreciate that your motivation is a feeling you can't control. Which does not mean that you don't have to work on managing your jealousy. I will send him a message and ask him to come here. But only if you promise to behave and stay in your study."

He exhaled slowly in relief. "I promise I will behave decently and not disturb you during your lesson. Should you decide, however, to move on to social interaction, I will join the two of you."

"What is it about Ram'an that you don't care for? Vern likes him, and so do I."

"He touches you too much. I find this inappropriate. And I have observed him, he does it only with you, not with other women. So don't even try to tell me that it must be cultural."

"He might be more reserved with the women who were born here. I lived in the Western Territories for a few years, so he probably assumes that I am more open or remember a thing or two."

Enric lifted a brow. "I don't think so. He keeps following you with his eyes, even if he is in a conversation with somebody else."

"That's complete nonsense," she sighed and shook her head. "I think the real problem is that you don't trust me not to run off home with him and you can't admit it. Probably not even to yourself. So you blame Ram'an, as it is his visit that makes you uneasy."

"What an interesting analysis," he replied in mock seriousness. "Do you mind if I try my hand at it as well?"

She leaned back and folded her arms. "Do go on."

"I suspect you are very tempted by the things he promises to teach you. And even though you have decided to honour our commitment and stay in the city, you're asking yourself what it would be like to go with him to the place where all the knowledge comes from. He has mentioned that the things he knows are marginal compared to what trained healers can do. You think of the things you might have learned there and that seem so very far away now. You may even be thinking of how to get there without being held back by the magical oath that binds you here."

"Stop this," she said quietly.

He noticed that she had gone pale. "My little guesses have obviously hit their mark," he said with narrowed eyes.

She shoved back the chair and got up.

"Now *you* stop." He quickly took her hand before she could leave. "I told you that there is one thing I will not tolerate, and that is running away instead of taking care of things. Sit with me, will you?" The last words were spoken more softly, less like a demand and more like a request.

"What do you want from me?" she called out desperately. "I have decided to stay here, to give up whatever there might be for me in the Western Territories! You can't ask me to be happy about it as well! Not yet - maybe not ever."

He sighed and pressed her palm against his cheek. "I know. I am grateful that you made the decision to stay here. With me. But I know it wasn't one that's made you completely happy, so I am eager to make it easier for you. Meeting the ambassador keeps reminding you of what you can perhaps never have. And I am still convinced that he would like you to accompany him instead of leaving here without you. He will try to make saying No to him very hard for you."

"And you are afraid that at one point it might be too hard for me?"

He closed his eyes. "It's something I dread every day, yes."

She smiled and lifted her second hand to his other cheek. "That is kind of sweet, actually. And a very powerful weapon you have just handed me."

He opened his eyes again and grinned feebly. "Because I would do whatever you wanted to make you happy, to compensate for the loss you have to live with?"

"Basically, yes."

"I hate to destroy your illusions, but that weapon has been yours all along. You are the one who keeps refusing my attempts to do things for you."

"Like buying me clothes?"

"Like trying to provide for you as best I can."

She released a long groan. "That is something I find really annoying. I was brought up to be useful, to take care of myself. My father had very clear views on women who take a wealthy companion and then be no more than an ornament for the rest of their lives."

"Eryn," Enric replied in his most reasonable tone, "I don't think anybody could accuse you of being idle or useless. I have seen what you are like when you have nothing to occupy yourself with. You are restless and moody. And I have never tried to make you sit back and stop you from your work, so I assume you are aware that it is not my intention to condemn you to a life of uselessness by buying things for you."

"You are doing this because I can't afford them! It's like I keep becoming more indebted."

He pinched the bridge of his nose. A new version of the clothes argument. Great.

"I am buying them for you because you would not do it yourself and you need them. Money is not a concern between the two of us, at least not for me. We have so much of it that it never has to be."

"*You* have so much of it," she countered.

"No, *we* have. Have you taken in the words of the commitment oath? That part about sharing. And I find it rather disconcerting that you keep refusing to take what I want to share with you. Am I to assume that you would keep your money to yourself if our roles were reversed?"

"Of course not!" she protested. "It's just that I don't like sharing if it only goes one way."

He smiled and kissed her on the knuckles. "It isn't, not for me. You now share a bed with me. To me that is worth a lot more than a few garments."

She had to smile, despite herself. "You have a way of making me feel small."

"You are. If you were any shorter I would get serious back problems when bending down to kiss you," he joked.

"Very nice. I'll have you know that I am taller than most women around here. I am not that much smaller than you, considering that you are unusually tall. Your back can consider itself lucky you got me."

"Not only my back, my love - all of me is." He pulled her from her chair onto his lap. "You should send your note to the ambassador now. We shouldn't keep him waiting, should we? And make him keep his hands to himself. And his eyes. Basically all his body parts. At least the ones he doesn't intend to part with."

She shook her head. "You won't mind if I don't use these exact words, will you?"

"No, not at all. As you have discovered your love for diplomacy, I dare say you will find more appealing ones."

* * *

"Eryn, dear," the ambassador said with his broad smile and was about to take her hands into his, when she quickly flourished them into a rather exaggerated gesture to invite him in. She caught Enric's almost indiscernible nod of approval.

"Ram'an, how very nice of you to be so flexible. I am sorry for the change of plan, especially as I am the one who will profit from this meeting."

"It is not her fault," Enric added generously and stepped next to her to put an arm around her shoulders and pull her close enough to plant a kiss on her temple. "I was so loath to part with her after our not seeing each other all day long that I pestered her into asking you to join her here."

"Of course," the ambassador said, making the ordinary words sound exotic with his lilt. "I can fully understand that."

"Well," Eryn smiled brightly and felt her cheeks start to hurt under the effort after just a few seconds, "why don't we get started? Enric, I seem to remember that you still have to take care of a thing or two?"

"Yes, my love," he smiled at her and lifted her chin to kiss her on the mouth. "How very thoughtful of you to remember." He then nodded once to the ambassador and strolled into his study, leaving the door ajar.

Ram'an looked around. "So this is what your quarters look like when you have not adapted them to make your foreign guest feel more comfortable at a dinner party."

She smiled and shrugged. "It must seem plain to you compared to what you are used to."

"No," he assured her. "Not at all. It is not as elaborately and openly decorated, but then there is more that meets the eye when one looks more closely. Your furniture, for example." He let his fingers glide over the drawers of the chest she had sworn to remove. "The carvings. We do not pay so much attention to details such as that, we catch the eye with boldly coloured fabrics that would not even let us notice little artistic touches such as this. Your fabrics are more subdued, subtler. It is a different style, but hardly less intriguing or plain, as you termed it."

She watched him for a few moments, trying to discern whether he was just telling her what he thought she wanted to hear or if he was serious.

"An interesting observation," she then said noncommittally.

"I wonder why you do not remember anything about your home, Eryn. You spent what is considered the most formative time of your life there, after all. You were already five years old when your father took you away. There should be some memories."

She frowned. "There are, but nothing tangible. The other day, when you served the drink, some of the ingredients seemed familiar, but it was more a feeling than a specific memory. I have pictures in my head, but only snippets of colour and shape, not even any faces I should probably have remembered. There is an image of my mother, but it is blurred and I am not sure if it really is a memory or if it is what my head came up with when my father told me about her."

"So he told you about your mother," Ram'an said and seemed surprised.

"A little, yes. This is obviously not what you expected."

The ambassador smiled and shrugged. "You could say that, yes. He took you away from your family, after all. So I would not have expected him to tell you about them."

Eryn shook her head in bewilderment. "Why wouldn't he? The family we left behind was not really close after my mother's death."

Ram'an stared at her for a few moments, then his eyes darted about in what seemed to signify quick thinking. "What has he told you about your mother's death, if I may ask?"

"Not too many details, I admit. He just said that he lost her only a few years after they were joined and that he was devastated by it. Why do you ask?"

He smiled, but there was no pleasure evident behind it. "Just out of interest."

She folded her arms. "I get the feeling that there is something you are not telling me. What is the matter with my family?"

"I am afraid I am not at liberty to talk about your family," he replied slickly.

Damn, she thought. What a handy sentence to trot out to somebody if there was something one didn't want to talk about and happened to be a diplomat.

"What a pity," she said, her voice empty of any emotion.

"Eryn," he pleaded and took one of her hands between his. "Let us not have this little matter between us, shall we? Come, I will show you what you are so eager to learn."

"Alright," she sighed. "Let me get my vials. I still have a few full ones left."

She went into the guest room and returned with a small, simple wooden box. When she opened it, Ram'an took out one of the six vials within and inspected the dried herbs inside.

"You need to mix this with a little water, otherwise it will not work," he instructed and she went to retrieve the water jug on the dinner table.

He uncorked the vial, added a few drops, then closed it again to mix it. "Water is necessary as we will not imbue the herbs with magic, but the water. Elemental magic is much easier to handle and quite effective."

She raised her brows in surprise. "We enchant the water, not the herbs? But why do I even need the herbs then?"

"You will not enchant the water to give up its primary purpose as carrier substance, but to enhance and strengthen the effect of the herbs it carries. The herbs act as messengers, they know what needs to be done, what their effect will be, and the water just boosts it," Ram'an explained.

"So I just feed the water with energy? Like I do with my muscles?" she enquired, never having thought of infusing something lifeless with magic.

"It is not quite as simple as that, I am afraid. You need to find out which attributes you would like to be stronger. Maybe some of the herbs have characteristics which should not be stronger or the patient would be in danger or suffer from unpleasant side-effects," he pointed out. "So you first see what needs to be enhanced and concentrate on that. For this you need to analyse the herbs and eliminate or reduce whatever substances are unwanted. Then you can infuse the water and thus only strengthen what you need."

She nodded slowly. Analysing the herbs wouldn't be much of a problem - she already knew how to examine plants. Cupping her hand, she emptied the herbs into her palm and closed her eyes. After more than a minute she opened them again.

"Why is this so hard to do? I get hardly any response."

Ram'an smiled. "Because they are dried, there is hardly any life left in them. Doing this with fresh herbs is much easier. You dry them afterwards."

Looking at the powder in her palm in dismay, she sighed. "So I have nothing to practise this on to see if I can do it. What a shame."

"Do not worry, it is not so hard and you can practice it alone and come to me if you have questions or need further instructions. To see if you can use the technique does not even require medicinal herbs. You can try it with spices, for example; your kitchen can surly provide you with some of those. Enhance the oils in them and you can then taste them and see if they are more intense than before. This is how we practise it at home. It is an easy and very quick way to see if there is any progress." He smiled. "If a student is particularly bothersome, he or she is made to test this with hot spices."

Eryn laughed. "That does seem a bit cruel."

"Yes, teachers are not to be trusted sometimes. Though I cannot really complain, I was always a very compliant student. I just watched my mates running for water after tasting their results. And as you surely know, water is not a good thing to drink after eating something hot. It just aids to spread the burning substance in the mouth more evenly. My teacher would of course only impart this little piece of wisdom afterwards and only then send them to have some bread instead."

She shook her head. "I can't help thinking that it was probably a good thing for me not to have grown up there, I would very likely have lost my sense of taste completely by now."

The ambassador raised his brow. "You were not an obedient student yourself then, I gather?"

"Yes, I think you could put it that way. At least not with the theoretical part, I was always more eager to do things, try them, make mistakes and learn that way. Which isn't, of course, always a viable line to take when it comes to healing. Some things cannot just be tried like that as the patient might not survive the experiment. Especially as we needed to keep our abilities a secret."

"But your studies did not end with your father's death, did they? He took a lot of books with him when he crossed the sea. I assume they are in your possession now?"

She nodded. "Yes, I used them to continue my training afterwards, but without anybody around to ask, many things were very hard to understand."

Ram'an scowled in sympathy. "I can understand that. I have only had some very basic healing training, but I do not think I would have managed to learn most of it only by perusing books."

Eryn sighed. "And now I am supposed to train other healers. This will be quite a challenge. Firstly, I have no idea how to train others except by showing them how to do it and give them books to read. And secondly, now that you are here I see what considerable gaps there are in my own knowledge."

He reached out to squeeze her hand. "Do not be discouraged by that, these are just little things, easily learned. I dare say your father has taught you quite a lot before he died, so you are surely skilled enough. Especially as you are in a country which provides no healing services at all at the moment. Whatever you do will be an improvement, whether it is perfect or not."

Smiling at him, she rose to refill their glasses, glad to have an excuse to remove her hand from under his. Enric wouldn't appreciate the sight. And sure enough, when she turned, there he was, leaning against the door frame of his office, arms folded in that position he liked to adopt when he was watching her. He had this uncanny ability always to turn up at the right - or in her case, the most inappropriate - moments.

"I assume your lesson is over?" he enquired. "Then I hope you will permit me to join you?" He raised his brow questioningly at the ambassador, who could hardly do anything but agree without seeming impolite.

"Of course, Lord Enric, it would be a pleasure."

Enric eased himself away from the door frame and joined Eryn, picking up the ambassador's glass and a clean one for himself to take to the table.

"Ambassador. Thank you for sharing your knowledge with Eryn. New healing knowledge is rather hard to come by here, as you might imagine," Enric spoke and placed a glass in front of Ram'an.

"No, of course not. But if your own and my country manage to reach an understanding, we might in the future be able to change that."

Eryn sat down at the table again, intrigued. "Really? What kind of understanding?"

"My attachés are both busy testing the ground for trade arrangements. And if we can trade goods, then why not knowledge as well?"

Her heart had begun beating faster. Healing knowledge from the Western Territories! She would maybe be able to learn new things without even having to leave the kingdom!

"Books," she murmured and stared at the table. "We could buy books from you. Healing books. The ones my father left me are old, and I am sure you have made new discoveries in the meantime. And books on art for Vern. You said artists are highly esteemed in the Western Territories, didn't you?" She jumped up and ran into the guest room, returning only moments later with what Enric immediately identified as the book Vern had given her.

She put it in front of Ram'an. "I gave him one of my father's books and this is what he gave me back."

Ram'an smiled politely and opened the book. Then he drew in his breath sharply through his teeth and stared at the detailed drawing of muscle fibres, then back at Eryn. "The boy did this? But he is hardly sixteen years old! Where has he learned this?"

Eryn laughed. "Nowhere! Magicians are not encouraged to develop artistic talents, so he has had no training whatsoever. This is just what happens when he picks up a pen."

"Extraordinary," the ambassador said in amazement and then looked thoughtful for a few moments. "Do you think the young man would agree to having another copy made for me so I can take it back with me? I am convinced that this will be eagerly received in certain circles. I would, of course, be willing to pay handsomely for it."

Enric smiled. "No, we would rather have you accept it as a gift. I will order another copy tomorrow and will ask Vern personally to take care of the illustrations. I am afraid the scribes would hardly do them justice."

"Thank you, Lord Enric. I appreciate this very much."

"This is great! Vern will be so excited! I can't wait to tell him tomorrow, I will let him know first thing in the morning!"

Enric shook his head. "I don't think you will, my love. Tomorrow morning you will have no time for social calls. You have a training lesson scheduled with me."

She sighed. "Oh. Again? Are you sure the training plan is correct? Still every second day, is it?"

"Yes. And we didn't have one this morning," he explained patiently. "You are not trying to wriggle out of it, are you?"

"No, of course not," she smiled though looking downcast. "Why ever would I?"

Ram'an frowned. "You are her teacher as well as her companion, Lord Enric? Please forgive my ignorance, but where I come from this would seem highly unusual."

Enric chuckled. "Believe me, until we found Eryn it was not common practice here, either. Firstly, because she is the only female magician we have and thus the question of companionships between teacher and student has never before arisen. And secondly, there is not much choice, as only Lord Tyront and myself are strong enough to teach her fighting skills without blocking her powers. Lord Tyront is a very strong magician, but his combat skills are not as advanced as my own. So I am practically the only one in the Order meeting both requirements."

The ambassador nodded. "I see. Of course you would continue to train fighting skills. It is a requirement to be a member of the Order of Magicians as I understand it?"

"Yes," Enric agreed. "Up until now we haven't really thought of using our powers for anything else." He slung an affectionate arm around Eryn's waist and pulled her down next to him.

"By the way, King Folrin is planning to hold another ball soon. I have scheduled dancing lessons for you. You are starting tomorrow afternoon."

She turned to him, frowning in dismay. "Dancing lessons?" She was about to protest but thought better of it. Maybe this was why Enric had raised it now, because he knew that she would not start a fight in front of their visitor.

Ram'an raised his brow in surprise. "You do not dance, Eryn? How is this possible? It is an expression of joy, of beauty and elegance! In my country not dancing is unthinkable."

"You have a look at the way people dance here and then tell me that again. It looked so boring last time. I don't imagine doing it is much more fun than watching. And I am not particularly fond of balls. And the last one was…" She stopped herself in time.

"Unpleasant?" Ram'an enquired and leaned forward, clearly very interested in how she had intended to end the sentence. "From what I understand your commitment ceremony was held at the last ball."

Damn, she thought and forced herself to smile. So he had his own sources of information here already. How very expeditious of him.

"Oh, yes," she said and cursed the high pitch her voice was now at. Her abilities to lie had turned out to be less advanced than she had thought. "Apart from that, of course. That was the only pleasant part. Really."

"Of course," the ambassador smiled back, clearly not believing a word of it.

CHAPTER 42

Learning Dancing

Enric glanced up from his paperwork when he heard the entrance door being slammed shut. He frowned and rose. That was rather early for her to return from her dancing lessons.

"Eryn?" he called out and went into the parlour, where she was lying on one of the sofas, legs up on the back rest, her head dangling down over the edge.

"That does not look particularly comfortable," he commented.

"Do you want to know what else was not particularly comfortable? Having a dancing lesson with your former lover."

She watched his upside-down form close his eyes for a moment.

"Pardon me?"

"Valcredy. She told me that you had been lovers." Eryn sat upright again, her hair tangled. "I have no problem with that. You have your past, I have mine. I appreciate that you do have one, actually. You are a skilled lovemaking partner and I am aware that this skill has to come from somewhere. But I really don't think I have to let myself be insulted by someone who clearly seems to be a very jealous and frustrated woman."

Enric exhaled and took a seat on a chair opposite her. "Are you telling me that she behaved in a disrespectful and inappropriate manner?"

She looked up at the ceiling in exasperation. "You bet!"

"More details would be helpful if you don't mind," he requested calmly, though he was clearly not looking forward to hearing them.

"She basically told me that you wanted to possess me, as having an exotic pet would increase your standing among your colleagues even further. And that apart from that I am also a convenient means to produce magically powerful offspring with you. Seriously? You people here don't even know how to heal a bleeding finger, so why is everybody suddenly an expert on whether and how magical abilities are passed on? And you couldn't even make me have children without my consent! I can manipulate my fertility cycle! I am the mistress of my progeny!" She had stood up and thrown up her hands.

Enric watched her, slightly amused. "Mistress of your progeny?"

"Yes! I am! And there is nothing you or anybody else can do about it," she snapped at him, daring him to contradict her.

"Well, this is a relief. As *I* have no intention of doing anything about it, I am glad to hear that nobody else can."

She narrowed her eyes. "Don't tell me you chose this moment to mock me! How in the name of everything that is good and decent does a man come to think that sending his current partner to take dancing lessons with his previous lover is a sensible idea? I mean, really? You could have prepared me a little at least! I stood there like an idiot, not knowing at first why she resented me so much!"

"I am sorry, Eryn. I had not expected her to be bitter about our affair. I never consciously fuelled any hopes, in case you are wondering," he added casually.

She lifted her hands, palms facing towards him. "I am absolutely *not* interested in what you did or did not do and said or did not say to her. I just want to make it very clear to you that I have no intention of ever having another dancing lesson with her, in case *you* were wondering."

He smiled. "I wasn't."

"Good. I cannot guarantee what will happen if she spews her bile on me ever again. I might throw some poison right back at her." Her smile held a wicked snarl within. "But not the verbal kind. The literal one. I know how to mix it, after all."

"Not jealous, are you, my love?" Enric grinned and leaned forward.

"No. A man as jealous as you is hardly inclined to return to his old lovers." She smiled. "I imagine you would be much more jealous of *my* former lovers, should you ever encounter them."

His smile vanished and he pursed his lips. She was damn right about that, he had to admit.

"Not that it would make any sense, though," she sighed. "I have always avoided forming any kind of attachment to my lovers. Too dangerous. Who would have thought I would one day be fettered to the most dangerous one of them all?"

He raised his brow at her. "I don't like the term *fettered*. But I approve of your assessment of my level of danger. Just don't forget it when the ambassador next feels the need to express his sympathy by touching you."

"Oh, please! I more or less jumped up to get out of his reach that time! And I don't see why you change the topic away from your idiotic musician bed partner and instead make me feel like *I* have to defend myself. Which I do not, as I have done nothing whatsoever to earn your disapproval. You, in turn, have done something very stupid, and I would very much like to continue talking about *that*."

"Alright, I apologise for putting you in this position. I am sure it was unpleasant and I grant you a wish to compensate you for my lack of providence."

She pursed her lips. "A wish? Alright. I would like to be the one to decide whether or not to spend time with Ram'an unsupervised."

He shook his head. "No, not that."

"Then I want to stay at home instead of attending the ball."

"Not that, either. The King would not be amused."

She sighed. "Alright, then I want to reduce the number of fighting lessons I have to take."

"Eryn! That would endanger your status as member of the Order. So no."

She threw up her arms in frustration. "Fine! Thank you so much for the wish! It's completely useless if you keep saying *No*."

"I was hoping for something like jewellery or other requests that can be satisfied with money."

She shook her head and scoffed. "Really now. How long have you known me?"

"I can still hope, can't I? Maybe you realise one of these days that a comfortable life is not something to be ashamed of, but may also be embraced to a certain degree without seeming frivolous."

"By letting you buy me earrings so you can clear your conscience?" She laughed. "Hardly."

Enric considered her for a moment. "If money is not the currency you are interested in, maybe I can offer you another one. Information."

"What information?"

"Let's just say Tyront has received an application for a healer trainee that he is not too happy about," he replied slowly, enjoying the spark of interest in her eyes.

"Who?"

"He currently holds a position that enables him to tip future decisions in your favour."

She frowned and her gaze wandered along the ceiling while she was thinking. Then her eyes darted back to his face. "Not Lord Poron, is it?"

"The very same," he said.

He watched her lean back after a moment and start laughing loudly. "Lord Poron! That is brilliant! And as he and I will both approve, there is not really anything that Lord Tyront can do about it. He is outnumbered! This means that we will really be able to make informed decisions about who to accept into the profession, if two out of three persons are aware of the requirements."

"Try not to be smug about this," Enric warned her. "You should be careful with Tyront - you don't want to be in his bad books. And there is still the tiny matter of your demonstration of your new bolt lying between the two of you. Even if you do vote in favour of Lord Poron's application, you should at least show the courtesy of hearing Tyront out and discuss it with him. If he has objections they very likely will be worth listening to."

"Alright, I will crush him gently," she said airily.

He shook his head in exasperation. "Why do I have the feeling that I should be present at this meeting to calm the waters?"

Eryn clucked three times and waved her index finger. "I regret to inform you, Lord Enric, that your presence is not actually required at this meeting as long as you have not been summoned before us. And I am not aware of such a summons having been sent to you."

"A summons? I am both your and Lord Poron's superior, so what would keep me from attending if I wanted to?" he enquired.

"Your rank hardly justifies sticking your nose in where it doesn't belong. You would make fools of us both if you accompanied me to my meetings. You heard Lord Tyront when he told you to let me undertake negotiations with the apothecaries alone."

"Yet you didn't really do them alone, as I recall. In fact, it seems as if you didn't do very much negotiating at all but more or less provided the legitimacy for Vern by simply being there," he retorted.

"Not the first time. He only joined me a few days later when they came back. And even though I admit that Vern was the one to thrash things out, it still proves that I can somehow manage without you. Even if it is only because I manage to find the right person for the task at hand."

"Yes," he snorted. "I must say you have a talent for finding them. Junar for organising your spontaneous dinner parties, Vern for doing your negotiating."

She beamed. "It is all a matter of delegating. Even you have turned out to be useful."

"I have? How delightful," he replied in mock surprise. "In general or with regard to something in particular?"

"Your presence lends me legitimacy when I need it. People tend to just swallow and nod when you stand there with your arms folded, giving that cold glare."

"*You* don't."

"No. Because I am not afraid of you."

"Not anymore," he pointed out.

"Who says I ever was?" she replied loftily.

"You used to run away or freeze every time you saw me."

She gave him a haughty look. "That was hate. Easily confused by somebody who prefers to be feared, I suggest."

"Yes, right," he said with a good-natured smile. "So, having abandoned your dancing lessons you have a free afternoon now?"

"Theoretically, yes. But I think I will take a walk and have a look at the healers' building and check on progress."

Enric nodded. He had already been there himself after his last meeting and had bumped into Orrin. The warrior was true to his word and walked by about twice a week. People found it generally disconcerting to be watched by Orrin for more than a few seconds. He, too, had a rather galvanising stare.

"And I suppose you will be teaching Vern after his lessons are over?"

"Yes, that is the plan. But he also has to draw the pictures for Ram'an's book, so he will probably not be very receptive today."

"Then you can spend one or two nice hours with Orrin..." He stopped himself and looked at her thoughtfully.

She frowned. "What?"

"I seem to recall that Orrin is an able dancer. I wonder if he is willing to work with you on that."

"Dancing lessons with Orrin? Seriously?" she moaned and let herself tip over to bury her face in a scatter cushion. "I have just escaped combat training with him!" Her voice was muffled through the fabric.

"Well, there is always Valcredy if Orrin is not an option for you," he remarked mildly.

She looked up and glared at him. "Oh, shut up. I don't even see why I have to learn this. Didn't Vyril say it is not a problem as long as I dance with a magician? I assume you can steer me with the right muscle impulses."

"True enough. But that is no long-term option. Firstly, you should also be able to dance with non-magicians, and a few of them are quite important and should not be made angry by a rejection. And secondly, I didn't have the impression that you took very well to your muscles being steered by somebody else."

She stared at him. Valid points, both of them. Damn. Sighing in defeat, she rubbed her face. "Then let's ask Orrin if he is willing to endure teaching me yet another undesired skill. He will be so thrilled."

Thinking of his likely reaction to that request made her smile lopsidedly.

* * *

The three musicians in the room stood together, casting furtive looks at the man and woman at the other end of the room. Eryn was watching them as well, though more openly, from her place next to a window, propped against the wall.

Valcredy looked sullen with folded arms, her head turned a little to the left and slightly down, not meeting Enric's cool stare. Her lips were pressed into a thin line. Enric was standing straight, his arms akimbo, legs broad and seemed to be doing most of the talking. And it didn't look like a particularly friendly conversation.

Eryn considered listening in, the way Enric liked to do with his little air trick, but decided against it. It wasn't as if she didn't have a pretty good idea what he was telling her. She didn't feel any need to revel in the other woman's discomfort and humiliation. And she was sure that it had to be humiliating to be reprimanded by a former lover, whom she was still attracted to, because she had behaved callously towards his companion.

After several minutes Enric grasped Valcredy around her upper arm and, none too gently, virtually dragged her to where Eryn was standing. He let her go immediately after she was standing where he had intended her to as if he wanted to avoid contact for any longer than was necessary.

"Go on," he instructed her with threat evident in his voice and posture.

Eryn rolled her eyes and pushed herself away from the wall. "Don't tell me you are making her apologise to me."

"It is the least she can do," Enric said calmly.

Valcredy closed her eyes, took a deep breath and started, "Lady Eryn, I..."

"Shut up," Eryn said mildly. "I don't want your apology. It would hardly be an earnest one. I would prefer a little deal instead."

Valcredy narrowed her eyes in suspicion while Enric looked on intently.

"If you ever again insult me the way you did last time or talk about me behind my back, I will drag you out into the open and give you a good whacking for everyone to witness. And I have to warn you - in the course of my fighting lessons over these last few months I have acquired some skills that might turn out to be rather painful for you to be on the wrong end of, even without using magic. Is that acceptable to you or do you feel any particularly strong wish to apologise to me instead?"

The other woman shook her head stiffly. "No, not really. I accept it."

"Good," Enric remarked with a smile in Eryn's direction, "now that this is settled, we can start the dancing lesson as soon as Orrin arrives." He turned to Valcredy, his expression turning cool again. "You may leave now. Don't return until Eryn is finished here. You may feel that you are being treated unfairly by having your musicians used without your consent, but it was your own childish and unprofessional behaviour that you have to thank for that. Be grateful that there are no other, longer term consequences for you."

The woman turned stiffly and walked out without sparing either of them another glance.

Eryn watched the swinging hips and long blond mane retreat and shook her head. "You know, I start to see a preference for difficult women here. It's sobering to realise that it was not my uniqueness that attracted you, but the fact that I match your preferred type of woman."

Enric grimaced. "Don't compare yourself to her. There was never more than physical pleasure between us. There was not enough depth in her for my liking for anything more."

She grinned. "Really? My depth is what attracted you to me in the first place? I thought it was a tight dress and music that freed inhibitions."

"No, my love," he said and took her hand, deciding against kissing her in front of the musicians. "That's just what made me take advantage of you much earlier than I would have done otherwise. I am a traditional man, basically. Normally I try to make a woman stop hating me before I coerce her into bed."

"Aww, an old-fashioned gentleman," she cooed and made to pinch his cheek. He leaned away and caught her hand instead.

"Absolutely. But somehow you make being old-fashioned very hard for me," he smiled and turned when the door opened and Orrin came in, seeming none too happy about his new assignment.

"I am leaving the two of you to your lessons now," Enric said with a broad grin.

Eryn narrowed her eyes at him. "Say, judging from your high and mighty standing in society, you would also have to be able to dance, right? Why aren't *you* teaching me?"

He laughed. "Because my high and mighty standing enables me to delegate tasks that will make you grumpy and irritable to other people. Power is a beautiful thing."

"Nice to see that you use your authority in such a responsible way," she sniffed and tugged her hands from his grip.

Orrin had reached them, bowed to Enric and nodded to her.

"Please don't look so sour, Orrin," she said, hooking her arm through his. "We both know how much you miss teaching me something, so stop pretending you are unhappy about it. And this time you even get to hold my hands, lucky you."

"Yes, right," he growled but his expression softened a little.

"You can leave now, Enric," she said and waved him away. "I am in strong, masculine, capable hands if I am to believe my good friend Junar."

She smiled sweetly when she saw his eyes narrow at her. So much for making her a task that had to be delegated.

CHAPTER 43

A None-Too-Subtle Warning

Eryn opened the door to their quarters, leaning against it after she had closed it again. It had been another long day. She slid down to sit on the floor and yawned.

She heard the chair in the study being pushed back. Enric appeared in the doorway after a few moments.

"So tired?" he asked.

"No. The floor just looked so immensely comfortable I couldn't resist," she grumbled. "I feel like I haven't slept enough in days. The current programme is probably a bit too much for me in the long run. Learning the stuff you feel is necessary for me to be a person of respect in the Order, combat training, dancing lessons, planning the whole setup of the healing services, teaching Vern, meeting the ambassador occasionally to keep him happy as well, preparing medicines for later use…"

Enric regarded her with a slightly concerned look. "Yes, that is a lot. You might want to prioritise."

"Prioritise? Really? That basically means neglecting the matters the Order doesn't consider very important. My priorities are healing and teaching, yours are teaching me this useless stuff from your ancient books, fighting, and dancing. I can't even remember when I last saw Plia! I suppose she has grown into a beautiful woman and has three kids by now."

He shook his head. "No, not quite. I saw her last week. Still a girl I'd say."

She grasped the door handle and pulled herself up again. "Good, that's comforting. If you will excuse me now, I have an urgent appointment with my bed and can't be disturbed for the next few hours."

"Have you considered asking Tyront for an assistant?" Enric said and followed her into the bedroom, watching her when she struggled out of her clothes and let them drop to the floor right where she was standing.

"No," she chuckled. "Not really. I have no great hopes of his granting me favours anytime soon. I am still waiting for his wrath to strike me down. Actually, I would like him to take his revenge rather sooner than later, as I find that rather a strain, to be honest."

"You have nothing to lose by asking him, then. Either he refuses and you have thus given him the chance for the revenge you want to get out of the way, or he grants it and you can delegate some of the organisational work for setting up the healing services," Enric shrugged.

Eryn pulled the nightshirt over her head and slid under her blanket, considering his proposal. "You know, this does sound halfway plausible. If this is not just due to my current status of tiredness and I still think so tomorrow morning, I will send Lord Tyront a note."

She yawned once more and turned to her side, pulling the blanket up to her ears. When Enric stepped next to her to kiss her good night, she was already fast asleep.

* * *

"How are your dancing lessons going?" Enric enquired while parrying a blow aimed at his ribs.

"Surprisingly smoothly," she replied and watched his moves to assess where best to strike next. "Orrin is a good dancer, which should not really surprise me. It's basically all about making your partner do what you want, and he has plenty of practice in that area."

He laughed. "Probably. The trouble is rather that you are not really used to doing what you are told, I would assume. So has there been any progress at all or are you just straining his nerves even further?"

She thrust her sword at his shoulder and blocked his answering strike.

"I think there is some progress, yes. Orrin is relatively relaxed, so that is a good indicator. And I have the feeling that he has fun teaching me this, even though he would never admit it." She cocked one brow. "But I am sure you didn't need to ask *me* to learn about this. I bet you are having Orrin send regular progress reports about my dancing lessons."

Enric grinned and she knew she had guessed correctly.

"What does he say, then? Is his evaluation of my skills anywhere close to what I said?"

"Fortunately, yes. He wrote that you have mastered three out of the four dances he planned to teach you and you still have two more lessons planned to take care of the last one before the ball."

"Good. I can't tell you how much I am looking forward to this ball being over. I assume my dancing lessons will then be finished as well, at least for the time being?" she asked hopefully.

He nodded. "Yes, for the time being. We will probably schedule a lesson or two between balls so you don't forget everything, but nothing regular."

She smiled in relief and Enric used the diversion to knock her sword out of her hand.

"Concentration," he scolded. "Don't let me distract you."

"Then stop asking me questions!" she complained and went to retrieve her weapon.

"No, that is the purpose of the exercise: resisting diversion." He waited until she was ready again, sword in hand, before he asked her, "Have you decided yet whether to apply for an assistant?"

Hopping back as he swung his weapon at her, she nodded. "Yes, I've decided to give it a try. I will send him a note after the ball. Maybe I can make a good impression on him there by dancing with him."

Enric whistled through his teeth. "Already using your newly acquired skills to plot manipulation? I am impressed."

"You are just saying that because I am not using my evil powers of manipulation on *you*," she said.

"True enough. But if you want to try dancing me into submission, I am at your disposal at any time for it."

"How sweet of you. But for you I have more effective ways at my disposal." She batted her eyelashes.

"That you do. And as you are doubtlessly aware, I am even more eager to be available for *them* whenever the mood strikes you." He hastily raised his sword, blocking her blow at the last moment.

Smiling, she mimicked his earlier reprimand. "Concentration! You are not to let me distract you."

He replied by sending her sword spinning out of her hand again. Damn.

* * *

Eryn turned in front of the mirror. The current ball gown was more to her liking than the last one. There was still a very generous neckline, but the cleavage was more or less covered with some gauzy, see-through material that at least gave an illusion of not being completely undraped in her upper regions.

"You know, I think you are getting the hang of this," she told Junar who rolled her eyes in reply.

"*I* am getting the hang of it? I was playing around with needle and thread before you were even born. But it does you credit that you finally start appreciating my work," she added generously.

Eryn grinned at her in the mirror. "Whichever version keeps you happy. I remember the last time we tried on a dress. It was for the banquet after the delegation had arrived. The white one. You were in a really bad mood that day. I think you said it was because of a difficult customer."

"Well," Junar grimaced. "That was a lie, actually. The difficult person I had to deal with was Orrin."

Eyebrows raised in surprise, Eryn turned around to her friend. "Really? He can put you in such a foul mood? What did he do?"

"He wanted me to expand my shop and offered to pay for another building in a better location. I was really angry at him for this. As if I was only spending time with him to make him buy things for me." She shook her head in disgust.

Eryn nodded in sympathy. She could remember that feeling well enough.

"So you refused, I assume?"

Junar nodded. "Of course." Then she grinned. "But thanks to my fabulous connections to a certain female magician in this city, I had so many new orders and have a lot of new regular customers, allowing me to pay for the new building myself in a couple of months."

"So you do like the idea as such?"

The seamstress shrugged. "Sure. I just resent his taking on the role of the big provider."

"Funny. When I had that same problem with Enric, you just laughed at me."

"That is something completely different. Lord Enric never wanted to buy a building for you, just some much needed clothes. And you are his companion. Orrin and I are not even close to that and will probably never be. I, at least, have had my share of being bound to a man." She shuddered and then looked at Eryn apologetically. "Sorry, you know how I meant that."

"I know your former companion was not up to much, but this does not mean that there is nothing better out there. I mean, Orrin is a decent man. And trust me, if somebody who has been forcefully trained by him for several months can say this, it is quite a compliment."

Junar shook her head in wonder. "Look at you. You finally admit to being happy in your companionship and even try to make others follow your example! And this after only one month."

"Nonsense." Eryn scoffed. "Being joined with him has nothing to do with it." She laughed when a thought came to her. "You know, I would probably still be living with Orrin if the King hadn't made me move in here. That would have made meeting him even more difficult for you."

"Yes," Junar said dryly, "having another, younger woman live with your lover is a very pleasant thing to imagine."

"Don't tell me you are jealous now!" Eryn exclaimed. "If I have to deal with another person suspecting Orrin and I of being attracted to each other, and after Enric finally got that notion out of his head, I am going to go crazy! Open your eyes! He treats me like a substitute daughter, which everybody but you and Enric seems to be aware of. And - no offence meant - but not everybody is into the whole generation-age-difference thing. My companion is seven years older than me, and that is about as big a gap as I would tolerate."

The seamstress gestured helplessly. "It's easy for you to talk, but how would you react if you learned that your lover had been on the verge of making a claim to the woman he supposedly treats like a daughter at her commitment?"

Eryn laughed out. "What? Now that has to be complete nonsense!"

Junar scowled at her. "No, it is not. Lord Tyront had to threaten him or he would have interrupted the ceremony."

"You are joking, aren't you?" She frowned. "That could not have ended well. Enric would have skinned him alive." She looked into Junar's eyes. "But you must be aware why he'd intended to do it. He knew that I was being forced into it and wanted to protect me."

"Yes, that is why you both still have your arms attached to your bodies," Junar grumbled.

"Well, well, I wouldn't have pegged you for the vengeful type. Funny, what romantic passion does to people."

The older woman eyed her speculatively. "Don't tell me you wouldn't mind if another woman dallied with your companion? I know that your commitment was not exactly voluntary, but your involvement with him was. So I assume there must be some kind of attachment on your side as well."

Eryn shrugged. "I don't think I am the jealous type. If he wants to run off with another woman, I think I would survive it somehow. Who am I to try and force him to stay with me if he doesn't want to?"

Junar pursed her lips and shook her head slightly. "Tough words. But I dare say that you only see it in such a relaxed manner because you know that he is crazy about you."

"So you think I might be jealous if he gave me more reason to? I don't know." She considered the possibility. "He had this affair with the musician, the one always attired in boldly coloured dresses."

"Valcredy? Yes, I know. She didn't really keep it a secret. He was a real feather in her cap, after all. And I suspect she had seen herself as his companion one day - until you came along. Why?"

"She insulted me when she was supposed to be teaching me dancing, and I was not jealous - not a bit. So I am either not the jealous type or I am not fond of Enric enough really to care about losing him." She frowned. The second option would be a very sad one indeed.

She felt Junar take her hand. "I have seen the two of you together. To my eyes you do not seem indifferent." She smiled then. "So she insulted you? I assume this is why Orrin switched to teaching you dancing instead?"

Eryn grinned. "Yes. It was Enric's idea. That proves that he is no longer afraid of anything improper going on between the two of us. I was pleasantly surprised at how well he dances. I dare say the ball tonight is my final exam, so to speak. How much time to we have left? You should probably get yourself dressed as well."

"Me? Why would I? I am not going."

"What do you mean, you are not going? Don't tell me Orrin hasn't asked you?"

The seamstress sighed. "He has. But it doesn't feel right to go to a royal ball just like that. Magicians, aristocrats and their companions. That's who is expected to turn up there."

Eryn shook her head and said mildly, "You are being an idiot, you know. But I won't try to persuade you if you really don't want to go."

"Good!" she replied emphatically. "Vern has been trying just that for the last three days, and I have started hiding from him."

"Pity. I would have enjoyed having you there. There are not that many women around I can talk to. Or would want to."

"Oh come on! Don't try to make me feel guilty!"

Eryn shrugged. "I am not. I will probably not have that much time for casual conversations anyway, as this is more or less my first big public appearance as Enric's companion. Maybe I can hold on to Orrin and Vern."

Junar smiled. "I wouldn't count on that. Now that you are available for dancing, quite a few gentlemen will use this opportunity to introduce themselves I'd wager. You are a very important woman now, after all. And still a sensation, a threefold one. Healer, female magician and companion to Lord Enric. There will be quite some demand for your attention."

Enric knocked at the open bedroom door. "Are you ready? We are due in only a few minutes."

"Yes," Junar said. "Just finished."

Eryn turned away from the mirror towards him and let her gaze wander over his tall form. He wore black, enhanced with a few blue ornaments the colour of his eyes. Something was unusual, though. It took her a few moments to realise what it was.

"Your hair is shorter."

"Yes. You don't sound too thrilled about it - am I to assume you don't like it?" he enquired with an expectant frown.

She walked over to him and motioned for him to spin. He obeyed good-naturedly.

"No, I do like it. It looks more formal."

He cheered up and took her hand to guide her outside. "That was the idea." He looked over to the seamstress. "Will I see you at the ball later?"

Junar shook her head.

Enric looked somewhat surprised, but didn't comment any further. Eryn gave her a look that conveyed the message *I told you so* as clearly as any words would have.

* * *

Junar's words had turned out to be prophetic. It seemed as if every single male guest was determined to dance with Eryn.

The first of them had been King Folrin himself. This time he had chosen her for the first dance that would open the ball. He strolled along his assembled guests, letting his gaze flit seemingly aimlessly. She had squirreled herself away as far as this was possible, while Enric in his front row position had held on to her hand to stop her from shuffling out of sight towards the back of the crowd.

When the King's gaze searched and locked onto her face, she saw a faint smile slowly broaden his face and she swallowed. She had tried to free her fingers from Enric's grip and disappear further back between the guests, but the King's voice stopped her.

"Lady Eryn, do me the honour of opening the ball with me."

Judging from the slightly malicious glint in his eyes he had been very well aware of his chosen partner's reluctance. But that would hardly keep him from asking, or to be more precise, *making* her dance that particular dance where they would for some time be the only ones on the wide dance floor, being watched by everybody.

She had felt Enric's tug at her hand to make her come forward and placed her fingers into King Folrin's hand with a bow.

The King was an able dancer, she had to admit. He would need to be, considering his duties. He of course obeyed all rules of propriety as regarded distance and where he placed his hands.

"I can see that Lord Orrin's dancing lessons were crowned with success." He smiled at her somewhat irked expression. "I think you must be the only person in the city still surprised at my being rather well informed."

She hadn't commented on that but he seemed happy enough to continue the one-sided conversation. "It is a good thing Lord Enric took care of this, or I would have suggested it to him today. Dancing is such an effective way of initiating, furthering and maintaining social connections. And you, dear Lady Eryn, are quite the important social connection a lot of people are eager to make."

She forced herself to smile at his words. An important social connection. Marvellous. As if she didn't have enough on her plate already.

The King, however, had not been duped by her smile. "This surely seems like an unpleasant duty to perform, but you might be surprised at how useful some contacts can turn out to be."

Eryn was relieved when the music stopped and the King released her again. Enric was there and took her hand for the next dance as soon as the King had accompanied her back to him.

Names, titles, faces became a blur - constantly changing dancing partners that whirled her around with different levels of skill. She closed her eyes to try and order the confusion.

"Orrin," she sighed when she opened her eyes and saw him standing before her, ready to take her hand for the next dance. "What have you done to me? I haven't managed to sit down for a minute; every time the music stops, somebody else rushes forward before I have a chance to flee."

He chuckled. "The curse of fame, I am afraid. Will you dance with me nevertheless or will I be the only one you refuse? Not that I want to put you under pressure, but to demur would probably inflict permanent damage on my standing."

Smiling despite herself, she took the hand he was holding out to her. "In this case I will take pity on you. But you need to promise me that you will lead me away to a quiet place afterwards. I desperately need a few minutes to breathe."

"Agreed."

The music started and he smiled. "I have been watching you dance."

She sniffed. "Yes, I felt your watchful eye on me. What do you say? Have I disgraced you?"

"Not yet. But I don't want to offer praise prematurely until I've tested you in a lifelike situation - so ask me again when I have danced with you myself."

She laughed. "Well, I am glad you came only now after all these poor men have served as warm-up exercises to get me in form."

"How are you doing, girl?" he asked, his voice serious. "They are swarming around you like flies."

"My feet are starting to kill me."

Orrin grinned. "Then it's a good thing you are a healer and can make pain disappear, eh?"

"Yes," she admitted reluctantly. "Still, a few minutes of peace would be nice."

"As soon as you have convinced me of your dancing skills," he replied. "You are doing fine so far, I should say."

"High praise indeed," she grinned.

"But don't hide for too long. There still are a few people waiting to dance with you. The ambassador, for once."

Eryn's brow rose in surprise. "Ram'an? He knows how to dance the local dances?"

"Yes, he has been taking dancing lessons with Valcredy from what I know."

A few heads turned when she laughed loudly. "Well, at least she has been able to use the time she would have needed to teach me."

Orrin twirled her elegantly when she lost the rhythm owing to her outburst of merriment.

"I tried to induce Junar to come to the ball, but she refused. Do you think you could talk to her about that?" he then asked.

She grimaced. "I am afraid I can't help you much there. We had a little discussion before I came here. She got rather angry when I tried to press her on it. And from what I have heard Vern has been trying in vain for some time as well. Maybe you should just let her stay away from these festive occasions. I know I would be glad to do so myself."

"Then I would suggest you are hardly the right person to try and convince her," Orrin remarked dryly.

"Don't blame *me*," she said. "I would have enjoyed having her here. Each person here who doesn't want to make polite conversation or dance with me helps me stay sane."

The music faded away and true to his word, Orrin held on to her hand to lead her away from the dance floor past two expectant men who had obviously intended to approach her but instead settled for following her with their eyes.

After they had turned a corner Eryn ducked behind a column and Orrin looked slightly alarmed as her hair suddenly turned blond.

"Trying to blend in? Don't you think people will still recognise the dress?"

She grinned. "You would be surprised at how little people notice when something doesn't fit their picture of the world."

"But people here might have heard about your ability to change the colour of your hair. Vern has been delighting his surroundings with exotic colours for quite some time now."

"You think so? Watch." She straightened and teased out a few strands of her hair from the elaborate hairstyle so as to make them frame her face.

When she stepped back into the ball room, Orrin followed her and watched the two men who had intended to ask her to dance with them before. They both turned away and kept on scanning the crowd, very likely for the brown head of hair they had expected to find.

"You see?" she whispered. "I am basically invisible."

"Yes," he murmured. "And I am sure soon enough people will start wondering where you are. How long are you going to hide like this?"

"Half an hour, probably. An hour at the most."

He sighed. "Suit yourself. As long as you are willing to bear the consequences."

"What consequences?" she frowned.

"How do you think the King and Lord Enric will react to your little game? Hardly very enthusiastically unless I am very much mistaken."

She put him off by waiving her hand. "They will not even notice it."

"What do you think you are doing?" she heard a calm voice at her side. She turned and saw Enric stand next to her, studying her with folded arms and an annoyed and disapproving look.

She heard Orrin chuckle quietly and gave him an icy look when he imitated her. *"They will not even notice it.* Right."

"I do not sound like that," she hissed at him and turned back to Enric when he cleared his throat pointedly.

"I need to rest a few minutes as it seems like every man here is determined to dance with me. I thought it would be more polite to make myself invisible for a while instead of declining offers to dance," she reasoned.

Enric shook his head at her. "I am not happy about this. You are basically anonymous now. This might end with people not treating you in accordance with your status."

She shrugged. "I have no particular need to be treated in accordance with what you call my *status*. I would, in fact, very much prefer to be treated like everybody else for a change."

She saw Ram'an walk past and slow to bow to Enric, when his gaze brushed her and he stopped and walked back, frowning at her.

"Eryn!" The displeasure was clearly audible in his voice and she sighed.

"It is just for now to get a few minutes of peace!" she explained. "Which is clearly not working, with the three of you around proffering criticism! So, if you don't mind, I will sit down for a bit. Alone," she added and gave them a glare before walking off towards an unoccupied sofa, letting herself fall onto it without much elegance.

She smiled contentedly when people walked past her without sparing her so much as a glance. Funny, she mused - how her fame depended on her hair colour as if it were her only distinguishing feature. It seemed as if people didn't look her in the face at all. This might have been a depressing thought at other times, but as it now earned her a little time off the dance floor, she felt contentment rather than annoyance.

She ignored Enric's gaze on her and continued watching the other guests. Vern was currently dancing with an older lady and looking bored, nodding at regular intervals to something she said.

The King was also dancing, though with an attractive young girl Vern would very likely have preferred as his dancing partner. King Folrin regarded Eryn for a moment and raised his brow. She looked away and ignored him as well. Disapproving male glance number four, she thought sourly.

"May I ask you for this dance?"

She looked up at a smiling man in his mid-thirties, regarding him thoughtfully. Had he asked her because he had recognised her or just like that?

He kept smiling at her politely while he was waiting for her answer.

She suppressed a sigh and made herself smile when she accepted his hand. "It would be my pleasure."

He led her to the dance floor and she caught a glimpse of Enric, who was smiling at the failure of her plan just to sit and relax a little.

"A very nice ball this time," her dancing partner commented and continued without waiting for her to agree or disagree. "Last time was a bit of a strain, to be honest. Though the commitment ceremony was rather entertaining. I see Lord Enric standing over there, I wonder where that magician woman is. Has been dancing a lot."

Oh, just tell *me about it*, she thought and merely smiled.

"I haven't seen you around here before," the man said and cocked his head.

"I was here at the last ball," she replied evasively.

"So you saw the spectacle, then? What did you think of it? I thought the Lady did not look particularly happy, but that might have been nervousness. I understand that the King's offer to join them then and there had been quite a surprise for everyone, also for the happy couple."

"Yes, I suppose it must," she said noncommittally and started to wish for the music to come to a close quickly.

The next move brought him closer to her than she felt comfortable with and she pretended to miss a step to increase the distance between their bodies again.

Her dancing partner, however, seemed unperturbed by this and repeated the manoeuvre several times. Then he changed his strategy and pretended to bump into her occasionally to brush against her breasts.

Oh dear, she thought. Subtle flirtation was clearly not this man's forte. She hoped that he would soon get the message of her disinterest or she would have to leave him standing here in the middle of the dance floor.

She sucked in a sharp breath when she felt his hand brush across her bosom in what he clearly tried to make look like a clumsy movement, but the glint in his eyes gave him away.

Very suddenly he was pulled to one side by a tall, familiar and very angry looking figure. She closed her eyes for a moment, dreading what was about to follow.

"Enric, no!" she shouted, terrified, and watched him draw back his fist before it connected with the man's nose only a moment later with a sickening crunch.

The man first staggered back a few steps and then fell to the floor heavily, all the time staring at Enric uncomprehendingly and in utter astonishment. A stream of blood began trickling down first one, then both nostrils.

The dancing couples had stopped moving and spectators were starting to gather in a circle around Eryn, Enric and the man on the floor. Keeping a safe distance, of course.

The ones who were lucky enough to have looked in the right direction at the right time to witness the incident started to convey it to those who hadn't.

Eryn, one palm over her open mouth, stared at the man, who was clasping his bloodied nose with both hands. Blood oozed from between his fingers and it seemed as if the pain from his injury was slowly starting overcoming his shock.

Enric stood only a few paces away from him, one hand still balled into a fist, and stared down at the man with a withering expression in his narrowed eyes.

Ram'an came running towards them and knelt next to the quietly whimpering man. A quick touch of his hand, then the ambassador looked up at Enric.

"You have broken his nose, Lord Enric," he explained calmly. "Will it be acceptable to you if I offer to heal him? I assume you would not wish for Lady Eryn to do it."

Enric breathed in and out a few times and closed his eyes for a moment before he nodded. "Yes, thank you. It is very thoughtful of you, Ambassador."

"Why?" the man wailed in a tinny, high pitched voice. "Why did you do that? What have I ever done to you?"

Enric looked up at the ceiling. "Eryn?"

She let out a long sigh and then changed her hair back to her natural brown colour, increasing the noise level of the murmuring and whispering around them once more.

"But I had no idea that it was her!" the man cried out. The stream of blood had reached his shirt collar, turning the bright blue into an unpleasant shade of mottled purple.

"I know," Enric replied evenly but not exactly in a friendly tone. "That's why your nose is the only part of your body that suffered damage and why I am granting any healing to be done to you at all." He then turned away from the man and towards Eryn, gripping her hand firmly in his.

"Come," he ordered. "We are leaving."

She looked back to the man who was still laying sprawled on the floor, staring at her hair. Ram'an crouched next to him, eyes closed, obviously concentrated on healing the damage Enric's fist had done.

One look at Enric told her that he wouldn't take kindly to any objections from her right now. Although he didn't seem to be on the edge of violence any more, there was still some tension in his posture and in the way he clenched her hand.

He didn't wait for her to agree but turned towards the exit, pulling her along with him. He stopped abruptly when he saw himself facing Loft, the King's advisor.

"His Majesty wishes a quick word with you, Lord Enric," he said factually.

Enric breathed a sigh of defeat and nodded. Of course, he thought bitterly - anything else would have been too easy. He wished he had managed to leave more quickly and been summoned to the King tomorrow instead of right now.

He kept Eryn's hand held tightly in his own as he followed the short, bald man to an unobtrusive door right next to the throne. Loft opened it and led them into a small room, in the centre of which King Folrin was waiting, his stance broad, arms folded, his face set in a clear expression of dissatisfaction.

Enric and Eryn bowed to him and waited for him to speak first. They didn't have to wait long.

"Lord Enric," he said with an undertone of forced patience, "I do not approve of how you treated the ball guests. It does show a certain disregard for your host, who happens to be *myself*."

Enric bowed again. "I apologise most sincerely, Your Majesty. I am afraid I lost my temper out there," he said slickly.

"Did you now, Lord Enric?" the King mused. "I wonder."

Eryn frowned and looked at her companion. What exactly was the King implying?

"In these last ten years nobody really seems to remember ever having seen you lose your temper. Your being angry, yes. But not losing control over your fury if ever there had been situations to put you in such a state. How very interesting now that a few inappropriate, if hardly more than annoying, touches from a man who poses hardly any danger to Lady Eryn, manage to trigger such a reaction in you." The King stared at the magician.

"I think I have in these last weeks since my involvement with Lady Eryn gained a reputation of being rather obvious in my regard for her, Your Majesty," he replied stiffly.

"No, Lord Enric," the monarch contradicted in a tone of grim amusement. "That is putting it too mildly by far. Your reputation is more along the lines of being possessive, jealous and imperious. And yet..." He pursed his lips. "It was a very interesting coincidence that Ambassador Ram'an was in a position to observe everything from such close proximity, was it not?"

Enric kept his gaze even. The man was good - really good. He had once more demonstrated how dangerously effective his brain was.

"Your Majesty?" he just asked.

King Folrin smiled. "You are very well aware what I am talking about. But I can see that your companion is puzzled. I doubt that she will appreciate your little manoeuvre, Lord Enric. I myself am impressed by your quick thinking and how you identified and used this situation to your advantage. But of course I can hardly admit this publicly, can I?" he added with feigned reluctance.

Eryn pulled her hand from Enric's hold and waited for one of them to explain to her what seemed to be so very obvious to the King.

"I will do the explaining. That is, if you don't object, Lord Enric. I wouldn't want to force you into either admitting your little scheme openly or lying to me." The word *again* hung in the air unspoken. The King turned to Eryn. "My dear Lady Eryn, I imagine you are aware of your companion's frustration when it comes to the ambassador's attentions toward you? Ambassador Ram'an's position protects him from the kind of dealing out of a physical lesson we just saw. It does not, however, protect him from witnessing it and drawing his own conclusions from that, does it? And then the ambassador even offered to heal the object of this little demonstration. What a very nice turn of events! It enabled him to not only see the warning carried out, but also to take in the full impact from a medical point of view." He watched Eryn grind her teeth and turn pale.

Breathe, she ordered herself. In and out. Don't shout at him in the King's presence. It's not professional.

"Thank you very much for sharing your view of the current events with me, Your Majesty," she replied and concentrated on the pain her fingernails caused by being pressed tightly into her palms. Pain distracted her from the anger that was building up inside her. She needed to get out of here. And soon, too.

The King's gaze flitted to the white knuckles of her fists for only an instant and returned to her eyes. He grinned. "It was my pleasure, Lady Eryn," he replied. "And now I am sure you are very eager to return to your quarters for the evening. Try not to damage anything on your way. Or any*body*."

CHAPTER 44

Ram'an's Questions

Enric opened the door to their quarters and let Eryn enter first. She had not spoken a single word since they left the audience with the King, and he didn't have any illusions with regard to the cataclysm that awaited him as soon as they were alone in their quarters. Which would be in only a few seconds. He braced himself and closed the door.

Her eyes almost shot out sparks when she turned to him with her arms folded.

"You manipulative, scheming bastard," she said, with surprising calmness. "What do you think it felt like to stand before the King and have him explain to unsuspecting little me what devious intrigues my devoted companion has just employed me in?"

"So you don't object to the deed itself, but that you had to learn about the particulars from the King?" he enquired, his brow raised. Maybe this wouldn't be so bad after all.

"Don't be an idiot!" she hissed. "Of course I object to it! It was an idiotic thing to do - completely unwarranted and an insult to the ambassador! Not to speak of the pitiful man whose nose you broke! The King's little lecture about your dark deed was just the icing on the cake!"

He sighed. So much for his hopes. "The *pitiful man's* nose has already been healed. And let's not forget what he did to provoke the injury."

"What he did to provoke it? You used him to try and scare Ram'an!"

"You may not have known me for very long, Eryn, but you can hardly be thinking that it would have been acceptable for me to watch another man paw at you the way he was doing. There would have been consequences for him whatever happened, believe you me. They have just been a little more severe in order to serve not only as a well-deserved punishment for him, but also as a little demonstration to the ambassador."

Eryn shook her head at him. "I told you before that I expect you to work on your jealousy issues. This is not what I had in mind!"

"My jealousy issues, as you call them, are well founded and thus my way of working on them consists of discouraging the ambassador." He lifted his hand as she was about to speak. "Yes, I am fully aware that this is not what you meant. And no, I have no intention whatsoever of changing my way of handling this particular matter."

"Fine," she said abruptly. "As you are so very accommodating of my wishes, I will take the liberty of repaying you in kind. I will from now on no longer consider your wishes when it comes to spending time alone with the ambassador."

"Eryn." She could hear the warning in this one quietly spoken word clearly, but was in no mood to acknowledge it.

"No! Don't you dare making me seem like the one who messed things up!" She stepped close to him, waiving her outstretched index finger under his nose. "Have you even considered that there might have been a thing or two that I wanted to do tonight? Like for example dancing my very first dance with Vern, or making a good impression on Lord Tyront so he is more favourably inclined towards granting me that assistant you yourself suggested I apply for? And instead of that you made me look like a woman who intentionally lures unsuspecting men by disguising myself so as to make you jealous! Thank you so much!"

"Now listen. If you hadn't changed your hair-colour..." he began and was interrupted almost immediately.

"Me? Have you gone completely crazy? Me changing my colour was the one thing that made your little scheme even possible, so it played right into your hands! If you try somehow to twist this into an accusation saying that *I* brought all this on, I am going to start throwing things at you!" she hissed. "It was *your* doing, yours alone! I would just have left him standing there and walked off!"

She turned and marched into their bedroom. Enric frowned when she returned a few moments later, her arms laden with a pillow and a blanket.

"Now, wait a moment," he growled. "You are not returning to the guest room. I told you that I will not have you sleep there anymore!"

She looked at him, annoyed. "Oh, but I won't. *You* will. Not that I particularly care what you will or will not have me do at the moment, mind you."

He stared at her in disbelief. "You are throwing me out of my own bedroom?"

"*Our* bedroom, as you do not tire of reminding me," she retorted and shouldered open the door to the guest room to drop her bundle on the bed.

Enric had followed her and stood in the door with folded arms, blocking her exit and staring down at her. "Don't you think this is something of an overreaction to this rather harmless matter?"

"Harmless?" she repeated incredulously. "You ask that poor man whose nose you broke how harmless *he* considers that! He may be healed by now, but that does not take away the pain of his nose's brief acquaintance with your fist! Do you even know who the fellow was?"

"No," he replied. "And it doesn't really matter. Though I assume we will learn about it tomorrow anyway. News tends to spread."

"It doesn't really matter?" She shot him an annoyed look. "Get out of my way! I want to go to bed now."

He didn't budge and continued looking down at her.

"I don't want to sleep in here alone," he protested.

"You should have thought about that before your little display of brutal manipulation. Why don't you take it as a reminder of how badly I take to being used for your purposes?" She smiled sweetly and squeezed out through the small gap between his body and the door frame.

He let out a resigned sigh and eyed the bed sullenly. At least *she* hadn't moved out of the bedroom, he mused. He would grant her one night of solitary annoyance, but no more. And for him to return to the bedroom was much easier than making her would have been.

*　*　*

When he emerged from the guest room the next morning, he could instantly see that she had calmed down enough for him to move back into their bedroom.

He went over to the table where she sat in front of her breakfast tray and sipped her tea. Her gaze was relaxed and he decided to see how close she would let him get right now. To his relief she didn't object when he lifted her chin and pressed a kiss onto her mouth.

"Good morning, my love. You are up early today. Would it be too bold of me to attribute this untypical eagerness to get up to your waking up alone instead of in my tender embrace?" He toyed with a strand of her hair when she smiled.

"That is rather bold, yes. We have hardly shared a bed for such a long time that I would be unable to sleep peacefully without your being in it."

He smiled and thought of his own rather restless night. "Whatever you say."

Eryn regarded him for a few moments before she asked, "Will the King make you apologise to the recipient of your attentions yesterday?"

Enric shook his head. "I seriously doubt that. Public apologies tend to leave an aftertaste of fallibility, and that is not an image the King or the magicians would wish to be connected with the Order."

She frowned. "So he will let you get away with it because the Order would look as though its members might be remotely human, thus prone to mistakes and uncontrolled bursts of violence?"

He shook his head. "He hasn't let me get away with it. He told *you* about it and you have made me pay. An elegant solution, I have to admit. If he punishes me openly, he has to admit that an Order magician has made a mistake, which is something he would want to avoid at any cost, as we established before."

She sighed. "He even takes the fun out of taking revenge on you."

"I don't think I approve of you enjoying it," he remarked dryly.

"I wouldn't have expected you to. You should be glad I only made you sleep in another room for one night."

He remembered her words about meeting the ambassador alone without any longer taking his concerns into consideration. "And yet I don't have the feeling that this will be all."

"Don't be difficult about Ram'an. You should probably see it as a kind of therapy. I meet him and you try not to throw a fit, to hit people or to come storming into wherever we are. This will be really good for you. A chance to develop."

He didn't comment on that and just gave her a brooding look, thinking of the two spies he had still following the ambassador and wondering if they were enough.

* * *

She saw Ram'an standing in front of the healers' building, looking up and observing with interest the activities that were visible through one of the windows on the first floor. He turned and smiled when she stepped next to him.

"Eryn, dearest! What a pleasure to see you. Where are you headed? Can I persuade you to spend a little time with me on this grey and cold afternoon?"

She couldn't help but grin. "I am on my way back to my quarters. I have just survived another day of battle strategy and wanted to check on the progress here. And yes, I would love to spend some time with you."

"Very good, you just made my day. I have to admit I feel rather betrayed that I did not have a chance to dance with you at the ball yesterday. I was really looking forward to that, to be honest."

With a sigh of helplessness, she took the arm he offered when they started walking back to the palace and nodded. "Ah yes, I heard that you had been taking dancing lessons as well. I am afraid the evening did not turn out to be as uneventful as I had hoped. Thank you for healing the man; that was very considerate of you."

"A minor thing, it was taken care of in a matter of minutes. I saw the little bald man escorting you to your King. I hope there were no unpleasant consequences for Lord Enric?"

Eryn hid a smile at the obvious insincerity of that last statement. "No, not really. Though the King was not exactly pleased, as you might imagine. He does expect a little more restraint from his magicians. And for good reason, too. We are a bit too dangerous to be running around hitting people whenever the fancy strikes us." She looked at Ram'an and wondered if he had worked out yet that it had been intended as a warning for him.

"I see. You must be very relieved."

She shrugged. "I don't know. Maybe a little royal reprimand would have motivated him to exercise a bit more restraint in the future. How was the rest of the ball? Did anything else happen that will keep the gossip going?"

"No, unfortunately not. After you left it was frightfully boring, to be honest. But at least you and Lord Enric gave people something to chatter about for a while. The man you danced with last was the nephew of one of the members of the Magic Council, I was told."

Eryn stopped and looked at him in surprise. "He was? Well, well, it seems that there might be unpleasant consequences for Enric after all, even if they only consist in enduring unpleasant Council meetings for a time." She smiled broadly. "That serves him right!"

Ram'an turned into the network of corridors that led to his quarters. "Will it be alright for Lord Enric if you join me for an hour or two?"

"It is alright for *me*, so how can he object?" She studiously ignored the ambassador's raised brow.

Ram'an opened the door for her to enter first and she unfastened her cloak and hung it neatly on a wall hook before walking straight over to the cushions on the floor. She sat down with folded legs and leaned back.

"Have I mentioned that I like your sitting arrangements? Though I fear that I would fall asleep a lot in a room like this. It's really cosy."

He smiled and went to the chest she remembered from last time, the one he had taken the very interesting drink out of.

"Ram'an," she sighed, "this is not a good idea. Last time you opened one of these bottles I returned home too late and rather drunk. You are turning out to be a bad influence on me."

"So you would prefer a less intoxicating beverage, I gather?"

She nodded. "Yes, if you don't mind. I need to get up early tomorrow."

"Fighting training with Lord Enric again?"

"Yes," she breathed. "And he makes me pay for it if I am not up to my full strength."

He returned with two glasses filled with a dark red liquid and pressed one into her hand.

She frowned. "This looks a lot like blood."

Laughing, he shook his head. "It is nothing of that kind, I assure you. It is a berry juice from home, one we also give our children to drink. You may rest assured that it will not have any effect on your sobriety. I promise." He raised his glass and waited for her to do the same.

"I drink to your happiness, Eryn. May you find it if you have not discovered it yet and treasure it if you have."

They clinked glasses and she carefully tasted the juice. It was very good - sweet and aromatic.

"Tell me, Eryn, only if you are able, of course. Is your King very powerful?"

She looked at him in surprise. "I am not sure I understand your question. I dare say he is. I mean, he is the King, after all. There is no other single person holding that much power in the kingdom."

Ram'an looked at her indulgently. "No, I meant as a magician."

"As a magician?" Frowning, she shook her head. "What might have given you that idea?"

The ambassador blinked several times before he carefully put down his glass and leaned forward, his gaze intent. "Are you telling me what I think you are telling me? King Folrin is *not* a magician?"

"That is right, he isn't. Why would you assume that he is one?" she asked in astonishment.

Ram'an didn't seem to hear the question. Still staring at her with an expression that looked a lot like rapture, he leaned back, grabbing the glass he had just put down and emptying it in one gulp.

"Please do correct me if I remember this incorrectly," he said after several seconds of silence, "but he was the one to join you and Lord Enric, was he not?"

"Yes," she said carefully. "Why do you ask?"

"No particular reason," he replied nonchalantly with a satisfied half-smile playing around his lips.

She narrowed her eyes at him, not believing him for a second. "Being diplomatic with me, Ram'an?"

He just smiled at her, very obviously pleased about something.

She glared at him in annoyance. How she hated being kept in the dark!

"Do not look so angry, dear Eryn. I was just wondering at your most powerful man having no actual power of his own, but just the power the system grants him. This is quite different at my home."

"It is? So the Western Territories are ruled by magicians?" she enquired curiously.

"That they are. At least most of the time. By three of them, to be precise. They rule together for a period of time and are then subjected to a form of assessment to see how well they have done their job. If the people are satisfied, they are granted another period of ruling. If not, then one, both or all three of them are replaced."

She bit her lip, intrigued. "That is an interesting concept." Then she chuckled. "I am sure King Folrin would not be too pleased about any attempts to implement a similar system here."

"Probably not," Ram'an agreed with a smile. "Let us refrain from proposing it then, shall we?"

"Definitely. He would withdraw the funding for my healing services immediately," she retorted, only half joking.

"Your healing services," he repeated and looked at her, the unnerving half-smile still on his face. "I think people here would profit very much if you came to my and - strictly speaking - also your own country for a while to learn about the things your father did not have enough time to teach you."

Eryn swallowed. She remembered the discussions with Enric, where he had warned her that the ambassador would sooner or later surely make her a proposal such as that.

Ram'an's piercing gaze remained on her face. "Why do I sense reluctance in you when I speak of this, dear Eryn?"

She forced herself to smile. "It is something I have thought about, believe me. But I discarded the idea again. I have plans here - things I want to do, duties, responsibilities. I can't just run off. I don't *want* to run off right now," she corrected herself.

"Really?" His voice was soft and she tensed when she felt his warm hand on hers. "And this is not just what Lord Enric would wish you to say?"

She sighed and rolled her eyes. "Enric. He would wish me to jump up indignantly and storm out at this point. And he would not look kindly upon any such offer being made to me," she added quietly.

"Yes, I assumed he would not. Then I should probably be more careful if I do not want *my* nose broken as well, eh?"

His telling smile eradicated any doubts she had had about the warning having hit its mark. She exhaled slowly and closed her eyes. "I think I should leave now."

"I wish you would not," Ram'an said and she saw him frown when she opened her eyes again. "My stay here comes to an end in only three days. And there are questions I have."

Eryn braced herself. She doubted very much that she would be in a position to answer his questions honestly. Or at all.

"From the things I have heard, it seems to me that your commitment to Lord Enric was not exactly a voluntary one, was it?"

She laughed nervously under his intense scrutiny. "Oh come on, you know how people talk!"

"No, I am afraid I do not know." He leaned forward, still holding on to her hand. "Kindly tell me what is true then, have you been committed to Lord Enric willingly and voluntarily, Eryn?" His voice was sharp.

She felt warmth seep from his hand into her skin and made to pull it away, but he strengthened his grip. Was he really using magic on her? What kind? When she opened her mouth to tell him that this was an absurd question, not a single word wanted to come out. Then it struck her. He was using a truth block on her!

His eyes flashed and narrowed at her obvious attempt at lying to him. Her thoughts raced. No! She couldn't let him leave here with that piece of information. She shook her head, willing her chaotic thoughts to obey and provide her with a quick solution.

Voluntarily. What did that even mean? She had made the decision to allow herself be joined to him, hadn't she? As long as Ram'an didn't ask her why or about the consequences of a refusal, it still was the truth, theoretically.

She drew in a deep breath, looked him straight in the eyes and spoke, "Lord Enric asked me to become his companion, and I agreed. The ceremony at the ball, however, was quite a shock to him and me both, as we had not been expecting it. I can see how people would construe this as reluctance."

He stared into her eyes for what seemed to her like an eternity before he nodded. "Well done, little Eryn," he said quietly. "Forming a lie with bits of truth is a formidable skill. Though none I appreciate your using on me right now." He smiled without humour. "But then it is also an art to ask the right questions, is it not? Why did you agree..."

She finally managed to dislodge her hand from his grip abruptly enough to surprise him into letting her go. She jumped up, breathing heavily and shook her head at him in disgust before bolting towards the door.

Her fingers felt the crackling of a shield when they reached for the door handle. She whirled and saw that Ram'an, too, had risen from his seat and stood with folded arms and an inscrutable expression.

"How dare you," she shouted at him, hands balled into fists. "What do you think you are doing? Interrogating me like a criminal! Do you have any idea what Enric will do to you if he ever finds out about this? What this could mean for both our countries?"

"Lord Enric," he spat the name, "seems to have done a few things already that might cause problems if they ever became known of at home."

She folded her arms, staring at him coldly. "And what is it you think you know, *Ambassador*? I have just told you under the influence of a magical spell you used on me without my permission, that I agreed to being joined to him."

"A lie - even though you managed to mask it with your choice of words, and we both know it," he spat back and started coming closer.

"Don't you touch me again or I swear to you, you will pay for it," she hissed.

He stopped again, watching her carefully. "Eryn. Let us not part like this. I apologise."

"Remove the shield," she demanded in as much of a matter-of-fact-way as she could muster.

"Not as long as you are furious toward me."

Nodding slowly, she turned towards the door and raised her own shield between them in case he wanted to try anything stupid. "Then I suppose this is where we find out which one of us is the stronger magician."

She raised her palm and shot a strong bolt at his shield, making it flicker but not collapse. Sending a second strike at it made it wither away completely. Her relief was so profound her knees threatened to buckle under her. She was stronger than him, but only barely. A tiny difference in strength that would enable her to walk out of here now.

"Eryn, please! Let me explain," she heard him calling after her as she ran down the corridor towards the palace gate. She could under no circumstances return home and meet Enric right now. She needed to come to her senses, to think and plan what to do next. There was only one place to go, of course. Orrin's.

CHAPTER 45

The Assistant

Enric looked up from his book when she entered the parlour.

"Good evening." He frowned. "Is everything alright? You look a little flustered."

She nodded. Flustered she could live with. Three hours ago she had appeared seething with rage, desperate and a little helpless. Orrin himself had barely been able to subdue his wrath when she told him about her visit to the ambassador's quarters. She had only just managed to stop him from storming over to Enric and telling him everything about it so he could teach the devious foreign upstart a good lesson in how to treat a lady. Pointing out to Orrin that Enric himself had not always treated her like a lady had done nothing to calm the warrior. That had of course been a completely different situation.

She had made Orrin promise not to reveal anything to anybody of what he had learned, also and especially not to Enric or Lord Tyront. He had argued that if asked directly pretending not to know anything would be a direct violation of an order, especially as both of them outranked her. After considering this she had conceded that she would be content if he at least didn't volunteer any information and only provided it if asked explicitly.

Of course, Orrin couldn't be the one to be made responsible for keeping this a secret - that was her decision entirely. They had agreed to treat this as if she had ordered him to keep silent. Should the Order decide to punish anybody for this omission, it would be her, just as it should be.

She had discussed with Orrin how much and what exactly to tell Enric. If he somehow managed to see Ram'an trying to talk to her and her cold reaction to him, he would know instantly that there was something she had kept from him, and he wouldn't give up until he knew everything. That was not good. So they decided that she would tell him about the offer and that he had not been very happy at her rejection of it. And nothing more.

"I visited Ram'an today."

He smiled thinly. "I know."

Of course he would, she thought grimly, he would still have his two agents set on the man.

"He proposed that I spend some time in the Western Territories to improve my healing knowledge."

Enric slowly closed the book and put it on the table. "And what did you reply, pray tell?" he asked with considerably more calm than he felt.

She rubbed her hands over her face. "I told him that I had things to take care of here, and neither could nor wished to run off to another country right now. He was not very pleased about that. We didn't exactly part on amiable terms," she finished wearily.

She felt his arms wrapping around her and pulling her close, grateful for the comfort and warmth. Leaning her head against his shoulder, she pushed aside the feeling of guilt at lying to him. It was for his own good as well, she thought. Enric storming into Ram'an's quarters and making him feel the full impact of a strong warrior's anger was nothing the King or Lord Tyront would allow him to get away with. Only three more days remained until the delegation left again. She could stay out of his way that long.

"I was wondering when he would ask you," Enric said. "He is running out of time, after all."

She looked up at him. "You seem remarkably calm about it. I would have expected you to be more agitated."

"I was prepared for this, it was not unexpected for me, as you know. I am sorry, though, that it seems to have been a very unpleasant situation for you. It does seem strange, though, that he didn't try to avoid angering you. It basically reduces his chances of persuading you to nothing." He studied her thoughtfully. "You are not keeping anything from me, are you?"

She made herself chuckle. "If I were, I would hardly admit to it now, would I?" That was technically not a lie.

He seemed satisfied with her reply and squeezed her close again. "I am very pleased at your refusal. And I have to admit that I am glad that he handled the matter clumsily enough to make you angry at him. I won't be sad to see him leave in a few days. You just need to get the farewell banquet behind you, then you don't have to see him again - at least for quite a while."

She closed her eyes. A farewell banquet. There had been a welcoming banquet for him, so why was she caught off guard by the news of there being another one to send him off on his way back home?

It couldn't be helped; she would have to face Ram'an one more time before he finally departed. But it would be amidst a lot of people, so at least he wouldn't have any chance to corner her there. Enric would be watching him like a hawk, especially if the King placed her next to him again. Which she fervently hoped he wouldn't.

Enric felt the tension in her muscles and tried to distract her. "I met with Tyront today. From what I gathered, you have not yet sent him that note with your request for an assistant. I tested the waters to gauge his general opinion, and I think your chances are pretty good." He smiled. "And I am sure he will consult me in this matter, which will increase even further the likelihood of his granting it."

"Then I better take care of this quickly." She slipped from his arms and walked towards the guest room to retrieve a pen and paper and write the note immediately before it slipped her mind again.

She returned with the writing utensils and took a seat at the dinner table. "Any recommendations of how to phrase this? Is there any formal address I should be using?"

"Addressing him with Lord Tyront will do. And as for the phrasing, he has a lot of things to read every day, so he will appreciate a short and simple letter, well-structured with plausible arguments, no complicated literary constructions or some such."

That sounded fine to her. She was in no mood to compose an epic masterpiece worthy of being turned into a ballad, anyway.

When she had finished her first draft half an hour later, she handed it to him and waited for his appraisal.

"Very good," he nodded. "I will see him tomorrow. Would you like me to give it to him then? Though it would look more official if you sent it to him by messenger."

"Then let's do that." She smiled and took the letter back, folding it. "I wouldn't want to abuse my own superior by making him deliver my requests."

Enric looked at the piece of paper and frowned. "I just realised that we haven't had a seal made for you. That was rather neglectful of me, I must say. You have nothing to stamp into the wax."

"A seal?" She blinked. "I wasn't aware that I needed one. I thought only the King and the Order used special ones."

"No - Tyront, myself and all other members of the Magic Council have their individual seals in addition. And there is the official Order seal, of course. I think we will use it for this message for now, as it is Order business after all. We will take care of having your own stamp made tomorrow. I suggest something similar to my own design with a few embellishments to make it individual."

"But still similar enough to remind people who I belong with?" she grinned and found the intention somehow endearing.

"Exactly," he confirmed and kissed her on the forehead, glad that she didn't object to his suggestion.

* * *

Once Enric had taken a seat in his study in front of the desk, Tyront picked up the message, which he had received the evening before.

"Correct me if I am wrong, but judging from our conversation yesterday, Eryn's request for an assistant is doubtlessly known to you."

Enric nodded. "Yes, of course."

The older man turned the envelope and rubbed his thumb over the official Order seal. "Don't you think it's time for her to get her own seal, my friend? She is about to become a very important person in the Order. Not that I mind her using the Order seal, but it might make her seem less exalted than she is, which will turn out to be a disadvantage."

"I have commissioned a few design drafts from young Vern. I think he will come up with something she will agree to. As soon as she has picked one I will have it sent to the engraver."

"Good." Tyront watched the younger man. "What do you think? Shall we grant our lady rebel an assistant?"

Enric nodded. "Yes, I think we should. I have first-hand knowledge of how swamped with her many tasks and subsequently exhausted she is in the evenings. Sometimes she comes home and collapses into bed without even eating anything. I am concerned for her, and an assistant could take some of the load off her. At least the things that are connected to the organisational matters around healing."

"Alright, an assistant for her it is. How far along is the healers' building? He will need a place to work and I would say that is the obvious choice."

"The construction is going very well. From what I have learned it will even be finished ahead of schedule," Enric explained with a lopsided grin.

"Indeed? And I suppose that has nothing to do with the steady stream of magicians who you happened to have drop by these last few weeks, has it?" Tyront asked dryly.

"Probably. Our presence does seem to spur people on for some reason."

"Says the man who broke a stranger's nose at the last ball. You are aware of who the man was by now, I assume? He is Lord Seagon's nephew."

Enric shrugged. "I don't really care who he is. He'd better learn to keep his hands to himself."

"Was that the primary objective of your small show of brutality?" the older man asked with a thin smile. "I can't help feeling that the ambassador was the main beneficiary of this spectacle."

The younger magician raised his brow. "Whatever would give you that idea?"

Ah yes, so they were playing games again. "Just a thought, nothing more. It has been brought to my attention that Eryn left the ambassador's quarters yesterday in what seemed to be a great hurry and a foul mood. You wouldn't happen to know anything about that, would you?"

"I do, as a matter of fact. It seems as if our honoured guest asked Eryn to accompany him back to the Western Territories and was not too pleased with her refusal." Enric's voice had gone cold.

Interesting, Tyront thought. So Enric's agents had not been close enough to overhear the noises of what seemed to have been a magical fight. Unlike his own. And Eryn seemed to have provided her companion with an edited version of the occurrences. He himself was also not fully aware of them yet, but he intended to find out. Either Eryn herself would confess, or he would make Lord Orrin talk. That was where she had fled afterwards, in any case.

"I see," he said. "So your concerns about her accepting an offer of this kind were unnecessary. That must be a great relief to you."

"It is," Enric confirmed. "Though I somehow have the feeling that he will not be leaving it at that. I will only feel completely reassured when he has departed from the kingdom. Two more days, and then we will finally get rid of him."

"Yes, we will. But you have to admit that we will have benefitted greatly from some of the agreements that were negotiated by the ambassador and his attaches. Let's not forget this - however great your personal aversion is to him."

The younger magician sighed. "I know. I will be civil to him at the banquet, but that's as much as I will do."

"And there's no more I ask of you. Just remember that the exchange of knowledge is also a part of the agreements, one that will enable your companion to increase her healing knowledge without leaving here for now." Tyront picked up the request in Eryn's slightly impatient handwriting and smiled. "I will send for her tomorrow afternoon to deliver the good news. And I think I have just the right man for the job."

* * *

Eryn looked out the window of Vern's room, watching the rain hit the cobblestones and roof shingles in their monotonous rhythm.

Vern was working on a street cat she had caught on her way here. It was missing half an ear and Vern's task for today was to regrow it.

He had been scratched several times and had let loose an impressive array of curses she wouldn't have expected a young man of his upbringing to be familiar with. After watching him for several minutes she rolled her eyes and suggested that he send the cat to sleep first. He had obviously been a little embarrassed at not having thought of that first himself, but he had only ever encountered willing patients who were *glad* to receive healing instead of fighting it with, well, in this case literally, tooth and claw.

When she looked back to the boy, he was still sitting motionless with his eyes closed, one hand resting on the cat's side. The ear was slowly reforming into its original shape, though it still looked fresh and pink, without any fur to cover it.

She watched the tip of the ear slowly round itself to match its counterpart on the other side of the head, and then she saw wispy hair growing unusually quickly on top of the bare skin.

When Vern opened his eyes again a few minutes later, she nodded approvingly and gently touched his work. "Very well done. Another challenge mastered, my lad. If you keep up that pace, I will soon run out of things to teach you," she smiled. "Have you done a check of the entire body or just the ear?"

"Entire body, of course," he replied as if even being asked was an insult. "There are quite a few things that would need taking care of. Broken rib, parasites in the intestines and what I think is a cardiac defect."

She touched the cat's paw and closed her eyes for a moment. "Yes," she confirmed. "I agree. I would say you get to work. Start with the rib and the parasites. Let me know when you move on to the heart, I will monitor that one. It is a bit more complicated than the rest, so I would like to make sure you don't do any damage. Well, any additional damage, that is. It might be a poor excuse of a cat, but it has as much right to live as you or I."

The boy nodded and returned his attention to the feline body on his desk.

She looked up when she heard a quiet knock at the door and rose to answer it. Vern was used to her taking care of any interruptions while he was working, so he didn't even bother opening his eyes.

Orrin wordlessly handed her a message. She turned it to have a look at the seal. Lord Tyront. Could he already have made up his mind about her request?

The message was short and requested her presence at his study after her lesson with Vern was finished. A hint of the topic would have been nice, she thought nervously, and smiled at Orrin to let him know that nothing dire had happened. Yet.

Vern finished his unsupervised repair work and then looked up at her. "Everything alright?"

"Lord Tyront wants to see me when we are done. It's very likely to be about the assistant I requested."

"Do you think he will grant it?"

She shrugged. "I have no idea. He is not my greatest admirer, but Enric promised to put in a good word for me, so anything is possible. I will soon know more."

"You can go there now, if you like. I don't mind."

"Surely not," she chuckled. "You will heal that poor creature's heart first. No wriggling out of that. It's time to move on to the more sophisticated procedures. You have drawn the human heart so many times, I am sure you know it inside out by now. A feline heart is not so different from ours - apart from its size, of course. You should thus find your way around easily. Ready?"

He sighed and nodded, then both of them closed their eyes and touched the cat again to let their magic flow inside it.

"It's the valve on the left side," Vern murmured. "It doesn't close properly. The blood doesn't flow where it is supposed to."

"It is too short," Eryn said equally quietly. "Make it grow a tiny amount."

Another few moments in silence, then she warned, "Careful, the growing must not stop the heart from doing its work. Slowly." She observed him adapt his technique and nodded. "Very good. Do you see how the flow from one chamber of the heart to the next works differently now? That's what it is supposed to look like. Well done."

Vern opened his eyes and sighed in relief. "I don't know why working on the heart makes me so nervous. It is an organ like any other, and yet…"

"It is a tricky one. If you stop it for too long, the whole body will shut off, just like the lungs or the brain. A certain degree of respect is definitely appropriate here. But also avoid fear; it will just paralyse you." She rose and stifled a yawn. "I hate this weather. It makes me want to curl up and sleep all day long." But her visit at Lord Tyront's would shake her awake in no time, she thought gloomily.

"Let me know what Lord Tyront said, if it's about your assistant. Be nice to him for a change," Vern warned her with a raised index finger.

"Thank you so much," she shook her head at him. "And get rid of that cat. Orrin will blame me if it chews, destroys or marks anything of his."

Vern ruffled the unconscious cat's fur a bit and looked down at it with a fond expression. "I will wait until he wakes up and feed him first. He has basically been abducted and experimented on. I feel he deserves some kind of compensation."

She laughed and ruffled his too long hair. "I like that you have a soft spot for your patients, no matter how many legs or fleas they have."

Leaving his room, she nodded to Orrin and grabbed her cloak on her way out. The new boots Enric had insisted on having made for her kept the water out just as they were supposed to and she silently sent him thanks for his providence. Wet, cold feet were something she could easily live without right now.

She was led into Lord Tyront's study and bowed when he rose to greet her. Enric was there as well, sitting on the sofa in front of one of the windows and looking relaxed as he flashed her a smile. She hoped that this was a good sign.

"Please take a seat, Lady Eryn. May I offer you a hot beverage? I assume you will need one after braving the rain," her host offered.

"Yes, thank you," she replied politely. If he declined her request, she could always hurl the cup at him, she considered.

Tyront waited for Enric to pour her a cup and hand it to her before he continued. "As you surely expect, I have asked you to come here to inform you of our decision as regards your request for an assistant." He watched her sit up a little straighter, holding her breath.

"It is my pleasure to inform you that your request has been granted. As soon as the work on the healers' building is finished and there is a place for him to work, your new assistant will start." He smiled when she leaned back and exhaled slowly, the relief evident on her face.

"Thank you very much, Lord Tyront."

He smiled benevolently, looking forward to what was to come next. "Here is the file of the young man I have chosen for this position."

She took the leather folder and looked at the first sheet of a collection of neatly stacked papers inside. Reading the name, she looked concerned.

"Rolan? The name sounds familiar, but I can't quite place the face." She looked over at Enric, who had closed his eyes and covered his mouth with one hand, though she wasn't sure whether to keep himself from speaking or to hide a smile.

When she looked back to Lord Tyront, she swallowed at the expectant and clearly mischievous look in his eyes. What was going on here?

"Enric?" she asked cautiously. "Would you help me out a little? I feel like the two of you are laughing at me and I think I should at least know why. Who is that man? Why have I heard that name before?"

Enric cleared his throat. "Rolan was the young man Orrin had you train with shortly after your arrival in the city, my love."

She stared at him, realisation slowly dawning on her. "But... I repeatedly kicked him in the..." No. Oh, no. Not him. Why? But the answer to that was obvious, wasn't it?

"This is your revenge," she said slowly, giving Tyront a look of incredulity. "You are punishing me by appointing *him* my assistant!"

The older man's smile was thin when he replied, "I am sure I have no idea what you are talking about, Lady Eryn. Are you telling me that you do not approve of my choice?"

She slowly shook her head and exhaled. "No," she forced herself to say, "of course not."

What else was there to be said? There was no doubt that he would not give her another assistant in place of Rolan. It was to be either the arrogant young half-wit who had sneered at her all the time until he requested release from training with her, or no assistant at all. She wondered which was the less painful option.

Glancing down at the folder in her hand, she gulped. It was not exactly thin. So this arrangement was probably not only a punishment for her, but for him also. That file would very likely provide for some very unpleasant reading material for the evening.

* * *

Enric watched her lying prone, the sheets from the leather file on her new assistant spread across her side of the bed.

She looked up when she felt his gaze on her and looked grim. "He has been kicked out of three positions already, and that within the last year!" Shaking her head, she scanned the jumble of pages around her for a particular sheet and snatched it up when she had found it. "It says here that he was impertinent, disrespectful, pert and insolent." She gave Enric a desperate look. "This is basically a description of *me*! How am I supposed to work with a man like that?

We will end up throwing things at each other within the first hour! I need somebody level-headed, organised and patient, somebody who has a balancing effect on me. Not him," she added with an all-embracing gesture at the papers around her.

Enric chuckled and came closer. "I warned you that Tyront has a very dangerous sense of humour. But do not despair, he wouldn't burden you with something like this without its having some chance of success. He has thrown down a challenge for you, my love. He is a chancer, and he sometimes enjoys losing as much as winning, especially when he feels that in losing he has enabled you to move on, to develop. Which would make him the winner again, in a strange way. So he basically can't lose, even if he does under the regular rules."

Eryn shook her head in confusion. "That did sound a little tangled. So you are telling me to make it work? How can I? I don't know how to!"

He smiled. "You don't? Then I would suggest you look back over these last months. You say you and he are rather alike. So, what has worked in making you cooperate with us?"

She furrowed her brow. "Good idea. So I am to coerce him into bed with me? An unexpected suggestion coming from you, but I'll take it into consideration."

"Very witty," he retorted, obviously not at all amused. "How about showing him that he can't really win by fighting you and instead demonstrating that he has a lot more to gain by working with you?"

"I see. So that was your great plan? And how does the King's little coercion fit into that very sensible scenario? Or is blackmailing one of the instruments you recommend using?"

Enric shrugged. "Why not? You said he's already lost three jobs in one year. Then I'd say it is in his own interest to keep this one. The Order's patience is not unlimited - that is something you can work with. He can't really afford to lose another job. And then it is up to you to make him respect you and find the right kind of tasks for him to take care of. Things he is good at, that he enjoys doing."

She raised her brow at him. "Don't tell me that is the strategy you are using with me, because swamping me with theory and combat lessons is not my idea of doing something I enjoy!"

"You may not be too happy about this for now, but at least the theory lessons will be completed in a few months. But the important thing is that you will be able to heal, isn't it? That is how we managed to persuade you to join us, after all - by letting you do what you value most. Think about it."

He turned and went back into the parlour, leaving her alone to give her time to think his words over. And think about them she would, he knew.

CHAPTER 46

Departure

She looked up when she heard somebody entering the library. It didn't sound like Lord Poron, his steps were usually less obvious, more suited to the surroundings. And indeed, it was somebody she had not expected here: Lord Tyront.

He lifted both arms and all three double doors leading into the room closed themselves as if by invisible hands slowly but with finality, shutting the two of them in.

A little alarmed, she watched him walk towards her and halt with folded arms before her desk.

"Lady Eryn. We should talk," he said without a greeting and she just managed to pull her hands away before the heavy book in front of her closed itself with an assertive thud.

"We should?" she replied with some concern. "What about?"

"About your little row with the Ambassador yesterday afternoon." He shook his head slightly when she opened her mouth. "Don't. No lying. Don't even *try* to sell to me what you told Enric." He smiled thinly when she gulped audibly. "Using magic in your dispute is a very serious matter and it is no longer one only concerning you and our visitor. It is now a concern for the Order. And as the leader of the same I hereby command you to relay what happened between the two of you yesterday in his quarters."

She stared at him for several moments. This was not good, not at all. How did he know about all this? Or was he just pretending to know, was he bluffing to see how much he could glean from her?

"What makes you think magic was used in our argument?" she asked carefully.

"Because the sound of a magical barrier being forced to collapse by two powerful bolts is a very distinctive and recognisable one. I should point out that you are not the one asking the questions here. I gave you an order." His eyes bore into hers without blinking. "I am waiting."

"He wanted me to come to the Western Territories to learn more about healing," she said nervously.

"Yes, I know that much. And you refused. But that was not why the situation escalated, was it?"

She tried to turn her head away, but found it impossible. His intent stare seemed to lock hers into place.

He slowly shook his head. "What happened in there, Eryn?" he said calmly, making the question more intimate by omitting her title. "Something you couldn't tell Enric, am I right?"

Almost against her will, she found herself nodding.

"Was *he* the one to use magic of some kind on you first?" Tyront asked and was immensely relieved when she nodded again, closing her eyes.

"You can't tell Enric about it. He might do something stupid," she said in what was hardly more than a whisper.

"Let me be the judge of that," he countered quietly. "What kind of magic did he use?"

"A truth block," she replied and found it almost a relief to share the information. It was like passing on the enormous responsibility to somebody else. A man many years her senior with so much political experience would surely be better suited to deciding what would be the most sensible course of action, wouldn't he?

She saw his eyes narrow. "A truth block," he repeated thoughtfully. "What did he want to know?"

"He asked me about my commitment to Enric. If I entered into it voluntarily."

"What did you reply?" The first signs of unease began to show on his face.

"To begin, I tried to lie to him. I hadn't been aware what he was doing or that lying wouldn't work. He noticed this, of course. I then told him that Enric asked me to become his companion and that I agreed to it. He accused me of using bits of truth to construct a lie and was about to ask me why I agreed to it." She raked her fingers through her hair and rose from her chair to pace the room agitatedly.

Tyront remained where he was and watched her taking a few steps away from him.

"What happened then?"

"I managed to pull my hand away and ran to the door."

"Where he tried to stop you from leaving with a shield, I imagine?" he asked calmly but with hard lines around his mouth.

She nodded. "Yes. I told him to let me go, but he refused. I attacked the shield and barely managed to break it with my second bolt. Then I just ran." Shaking her head, she looked up at him again. "I don't know how else I could have handled this situation."

He watched her thoughtfully. "Don't worry about that, you did well enough. So he was interested in nothing else but your commitment to Enric?" Tyront stared up at the ceiling pensively after she nodded. It seemed as if Enric's jealousy was more than justified and had been from the beginning. The ambassador could have asked her about many things - matters pertaining to defence or politics - but he had risked a lot by using magic against her in what could easily be seen as an assault just to learn about her personal connection to another man.

He looked back at her. Her decision to withhold that information from Enric had been a smart one. Though there was another magician to worry about.

"You shared all this with Lord Orrin, I assume?"

She hesitated for a moment before she nodded again. "I asked him to keep the information to himself unless you or Enric distinctly ordered him to speak of it."

"Good. I agree with you, Enric cannot be told about this, especially as long as the delegation still is in the city. He might do something to endanger the peace we are trying to establish and maintain. It seems to me that the Ambassador's interest in you is considerable, and I suspect it is for mostly personal reasons."

"I have never intentionally encouraged anything of that sort!" she exclaimed with wide eyes. "Enric would lock me up for showing any sign of interest in another man!"

That last bit was probably very true, Tyront knew. "Calm down. I know you didn't. Your conduct with Ambassador Ram'an is beyond any doubt, and it is understood that there was never more than friendship offered on your side." He leaned forward. "I am aware that you are hardly keen on meeting him again before his departure, but I must insist on your attendance at the farewell banquet. Otherwise you would have to provide the King and Enric with a very good reason, and even though you do have one, we do not want that to become public knowledge at this point."

Even though with the King it was hard to tell how much he knew, he thought. But knowing it and being officially told were two completely different matters. Only the second option required a public reaction, for once.

"Has he tried to contact you in the meantime?" he asked.

"Yes. He sent me two messages, urging me to meet him so he could explain everything to me. I ignored them both."

"I see. Should you change your mind about meeting him, make sure not to be alone with him. You would seem to be a little stronger than he is, but I would still advise you to have another magician accompany you. Lord Orrin is aware of the situation, so he is the obvious choice for you. And there is myself, of course, though we might want to keep the Ambassador in the dark about how far up in the Order the particulars of this situation are known."

Eryn nodded tiredly. It seemed as if the lying and deceiving was about to go on for a while yet, and the regrettable thing was that it was her own companion who she was inflicting it upon. She and Lord Tyront working together to withhold information from Enric. What an absurd situation.

* * *

Eryn stared into the mirror with unseeing eyes.

Junar studied her with a worried expression and tugged the sleeves of the dark red dress into position. No bickering, no token complaints about the dress, no joking, nothing. This was highly unusual.

"You are not worried about the banquet, are you?" she enquired cautiously.

"What?" Eryn blinked a few times while finding back to reality.

"The banquet," Junar repeated patiently. "Are you worried about it?"

"No, of course not," the magician fibbed without batting an eyelid. "I am just tired and it's keeping me from going to bed early."

The seamstress sighed and decided to leave the topic alone. Her friend was obviously not ready or willing to share whatever was on her mind.

"Well, from my point of view you are ready to dazzle them all. Let's give the Ambassador something to remember when he returns home, right?"

Eryn closed her eyes for a moment. That was exactly what she wanted to avoid tonight. Ram'an's attention. She had managed to stay out of his way for these last two days and had even considered not attending the banquet. But of course she would have to give the King a very good reason for not attending, just like Lord Tyront had pointed out. Feigned illnesses would somehow ring a little untrue if they were claimed by someone known to be able to heal themselves.

"Thank you, Junar," she said and turned around. "The dress is beautiful." She made herself smile.

"Are you ready, my love?" Enric's voice came from by the door and she nodded. "You seem unusually quiet," he commented as they were walking along the palace corridors to the banquet hall. He had taken her hand in his and pulled her to a halt. "Are you that uncomfortable about seeing the ambassador again?"

She sighed. "Yes, I am. I mean, we were getting along very well and he somehow then destroyed it all. And looking him in the eye again is just not the most compelling thing I can imagine right now. He was like a connection to my place of origin, of what used to be my home, but now..."

Enric nodded slowly. "I see. But don't let the words of one man ruin this for you, my love. I am sure you will in time meet more visitors from the Western Territories and renew this connection. Come. Let's get this behind us."

She felt Ram'an's gaze on her immediately as she entered the hall. Carefully avoiding his eyes, she first greeted Lord Poron and then Orrin, talking to both of them as long as possible to bridge the time until they would be escorted to their seats by servants circulating around them. With a little luck she would be seated far enough away from Ram'an this time to be able to completely ignore him the entire evening.

She heard the signal, and when a servant in livery politely asked her to follow him, she detected her heart beating faster and suppressed a groan when she saw from the corner of her eye that Ram'an was being led in the same direction. And indeed, they were to be seated next to each other - again. Rotten luck if ever there was.

"Eryn," he said quietly enough only for her to hear. "We must talk."

"There is nothing to talk about," she replied frostily without even looking at him. "I will not regret seeing you leave tomorrow after what you did."

"I must explain this to you. Please," he urged her.

She ignored him and took a seat, looking around to see where Enric, Lord Tyront and Orrin were seated. Unfortunately, none of them was close enough for her to talk to. Ram'an sat down on her left, and she suppressed an agonised sigh when she saw who her right hand neighbour was: Lord Seagon. The uncle of the man whose nose Enric had broken. Brilliant. It looked like this was going to be a very long evening for her. Who planned these bloody seating arrangements? Doubtlessly somebody with either a talent for making people ill at ease or a strange and misplaced sense of humour.

The guests rose when the large double doors at the far end of the hall were pushed open and King Folrin entered. He strode towards the head end of the large table and took his seat, thus permitting the assembled guests to sit down again.

He let his gaze wander around the table, observed who was in conversation with whom and any other tell-tale signs of alliances and enmities around him. Of course he was aware that the relationship between Eryn and the ambassador had suffered considerable impairment for some reason. The official version was that he had proposed taking her on a visit to the Western Territories and had been greatly displeased by her refusal, but the King had discarded this almost immediately as the reason for the change between them. And watching them now confirmed his prior assessment. The ambassador was trying to get her to talk to him, but she kept ignoring him or just hissing some doubtlessly not very friendly words to him under her breath. Why would *she* be angry when he was supposedly the one to be unhappy about her refusal?

Whatever had happened between them, he needed them to patch it up before the delegation's departure. He had seated them next to each other with that end in mind. Lord Enric he had placed further away this time. The Lord would hardly be very keen on seeing his companion and the ambassador make up again, and might turn out to be a hindrance. The King had even placed Lord Seagon on her other side to make it even less likely for her to talk to anybody else but her left hand neighbour. So far, however, his efforts did not appear to be rewarded with success. He would give them another hour before he intervened.

Eryn dutifully lifted her glass when the King did and listened to his words of praise, hope and a new age. Along with the other guests she sipped at the wine once he had spoken his last words, and waited for the first course to be served. People around them resumed their conversations and it seemed that she and Ram'an were the only quiet ones on this side of the table.

"Eryn," he implored again, "do not do this."

She sucked in a quick breath when she felt his fingers closing around hers. A quick move broke the contact and she gripped a fork from the assortment of cutlery in front of her, driving the prongs smartly into the flesh of his thigh under the table.

She felt dark satisfaction rise inside her when she heard his shocked gasp. It was impressive, she had to admit, that he managed not to let the tiniest sound escape from his lips. That jab must have been rather painful, after all.

Observing the jerky movement of his arm, she saw him replace the fork with the bloody prongs back to where she had taken it from the table. He stilled for a moment, closing his eyes. Doubtlessly to heal himself.

Eryn picked up the now red-tipped fork and motioned for a servant.

"I need another fork. This one is dirty." She pressed the piece of cutlery into the servant's hand and turned back to the table. She could feel the King's gaze on her as clearly as if he had placed a hand on her shoulder, and decided not to meet it for now. At least Enric was far enough away not to have seen what she had done.

King Folrin watched her and waited for her to look at him, but she was obviously determined to ignore him. He had to warn her somehow. Stabbing the ambassador with cutlery was not acceptable. With words, well, if they were well-chosen, why not. But a fork attack was definitely not at all diplomatic enough in a banquet.

And it seemed as if an earlier than planned intervention was now called for. Letting her carry on like this for another hour was probably not a wise move.

"Lady Eryn," he said and thus forced her to look at him finally. "Come and walk with me, will you."

"Please, Your Majesty, I would be horrified if this little mishap among friends had unpleasant consequences for Lady Eryn," the ambassador interjected quickly.

The King watched him with a slightly raised brow, clearly intrigued. A fork had just been jabbed into his thigh, and yet he was defending her. Whatever he had done or said to upset her must have been rather severe.

"I admire your very generous attitude in approaching this, Ambassador. I admit I was rather worried that the status of you two as *friends* has been somehow compromised," he spoke calmly with a smile that wasn't really one.

Ram'an's answering smile looked rather more forced when he replied, "No, Your Majesty, not as such. There was just a little matter I was hoping to resolve before my departure."

"Indeed, there is obviously some need for that," the King remarked without a trace of irony. "I do admit that I prefer the two of you to part as friends."

Eryn worked hard at keeping the curse that sprang to her lips unbidden inside instead of unleashing it. Great. So the King wished for her to make up with Ram'an. He didn't even have a clue what all this was about, or did he? Almost certainly not, she decided. Ram'an had been about to find out that the King himself had forced her to commit herself to Enric, and that could hardly be in his interest.

She met the King's icy gaze and held her lips together. What might have seemed like a casual suggestion was in fact a royal order and he wanted to make sure she interpreted it as such. Only when he kept staring at her, did she realise that he expected an immediate reaction.

"Ambassador," she managed to utter between clenched teeth and without looking at Ram'an, "we can meet tomorrow morning after sunrise in Lord Orrin's quarters, if this suggestion meets with your approval."

"Of course. I will be there. Thank you," he replied softly.

She looked back at the King with her brow raised in enquiry and he nodded once. How delightful.

* * *

Orrin looked at her and went to open the door. So he had arrived. He saw Eryn breathe in and out a few times and brace herself. They had agreed that he would be in his study with the door open in case the ambassador tried anything foolish.

"Lord Orrin," she heard Ram'an say. Somehow the name sounded especially exotic when pronounced by him. "How very good of you to provide this neutral meeting space for us."

He entered and his eyes searched and found Eryn.

"Eryn, dear," he said softly. "I am aware that you are not pleased with your King's interference, but I have to say that I am glad that he gave me the chance to converse with you once more. I deeply regret that he had to compel you to do it, I would have preferred a more amiable arrangement."

She looked at Orrin and nodded to him, confirming that it was alright to leave her alone with Ram'an now. Or as alone as an open door would grant.

"Speak then," she said briskly and remained standing to indicate that she did not intend for this encounter to be a very long one.

"Eryn," he sighed. "I did not intend to harm you or force you into anything. I was worried. The notion that you might have been strong-armed into giving yourself to Lord Enric is one that truly terrifies me. And I have to tell you that your answers did not exactly dispel my concerns. Quite the opposite, in fact." He took two steps towards her but stopped immediately when she made to retreat to stay out of his reach. "If they are keeping you here against your will," he said quietly with a glance towards the open study door, "you can tell me. I will assist you, I promise. I can take you away from here. You would be welcome back at your home, Eryn. Very much so." He shook his head and looked at her with a pained expression. "How can I leave here with the suspicion that you are a prisoner? I mean, look at the timing! It was only days before our arrival that you were joined with Lord Enric. And people are talking, saying how pale and frightened you looked that evening at the ball. What else am I to think?" He threw up his hands in frustration.

She let out a long breath. "Ram'an, I do understand your concerns, but let me assure you that they are unfounded. I am happy in my commitment with Lord Enric. You must have observed that he does not treat me like a prisoner of any sort but with warmth and affection. As for the Order, I do admit that I find some of the demands rather wearing and unnecessary, but they let me do what I have always wanted to: heal people. So there is no reason whatsoever for you to worry about me." Her tone changed and became hard. "I might appreciate your concerns, but I strongly objected to your methods. You used magic to interrogate me without my permission. *You* were the one treating me like a prisoner, Ram'an, not them."

He closed his eyes and shook his head. "Yes, I was. And I apologise for it most sincerely. It was fatuous of me to do, but I tried it only out of concern for your welfare, dear Eryn. Will you forgive a poor fool for treating you this way? Let us not part on these terms. I would like you to think of me fondly, not with anger in your heart when I am gone."

Eryn stared at the hand he held out to her. Her thoughts raced. Staying mad at him wouldn't win her anything, especially as he was leaving in only a few hours. He had been right with his suspicions, after all - she *had* been blackmailed into her commitment. Being angry at him for figuring it out seemed rather petty. And at least he had apologised for using the truth block on her.

Sighing, she took his hand and saw the relief in his eyes when he pulled it to his lips to press a firm kiss onto her knuckles.

"I hope I will see you again one last time when we are leaving?"

He waited for her to nod, then bowed and left.

She turned towards Orrin's study and called his name.

"How did it go? I didn't hear any screaming or fighting, so I assume you have forgiven him?"

"Basically yes. I am still a bit angry at him, but at least he has apologised. And it's not like he will be a danger to me in the future. He will soon be gone, and the King has made it very clear that he wanted me to take care of this before his departure. All in the interests of diplomacy, no doubt."

Orrin snorted. "Yes, that's what you need to remind yourself of when you would rather kick somebody but have to smile at them instead."

* * *

The King, the Magic Council and other people who had regularly met with and negotiated with the delegation had made their fare-wells in the throne room. Eryn and Enric were to accompany them to their mounts.

Their belongings had been packed and strapped onto the horses, and Ram'an was the last one who had yet to climb into the saddle.

"Good bye, Lord Enric. It was an honour to meet you," he said, and both men bowed to each other. Then he turned to Eryn and smiled warmly. "Eryn, what can I say to you but that it pains me to leave here without getting to know you better and without knowing when I will see you again." He went to his horse and took a small parcel from one of the many bags. "I would like to give this to you. Something from the place where you were born, even though you do not like to call it your home anymore."

She took it cautiously and opened the box, looking down on a silver necklace with a pendant that seemed to consist of two crests, one larger, the other smaller.

"What is it?"

"It is what members of more influential families like to wear for official occasions." He took the pendant in his hand and pointed to the larger crest. It contained a small sun, trees of some sort, a circle containing a flash of lightning, and a bird.

"This is the coat of arms from your mother's side of the family. The symbolism is as follows: The sun is our symbol for leadership. Your family has in these past centuries been at the top more than once. The trees show wealth, as the climate in our land is rather harsh at times and owning fruit-bearing trees is a good way to become wealthy and remain so. The circle here is our symbol of magic, and this particular bird is a symbol for wisdom." He smiled at her. "It is a powerful House you stem from. One that did not take losing you lightly."

She swallowed and looked down at the pendant again. "And the smaller one is from my father's family? Why is it so much smaller?"

"Because the mother's family is the one which has greater influence on the path the child's life will take. All major decisions are made by them."

So her mother's family would have been massively displeased not only to lose Eryn, but lose her to a father who was not even entitled to take her away, according to their system. She wondered what they would have done to him had they ever caught him.

She looked at the symbols of the small crest. The circle that showed magical abilities, the sun again, but smaller and with a hand underneath, and a second hand with what looked like rays emanating from it.

"The symbols of your father's family speak of magic, being trusted advisors to the leaders, even though with no inclination towards being leaders themselves. And the last one here, the shining palm, is a symbol of a long tradition of healing."

He watched her smile spread at his last words and her index finger touched the tiny symbol.

"A family of healers," she sighed and looked up. "Thank you, Ram'an. I have finally found something to connect me with that place that still seems so very foreign to me."

"I am happy to hear that, dear." He took her free hand and lifted it to his lips, ignoring the stern gaze of the tall magician next to them, before he turned and mounted his horse. He waved a final goodbye and the small group began on their long trip, leaving the city.

Eryn watched them receding until they were no longer visible and wondered if she would see the ambassador again one day. To her surprise, she hoped that she would.

www.ingramcontent.com/pod-product-compliance
Lightning Source LLC
Chambersburg PA
CBHW070539030726
47505CB00001B/85